I0647145

Omnibus Edition

The versions included in this edition of
The Human-Hybrid Project contain the
complete and unaltered text. Additional maps
and other items are found only in the
individual books.

See our website for the complete story behind
the characters, the locations, and the events
surrounding Bay City and the human-hybrid
project.

www.TheHumanHybridProject.com

The Human Hybrid Project

FARLEY L DUNN

THE HUMAN-HYBRID PROJECT

Books 1-10 in the Series:
THE HUMAN-HYBRID PROJECT

Including:

Shattered by Glass
Inside the Darkness
The Mirror Cracks
Reflections of the Silverback
The Glass Siege
Taking the Tower
The Rage
Sunchaser's Gambit
The Electrified Sword
The Russian's Revenge

Published in Fort Worth, Texas

 THREE SKILLET

www.ThreeSkilletPublishing.com

Three Skillet Publishing
PO Box 162194
Fort Worth, Texas 76161

ISBN: 978-1-943189-94-6

Third Printing October 2021/Printed in the USA

The Books

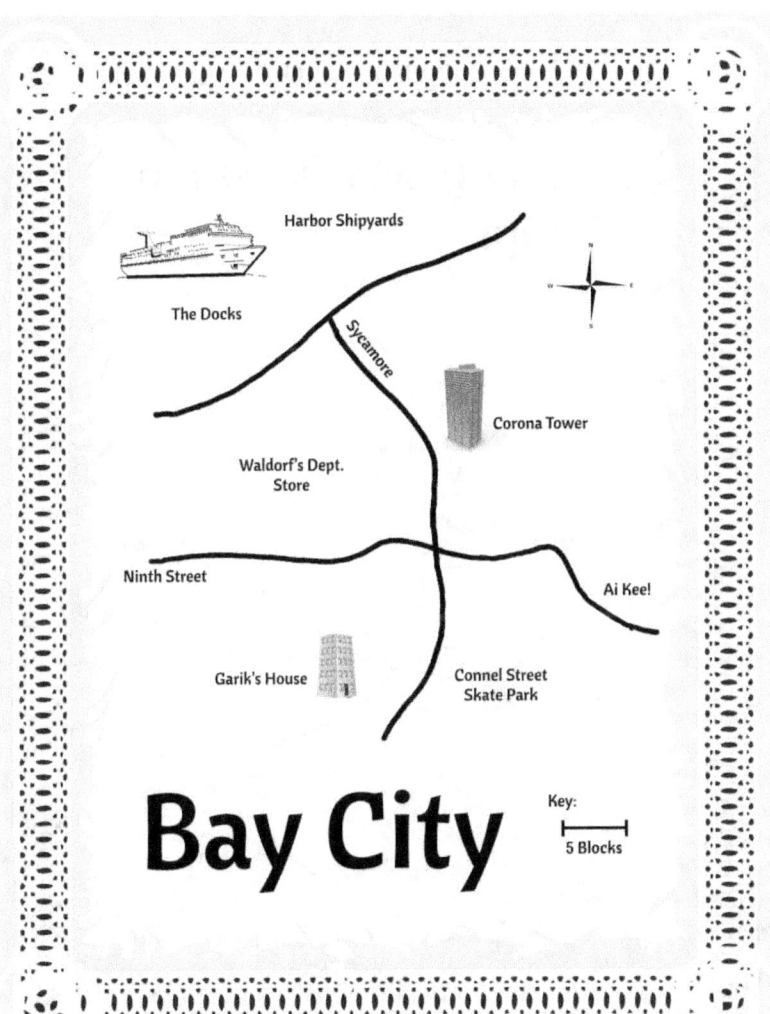

Harbor Shipyards

The Docks

Sycamore

Corona Tower

Waldorf's Dept.
Store

Ninth Street

Ai Kee!

Garik's House

Connel Street
Skate Park

Bay City

Key:

5 Blocks

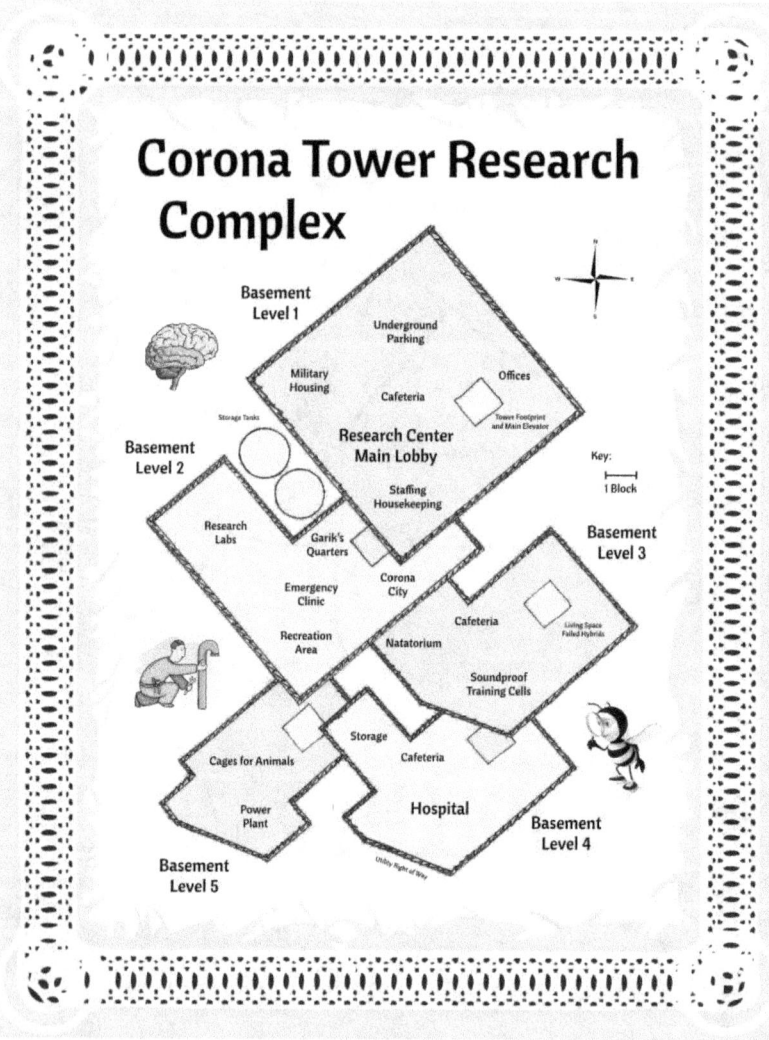

Corona Tower Research Complex

Basement Level 1

Underground Parking

Military Housing

Offices

Cafeteria

Tower Footprint and Main Elevator

Storage Tanks

Basement Level 2

Research Center Main Lobby

Staffing Housekeeping

Key:
1 Block

Research Labs

Garik's Quarters

Basement Level 3

Emergency Clinic

Corona City

Recreation Area

Natatorium

Cafeteria

Living Space Failed Hybrids

Soundproof Training Cells

Cages for Animals

Storage

Cafeteria

Power Plant

Hospital

Basement Level 4

Basement Level 5

Utility Right of Way

Book 1

SHATTERED
by
Glass

— 1 —

THE SKYSCRAPER continually collapsed and rebuilt itself.

Forty floors of industrial steel and glass, the black, silicon fist thrust angrily into the night sky. It stood, immutable, then the glass walls flexed, burst into a billion shards of immensely beautiful silicon glitter that showered onto the Bay City streets below, obscuring the walls of the building as they shattered and fell.

The crowded mall at its base held open arms to the sky, and the splinters of light showered the midnight revelers in a feast of mind-bending beauty before coalescing into the great, glass behemoth once again. A massive sign read SOLD OUT and revealed tonight's featured Rez band, the Howling Pterodactyls, sporting green sequined high-heeled boots and matching bird masks. Their instruments pumped out discordant and unearthly harmonies like a raging nor'easter coming in across a churning sea.

Costumed revelers in outrageous dress, or some hardly dressed at all, throbbed or spun or leaped impossibly far into the air as the music dictated the evening's fanfare. Winged or masked, bare skin or leather wrapped, the assortment of variations on the human form was a sight to behold.

Garik Shayk did a 360 as he topped the hill at First and Syca-more. The chill air pummeled his dark hair as his jet-assist Street Strider leaped to grab the night sky, revealing the black silhouette of the city with the pliable Corona Tower at its center blazing in a spiraling windstorm of light. The ever-fluid building was mesmerizingly malleable as it grew and shrank, pulsing against the eternal backdrop of the Milky Way spanning the midnight sky.

Garik pulled on his makeshift brake and skidded to a stop. His machine rumbled between his thighs, occasionally burping a black cloud of indigestion. The quivering machine vibrated his arms, sending small earthquakes down his torso and into his legs. His clothing rippled next to his skin, more revealing than the slender 17-year-old might have wished, belying his big hands and strong features.

The sight of the Tower sliced his soul with brokenness—no, with anger. His bronze skin kept him from joining the festivities. He was excluded, and for that, he felt he was about to erupt in fury.

"No," Garik whispered into the darkness. "Anger gets me nothing. I must use my hands, my mind, my desire to achieve what I want. Like my Street Strider."

He patted the core of the machine, the jet turbine running between his legs. He had discovered it rotting away behind Kang's Garage underneath a shredded tarp. Kang had offered it in exchange for grunt work around the shop, Garik had begged a few dollars from his aunt for used parts, and now it was his.

The Street Strider coughed, and with a backfire, the darkened intersection went silent.

"No!" Garik hit the kickstand with his heel, jerked his tight, muscular frame erect, and stood with his arms crossed, scowling at the bike. "How can you do this to me again? Every time."

And his watch had been confiscated by his aunt—well, by her no-good boyfriend. He couldn't even call home, not that he would. He loved Irina, but she told everything to Arik, and Arik didn't approve of his freedom on the Strider. Envy, Garik had decided long ago. It was Marisa he trusted. She was like him, a fighter, and like him, she was frustrated by her lack of power to fight the "system."

The "system" was down the hill, parading over the city, melting and reforming on a cycle that was as predictable as rats producing new litters of pups. It taunted him, locked him out, and said that he wasn't good enough to be part of them.

Garik knelt by the cycle and he worked the cover off the high-voltage connectors. Often, this was where the problem was. He flipped the whole-bike breaker, waited to the count of ten, and flipped it back on. He remounted, rested his thumb on the starter switch, and closed his eyes.

Sometimes it started, sometimes it didn't. Garik whispered, "Dear God, Holy Jesus in Heaven," hoping someone up there was paying attention, and he pressed the button.

Nothing. The faint hiss of the Rez band at the Tower rippled around him, but his bike remained silent. The bike was powered, or so resetting the breaker might suggest, but he had forgotten that the jet assist needed to be kick-started using a spark capacitor and a jet-fuel injector. The built-in injector was fried, which meant he had to do this manually.

Garik pulled a small injector from the pack behind him, attached a fuel cell, and inserted the end into a hole he'd drilled in the side of the jet-assist module. He pressed the start button again, triggered the injector, and whispered again, "Dear Holy Father—"

The bike coughed hard enough that he almost lost the injector, but the assist was flaming beautifully. He breathed relief and disconnected the fuel and stored it in his pack. For a moment, with the cold night, he regretted the ceramic shielding insulating the furnace inside, but some warmth escaped. The night would be bitter before he returned home, and by then, no matter how cold the night, he would be grateful the warmth between his legs stayed between his legs.

"YOU KNOW it's not real." Marisa Bruni, petite with Asian features and giant eyes that belied her fierce determination to win every time, drove her stylus hard into her MicroArt tablet. She sat with Garik Shayk on the roof of the building their families shared, wrapped in blankets under the stars, with the howling remnants of the Pterodactyls filtering through the buildings to their ears. "They don't even sound good."

"Still." Garik squeezed his arms around himself, wishing his blanket were heavier. "I wish I were there."

"Well, you're not. Here, what do you think?" Marisa held up the tablet, its tight pool of glowing light shifting from her face to his. "Is it funny, almost funny, or should I just start over?"

"No, no. Don't start over." He took the tablet and worked it into his lap, keeping everything except his fingers inside the blanket.

"Yah! You haven't even looked at it." She was clearly laughing at him. "You are so clueless with the real world. Press here to go to the next image."

Garik watched Marisa's face, mesmerized. She was beautiful, though he had yet to tell her that. She was so focused, knew what she wanted from life, and he was afraid he might lose her if he got in her way. This, well, she wanted to be a graphic artist, and she was always creating storyboards to show him. Sometimes she wiped them all away, gone as soon as he looked at them, saying that she would earn a place on a Mars flight, and her drawings were just for fun. Other times, he saw her look wistfully at the tight and trim people coming and going from The Martial Arts Center, even though she never talked much about the classes she regularly attended at Ai Kee!

Garik? He wanted into the Corona Tower, at least into the mall on an event night. To sit front row to the Pterodactyls, well, maybe not the Pterodactyls, but the group of the week was his dream. To be there when the building shattered into glitter and to look up with his hands in the air as the glitter fell all around him—

"It's not real, Garik. Aren't you even listening?" Marisa pulled the tablet from his hands. "I don't know why I show you my best when you won't even look at it. See? Look at this frame. I have Halo Sunchaser with her electrified sword. She's about to cut off the head of the gorilla thing. I tried to draw a silverback, but I'm not sure I got it right."

"It looks right to me. You're good, Marisa. Don't doubt yourself."

"Oh, you're looking, now?" She laughed. "And that's real, by the way."

"What?" The tablet, the drawing, or what she had drawn?

"The electrified sword. I've seen the schematics for it. If you add ESS when you search Corona Tower slash Halo Sunchaser, you can pull up the working plans to build it, although no one's been able to. I think the schematics are incomplete, and it's so complicated that no one can tell." She giggled, sounding as innocent as she looked.

"No one can tell what?" Garik took the tablet back and expanded the image of Sunchaser with the sword, the ebony face baked into hardness by the white-hot sword vibrating with the unshielded energy of the sun.

"What's missing, that's what. Well, I could tell. No one will be able to build a copy, because they don't want you to."

"How did you know about adding ESS to find the schematics?" The sword in the drawing did look cool. Garik had to admit that.

"Electrified Sword Schematics. E. S. S. Duh. I thought anyone would know that. I tried it with the Tower, but no luck."

"The Tower?" She had his attention, now. If he could get the schematics, perhaps he could find a way for it to let him inside.

"Yep and nope. No go, Bozo. They are secured tighter than a freezer pack of peas. Nothing escapes they don't want to escape. There's got to be a reason for all that security."

"That's easy." Garik had moved on past the electrified sword, and now he was seeing other creatures Marisa had drawn into her graphic storyboard. Winged people, one person dissolving into a purple mist. Others, too. He looked up. "Rich people. Everyone knows the floors up to six are a fancy hotel. Some people live there full time. That would be nice, to be waited on hand and foot. Anyway, they have to provide security for them. That's what it is."

"What's that bird that flies over the water?" The tablet was back in Marisa's hands, and she was leaned into it, drawing away.

"A, um, gull?"

"Yeah, you. Gull-i-ble. What about the other floors? Buildings like that have basements, too. What's so secure about a basement? I say something's fishy."

"Didn't your sister—" As soon as he said the words, he knew it was a mistake. Marisa had never talked about her sister who had supposedly disappeared inside, and everyone had told him she never would. He watched her hands freeze on her MicroArt tablet, and she laid the stylus to the side and clicked it to a special clip, causing the screen to go black.

"All that stuff you see the Tower do isn't real. It's an illusion." She sounded flat, as though she was shifting the topic, nothing else.

"The glass breaking. Sure, I guess I knew that. Still—" He was stupid, and he couldn't believe how much. Stupid, stupid Garik.

"No still, Gari. It's just a building, and the walls are just glass, and they use projectors and such to make it look that way. It's a security distraction to keep you from looking closer. That's all. You're supposed to see the lights, the glitter, the parties on the mall and not notice what they don't want you to see."

"The food court? I mean, that's real. Anyone can visit the food court." At Chow Down, they let you in no matter who you were. He had been there looking for clues, only there were none. Just other city kids, wannabes like him, people who wanted to move into a better life but didn't know where the ladder was.

"And spend money to enrich the people who already have it. I have to work in the flower shop in the morning. I need to get home." She stood, tucking her blanket tighter when it pulled loose on one side. "Your bike, did you secure it?"

"No one would want it." Still, he held up the fob to the cable that looped through the spokes on the wheels and snaked through the hollow jet assist.

"Good. I want to go for a ride on it someday." She looked off across the city. Most lights were off, and the streetlights didn't reach them. "This is my home, but sometimes I don't feel that way. See you later."

Garik watched her tug on her blanket where it was dragging on one corner. She hiked it up, but when she turned it loose, the corner fell back down and trailed the roof anyway. He wanted to offer to help, but he didn't know what to say. He'd already messed up once tonight, and he couldn't risk another misfire.

As he stood, he realized he was still wrapped in her blanket. He smiled and tugged it tighter. One day, he thought. One day, I'm getting in Corona Tower, and when I do, I'm taking you with me. We'll find out what's going on in there, and I bet we can even find that electrified sword. Won't that be cool?

Well, the air was no longer just cool, it was definitely cold. When he began to shiver, Garik made his way to the door into the building. Once inside, he headed down the stairs, light of foot and light of heart, certain that Marisa was as anxious to get inside the Tower as he was, and they would do it together.

Inside his bedroom, he spread the blanket over his bed. He would have to return it tomorrow, but for tonight, dreams of Marisa would keep him company all night long.

— 2 —

"IRI, I'M OUT for the morning." Garik worried the lock fob for the Strider with his thumb. It wouldn't unlock from this distance, but still, he was careful. The small screen showed no attempts to steal it, but he had meant what he said to Marisa. It barely ran and looked worse. Some days, it was hardly worth taking out, as walking was quicker than the time he spent on his knees with the power couplings exposed and his tools deep in the workings of the finicky bucking bronc. "Irina, did you hear?"

"Sorry, Gari." Irina appeared, cocooned in a terry wrap, rubbing her hair with a towel. She kicked aside yesterday's towel, revealing a damp spot on the concrete where last century's linoleum had peeled away. "Do you want breakfast? Arik had to leave early, and I think he ate the last of the eggs. I might have some Crispies."

"Milk?" If Arik had finished off the eggs, likely he'd done the same with the milk.

"Yah! Will I never remember?" Irina hit the heel of her hand to her forehead, shaking her head and rolling her eyes. Her black hair, crimped, wet, and clinging to her neck, took on a life of its own as she hit her forehead a second time.

"It's okay, Iri. Maybe I can snag some fries at the court." It hadn't been a plan, but now maybe it was. After the previous night, and Marisa, and watching the Rez concert from First and Sycamore—

"No, no, my baby nephew." Irina was already in the small kitchen. She dropped her towel on the counter, covering a portion of last night's unwashed plates, and she rummaged through a cabinet. "I have some powdered from last month's box. I know it's here."

"It's okay, Iri. I have a couple dollars, and anyway, people leave fries all the time. I don't mind, especially when they're free." He grinned.

"Here, I found it." Irina held up a clear pouch filled with white powder. Then she looked at it more closely and smiled apologetically. "Ah, I'm sorry, Gari. This is potatoes."

"I like potatoes, just not for breakfast. It's good, really, Iri. I'll get something later."

"Wait, before you go. I don't want you going all the way down to the Tower. See?" She smiled brightly. "I keep up. I know where the court is. It's where all you kids hang out. Do you still call it that, hanging out?"

"Yes, we still hang out." Maybe not hang out. Network or chill, but it was pointless to correct her. Iri still used all her words from when she was seventeen. He had heard them so often that it was like knowing a second and very secret language.

"I don't *want* you to go there, because I don't like what happens there, but *if* you do, you'll go right by Masti's Deli, won't you? I have a twenty. Bring home a pint of milk, will you do that?"

15

Irina rooted in the cabinet and pulled down an old Hersey's Chocolate Powder can, worked the little lid loose, and fished out two bills. She peeled one off, folded it twice, and held it out to Garik. He took it, slipped it into a small pocket, and gave his aunt a kiss on the cheek.

"Bye, Iri. I'll be back before dark."

"Be safe! Arik will be home at four. Be kind, Gari, and don't do anything that's not good."

"Do I ever?" He grinned, waved, and pulled the door open. He understood her warning. Arik would be back at four, and that wasn't a good time for Garik to unexpectedly appear. The two were better apart, especially on days when Garik's Strider was running properly, and he was out and about.

The top of the one tree on Maple Street sported a handful of scraggly leaves just off the balcony leading to the stairwell. Garik leaned out and brushed the one leaf he could reach. Not maple, he was certain. Alder, likely. Anyway, he was glad to have it outside their apartment, and he always told it good morning.

"Good morning, beautiful," he called.

"Thank you. I'm glad you think so."

He leaned out and looked up to see Mrs. Waggoner, the old dame of the building and one of his few friends besides Marisa. "What, the day or the tree, Mrs. Waggoner?"

"Neither, sweetheart. Me, of course. How's that aunt of yours doing? I don't see her out much," Mrs. Waggoner asked in a bright voice. She had a plastic watering can, and she was tipping green-tinted water into each of her hanging pots.

"She doesn't get out much, Mrs. Waggoner. I'll tell her you asked."

"And that boyfriend?" She asked the question hard, and that caused her to tip her can too far. "Oh, my. Didn't mean to do that."

"Arik's at work today." Probably not, but he wasn't here, and that made the day better than it had been.

"Arik?" She inspected one plant for a moment. "Oh, the boyfriend. Where are you off to if you don't mind me asking?"

"Uptown. Might visit the Tower. Got some friends heading that way, see what's left from the concert last night."

"No good. That's what's left. You taking that Marisa with you? Is she your girlfriend, yet?"

"Nah." He felt his face grow hot. It was what he wanted, but she didn't seem to want anyone. Water overflowed one pot, tumbling in a waterfall towards Garik. He drew back and watched it spatter the railing beside him before continuing on its way.

"Did it miss, Garik? Fertilizer. Be careful. You might grow fresh roots."

"Mostly, Mrs. Waggoner. I'll dry, thank you. You be careful with that watering can. You can't be wasting the complex's water."

"Now, now. It'll rain again someday. The catch tanks always fill up again. Always have, always will."

And I would like a real shower, he thought, but he said, "That's right as rain," and he laughed as he took off toward the stairwell.

Mrs. Waggoner was cackling and repeating, "Right as rain," as he slipped inside the door and tripped down the steps. Third floor to ground, at least he had strong legs. He jumped down them four at a time to make the descent go faster. He barely missed a dirty diaper on one step and two broken bottles on the first-floor landing. A new word was scrawled in orange-glow shimmer gel on one wall, crying, "The Tower steals our lives." Garik shrugged. They could steal him if it got him inside. He could always break out again, no matter what people said. If you were clever enough, you could Houdini out of any tight spot.

He wondered who risked gelling the complex's walls. That could get your family kicked out. But the message was forgotten as he vaulted past. The walls were coated with paint repellant. That's the reason for the gel. It would oxidize and turn to powder in a day, leaving no reminder it was there, other than fine orange dust along the baseboard.

On the last run of steps, Wajeha Nayef and Robbie Icardi were lip-locked in an embrace. On the way past, Garik clapped Robbie on the shoulder, hissed, "Bro, really? You're fifteen," and winked at Wajeha. "Get a room," he called back.

At the bottom, he hesitated before throwing back the heavy fire door. He always did this every time since dragging his bike home from Kang's. Sure, he cable-locked it, and he kept the fob safe, but hackers could hack, so nothing was certain safe. You did the best, and you hoped for the best—

Then the door was yanked from his hand, and sunlight flooded in.

"Bout time, Garik."

"Yeah, dude. How come it takes so long for you to come down

17

the stairs? That was at least fifteen seconds this time. We been waiting on you."

"For what?" He stepped outside, blinked as his eyes adjusted, and felt his stomach settle when he found his Strider right where he'd left it. "Yo, Shrimper. What's you doing on my bike?"

Shrimper was about eight, and with skin hard to see in shadows or in the dark, he was the go-to gofer for the wannabe gang of preteens chilling in the parking lot.

"We going for a ride today?" The little guy had his hands on the bars. He could barely reach them, but he was imagining he was the king of the road, at least until he had to brake or shift gears.

"Places to go." Garik lifted the fob, placed his thumb on the screen, and heard the sharp click as the lock released. A second click, and the cable wound into the locking mechanism and the unit tumbled to the ground with a clank of hollow metal against solid concrete. "Maybe to the court. Fries for breakfast."

"Nah." A thin blond about eleven named Winter scoffed. "Heard they had a concert last night. Dactyls. Probly still stringing the last wails from their guitars."

"I heard them." Garik knelt and opened a compartment in the bike and slipped the lock inside.

"You was there?" The rest of the boys drew in like they were links in a chain, pulled forward by the teeth of a turning crankset. "You saw the Dactyls? Cool."

"Maybe." Garik pulled out a pair of fat eye shields and closed the compartment. He stood, trying to act as if last night were nothing.

"Saw you with Marisa on the roof." A small redhead who went by Firestarter piped in. "While they was still playing."

"Can I get a break? I got my Strider. How else you think I got there and back?" Garik laughed and swung his leg over and kicked up the stand. He set his eye shield on his nose and strapped it in back. He would be blinded in the sun otherwise.

"Ain't letting you in. Only richies get into the concerts." Winter. "Bet you was liplocking on the roof."

The boys began to chant, "Liplocking, liplocking. Garik's been liplocking."

"Didn't say I was at the concert." Garik gave in a tiny bit to divert their attention from their little game, while admitting more of the truth than he'd hoped. "Said I saw the Dactyls, and that's the

18

truth. But if you're going to be like that, I'm going now, cause the court's open to everyone. I'll eat a fry for you and you and you." He pointed at each of the boys, laughing. "Out of the way. Don't want you to get burned."

Garik held his breath and hit the starter twice, hoping the Strider didn't embarrass him. It was bad enough when he saw other riders give him the stink eye because of the rust, but to not start with his little "hood" standing around watching? That would be mortifying.

The Strider fired up perfectly, and Garik let himself breathe again. He grinned and nodded at Shrimper. "A fry for you." He fed excess fuel into the jet, and it roared. Then, looking up to see Mrs. Waggoner on her floor's balcony leaning out and looking down at him, he backed off, released the makeshift brake, and let the vibrating machine trundle out of the lot and through the heavy iron security gate.

"Even we gotta have protection," he said, spinning up the jet's turbine and bumping along Maple, what seemed to be the city's most poorly maintained road. "Always people poorer than you are, no matter who you are. Richer, too, though I wouldn't mind that."

Too bad Robbie was liplocking. He mighta liked a free ride to the court, that and free fries.

He tried to picture who might show. Maria Putin, with her black bobbed hair and big earrings, Regina Kournikova, lithe and blonde, a cheerleader back in high school, maybe Vladimir Varlamov, the weightlifter of the group, and Giorgio Versace, wannabe fashion icon. Vladimir and Giorgio were always hip-to-hip, different as night and day but in each other's pockets everywhere the group went. Where Vladimir was found, Giorgio wasn't too far away, yeah, like that.

On Sycamore and crossing Third, with seven blocks to go, he saw three of the "posse" heading in. Ibn Hariri, with flowing locks and the start of a scraggly beard, Muhammad Saud, wearing a skull-cap with a skull stitched into the fabric and a tattered knit sweater, and Hayat al-Haber, in his headscarf and robe, were on their long-boards, skipping off curbs and back on again. Garik slowed enough for Ibn to grab hold before he gunned the jet assist, and the bike began to fly. It only coughed once, and it didn't cut off at all. About halfway to Fifth, Ibn released his hold, flew up a handicap ramp, and did a 360 around a light pole.

Garik was stoked. Not having to see Arik this morning, and now, his friends at the court? This might well be the best day of his week.

— 3 —

GARIK PRESSED the thumbscreen on his lock's fob and looked skyward. Corona Tower. Forty stories of mystery, fascination, and wealth drawing in the city's elite and wannabes, all hoping for access to the inner sanctum of the powerful and the great.

"Garik, what's with you?" Ibn Hariri bumped his shoulder with a fist. "The court's down *here*, my friend. Up there, that's not a place we will ever go."

"Yeah." Garik shrugged, hardly able to tear his eyes away. How did they do it, he wondered? The lightshow, the black glitter, the diamond sparkles flowing down the building, the entire thing *gone*. Then, it was back again, whole, ready to do it all over again.

"So, your attention. Huh, Garik? Let me join you." Ibn pressed his shoulder to Garik's and stared skyward. He balanced his board upright, bright yellow with an Arabic graphic scrawled down the center, one truck black and the other gleaming silver, both scuffed with road and rock and steel, one end on the ground, and the other loosely in his downturned palm. The board complemented Ibn's shiny locks, sometimes in dreads, now free to blow in the breeze.

"What's this?" Hayat al-Haber's board was still grounded, one foot controlling its motion, and he rolled forward to stand with Garik and Ibn. With his headscarf and rope, he leaned especially far back to see what the attraction was so far overhead. "I see clouds, but only a few. What, what? This is interesting? Come, Muhammad. We have found something to look at."

The board under Hayat's shoe was a gridwork overlaid with unicorns and fairy dust. His older sister, Akilah, had skated before she married, and it was a good board, so why let it go to waste? It still had its neon pink wheels. Muhammad Saud walked up, his board under one arm, revealing skulls and bones on the bottom and painted blood splatters on the top. His wheels were burgundy, like blood flowing from his white-painted trucks.

"Dundersaps. The real vision is *there*." Muhammad pushed himself through the trio blocking his way, making room for his skateboard with a big hand, and he took the steps up to the mall's main concourse three at a time. At the top, he turned and laughed. He nodded his head to the open area of the food court. "Coming? Or you want to gawk while I grease my chompers and fill my belly?"

"Come, Garik. Breakfast." Ibn laughed, yanked his board upward and caught it under his arm. He only managed two steps for each leap. The morning sun cut through the city's buildings with laser slices of light. One caught Ibn's silver truck as he leaped, flashed, and then was gone.

Garik shifted gears more slowly. His stomach growled, and he thought of his aunt's twenty. That would buy a full stomach, but then he had to return home. Arik. Irina would tell him, "Gari's bringing the milk. I gave him the money," and Arik would be angry that Irina had saved back some, but he would be angrier that Garik spent any of it on something for himself.

He decided that he would have to be especially quick. There would be abandoned fries on the tables and probably on the floor, but he would leave those. The tabletop fries would be enough for him to not leave hungry. He took the steps in a rush to find Ibn already locking his board into the secure racks on the mall's perimeter. Boards were ubiquitous. Everyone rode them, yet they weren't welcome in the food court. No one would come to the food court without their boards, so the secure racks, exposed wire cages fitted with built-in locks, were the answer. Insert your board, take the key, and pick up your board when you returned.

Beyond the racks, the mall stretched for blocks, enough for an entire Dactyls concert, as Garik had seen last night from First and Sycamore. Now, there was no sign any such event had occurred. The platform, sure, that was permanent, but the tables, the chairs, the open bar that had livened up the patrons. All gone.

At the center, Corona Tower reared its massive bulk on giant steel and brick piers, hulking over the mall like an enormous spider about to strike its prey. The food court underneath was open on every side, already filling with diners of all colors and ethnic backgrounds. Kaftans, robes, and saris glittered alongside studded leather jackets, miniskirts, and neon boots. Even a cowboy hat or two. One table was crowded with crop-haired military types in casual fatigues and heavy boots, not surprising with the Air Force base just to the west of Bay City. They wore matching mirrored shades, even in the false lighting of the towering structure overhead.

Along the back wall, where the sun crashed into the building and promised a searing day, the darkened glass walls remained fixed in place. As the sun crawled from dawn to noon to dusk, the glass walls would follow, slipping up into the mass of the building, or folding out of the way, as dictated by the design of the mall. The food court was nominally at the core of the Tower, tucked into the central nexus of the leviathan, but on mornings after a concert, the city around the Tower vibrated with anticipation, as if each person felt a new connection with the mystery behind the Tower's elaborate security that overshadowed every other endeavor. The food court grew to encompass the mall, with additional tables, mobile servicing kiosks, and teams of cleaning crews to keep it all spotless. The people of the city, disenfranchised and otherwise, wanted to be here, to join in, even if they knew they would never score admission into the real party when the walls around the mall rose up, blocking the rabble from entering, so that the elite, whoever they were, could dance and drink to excess all night long.

And so, there it was again, the wall, city people on the outside, Tower people in, with the message, "You can have a taste of what we offer, but only in the food court. The rest is private, so vamoose, you leaden deadbeats."

The four youths dispersed into the cave-like court, a wave of interconnecting action, taking advantage of the tight groups, those with hangers on, and others who were lone diners. They eyed people standing, walking away, some policing their own tables, and others leaving their detritus to the cleaning crews. With practice, it was easy to tell which was which. The carelessness of a cup set to the side, forgotten in a moment of discussion, scattered fries, a breakfast burrito half eaten and returned to a tray. In ten minutes, they had a tableful of food. They pooled their change, and two drinks, two empty cups, and they had four drinks all around.

The conversation was a cyclone of boarding, girls, and was anyone going back to school when the session started up again? Girls were on everyone's mind, and not returning to school? It might be wishful dreaming, but to say it meant they could imagine.

Garik studied the perimeter of the court and what he could see of the massive legs holding up the Tower. He thought of the Dactyls the night before and what Marisa had said about the black glitter. He popped a cold fry into his mouth, and as he chewed, he blurted, "How do they do it?"

"You must be clear, my Russian friend." Muhammad reached to Garik and pushed him on the chest. "Do what?"

"Skateboard, of course. What else? Why, it is speed, my friend.

Quickness and speed. It's the only way to get that much height." Ibn grinned at him. "Me? I just find a steep hill, and then I hold on for the ride."

"Hold on to what?" Muhammad licked ketchup off one finger, and he poked Ibn in the arm. Muhammad and Hayat laughed, while Ibn flushed.

"I mean the building." Garik thought his question was obvious. He pushed the wrapper with its cold fries away and took the good end of a half-eaten breakfast burrito from in front of Hayat, tore off and dropped the chewed end back to the table, and sank his teeth in. He spoke carefully around his food. "Last night, Marisa said the tower at night is all fake."

"What, like, like not real?" Hayat pushed his robe from his wrists and took the burrito back from Garik. He offered a trade. "You take the danish."

It was a rule of thumb that they never scavenged anything liquid like soups or wet cereal. Only things they could break off or separate out. The danish had been untouched, still wrapped, and they had nearly passed it up. It was a prize.

"You've seen it during concerts. Well, any night, but all out when there's a band." Garik didn't want the danish, but he pinched off a bit as a peace offering for taking Hayat's preferred burrito, and he popped it in his mouth.

"Nope, my friend!" Ibn flicked a tater tot upward and caught it on his tongue before pulling it into his teeth and biting into it. "No one sells *me* tickets. You, Hayat, Muhammad? You ever had a ticket appear in your hands?"

"Not from inside, Ibn, but we've all watched from the city." Garik had asked a real question, and a stab of anger made him want to slap the tater tot from Ibn's mouth. He bit his rush of irritation back. My mind, my reasoning, not anger. Explain, Garik, that's all you need to do. Yet, sometimes, it was hard.

His life. How could anyone not be frustrated with a life like his?

"You all know," Garik encouraged. "Look out any window, and you'll see it, even if they don't let us into the events."

"Not from my apartment." Hayat made a dismissive gesture. "We see nothing but a blank wall. Every window, blank wall for a view. I thought America was land of the free, with waves of grain and purple mountains. I have never seen one of these."

"Well, I'm not locked in my aunt's apartment. I get out, and I see things." Garik's frustration wasn't with his friends, but with the Tower overhead, yet he was tired of patience, being pushed aside, and feeling he was never good enough.

"And you have a Street Strider." Muhammad tucked into a fry, looking at his hands and brandishing the skull on his cap where his face belonged.

"That I found broken and worked to bring back to life."

"Sometimes back to life," Ibn cackled. "When it's not broken again on the side of road."

"Seriously, about the Tower." Garik felt a bit of a sulk coming on, and he quelled it with a grimace. "I don't see any projectors, and Marisa said it's all done with projectors. Do you guys see anything like that?"

"Ask the man upstairs." Hayat pointed to the ceiling overhead. "They know."

Across the food court, the closely cropped crew in military fatigues had finished, and they were walking toward a trash bin. Being military, they had, of course, policed their table, and it was bagged and in their hands. A solidly built man with the name Han stitched onto his shirt nodded at the boys. He held one brightly emblazoned Chow Down bag that seemed especially full. He said something to the rest of his crew and stepped the boys' way.

"Need more?" He held out the bag, his face expressionless but not unkind. When the youths remained silent, he said, "I saw you scrounging. Well done. Most people didn't notice. I did, and this is extra. Do you want it or not?"

"Thank you, Mr. Han." Garik stood and accepted the bag.

"Wu Han, Airman First Class. And you?"

"Garik Shayk, and my friends are Ibn Hariri, Muhammad Saud, and Hayat al-Haber in the headscarf." Hayat held out one corner of his headscarf as if to preen. "Are you going to rat us out to them?" He thumbed upstairs.

"Not if you're the one with the Strider outside." He pointed to Garik and winked, letting the youth know that he'd been watching them since they arrived. "I'm a cycle man myself, and that Strider's a classic. Haven't seen one of those since I left South Korea. Annyeong, my young friends. Good-bye."

Han turned sharply, and in moments, he had caught up with his friends. Garik and his crew? They tore into the Chow Down bag and discovered more good treats than even Garik's twenty would have been able to afford.

4

THE BOYS, now sated, took their time picking at the food littering the table.

The sun had started to climb into the sky, becoming an overhead furnace and blistering the outside portions of the mall. Those who had been seated in the open air earlier in the morning had begun to migrate underneath the building. With a click and the rattle of gear-driven chains, the fourth wall of the court began to lift into the superstructure, leaving the entire span underneath the Tower open to the city, except for the center where the food court hawked its wares with neon signs that flashed brighter and brighter even as the sun tried to wash their messages away.

Outside, the giant sign for publicizing the Tower's next big event and broadcasting the remaining available tickets was dark, except for the Tower logo at the top, blazing even in the glare of the midmorning sun as the image of the Tower exploded and rebuilt itself over and over in a kaleidoscopic display of color. Above the boys' heads, on multiple screens lining the interior of the food court, cartoon characters sang and danced. Later, when the lunch crowd arrived, the screens would shift to clips from current movies or from video games, teasers to tempt diners to part with their money in the Tower's 10-Plex before they made their way home or to go online and download the latest Tower games. 30 days for free, and only a small, weekly charge to continue playing your NEWEST FAVORITE GAME.

In the mornings? The court touted their menus instead of ads, offering chicken bits, tacos, or tasty French toast bites with honey. Occasionally, the Tower's upcoming concert attractions flashed across the screens, with ticket prices, remaining available seats, and reservation numbers to call NOW, NOW, NOW.

Three adults stepped in out of the sun, trailed by several children in party hats. Two more adults joined them, towing several more children with balloons, and between them, they filled several tables. A cake with eight candles appeared out of a brightly colored box.

"Look, look." Hayat pointed. "That, I could like a taste of. No one leaves cake. Just old fries." He shrugged as if vastly disappointed.

"Here." Garik pushed the danish from earlier his direction. "Why wait? Have it now." He set the bag from the Airman aside, brushing two empty cups, and barely catching one when it almost tumbled. The danish had been ignored in the excitement of the Airman's mystery bag.

"Have it now." Muhammad repeated Garik's words, slapped the table excitedly, and pointed to one of the large screens lining the inside perimeter of the underbuilding portion of the mall. "Have it now!" blared an invitation to everyone in the food court. Visit the Tower's luxury Stamford Suites, spanning the second through sixth floors, with direct, exclusive access to the hotel through the Corona Tower Parking Garage, with FREE PARKING validated for all hotel guests. The words changed to a picture of the garage and the double glass doors that accessed the Corona Tower's luxurious first floor. Then it flipped to the pool (that no one in the food court had ever visited in real life), the tennis court, sample rooms with luxurious fabrics and vast walls of windows, and finally a smiling face. A bright, cheerful voice called out, "Gunther Diehl, your concierge, is waiting on YOU. Come see him to make your reservation today!"

The camera backed out to reveal Gunther at a black granite desk, with a glass-covered atrium rising around him on three sides. The blue sky beyond the glass was too perfectly painted with a color that barely looked real, and wispy clouds made the blue deeper and richer than any sky ever was.

Then all the screens flashed at once, going white and fading to purple and finally black. Small neon diamonds flooded in from the edges, blinking rapidly in a staccato barrage of colors. The Corona Tower logo flashed on each screen, each one identical, with the black diamond glitter falling from a velvet sky.

"Welcome, Diners." Speakers blasted the salutation throughout the court. "Thank you for visiting the Corona Tower food court. We have what you need when you need it. Why wait, when you can get it now?"

The voice was accompanied by booming music, not as discordant as the Pterodactyls' wailing chords but too loud for easy conversation. The boys at the table with Garik watched the screens, as Garik was sure the advertisement intended.

"Corona Tower would like to announce, coming this Friday night, for your enjoyment at the Corona Mall—" the voice and music growing louder with each word, "—the sensation of the summer, the great, the wonderful, the amazing—"

"Cord and Roy!" Muhammad hooted the words. Cord and Roy were street fighters. Muhammad had posters of them on his walls at his grandmother's apartment.

"Jezebel and the Sticks." Ibn thumped the table, then he said it again several times. "Jezebel and the Sticks. Jezebel and the Sticks." Jezebel and the Sticks was an alternative band Ibn had heard in Azerbaijan while staying with his uncle the previous summer.

Garik and Hayat watched each other, a grin of anticipation revealing the whites of their teeth.

"Jantzen Hefferly and the amazing Purple Mist!"

"Huh?" Garik and Hayat shrugged, but the screens had jumped to a man in black, hooded, with black gloves covering his hands, and they turned to watch, along with everyone else in the court. The man in black stepped out of swirling purple fog and tossed his hood back to reveal a narrow face with black hair and a tight beard. His eyes glittered the same purple as the fog.

The voice swelled, "Get your tickets now for one night only, this Friday at the Corona Mall!"

The man in black evaporated into purple smoke. His gloves, coat, and hood crumpled to the ground, disappearing into the fog as the smoke swelled out of the openings in the cloth and coalesced into a man-like form before whipping away like it had been caught in a stiff breeze.

Reservation information flashed on the screens, and outside, the giant sign blared on in a flash of chaotic color before the words, "Jantzen Hefferly and the Amazing Purple Mist," rolled into position at the top, and "Friday Only" at the bottom. In between, a two-meter-tall number pulsed.

"Ten thousand." Ibn looked around at the people sitting underneath the massive tower, taking advantage of the shaded food court. The adults with the birthday party had barely glanced at the promotion for the upcoming Hefferly event. One of the little partiers was running free with a balloon in her hand, and her mouth was plastered with white and blue frosting. Two adults were chasing her, not with much luck.

Past the central nexus with its blazing neon signs, a group of well-dressed and obviously well-heeled citizens with heavily stitched boots, diamond-studded leather satchels, and elaborately styled hair lounged over a small cadre of tables. Before the announcement was over, they had their smart watches logging on to the Tower's webpage for a link into the Corona Mall's available ticket database.

"Ten thousand, what the mall can accommodate." Garik whistled. "And it'll be full at that."

"What if we could score a ticket?" Muhammad's eyes twinkled.

"Even better, a dozen. See? We're here, now. This is our Allah-given opportunity. Just go online, and we're in."

"And do what? You have a couple thousand you can shred on that, a magician?" Garik scoffed, although yes, he would if he could. But the twenty in his pocket, the tickets were ten times that for the cheapest, and the best? So far out of sight it might as well be green cheese from the moon.

"I get it," Ibn said. "Not buy, Garik. Scalp, make two for one. Spend three, make six, keep three. I'm in. Who's got a watch?"

"Yo kay. As always, I got this, you dunderdudes." Muhammad sighed and reached inside his tattered knit, and he pulled out a leather pouch attached to a cord around his neck. He unzipped it, pulled out an earbud and slipped it in place. He held the watch just above the table and said, "On, Ratchet."

Outside, the sign had begun to change. What had been ten thousand minutes before was now below eight and blinking fast.

"Faster, Mo," Hayat encouraged. He pointed to the sign, the arm of his robe like an angel wing as he flapped it emphatically. "Everybody else will be there before us. All gone." He waved both arms, and with the sun behind him, his thin body was a skeleton animating his white wings.

"Hush, dunderpuss. Ratchet only goes so fast." Muhammad's eyes remained fixed on the watch. He touched it once, then leaned in, speaking slowly and enunciating clearly. "Corona Mall tickets, Friday, Jantzen Hefferly. Twelve, please." He looked up and grinned. He glanced back at the watch and frowned. "No, twelve." The watch said something to him over his earbud, and a look of irritation passed over his face. "Oh, sorry. I didn't realize there was a limit. Four, then. Sure. Let me thumb you the approval."

He reached to place his thumb on the watch face when Hayat jumped from his seat, yelling, "It is almost zero!"

Garik's eyes were locked on the sign. In a matter of minutes, it had gone from ten thousand to only hundreds. He didn't know how he would pay for his share of the bill, but he would if he had to wash windows for Mrs. Waggoner. He'd even water her plants, for a year, even if it killed him.

"Faster, Muhammad," he said under his breath, afraid to commit to how much he wanted this, because city people never scored tickets to the events at the mall. The wall came up and they watched from the outside, if they could see anything at all. "Please."

Garik turned to Muhammad, unable to watch his dreams count down to nothing on the board, and willed Muhammad's thumb to connect before the last tickets were gone.

Then all the screens in the food court pulsed in a flashing cacophony of light, with Sold Out on each one. The sign outside now boasted a big fat zero, then with a twinkling spray of fireworks light, the zero changed to SOLD OUT.

"Mo?" Ibn held his breath, his cheeks red, as he looked at his friend with his thumb pressed against his watch.

"Move, move your thumb." Hayat twisted one corner of his headscarf. "We wish to see, Muhammad."

"You're the dunderpuss," Garik teased, his stomach sick with hope. "Come on."

"Here's the truth. Four tickets. Of that, I am sure." He pulled his thumb away, and his face fell.

"What?" Ibn leaned in and pulled on Muhammad's hand. "Show us."

Muhammad turned the watch around so the others could see the screen. It was as Garik had expected, though not as he had hoped. They were right here. No one could have tried any harder or faster, and the tickets were all gone.

Then cheers of triumph erupted from across the court. The well-heeled, diamond-studded fluencers were cheering. Once man wearing a studded belt and a diamond in each ear pumped his hand in the air and yelled out, "Fifty! For me and all my friends!"

Garik glanced outside at the sign and the words SOLD OUT and back to the upper-crust Tower type cheering his fifty tickets. He caught Muhammad's look of disgust as he stuffed his earbud and watch away and dropped the leather back down the neck of his shirt.

It was as always, Garik thought, deflated despite not really expecting to get in to see Jantzen Hefferly and his amazing mist, whatever that had been. Video trickery, but cool, anyway.

"Let's go, my friend." Ibn slapped his shoulder. The others were standing, already. "We are not Tower people. This is more proof. But we are friends, and that is better than a purple mist any day."

"Right." Garik grinned. Still, though. One time. He wanted to be *in* just *one time.*

5

GARIK SNIFFED of the underside of the small refrigerator in his aunt's apartment and jerked his head back in disgust.

"So, my sweet nephew. Is it dead?" Irina held a bottle of milk, half empty, and she removed the lid.

"I hope not, Iri. I may have to see if the junkyard has a new compressor. Did you know you have dead rat babies in here? I think the momma ate through the wiring."

"Rats? Probably from Shelina's next door. She's always catching rats in her traps. She puts them on the super's doorstep. Is this spoilt? Arik will be crazy if there's no milk for his Posties." Irina held the milk Garik's direction.

The fridge was in the middle of the kitchen, tilted forward and leaning face down on a chair. Everything from inside covered the counters and spilled over onto the small dining table. Water dripped from the freezer compartment, and Irina pushed a soggy towel into the spreading puddle.

"Not if it's cold. Or cool. Nothing's cold. Sorry. This rat nest smells. I don't think I'll be a good judge for your milk." He reached inside the broken appliance with a small wrench and worked to free the broken part.

"Maybe Arik will be late today. He doesn't need to know about this." Irina sloshed the milk hopefully, screwed the lid back on, and set it in a bowl of ice on the table next to a nearly full bottle of ketchup. "Or the fridge, if you can get it fixed, Gari."

"Maybe he won't come home at all," Garik muttered. He didn't mind being the fix-it guy for his aunt. She usually said thank you and seemed appreciative when he repaired things around the apartment. She also helped him with his own projects when she could squeeze a few dollars from the household budget. Arik? Garik didn't enjoy helping him at all. Even when he did things right, like when he got the television working last month after it had been cutting off during Arik's favorite shows for weeks, all his aunt's boyfriend had been able to say was a growled, "About time. If we're going to provide a room for you to park your lazy backside, the least you can do is keep things working around here."

Well, it wasn't his fault that Arik couldn't hold a decent job, or that old televisions went out, or that there wasn't enough money to replace the fridge or the toaster, or any of the other things Garik had worked on the past year.

"Got it free." Garik sat up and displayed the small compressor. He picked off the part of the nest he'd pulled out with it. He stood and slipped it into a purple-colored, wrinkled plastic bag with Fasst Market on the side in white letters and tied the built-in handles together. "I'll be back with a new one quick as I can. Do me a favor, Iri. Clean the nest and chuck it all. Will you, for me?" He smiled and kissed her on the cheek. He didn't wait for her answer before disappearing out the door. Irina would do it or not, depending on how distracted she was. She would agree because she wanted him to be happy, but he didn't want her to feel like she had lied to him if she didn't get it done.

Garik didn't try to peg his aunt to too high a bar. It hurt too much each time she fell off.

Once outside, he checked to see that Mrs. Waggoner's plants weren't flooding his escape route, flew down the stairwell—only watching enough to avoid stepping into something he might have to wipe off his shoe—and burst out of the building. No preteen crew to greet and tease, something he enjoyed, but just now hoped to avoid. Tonight was about meeting up with some of his friends. He could only pull that off if he could avoid Arik, and in the tiny apartment, he could only avoid the man if he was gone when he got home.

He weighed taking the Street Strider. It was faster—if it worked there and back, but he couldn't leave it on the street if it broke. He touched his fob, thinking of the time gained. Even if he locked it, there were people that knew how to pick locks, given time, and even if his lock notified him his bike was being stolen, he wouldn't be able to do anything about it except watch it be carted away.

He stepped back inside and behind the stairs where a long corridor revealed chain link lockups for the residents, the one good thing about living in City View Apartments. Maybe the only good thing, except for Marisa. He keyed the four-digit code, pulled out his board, a Santa Cruz Classic Dot deck in blue, yellow, and red with black wheels. It had been his only wheels before the Strider. He still rode, though he borrowed at the skate park mostly—Muhammad's wicked skulls or even Hayat's unicorns. He slammed the gate, checked the lock, and fell onto his board once he hit the parking lot, brushing by the Strider and trailing four fingers along the jet-assist tube before vaulting out of the lot and onto the sidewalk beside Maple.

"Hey," a male voice called as Garik pushed himself forward.

Garik gripped his plastic Fasst Market bag tightly and turned to see Robbie Icardi, with his shined hair and dark sunglasses waving.

"Later, Robbie," Garik yelled with a wave. He looked forward just in time to dodge around a brown Lab doing its business on the sidewalk, and Garik laughed as the dog's eyes grew wide and it tried to scoot sideways to give him room. "Sorry, Catnip. Catch you later."

He was already out of sight, and Garik leaned into his board, pumped with his feet a couple of times, and flew across Avenue C at a crosswalk light that seemed to know he was coming.

"Thanks, light," he called.

It was mostly downhill, though gradual. Past Ninth and the train station, Bay City dropped off toward The Docks another twenty blocks away. He was only going as far as Eighth, and he pumped as often as he hunched down and flew, weaving around pedestrians, and only once stopping when a light refused to give him permission to cross without paying the penance for arriving too early. Flying through Washington where it turned into Eighth Avenue, the sign for We Got Junk appeared halfway down the block.

Garik skidded through the tall industrial doors that opened to a vast array of disassembled machines where he stepped off his Cruz and kicked one end up into his big hand. He looked around, saw who he was looking for, and called out, "Hey, Wesji. Got something I need you to help me find."

"Yo, dudette. You help me, I help you. Deal? What's it today?" The big man wore greasy coveralls, and his head spouted a denim hat with the We Got Junk logo on the front.

"This." Garik held up the purple Fasst Market bag. We Got Junk was how Garik had repaired his bike on the cheap. Wesji let him trade off around the shop, disassembling or sweeping up for the used supplies he needed. "It's a compressor for an EverKool 7.0."

"EverKool." Wesji pulled a rag from a back pocket and wiped his hands. "Bottom freezer?"

"Top." Wesji's question gave Garik reason to hope. If he was asking, then he knew what Garik needed. If he knew, then he likely had one, and EverKools were as common as trucks on a skater's board. Like, two-to-a-person.

"You disassemble five EverKools and sort the parts, and I can give you one compressor guaranteed to work when you walk out the door." Wesji took the bag and pulled out the broken compressor. He hefted it and sighed. "You need coolant, too?"

"Maybe." Garik grinned. Good ol' Wesji. Coming through as always. "Can I do the fridges in a couple days? I got things planned, you know, with friends."

"Ah, to be seventeen again. Sure, kid. This salvageable?" He held out the compressor, eyeing it critically.

"I think it's just the cords. I found a rat's nest packed around it." Garik pointed to one wire where it exited the unit. Toothmarks showed through the black insulation, and one wire was severed.

"Ah, easy as grandma's pie. Sure, three EverKools by Tuesday, and we're even. How's that, Garik, my little friend?"

"Thanks, Wesji. You're awesome. Are the compressors still in the back by the bathtubs?" Garik was already backing away, aware that time was of the essence if he wanted to make his escape from the apartment before Arik claimed his evening.

"No one's moved them. Go. Get a can of refrigerant at the front desk." Wesji waved him away with his rag and turned without waiting on Garik to see where he headed.

Garik leaned his board against a rack of doorknobs and bathroom faucets, and he tore down the open aisle, barely catching himself, slipping on the gritty floor, as he dived into the compressors. Breathlessly, he scanned the shelves next to the bathtubs, his eyes jumping past piping, used toilets, and a scattered array of disassembled appliances. The compressors had been moved from the middle shelf to the bottom, despite Wesji's reassurances, replaced by a rack of sealed-glass stove burners. Garik squatted, ran his hand down the dusty compressors until he found one that looked right. A paper tag attached with a string said, "EverKool 5.5-9.8."

"Gotcha." He snatched it up and tucked it under his arm. On the way out, he waved to Ulldressa, high on a ladder behind the payment desk. He started to explain that he had permission from Wesji to take the compressor and can of coolant, when she called down, "Refrigerant is in the yellow bag. Just plug it into the port once you get it attached. Be careful on that skateboard."

"Bye. I will." And he was gone, his wheels miniature tornadoes pushing him along.

"HEY, MARI." Garik held his board in one hand as he burst through the stairwell door and the yellow bag with the compressor and refrigerant in the other. He was surprised but pleased to see her sitting in the stairwell.

"No wonder I couldn't find you." She pointed to the board.

He shrugged. "I've got a fridge to fix, hopefully before Arik comes home." He held up the yellow bag.

"Too late." She smiled apologetically, the bearer of bad news. "I thought you'd forgotten how to ride the old Cruz."

"Never. Couldn't risk the Strider breaking down." He looked upstairs, his heart sinking, and his stomach churning. "You saw Arik?" He wanted her to say she was teasing. Please, he begged. Teasing, Marisa. Teasing.

"I'll carry this." She reached for the board and headed towards the storage lockers. "I hoped you'd come with us to see if we can see any of the show at the Tower."

"The show at the Tower?" No! Unfair!

"You repeating me, now, Gari?" She rapped his forehead with her knuckles.

"Hefferly, right? Isn't it purple fire or something? How, I mean, if it was music, you could hear everything, but a magic act? You won't be able to see anything, and there'll be nothing to hear." Still, to go, to at least try to get a peek.

"Alexi's uncle has an apartment on Sycamore. We're meeting there. From his roof, Alexi says you can see the mall."

"Alexi's in detention." They were at the gate, and Garik entered the code twice before it took. He opened the gate and turned to Marisa before stepping in. "How are you meeting at Alexi's uncle's if Alexi's in detention?"

"Not exactly at his uncle's. His uncle's out of town. Alexi knows the passcode into the building, that's how."

"Oh." He worked his Santa Cruz into the piles of stuff and pushed the gate to as he exited, rattling it to be sure it was locked.

"I have to . . ." He reached for the sack.

"Fix the fridge, I know. I was up to see your aunt. When I found your bike still here, I hoped you were back. I stayed in the stairwell to warn you about Arik."

"I—" His voice broke. He wanted to go, to see the show, to look down on the mall if he couldn't be on the mall, to try to see Jantzen

Hefferly do his purple thing, the one that had looked so cool on the promotion at the food court. "I—I have to go upstairs and fix the fridge."

"You want to borrow my electrified sword?" She pulled a folded page of paper from a pocket. "I brought it to give you power, if you think it will help. I think I got the schematics figured out, so it's fully charged and operational."

He laughed and accepted the offering, unfolding it. She had drawn herself as Sunchaser, with two electrified swords on her back. He looked up and grinned. "Thank you."

"Maybe this will help. Kevin Lee from Ai Kee! is auditioning for a film role tomorrow at The Martial Arts Center. One o'clock, and the public is invited to watch and cheer. I scored two tickets. Want to go with me and meet him? He might even show us some moves." She smiled, her eyes a peace offering, soothing the knowledge that his aunt's boyfriend would likely make Garik's evening a brutal nightmare.

"Thanks, Marisa. Okay. Sure, if I survive the night with Arik eating all my happy thoughts and vomiting them all over me."

"Baby. You're tougher than you know. Get up there and cool your aunt's milk. She's afraid it will spoil, and no one likes spoilt milk."

"Least of all Arik." He grinned. "See you tomorrow."

Garik took his bag and leaped up the steps, taking them three at a time. If he was to be dinner, he might as well get started and get it done. Maybe Arik would fall asleep in front of the television, and he could disappear to his room, stuck at home, but so clearly not stuck in the same room with his aunt's grumpy boyfriend.

— 6 —

THE NEXT morning, Garik flew down the steps in the stairwell, grateful not to have seen anyone up and about in the apartment. It was far too early to meet up with Marisa, but that didn't mean he had to sit in the apartment and stare at Arik's bristly mug while the man slurped his milk out of his bowl as he ate breakfast. Better to be out and about in the city, maybe on his bike.

He had his watch back—*thank you, Arik, but not really, you big lump*—and could call to see who could meet up with him to do something. Too bad it couldn't be Jantzen Hefferly and his purple

35

fog, but maybe he could hear about it. When second best was dished your way, sometimes that's what you had to take.

He burst through the door to the parking lot and drew up short. Arik sat on his bike, sideways, one leg propped up on the jet-assist tube, and a smoke dangling from between two fingers. When he saw Garik, he blew out a twin stream of smoke through his nostrils.

"What are you doing down here?" Garik couldn't think what else to say. Arik, *Arik was sitting on his Street Strider.*

"Better said, I knew you would be down here, and now you are. I need this bike unlocked."

"What for?" Garik felt of the fob around his neck. It was his, his fob, his bike, his thumbprint to unlock the lock. Arik had *no right.*

"Now, kid, easy or hard, which way do you want it? It's not my fault you let the fridge break, not my fault that you took that dinky skaterboard looking for parts, not my fault that you're such a good-for-nothing that this *whole complex is falling apart brick by brick.*" The man had gone from a light rain to a thunder squall in the space of one sentence and was now yelling.

"How am I responsible for how the complex is maintained?" You, he thought. You're the one who won't look for a new apartment. You're the one whose credit keeps my aunt and me living in this hovel. *You, Arik.*

Anger boiled, but Garik dared not breathe those words, not if he wanted any freedom at all. He'd be grounded for the rest of the summer if he gave Arik the least reason.

"Unlock, please." Arik was calmer, even placating, but that was like him, softening up his prey so he could strike again. He crooked the two fingers holding his smoke and pulled them to him several times in rapid succession. "Now."

"Sometimes the bike breaks, Arik. It just stops dead, and I have to pull over and repair it." And Arik wouldn't know how, would walk off from it, and it would be unlocked and easy pickings for anyone who happened to be interested.

"Should'a thought of that when you let the milk spoil. And I ain't walking. Now, little man, or I might decide to take this bike away, just like I did that watch."

Arik nodded at Garik's wrist, and Garik tried to hide it before he caught himself, realizing that's what the man wanted him to do.

"Just because you put it behind your back doesn't mean I don't know it's there, *Gari.*" He spit the name like soured milk. "Don't insult my intelligence. Now, the bike, cause I'm hungry, and that milk's not getting here on its own."

"I'll go for it." Desperation clutched at Garik, pounding in his head. "Right there and back."

"Not with my money." He swung one leg over the jet-assist tube and squirmed to settle himself in. "Never ridden it. Might be fun." He leered at his girlfriend's nephew, and he winked like he intended to treat it like he stole it.

Which was what he was trying to do.

"Arik?"

They both looked up. Irina was in her robe, her hair in a tangle, with Mrs. Waggoner's greenery above framing her into a sleepy garden nymph.

"Gari, here." She held out a twenty, the twin to the one from the day at the food court. "You forgot this on the way out the door. Besides milk, can you get me a candy bar? Coconut, if they have one. At Masti's?"

"At Masti's, right. They have them. Only one?" Thank you, Irina, he breathed. Thank you, thank you.

Without waiting on Arik, Garik darted into the stairwell, took them three at a whack, and tried to walk calmly down the balcony to Irina. When he reached for the bill, Irina pressed it into his hand and wrapped both hers around his.

"Sorry, Gari. I want Arik to be a good man. I know you do, too." She smiled weakly, and her eyes watered. "This is my last one. Get yourself something, too, cause I don't know when I'll have more. Arik, well, Arik can't find a job, and he needs money, sometimes."

"I love you, Iri. Thank you, thank you. I'll be right back with the milk. And your candy bar." He grinned as he turned to walk away. "Thank you again," he said, blowing her a kiss.

Downstairs, Arik was leaning against a post, a blackened and discarded fag on the ground at his feet. He ground it into the pavement with the sole of his shoe. His shoulders were hunched, and he drew in a deep breath. A fresh smoke brightened between his lips.

Garik felt the man's eyes burn into him as he tucked the twenty into a pocket and buttoned the flap. He thumbed the fob, caught the lock as it released, and stowed it away. The fuel pack and the injector were a nuisance mostly, but today, he fiddled with them, taking longer than necessary, and making a point of how much trouble his bike was to operate. He thumbed the starter, inserted the injector and thumbed it again, only relaxing when the jet tube burst into flame.

Arik pulled away from the pole, walked by Garik's bike, and blew smoke into Garik's air. Garik coughed and cleared his throat, trying to stay focused on the machine rumbling between his legs.

"This time, boy." Arik flicked ash at him, sauntered away without looking back, and disappeared into the shadowy stairwell.

"AND AFTER that? You smashed his face, right?" Robbie Icardi grinned as he dangled his legs off the side of the bowl nestled in the corner of the Connel Street Skate Park. He wore crisply creased yellow shorts, a bright blue polo shirt, and his shoes were brilliantly white and spotless. Needless to say, Robbie had never mounted a skateboard, and as he would tell anyone who ribbed him about it, he hoped he never did.

He flinched when Muhammad Saud flew up and caught the rim with his board, yelling out, "Dundersaps," before dropping back into the bowl.

"Yeow, I wish he wouldn't do that." Robbie straightened his shirt. "I would have, you know, smashed his face if my brother did that to me."

"He's not my brother. He's my aunt's boyfriend, and yes, I have to take it." Garik waited his turn for Muhammad's board. His Strider hadn't restarted after his milk run, and he hadn't wanted to give Arik the satisfaction of inserting the knife and twisting it, too. He had locked it and left on foot, too embarrassed to even retrieve his board knowing Arik might be watching.

"He's only five years older than you. My brother, Lawrence, is seven older than me, and I don't do anything he tells me to do."

"Well, so—" Garik raised an arm and called, "Mo, my turn." He clapped Robbie on the shoulder and leaped to his feet. "Sorry, Robbie. My turn."

He was tired of talking about Arik. He couldn't do anything about Arik. Nobody understood. So he did what he could, leaped on Muhammad's board and dropped into the bowl. On the other side, he worked himself over a protruding hip, down a sloped rail, and dropped into the funbox to grind along a steel-edged bench. He came off and hit the ground running, popping his board up and grasping it in his arm, panting.

"Wahoo!" he yelled, pumping one arm into the air. His watch began to chime, and he popped an earbud into his ear. "Yeah, who is

38

it?"

"Me, you ridiculous ape. Who do you think? I heard you and Arik going at it this morning. You grounded?"

"I think everybody heard it." Garik dropped to sit on a rail that was vacant of riders.

"Yah, and your aunt was brilliant. Did Arik enjoy his milk?" Marisa tittered.

"Probably. I didn't stick around." Muhammad waved for his board, and Garik pointed to his watch and motioned for him to come get it.

"I hear wheels. Are you on your skateboard?"

"Nah. I walked. But I am using Mo's. Are we still on for our date?"

"Date?" Marisa laughed. "What date? But yes, we're still meeting at Ai Kee! Do you need a ride? I bet I could drum up a skateboard somewhere."

"You don't ride." He pictured her falling off every four feet.

"Walk, then. I'll be at the skate park in an hour."

Garik pulled out his earbud just as Muhammad strolled up. He kicked the end of his board and caught it, then he dropped beside Garik.

"Allah be praised. Garik's talking to a girl." He grinned.

"You don't know." He tucked the earbud in his pocket and looked across the park. Robbie was following a skinny girl in green tights and a clingy skirt. She looked about thirteen and very uninterested.

"You and Marissa still on for the thing at Ai Kee!? What, a movie or something like that?" Muhammad grinned.

"Something. Not a movie. You know Kevin Lee?"

"A trainer, er, instructor at the Center?" He was tracing the skull on his longboard with his finger. He wasn't into martial arts, as he insisted to anyone who asked, but to watch, that was okay.

"Plus, he competes—"

"Won at Nationals last year, right? See, I do know a little about him."

"He's auditioning for a movie role. Marisa and I are going to be part of the audience." It felt good to Garik to put them together in a sentence, *Marisa and I.*

Still, the sun had found a spot just overhead to pummel the skate park, and Garik made his way to the shaded pavilion on the east side

39

of the park. A water fountain, a quarter hour of roughhousing, and several wet shirts passed the time until Garik saw Marisa waving from the entrance, their two tickets in her hand.

"Yo, guys," he called, leaping to his feet. "Pray I get a movie role. I'll move to Corona Tower in one of the fancy apartments, and you can all come visit."

"Yeah, pah!" Muhammad waved him away with a languid hand motion. "We be moving in *with* you."

He and Robbie laughed, and Garik took off running. Kevin Lee. The movies. Some people got all the luck. But he had Marisa. He leaped over a low wall, and he slowed down as he reached her.

"You ever talk to Kevin?" She was a martial arts freak. If she'd been to the Center, Garik knew she must have.

"A few times. Once he helped with how to hold my hands." She shrugged, pleased.

"So, he knows your name?" Garik grinned.

"Pssst!" She elbowed him in the ribs. "He's got better things to do than know my name. You know, if you want an autograph, now's the time. By next year, he'll be too famous for us, by far."

"Not too famous for Halo Sunchaser." Sunchaser, a Tower elite, the wielder of Marisa's electrified sword. "Doesn't she visit the Center? I hear she's a martial arts nut like you."

"I'm not a nut, just interested. And I take lessons. I've seen her there."

"What I can't figure out, why would she need to learn martial arts? She has that sword. Does she carry it at the Center?" Garik grinned. He imagined an old-time cowboy, his whip attached at his waist and a rifle on his saddle, ready to take down any bad guy that came along.

"Dreamer." Marisa shook her head and laughed. "She might be there. You never know. She trains with Kevin some days, but I heard who Kevin Lee has eyes for."

"You?" He grinned, teasing, and made a heart with his hands.

"Callie Fornya."

"Wasn't she in the Olympics?" Even Garik had heard of her.

"Got injured and now works at the Center. Ai Kee!'s poster girl. Except she never gets on the floor. She does the financial books and poses for the advertising stills."

"She's the girl on the billboards?" She looked ready to take an opponent down.

40

"Talks the talk, but she can't walk the walk. *Once a member of the U.S.A. Olympic team, Callie Fornya says . . .* well, she doesn't get my respect."

"How sad—" Garik was picturing Kevin Lee, and well, Callie Fornya was beautiful, even if she couldn't compete on the floor.

"I respect Halo Sunchaser more. That sword could take down anyone, no effort required. It's not carrying it—"

"It's knowing she can." Garik finished her sentence.

That was much better.

— 7 —

THEY HAD talked out Halo Sunchaser by the time they reached The Martial Arts Center and Ai Kee! The street was filled with cars and pedestrians and several black SUVs. This was clearly an event. Thank goodness for their tickets.

They were asked for them at the door. The doorman looked at them carefully, studied Garik and Marisa's faces, and without saying anything, tore the tickets in half and returned one end to them, allowing them entrance.

"What was he about?" Garik turned and frowned.

"I don't care." Marisa laughed. "Follow me. I know where they are having the interview. We can still get good seats."

Garik followed close on her heels.

The audition was in the Center's competition gym, a room with a vast ceiling and a bank of risers along one wall with narrow windows bordering the ceiling. Callie Fornya's picture covered a large section of one wall. In it, Callie wore a black robe tied at the waist with a cloth belt. Her copper-colored hair was in a sensible bob, and her green eyes jumped out of the image. The Ai Kee! logo filled the background, and below her, it stated, "Olympic Quality Facilities. For the Olympian in You!"

Marisa explained that normally multiple mats were set up. Numerous people trained at the same time, but today, only one was in the middle of the room. Props had been brought in, with a temporary backdrop that looked like a scene from an old-fashioned Chinatown film.

"The lights," Garik asked, pointing around the massive room. Large lights were on tall stands, some reaching nearly to the ceiling. They seemed overkill for the well-lighted space. "Don't those get in

41

the way?"

"Yes, they would," she explained, "but the lights aren't normally in the gym. This is a special setup all for Kevin's audition."

"Ah. Hollywood." Garik pictured movies he'd seen. He guessed this was how they made them. Several bulky cameras on rollers had cables running to an electronics-filled table off to the side, yet more movie-specific additions to the gym.

Sitting a row in front of them and down some, Marisa pointed to a woman with bristly short hair and dangling earrings. She wore a lime green flowered top and black lycra pants. "Vegan Flo." She giggled. "She never eats meat because it's not neat."

"Vegan Flo?" Garik thought Vegans dressed in shiny silver. "Where's her outer space gear?"

"Shush. Not so loud." Marisa put her finger to her lips. "Not like the star Vega. It's a diet thing. She tells everyone that she never touches anything that touches animals. She wears cotton or synthetics—" she giggled "—or nothing at all, I guess."

"Doesn't oil come from animals? That's how synthetics are made."

Marisa shrugged. "Talk to Vegan Flo about it. Oh, and there's Jung Il-woo."

"The Chinese guy?" A tall man with long arms and short black hair walked in. A pretty face, he was cleanly shaven with a black tee, tan chinos, and sneakers.

"Yes, but South Korean, I think."

He was followed by a shorter, heavier woman a few years older, in a business suit in a good cut, with a similar ethnic cast to her face. "Who's the other one? Anyone you know?"

"Drinking companion at Kerre's Dive, the gossips say. Shin So Min. Always pays for his drinks." She snickered and linked her fingers, then shrugged. "I don't think so and don't care, because I think she's a foreign agent for the Chinese government. Maybe Il-woo is infiltrating Vegan Flo's vegan lifestyle so they can monetize it for worldwide export. It'd make a bundle."

"I don't think so. No one would want it. She could be Korean, too. Maybe she's his mother."

A door off to the side opened, and a boy who looked about sixteen leaped through in full martial arts dress. He landed with his feet spread and his hands high, making a chopping motion, as he yelled out, "Ai Kee!"

"Not Daniel." Marisa sank into her seat and put her hand over her eyes.

"I thought his name was Kevin." Too many names for too many people, and Garik was getting lost, but he remembered Kevin Lee's name.

"That isn't Kevin." Marisa spread her fingers just wide enough to see Daniel Kim walk onto the set and pretend to karate chop one of the props. He hit it, and as it toppled, a woman wearing one of the studio's lookalike outfits dropped her tablet onto a table and made a beeline for Daniel. Daniel held up his hands to the risers, as if waiting for the audience to acknowledge his amazing performance.

"Not Kevin." Garik watched as the woman took the boy's arm and maneuvered him off the set and set him in a chair behind the studio equipment. She waggled a finger at him as if admonishing him to stay put. "Who is he?"

"A boy. I don't know why he's at the Center."

"He shows up and just chills, then." That was okay with Garik. If they let people chill at the Center, maybe he could, too, at least some. He was having fun.

"No, he gets paid, but I'm not sure what for. Perhaps to clean up. Janitor, maybe."

"Oh." Then it hit Garik. "I've seen Daniel at school, I think. He's in Wajeha's class."

"Yeah, Daniel Kim. At least he tries, I can respect that. And the changing rooms are always clean. Shush. I think we're starting."

The banks of lights clicked on, and the gym brightened as they began to warm. Cameramen nestled into the seats on the camera rigs, and several martial arts performers Marisa didn't know took their places in front of the backdrop.

Kevin Lee appeared in loose pants and a bare torso, tight and fit. A blonde-headed director walked around the mock set, described what she wanted, and called, "Action!" She had them repeat several short takes, and after less time than Garik and Marisa had waited for the hoopla to start, the director called, "Cut," and the studio team began breaking down their equipment.

The owner of Ai Kee!, Mr. Mandering, got on the speaker system and announced in a crisp and clean-cut Des Moines accent, "Visitors, guests, and those of you who are patrons of our facility, as the owner of Ai Kee!, I would like you to join us at the Corona Tower food court to visit with our movie hopeful, Kevin Lee. Kevin will

43

be available for photos and autographs, twenty dollars each. Come on down. We'll start at two. No refreshments provided by us, but it's the food court! You can purchase whatever you want. I've arranged for a twenty percent discount on any food purchases from Chow Down between two and three. Tell the cashier that you're with Gerry." Gerry laughed as he disengaged from the microphone and waved at the audience on the risers.

As the people around Garik and Marisa began to stand and work their way off the risers, a pretty woman wearing a shirt emblazoned with Kickstarting Life and stylized versions of an adult holding the hands of two children walked up to Gerry. A boy about eight tagged behind her, holding to her purse strap. She reached to Gerry's arm in a familial way, and they laughed about something.

"His wife?" Garik nodded their direction.

"A parent, I think, but the kid's not from here. Kickstarting is an after-school program for troubled youth." She shrugged and stood.

"The boy doesn't look troubled."

"You can't always tell. Look at us." She winked at him. "Do you want to go for 'photos and autographs' or do something else?"

"Of course." Garik stood and grinned. Meet Kevin Lee— maybe—and spend more time with Marisa. That was always a good way to spend the day.

A SECTION of the food court was roped off with a long table draped with fabric sporting Kevin's name. There were the expected kids, many who took classes at Ai Kee!, and others who had shown up because of the news announcements about the audition. Kevin was a minor local hero, especially to the younger crowd in the city. They crowded around, wide-eyed and adoring. Kevin charmed them. He walked around the table and knelt at their sides for photos; and he signed tee shirts, paper receipts, and even sold a number of Ai Kee! autographed photographs.

The adults took over after the kids dispersed to a late lunch or early dinner, several well-heeled by their dress, and the free autographs ended. Gerry set up an Ai Kee! backdrop and began taking money, pushing Kevin to go faster, to keep the photo conversations brief, and not to autograph anything people didn't pay for.

Garik and Marisa combined their change and, with Gerry's discount, were able to share an order of fries and two glasses of water. The rest was entertainment. After three, the ropes were removed, and the regular visitors that weren't at the audition and had no clue what was going on without Kevin's sign began to filter in, diluting the familiar faces. Garik was surprised when a hand reached between them and placed a huge order of nachos on the table.

"I saw you two at the audition." Kevin carried a glass to the other side of the table and sat. "I didn't get to eat, and since you guys are familiar faces, I thought you might not mind sharing." He pushed the nachos their direction.

"Seriously?" Garik's fries had only made him hungrier, and he grinned, taking one and biting into it.

"You're welcome. I'm Kevin." He held his hand over the table.

"Garik." He wiped his hand and shook. "And this is—"

"—Marisa, I know."

"See?" Garik cut his eyes to Marisa. "He does know your name."

"What?" Kevin asked, his eyes twinkling. "I'm a topic of discussion between you two?"

"Yah," Garik said. "All morning. You signed a lot of autographs, huh?"

"More than Mandering expected. Did you see the richies? Money, money. I could use some of that, but I don't know about the Hollywood thing. So boring. Did you see how many times they wanted me to do each scene? And each one was perfect. I want to do, not wait and redo so they can have ten identical takes to slice and dice." He took two nachos at a time, one in each hand, and bit into one, dripping cheese that he caught in the other.

Richies! That topic interested Garik. "Did you know any of the richies?"

"Maybe." Kevin licked one finger. "Did you see the blond guy with the hair?" He touched his hair and flipped his fingers up.

"The blue?" When Kevin and Garik looked at her, Marisa shrugged. "I notice those things."

"Then you must have noticed his girl. Boris and Kirsten. He's with Lindemann Airways and she's an heir to the Kaudlitz hotel chain. One of many, I'm sure, but worth a lot. They have one of the apartments upstairs. Lindemann likes to tell people that there's something going on in the sub-basement, but what does he know? Nothing, probably. They were instrumental in connecting me with the Hollywood bunch."

"It's cool that you know them." Garik remembered the group

45

that had scored the fifty tickets for Jantzen Hefferly. Had Boris Lindemann been there? With the blue tips in his hair, surely he would have stood out.

"I don't, dude. I know *of* them. They like my local fame. That's rich people. They have money, but if they're smart, no one knows who they are. I suppose they like that, but they feel bigger if they are connected to people with a little star recognition. We all do, I guess. Gives us a sense of value. Me?" He chuckled. "The person I want to connect with doesn't know I'm alive."

"Callie?" Garik had the name out before he realized what he'd said. Marisa kicked his shin, and he leaned down to rub it.

"So, everyone knows." Kevin laughed sourly. "Except Callie. Maybe if I do the movie thing, then she'll notice me."

They turned at a sound from the street running alongside the mall. Several car doors slammed one after another. Two black SUVs drove off, and a half-dozen military types in dress blues and dark sunglasses strode into the shade under the Corona Tower, walking right by their table. One solid-looking man brushed Garik's elbow, and he paused, turned, and said, "My apologies, sir."

"No problem." Garik looked up with a smile.

The military type removed his glasses. "I thought I recognized that voice. Garik, right? I didn't see your Strider outside." The man reached to the other two and shook hands. "Wu Han, U.S. Air Force. If you're with Garik, I'm glad to meet you. I would stay for introductions, but I must go. I'm expected at a meeting."

With a nod, he returned his sunglasses to his nose and headed toward the elevators.

Kevin reached to Garik, rubbed the back of his fingers down his shirt front, and grinned. "Now who's the important one?"

"Garik?" Marisa pushed him on the shoulder. "How did that happen?"

Garik felt his face warm. He wasn't used to being the center of anyone's attention, not in a good way, anyway. He pointed to the bank of elevators by the food court kiosk. As the doors opened for the military types, the down arrow was clearly lighted.

"What's in the basement, do you think?"

"Ask Lindemann. He knows." Kevin laughed, took another nacho, and invited his two newest friends to do the same.

HALFWAY THROUGH a second bowl of nachos, Kevin Lee leaped to his feet, paused long enough to say, "Wait here. This is so exciting!" and vanished into a wall of Japanese-speaking tourists complete with broad-brimmed hats, colorful shirts, sunglasses, and phones snapping photos of the mall and the food court.

"That was sudden," Marisa said. "Perhaps he has to go. I wouldn't think of that as exciting." She grinned.

"No, but look who's here." Garik pointed to an ebony face with a towering headwrap in vivid jungle colors clearly visible among the colorful tourists. Halo Sunchaser, a recognized researcher and martial arts aficionado, respected around the city, and occasionally seen transiting the food court, was eminently recognizable, even to someone like Garik, who never did anything martial arts at all. She was draped in a kaftan in shimmering orange and green.

"She's here?" Marisa sat up, now interested. "I've never seen her outside of Ai Kee! Does she have her sword?"

Garik gave Marisa a puzzled look. Sunchaser would actually wear it around the city? When he saw her wink, he laughed. Teasing. She was goading him just for fun.

"Maybe," he teased back. He stood partway. "I can't see her that well. Oh, Kevin's with her. I forget that you said they know one another. She's one of his students."

Sunchaser seemed giant next to the tourists. Her headwrap accentuated her height, making Kevin short by comparison. Garik watched Kevin point, and Sunchaser turned their way and smiled. She nodded and moved their direction, parting the sea of Japanese tourists like an African goddess.

She almost was, Garik acknowledged. An electrified sword? The weapon of a goddess, if there ever was one. He wondered how that worked. Could anyone use it, or was it based on fingerprint or DNA recognition? Too bad Marisa hadn't been able to find the final layer of schematics for the sword.

As she drew closer, Garik was impressed by her hawk-like nose and sharp, piercing eyes. She smiled as she spoke with Kevin, but there was something predatory in her expression. Just for a moment, he shivered, then she was at their table holding out a hand with long fingers and talon-like nails in bright red.

"I had forgotten about Kevin's audition, or I would have been at the Center earlier. I'm so glad he caught me. You must be his friends. Garik, I would recognize you in an instant. Such beautiful bronze skin. You lucky boy, you, even if no one tells you." She shook his hand, dragging her nails across his skin for a moment as she released her hold on him. She turned to Marisa. "I've seen you at the Center. We've not met, but you can only be Marisa. Such a pretty face. You must be the rage among all the boys. Probably hated by all the girls."

Sunchaser laughed, and for a moment, Garik didn't know how to take her veiled compliments. Her next words took his worries away.

"I have a competition in South Africa next month, and Kevin has been honing my meager skills. Then, we can't all be national champions like Mr. Lee, here." She took Kevin's hand and patted the top of it before releasing it. "I hope for the best for your movie career, but I hate that I might be losing my best teacher. And your friends, thank you for introducing me. I love young people. New blood, fresh. You are all wonderful."

"Ms. Sunchaser?" Marisa had her arms on the table, and she took a deep breath. "You work here, don't you?"

"In the Corona Tower? Of course. Why?" She glanced behind Marisa, whether looking for someone, it was hard to tell. It seemed that her eyes did something and then refocused on the table and the three friends.

"My sister." Marisa looked down before seeming to regain her confidence and holding up her head. "My sister, Marina. She came to work for the Tower two years ago, and my family hasn't heard from her since. I thought, well, since you work here, you might know something, maybe you've seen her."

"Marina? I can't say that I have—"

"My mother says I look a lot like her." Marisa's eyes pleaded.

"Now that you mention it, I thought you looked familiar, even at the gym. Maybe I can check on that for you. Nelson Tutu keeps up with our itinerant workers." For a moment, her expression shifted, her eyes hardened, perhaps, and then her smile returned. "Bruni, right? I'll ask Nelson about a Marina Bruni and see if he knows anything. I must run. Thank you, Kevin, and I'll see you in our next session at the Center."

She turned, stately in her height and flowing kaftan, and smoothly moved away, almost as if not moving at all.

"I'm surprised but happy." Garik grinned at Marisa.

48

"Oh?" Marisa licked her lips and seemed jittery.

"Your sister. You never want to discuss her. Now you might find out something."

"Right from the source," Kevin added. "I didn't know you had a sister."

"She doesn't talk about it." Garik stage-whispered the words, grinning.

"I still don't plan to." Marisa's eyes narrowed. "So, Gari. You can have an opinion, too, Kevin. Let me ask you this. How did she know my sister's last name would be Bruni?"

"Kevin?" This answer seemed easy to Garik. "You told her, right?"

"No." He shrugged. "Maybe from the gym?"

"I don't think so. She said she'd seen me but that we'd never met. There's no reason for her to know my name."

Kevin's watch chimed, and he glanced at it. "I have a client at the Center in half an hour. This is my signal to leave." He shoveled one last nacho in his mouth and stood, still crunching his final bite of chips, the side of his face shifting as his jaw moved up and down. He cleared his area and stacked the refuse from their late lunch on the food court tray from the kiosk.

"We'll get that, Kevin." Marisa gathered several small salt packets scattered around and added them to the tray.

"Leave it like you found it is my motto. Cleaner if you can." He grinned. "I'll see you at the Center, Marisa. Feel free to say hi even if I'm giving a lesson. I can introduce you to people. And you, Garik, come on down. We might get you interested. What do you say?"

Garik shook his head emphatically, and Kevin laughed before waving and heading off. The gaggle of tourists had clustered around the central kiosk for a time, but now they were spread about, seated and eating or visiting. Kevin made his way through them without having to request a one to move.

"Thank you for inviting me today." Garik peered into the nacho bowl, but he was stuffed, and although they still smelled good, the thought of anything else in his stomach was unbearable, and he pushed the bowl to the other side of the table.

"After last night," she rolled her eyes, "you needed a break from your aunt's boyfriend. If you want, we could visit the Harbor Yards. There's a new ship in, a yacht transport. They say it has boats on board worth more than the entire Corona Tower."

"Pshaw. Worth more than the Tower?" The Tower was enormous, forty stories. And the things it could do, melting into black silicon glitter at night and turning back into a gleaming glass skyscraper. Garik still hadn't discovered how they did that. Maybe it was a security measure like Marisa had suggested, but it was cool. "Sure, let's go." A boat worth more than the Tower? Who would want to miss that?

THE HOTTEST part of the day had passed, but the sun was still bright, and once they crossed the vibrantly hot mall, they took the steps down to the city sidewalk and the streets proper. As they crossed the recessed barrier that would leap sixteen feet from the ground during Corona Tower concerts and events to keep the "riff-raff" out, they found it cooler to keep to the shady sides of the streets.

Still, Sycamore was four lanes, plus a turn lane in the center, and they had to walk to Beacon to catch an elevated pedestrian crossover. The shade from the Tower was falling to the east, and that meant Sycamore was still in full sun, at least on the Tower side. The Beacon Street Crosswalk had a small, covered shelter in the center, a bench, really, with a tinted glass top, and they paused there, looking at the cars driving below them, joking that if the cars with glass roofs opened them, they could drop in water balloons, and wouldn't that be fun. Beacon ended three blocks over at Waldorf's Department Store. Garik watched the glittering displays in the windows hungrily. He'd never been to Waldorf's, and he'd lived in the city ever since coming to America. Then, Waldorf's was for the richies, and that would never be him.

They turned right at Waldorf's on Bleaker, running down the line of manicured shrubs and the tinted SUVs, and at the corner, they crossed against the signal, laughing when they thought they saw a flashing light. It was only the signal blinking to warn the pedestrians heading the opposite direction that the light was about to change once more.

Another four blocks, and two lights later, and they had to go left on Williams and right on Welton, cutting between the massive buildings of the Williams Street Apartments towers. At the end of the block, they looked both ways along Shorefront, waited for a break in traffic, and ran full out to The Docks. They could see Harbor Shipyards to the right, with towering gantry cranes looming over the wa-

ter like muscular arms waiting to snatch up anything that came within reach. In front of them, four massive piers labeled A to D jutted
into the water, perpendicular to the wharves hugging the shore. Several tugboats pushed bigger ships through the water, and at the largest pier, just to the left, was a massive floating superstructure that
hardly seemed real.

"It's an entire city on the water!" Garik was impressed. He
leaned his elbows on the railing alongside the wharf. The vessel taking up the entire length of Pier A was filled with large and small
boats of all shapes and sizes. Men were like ants scrambling over the
deck, and they made the ship look even larger.

"Not quite." Marisa turned and rested her elbows on the rail,
looking back at the real city layered behind them, to Corona Tower,
and higher, past the Old City Hall on Sycamore with its gold dome,
to the Ransom Communications Building way up on Stanwick Hill.
The cell tower at the top was all she could see of the Ransom, but
still. Their apartment building at Maple and Avenue D would be
across Sycamore from the Ransom but not tall enough to see from
The Docks. Conversely, they couldn't see The Docks or the water
from their building, not even from the roof.

"How many . . ." Garik began to count the boats clustered on the
floating barge. "One, two, three—"

"Too many to count. That big sailboat on the left? I read it's
worth over fifty mil."

"Million? Dollars?" He felt lucky to have his Street Strider, and
it had been abandoned in an alley.

"No respect, though." Marisa thumbed her nose the direction of
the massive ship holding dozens of other massive ships.

"Why's that?" He grinned. Nothing much earned Marisa's respect.

"Lazy. Anyone with that much money has enough time on their
hands to sail it themselves. After all, boats aren't made to hitchhike
on other boats. They are made to be in the water."

"Still, it's cool, even if they're fools." Garik was feeling good.
"Hear that? I made a rhyme. Give me a dime."

"I might walk home without you if you make another one."
Marisa hit her shoulder against his arm, and she plunged her hands
into a set of pockets, setting her elbows akimbo and giving her pockets a full appearance. She pulled one hand out to shade her eyes from
the western sun, and she called, "Let's go the back way. We can stop

by Argyle Station if we have time."

"Okay." As long as Garik was tagging along, he'd go anywhere Marisa suggested.

Just down from Pier A, Plymouth Avenue cut back into the city. It was seven blocks to Shady Ridge Acres, a richie's area, with winding streets and cul-de-sacs, with Argyle Station one block west. Plymouth changed to Vista at the Ninth Street walkover, the houses even ritzier than Shady Ridge, seven blocks long and winding, making it seem even longer. They had another walkover at First where the street changed names once more to Cedar, then four more blocks to Avenue D, left, and they were nearly home.

All that, and it was still too close, because at the end, Garik would have to say goodnight to Marisa, and he would get to listen to Arik grind on him all evening long, ruining his one good day and making it into nothing at all.

Garik refused to think about Arik or how much milk there was in the fridge or if the fridge even worked.

"Hey, doofus. I'm talking to you. Where's your head?"

Garik grinned. They were two blocks up Plymouth, the street lined with crape myrtles, and they were brilliantly in bloom. It would take an hour to get home. He said, "Argyle Station. I vote we stop and see what kinds of trains are in." And pretend we're taking one and leaving Arik behind forever.

"Just what I was saying, doofus. At least we're on the same page."

Yep, Garik thought, watching Marisa talk. Just what I was thinking.

— 9 —

GARIK OPENED his eyes to the sun cutting into his small bedroom.

"Summer," he moaned. His time was his, but then there was this.

He rolled over, twisted from under the sheet, and sat up. It had been cold during the night, but he expected the afternoon would blister the city. He reached to the old crate that was his bedside table and touched the framed photo of his parents.

"Mama, Papa."

At St. Anne's, just last Sunday, the smell of the old wood on the floors and the incense from the braziers had stirred a windstorm of memories—his mama and papa—and tears had almost filled his eyes. Irina hadn't attended with him. Garik preferred not to go alone, but his aunt had said she had enough demons in her life, and she didn't need any of the Christian kind. He loved Iri, and so he kissed her cheek and left the apartment alone in the early morning light and made his way to the church. In the picture, behind his parents, the old stone house, his grandpapa's, built by his own hands, where Garik had learned to walk and wished to return one day, reared out of the soil, the dirt-colored stone a permanent part of the earth in his mind. Eck, he considered, with a wistful grin. Maybe not return to live, but to hold his mama and be patted on the head once more by his papa.

"I miss you." He released the picture and blew them a kiss before leaping to his feet and taking the one step across his room to the door. He peered out, uncertain who was home. His aunt, certainly, but Arik was his concern.

"Iri?" He called Irina's name, not too loudly, as not to irritate Arik if he was still sleeping. He turned as something pinged against his window. Stepping on his bed, he turned the crank and leaned out when the window opened enough for him to work his shoulders through. A small stone hit him on the forehead. "Hey!"

"Garik, come down." Winter, thin as a rail and his hair bright against the dark soil and gravel grounding the backside of the apartment building, waved to him. "It's important."

"Tell me from there." Bathroom. Breakfast. Dodging Arik. Recalling his dreams of Marisa. That's what he wanted to do.

"Ah, come on. Don't be a pansy. Hey, did you just get up?" Winter laughed. "Sleep tight. I guess the bedbugs didn't bite."

"Arrgh, you little ape. Okay." Garik twirled the crank and resealed the window. Hooking yesterday's pants with his foot, he kicked them upwards and grabbed them, a move very much like a skater's. He shoved his feet into his shoes and pulled a fresh shirt from the back of a chair and tossed it on. Slipping into the hallway quietly, he made a pitstop before exiting the apartment and tripping down the stairs. He found his way through the storage cubicles to the back entrance, pushed the door open and stepped outside, only to be startled by a bucket of water dumped on his head.

"Ha, ha, we got you!" Winter, about a dozen feet away, held his stomach and laughed.

Beside Garik, Firestarter was backing down a wooden stepladder with a red plastic bucket in one hand that said IN CASE OF FIRE on the side; and little Shrimper, a shadow among the morning shadows, held tightly to the legs of the ladder to keep it stable.

"Why, you!" Garik made as if to grab the boys. Firestarter leaped from the fourth step, falling, too wrapped up in laughter to manage running and keeping hold of the bucket, and he was off to the far side of the weedy plot. Shrimper wasn't so lucky. Garik caught his leg and wrapped him in one arm and tossed him over his shoulder.

"Wasn't my idea, Garik!" The boy laughed as he fought for freedom.

"You're the one who's going to pay." Garik snagged the bucket, set it under the outside faucet, and turned it on. "It's worth a little of the building's water to see some paybacks come your way."

Garik didn't slosh it over him. Instead, he moved the bucket to a clear area, held Shrimper upside down, and dunked his head in the water. By the time Shrimper came up the second time, the other two boys were pulling at Garik's shirt, pleading for a turn.

Looking up at his window and to the one just down that was his aunt's room, he decided he could do without risking an altercation with Arik. Marisa was likely working at the flower shop for the morning. He felt for his fob and groaned to remember it was on his bedside table. The shop was only four blocks away, fronting on Sycamore, with back and side doors butting up to Elm and Avenue C, a little triangle of a city block left after they had widened Sycamore at one point.

Popping the backs of each of the heads of his "hood," he instructed them to return the red bucket to the fire shelf and leave it there, and if Irina should ask about him, he was at the flower shop. He unlocked his apartment's storage and worked out his Santa Cruz, and he dropped it in the parking lot next to his bike and caught it with one foot. His Strider reminded him of Wu Han. The Airman had admired something that belonged to him. He smiled, feeling good for a change. His hair dangled wetly against his neck, his shirt still damp enough to keep the morning's rising heat in check, and the sun through the lone not-maple tree splattered charcoal-colored splotches across the sidewalk. A good skater day.

He came out on Maple, giving a push with one foot, while keeping an eye out for Catnip and Catnip's business. He waved and called to Mr. Larkin across the street. He was pulling a small wagon toward Avenue C.

"Hey, Mr. Larkin." Garik stopped when the old man looked up and waved back.

"Garik! Good morning. Where's your bike?"

"Eh, I'm just headed to the flower shop. It's only a couple blocks. Are you off to Fasst Market?" Garik liked Mr. Larkin, and if he was, he didn't mind helping.

"Yes, I am. Does your aunt need me to bring her something?"

"Nah, Mr. Larkin. Do you need help with your wagon?"

Mr. Larkin laughed. "I know who works at the flower shop. You go see your girl, and I'll manage my wagon fine." Mr. Larkin waved again and returned to plodding down the sidewalk.

My girl. Garik grinned, especially pleased with his morning, and he pushed off, hooked a right at Avenue C, and pushed hard to build up his speed. At Laurel, cars blocked the curb, and he had to ride down the handicapped ramp from sidewalk to street and back up again on the other side, but on Ash and Beech, he was able to jump the curbs, once kick-flipping his board before skid steering around a lamppost and up to the flower shop's back entrance as he crossed Elm.

Garik kicked his board up to grab the end, and he caught his reflection in the glass door. Medium height, slender but tight, muscular frame, oversized hands. Thick, dark hair more wild bush than controlled mane, but that was from skating for four blocks. Big features, bronze skin, his Armenian heritage out there for the world to see. He thought nothing of it, just recognized himself as who he was, and put his hand on the metal bar spanning the door. The backside of the glass had a large red arrow and said, "Entrance Around the Corner," being the delivery door, but Garik had entered this way so many times that the sign didn't register.

The door dinged as he entered, and he found himself in the bowels of the shop. Bundles and buckets of flowers, banks of glass-fronted coolers, and rivulets of water running across the sloped floor to a drain in the center. A compact Asian man in a leather apron spouting a bit of a belly pushed through a plastic curtain from the front of the shop and looked over his glasses at Garik.

"Mr. Bruni, hello." Garik ran his hand through his hair, aware of its disarray. "I'm putting my skateboard here. Okay?" He leaned it against a waist-high portable white cabinet covered with buckets of greenery.

Mr. Bruni brushed the air with his hand, sighed, and said, "Mari

55

is in the front. She is with a customer. Perhaps you wait?"

"Sure." Mr. Bruni disappeared back through the curtain, and Garik browsed the stocks of blooms filling the humid space. He heard Marisa's laugh, and in response, he heard another voice he recognized. He poked his head through the curtain and called out, "Marisa?"

Her father answered. "No, you, Garik. You say you wait. You wait." Mr. Bruni walked his way, brushing him back into the stock-room with his hands waving in the air.

"Oh, hello, Garik." Marisa intervened. "Father, it is okay. Mr. Lee and Garik know each other."

"Mr. Lee? This is so?" Marisa's dad looked to Kevin for affirmation.

"Hi, Garik," Kevin called. "We're old friends, Mr. Bruni. No problem."

"Well, then." Mr. Bruni cleared his throat, obviously not happy, and began pulling flowers from a refrigerated glass case.

"Hey, I didn't expect to see you here." Garik was suddenly aware of his rumpled appearance in contrast to Kevin's neat black turtleneck. He wondered if Kevin now liked Marisa. He would be devastated. "It's good, though," he said, not entirely convinced.

"We were talking about you." Kevin grinned. "You remember, from at the food court."

Mr. Bruni had edged closer, glancing at the young people from time to time, and Marisa called, "Father, this is private. Mr. Lee has already selected an arrangement. Maybe you could assemble it in the back. Please."

"I'm sorry." Garik squirmed as her father collected several blooms and a small pair of snippers and disappeared through the plastic curtain. He felt out of place with this unfamiliar situation in this very familiar place. "I don't want your father to be upset."

"He's just nosy. He doesn't need to overhear this. Tell him, Kevin." Marisa had a gleam of anticipation in her eyes.

"I was just thinking last night about Marisa's question to Ms. Sunchaser." He dropped his eyes, looking almost embarrassed. "It doesn't feel right to call her Halo outside of our lessons, though she insists there."

"About Marisa's, um—" Garik hesitated.

"My sister. You can say it. I opened the can yesterday, and it's not closing anytime soon. It's why my father doesn't need to overhear. It will upset him."

"This is about your sister?" Garik saw no way this could be good.

"See," Kevin said, "I know Ms. Sunchaser, and she seemed very interested in you two—"

"And too informed about who I was, but that's not the point—"

"The point is," Kevin jumped back in, "what if I talk to her, tell her how interested you two are in learning about the Tower? Just perhaps that might get Marisa through the door."

"You don't need me for that." It was exciting, imagining pushing the elevator button, seeing the up arrow light up, knowing it would be him getting on. Garik wanted, but he could hardly dare hope for something so impossible.

"But you see, you doofus, we do need you." Marisa put her hand on his forearm, sending a tingle through Garik. "If it's just me, that will sound like I don't trust her to inquire about my sister. If it's all of us, then we're doing nothing suspicious, simply being curious. See, Gari, you've got to be part of this."

"If it works," Kevin cautioned. "Maybe this Hollywood thing will turn into something good, after all. People might open doors to me because of it."

"Sunchaser, you mean. Ms. Sunchaser will open doors." Inside Corona Tower. Wow! Garik could hardly think it.

"Not just Ms. Sunchaser." Kevin grinned, his face flushing.

"Can I tell Garik?" Marisa looked like she intended to, anyway. Kevin shrugged. "His flowers are for Callie. He's ordered the biggest arrangement we make. My father is very pleased."

"And probably very busy." Kevin smiled broadly in his high-energy, tightly tuned way. "So, should I ask Ms. Sunchaser? We have a lesson this afternoon, and I can mention it then."

Garik searched Marisa's face, and her eyes pleaded with him. How could he say no to that? "I'm in. I might need to wear something better, though."

"You are a bit of a mess," Marisa agreed.

Garik didn't even mind. It was the way she said it that warmed him inside.

— 10 —

GARIK TUGGED at the cuffs of his jacket.

Well, at the cuffs of Kevin Lee's jacket. He didn't own one, and Kevin had brought one for him to wear. Garik stood in front of a full-length mirror in the changing room at Ai Kee! and could see Kevin behind him, seated and tying his shoes. Kevin had called the previous evening, excited that Ms. Sunchaser had seemed pleased that the three youths were interested in Corona Tower.

"How did you, I mean, what did you say that she agreed?" Garik had been beside himself at the news.

"Well," Kevin had admitted. "It's only the hotel portion, the lobby, which really almost anyone can visit, but she said she might arrange to get us into the actual hotel."

"And the pool? We can see that?" Garik had pictured the scenes from the screens in the food court, the shimmering water, the glass atrium, everything that always looked so rich to him.

"Here's the thing," Kevin had said, clearing his throat to break the news. "I kinda suggested the two of you might be interested in a job . . . well, more than kinda. But this isn't an interview. More like a pre-interview, so that makes it okay."

Garik had been less sure, but Marisa had no reservations. This was her chance, however slim, to find out something about her sister. She would go under any conditions.

They had met at Ai Kee! Kevin had two classes that morning, but he would bring Garik a jacket, and Garik only needed to wear pressed jeans, clean shoes, and a plain tee. Kevin would change into fresh clothes after he showered, so they could come dressed or plan to change, also. Their appointment was for twelve.

The pressed jeans had required a trip to see Mrs. Waggoner for an iron, and she had made him a cup of tea while she pressed his jeans.

Garik's hair was something else. He turned sideways to see it in the mirror, unsure if it was better than before or worse. Marisa had pulled it to the back of his head and knotted it at the base of his neck. Small tufts had refused to be trapped, and they curled at his temples and ears, shouting the truth, that Garik was a wild boy at heart, a denizen of the concrete jungle that was his home, and no amount of effort was ever going to polish that out of him.

"Ready?" Kevin stood, brushing down his black turtleneck, and clapped Garik on the shoulder. "You look fine. The jacket suits you. Maybe a little loose, but it's always been tight on me. I like the look."

"Sure, I mean, thanks. Do you think Marisa will like it?"

"Dude, she hangs out with you. Yes, Marisa will like it."

Marisa was in the lobby, dressed simply, a flowered summer jacket over a yellow tee and tan pants. Unusual for her, she wore flats rather than sneakers, giving her petite frame a daintier look than usual. She smiled when she saw Garik, and her eyes seemed to open to her soul.

"Hi, there. Don't you two look the part." She ran one hand through her dark hair, letting it fall back in the exact same place, before looking out the window. "It's almost noon. If we're doing this, let's get started. Ten blocks."

"Only fifteen minutes." Kevin pulled out sunglasses, two tight round circles, and set them on his face. "And a beautiful day."

If you like sunshine and heat, Garik thought, and wearing other people's clothes and going in the admittedly intimidating Tower, all while not being exactly honest about why they were visiting.

Yeah, it was a beautiful day.

They followed Ninth the two blocks to Central Park, around the curve leading along the duck pond, where a visiting daycare class tossed bread into the water for their winged patrons, and then four more blocks to Forest, turning right toward the Corona Tower by Swizzel's Shoes, across Forest from The Luncheon Lady, a boutique deli that catered to the City Hall crowd just across Ninth. From the steps of City Hall, it was a straight shot to Corona Tower. They would pass Masti's Deli on the way, except four blocks over on Sycamore, but Forest was the most direct route. From City Hall to the Tower, the elevation dropped sharply. Several blocks beyond the Tower, the marshy area bordering Harbor Shipyards and the water beyond stood out as a pointillist backdrop to the towering structure claiming the nexus of power in Bay City, both politically as well as financially.

Corona Tower, their destination, and the cause of the pit in Garik's stomach.

Everything he had heard about the Tower was lodged in his throat: the electrified sword; Jantzen Hefferly and his mysterious mist; Halo Sunchaser and her hawk-like gaze; the engaging Airman Wu Han; and most of all, the rumors of the head of it all, Weston Rodheimer, the man behind the super-secure Corona Tower and the strange lightshow that entertained the city each night.

If they were caught, Garik was certain that Boris Lindemann

would be proved right, and the thing going on in the basement would be them, in security lockup, answering to Weston Rodheimer for entering the city's most secure and private building on falsified purposes.

It was almost more than he could bear.

KEVIN LEE pushed the big, round circle beside the Corona Tower elevator, and he turned and smiled. "First time for you two."

Garik grinned weakly. He was surprised to see there weren't separate buttons for up and down. The up light came on, and a few moments later, a speaker dinged. The doors slipped silently aside to reveal Ms. Sunchaser standing smartly on the other side.

"Very prompt." Sunchaser nodded approvingly. "A very good trait here at the Tower. Step in. You'll note first of all that the air in our elevators is fully conditioned. Our filtration systems are next to none in providing the purest and most odor-free environment possible."

A sales pitch or a warning? Garik felt a shiver down his back.

Marisa's eyes were taking in everything, as Kevin replied, "Thank you, Halo, for letting my friends have this opportunity. They still have another year in school, but it never hurts to consider your options in advance. Otherwise, how will you know where you want life to take you?"

"Quite right, Kevin." Sunchaser smiled. Her headwrap was in a shimmering black today, and it complemented her gray and black formal suit. When the door opened to the lobby, she touched an icon on the panel beside the door, and a small metal passkey with a thumb-size screen on one side ejected. She removed it and dropped it into a pocket at her waist. "Let me introduce you first to our Front Desk, Charity Cellers."

The three visitors followed Sunchaser into the lobby. Across the marble-tiled, brightly lighted space, a wide doorway revealed the glass-walled atrium. Low sofas and broad tables were arranged in an artful and inviting manner, and at various locations, oversized artworks burst from the floor, sweeping shapes that seemed to cry, "Notice me!"

"Miss Cellers, here are the young people I told you about. They will be with me for a partial tour of our facilities. You know Kevin, and this is Garik and Marisa. Do you have their passes ready?"

"Certainly, Ms. Sunchaser." Charity, slender and super-chic in an A-line dress in a bright geometric pattern with matching hoop earrings, sported long, straight blonde hair.

"I believe I should have a packet of tour materials, something to send home with our visitors."

"I have that right here." Charity handed a leather satchel to Sunchaser, pulled open a shallow drawer, pushed aside several passes, and selected three with long lanyards attached. She lifted them out and smiled. "Will there be anything else?"

"A tablet and a stylus. The passes go to our visitors. Thank you, Charity."

"Of course." She set the passes down, retrieved a small tablet and a stylus from a rack behind her, and held them out for Sunchaser. Sunchaser slipped them into the pocket with her passkey. Charity laid out the passes on the counter one at a time. "Slip these around your necks. Here's yours, Kevin. And Garik." She paused at Marisa's, looking at her and back to the pass. "Have you visited with us before?"

"Charity." A shadow passed over Sunchaser's smiling face. "The pass, please. We have limited time."

"My apologies. Marisa?" Charity slipped the pass to her, before turning to her screen and seeming to intentionally occupy herself.

Sunchaser invited them to step into the atrium. Several guests milled around, two idly enjoying a drink in front of the massive windows that opened to The Docks and the blue expanse of water and sky reaching to the horizon. A smaller desk was off to the side, black granite, one Garik had never seen in real life but recognized instantly. Above, recessed into the wall and backlit in warm, golden tones, black granite letters spelled out Stamford Suites, and underneath that, in smaller letters, Exclusivity Is Job #1. Just to the side, a set of elevator doors said: Private. Stamford Suites Guests Only. An adjacent set of double glass doors led to the upper floor of the Corona Towers parking garage.

Gunther Diehl stood behind the desk, his eyes down, focused intently on some unseen job. Occasionally, he moved a hand and tapped something, and he glanced up with a smile as the party approached his desk.

"Good afternoon, Ms. Sunchaser. I see our guests have arrived." He nodded at the three visitors as if he knew them intimately. "Will any of you be wishing to swim after your tour? Mr. Lee, I believe you've enjoyed our athletic facilities on occasion. May I encourage you and your friends to join us today?"

For the first time, Kevin seemed flummoxed. He glanced at Sunchaser, who seemed to consider the question, and with a slight frown, she nodded. She leaned slightly toward Gunther and spoke in a voice too obviously loud to be a real whisper, "For a short time, Gunther. I suspect you will need to provide suits."

"Very well. Three suits for the pool. During your time in the hotel, please keep these with you." He laid three passkeys on the granite surface of the desk, looking very much like the one Sunchaser had removed from beside the elevator door. "Your thumbprint on the screen will activate them for twelve hours—"

"Twelve, Gunther?" Sunchaser interrupted, clearly considering twelve hours excessive.

"It is the default setting." He shrugged. "I can assign Jerry as a chaperone, if you prefer. He is on duty until midnight."

"Jerry?" She considered. "Is Kang Song available? No, I remember, she has the weekend's event on the mall coming. Song is out of the question. I do not think Jerry Lantana is suitable, either. He has maintenance duties that he must attend to." She cut her eyes toward the lobby. A tall man, wider in the shoulders than it seemed possible, stepped from the elevator. As he moved forward into the lobby, his presence was magnetic, and everyone within eyesight shifted their attention to him.

"Who's that?" Marisa whispered.

Both Garik and Kevin shrugged.

Halo Sunchaser provided the answer. "No one informed me Mr. Rodheimer was making an appearance today." She placed the satchel on Gunther's granite counter, the movements of her hands revealing her flustered condition, and before walking off, she emptied the tablet and stylus from her pocket and hurriedly put them with the satchel. Something clattered, metal on stone, and she moved the satchel aside. A metal passkey appeared, and she swept it up and slipped it back into her pocket. "Gunther, I'm leaving this in your hands."

"Ms. Sunchaser, you can count on me."

"My apologies, children." Sunchaser smiled. "I have other duties to attend to." She turned, letting the smile fall away, and was gone to attend to her boss.

"What have you seen so far?" Gunther reached for the passkeys, found only two, and frowned.

"Here," Marisa said, slipping one from underneath the satchel. "I

62

moved mine. I hope that's okay."

"Ah," he smiled. "Now we're ready. What have you seen so far?"

"Just the lobby," Garik ventured. "We only just arrived."

"So, we need to see everything, well, everything that you *can* see." Gunther chuckled. "I can't accompany you to everything, but I can take you on a short tour and give you a map for the rest. Your passkeys will keep you out of anyplace that's off limits. Now, if each of you will take one and press your thumb to the screen. When you're ready, I'll hit accept on my computer, and you'll be all set."

Garik noticed Marsia's smile when she placed her thumb on the screen of her passkey. He was pleased she was having a good time.

And the pool? To actually swim? That was a special bonus that he hadn't even thought to dream. What a day this was going to be!

— 11 —

GUNTHER DIEHL was more than good to his word.

They met Choi Bak as they entered the Stamford Suites "Guests Only" elevator. Mr. Choi was liveried in the Corona Towers cream top and tan trousers, with a microfiber cloth dangling from his back pocket. They waited as he pushed a polished brass cart loaded with two oversized suitcases from the elevator. Gunther called his attention to his visiting guests.

"Bak, meet our visitors. They are with us for a short tour. Kevin, whom you may know, and this is Garik, and—"

"Ah, yes." Mr. Choi took Marisa's hands in both of his. "Miss Bruni. I am glad to see you again."

"But we've never met." Marisa glanced at Garik and Kevin, then back to Mr. Choi, questioning.

"No, no, we have met, many times. I do not forget a face." Mr. Choi smiled, removed his microfiber cloth from his pocket, and held it for a moment. "Is okay, Mr. Diehl?"

"That is all, Bak. Thank you." Gunther nodded in dismissal.

Mr. Choi ran his cloth over his gleaming cart handles, returned it to his pocket, then moved toward the parking garage. The doors opened automatically when he approached.

"My apologies, Marisa. We have many returning guests, and Mr. Choi is wonderfully friendly to all of them. I'm sure he has mistaken you for someone else."

"I'm sure," Marisa murmured. She pulled her passkey from her pocket, frowned and rubbed it a moment before returning it to her pocket.

"All right, everyone aboard." Gunther moved them ahead with a wave of his hand. He inserted his passkey, and the elevator doors sealed them in. With barely a sensation of movement, the numbers beside the door began to change.

BY THE time they reached the pool area, they had crossed paths with Jerry Lantana carrying a red, metal toolbox labeled CT Maintenance Only. He wore tan coveralls in the Corona Tower colors with the Tower logo on the breast of the coveralls and JERRY stitched in a cinnamon color just below. When they were introduced, Jerry removed the disposable gloves he was wearing, pulled a new pair from a package at his waist, and slipped them on before reaching to shake hands.

They also visited the Stamford Suites Grill, just for hotel guests, and were introduced to Ted Charles, the restaurant manager, smartly suited in formal black with a red tie. He boasted a wide smile, but one eye seemed to develop a tic when Gunther asked him how his day was going and whether he'd had many guests in for lunch.

They stopped by Kang Song's office, but Bom So-hye, Song's secretary, her hair a whirl of pink cotton candy, said she regretted that Miss Kang was out for the afternoon, but she would be glad to let her know they had stopped by on their tour.

Once more in the elevator, Marisa specifically asked about Nelson Tutu, telling Gunther that Ms. Sunchaser had mentioned that he kept up with the Tower's itinerant workers.

Gunther smiled at the question. "I believe you mean temporary workers. Yes, that is in Mr. Tutu's job description. Workers at the tower are only considered temporary until they have completed their training and probationary hours. Normally that would be about six weeks. It is unusual for anyone to remain under Mr. Tutu's umbrella of influence after that. I'm sure he would be glad to schedule you in a visit, but it will need to be another day. Would you like me to set that up once you three are on your own? I can approve your visit with Ms. Sunchaser once she has concluded her business with Mr. Rodheimer."

"Can I think about it?" Her eyes said that six weeks wasn't very long against the two years her sister had been missing.

"Of course. We've reached the pool." The elevator doors opened, Gunther removed his passkey, and they stepped into a marbled foyer that sparkled with reflected light from the pool just through the glass doors ahead of them. To their left, a twenties-something man in a polo and shorts with canvas shoes in the ever-present Corona colors sat on a tall, modern stool at a glass reception desk. His tight hair was cut in a row-like pattern to imitate harshly braided hair. "Ah, Kofi. I'll leave our guests with you."

"Certainly, Mr. Diehl." The man stood respectfully and waited for further instructions.

"Let me introduce you to Kofi Mandela, the best pool boy in the Tower."

"The only one," Kofi inserted with a grin.

"And therefore, the best." Gunther and Kofi seemed to enjoy one another's banter. "Kofi has your suits and a towel for each of you. Enjoy the pool as long as you like. Feel free to explore afterwards using your passkeys. You can drop them off with Charity at the reception desk as you leave. Are there any questions?"

"You mentioned a map?" Garik heard his voice turn the sentence into a question, a silly boy thing.

"Kofi, you have the maps for our visitors?" Gunther was all warmth and friendliness.

"As you requested, Mr. Diehl. With their suits."

"I'll leave you to it, then. I have enjoyed our tour. If you should decide later to apply for a position, mention my name, and I'll be happy to expedite your application."

Gunther returned to his elevator, and Kofi had three sets of kit waiting in the changing rooms. It was only minutes before they were in the pool, with Garik so excited that he broke the smooth water into a million fractured bits with the biggest cannonball he could manage.

BACK IN the elevator, with Kevin's hair as neat as always and Marisa's mostly dry, Garik looked up to see his reflection in the smoked overhead mirror. His tight bun was long gone. The pool had turned his hair into a brown torrent of a waterfall bursting from his scalp in a wild twist of curls. Kevin had his map in his hands.

"There's a lot of this I've never seen. The inhouse laundry." He looked up and laughed. "Who would want to see that?"

"Someone with dirty clothes?" Garik felt in his pocket and produced his passkey. He stepped toward the elevator panel. "Which floor?"

"Let me try mine." Marisa smiled innocently.

"Okay," Garik agreed, and he held out his hand. "I'll insert it."

"I think I have to. Sorry, Gari." Marisa placed her thumb on the screen, pushed the passkey into the slot, and the entire access panel lit up.

"That's not, um, right." The light on Kevin's face changed as the door silently swished shut and caught him at an angle that revealed his astonishment. He looked at his key and back to the panel.

"I guess I got lucky." Marisa's eyes were wide with innocence. "I don't think I need to see anything else. You two, you can stay, but I think I'll head back to the flower shop. Father is probably overwhelmed with orders today."

"Kevin, I've also seen enough. Thank you for getting us in past the guards." Garik grinned. His mind was full of Corona Tower. He had learned it was just a place. Fancy for the richies, sure, but nothing especially mysterious, and everyone he had met had been especially friendly. *That* he hadn't expected.

"I'm just glad I was able to get you guys inside." Kevin grinned. "Do you want to do it again sometime?'

"Apply for another job? No." Marisa had already tapped the lobby icon, and the panel by the door now showed a green L. The elevator door dinged and opened.

"I mean the pool and seeing all the stuff. We didn't even make it to the gym. They have every kind of workout equipment." He punched Garik on the shoulder. "You would love it."

"It has been fun, but I don't really belong here." Looking out into the atrium past Gunther's vacant desk, he was reminded of the difference between his life and the one the patrons of this hotel lived.

"As long as you leave it cleaner than when you came, these people are all right." They moved toward the lobby. Charity was helping a mother with two small children. Choi Bak was loading their luggage onto a cart. He smiled and pretended to tweak one of the children's ears, and the mother laughed. The father was exiting the elevator with a roll-on case and two garment bags, and he seemed to be struggling getting through the door. "Anyway, think about it."

"I have." Marisa had a fresh look of determination on her face. "I'm sorry, Kevin. You, especially, Garik. I hope I don't get either of you in trouble."

"Trouble?" Garik's heart pounded. He knew Marisa. "What are you—"

She didn't wait. She walked rapidly toward the open elevator as if to help the gentleman, and then she stepped inside.

"Your passkey," Kevin called.

She held it up, smiled, and reached for the control panel. Garik burst into a sprint, falling through the door just before it closed.

"What are you doing, Garik?" Marisa slapped him on the shoulder before helping him to stand.

"Your sister." He grinned and rubbed his hip. He had hit the floor hard. His shoulder? Marisa could hit him anytime. "You forget I'm your best friend. If you're looking for her, I'm going, too."

"I don't want to get you in trouble, and this might get us in deep, like, bad trouble." Her eyes were moist, and she pointed. "Look."

"What?" He glanced to the elevator's control panel, and his eyes went wide. It didn't show just the food court and the lobby. There were forty floors and five basement levels. A green light was blinking, and a neutral voice intoned, "Palm scanner access granted two hours forty-six minutes ago. New access approval required in fourteen minutes."

"See what I mean?"

"It's okay. Gunther said our passkeys wouldn't take us anywhere we aren't supposed to go. It just means our visit is about up." He shrugged.

"It's not mine. It's Ms. Sunchaser's. I switched them."

"Oh, Marisa." Garik felt his stomach turn over. He tried to come up with a quick solution. "We can turn it in and pretend we didn't know."

"No! I'm finding Marina!" She reached past him and hit the Basement 5 icon, and the elevator floor fell from beneath them.

GARIK FULLY expected a SWAT team to be surrounding the elevator door when it opened. Boris Lindemann was endowed with prescience. And Garik and Marisa were about to be locked up and hauled away to the Bay City Police Department for breaking and entering, or at least entering the part of the building that was OFF LIMITS TO THEM.

Arik would never let him live this down.

His initial apprehension evaporated into nothing. The doors opened, and cool, impersonal light flooded the elevator. There was no one waiting on them. Not a gun, no SWAT officers, not even Gunther Diehl with a kindly, "I believe you've taken a wrong turn. This way, please. Let me show you to the exit."

Instead, there were vast corridors filled with cages with concrete walls and stainless bars or glass fronts. Light rippling across the floor in front of many of them suggested water. Marisa stepped forward first, looking back at Garik, then took his hand and pulled him into the vast space. The ceilings were twenty feet away, and catwalks above their heads doubled the space.

"Gari, these cages are filled with animals." Marisa touched the front of one. The creature inside mewled at her, reaching out a foot that was more palm than paw. She moved to the next, then the next. "What is going on? Look at these. They are all deformed."

Garik saw the deformities, but he saw more. Many of them were easily identifiable as cats, dogs, bats, even underwater creatures, such as jellyfish and squid. Others wore expressions he had seen before, in his mirror on a bad morning, when Arik was disgusted with him, or in the moments when Irina despaired of Arik's shenanigans and reached the point of giving up. Many crawled, swam, or clung to the fronts of their cages, reaching out to them as they walked by.

He didn't want to be here, to see this, to be part of this. It couldn't be real, not in Bay City, not under the feet of the people who were living out such ordinary lives right over their heads.

They were several turns in when a voice yelled, "Hey, you!" They turned to see a technician in a white coat pushing a cart loaded with food buckets. He shoved the cart aside roughly, and one bucket crashed to the floor, sending food everywhere, initiating a discordant ruckus from the nearby cages. He tapped his watch with one finger, talking into it as he walked quickly their direction.

"Run," Marisa hissed.

"Not without you." Garik grabbed her hand, and together they ducked around the end of an aisle, darted past three rows of stainless-fronted cages, and knelt, facing each other and breathing hard. "What now?"

Marisa held out the passkey. She grinned. "Back to the lobby?"

Garik didn't get to answer. An alarm sounded, setting the rest of the cages to howling, yelling, splashing, or whatever each occupant did. Pounding feet echoed, felt more than heard over the ear-splitting commotion.

"Go," he mouthed to her. She took off, and he turned, prepared to follow, when something hit him. As if in slow motion, he became the villain in a Batman comic, caught by the arms of a BolaWrap, and he tumbled to the floor. At first, he pictured himself getting up and hopping after Marisa. She would help him remove the lines from around his feet, and they could exit the elevator as if nothing had happened, leave Corona Tower and be free.

Then, his head hit the concrete floor a second time, and he fell into the depths of a blackness he was certain would never end.

— 12 —

GARIK'S EYES opened to a world of white with a bright light in the center. It was too bright for his eyes to focus on.

"It's true," he thought he whispered. He didn't hear his voice, and that was odd. The white light was odder.

"No," he moaned. He was dead, and Heaven was a real place. And Marisa wasn't here to share it with him.

Marisa! He remembered the alarm sounding, telling her to *run*, and then . . . and then what?

He blinked, and the white light coalesced into an overhead fixture. A simple bulb in a simple glass fixture. It even had a metal band surrounding the glass where it attached to the ceiling. Listening closely, he heard the light buzz slightly, as though the ballast in the fixture was well used, and it would soon need replaced.

Like today, Garik thought. I need a do-over.

He tried to stand and couldn't. Not even lift an arm. He looked to his side, then his feet, tugged harder, and realized he was strapped to a . . . hospital bed? Around him he saw white, unadorned walls, and a door with a small wire-reinforced glass window and a silver lever for a handle.

"Anybody?" This time he knew his voice worked. He called louder, "Hey, I'm in here. Where are you?"

"One moment, Mr. Shayk. Be patient."

The voice came from nowhere. Garik looked around, hoping to see someone through the reinforced window in the door, but without luck. He noticed a white grille in the wall beside the door, with a small, gray button. A speaker. Surely a microphone, too, and he bet there was a camera somewhere in there.

Metal sounded against metal, the sound reminding him of a deadbolt thumping back into its housing. The door lever twisted, and the door opened a fraction, nearly closed again, then pushed wider. He heard someone say, "I've got this one. He's fully strapped down. I'm not worried." Then the door swung wide, and a medium-size woman walked in, neither old nor young, with neutral brown hair and little makeup.

"Where am I?" Garik watched her reach behind his head. He tried to see but couldn't bend his neck that far back.

"Where you wanted to be, Mr. Shayk, and we're so glad to have you join us." She stepped back and smiled, and her face softened. "In case you've forgotten, I'm Leah Fortinier. You've also asked me that every time you've woken."

"Can you unstrap me?" He tugged his arms, the straps on his wrists refusing to move.

"That would not be wise. We have removed most of that hair. I do apologize for that." She chuckled and touched his head. "It was beautiful, but it would only get in the way."

He turned his head back and forth, letting his scalp rub against the pillow, not believing they had *cut* his *hair!* They had no *right!* His heart pounded, and he began to thrash his arms and kick his legs, screaming, "Let me out of here!"

"We've done this before. You know it doesn't get us anywhere. Okay, my young friend. Back to beddie-bye land once more." She pulled out a syringe and wiped his arm with a moistened pad.

"No," Garik whispered. Then louder, until he was yelling, "No, no, no!"

Then the needle pierced his skin, and the bright light in the center of the ceiling washed every problem away.

GARIK REMEMBERED a hazy vision of a medium-size woman who was neither young nor old. He recalled more clearly the needle.

He shifted his head, and yes, his hair was still gone. It was now bristly against the pillow. He could lift his arms this time, but when he did, people on either side of him caught his wrists.

"Now, now. Lie still. We've had too many episodes already, and Mr. Rodheimer wants to move this forward. Leave your arms right here." The woman. The . . . nurse? He couldn't remember her name.

"What's going on?" He remembered the needle. He left his arms where they put them. "Move what forward?"

"You can open your eyes." Chuckles, and a man's voice. "You are very lucky, you know. We have applicants from numerous countries all over the world vying for inclusion in our research program. You've been shunted right to the top."

"Who are you?" This time when he opened his eyes, he was no longer in the empty white room. He looked down to see himself in a hospital gown, with medical machines surrounding the bed. More hulked against the walls. Double doors with the upper parts finished in the same wire-reinforced glass completed the picture.

"Dr. Jamie." The name Jimenez on the man's lab coat suggested Jamie was his first name. "I'll be with you throughout today's procedure, and if this goes well, we'll be seeing each other quite often. How's that?"

"What procedure?" Garik didn't like being in this room, he didn't like his hair being messed with, and he definitely didn't like the sound of the word procedure.

"Not to worry." The doctor patted his arm warmly. He looked across to someone Garik couldn't see. "Leah, how's the DNA material coming along? How much longer until it's fully at body temperature?"

"Another ten minutes, Dr. Jamie." The needle voice. Leah. Fortinier, Garik seemed to recall.

"Thank you. Now, Mr. Shayk, do you want to know what you're going to become?"

"An adult?" Become? He already *was*. He jerked his legs. *They* were strapped to the bed. That was when he realized he was on an operating gurney.

"True, true, but *more*. So much more." Jimenez's eyes gleamed with excitement.

"What was in those cages?" Garik remembered the stainless-steel bars, the man with the cart, and telling Marisa to *run*.

"Ah, that. We've explained this before. Alas, the sleepy medicine tends to mess with short-term memory. Not the best experience for you to learn about who we are. It was unfortunate for you to start your time with us there, but no matter. You won't have to see that again—"

"Explained before? Leah, I think it was, said something like that. How long have I been here?" He thought of Marisa. *Run*. What had happened to her? Did she know where he was? Was anyone looking for him?

"We needed time to extract your DNA, and it's not simple splicing two different DNA strands into one distinct and completely new structure. The failure rate for that is quite high, but once we reach success, we move forward!" He clasped one hand into an excited fist. "We are now ready for you to move forward. This will need to drip for a while. Nurse?"

She handed him a needle attached to a short IV tube with a cut-off valve, and he lifted Garik's arm, gripped it tightly, and inserted it.

One of the doors burst open, and three men walked in. The first was in military attire, solid, white-haired, with a firm step and a straight back. The next two were dressed as civilians. Jimenez pressed a pad to Garik's arm and stepped back, putting his hands behind his back respectfully. The nurse also fell silent.

Jimenez nodded and acknowledged them. "Colonel Brace. Director Rodheimer. Asst. Director Hefferly."

Garik recognized the big man, Rodheimer, with his wide shoulders that were incongruous in the man's expertly tailored suit. He had been in the Tower when Ms. Sunchaser was introducing them to Gunther. The other man, with his dark, slender face and closely trimmed beard, he had seen him on the screens in the food court, advertising the mall event with the purple mist, the one Arik had caused him to miss.

The colonel was new to him.

"So, this is our young man." Rodheimer stepped to Garik, even more massive when seen from Garik's vantage point on the bed. "What enhancements do we hope to achieve with this one?"

Enhancements? Garik's temples throbbed with fear and anger. He was certain they could see. Like, prosthetics or tattoos? And then he remembered the doctor's words. DNA. No!

Still, his legs weren't free, and he had no idea where he was. Arrgh!

The slender man—Jantzen Hefferly—answered for the doctor. "Cunning. Strength. Quickness. We expect a high level of intelligence from this subject, one of the best." Hefferly lifted Garik's wrist. The pad covering the needle fell away, and blood seeped from the site. Hefferly returned the arm to the gurney. He looked in Garik's eyes, not unkindly. "Your body will be greatly improved."

"Intractability?" Colonel Brace looked up and down Garik in a cold and calculating manner. "We've yet to achieve those qualities in a compliant subject. What is the subject to be partnered with?"

"We considered several combinations, first comparing various breeds of dogs for compliance, but the cunning and quickness weren't there. When we looked further, the wolf rose to the top. Which breed did we settle on, Dr. Jamie?"

"Timber wolf. Caring with their own, extremely competent at survival skills, and the biggest and strongest of the breed."

Garik pictured the creatures from the basement cages. Surely they weren't making people into those. He spat his words, anger boiling out of him, "You can't do this to me. People will know. I've got friends. My aunt will come looking for me."

"Maybe *had* friends, Mr. Shayk." Rodheimer smirked. "Remember, you broke into a secured building. And your aunt? When you were caught breaking and entering, you were deported right back to Russia where you could no longer cause our good country additional problems. No one will come looking for you."

"My—" Garik almost said girlfriend, but what if they didn't know she had been with him? Or had they captured her, too? Was she also going to have wolf injected into her to become something strange and probably unrecognizable?

"Your what, Mr. Shayk?"

"I have a girlfriend. Does she know where I am?" Garik looked for a way to fight back, but how? Please say she is safe. Please.

"Ah, Marisa with the missing sister. How did that play out, Jantzen?"

Jantzen Hefferly cleared his throat, looking a bit uncomfortable. "We, um, had her sister, Marina, contact her with an explanation, telling Marisa that she was now living overseas. Marisa will no longer have any reason to suspect her sister is one of ours. Of course, we explained to her the reasons you were deported and that if she should decide to reveal that she had entered our secure facilities illegally, her family's flower shop might face difficulties relocating when the adjacent intersection is widened."

"That's unfair!" Garik jerked, trying to sit up, and he slipped sideways, coming partially off the gurney. The doctor on one side and Jantzen Hefferly on the other steadied him, forcing him back to the table. Garik jerked one arm free and grabbed Hefferly's wrist, twisting the man's arm. Hefferly jerked back in pain, leaving Garik grasping nothing but air.

"Ah, Mr. Shayk. We thought we had learned this lesson. We shall have to return to the straps." Jimenez motioned to his nurse to help him.

It was as they were strapping his arms and chest down that Garik understood what had happened, and even then, it was too bizarre to be true. Jantzen Hefferly hadn't twisted out of his grasp. His arm had become smoke for a moment, purple smoke, becoming solid once again as soon as it was free of Garik's hand.

How was that possible?

"Perhaps a little sleepy juice to make this easier, heh?" Jimenez smiled agreeably. "We all want this to be as pleasant an experience as possible."

"No, please," Garik begged. He was desperate for this not to happen, and he pulled against the straps. He watched Nurse Leah press a needle into the end of the IV tube, and the tube filled with liquid. She turned the valve, and he felt his muscles begin to relax.

Rodheimer and Hefferly had already exited, but Colonel Brace stood to the side and watched with a proprietary air, as though this was his money, his project, and his results. He wanted to see that it was done at the highest level of expediency.

Jimenez patted Garik's shoulder. "Better already, isn't it?"

As he closed his eyes, Garik thought of his Street Strider and Arik sitting on it with a glowing fag hanging from his lips. Except for the medicine, he would be angry all over again. Instead, the best he could do was smile at the thought of his aunt's boyfriend on the side of the road, broken down and not knowing the first thing about how to repair the bike.

"Serves you right, Arik."

He thought he spoke the words, but maybe he just dreamed them. In moments, he slipped into himself and no longer thought of anything at all.

Book 2

Inside the Darkness

— 1 —

DARKNESS SWIRLED, reaching for Garik Shayk and spinning him in a tornado of images.

Like Dorothy, he imagined, trying to focus and locate something familiar. He would rather find Marisa. He pictured his petite girlfriend, reached for her, searching for her hand, and she was gone, swallowed in the inky otherness.

He thought he glimpsed Ibn, Muhammad, and Hayat, skaters all, his friends through thick and thin. They were used to being upside down, their world catawampus, skating the streets of the city, performing their trick moves as though an adoring crowd cheered them on, prowling to brush their trucks against every curb and bench hidden by the shadows in the dead of night.

If Garik could find anyone in his tornado, they would be there.

Abruptly, he gasped, newly dizzy, and he sat up, throwing sweaty sheets and a blanket to the side, still falling, falling. He tossed his hands to his head to thrust them into his hair, only to find freshly shorn bristles covering his scalp. Reality rushed over him like a broken floodgate emptying the cesspool of his world into his head.

They had cut his *hair!*

He opened his eyes, and the falling room righted itself, shifting around him into a cohesive box of walls and windows and a floor and a ceiling. "Not Oz," he accused the room, and he released a hard breath, puffing his cheeks out, not remembering everything, but he remembered the needle.

Over and over, the needle.

What had they called it? Sleepy juice. Nurse Ratchett, er, Nurse Leah, placing the needle to his skin, and slipping it so effortlessly inside. He ran fingers down the smooth crook of the inside of his elbow. So many puncture marks. How many times had he fought back? How many times had they given him the sleepy juice? Too many times. Why? *Why?* He did grin, though, remembering one thing. The straps. It seemed he'd fought back, even if he didn't remember all of it. "Good for you, Garik," he whispered to himself. "That's showing them."

The room was cold. He tested his feet to ensure they weren't strapped down. They had been the last time he remembered anything at all. Nurse Ratchett and Dr. Strangelove, aka Dr. Jamie. He shivered at the memory. *"Do you know what you want to become?"* Then, *"We thought we had learned this lesson. We shall have to return to the straps."*

Garik's feet moved just fine, and he threw aside the bedding and drew up his knees. His ankles, the familiar bronze skin snaking out of loose, full-length pajamas in an animal print. His upper body was bare. Loosely tied cords at his waist secured the pants, and he swung his legs over the side of the bed. His toes just touched the floor, and he was surprised to find it pleasingly warm.

He pushed himself to a standing position, fully prepared to catch himself. He remembered the tornado. He must have been on something, the sleepy juice, perhaps, and it hadn't completely worn off. His thoughts felt wonky, like he was still caught up in it, and his thoughts were constantly being twisted inside out. What he wanted to find was the exit, a way out of here.

The room contained several doors, the main one closed. A darkened doorway revealed a glimpse of porcelain fixtures. He took one step toward the black space, found he was stable, and took a second.

Walking. He breathed in deeply. It felt good to walk, like he hadn't done it in a while.

He rubbed his scalp again. How long *had* it been? Too long, clearly. Inside the small bathroom, he turned on the light to reveal himself in front of a full-length mirror.

That's me? Garik wasn't sure for a moment that he was seeing himself. Then, in his aunt's apartment, the mirror over the small sink in the one tiny bathroom was postage stamp size, and when he brushed his teeth, he could barely fit in all his face at one time. Still, there were glass doors and plate glass windows around the city, and he did have pictures of himself on his watch.

Studying his shorn head and his sparse mat of newly grown hair, anger welled up in him. This wasn't the person he was supposed to be. He tightened his jaw. My mind, my reasoning, not anger. He forced himself through his self-styled mantra.

His watch! He involuntarily checked his wrist, even as he knew it was bare. All of him was, except for his borrowed pajama bottoms. They had even taken his watch, though he knew they would. How else would they keep him from calling for help from everyone he knew?

He pictured himself the last day he remembered before waking up here. He had stood in front of the flower shop doors reflected in the bright sun against the dark interior. It seemed just yesterday but was certainly weeks ago or longer. A thick, wild-boy mane of dark hair tossed into windblown disarray from his skateboard ride across the city looked back at him. He had been slim but muscular, and he was dismayed at how soft he now looked. And his *hair!* How many weeks had it been for his hair to regrow this long?

He jerked around and let his eyes roam the room, searching for clues. For anything that would give him fresh information. A bedside table with a lamp and a clock. A small desk across the room holding, and this surprised him, a computer monitor and keyboard. There was even enough space for a small sofa facing a good-size television. Across the room, the bed, rumpled, his shape still in the sheets, a slender youth of average size, revealing the impression of two arms and two legs, and yes, that was important, because he also remembered Dr. Jamie's other words: DNA. *"How's the DNA material coming along?"* And later: *"This will need to drip for a while."* Drip where? The answer was plain as orange-glow shimmer gel splashed across the walls. *Into Garik's arm.*

Who knew what that would do to his body? What had they said? Timber wolf? Garik didn't feel any different, other than frustrated from not *knowing,* from not being *told.* This was his life. They should let him know what they were doing with it.

He turned back to the mirror and moved close to inspect himself.

He lifted one eyelid and peered inside. What did wolf eyes look like? They were dogs, so there was that. Didn't some breeds have eyes of different colors? If so, his hadn't changed yet. His were still clear gray speckled with gold.

A thumb told him his teeth were still even and flat. No canine incisors to rip and tear raw flesh. His ears? Should they be pointed on top? Or was that just for werewolves? No fur on his skin, just the thin growth he was used to when he lifted his pajama legs and inspected his shins.

It seemed he was still all Garik, and that was a relief. Maybe whatever they were doing hadn't taken, and they would have to show him the door, saying, "Sorry, kid, things didn't work out. You're not the one, but then, we didn't really think you were." He could return to his small bedroom in Irina's apartment and head back to school in August. He was a senior—something he had looked forward to for three years—and while he didn't want to sit in class, he had lots of friends he missed, and he would enjoy his time with them.

"Hey," he called out. He remembered the first room, the all-white one with the wire-reinforced glass in the door. That room had spoken back to him. "Is anyone listening? I'm awake if you're there. Are your cameras on? Are you watching what I'm doing? Woo-hoo, wolf boy, waiting on instructions."

He grinned. If they were there, that would get their attention.

He checked a slim door and found a closet. The light clicked on automatically to reveal clothes, shoes, and a shelf with tees, underwear, and socks. He checked the waist of a pair of pants, and yes, they were his size, or had been before he turned all soft. Someone had been checking, doing their stuff.

The door to the room clicked, the sound of metal against metal, reminding Garik of the lock on his Street Strider when he thumbed his fob to unlock it. He stepped out of the closet to await whoever—or whatever—might be coming through the door.

THE DOOR opened wide, and a rolling metal cart with several covered items came through, followed by what Garik was relieved to see was a familiar face.

"I'm glad to see you up and moving." Nurse Leah Fortinier used her shoe to pull down a doorstop on the outside of the door. With the door secured in an open position, she worked the rest of the cart

78

through before turning back to the door, where she wrapped one hand around the edge and released the doorstop with her foot. Before the door closed, Garik caught a short corridor and a wide doorway opening to a vast space. The exterior of the door had large letters identifying it as B2-17.

"What's that?" He nodded at the cart.

"More questions?" Leah smiled pleasantly, as she began uncovering steaming portions of food. "Now, don't expect this every day. We have a cafeteria on the first level, well, on almost every level, but you'll be expected to use the one on the first level mostly. This is because this is your first day in your new room."

Leah had moved the chair from the desk to the cart, and it now looked like a high-tech dining table on wheels.

"My room?" He wanted to say, *I have a room, and it's at City View Apartments, not this,* but he was out of his element, and he had less power here than he did when dealing with his aunt's boyfriend, Arik, meaning none at all.

"Yes. I can see you've been exploring. All those clothes are sized for you, so feel free to choose what you like."

"The weather?" He made a point of rubbing his head. "I don't know if it's even summer any longer."

"I am so sorry about that. Your hair was beautiful, but it will regrow. Don't worry about the weather. You'll be inside for the time being." She patted the back of the chair. "While it's hot?"

Garik glanced at the food. It did look good, and it smelled better. He glanced back to the closet. Clothes, yes, that would be nice, too, especially with Nurse Leah standing there watching him, as if checking on whether he had begun his transformation from normal boy to teen wolf, ready to leap across the room and bite her on the ankle.

"Okay, suit yourself." Leah didn't seem upset. "I have one question for you. Do you remember my name?"

"Nurse Ratch—" He caught himself. "I'm sorry. I mean, Nurse Leah. Fortinier is your last name."

She chuckled. "Your memory is returning. I've been Nurse Ratchett to you more times than you remember. Leah is fine. Enjoy your breakfast."

She turned to leave, and Garik stopped her.

"Leah, are you locking the door again?"

"I know you want to know everything, but you can't just yet. And we can't have you wandering the facility until you've been through orientation. There are things here—good things, we think—that need to be explained before you make up your mind."

"Will I ever be able to leave?"

"Certainly." She frowned as if surprised at the bald question. "We don't keep our project participants locked in their rooms."

"Like on the bottom floor." Garik felt his face harden, and he saw Leah wince. "I mean from this place, from all of this. Or will I wind up in prison like them?"

"Patience, Mr. Shayk. I don't have all your answers now. That's what orientation is for."

"Garik. My name is Garik." His father was Mr. Shayk, and he lived in Russia on the other side of the world, a place Garik would be glad to be right now, even if he had been grateful to leave when he did.

"Thank you, Garik. I will remember that. For now, concentrate on breakfast and clothes."

"One more thing." This was vital. Garik had to know. "Cameras? Microphones? Is that how you knew I was up?"

This time Leah laughed. "We don't *spy* on our people, Garik. You do have your privacy, or as much as we can allow when inside your room. We do have heat sensors that tell us when you begin to move about. With our line of research, it's important to monitor body temperatures at all time. For your health, of course. Enjoy your morning, Garik. This afternoon we'll get you out and hopefully up to speed."

The door closed, too quickly for Garik to sound off another question, and yes, he listened for the thud of metal against metal. It came, solid and reinforced, if he was any judge.

Answers? Up to speed? How about out of here? That was the one and only answer he was certain he needed.

— 2 —

THE WINDOW. Light streamed against the outside of the blinds, the casements outlined in darker patterns. Could he crawl out? If he had to.

"If it doesn't fall out of the frame and knock me out," he joked. He remembered that part of the old movie, too. "At least I can see where this place is." He imagined the upper floors of the Tower if he hadn't been moved to some distant and secretive test facility. Area

51, perhaps. He didn't see how he could scale down the side of the building, though, unless he could shimmy down the glass exterior with his bare hands and feet.

He reached to the blinds, lifted one slat, squinted, then spread it wider. Nah, it couldn't be. That was his parents' old rock house in Russia, built by his grandpapa's hands years before he was born. The wind blew, the tree he used to climb as a small boy swayed, and a bird alighted into the sky.

"What do you think, Garik, my boy?"

Garik turned, saw a face he remembered, and dropped the slat to turn completely around. He felt caught out not to have noticed the door unlocking. "About what?"

"The view." Dr. Jimenez walked fully into the room, his hands behind his back, allowing two people to follow him in. Jimenez smiled, made his way to the window, and reached to a clear rod hanging from one side. He twisted it, and the scene jumped fully into the room. Slats of sun slashed across the floor, the warmth cutting across Garik's bare feet. "Is it as you remember? Your home, that is your home out there."

"My parents' home. I live with my aunt, Irina." Still, Garik glanced out the window, squinting, hoping to see his papa and his mama, for a moment longing for their familiar faces.

"Have you forgotten?" Jimenez grasped Garik's bare shoulder in one hand, squeezed it warmly, and dipped his head to peer at him in a fatherly manner. "You have been deported. I believe Mr., um, Hefferly apprised you of your current situation." Jimenez glanced at one of his associates as he mentioned Hefferly's name, only moving on when the associate nodded.

"The black-bearded guy." Garik wanted to shrug off the doctor's hand, but he remembered Hefferly's wrist. Garik had grabbed it, twisting hard, and then he had held nothing. The man's wrist had turned to empty air, to *smoke* in his hand, before becoming real flesh once more.

Who could do that? Better, *what* could do that?

The event . . . with Hefferly on the mall . . . surely that hadn't been real, a man turning into purple smoke. That was impossible. It must have been video fakery . . . except, Garik had held his wrist, and it had *vanished* right out of his grasp.

"What about Mr. Hefferly?" Garik felt his chest tighten. Nurse Leah. Colonel Brace. The massive shoulders of Weston Rodheimer.

The needle. And now, memories of purple smoke. His childhood home outside the window. The *tree* he had climbed as a child.

"You were deported because you broke into our secured facilities. Do you remember that?" Jimenez wasn't unkind with his words, more as though he wished to prod Garik's memories.

Garik looked back through the window, the hand on his arm keeping him connected to this room, and his thoughts flew backwards to a childhood storm. He had huddled in his bed in his room under the eaves, and lightning had punched through his small window. The crack of thunder had shaken him off his mattress, and he had fallen to the floor and rolled under the bed, pulling his blanket in after him. The next morning, the top of the old tree lay on the ground, a gaping wound in the branches, a reminder that the fist of God could strike anywhere, even just outside your window if you weren't careful.

The old tree had never been the same.

"That's not real." Garik cut a glance to the doctor, and before the man could stop him, he reached through the blinds and rapped the surface of the "window."

"Now, don't do that." Jimenez pulled him back. He grasped both his shoulders and studied Garik's face. "That was a very quick interpretation of your surroundings, and with no explanations. I didn't expect to see adaptations in you so quickly."

"Adaptations? What's that supposed to mean?" Garik shrugged off the doctor's hands. "Leah said I'd have my privacy. Can you people maybe give me some? I want to get dressed."

Garik's hope for escape was crushed. It was not a window. He wasn't in the Tower, then. Not in Russia, either. Not . . . what did he mean, adaptations? In the mirror earlier—what had he seen that Garik had missed?

"Mr. Shayk, let me—"

"Garik. I told Nurse Leah that. Do you people listen?" Garik trembled inside with frustration. He wanted to yell at the man, *Let me out of this place,* but the needle, he didn't want that again.

"Ah, yes, Garik. I will do well to remember. Let me introduce my associates, well, soon to be your associates, also, as we're making excellent progress in your case. Mr. Rodheimer is very, very pleased." Jimenez didn't seem taken aback by Garik's outburst, and he slipped an arm loosely over his shoulders and prompted him away from the window. "We can let you dress if that would make you more comfortable, but names, that won't take but a minute. First, T'Wana. T'Wana will be your physical therapist. T'Wana?"

"Hello, Garik." A woman with big features and a pronounced jaw who carried more weight than she seemed comfortable with stepped forward, offering her hand. "T'Wana Dolalas."

"Hello." When Jimenez squeezed his shoulder and nudged him forward, Garik held out his hand. "How are you?"

"I'm glad to meet you, Garik." She took his hand and gave it a squeeze, almost as if she were testing his grip, before releasing him.

"Why do I need a physical therapist? I'm fine."

T'Wana smiled, but it was Dr. Jimenez who answered. "Fine, now, my boy," and his hand squeezed Garik's shoulder reassuringly, "but the future, well, who knows? We want to keep you fine as you progress in the program. And next we have Van. Van will soon be a regular in your day. Van?"

The second person stepped forward. He wasn't old, but older than Garik—a regular adult—with good hair but a rough, pocketed face. His skin was darker than Garik's. His shirt flexed as he moved, and Garik wondered what he did, martial arts, bodybuilding, or what? He decided not martial arts, because Kevin wasn't bulky like that.

Kevin! He had been in the Tower with them when Garik and Marisa disappeared into the basement. It was a needle in his heart. He liked Kevin, felt attracted to someone who had instantly treated him as a friend, like he was important, and even invited him to take lessons at Ai Kee! Now he wished he'd had the chance to take him up on that offer.

"Garik, are you with us?" The doctor gave his shoulder a gentle reminder, a quick pump of his hand against his arm.

Garik shook his head, wiping the fog of longing from his thoughts, to see a hand reaching out to him.

"Van, Van Hermoso. I'm glad to meet you, Garik. I'll be your occupational therapist."

"I don't have an occupation." Garik took the man's hand. "Other than high school, but that's not really an occupation."

Van chuckled. "I'm here to help you develop your occupation, or, rather, the skills you will discover in the coming months. I'll also help you maintain what you already have. No sense in letting those go to waste." He released Garik's hand and stepped back, his movements quick, spare, and assured.

"Oh." Garik let that sink in. DNA. Timber wolf. *"I didn't expect to see changes so quickly."* Were they inspecting him as they watched him from across the room, the way he wriggled his nose, maybe an extended jaw, tufts of hair on the tips of his ears?

Garik shivered in the growing silence.

Rapping on the door broke the moment, and they turned to see Nurse Leah peering inside.

"My goodness, girl," T'Wana let out, her body melting out of its formality for a moment before straightening. "You nearly took my breath away."

"My apologies, Tee. Dr. Jamie?" Leah smiled brightly. "You remember Justin. Michelle requests a few moments of your time. It seems Justin has been acting out again, and, um, well, Michelle seems to think this is pretty urgent."

"Michelle?" Garik frowned. He didn't like names being bandied about, like he was an experiment in a high school petri dish, and it didn't matter what they said around him, because they would throw him out as soon as he failed to produce the desired effect.

Jimenez groaned. "Leah, has she tried calling Justin by his name? That's all he wants, for her to remember his name and *use it,* for goodness' sake."

"I think she will listen to you better than to me." Leah smiled. "Can I tell her you are coming?"

"I'll be right there. Thank you, Leah. Now, Garik," and he released Garik's shoulders with a bright sound in his voice, "I'm leaving you with T'Wana and Van. They have some things to discuss with you. If you have any questions, feel free to ask. They know what they can share with you, and anything else, well, organize your questions, and I'll see you again, perhaps even later today. Okay?"

Garik shrugged. He was glad the man's arm was gone, but he also missed the small familiarity, even if he knew it was false. Through the window, if it was even a window, the image of his childhood home had touched a tender spot inside. His mama's hug, a pat on the head from his papa.

"Okay, then." Jimenez shifted his attention, moving on from Garik. "T'Wana, Van, you've got this until I can get free, right?"

"Certainly, Dr. Jamie," the two stumbled over themselves to say.

Jimenez disappeared out the door, kicking up the doorstop and letting the door click shut behind him. The sound of the latch clicking was a jailer's key to Garik's ears. When Van checked his pocket and pulled out a passkey, smiling and taking a breath of reassurance, it seemed to say that he was glad he wasn't locked in, and the truth washed over Garik like hot butter over a prepackaged waffle.

He was lunch. That's all there was to it, ready to be eaten up, regurgitated if he didn't go down well, and tossed out with the rubbish.

And no one would know, because no one knew he was here.

GARIK PULLED a shirt over his head, a plain gray tee with a flat, woven collar around the neck. T'Wana and Van had allowed him to select an outfit from the closet and dress, for which he was grateful. If he was going to sprout wolf fur from his back, he'd as soon have it covered as out for someone to observe, document, and record in a computer file somewhere that he would never be privy to.

Wolf boy in human clothing. Watch out, watch out! It might be his canines, next. Open wide. What big teeth you have, Garik, my boy!

He rolled his pajamas and tucked them under the sink. He didn't know how often he would receive fresh ones, and none of the doors in his room had revealed any laundry facilities, yet.

He studied his face in the mirror, wished for a cap, and remembered Marisa tying his hair into a bun for their visit with Ms. Sunchaser to tour Corona Tower. He blinked his eyes to clear them, then pressed the back of one hand to each side of his face, sniffling.

Marisa. He took a deep breath, lifted his right shoulder to his face and dried that eye, and then his left.

He shook his head in dismay when he saw two damp crescents on his shoulders. Okay, let them see. They needed to know what this was doing to him. He turned, pulled the door back and turned out the light.

"First," he demanded, determined that this time they would listen to him, "I have some questions."

T'Wana and Van were seated on the small couch, and they smiled and nodded. Van said, "We expected you would. Shoot, my friend."

"That's not a real window." Garik pointed to the obvious.

"Dr. Jamie was surprised you saw through that so quickly." Van smiled.

"Nothing to see through. That tree was struck by lightning when I was seven. Half of it was gone. It never grew back."

"Oh." Van and T'Wana glanced at each other with raised eyebrows. "You said questions. Next?"

"Who is Michelle?"

"You'll meet her later—"

"You'll tell me now." Garik crossed his arms. "I'm tired of being treated like I'm an experiment. Who's Michelle?"

"Michelle Vasquez." T'Wana stood, and she glanced from Van to Garik, obviously considering how much to say. "A nurse, like Leah—"

"Except not like Leah." That was plain to Garik. "Leah does medical things, like give me shots when I fight back. She was clear that Michelle wasn't doing that, so why isn't Michelle giving *Justin* a shot? Just knock him out? You people did me more than once, as everyone keeps telling me." He rubbed the stubble on the top of his head. "I don't even remember this growing, but I remember when it wasn't there at all. So, who's Michelle?"

Van stood this time, and he touched T'Wana's arm. "I'll take the blame for this. Garik, some of our research subjects need help adjusting, and not just with developing their skills. They need more." He grimaced and touched his temple. "Michelle is our . . ." he hesitated, then blurted out, "psychiatric nurse."

T'Wana made a face when Van said the words.

Crazy people, Garik thought, and dread flooded his brain with an explosive rush. What they do to people here makes them crazy.

And they'd already done it to him. Sheesh!

— 3 —

GARIK LOOKED upward, his heart pounding. *This? They had a climbing wall?*

He was on his "orientation" with Van and T'Wana, and they had been joined by a short man with Cambodian eyes but an Irish complexion, crisply turned out in a military uniform and excessively polite.

"Do you like?" Senior Airman Shan Vang smiled at Garik, the perfect blend of manners and consideration for the young man's exposure to the new world of the Tower's basement research complex.

"What's not to like?" Garik had never used a climbing wall, so he wasn't entirely sure how they were supposed to be laid out. Arik, his aunt's boyfriend, liked to watch Wall Warriors, a competition series on television. Their climbing walls were nothing like this.

This one shot up through the floor above—Basement Level 1, if the sign on Garik's door meant anything—and the upper portion was filled on three sides with observation windows, where, Garik assumed, people on the upper floor could view the goings on up and down the climbing wall, including goof-ups, like his. He felt the hairs on his arms stand up just thinking about it. Higher were loops, straps, and harnesses hanging from ceiling gantries, several which appeared motorized. Half the wall had grips spaced impractically far apart.

"There, how could anyone climb that?" Garik nodded his head at the portion of the wall with the crazy distances between the grips.

"You've climbed, then?" Vang glanced at T'Wana and Van, slightly disapproving, without answering Garik's question. "I wasn't told."

"Are you kidding?" Garik laughed. Him? He was lucky Bay City had built the skate park. If they had built a climbing wall, he was certain he would have been on it—and broken an arm or leg or two. Besides, he didn't have to climb to see that no one's arms were that long. Unless someone could fly, well, and that was impossible. "I skate."

"Ah. That I knew." Vang's forehead smoothed, and Garik's two overseers began to breathe again. "Would you like to try?" He motioned to the wall.

"Can I?" Garik looked to Van. Dr. Jamie hadn't returned, and T'Wana seemed kind but afraid to decide without him. Van had told him about Michelle, and that had created a link, however tenuous, between the two. He didn't trust the Senior Airman, not that he distrusted him. He didn't *know* him.

"I'm sure Dr. Jamie would appreciate knowing if these are skills you might develop. Climbing, you understand. And I'm sure he will accede to my authority. I am, after all, your occupational therapist. We'll never know what occupation you can pursue if we never pursue one, will we? Besides, it's good exercise. Keeps you fit."

Van clapped Garik on the shoulder, hard enough to make him stumble. Garik frowned, but Van was smiling, not in an unfriendly way, and T'Wana nodded her agreement.

Vang gently touched Van's sleeve and said with an even, polite undertone, "Careful with the subject, Mr. Hermoso. We don't know his limits, yet."

Subject? Garik glanced at the Airman, ready to retort that he had a name. Vang was leaning in close to Van's ear, and T'Wana wore a pasted-on smile, waiting to see what was next on the "orientation" agenda, patently oblivious to the Airman's caution. Yet, Garik had heard him fine. Had he intended for him to hear? If so, why would he call him that? Maybe the man wasn't as kind as he seemed. Garik shivered.

Then he latched onto the rest of what the man had said. *We don't know his limits, yet.*

That was funny. He was seventeen, only recently a senior at Bay City High, and that was only if they ever let him out of this place. The unexpected reminder of his life outside his new prison—however fancy it might be—made him long for Ibn, Muhammad, even the three shrimps, Winter, Firestarter, and Shrimper. Especially Robbie, who was like a little brother. Garik had stayed over his place like a second home on nights when his aunt worked late before she went on assistance.

"Can we do this?" Garik drew in a deep breath, hiding his emotions behind a wall of action. He pointed upward. "Do I need one of those?"

"A harness, yes." Vang smiled. "Mr. Hermoso, we should give the boy a chance to experience some of what we have to offer. This will be a good test of his progress. Ms. Dolalas? Is our young man ready?"

"I suppose so, though I haven't personally evaluated him. Dr. Jamie only introduced us this morning, and then he was called away."

"Yes, with Justin. We are all aware. Still, you are unaware of any reason we shouldn't proceed? He will be in a harness and unlikely to fall."

"I don't fall." Garik said the words hard, angry bravado overriding his sense of caution. He was deciding he didn't like this Airman as much as the one he already knew. He would show him.

"I am pleased to hear that." Vang tapped his watch, and Garik noticed a flesh-toned earbud in his ear. "I need Maye here. We require the climbing wall." After a moment, he said, "We're here now. So, stat."

The Airman looked up, pleased. He motioned to Garik, walked with him to the wall and grasped a plastic protrusion bolted to the undulating surface.

"This is us." He wrenched the grip in several ways, and it failed to budge. "You are you. We remain the same." He rapped the grip with his knuckles, a hollow plastic sound, for emphasis. "You must adapt to us. It is easy. We provide the structure; you learn to make your way forward. Do you have questions?"

Structure? Adapt? Garik wanted to laugh. He also wanted to climb this wall, and that wouldn't happen if he offended this man.

"Can we do this now?" That would have to do—for the moment.

"Certainly. I see Mr. Maye arriving. I will put you in his capable hands. I'm looking forward to this demonstration, and I'm sure you will perform admirably."

Vang stepped back, and Garik turned to see a tall, fit, blond man striding his direction with a broad smile. Nordic in skin tone and facial structure, he carried a climbing harness with a waist belt, two leg loops, and several metal eyes to attach gear and the safety lines hanging from the ceiling.

"Garik!" The man raised one hand is an open-palm wave, his five digits like a gleaming star, as if they were old friends. "I hope you like first names. I'm Devon, the recreation coordinator and activities director around here. I've been hearing good things about you."

"Sure." *Hearing good things about me?* Garik had no idea what that meant. "You are going to help me climb this?"

"Right-o, kiddo." Devon grinned. "Let's see how well I chose your harness."

Devon knelt, held the harness to Garik's waist, and checked each of the leg loops. He adjusted the buckle on the waist belt, shortened the leg loops slightly, and stood with a grin.

"I need to put that on?" Garik glanced to Van for confirmation, to see him nod.

"Devon knows what he's doing. I'm here to observe how you perform, but Devon's in charge of this. Just do what he says."

"Okay. Do I keep my shoes on or off?"

"Ack!" Devon hit his forehead with one hand, causing Garik to notice a pronounced cowlick at his left temple. He laughed, not at all irritated. "Shoes, shoes! No one tells me they need shoes."

"I'm sorry," Garik said, apologizing for something that wasn't his fault but that he felt was his responsibility, somehow.

"Here." Devon grinned expectantly as he unzipped the largest fanny pack in the world. "I might have an extra pair in here." He pulled out a pair of thin, rubberized shoes, with a wide, Velcro flap to hold them on.

Garik turned at a hand on his shoulder to see Van at his side. Van said, "See? Devon has you covered."

The touch of the hand, the magic pair of shoes, and the climbing wall at his side . . . Garik's frustration and anger softened a bit, and in that moment, he felt a surge of anticipation.

I can do this. I know I can.

He looked up at the wall, excited, and he was certain he would reach the top and be better than anyone ever had before.

Just watch, Airman Vang. I'll show you.

GARIK GASPED as he hit the bottom of the safety line's arc. He had fallen five times already, and his legs were sure to bleed bruises before morning.

"I'm all right," he called to those below him. Devon held the end of the safety line where it looped up through a pulley attached to a ceiling gantry and anchored to Garik's harness on the other.

"We'll move you over and try again," Devon called. "Hold steady while I shift your position."

A machine attached to the pulley began to whine, Garik felt the carabiners at his waist shift and jerk, and the wall moved closer. Vang had abandoned the demonstration, except for cursory attention from time to time. The man normally lifted his head and spoke down his nose, and he wasn't doing that now, which meant the man wasn't interacting with or showing interest in Garik's current progress.

What was Garik saying? *He* wasn't interested in his current progress, because he wasn't making any.

Van still called out encouragements.

"Swell job," and, "Way to go, Garik." Garik knew better. Swell meant you didn't fall six times, and with everyone watching, too.

Dr. Jimenez had joined them about the third fall, cutting Garik's humiliation even deeper and adding raw sandpaper to the mix. And the things they'd been saying to one another. "The Director will be disappointed." "He should be making progress by now." "Even Marco could do the climbing wall after only three weeks."

Three weeks? This was Garik's first day, at least the first day he was off the "sleepy juice." He'd show Marco in another three weeks.

Then someone, Van, Garik thought, said, "Marco? Marco Lopez? Whoa, I didn't know that."

Devon said, plenty loud for Garik to hear, "Yes, and he's a confirmed failure."

Garik had no idea who Marco was, except a confirmed failure, but now he knew he was worse than Marco. What was less than a failure? A slug? A blight on the research program's record? One of the "things" on the Basement 5 level?

Is that what would happen to him? His body would degenerate into something soft and unrecognizable? He'd already lost muscle tone. The mirror that morning had proved that. Would he even recognize himself in the morning?

He looked up, the glass and hard surfaces surrounding him causing the conversations below to reverberate in his ears. He heard Vang, and he glanced down to see him at the doctor's side, his mouth covered like that made it alright to talk so loudly.

"This is not what I hoped to see. I trust we don't need to write off another of your subjects."

"I still feel hopeful," Jimenez replied. "The Director's transformation spanned six months, and much of that was touch and go. Look at him now."

"Agreed. This one? He's too soft—"

"I can hear you," Garik yelled down the shaft to the floor below.

They looked up. Jimenez smiled. "Then there's that."

"Yes, there's that." Vang dropped his hand, lifted his nose, and said the words grudgingly. "If it's anything."

Garik shook his head in dismay.

"Use the red grips this time," Devon called, his voice light and positive. "We'll try a different route."

Garik, hanging from the ceiling, the straps on his legs making them into segmented sausage links, looked at his hands. The grips smelled . . . like people. Who, he didn't know, but he had identified sixteen different people who had climbed the wall since it was last sanitized. Or maybe it was never sanitized. Who cared if confirmed failures transmitted viruses or other germs via the grips on the wall?

He knew one thing: Devon had climbed the wall, and he was good. Devon had helped attach his harness, tightening it around his waist, then giving him instructions on how to tighten the leg straps. At one point, he'd taken Garik's hand and shown him how to place his fingers and grip the plastic protrusions on the wall. The aroma left on his skin was clean and fresh, a whiff of spruce and flowing mountain streams. His smell was all over the blue and nowhere else, meaning he was better than good, but not even Devon seemed to have made it to the part with the impossible grips.

Garik began making his way along the red route, stretching, suspecting that only *tall* people could do some of the routes, and that wasn't him. He caught more odors, individual smells that were as distinct as the fingerprints on people's hands, but not any he was familiar with. What did that mean? When one hand slipped off the same grip twice, he gasped, thinking, *C'mon, people. I know how tall I am. Can't you tell? Give me something I can do.*

In a last effort to prove himself, he stretched and leaped for one of the "impossible" handholds. They were there for some reason. They couldn't be just decoration. Maybe this was the way. He touched it, felt it slide through his fingers, and he was airborne, in freefall for what seemed forever, then the safety line caught him, jerking hard against his waist and legs, and he hung, limp, sweaty, and exhausted.

Devon caught him, let out a poorly disguised, "Oomph," then muttered, "Man, even Amy could do the red route."

Garik felt his eyes water, and he didn't want tears. He squashed them shut. Even *Amy* was better than he was, and he didn't even know who Amy was. Frustration and self-loathing seeped from under his eyelids. Devon was disappointed in him, Vang said he was too soft, and Van. Even Van had stopped calling out his bright if banal encouragements.

Leave me here, he thought. I can't come down and face you people.

But he wasn't so depressed that he couldn't hear Vang say, "I can't see anything positive in this subject."

"I can still hear you!"

Were they *trying* to make him more miserable than he already was? Good luck with that!

— **4** —

GARIK STRIPPED away the climbing gear, a volcanic level of shame and embarrassment at his abject failure forcing his eyes to the floor, where they caught nothing but feet, feet, and more feet, all of people who had found their niche in whatever program he had been sucked into in the dank bowels of the Corona Tower basement.

Deported. He was here, wasn't he?

Marisa had been lied to, and *there was nothing he could do about it!* He couldn't even climb the wall that *Amy* could do. What was he going to do, shout at them, force them into letting him go? *They* had the needle. *They* had Nurse Ratchett. *They* had all the power, and he had none at all.

Garik held the climbing harness, the magic that he had so recently strapped to his legs while his heart had raced with excitement. He fumbled with resetting the buckles, unable to get them to readjust to their original settings. He was going to show Airman Vang. He was going to be the best, maybe even be a success at the part of the wall that was impossible to climb. Now, his throat was a knotted rope, and it squeezed moisture from his eyes.

He wadded the harness in one fist and knelt to remove Devon's shoes, forcing his shoulders to his face, pressing one to each eye, and he tried to stifle a ragged breath as he involuntarily sucked air down his windpipe and into his burning chest. He remembered the damp crescents from that morning. They would know. They *would know* he had been forced to tears. It was yet another mortification on top of every other failure that had bitten into his day and spat him back out, ragged and exposed for everyone to see.

A hand clasped him on the shoulder, and an open palm interrupted his misery. "Harness?" Four fingers flexed, reminding Garik of Arik when he wanted to confiscate something that didn't belong to him.

"Harness," Garik repeated and felt a tear run down one cheek, once more mortified. Just the one word had revealed his ragged emotions. His chest shook as another stumbling breath fought its way down his throat.

"Hey." Devon's face appeared at his side as the tall, blond man knelt beside him, leaning in and speaking in a whisper. His hand found the back of Garik's neck. "It's okay, kiddo. It's your first time on the wall."

"Amy could do it." Garik felt his nose turn loose, and he brushed it with the back of his wrist. He refused to look at the man.

"You heard that." Devon sat up and blew out a hard breath.

"Yeah, and Marco, and the Director will be disappointed. And Airman Vang wants to write me off." Repeating it made him angry. "Is that what you think? And Van, he thinks I'm a disappointment, too?"

Devon leaned back in, his hand still on Garik's neck. "No one thinks you're a disappointment."

"Van quit encouraging me, and now they're all over there, probably deciding to kick me out the door."

"You're not lucky enough for that, I'll promise you now." Devon chuckled, and he squeezed Garik's neck before patting him on the back. "C'mon, while they aren't looking, and we'll get you somewhere you can clean up. No sense in being more embarrassed than you already are."

"Okay." Garik glanced over to see Airman Vang looking down his nose and saying something to Dr. Jimenez. Neat, polite, but not nice. Garik frowned.

"What?" Devon stood, and he looked that direction.

"Terminate. What does Airman Vang want to terminate?"

"You can hear that?" Devon wrapped his fingers around Garik's arm and pulled him to his feet. He called to the others, "Showers! I won't let him wander off."

Devon waited until Jimenez looked their direction and held up a hand in recognition before he dropped his arm. The good doctor was making an animated point with the calm, ever-polite Vang.

"So, what was the doctor saying back there?" Devon took Garik's harness and the shoes. He tucked them into his fanny pack and held out Garik's shoes. "You can carry these."

"What do you mean?" Garik tucked the shoes under his arm. Devon had started moving, and he matched his pace.

"Just curious. I want your opinion."

"You, first." Garik was warming to the man, and he wasn't sure he liked the feeling. No one here, *no one*, meant good to him. They were all part of locking him away without his permission and lying to everyone about where he was. Every one of them.

"Right-o, kiddo." Devon laughed as if this were an inside joke, one they had shared before. "I think they were saying they were wrong, and they expect you to exceed on every test they give you, put you at the top of every leaderboard in the facility."

"Right. As if." Garik caught Devon's wink, the blond cowlick making him boyish and approachable, like Devon enjoyed a good time more than he enjoyed the people who were over him in this place.

"Your turn. Spill." Devon grinned. "Give up the goods on the good doctor."

"He told Vang I'm double fortunate to be in the program, and he would terminate me only when I proved I was a failure."

"Ouch." Devon stopped, causing Garik to almost run into him. They had reached what served as the locker room for the climbing wall, and Devon paused before opening the door. "I'm sorry you heard that. Hey, look, I don't tell everyone this, but my mother died of ALS. Do you know what that is?"

"That baseball player's disease?"

"Yes. It causes your muscles to waste away. And I'll tell you this, my mother was no failure. Forget them. You come back to the wall anytime. You'll get it eventually."

"You'll teach me? You're good. You've done every blue route. I could tell." Garik grinned. "Just none of the impossible ones."

"How could you tell that?" Devon frowned.

"Your smell. It's trees and water." *None of the impossible ones.* Would he never learn? Garik pleaded with his eyes for Devon to forgive him.

"I—" Devon smelled of his hand. "I don't—" He shook his head. "And you heard the doctor back there."

"You did, too," Garik said. "You must."

"Have they told you what they, um—" He paused and looked around. "—what they *mixed* you with?"

"Oh, timber wolf."

Devon shook his head and closed his eyes, and when he opened them, he smiled.

"What?" Garik felt his frustration building. *Just say it!*

"Timber wolf. That explains a lot. I'll need to watch what I say *and* the soap I use."

"What does that mean?"

"Nothing, kiddo. Wolf is good, better than what Hefferly got. I might even like you if you stick around. So, stick around. Now, inside and get cleaned up. Here, I even have a change of clothes for you." He dug in his pack and pulled out a tee, pants, and underwear, all in Garik's size.

"Mine are clean." Garik accepted the clothes grudgingly only when Devon forced them on him.

"Not after that in there. Go all the way through. The shower room is in the back. Soap and towels are inside. I'll wait here. Make it quick. *They* want you back again, and we don't want them to wait too long. Right-o, kiddo?"

"Right-o," and Garik slipped inside the door and let it close behind him.

WHAT HEFFERLY got. The words churned in Garik's mind, leaving red-hot embers in their wake.

What did Devon mean? Garik had grabbed Hefferly's arm, twisted, and the man's arm had evaporated in his grasp.

Hadn't it? Or had it only seemed that way?

Then, there was Amy, an unqualified success at the red route. Was she a "subject" also? Or Marco. He was a failure, and he had been a success on the climbing wall.

And why would Devon need to watch what he said around him? Or his soap? Garik was just Garik, with no differences, none except what these people had done to him.

He dried his face and, with the towel, cleared a small circle in the mirror. He studied his eyebrows, his nose, and his chin. He could hardly forgive them for his hair, but that was something *they* had done, perhaps to disguise his appearance. Who knew? The rest of him? Softer was from lack of exercise, that was all. With Van's help, and now that Devon was offering him extra time on the climbing wall—

Still, through everything, Vang's words kept toying with his mind. *"The Director will be disappointed."* And, *"I trust we don't need to write off another of your subjects."*

Him. He was talking about *him*. Garik.

He pictured himself in one of the cages on the Basement 5 level, the sad eyes looking at him and Marisa, the grasping hands, and the hopelessness they'd seen there.

Marisa! He wanted to protect her as never before, and he couldn't, not locked in here. They had lied to her, threatened her family, said they would destroy her family's business if she said anything about the Tower's basements and what they had found inside. It wasn't fair!

He couldn't bear to see himself in the mirror—helpless and soft and weak—and he wadded the towel and forced it to the glass, pressed hard, trying to make himself disappear into the steam and fog in the shower room.

Rage crawled out of him in a scream as he began to pound the glass. He wasn't sure if it was his voice or the glass breaking, but before he exhausted his fury, warmth flowed down his arm, and sirens wailed around him. Devon burst into the room, groaned and said, "I'm in trouble now," and he reached into his pack, pulled out a syringe, and plunged it into Garik's arm.

Garik wasn't sure if things were better after that or if he just didn't care. He looked into Devon's face, thought he saw his lips say, "I'm sorry," and the alarm and lights faded away.

THIS TIME when Garik woke, he recognized the light. *Not Heaven.* He waited for it to morph into the familiar light fixture before looking around.

The machines. The clinic. He heard a sound behind him. "Am I getting another injection?"

"Why would you ask that?" A pretty voice, with a familiar undertone.

"Needles, needles, needles. Anything that happens, you people poke me with a needle. What was it this time?"

"You don't remember?"

The unfamiliar voice moved into view, and for Garik, the room narrowed with shock. He tried to sit up, only to be gently pressed back to the bed.

"Not okay. You're not badly hurt, but you are hurt."

"I'm not strapped down?" He looked at his feet. His ankles were bare, but no straps. His wrists, none there, either.

"Not if you behave, and I suggest you behave." She took his arm and held it to where he could see the bandages. "I don't know how many stitches, but many. Now, lie still. Head back. Less talking."

"I know you." Big eyes. Black hair. Below her chin, though, things weren't so normal. Scales on her neck, flaps that were perhaps gill openings, bigger on her right side, and webs between her fingers on her right hand. He noticed she continually kept her left side turned his direction, as if the changes bothered her. "You're Marina."

"Yes." She smiled.

"Your mother was right. Marisa looks a lot like you." Garik watched her face, seeing Marisa in her sister, and suddenly more heartsick than he had been yet.

"You'll make me cry." Marina looked away, and she patted her face with her fingers, finally wiping her cheeks. "I know of you, that you were captured to allow Marisa to escape. Thank you."

"Okay." He hadn't thought of it that way at the time, but it made him feel a little better that she had escaped because of him, even if he'd rather that he'd escaped with her.

"You don't seem surprised to see me." Marina smiled, clearly teasing him, so much like her sister.

"Mr. Choi thought Marisa was you, and when I saw you, I immediately understood."

"That's the wolf in you."

"Aargh! Does everyone know?" Garik threw his head back and slammed his fists down on the bed. His right hand began to throb.

"I suggested you behave." Marina patted his throbbing arm. "I really liked Mr. Choi. Thank you for telling me that he remembers. Now, we can head you back to your room. B2-17, right?"

"You even know that. Don't I get any secrets?"

"I sincerely hope so. Here's one you can appreciate. Wolf is very good, better than what they've tried on some of us. Enjoy your differences. If you see Marisa again—" She took a deep breath, smiled, and said, "Never mind. Stand up. Let's get you to your room. It's two floors up. I'll be going with you, just to see that you arrive, okay?"

"My jailer."

"Your friend, if you want me to be."

He grinned. "Any friend of Marisa's—"

"—is welcome to be a friend of mine." She pulled out a passkey, slipped it into the door mechanism, and when the metal deadbolts thumped noisily, she removed it and opened the door. "With me, please."

Garik did look at his arms as they passed the climbing wall on the way back to his room. Two hands, one wolf and the other human. Is that how his life would play out? Is that why Marina was hidden away? Clearly, she was fully functional.

He didn't want to be locked away in the basements of Corona Tower for the rest of his life. Surely there was a way out.

He just had to find it.

— 5 —

"MARINA, DO I have to go back inside now?"

The sight of his door—B2-17—made Garik's skin crawl. It might be filled with everything a body needed to live, including furniture, good electronics—if he ever got the chance to use them—and a closet filled with clothes, but it also had a lock on the door, one that he didn't have a key to.

A prison was a prison was a prison, no matter how they styled it up to look like a place someone might want to live.

She had her passkey out, Garik noticed. It was required from the outside as well as the inside. He couldn't get out, but by the same measure, no one could get in, not unless they had the magic stick.

What did that mean? What would they want to keep out of his room that might want to get in?

He was no longer thinking *who* might want to get in. He had seen too much. DNA. Timber wolf. Marina in her fish clothing. Jantzen Hefferly's effervescent wrist, evaporating into smoke at the touch of Garik's hand.

It was no longer *who* might want to get in his room but *what*. Garik's thoughts had shifted as easily from one concept to the other as a man might slip down a greased pole from one level of a firehouse to another, disappearing into the dark hole in the floor to face whatever awaits him, good or bad.

"Where have you been allowed to visit so far?" Marina paused, wrapped her passkey in her hand and, after a moment, turned toward Garik.

Her eyes, a slight shifting of her lips, the anticipation of his answer. Garik remembered that night on the roof with Marisa. They each had wrapped up in blankets against the cold dark, and the sound of the Dactyls had filtered through the night air. Marisa was focused on her MicroArt tablet, furiously scribbling away on her latest graphic storyboard, and she had handed it to him to see—

"The electrified sword. I haven't seen that." He said it with an assurance he didn't know he possessed. It was thinking of Marisa. She had been captivated by the idea of the sword, even giving him a drawing of her wearing two of them when she knew Arik was coming down on him. Well, was about to come down on him, but it was the same. She had offered him protection from what she knew was coming, even if it was only ink on paper. He wanted to reach out to her and protect her now, and he couldn't.

Still, the sword was a connection to her. If he could see it, know where it was, even—though he couldn't imagine this would happen—touch it, hold it, wield it to fight his way out of this place—

"I was told you were a bit of a dreamer." Marina touched his arm. Garik jerked back to the corridor, startled to see the ordinary lights overhead, his door, B2-17, beside him, and Marina looking at him with a smile that reminded him of her sister.

"Dreamer. What do you mean?" His heart wasn't yet settled from his conquest of his dungeon prison, and he realized he could identify Marina's fragrance. "You are seaweed and the beach, did you know that?"

"What?" She laughed, pretty in the moment, and clear and guileless in her surprise. "Where did that come from?"

"I don't know." Garik shrugged. "You just are. It smells good, you know, the shore. Marisa and I used to walk to The Docks—"

"Don't tell me I smell like The Docks." Marina chuckled, her left hand at her mouth to quiet the sound. "I've lived in Bay City all my life, and that place is diesel and death. Yuck."

"No, wait." Garik would be irritated at himself for his clumsiness, but Marina seemed not to mind. He grinned. "Not The Docks. We would walk down Shorefront to Cassel Dunes and watch the surf come in. The wind would come in from the water, always cold, and the smell was like the world was brand new, and we were the only people in it."

"Seaweed, though?"

"Seaweed's not a bad thing." Garik shrugged again, though not as big as before. "It's just part of it. I like seaweed."

"Okay, then. I just never thought I smelled like seaweed." She lifted the inside of her wrist to her nose and drew in a dramatically deep breath before moving her arm away.

"And the beach," Garik reminded her.

"And the beach, so that makes seaweed okay. I can live with that." She glanced down the corridor both ways, as if deciding what she might be permitted to show him. Her eyes settled on the large room Garik had seen earlier from through his door. "Follow me. I don't think I can give you the sword, but I can show you a few other things. You must promise to behave."

"I promise." He lifted his arm to pledge his cooperation, saw the bandages, and changed arms. "I don't guess my bandages are much reassurance."

"Your promise is enough. Just be good." She waggled a finger at him before turning to lead him through the opening into the vast space beyond. "I'll need to pick up a tablet. I can get one in the clinic."

MUCH OF Basement Level 2 was off limits to Garik, he quickly found. Marina showed him the small clinic first, where she put in a code and withdrew a tablet and a stylus from a cabinet and signed in.

"What's that for?"

"I have to let them know you're with me. Have they told you about the heat sensors?"

"Yeah. They supposedly don't spy on me, but they do. What about them?"

"Don't be too harsh with them. They might save your life. It's not my place to say too much, and I'm not an expert on what will happen to you in the next few months, but you will change. Anyway, this way they will know why you aren't in your room."

No one was inside the clinic, so they only glanced around. Marina left the lights off, as they had found them. "The clinic is only for emergencies," she said, and Garik pictured his bandaged arm, wondering what constituted an emergency.

He did notice that Marina signed out a small container of lotion, and as they continued, she opened it and began working it into the skin on her right arm. She didn't explain, and pretty soon, Garik's mind had turned to other things.

The climbing wall was only one part of a much larger recreation area, with running tracks, boxing rings, and gymnastic equipment. One wall of glass fronted a water-filled room.

"That's recreation?" Garik walked to the wall, looking into the blue-tiled cavern, seeing resting places and tables underwater. It didn't look like the pool in the upper floors of the Tower that he had visited with Marisa and Kevin Lee. "Who uses that?"

"Me."

Garik turned, mortified at his continued clumsiness. "Oh. I didn't think. I'm sorry. I forget—" He cut off his words before he said something else he would regret.

"Don't apologize. I'm glad you see me and not what I've become. Let's move on."

They were walking past a long set of interior windows, plain glass backed with blinds, when Garik asked, "Why did you call me a dreamer?"

"That?" She laughed lightly. "I'm sorry. I should have watched my words. It's nothing."

"Marisa calls me a dreamer." He felt his eyes tighten with memories and shook them off. "So, why am I a dreamer, and who's been telling you that?"

"It's the way you pause, lost in your own world, and you have to be reminded that someone's talking to you—"

A loud, unexpected voice interrupted her. "There you are! Marina, wait!"

"Caught out." Marina wrapped her hand around Garik's good wrist and whispered as she laughed. "This is likely the end of our tour. It's Jantzen."

"Hefferly?" Garik knew who she meant. He just didn't know if they would meet the man from the video screens in the food court, the man who had seemed compassionate in the hospital room, or the one who had jerked away in pain when Garik had grabbed his wrist. He felt his body tense in anticipation.

"You promised." Marina gave his wrist another squeeze before releasing it.

"Be good. Right." Garik tried to relax, but the memory of the needles wasn't a good one, and to him, even though the man had seemed to have kind eyes, he also hadn't hung around to stand up for him when Dr. Jimenez had instructed Nurse Ratchett to shove the needle back in his arm to send him off to sleepy land.

"Thank you." She turned, lifted her left hand to her hair, pushed it through, and let it fall back in exactly the same place as before. "Jantzen, hello. What can I do for you? I'm taking Garik on a walkabout—"

"I know. Thank you." Jantzen stopped at their side with a smile. He straightened his dark-gray shirt with its long sleeves and shook one leg to line up a crease to center on a gleaming leather oxford. As he brushed the front of his pants flat, the black face of his watch peeked from inside his sleeve before disappearing once more. He looked almost ordinary, but his dark hair and tight beard did nothing to disguise the glint of purple from his dark eyes. "I would like to borrow Mr. Shayk for a time."

"Garik." The word was out before Garik took time to think.

"I remember. My apologies, Garik. I wasn't sure if Marina . . ." He looked at her and back to Garik. "You are familiar with one another?"

"Yes," Marina replied, leaving it at that.

"Then, Garik, you will understand that Marina needs to hydrate. I was surprised to see her leading your tour. Marina?" He smiled at her, nodded his head, and clearly dismissed her.

"Of course. Enjoy the rest of your tour, Garik." She smiled and stepped back. As she walked away, she pulled out her tablet and marked on it, holding it very much as Marisa had held her MicroArt tablet that night on the roof.

"Let's visit the break area. Meals are always taken on the floor above, but we don't want you to starve." Jantzen was ebullient, as if wishing to put his best foot forward. "This way. Very well stocked, even if I prefer regular meals over snacking."

"If my door's always locked—"

"I know." Jantzen grimaced. "But, you understand, this is a research facility, and for now, you're an unknown. But you have T'Wana and Van assigned to you—"

"Assigned to me?"

"Of course." The corridor opened up on one side to a large space with tables, chairs, and lounging spaces, a large screen on the wall, and a kitchen area and refrigerator hunkering in one corner.

"To only me?" As what, monitors, overseers, or even guards?

"Yes." Jantzen's answer was blunt, and he let his word hang without elaborating. He pulled two canned drinks from the fridge and motioned to a table. He handed one drink to Garik before pulling the tab on his. Once Garik was seated, Jantzen pulled out a chair and seated himself casually.

"Okay?" Garik could wait. Answers were what he wanted.

Jantzen let out a sigh, licked his lips, and took a sip of his drink. He leaned forward and placed both arms on the table, as if about to reveal something important. "This can't be easy for you—"

"Yah!" The word burst from Garik. "You figured that out? It took you this long? Sheesh! Stupidity fills every corridor in this place."

"Okay. I deserved that. *We* deserved that." Jantzen leaned back, took in a deep breath, and grinned sheepishly. He tapped the table for a moment with his fingers before saying, "I am sorry—"

"Just not enough to let me go." Garik's words came out like a fist into a punching bag.

"Some things I can't control. Some things I can. I can take you on a more exhaustive tour than Marina could. Does that interest you?"

"Maybe. Tell me this, first. You know Marina. Upstairs, Ms. Sunchaser acted like she never heard of her. Is everything here lies?"

"They're wrong about you." Jantzen studied Garik out of his purple eyes.

"How?"

"You're not a failure. I can already see you are becoming exactly what you are meant to be."

"I'm meant to be seventeen. I'm meant to be a senior at Bay City High next year. I'm meant to be me, Garik, not some monster you lock in a cage." By then, Garik was furious, and he pictured the cages on Basement Level 5, but he couldn't say that. It might make it true, and that was too much to stomach right then.

"How about that tour?" Jantzen stood, leaving his unfinished drink on the table. "Maybe some time to cool down will be good for us."

"Hmph." Garik refused to reply.

Jantzen looked at him, and as he stepped back to push in his chair, he murmured, "Maybe more than they intend him to be."

"I heard that," Garik said, trying to decide if he should like this man or not.

Jantzen paused a moment, as though to soak in something he hadn't expected. Finally, he grinned. "As I said, my young friend, no way are you a failure. You might be the best one yet. Follow me. I've got some things to show you."

Garik joined the slim, well-tailored man with his tight beard and dark looks, and they stepped out of the break area. The man had clearly whispered his remark, but not quietly enough. Had he intended for Garik to hear? Whatever, he had heard him fine. There, Mr. Hefferly. My secret's out. I heard every word you said, whether you wanted me to or not.

It didn't make Garik feel much better, but it was better than nothing, so he guessed it would have to do.

— 6 —

JANTZEN HEFFERLY'S first stop was at a door flanked by long walls of plate glass. The door boasted the tag, B2-Facilities Mgt. He leaned into the doorknob, faced Garik, and shrugged. "Even I have to report in." He winked and grinned before opening the door and pushing partially through. "Rachel, I've got the new kid with me. Code him in so we don't get any alarms."

Garik flicked his eyes down the identical windows with the same identical blinds—all closed—filling the corridor. He couldn't see who Jantzen was talking with, but he could hear her fine.

"I've got it already in the works. Marina had tentatively shifted him to you at the, um, yes, it's right here, at the break area. He's been with you since?" Rachel sounded very bright and efficient.

"Yes. If Weston asks, I need to acquaint myself with him, and," his voice dropped in volume, but not too low for Garik to clearly understand, "we had an incident earlier. I want to resolve this so Devon, well, it wasn't Devon's fault, and he doesn't deserve the reprimand I suspect is coming."

"Certainly." Garik heard the rapid staccato of a keyboard's rhythmic music. "There. That should give you as much time as you need."

"Thank you, Rachel." Jantzen pulled out of the doorway, and without any intervention, the door began to close, giving off the heavy metallic thump, thump of every door in the place when it closed and locked.

Garik had loved the sound when locking up his Street Strider. It was the sweet music of safety and security, of, "I'll still be here in the morning," but this was completely different. This metallic thump, thump now sang of abandonment and anger and the tedious existence of people who were no longer free.

"My apologies for excluding you, there." Jantzen nodded his head down the corridor, and he started forward, slower at first to let Garik catch up. "A little private time to handle a little necessary business. Now we can take the time we need to explore. How is your hand doing?"

"Okay." His conversation hadn't been exactly private. Garik had heard every word, but Jantzen's comment suggested he hadn't been meant to. He wondered why Devon would be in trouble. Sheesh. Nothing made sense down here.

"If that arm starts to bother you, let me know. You should heal pretty quickly, but you've just stepped on the first rung of the ladder. I don't know what changes are accelerating initially and which will take a while. It's been a few days since I've scanned your file. Devon said you mentioned Amy, and Dr. Jamie said Justin came up in conversation this morning."

"If you like." Jantzen moved quickly, and Garik was working to keep up. "Can you slow down? I haven't eaten lunch, and this is pretty quick."

"I forgot. Your first real day up and about. I'm guessing that's part of the reason for the disaster at the climbing wall." Jantzen cocked his head sideways and cut his eyes Garik's direction, his words a hot poker as though he wanted to see if any sparks flew.

"Maybe." Garik shrugged as if it didn't matter, and he attempted to thrust his hands in his pockets. One went in fine, and the other jammed on the bandages. Flustered, and embarrassed, he curled his bandaged hand at his chest and held the arm with his good one.

"Something else, then?" They had slowed, but now they approached an elevator, and Jantzen stopped and withdrew his passkey.

"Is that taking us to food?" Garik asked a real question, and he hoped he got a real answer. He *was* hungry, and he didn't know if he could find the break area, but he'd be glad to try. That required freedom, though, and Rachel had assigned Jantzen as his jailer.

"Certainly. The cafeteria up on One. You'll be expected to eat there once we feel you can wander the facility without supervision." Jantzen slipped in the passkey, the elevator came to life, and he withdrew the key. "After you," he motioned, when the doors opened.

Without supervision. Garik almost laughed. If you mean when I won't try to escape, that'll be never. Still, he was hungry, and he moved into the sumptuously quiet elevator, with its freshly deodorized and purified air. The panel by the door illuminated when he entered. It was so close. He wanted to reach out and touch it, tell it to take him to the lobby, but this didn't look like the one he had been in that fateful day when Marisa had taken them from the real world above into this warren of rooms and corridors that had trapped him in its spiderweb of lies. It was likely a basement-only elevator. They weren't apt to let him near one that might lead up into the light of possible escape or recognition by anyone he had known before.

His mind leaped to his hair and to school. He glanced up for the mirror that had been on the ceiling of the elevator that day only to see recessed panels of wood. With the current length of his hair, Bay City High was likely back in session. He wondered if his friends missed him, or if they had made new friends and he would soon be forgotten.

A familiar voice brought him back to the moment.

"Thank you, Dr. Hefferly, for holding the door. Up or down?"

"The cafeteria, so up. You?" Jantzen sounded courteous and patient, as if he knew the man approaching, and he was happy to share his elevator.

Garik wasn't so happy. He recognized the voice and involuntarily pressed his shoulder to the wall. It was Airman Vang, and he didn't want to be in this elevator car with him, not now, not tomorrow, not ever.

And there was nothing he could do. It was about to happen whether he wanted it to or not.

AIRMAN VANG stepped through the door, hesitated a fraction of a moment at the unexpected companion riding along, and nodded before turning to face the door. He was followed by a tightly built man with thinning hair and delicate features. His arms looked like they could bust bricks. Jantzen made the introductions as he inserted his passkey and pushed the button for Basement 1.

"Airman, I believe you've met our newest young man. Second Lt. Wilder, meet Garik Shayk, a recent participant in our studies."

"Shayk." Wilder nodded, acknowledging Garik. He glanced at the bandaged arm before turning to the front to stand by Airman Vang as the doors silently sealed them in.

"That's the one that went off on himself?" Wilder.

"Yes, but the runt has ears like a bat. Can hear you across the room." Vang, subvocalizing, but perfectly clear to Garik.

"Didn't know they were using bats. Thought that was too much of a Dracula thing." Wilder visibly shivered.

"Timber wolf. They hear almost as well."

"So, no Dracula, but werewolf is fine. Whatever floats their boats. Mongrels, each and every one." Wilder chuckled.

"Got that right," Vang replied.

The door opened, and the two stepped out without acknowledging the two people standing behind them. Garik shook his head in amazement. Vang should look in a mirror. That's where he would find a mongrel, as if he would even know what one was.

"Garik?" Jantzen stepped forward and turned when Garik didn't move.

"Why didn't you say something?" Garik wanted to smash the wall, but he had tried that, and now look at his arm.

"Okay." Jantzen frowned. "I introduced you. Lt. Wilder's first name is Ron. I was assured you knew Airman Vang."

"No. What they said about me. Why did you let them say that? I'm a person, not a mongrel, a werewolf thing. Why didn't you tell them to shut up?" Garik felt his world tightening, his focus narrowing, the heat of his anger rising in his face.

"You heard all that?"

"I'm not a liar. You're telling me they didn't say it?"

107

"No, I'm telling you I didn't hear it. What else did they say?"

"That you don't use bats because it would make people think of Dracula." Not exactly, but that's what they meant.

"Okay, that's a near quote. Your hearing's better than I thought. I wouldn't share that ability with just anyone." Jantzen placed a finger to his lips and smiled.

"But why would they say that with me right here?"

"Because they thought you couldn't hear them. That's a pretty good trick you have, so don't give it away. Am I making myself clear?"

"Like your arm?" Garik started to put his hands in his pockets again, looked down at his bandaged one, and didn't know what to do with them.

"I didn't hide that very well, did I?" Jantzen laughed. "You'll feel better with food. I'm serious about how well you hear. No sense in giving away all the good stuff."

"Sure." Garik touched his lips and zipped them. "Can I get nachos?"

"Sure. And if they don't have them here, I can order from Chow Down. See? We get everything down here."

"Except a passkey." Garik whispered it, looked at Jantzen, and was convinced he didn't hear. He was learning. They were teaching him, and like he had said once before, if he ever got in the Tower, he could Houdini himself out.

Give him time, and he'd be gone.

GARIK DIDN'T get nachos. He learned the cafeteria wasn't always open, and he didn't want to wait on Chow Down, so Jantzen used his passkey to enter the kitchen, and they found fruit and pie and helped themselves.

Eating did help, though it did nothing for Garik's life that had been torn away. Basement 1 was overrun with military types and people who looked like everyday workers from Bay City, and Jantzen explained that some of them were, and many of the military personnel were housed on this level, and most of them had no reason to visit the lower levels. When asked why Vang and Wilder were down there, Jantzen shrugged, suggesting they might have been there to observe Garik, and now they were through. Garik thought, good. He wouldn't have to see them again.

They bypassed Basement 2 and went directly to Basement 3 after eating. Jantzen had someone he wanted Garik to meet, Hector. When the doors opened, Garik was surprised. Basement 2, where his quarters were located, was spacious, with high ceilings, and it seemed it would make a nice place to live, if it weren't a prison. Basement 1 had been almost like outside, with an enormous ceiling. He understood why the climbing wall could extend so high up. Basement 3 felt diminished, like the weight of the entire Corona Tower was pressing down on it, stunting the walls and eating away at the headroom.

Jantzen pointed out how each basement level was smaller than the one above it and the sections that were truncated in comparison to those above. But without any real reference points except his room, the climbing wall, and the elevator, the explanations didn't stick. So what if the top basement level had parking that extended another three blocks in *that* direction, and this floor had only a blank wall? To Garik, it was all impossibly large, and the comparisons were like comparing Jupiter with the sun. When you could fit a million earths inside, all sense of scale was rendered purposeless.

Hector Mascari made more sense. When they entered his massively overcluttered apartment, Garik understood immediately what he had been paired with. He boasted a stiff but sparse mustache, light down over his body, and a very pointed face. He was exceptionally friendly and seemed to take a liking to Garik, shaking his good hand and sniffing of his bandage.

"Very good, very good," Hector had muttered to himself after shaking hands. "Nice boy, friendly boy. Must come visit again." He had moved to the sink, and as he was talking, he scrubbed his hands with hot, running water and soap.

After their visit, once they were back on the elevator, Jantzen casually asked Garik, "What about Hector? What could you tell about him?"

"He had a lot of stuff."

"Fair enough. I should be more specific. He's a failed hybrid—"

"Obviously." Garik pictured the man sniffing his bandaged hand. "He's rat, but he's too much rat, right? That's why he's a failure. You got too much of what you wanted."

"Good guess—"

"Not a guess. The hand washing gave it away. Rats aren't dirty at all, not unless we force them to be." He almost felt sorry for the ones he'd discovered nesting under his aunt's refrigerator, except for the way they'd eaten the wires, forcing him to replace the compressor and causing Arik to come down on him hard.

"Okay, then, not a guess. And yes, getting the correct ratio of DNA has been a challenge, although we're better at it now. Why rat, though? Why would we choose that?"

"They survive everything, better than almost anything else. If the world ends, the rats will still be here, and they multiply quickly. They'll be everywhere."

"Close." Jantzen chuckled. "Cockroaches would survive better, but we haven't attempted that, yet."

"Please say you won't." A cockroach man. It boggled the mind.

"Okay. Then I guess I shouldn't suggest that we might have already done worse."

Garik cut his eyes to him hard. What did that mean? He pictured what he and Marisa had seen on Basement Level 5. Was that what he meant? He was certain he would soon find out.

— 7 —

THE NUMBERS glowing beside the elevator door shifted from three to two, and the muted steel box eased to a stop like a well-oiled piston. The door released with a ding and began to slip aside, revealing where they had started.

Where Airman Vang had invaded his life and stomped on his day, Garik thought, as he felt his eyebrows crease into a frown. He watched Jantzen pocket the ever-present passkey and nod to him to exit the elevator.

"Back to my cell?" Garik relaxed the lines in his forehead to hide his irritation. Jantzen Hefferly might be part of his inquisition team, willing to keep the handcuffs on like everyone else, but he hadn't been mean to him—or barked at him when Garik had expressed his opinion. That was a strong plus in the man's favor.

"Remember? Rachel checked you out to me, like at a library." He grinned and chuckled. "I don't have to check you back in until I'm through with you. Are you ready for me to be through with you?"

"Back into a room with four walls and a fake window?" Garik made a disparaging sound with his lips, very near to spitting, which he might if he wasn't inside this very fancy moving box of a floor carriage. He lifted a hand to run through his hair, a familiar gesture from before. When his hand met only the remnants of the curls he'd once worn, it reminded him of everything else that had changed about his life. He glanced around the wood-lined metal box, so nicely finished-out and luxurious. Elevator roulette. Which floor next? Pick and choose, B1, B2, B3, or! Drum roll . . . B5! He had no idea what was on B4, except for the hospital, and only because he had CUT OPEN HIS HAND AND LANDED THERE.

Okay, met Marina there, and that had been a surprise. At least now he knew, and when he escaped, he could let Marisa know.

"So, you're a go for more adventures?" Jantzen stood patiently, backlighted by the overhead fixtures lining the ceiling outside the elevator. The doors, blocked by his arm, moved as if they wanted to close, dinged, then became flush against the sides once more. Jantzen seemed to be genuinely considering what might interest Garik.

"Amy, is she one of your experiments?" She had done the red route, by Devon's account. The humiliation still stung, and he could feel the final grip he had reached for slipping through his fingers once more, then falling, only to be caught by the safety line.

Amy hadn't needed her safety line. He wondered what she was like. Perfect, like everyone else in this place.

"Amy is someone you will enjoy. I can check if she's available. She lives on your floor." Jantzen nodded his head toward the corridor where a giant B2 testified to the location.

"Okay, if it will keep me out of prison."

"A pretty nice prison." Jantzen turned right, and their feet began to eat up the distance. The corridor was especially spacious after coming from Basement Level 3. He shifted his sleeve, touched his watch, and said, "Rachel, locate Amy for me, please."

Garik didn't hear a reply, but he didn't expect to. His companion likely had an earbud in, which is what he would wear, if they ever gave him his watch back.

JANTZEN HEFFERLY and Amy Howe together were like a flash-bang grenade, stunning Garik to the possibilities of what the research in the Corona Tower basement was capable of.

Walking down the corridor from the elevator, Jantzen had touched his ear, paused, and said, "That's fine. We'll meet her there," and he turned to Garik and said, "Want a ride?"

Garik glanced back down the corridor to where the elevator was barely visible, and he said, "Perhaps. I don't know what you mean."

"Sorry." Jantzen shrugged. "I'm throwing a lot your direction on your first outing. This is a big place. Amy is in the gaming center, about five blocks away, if we count by the city above us. We can walk, but if you want a ride—" He let the offer hang in the air.

Garik returned Jantzen's shrug, and the man walked to a wide door, slipped in his passkey, and it clicked, thump, thump, and released. Inside were Segways, Onewheels, a Hovertrax, and others. Even a golf cart, and everything was neatly lined up and plugged in.

"Don't they overcharge? They can't get used that often." Garik touched the handle of the Segway, rocking it back and forth, and knelt at the Hovertrax, wondering if he could control the bright red and black device.

"Safety overrides on the chargers. You might like this."

Garik turned to see Jantzen holding something that interested him even more than the Segway or the Hovertrax. "A ZBoard!" It was an electrically powered skateboard. He recognized it instantly, even though he'd never seen one in real life, and had never hoped to ride one. He reached for it, set it on the floor, and stepped on it.

"You'll need this." Jantzen held out his hand, and in his palm was a black remote control. "Do you need me to—"

"No, I won't." Garik cut him off. "ZBoards don't use them. I've read up on these and watched online instructional videos. I know how this works."

"That's right. The remote is for one of the other types. Anyway, I'm on a Segway." Jantzen thrust the remote onto a shelf, pulled a Segway from the line, and stepped on it. With a whine, it propelled him through the door. Garik pushed off, like a regular skateboard, and he grinned as the board began to carry him along without any effort at all.

With their exit, the door behind them began to swing silently closed. When it connected, the lock secured the devices left inside with a firm double thump.

"Cool," he murmured, no longer interested in the door. Finally, something good about this place, something he could actually do. Too bad Muhammad wasn't here to see him. He was certain he would be jealous as a green bean next to a ball of falafel wrapped in flatbread.

The gaming center arrived entirely too soon. Garik hardly noticed the way the corridors opened up, the walls turned into individual building fronts, and people began to appear. The sensation of riding the powered skateboard seemed to peel away the fog of despair that had dogged him all day.

The gaming center was a wide doorway into a darkened, flashing cauldron of activity. Jantzen stopped his Segway just outside against a honed steel and bright red wall and stepped off. He waited for Garik to join him, indicating a rack with several other mobility devices.

"Should we lock them up?" Garik was just noticing the people, and several, although not most, were using various powered devices like theirs.

"Everything belongs to Corona Corporation. Nothing to steal. Leave it and follow me."

Garik had expected the gaming center to be a warren of electronics, with virtual platforms, old-style digital arcade games, and even role-playing games. Well, yes, it had all that, but that was just scratching the surface. The real trick was the *people.*

To Garik's eyes, every other person inside was hybridized, and they were doing the *coolest things ever!*

"IS THIS how you people train?" Amy had joined them, and Garik leaned in to talk over the noise of the gaming activities around him—birdlike screeches, the crash of what looked like bowling balls and the fur-covered creatures yelling as they dodged them, a table of drinks knocked over when a hybrid with what must be wings tried to leap into the air and failed, others with extra digits, and a few mutations that Garik didn't know how to describe.

"Training is a floor down, for those of us who need it. We come up here to challenge one another. Besides, it's fun."

Amy was petite, especially compared to the hybrids filling the gaming center, and more than he had expected—having completed the climbing wall *even though she had only done the easy route*, she insisted on telling him. Her hair was streaked yellow and brown, a fashion choice, Garik assumed, and her eyes sparkled with green.

He also noticed a slight buzz when she talked—and then there was her left arm. It was slightly shorter than her right. That hadn't kept her from being effervescently friendly when she was introduced to him.

Her big eyes and tiny jaw and mouth gave her an insect-like appearance.

"Don't people get hurt sometimes?" He watched the bird-like man climb off the floor. He didn't seem bothered, and his companions brushed broken glass from him.

"Sometimes," Amy said. "That's part of the fun."

"See there, Garik." Jantzen touched his arm, and he pointed to an elevated ring, like those used for boxing. "This person might interest you. Watch the man in the leather duster."

A man and a woman climbed over the ropes. Lights throbbed overhead, in purple, red, and yellow. Music thumped, and Garik could feel it through the floor. They didn't wear any boxing gear that he could see. Then the man pulled off his duster and revealed incredibly long arms with an extra joint in his forearm. He snapped one arm around, flexing it in a way no normal arm could flex, and suddenly he held a knife.

"How did he do that?" Garik had seen his arm move, but the knife? It hadn't been there, and then it was.

"I'm cheering for Alyna." Amy raised her short arm and called out, "Hoot! Hoot! Alyna!"

"She looks normal—" Garik shot Jantzen a question with his eyes.

"Not quite. Watch." Jantzen twirled his finger for Garik to turn his face toward the ring.

Alyna pulled off gloves, flexed her hands, and she unsheathed massive claws.

"Komodo dragon," Amy breathed. "I should have been so lucky."

The crowd throughout the gaming center had slowly focused on the two participants in the ring. Now that their weapons were exposed, repeated chants calling their names began to swallow the thumping music.

"Is that the man you asked me about earlier?" Garik nudged Jantzen with his elbow. The noise had grown deafening, and they could hardly speak and be heard.

"Justin Kurtew. What do you know about him?"

"Nothing. Dr. Jamie was called away because of him."

"I'm not surprised. He's up from Three. He knows not to bring blood, but with this crowd, who can tell?" With the chanting, Jantzen had become hyper alert, and his eyes scanned the crowd. "Amy, can you help me look?"

"I have been."

Garik looked at her, studying her eyes. She was still focused on the ring and occasionally cheering for Alyna No-Last-Name. In Amy's eyes, Garik caught something else. Each large eye was filled with green crystal structures, each one reflecting something slightly different, as if she could see a hundred different images all at once.

Like a bee, Garik thought, certain he had nailed her hybridization.

A frenzied cheer erupted from around the ring, and Jantzen vanished, his clothes dropping to his chair, and a dark purple smudge flashed through the air between their table and the two combatants in the ring. Garik blinked to see Jantzen's head and shoulders behind Justin Kurtew, with his arms underneath Justin's and holding them up over his head. Justin's hands kept whipping back and forth but were unable to touch anything with his knives, and across from him, Alyna held her forehead, her claws sheathed, and blood seeping from between her fingers.

"He'll want these." Amy sighed and gathered up Jantzen's clothes. "Every time, this is what happens."

"He, um, that was real?" Garik looked from the empty seat and back to the ring, where he could just see Jantzen's dark hair as he helped Justin back into his leather duster. He remembered the video promotion showcasing Jantzen on the mall, the event Arik had forced him to miss. Camera angles and magic fakery, he had thought then. Now, he was thinking, maybe the wrist thing had actually happened.

Jantzen and Amy reappeared, and Jantzen was pulling his shirt over his head. He looked exhausted, but he grinned at Garik. "Not quite the show I intended to offer you, but as you can see, maybe we've done worse than combine a person with a cockroach."

Amy rolled her eyes. "Not that old story again."

"Are all these people, um, like that? You know, that different?" Bloodthirsty, he almost said. The physical differences were a given. They just *were*. "And why were they fighting?" Garik watched Jantzen carefully as he walked around the table and seated himself, just making sure he was as solid as a real person should be.

"That's the reason for the events on the mall. And probably the reason the good doctor was called away to see Justin." Jantzen looked down to line up a crease on one leg.

"It gives everyone a chance to burn off energy. It's the only time many of them can go outside," Amy added.

"Outside." Garik pictured the tickets no one could seem to get, the twelve-foot wall that lifted from the sidewalks to keep the city folk out, and the light show that simulated the building crumbling into silicon glitter over and over. Wouldn't Marisa love to know how close to the truth she had been?

Had been. *Was.* Marisa wasn't gone. *He* was. She was still just as right as ever.

"Can I go to one?" They had to let him. They must.

"Go to one what?" Jantzen patted his face with a napkin. He was perspiring, and he looked like his vanishing trick had been painful.

"An event. I've always wanted to. Can you get me in?" He had to do this, and before he Houdinied. He might never have another chance.

Jantzen looked hesitant, but Amy said, "Friday night, Jantzen. The Howling Pterodactyls are performing. What do you say?"

"I should say no, but after that exhibition, I don't think much will surprise you. Okay, but you're to stay with me the entire time. No impulsive stuff." He looked hard at Garik's bandage before jumping his eyes back to his face.

"On my honor. I promise." He held up his hand, almost dropped it because of the bandage, then kept it up. "No more of this."

The mall. He would be attending a Tower event, and with Jantzen Hefferly. The Dactyls weren't so wonderful, but to look up and see the silicon glitter tumbling from the sky?

How lucky was that?

— 8 —

GARIK SQUEEZED one eye open and glared at the fake window taking up much of one wall in his room.

Fake window. Fake scene outside. Fake morning sun. At least the blinds were real, even if they only muted the blaring trumpet of the sun's fake rays.

The clapper of the bell at St. Anne's kept going off in his head, and he twisted his face into the pillow, forcing the morning back through the window so he could wrap himself in the comfort of the dark and return to blissful sleep.

He twisted, the sheet binding his legs, and he kicked his feet, sending the sheet sliding to the floor. His skin prickled in the room's cool air, and he moaned with self-pity.

His night hadn't been comforting and blissful, and that was the problem. Dreams of people with dragonfly eyes, lizard tails, and massive canine teeth had haunted him. He saw Marisa's drawing of Halo Sunchaser slaying a silverback gorilla with her electrified sword, and in the dream, the gorilla had grown larger and larger, smashing the sword and Halo Sunchaser, and then coming after him.

In his mind's eye, the gorilla had become King Kong, a fur-covered Hulk, ever larger, and raging after him. He had jerked awake just as the gorilla's massive hand had wrapped around him and begun to squeeze—

Garik jerked up, sitting, his heart rumbling in his chest like the Bay City trains he sometimes heard at night from his bedroom. They squealed along the tracks to Argyle Station, inescapable, rattling the picture of his parents he kept alongside his bed. Sometimes they caught him unaware in the darkness, and they were an earthquake, about to bring the ceiling down on him.

Garik's nightmare, the gorilla. A silverback, the largest and most powerful of them all. Garik made his way to the window, opened the blinds—squinting at the brilliance slicing into the room—and studied the bird that always flew from the tree outside his parents' rock house. He wasn't warmed or reassured by the scene. His night had done that to him, and he reached to the side and toggled the selector switch. The scene flickered and became a snow-covered mountain pass, the sky filled with clouds, and falling snow obscuring much of the image. The room darkened. He relaxed his eyes and turned away from the computer-generated scene.

The mall. The Howling Dactyls. Tonight was the night. His heart jumped, faster, although for a different reason. He rubbed his arms, the prickles like sandpaper, the feeling of excitement forcing the traumas of his night into the background.

And with Jantzen Hefferly and his purple mist. He wasn't going to *see* him. He would be *with* him.

He could hardly wait.

ARRIVING AT the event might be the focus of the day but preparing for the evening on the mall promised to consume Garik's time and attention.

Jantzen arrived to escort him to breakfast. He was now regularly eating in the cafeteria on Level 1, sometimes escorted by T'Wana or Van, but today, Jantzen assured Garik he had checked him out "like a book at a library" and they would spend the day together, unless Garik wanted some alone time in his room.

"No way," Garik had retorted. "I'm with you."

Jantzen had laughed. The man was freshly crisp, unlike after his transformation and altercation with Justin Kurtew and his flashing knives. That evening, Jantzen had offered to give the ZBoard a permanent home in Garik's room, if he wanted.

Two men who introduced themselves as Joseph Howard and Tyrone Brown had arrived the next morning and installed a permanent charging station for the ZBoard. Both men's shirts said Maintenance, but Joseph was the older and came across as the leader. Tyrone smiled a lot, flashing white with his grin. Now, when Jantzen arrived, if he had his Segway, Garik automatically pulled his powered skateboard from the wall. They would be heading on an excursion through the massive basement complex of the Corona Tower, wherever the adventure might take them.

At breakfast on Friday, Jantzen suggested Garik consider the weather for their night on the mall. Today was hot in the real world—meaning summer wasn't yet over—and while it would cool quickly once the sun was down, powerful patio heaters would be set up around the mall. They weren't likely to get cold before the event ended.

Garik wanted to look his best, and with Jantzen's advice, he chose a lightweight, flower print button-up shirt with a black background, dark gray summer slacks, and black loafers. Jantzen arrived at his door in a thin, long-sleeved black pullover with a hood at his back, black gloves, and lightweight black slacks. His black brogues were polished to a shine. With his tight black hair and closely cropped beard, he was transformed into the man Garik had seen so long ago on the food court screens, promoting his upcoming event on the mall. To be here, to be part of it, and with the man himself, was as exciting as Garik thought his week could be.

He couldn't wait to get upstairs—under the stars, if there were any—and be a part of something he had been excluded from his entire life. He didn't know if he would dance like he'd seen people do from his voyeuristic forays from atop his Street Strider, but he was certain he would stand with his arms to the sky as the silicon glitter tumbled around him, and it would be the best night of his life.

Then, tomorrow, he could start in earnest on his Houdini project . . . to get out of this place and back to the life the Tower had stolen from him. He had come to look forward to spending time with Jantzen Hefferly, but that wasn't enough. He missed Marisa, even Irina, if Arik not so much. He hadn't known how much he loved his life until he was inducted unwillingly into whatever they were doing to him here.

He refused to think about the changes he had seen in the people living under the mall in the Tower's basement. He was still Garik. He looked the same, except for his hair. He had been to the activity center with Devon twice, and he was sure his body was tightening up. No fantastical teeth, no fur down his backbone, no nothing, except for the bad dreams.

He wanted his life back, but if he had to be here, it couldn't hurt to end it with a night on the mall.

Bam, this could be exciting, and Garik felt it in every fiber of his being.

THEY RODE to the mall, Jantzen on his Segway, and Garik atop his powered skateboard. They passed the elevator they normally used, and Garik did his best to remember the twists and turns to reach the main elevator, the one he and Marisa had ridden the day they dropped into the cesspool he was trapped in. It figured large in his plans to disappear from the Tower's clutches.

Like a Houdini, or a Hefferly. Flash, vanish, and he would be gone.

Garik noted the military personnel at the doors, an extra guard, one at each of the two elevator cars, even with Jantzen's passkey required for access. At the mall level, the elevator doors opened, and they stepped out into the food court. Garik glanced at the food kiosk where he had so many times purchased a drink or fries, surprised, somehow, to see it shuttered. That small moment cemented the difference between then and now. He wasn't stepping back into his old life but living in this new one, even if this was an old, familiar haunt. Around him, the glass walls enclosing the food court were still retracted, leaving the giant glass Tower in its permanent spider mode, hunched on its steel and brick legs, ready to feast on whoever or whatever came within its reach.

It had sure feasted on him, Garik thought dryly, even as his new shirt caught the light breeze and moved across his chest, the touch of the soft fabric reminding him he was arriving first class, unlike what he would have done if Muhammad had been able to land tickets that unlucky morning.

The mall was tantamount with attendees, few of them as tamely dressed as Garik and Jantzen. A military presence was also scattered around the walls and at various places throughout the event. The Dactyls were in full regalia, with their feathered masks and sequin-encrusted boots, and they were tuning their instruments. It was as discordant as if they intended to hurt people's ears, but it was a Rez band, and that's what Rez bands sounded like.

As the music began to come together, Jantzen walked the mall, greeting people, laughing with a few, and introducing Garik to faces he'd never seen. He looked for Airman Wu Han but didn't see him. There were so many military personnel in attendance that he would have been surprised if he had. Of course, Devon was present, with his blond cowlick, but in party mode, with a giant balloon crown topped with a sea serpent. And Amy, in yards of luminescent material, dancing in circles as though flying. Even Marina and Hector. He didn't recognize Marina until she spoke with him. She had on a party mask that covered her eyes, but he knew her voice when she called out to him. Hector seemed to be pickpocketing careless attendees, and Garik understood the reason his apartment looked the way it did.

As the night got wilder and the sky drew darker, Garik kept waiting on the silicon glitter to fall from the sky. Finally, Jantzen asked what he was looking for, and he laughed, explaining that the visual effects didn't extend to those in the mall. They were in a "glitter-free zone." He seemed to find it as amusing as Garik was disappointed.

The names Garik learned that evening stacked up in his mind: Paolo Leveen, with the ends of his fingers in long, claw-like nails. Joanie McDonald, who sported a mohawk. And Julia Cantos, unearthly tall; Giselle Harmon, wearing a pirate mask; Leigh Jose, with her arms crisscrossed with leather straps; and John Carter, who seemed to be a larger-than-life blond god, even fitter than Devon Maye.

At one point, Weston Rodheimer with his broad shoulders and Halo Sunchaser in her headwrap appeared. The excitement of the revelers seemed to diminish when Rodheimer drew near, but they didn't come their direction and left shortly, at which point the noise level and partying ramped back up.

Justin Kurtew was there, but he didn't come and introduce himself. He glared at Jantzen, took in Garik, and walked away. Jantzen pointed out Marco Lopez, wearing a large tail and finding it convenient to climb anything to get a better view. When Garik started to ask, Jantzen shook his head but mouthed, "Lemur."

Garik understood. No discussing DNA mixtures or hybridizations on the mall. There had to be a place where what they had become was normalized. They could be as they were, not specimens to be poked, prodded, and evaluated.

Here, they were normal, because the not-normal ones were like Garik—and Jantzen, Garik supposed, although he could morph into purple mist, even if he looked totally normal otherwise.

Like me, and in that moment, Garik suffered an epiphany of despair. He was no longer normal, or he wouldn't be eventually. What had Jantzen said? He didn't know what changes would accelerate quickly and which would take a while. That meant that Garik wasn't finished becoming whatever he would one day be.

Like these people. His head tightened, and he suddenly wanted to be away.

"Is there a problem?" Jantzen touched his elbow to get his attention.

"I used to think these were costumes. They're not, are they?" Garik's trust in the reality he used to take for granted teetered, his enthusiasm melting into a lump of soul-robbing despondency.

"Most are, but this is where our less favorable transformations can be themselves. Does it bother you?"

"No . . . yes! I don't know." Garik felt the gorilla's hand whipping him back and forth, and he didn't know what he thought any longer.

"Come, I want to tell you something that will help, I think." Jantzen led him under the Tower to a vacant table marked on the top with Chow Down. He pulled out his earbud and turned off his watch on the way. The video screens around the underside of the Tower flashed and sparkled with the Dactyl's flamboyant style. Several people were also taking a break under the tower, but they were nowhere nearby.

"So, what?" Garik felt his Arik voice coming out, and he sat up and apologized. "I'm sorry. I'm just grumpy. What did you want to tell me?"

"Grumpy, maybe, but you have good reason. Your life's been stolen, like mine."

"Like yours?" That caught Garik off guard. This was Jantzen

Hefferly. Surely, he liked his life. He lived in the Tower, had power and respect, and he could change into purple mist at any time.

"You noticed the Director didn't come our direction. We've had differences."

"I'm sorry."

"I cared for him once, really cared, before all this." Jantzen motioned to the Tower above their heads and the people dancing in a frenzy on the mall. "I couldn't tell him how I felt, so I supported his research. When his wife died, he changed. Now you see what he is."

"No, I don't see. What is he? He's the boss, isn't he?"

"Much more than that." Jantzen laughed sourly and looked away. "He's like us, you and me, except his transformation, well—" Jantzen paused and cleared his throat, "—maybe that's not the best topic for discussion."

"What? He looks okay to me."

Jantzen tightened his jaw and looked out over the crowd. "Looks can be deceiving, my friend." The man seemed to sink into himself, and Garik had to listen hard to catch his next words, ones he was certain the bearded man didn't intend him to overhear. "For six months I nursed him, thinking he wouldn't survive. Then I begged to be the second trial subject to have something in common with him. Now, it's gone all wrong."

That left him thinking. What's gone all wrong? And how bad could things get? And finally, would it happen to him? He shivered, and he had a patio heater blowing right on him. With the night, it wasn't hot enough to drive away his chill, and thinking about Jantzen's words, he began to doubt that it ever would.

— 9 —

GARIK'S PARTY ended long before the bigger party did.

He and Jantzen sat for a time, Jantzen wrapped in his thoughts, and Garik not knowing how to respond. Out on the mall, people were doing impossible stunts, twisting and jumping, perhaps even flying, although the stunts Garik saw couldn't surely be real. People using drones, or perhaps leaping while attached to wires hooked to the building.

Eventually, Dr. Jimenez appeared out of one of the two elevator cars, pausing as if taken aback by a scene of unimaginable trauma and devastation. Perhaps to him it was. He was still neatly dressed in a hospital jacket, and he even wore a stethoscope around his neck, like he'd just come from the surgical ward.

Or it could have been his costume, but Garik doubted that.

Jimenez looked around, searching, and when he saw Jantzen, he nodded his head, satisfied, and walked briskly their direction. He was almost there when he realized Garik was with him, and he frowned for a moment before replacing it with a smile. Surprisingly, he acknowledged Garik before Jantzen.

"How are you doing, my boy? I didn't expect to see you here. But then, seeing you're with Jantzen . . ." He looked Jantzen's direction and raised his eyebrows.

"Yes, Doctor, he's with me."

"Ah, then I'm not surprised."

"Don't start, Doctor. Now's not the time."

"No, no, I'm sure this is a good thing, get our young man into the gritty undersides of the beast as soon as possible. Does it feel gritty to you, young man? Or are you liking what you see?"

Garik didn't know how to answer, but he could tell there was something going on between them that they weren't saying. He responded in a way that he had mastered with Arik, answering without answering.

"I'm meeting lots of new people." He gave him a smile, knowing the man would expect one.

"A good answer. Now, Jantzen," and Jimenez turned from Garik, done with him, and addressed the other man. "I'm afraid I have a situation that requires higher authority than mine to resolve. Are you free?"

"I'm supervising Garik. How important is this?" Jantzen visibly pulled himself together. When his eyes passed over Garik, he seemed to fully see him for the first time since their conversation.

"Utmost." Jimenez glanced at Garik, paused, then said, "If you trust someone to take over, I can wait, or we can drop him off at his room."

Garik caught Jantzen's eye and shook his head no, not wanting that almost more than anything, and Jantzen nodded and said, "Let me think, Amy's here, no, let me locate Devon. This is his chance for redemption. He will appreciate that. He didn't deserve his reprimand."

Reprimand. Garik glanced at his hand, seeing the butterfly stitches still crisscrossing the cuts from the glass. He would feel sorry for Devon, but just now he was preoccupied with not being locked up back in his room. He waited, hoping, as Jantzen reinserted his earbud, tapped his watch, and spoke.

"Devon, it's Jantzen. I'm in the food court with Garik. Are you free to supervise?" He paused, then said, "I don't know the situation, so I can't answer that. Thirty minutes, an hour, maybe longer." Another pause, then, "Thanks. Eyes on at all times, Devon. I'll be waiting."

Supervising. Garik narrowed his eyes at the bearded man. He acted like a friend, then he was "supervising." Garik was his "responsibility," to be passed on to someone else. Garik chanted in his head, Eyes on at all times, Devon. Don't let him get out of your sight, Devon. Keep the leash tight, Devon.

And it was all true. He would escape now, if he could. He'd tried it from the other side often enough that he knew the wall was as impermeable as glass to water. He wasn't getting through, not with the wall up, and he wouldn't be allowed out of the basement with the wall down.

Catch-22, it was called. No matter what he did, there was no solution.

Devon showed up, finally, in full party mode, his balloon crown long gone, and his shirt untucked. He held out something shiny and called from fifty feet away, "Look what I found. Will this do?"

It turned out to be a pair of handcuffs, and Garik thought, not on my wrists!

Jantzen laughed, took the cuffs, and clasped Garik on the shoulder. "Do what Devon says. He's helping me out, and more importantly, you're helping him out." He leaned in close and whispered his final words, "For the arm," then he called to Devon, "Remember, eyes on!"

"Gotcha, Mr. Hefferly. Eyes on." Devon tapped under his eyes with two fingers spread wide. Then he laughed. He threw an arm around Garik, gave him a harder-than-necessary squeeze, and said, "This will be fun. Right-o, kiddo?"

Garik shrugged and let himself be dragged into the melee.

GARIK FINALLY convinced Devon to let Amy take him to his room, claiming he hadn't recovered from his "induction" enough, and he felt weak.

Devon dropped his party persona long enough to look into his eyes, put his arm over his shoulders again, and say, "I know how you feel, little man. The party scene is too much for some of us. You'll get here someday, and that's the truth. Go with God and be a kind person. Okay, kiddo?" He smiled, put his fingers to his lips, blew him a lighthearted kiss, and released him to Amy, before turning back to the festivities and yelling, "Hoot, hoot! Don't be a fruit!"

Anyway, the weakness was true enough, if not exactly the picture he painted for Devon and Amy. The Dactyls were howling, the air had grown cool despite the heaters, and the real problem was that Garik couldn't tell who was real and who wasn't.

Of course, they were all real, but which strange and eye-bending adaptation was part of the person, and which was costuming to disguise what was underneath?

It was like the Tower. He had dreamed of standing in the mall and seeing the glittering Tower crumble around him, and once he was there, it was all a lie, and not just like Marisa's lie. He had expected it was to hide some Tower secret, but to not be there at all once he was part of the inner circle?

Then, Jantzen, all friends, and shuffling him off to another "supervisor" the first chance he got.

Did Amy also hate him? Was she playing happy face and then saying ugly things about him?

Airman Vang was better. At least he knew the man hated him, and he could deal with that.

Inside his room, he listened to the thump-thump of the lock, and it closed him in worse than any lock he'd ever heard before. He peeled his party clothes off, wishing he'd worn something comical or outrageous. At least, people might have laughed at him, like Devon, being crazy just because he could. Devon had been having a great time.

And why wasn't the doctor surprised Garik was at the event when he learned he was with Jantzen? What reputation did Jantzen have? Good? Bad?

And the Director? How was he messed up? And did that mean Halo Sunchaser was something other than she seemed, also?

He found his way to the shower and stood under the hot water, letting it beat at his shoulders. When he knew his skin was red, he killed the water, dried off, and pulled his pajamas from under the sink, slipped them on, and stepped to the "window." It showed nighttime, but it wasn't the nighttime happening just over his head.

Even the window was a lie. He toggled the switch to change the view, saw stars, then rain, and finally a city scene, but none of them were of Bay City, no "event" or the Dactyls or the sky that should be above him.

Not even the Corona Tower, continually shattering into silicon glitter and reforming to reveal the finished glass skyscraper ready to be destroyed all over again.

None were of his home.

And he couldn't turn it *off,* just like he couldn't turn his head off. He balled his fist and pounded the wall one time before turning to his bed, falling inside, and hitting the light switch on his bedside table.

By the door, the power connection to the electric skateboard glowed green. It was ready to go play, and yet it had never seen the light of day. Even that was a lie, not a real skateboard, just a toy to chase up and down the corridors inside the basement, following Jantzen, and never turned loose to explore on his own.

Garik squeezed his eyes tightly in the darkness, glad no one was around to see, and he brushed his face with the backs of his hands. He pictured his aunt looking into his room and seeing nothing but an empty bed, Marisa at the flower shop, cutting a fresh arrangement to fulfill yesterday's order, and Robbie on the stairwell, his arms around his latest girlfriend. Did Robbie wonder what had happened to him? Did Irina? Did Marisa?

Or did they all believe the lies, lies, and more lies, that he was in Russia when he was right here, right where he belonged—except where he belonged was not in the Corona Tower basement. He didn't belong here at all. He was in too deep. How could he ever get out now?

EVEN GARIK'S churning thoughts couldn't keep him awake all night. They could, however, form the groundwork to banish him to a nightmare world as his mind tried to make sense of the things troubling him. That night, he dreamed of the silverback again, a great, hairy beast with eyes that flashed with white light. Laser beams, scorching everything they touched. Garik was more scared than he had ever been, and he knew he could never win against such a frightful opponent.

A black-clothed man appeared, and he pressed something into Garik's hand, saying, "Use it."

Garik held the pommel of a sword, and as he lifted and turned it, it became part of his arm, an extension of his hand, as natural as curling and uncurling his fingers.

The silverback growled, beat its chest, and lifted a boulder that turned into a car. The massive animal hefted the car, locked its eyes on Garik, and chucked the machine into the air.

In his head, Garik heard, "The sword! Now!"

He thrust the pommel into the air, and from the end leaped lightning. It wrapped around the car and held it heavenward, suspended, and doing no harm to anyone at all.

The silverback beat its chest again, howled, and danced from one foot to another. It was furious, betrayed, and intended to make someone pay.

Garik trembled, even as he held the sword that had the power to keep everyone safe. Yet, for how long?

How long could he hold on before the truth came out? He was just Garik, seventeen, weak, and not prepared for this at all. He just wanted to go home.

In that moment of longing, Garik's arm fell, the electrified sword's light and power went wild, and the car fell tumbling to the ground. The silverback beat its chest once more, hooted in triumph, grew ever larger, and with an open fist, ran at Garik, becoming more massive with every step. Its arms were twenty feet long, its fists as big as a house. When the fist wrapped around him and began to squeeze, Garik jerked awake, back in his room and covered in sweat.

He opened his eyes and stared into the blackness, waiting too long for his heart to settle and his chest to stop heaving.

The man in black. Someone had tried to save him. Yet, Garik saw the truth the way it really was. Only one person could save him, and that was himself. And he had failed. He had dropped the sword and let everything come undone.

— 10 —

BREAKFAST DIDN'T have the usual appeal the next morning.

Not only was Garik's mind awash with the residue of his dreams, Jantzen appeared preoccupied.

"What?" Garik prodded him, wanting the joking, warm mentor back. He didn't know it until then, but he had come to depend on the dark-haired man as a friend-surrogate. He didn't know if he could ever consider him an actual friend, but he was as close as Garik was getting in this place.

"A situation." Jantzen diddled with his food, cutting his breakfast burrito with a fork, then pushing it back, uninterested. He looked off, scanning the other diners in the cafeteria but specifically not at Garik.

"What?" Garik hit the word hard, and he felt last night's despair rising like bile in his throat.

"Something I have to work out." Jantzen glanced at him, caught his eyes, and turned away.

"What happened last night? That's it, isn't it? What can't you say?"

"How about," and Jantzen let a smile spread across his face, "we give you broader opportunities today?"

"My own passkey?" The possibility sent Garik's heart into double time.

"Not so fast, my little highballer. Passkeys require directorial approval. I am working to get your door unlocked—"

"You can do that? I thought the doors always used passkeys." No passkey, but being able to come and go? The possibility of the unexpected freedom seemed a godsend.

"Only for newbies." Jantzen placed his hand on Garik's wrist, winked at him, and drew his hand away. "I have something else for you today, something you might enjoy. Are you interested?"

"I don't know, but if it keeps me from being locked in my room, probably."

"Hold on a moment." Jantzen stood and walked away from the table, leaving Garik stunned. It was the first time his leash had been unclipped since arriving in this place.

What did it mean?

He watched the man choose a table with several people he recognized from the previous evening. One was the woman with the mohawk, Joanie. He leaned over, spoke with her, and at one point, turned Garik's direction and showed her where he was sitting.

She smiled, nodded, and stood. Two other people stood with her: Paolo, the man with the claw-like nails, and a pretty woman Garik didn't recognize. They headed his direction but, notably, Jantzen didn't.

Again, he failed to see a pattern that made sense to him. These people looked mostly normal, well, as normal as a mohawk and claws could allow a person to be. The third person, well, he would have to wait and see.

Joanie arrived first, carrying a bit of a swagger, and she pulled out a chair roughly, dropping into it. She studied Garik's face as the other two arrived.

"Peach fuzz." Joanie leaned forward, her forearms on the table, and she smirked. "Baby barker."

"Be nice, Joanie." Paolo pulled out a chair and slipped sinuously into it, spreading his hands on the table in front of him as if to announce his differences, the transformation brought on by the mixture of his DNA with another creature. He brought with him a clean, ocean smell.

"Am. Was. Will be." Joanie's eyes were still fixed on Garik.

"What?" Garik spat the word. It was like she was evaluating him, deciding if he was human or not, and his anger jumped to tornado level.

"Joanie," Paolo warned a second time.

"Too human," Joanie said, and she broke her gaze, like she had taken in all the variables, and she had made her decision. She slipped a pack of mints from a pocket, and without looking, slipped one between her lips and made the package disappear.

"Seems like a good thing to be," Garik hurled back. He looked to the third person, trying to place her, and when she put her hand under her chin with her elbow on the table and winked at him, he knew. "Giselle, right?" He had seen her do that to Paolo last night, giving him her rapt attention. He'd wondered if they were a thing at the time, but now she was doing it to him.

"You remember. You are a sweetie, if a bit of a boy." She winked again, and she glanced at Paolo to see how he responded to her tease.

He didn't seem to notice.

"So, what's wrong with being human? I thought that was the plan, to make people who are different but can pass for human." He thought of the scene in the gaming center. Justin's arms and Alyna's retractable claws. Alyna might pass, but Justin, never.

Wasn't that why he was a failed hybrid?

"Pass, not *be*." Joanie turned her head to look back at their previous table. Her mohawk shifted, flexed, and resettled itself where it belonged. Jantzen was gone, but there were others still at the table, watching them, waiting, it now seemed, on Joanie. Joanie jerked her head in a "come on over" motion, and they erratically stood like pop-up toys, gathering their food trays for disposal before heading over.

"More of you?" Garik heard himself adopting Joanie's clipped style of speech. It gave him a bravado he didn't really feel, one he needed to face this overwhelming assault of the Tower's denizens. He recognized John Carter, with his height and blond hair, and Leigh and Julia, but a gothic queen he didn't remember from the night before was new to him.

"So," Paolo began, "what are you?"

Garik was aware of the faces, the new people standing behind the first three, the gothic queen with one elbow resting on Giselle's shoulder, all waiting on his answer.

"I thought we weren't supposed to discuss it." Last night, Jantzen had hushed him. Now, Garik wasn't sure.

"Only at the events." That was the tall Julia. "Down here, no secrets."

Still, Garik thought, why did it matter?

"Okay, baby barker. Already know. For you, I'll squeal. Jellyfish." Joanie didn't exactly smile, but it was likely the closest Garik would get.

Garik laughed. "What's the point in a jellyfish? They don't do anything."

"Except live forever." That was from Julia, and she popped a square of gum in her mouth. Joanie smiled, a real one this time.

"Sea cucumber." Giselle winked and pursed her lips in a kissy-kissy tease.

"And?" Garik wanted to hear this. He didn't think sea cucumbers were good for anything, either.

"I'll show you sometime." Giselle laid a pretty hand on his arm.

"Liquefaction. She can turn to water and back again." Paolo sighed. "It's not a secret."

"I wanted to show him," she pouted. "Besides, I don't really turn to water."

"It looks like it," blond John barbed.

"Tell him yours, then," Giselle vamped, sending him one of her kissy-kissies.

"Wood frog." He looked down as if embarrassed. "I can freeze my own blood and survive in subzero temperatures."

"Thrive, not survive, iceman," Giselle tittered.

"Deal with it, Giselle," John muttered.

"Enough," Joanie barked. "Next?"

Garik's head was spinning. Live forever, turn to water, freezing your own blood? It was craziness!

Still, the revelations continued.

Tall Julia was blended with a boa constrictor. She boasted a built-in infrared heat detector for locating living tissue in the dark.

The gothic queen was Laura Lassere, now half dragon millipede, giving her the ability to breathe out puffs of hydrogen cyanide from specially developed pouches in her throat.

Leigh Jose was part dolphin, though she didn't have a blowhole or the ability to swim underwater for extended periods. She could communicate via ultrasound, however.

"You," Garik nodded toward Paolo. He looked at the man's hands. "What caused that?"

Paolo lifted his hands and twirled them before smiling. "The remnants of my pinchers. I'm part pistol shrimp."

Ah, the ocean smell now made sense. But pistol shrimp? Garik must have looked puzzled, because Giselle offered a teasing explanation.

"Makes him too hot to touch, if you get my meaning." She winked at Garik even as she placed one hand on Paolo's. Garik noticed that he pulled his from under hers and set it aside.

"I can eject boiling water from my fingertips." He shrugged. "Your turn." He tapped one long fingernail and pointed it Garik's direction.

"Timber wolf." Garik shrugged. It seemed simple and non-evasive, compared to what he had just learned about these people.

"Lucky boy," Julia muttered, looking away, before turning her eyes back to Garik.

"Precog?" Leigh leaned in towards Laura, whispering, but Garik caught her question. Precog, like precognition? That was a wolf thing?

Laura's reply was even more puzzling. "The dog thing hasn't gone so well for Christian, and he's definitely precog."

"True," Leigh nodded. "Seeing the future is seeing your pain."

"Cease!" Joanie stood. "Come." She nodded her head, walked away, and the rest of the group moved with her. Paolo rapped the table, crooked his fingers at Garik, and waited for him to join the group.

Garik scooted his chair back noisily, wondered if he should police his table, and decided there was no time. These people would leave him behind, otherwise.

And he was interested. He wanted to know more.

GARIK'S DOOR double clicked, the thump-thump that told of the lock mechanism releasing.

He was on his bed, still clothed, and too filled with the day to do more than look at the ceiling and try to make sense of everything. Hot water expulsion, sonic communication, and turning to water. What else was possible? Next to those guys, he was nothing. He could hear a little better than before, and maybe his sense of smell was improved, but nothing else. He was still just Garik, Bay City teen on loan from Russia, and living on the struggling side of town. He would never be special like those people.

He wasn't sure he wanted to be. They seemed to have formed a team of sorts, friends, certainly, but they were also skittish about their lives down here, as if their future was uncertain, and they were looking for a way to ensure their survival.

Did he need to worry? It seemed he was being given everything he wanted, even watched over by the second-in-command, a man who seemed to like him and want the best for him.

Jantzen had even gone to bat for Devon when it was Garik who had messed up. Garik still felt bad about that, although there was little he could do to change past events. He would simply have to make better choices in the future.

Jantzen walked in, surprisingly more rumpled and tired than Garik had seen him before. Jantzen smiled, the expression dulled by whatever the day had done to him.

"Hello." Garik sat up. "Thank you for my day."

"I thought you might like them." Jantzen kicked off his shoes, carried himself to the sofa and dropped, leaning his head back. "I'm glad someone had a good day."

"I did. I can't believe all the stuff they can do."

"I can't either, sometimes." His eyes were closed, and he took a deep breath and released it. "What did you pick up from them?"

Ah, a test. Garik deflated. He'd thought . . . maybe hoped that Jantzen had returned as a friend, and now, he was asking him to evaluate his day, as if the people he'd been with were what mattered, and not Garik or his feelings or what the day meant to him. The disappointment cut, and the thought flashed through him that Jantzen should leave. He didn't need him here, because he was fine on his own.

"Did they say anything?" Jantzen rolled his head sideways and looked at Garik, not irritated or pushy, just reminding him that he'd asked a question.

"They're scared." Garik hadn't thought it just like that, but when it came out, he knew that was it.

"Why? Tell me what you got from them that told you that." Jantzen seemed more interested, as though Garik had noticed something important.

"Their skills aren't good enough." Garik expected Jantzen to agree with him, but the man continued to watch him, not responding, other than a tightened expression around his mouth.

"That's it?"

"No, that's not it at all. They are good, can do amazing things." He thought of Airman Vang, and Colonel Brace from the hospital room flashed into his thoughts. *We've yet to achieve those qualities in a compliant subject.* "They don't play the game, not the way they're expected to. That's what you wanted me to see, isn't it?"

"Last night, I had to initiate a reassignment for one of our failed hybrids to Basement 5. You know what that means, don't you?"

"Yes." Garik pictured the cages, the mewling creatures, the desperate eyes.

"This one didn't show quick enough progress for Weston, or at least not the kind he wanted."

Progress. Garik thought back to Leah Fortinier's words. *Mr. Rodheimer wants to move this forward.* Airman Vang had been concerned about his lack of progress, also. Then, this morning, Joanie's evaluation. *"Too human."* Garik felt the bile rising in his throat.

"What does that mean for me?" Even to ask it meant it wasn't good.

"That's what I'm trying to work out. Maybe . . . no, it's too early for that. Just know that I'm on your side. I'll do what I can to protect you."

Jantzen stood wearily, sighed heavily, and made his way towards the door. He slipped on his shoes, pulled out his passkey, and inserted it into the lock. Thump-thump, and without looking back, he was gone.

Garik pulled his knees to his chest and wrapped his arms around them. Try to protect him?

He didn't feel better, not any at all.

VAN HERMOSO was the first one in Garik's door the following day.

"Good morning, Garik." He smiled too broad of a smile, as if he hoped to cover up something he didn't want to say. "I see you're up and dressed. T'Wana will be joining us for breakfast. We have a full morning scheduled for you, so you'll be getting a break from your room this morning. How does that sound?"

"But . . ." Garik held his hand over his computer keyboard in the middle of typing a search query.

"Go ahead, shoot. I'm listening." Van smiled, but Garik noticed it was a little less broadly than before.

"I have a full morning already scheduled." He motioned to the computer. It was on and connected to the research center's educational site. He was expected to keep up his studies, even though it seemed irrelevant with being locked away in this basement PROBABLY FOR HIS ENTIRE LIFE. "And this afternoon, Devon said I could spend some time climbing with him. Can't this wait?"

"I'm afraid not." Van walked to his closet, opened it, and pulled out a pair of athletic shoes. "Excellent! These should do. If you will get these on, we'll head to breakfast. Get you all sorted out, all that stuff. I wouldn't plan on making it to Devon's, but we'll see closer to lunch. T'Wana will update you with more information at breakfast."

"Okay." Garik shrugged. He didn't mind missing the school lessons, but his climbing lesson with Devon? That was less comforting. And Van's overly upbeat attitude? It was like leading a puppy to the pound and repeating, "Here, puppy. Good puppy." It sounded nice, but the results wouldn't be agreeable.

Rather than argue, Garik worked his feet into the shoes and stood. He touched his keyboard to bookmark his place and shut it down. He had pants and a shirt on and nothing else to take with him. He glanced longingly at his ZBoard, but Van liked to walk everywhere, so the skateboard wasn't an option.

Both T'Wana and Van joining him for breakfast? The bad vibes were off the chart, and Garik wondered how his life would be different after today.

GARIK REACHED the side of the pool, barely, and pulled himself far enough out of the water that he could breathe. His chest heaved, and he expected the volcanic upheaval in his stomach to breach the levee as soon as he quit wheezing. He was fully clothed and had been wearing a pack with weights on his back *for twelve laps of the pool.*

Were they trying to kill him?

All morning, he had sat in a room on Basement Level 3 guessing what was on cards, prompted by a band wrapped around his arm that gave him a mild shock with each wrong answer. They kept upping the shock value with each question.

His success rate had been nearly nil.

He guessed Leigh and Laura didn't know as much about Christian as they thought. Precog? There was no such thing in Garik's brain, and he had the scorch marks on his arm to prove it.

Rapid reading skills, flashing words in front of him until they blurred. His head had been spinning before they finished. Then he had been placed in a maze, inside a soundproof room, he thought, because it had gone deadly silent when they closed the door. Inside was a full-size, walled-in maze, and once he was inside, they had turned out the lights. It didn't stay quiet. They expected him to find his way out WITH REZ MUSIC BLASTING THE ENTIRE TIME.

He left that one with his head splitting open.

The pool was the culmination of sprints, one after the other, chin ups that required his chin to reach past the bar, two-minute non-stop crunches, and a full minute of pushups. He had to restart three times on the pushups, each time more exhausted and more determined to finish than before.

Airman Vang and Colonel Brace had shown up during his weight training test, and they had a phalanx of six others with them, one of which Garik thought might be Wu Han, the Airman he had met in the food court. He didn't understand the reason for the basketball throw or the kettlebell snatch. He hadn't even known there was such a thing as a kettlebell snatch, and he dropped the heavy weight several times before he got the hang of it, and with everyone watching, to his mortification.

Dr. Jimenez was there the entire time, with Nurse Ratchett, observing, marking things down, occasionally saying just loud enough for Garik to make out, "Enough, gentlemen. We don't want to kill him."

Thank you, Garik thought, though he didn't expect it was out of personal concern for his welfare. More likely, they didn't want to have to carry his dead body out of wherever he expired. If he was alive, he could walk out and die on someone else's time.

After they watched Garik pull himself from the pool and shuck off the weighted pack, kneeling and trying to figure out why he wasn't dead already, Dr. Jimenez appeared with a tablet and a stylus and directed him to a bench off to the side.

"Come, my boy. We're learning much today. Let's have a seat over here."

"Garik," he growled. "I'm not a boy. I'm me."

"So I see. Let's sit and have a talk."

"Sure." He was sopping, his shoes were filled with water, and he'd completed twelve laps of the pool. How about you, Dr. Jamie? Want to give it a try? Still, he stood, walked as steadily as he could, gently lowered himself to the bench.

"Did you see the Colonel earlier?" Jimenez sounded kinder than Garik had expected.

"Yes." Garik used his hand to wipe the remnants of pool water from his face.

"And Director Rodheimer, did you notice him?"

Garik hadn't, and he looked up and across to the observers at the far side of the pool.

"Oh, he's gone, now. I dare say he's not impressed with your progress."

"What's not to impress? I completed everything you people gave me to do. What do you want from me?"

"Clearly, more than you're giving us. We expected much more from you by this point. It seems the DNA enhancement hasn't taken with you as expected." The doctor seemed almost wistful.

"So I can go home?" If so, the tests today were worth it, just to get out of here.

"Oh, you misunderstand me. No one who starts the program ever gets to go home. You are a permanent part of the facility's residents. There are, um, other avenues for your skills, those you are able to maintain."

Like Marina and Hector. They got more than they wanted from them, and now they were useless to them except as grunt labor. What was Garik, less than useless? He still had his arms and legs. He could run, jump, and swim. Wasn't that worth something?

Would he end up like Devon, instructing those who might show prospective skills? Or like T'Wana or Van, nudging other inductees, unwilling or otherwise, into the best their newly hybridized bodies could be?

"Can I change into dry clothes?" Enough was enough. For once, Garik could be locked in his room for two days and he wouldn't care.

"Let me ask you this, Mr. Shayk. Do you have anything else to give us? Are there reserves in there you haven't tapped, yet?"

Garik heard the man's words. Mr. Shayk. He had been demoted to a last name. If that didn't mean he was on the way out, what would?

"I'll all used up, Dr. Jimenez. I don't have any more to give you."

The man jerked his head up at the use of his last name. He started to say something and instead hardened his jaw and took a deep breath.

"Then, Mr. Shayk, you may get into your dry things. Put all this away first, so that Devon doesn't have to." Dr. Jimenez stood, adjusted his lab coat, and with firm steps, walked away without looking back.

GARIK SET the plastic bag with his clothes on the counter in the changing room. Rooms, because there was space for twenty people or more. It was all his, today.

The sound was as muted in here as it had been in many of the other rooms, and he suspected it was sound dampened and insulated so that whatever happened in here never made it past the door. That was as unnerving as everything else that had happened to him since arriving here.

What could happen in here that needed total secrecy? How bad could it be?

He left the wet clothes in a pile in the corner. He had policed the outside equipment. They could carry this away. He worked his dry clothes on, looking at his arm before slipping his shirt over his head. The red whelps from the glass hadn't disappeared, not quite. He was surprised how quickly it had healed. Even the butterfly stitches were only on for days. Shrugging, he pulled his shirt over his head, worked his arms through the sleeves, then pushed the sleeves up to his elbows. At the bottom of the bag was the passkey they had given him. Van had said it only worked the one elevator from Basement 3 to Basement 1. Breakfast to training, the two places he was trusted to go.

And access to knock on everyone else's door on Basement 2. He knew some people now, and with this, he could look them up, maybe even make some friends. Perhaps even Houdini out of here someday, although the chances of that seemed to be getting slimmer and slimmer.

He thrust his hands into his pockets as he charged out of the changing room, angry at the Tower, angry at the doctor, angry at the turn his life had taken, and especially at his helplessness to do anything about it. As the door slammed back, hitting the wall and echoing into the vast space surrounding the pool, he was surprised to see a familiar person leaning casually against one wall, his feet crossed at the ankles, and his arms crossed at his chest.

Jantzen unwound himself and said, "So, how did it go?"

Garik's throat filled up, his eyes filled up, and he fought to keep his face straight. Worse than awful, he wanted to say, but he was afraid he would fall to pieces if he did.

"That bad, huh? Well, I have some people who might like to spend some time with you. Do you think you, maybe?" Jantzen held out a hand, palm up, and crooked his fingers. He began to back away, leading Garik somewhere, who knew where.

Garik felt a grin break on one side of his face. He sniffled, shook his head yes, and pressed his shoulders to his eyes. Yes, he knew there were wet crescents, but the suddenness of Jantzen's unexpected invitation was a surge of warm molasses covering his bitter interaction with Dr. Jimenez.

Maybe he did care. He was here, wasn't he?

Garik kept his head tucked, and he still sniffled, and his hands were thrust deep into his pockets, but he wasn't alone, and right then, that counted for everything.

— **12** —

THEY EXITED the natatorium, leaving the shimmering pool behind, and passed by a dining hall—smaller than the one on Level 1—where the lights were on, but only a few tables were occupied. Jantzen waved, called out to two people named Heath and Chad, neither of whom were familiar to Garik. Chad was in a motorized chair and appeared to be disfigured in a way Garik couldn't define.

Several tables away, Justin Kurtew sat alone, this time in a tight shirt, revealing more differences in his physique than Garik had noticed in the gaming center. He was hunched over his table, his back especially long and convoluted, and his arms with their extra joints rapidly reordering the pieces of a game, also unfamiliar to Garik. He glanced up at Jantzen and Garik, his face darkened, and he went back to reordering his pieces without speaking.

"He's in a bad mood." Garik's hands were still thrust into his pockets, but he was interested in their destination. They had already bypassed the elevator, and he couldn't make sense of why.

"Justin hasn't dealt well with his slot in the program's hierarchy. He was too early in the program for us to have the kinks worked out."

"The reason he got the arms." And they had been too cautious with Garik, and he had gotten nothing, nothing worth crowing about. That would be fine, except now he would be locked away in this place forever with nothing to show for it, not even a deadly weapon he could use to display his massively successful combat skills, always at the bottom of the totem pole.

No one would ever bet on Garik because he was nothing worth betting on.

"Yes, but mostly he hasn't come to terms with his new self. That's a parameter only the volunteers in the program can control."

"He volunteered?" Garik recalled several comments he'd overheard suggesting people wanted to submit to the DNA melding process, but he'd not put it together that someone would choose to be changed into something so not normal.

"Most of our hybrids have." They had walked some distance to the area near where they had visited Hector Mascari. Jantzen stopped at an unlabeled door. "That surprises you, doesn't it? I hadn't considered that."

"Even the rejects."

"The hybrid failures, yes. They are the ones that live around here. They know the risks when they join the program." Jantzen had out his passkey, but he hadn't inserted it.

"Like Christian."

Jantzen's eyebrows went up. "What do you know about Christian?"

Garik pushed his hands deeper into his pockets. Stupid Garik. Saying things without thinking. It was his ears, hearing things people hadn't meant for him to know.

"Spill the beans. Has someone been talking to you about Christian?"

"Will I be sent to Level 5, too?"

"What?" Jantzen's passkey disappeared, and he grasped both of Garik's shoulders. He looked him hard in the face. "What's this about?"

"They said—"

"They?" Jantzen's purple-flecked eyes bored holes into Garik, searching as though he could reveal the answer he wished to hear by intent alone.

Garik couldn't tell, not if it would get Leigh and Laura in trouble. He remembered Devon and his reprimand, so he repeated his previous word, spitting it hard to ensure the man accepted it as all he would get. "*They* said he was combined with a dog. A wolf is like a dog, and I think he's in the cages down there."

"Okay, I don't need to know their names. It must have been someone in Joanie's group. I didn't expect them to be so careless."

"They weren't." Garik wanted to kick himself. "I overheard it, and they didn't know I could."

Jantzen sighed. "Accepted. I forget that you can do that. What else did they say? Anything I need to hear?"

"Did Christian have precog?"

Jantzen released Garik's shoulders and closed his eyes for a moment. "Not had, still has. He's alive and well, just up for reassignment. You're going to meet him tonight." His passkey reappeared, and he pushed open the door, revealing blaring music and flashing lights on the other side. Marco Lopez was hanging from the ceiling holding a bouquet of flowers and chewing on a yellow carnation.

Garik burst out, "What?"

"I thought you would say that." Jantzen grinned. "This is Christian's apartment. Hurry before we draw attention." He pulled Garik in and closed the door behind him.

"CHRISTIAN MAGUIRE." A tall man with black eyes inside deep blue, and those surrounded by lighter blue, like those of a husky, peered down at Garik with his hand held out to shake. He was shaggy and tousled, with coarse hair that didn't look as though it would accept a comb. His outsized arms and legs gave him a playful, boyish appearance. His rough-knit sweater was littered with wisps of hair that matched that on his head.

"Hello, Christian." Garik felt overwhelmed, even more so than when discovering Justin's crazy arms or Alyna's retractable claws. The man seemed friendly enough, but his size was daunting. When he shook, Garik's hand was swallowed in the man's big paw.

Paw. The thick hand did resemble a paw. He wondered how long it had taken the man's hand to change from normal to that, and if his own would someday look the same.

The apartment was small, one room, about the size of Garik's, and everyone he knew from the project was crammed inside, the hybrids he'd befriended, anyway. The non-hybrids—Van, T'Wana, Devon—were off doing whatever they did, which was likely something very non-hybrid. The room did have a small kitchen, which Garik didn't have, but no bed. Instead, cushions filled one corner. Marco had returned to the floor to pilfer more flowers, before leaping to the top of the doorframe. He was now perched on a handhold Garik couldn't even see.

"I thought you were, um—" Garik wasn't entirely sure *why* they were here. He hadn't expected to meet Christian, and for everyone else to be here?

"Reassigned? Not yet. Jantzen is working on a solution."

"I don't understand why everyone's here. They are, like, having a good time. How, I mean, I guess I'm asking, shouldn't everyone be sad?"

"Give Jantzen time. He will explain." The oversized man had bypassed the couch for the floor and sprawled like a large pet. He rested an arm and his head on a cushion and nodded his head at the people eating, drinking, and laughing at each other's antics. "They're here for support."

"Okay." A farewell party? No one seemed especially concerned that the man would soon be assigned to one of the cages on Basement Level 5. "Are parties like this allowed?"

"Not forbidden, but yes, we would be in serious trouble if they knew why we're here." Christian seemed amused. "We won't be, though."

"How do you know?" After today, Garik didn't need more trouble. What would happen, another twelve laps in the pool, this time with bricks in his pack?

"I can see it, twelve hours out."

"Your precog ability." Garik closed his eyes. He had done it again. He wasn't supposed to know.

"They hope for better in you."

The tests that morning with the cards suddenly made sense . . . the electric shocks on his arm . . . all motivation for him to make the right connections.

"Unlucky them. I'm not anything."

"I know. Not yet, anyway." Christian nodded as if it was obvious.

"How—" Garik stopped. Christian looked at him with an *are you kidding* roll of the eyes. "Precog, right. I didn't know you could tell things like that about other people. I thought precog was about what happened to you."

"And here you are telling me this." Christian pointed. "There's our friend. I'm glad we got to talk."

Garik felt Jantzen at his side. The bearded man clapped him on the shoulder, nodded at Christian, and leaned in and said quietly to the big man, "Give me time, my friend," and motioned to Garik to follow him.

They headed across the room to where Joanie was having a spirited conversation with Alyna. Whenever Alyna moved her hands to make a point, the tips of her claws extended, like a cat when flexing its paws, only these were daggers that could slice like razors. Garik noticed a flash of silver in one of Joanie's hands and realized she was popping mints like candy.

Giselle was at Paolo's elbow, watching him with adoring eyes, and Laura, by that time, was yelling at Marco to BRING BACK HER DAISY! IT WAS DECORATION FOR HER DRINK!

"Why has he given up?" Garik couldn't believe they were all having a good time when a friend was about to be sent off to whatever would happen to him on Level 5. He had been there. He had seen the results in the cages. He glanced back at Christian to see several others had gathered around him, and they were making the man laugh.

"He hasn't. That's his nature. Kind, generous, quick to warm to strangers. It's also why the military doesn't need him."

"Military?" *Stop repeating people*, Garik scolded himself.

"You haven't seen them?" Jantzen gave Garik a mock stare.

"Sure, yes. All the time when my friends and I were at the food court. But what do they have to do with Christian?"

"This I'm surprised you don't know. That's where our money comes from, the military."

"Oh. That's why I've seen so many uniforms going into the Tower."

"You never put it together?"

"No." Garik shrugged. "I never had any reason to."

"Exactly what they intend. Any other questions?"

Garik looked back at Christian. "What will happen to him? The things I saw down there were broken-down leftovers. Christian's a person. Can't he live here like Justin and Hector?"

"He's considered more valuable for genetic material. For research purposes." Jantzen looked around the room at the group of genetic hybrids interacting with one another as if evaluating their worth against Christian's. "He's not the first to be scavenged for body parts. That's what the research is about. We're building better soldiers, an army that can out-think, out-maneuver, out-kill any enemy that comes our way."

"No!" Anger surged through Garik. It wasn't fair, not for anyone. To think of a man being sacrificed for that, even if he barely knew him—

"That's how I hoped you'd feel, why I invited you tonight. You can help if you will. After this morning, you might be Christian's salvation."

"I don't see what you mean." His *disaster* of a morning? How could that help?

"Are you willing? That's all I need to know."

How could he refuse? Garik jerked his head in a quick nod.

Jantzen grinned. He interrupted Joanie's animated conversation with Alyna. "Joanie, I think we have a willing helper."

"For Christian? Rockin!" Joanie pumped her fist. "He deserves all the help he can get."

"Eh, eh, e-hay, little man! First time to meet. I'm glad to have you on the team!" Alyna reached to take his hand, her claws disappearing just before she grasped his palm to pump it enthusiastically. "It's gonna be a fun ride!"

"Team? What ride?" Garik looked around, now suspicious that this gathering was less about Christian and more about him. What had he joined? And did he want to be part of it?

Jantzen held up a hand, and he explained, "I told you Weston and I have had some differences."

143

"You and Mr. Rodheimer when we were on the mall. I remember." Garik saw Jantzen's eyes harden.

"It's bigger than that. Too many people are being cast aside in his quest for perfection—"

"Yeah, us," Alyna called, pumping one arm. "Down with the oppressor!"

"Not too loudly," Jantzen cautioned.

"Who can hear us in here?" She grinned gleefully. "Turn up the music!"

"More seriously, he needs to be pulled off his pedestal and given time to rethink the goals he's pursuing."

"Okay, but what about Christian?" Rodheimer's pedestal wasn't Garik's concern. The thought of Christian being cast aside for *research* was. The man might be a new acquaintance, but they also shared canine DNA. What happened to Christian could as easily happen to him.

"Go ahead." Jantzen encouraged him to continue.

"Christian can't be sent down to the cages. He just can't. You've got to rescue him." He didn't add, *and me.*

"We have a plan. And that is why we need you. You're still with us?"

"What do I have to do?" Garik let his eyes skip from face to face, his heart filling his chest with anticipation and dread. He thought of the bricks if he were caught.

"Play a lie, at least until it becomes the truth."

"Play a lie—" Garik squeezed his eyes shut. *No more repeating people.* Still, a plan, and they needed him. He looked across the room to Christian reclining next to Marco the lemur man, thinking about what might happen to the big man if he didn't help and the consequences if Garik's lie were discovered. He nodded. "I can do that." *And swim with bricks if need be.*

Jantzen leaned in. "Here's what we're asking you to do . . ."

Book 3

The Mirror Cracks

— 1 —

GARIK SHAYK pressed his shoulders into the iron bar, his leg muscles quivering, uncertain now if the extra weight his spotter had added at the ends was wise.

"I've got you." The shadows of his spotter's arms danced across the floor.

"Are you—" Garik strained, groaning with the effort of lifting the bar, and he yelped, "—sure?"

"Yes, sure. Don't be soft. You can do this. What's a few extra pounds? Such a tiny increase. Up, softie! Success is yours." The spotter tapped the undersides of Garik's arms, then harder when he failed to get an adequate response.

"So you say." Garik gave a final push, felt the bar slip into the forks on the top of the stand, and he leaned over, his hands on his knees, his legs quivering and barely able to breathe. Sweat coated his face and burned his eyes.

"Your towel." The towel appeared in front of him.

Garik opened it, pressed it to his face, and almost immediately jerked it away, spitting. "Aw, Christian, you've been shedding all over my towel again. Gross! What did you say your gene splice was with? Llama?"

"Wolfhound. I'm sorry. We shed."

To Garik's way of thinking, the man didn't sound sorry at all. He thought back four weeks to the reason he was working out with Christian at all.

"LEAH, GOOD morning. May I come in?" Garik was at the hospital on Basement Level 4. He was here to see Dr. Jimenez.

His passkey only allowed him access to the cafeteria on Level 1, his quarters on Level 2, and the training center on Level 3. Van Hermoso, his occupational therapist, had been doubtful about his request to visit the hospital.

"You do know I was tested yesterday, right?" Garik was very polite, making sure he appealed to Van's compassionate side. He was also very sore, but he didn't mention that. He certainly didn't want to offend him. If he did, his plan would be scorched before it had time to rise in the oven.

"Of course. I was there." Garik had caught Van at breakfast, and the pock-faced fitness nut was spooning shredded wheat into his mouth, a substantial spoonful at a time. He talked around his food. "What does that have to do with visiting the hospital? The emergency clinic can be accessed by your key. Go there to get what you need."

Ouch! After the tests he had been put through the day before—and his supreme failure—Garik knew he was beneath anyone's notice. This was proof.

"I, um, well—" and Garik put a quiver into his bottom lip, "—see, I lied to Dr. Jamie. I'm sorry, Van. I couldn't help myself, and I want to apologize."

"You *lied* to him?" Van grinned. "You freakin' *lied* to the man? That's rich. He's gonna roast you. What did you lie to him about?" He took another wheat biscuit and began to shred it into his bowl.

"I said I was doing my best, and really, I was just tired and wanted to go back to my room." Garik tried a half smile, the sort that sometimes worked as an apology at school when he didn't have his homework. "You know how it is."

"No, I don't know." He took his spoon and dipped up another chunk of shredded wheat and pushed the entire thing in his mouth.

Over the food, he said, "I don't get tired. I get fit. But I want to see you get ripped apart by the doctor."

That had gotten Garik to Level 4, and now he had Nurse Ratchett, his nickname for Leah Fortinier, Dr. Jimenez's personal nurse, to navigate.

"Yes, Garik, come in. I see your hair is improving. Yesterday, well, that was a shame. We all had such high hopes for you. I'm sure the research center will find a good place for you." She smiled, as bright and sunshiny as ever, even as she told him she now knew he was a loser, and she was disappointed, but not too much to continue with her everyday life bringing new human hybrids into existence, either with or without their consent.

"That's just it, Leah. You see, I need to apologize to Dr. Jamie." He smiled his apologetic smile. "I know I let him down, and it didn't have to happen that way. I know he expected more of me, and I failed to give it to him. I can be so much better. I was certain I could fool everyone into going easy on me, and now I know you saw through me. I've learned my lesson, and I'll give a hundred percent if you'll let me try again."

"Oh, this is a change of attitude." Leah smiled, very pleased. "I'm sure Dr. Jamie would like to hear what you have to say. Please wait right over there." She pointed to a set of two chairs with vinyl seats and backs, the sort that were sticky to sit on and worse to stand out of.

Garik smiled, said, "Thank you, Leah. I appreciate your help," and he gently lowered himself into the chair farthest from the door, so that anyone else who came in could have the best seat.

"SO, MR., UM—" Dr. Jimenez paused, undecided on the proper form of Garik's name to use. He looked up with a half-hearted smile and chose to use neither his first name nor his last. "Yes, my boy. What can I help you with?"

Leah had been very insistent over the intercom that *the young man from yesterday* was here to *apologize to you, Dr. Jamie.* Now, he didn't seem to know if he should call him Mr. Out-the-Door Shayk or good-friend Garik. Garik was amused, but not enough to risk his plan.

First, he repeated his apology, using his most contrite face, the one most apt to get him out of sticky situations in the past, and then he moved on to the heart of his proposal.

147

"See, Dr. Jamie—" he knew the man would warm up to Garik using his first name, "—I know if I trained more, really put my best effort into being all you want me to be, I can be a success. I want to make you proud of your efforts with me. The thing is, I've never done this. I've been going it alone, and I feel like I'm flailing around. I'm hopeless at this sort of thing."

"Hopeless, huh?" Dr. Jimenez leaned back in his chair. "Flailing, you say? Do you have any ideas on how you plan to change that?"

"I'm glad you asked, Dr. Jamie, because I've been thinking about that. I need a trainer—"

"You already have Van and that, um, Devon boy. Have you asked them?"

"Here's how I see it, Dr. Jamie." Garik saw the man's expression warm up every time he used his first name. "I need someone like me, someone who's had the same thing done to them that you guys are trying with me."

"I don't see how—" The doctor leaned forward, frowning, and Garik interrupted him.

"That's just it, Dr. Jamie." Bingo! The man smiled. "If there was someone who was DNA adjusted for exactly what you're looking for in me, then they would know exactly how to train me."

"I, um, think I see what you mean."

"Is there someone, Dr. Jamie? I hope so. I so want to be everything you hope I can be." Garik put his desperate face on.

"Well, there is one man, but he's scheduled to be reassigned. I don't know if it's too late—"

"Will you try, please?" He was talking about Christian. He had to be, because that was Garik's plan, to save Christian from being reassigned to Basement Level 5 where he would be genetically harvested for research. There was no reason to grovel like this, otherwise.

And that was why Garik Shayk was lifting weights he didn't want to lift, to give the research team a reason to value Christian Maguire's presence in the human-hybrid project and keep him on until Jantzen Hefferly could concoct a plan to rescue the failed hybrid from being terminated.

In the meantime, Christian knelt by the pool with a whistle in his mouth. Garik could now do far more than twelve laps fully clothed with a loaded pack, but they were working on underwater breathing skills. The pool was a full fifty meters, and Garik was on his fifth lap without coming up for air. With four weeks of practice, he was amazed how easy it had become. At the end of his fifth lap, he heard Christian blow the whistle, and he paused, looked up at his workout trainer, waved at the wavering image he could see motioning him to the surface. He smiled, pushed gently off the bottom, and let his face break the surface of the pool. Only then did he let out the breath he'd been holding.

It hadn't even been hard.

"How did I do?" Garik moved his arms back and forth, treading water.

"Don't start. You know you broke every record set on every leaderboard here."

"I know." Garik swam to the side, and he pulled himself up on his elbows, with his forearms overlapping on the coping. "I just wanted to hear you say it."

"Now's the real test. You're going up against Justin Kurtew. Are you sure you want to do this?" Christian was a kind soul, the reason the military didn't appreciate his skills. His DNA recombined with that of a wolfhound had been eminently successful at one thing, however, precognition. The only way to harvest that was to harvest the man. Only pulling him in to train Garik was postponing the inevitable, that was, unless Jantzen Hefferly, the number two man in charge of the human-hybrid program, could effect his escape.

They hadn't yet figured out how to work that out.

"I don't have a choice, Christian." Garik dropped back into the water, then with his hands on the side, he vaulted forward, surging out of the water and bringing about a quarter of the pool with him. "You've seen the outcome, though. Right?"

Precog. Christian had a twelve-hour window of events that centered directly around him. The military overlords had hoped for more, and that's why Garik's DNA was intermingled with that of a timber wolf. He was to be the success to Christian's failure.

"Not without injury."

"Grr. That's not the future I wanted you to imagine for me." Garik's precog ability was zilch. Nada. No such thing. Today, Colonel Brace and Senior Airman Vang had scheduled a second round of tests for Garik, to see if he had improved from his first. Garik had failed that one miserably. This one had to be successful. Otherwise, both he and Christian were likely to be written off.

"I've explained," Christian said, as he handed Garik a towel. "I

149

don't imagine the futures I see. They are just there."

"I know." Garik toweled his hair. Another four weeks had given him at least enough to hide his scalp. He still couldn't believe they had *cut it off* when they inducted him—*kidnapped him*—into the human-hybrid project. Of all the things they had done to him, that had been the cruelest.

At times, he wished his girlfriend, Marisa, had never hit that button on the elevator that took them down into the bowels of the Corona Tower basements. He could be enjoying his senior year at Bay City High, instead of swimming laps in this pool and preparing to fight a killer with extra joints in his arms and the ability to sling knives faster than the eye could see.

He could only pray he would survive.

Well, that and trust Christian's precog. He didn't look forward to his injuries. He did notice one thing Christian hadn't shared with him.

What damage would Justin inflict? Garik hadn't asked, because if he knew, he might not show up for the fight at all.

"MOVE INTO the ring, if you will."

Garik took a deep breath and caught Justin's aroma. Anger flowed from the oddly jointed man in brown soil and green plants, dead leaves and growing things. Justin Kurtew scowled at him, for once not wearing the leather duster that seemed to be his standard item of clothing. Garik glanced around the gaming center to see who had spoken. Sitting in a row of chairs, a posse of evaluators, including Weston Rodheimer, Colonel Brace, Airman Vang, and Dr. Jimenez, was poised to critique the competition, to judge whether Garik could continue in the program or be thumped aside like a noisome insect that had buzzed the inside of the screen far too long.

"Now, please." This time, the "please" punched the air a little harder, its impatience showing its face.

Garik realized they were talking to him, seventeen-year-old Garik Shayk, who should be a senior at Bay City High and living with his aunt Irina and her boyfriend, Arik Oblonsky, not here preparing to battle a deadly opponent. He should be getting ready for a skateboard competition, doing his homework, or spending the evening with his girlfriend, Marisa, not trying to save the life of a friend by fighting a deadly assassin.

Garik's first visit to the gaming center surged into his thoughts, reminding him how deadly today might be. Justin Kurtew had been in the ring against Alyna Lindberg, who was modified with a Komodo dragon, giving her retractable claws that were more steel knives than bony keratin. Justin had bested her, and she had walked away with minimal injuries only because Jantzen Hefferly had restrained him, forcing him to call the battle a draw.

Today, only Garik and Justin were present, both in boxing robes, although this was less boxing than bare knuckle fighting. Well, on Justin's side, bare *knife* fighting. It was Garik who was restricted to his knuckles.

Justin had come alone. Garik was accompanied by Christian. Justin's motivation today was validation. He wanted to prove his position in the hierarchy of the project—and perhaps eat Garik if he bested him. That was the mantis in him. Justin had already been thumped aside as a hybrid failure. He had nothing to lose. Garik was the one with his future on the line. His and Christian's, making his showing in the upcoming foray a vital link to his continued existence.

The two contestants dropped their robes, revealing very different fighting stances. Justin, mated with the DNA of a praying mantis, had a long, almost segmented body, and his forearms had extra joints, allowing him phenomenal fighting speed. Garik's was the tight body of a honed seventeen-year-old. His four weeks under Christian's tutelage had changed him from casual skateboarder to hardened athlete.

Garik's trump card would be the endurance that was a byproduct of his DNA infusion, timber wolf, which Christian had assured him would turn the tide in this battle against his very formidable foe.

At the starting signal, Garik didn't even see Justin's hands move when he felt something bite into his right arm. A gash opened in his skin from the wrist nearly to his elbow, and a volcano of blood welled up, spewing anger like molten rock. Garik stood frozen in shock for a moment, chanting to himself, "Anger gets me nothing. I must use my hands, my mind, my desire to achieve." Then Justin drew his arms back for another strike, sank the tip of a blade in Garik's shoulder, and Garik said, "Forget using my mind." He whipped around and smashed a foot into Justin's ribcage. As his opponent doubled over, he leaped on his back, repeating what he'd watched Jantzen Hefferly do. Justin seemed frozen in a rainbow haze as Garik wrapped his arms under Justin's and pulled them upward, holding the man tight, letting his opponent's arms beat the air, his knives useless against someone he couldn't reach.

There was no bell. No one called time. The rainbows faded as the observers let the moment go on, and on, and on, until Justin, quivering with exhaustion, dropped his knives and bled the words, "I give."

Garik was drained and his muscles burned. He dropped Justin and offered him a hand to stand. Justin glared, but he took Garik's hand before limping away, rubbing his shoulders.

Garik's arm and shoulder? Pound for pound, blood for blood, the price was one he was glad to pay.

— 2 —

COLONEL BRACE, with the solid, white-haired grace of a Southern gentleman, stood and took a firm step toward Dr. Jimenez. He took his hand and pulled him in close and whispered, "Any evidence of the precognition we saw in the other one?"

Garik felt his knees cut from under him. Didn't they see *anything?* He had taken down Justin, one of the deadliest hybridized humans in the complex, well, except for Laura, with her hydrogen cyanide breath, but he'd never seen her actually use it, so he supposed that it didn't count, yet.

He also had never faced her in combat, and he crossed his fingers he never would.

Still—

Christian took his injured arm, lifted it, and pressed a damp cloth against it. Garik turned to him, "Can you believe that man?"

"Justin? It's what I predicted—"

"No." Garik pulled his arm away and pointed to the men across the room who had come to evaluate his progress. "That one."

Colonel Brace had his back to them in an intense discussion with Weston Rodheimer, the director and head researcher at the Corona Tower research complex. Neither man seemed to be aware of Garik's fury.

"Your arm, please." Christian grasped his wrist, worked the cloth over the red area, and pulled it back, perplexed. "I do have the correct arm, yes?"

"Of course, you do. I'm sorry I pulled it away. I get angry, and I don't think. Thank you for helping me." Garik was sorry if he had offended Christian, but still, how inconsiderate and pig-headed could a person be?

"Your other arm, please." Christian held out one of his pawlike hands, waiting patiently.

"He didn't hurt it. It was my shoulder—" Garik looked down, reached his hand to where he'd felt the knife, and pulled it away. There was blood, but he couldn't find the wound. He looked at his other shoulder, and that was when he caught his arm. The red whelps from his fight with a mirror had long since faded, but he had distinctly felt the blade of Justin's knife slice through his skin. He rubbed the skin with his thumb, and he could just see a white line, like that of an old scar, that quickly faded away.

Garik looked at Christian, then at the men across the room. He remembered Jantzen's caution: *Don't give away everything you can do.* This was something new, and they didn't know. He didn't think they needed to, either.

"Wrap it, Christian." Garik turned to hide the arm from the other side of the room.

"No need. Let me clean away—"

"No. Now, Christian. Wrap it. You saw the wound. They did, too. Now, wrap it."

"Okay . . . *oh, I see.*" The big man pulled out a large swath of bandaging, and he began to bind Garik's arm, covering everywhere the skin had been sliced.

"Hurry. My shoulder, too. Here they come." Garik glanced at the colonel, still in earnest discussion with Rodheimer, but definitely headed his direction.

"Here." Christian cut a thick square of padding, added tape, and handed it to Garik. "Put that on your shoulder."

"It's too clean. It won't look real." Garik handed it back.

"How am I supposed to fix that?"

Garik didn't know. "Bloody it up, and fast!" He could hear the men talking, and they were discussing how fast they could expect Garik's injuries to heal.

"Why me?" Christian's shoulders dropped, and it seemed his whole body deflated like an old balloon. He took the scissors, jabbed it into his palm, and pressed it to the outside of the bandage. After a moment, he smeared it around and handed it back to Garik.

"Perfect. Thanks." Garik pressed it to his shoulder just as Weston Rodheimer began to speak.

153

"I've seen Justin in bloodlust before." Rodheimer glanced to the shoulder, nodding at the blood, and he dropped his eyes to Garik's arm. Garik held it against his chest, covering it with his other hand and trying to disguise the lack of blood. "Only one man's been able to stop him before. Impressive, no, Dr. Jamie?"

"But the other matter we discussed—" Brace dismissed Christian, his disappointment clear, and he shifted his eyes to Garik. "We must begin to see evidence of—"

"Enough for now, Colonel." Rodheimer held out a massive hand, with a palm almost apelike in its girth. "He anticipated an attack and thwarted it, even if he didn't realize what he was doing. I'd say that's proof enough, at least for now."

"Yes, Director, but I expect more."

"And I'm certain you will get it. Now, follow me," and Rodheimer turned his attention from Garik, walking away as he broached a new subject.

"Your robe, my liege." Christian stood, and he bowed slightly, offering the boxing robe opened and ready for Garik's arms. He had his injured hand wrapped with a large strip of bandaging tape.

"I know what a liege is, and I'm not your superior—or your boss." Garik backed into the robe anyway, trusting it to hide his pretend damage. He pushed his left, unbandaged arm through, and he let Christian drape the robe over his right shoulder, leaving the sleeve hanging loose. Christian tied the sash, leaving just Garik's hand exposed.

As they exited the gaming center, Garik thought about Joanie. Her DNA was mated with a jellyfish to enable longevity. Even eternal life. They had no real way to test it, other than killing her, and they hadn't chosen to do that, thank the afterlife gods that be.

He cringed to think how they might try to test his new skill, and every way he imagined was worse than the death it might bring.

GARIK SAT atop the examining table with his shirt off and swung his feet back and forth, a double pendulum, each foot providing a counterbalance for the other. He pushed harder, bored, wishing he could get back to the part of the complex where he belonged.

The door opened.

"Mr., um, Garik, my boy." Dr. Jimenez painted a wide smile on his face. "At least your legs work. How's that arm and that shoulder?"

"Fine, Dr. Jamie." He smiled and slowed his legs. He didn't need Jimenez to be too concerned or too inquisitive. "Christian re-wrapped it just before I came down. He says it's healing perfectly."

"Okay. I don't see any seepage, so that's good. I didn't see the cut on your arm when it happened, but I saw the one on your shoulder. I should look at that one. If the muscle was torn—"

"I don't feel anything." Garik lifted his arm and rotated his shoulder in its socket. He definitely didn't need the doctor removing the bandage to find no damage underneath at all. "Christian is great at this stuff. He's taking good care of me. Thank you, Dr. Jamie, for letting him train me. My success is your success. Without you, I probably wouldn't be here any longer." He smiled brightly. Convincingly, he hoped.

"At least let me check your range of motion." Dr. Jimenez took Garik's left wrist in one hand, his upper arm in the other, and forced the limb as hard and far as he dared. "That doesn't hurt?"

"Not at all, Dr. Jamie. Do you want to try the other arm, too?" Garik tried to keep anticipation on his face, a hopeful look that the doctor might find something wrong that needed fixed.

"No, that's fine." Jimenez stepped back, pulled a tablet and stylus from a pocket, and marked several things. He glanced at Garik, motioned with the stylus, and said, "You may go. Tell Christian he has my approval."

"Thank you, Dr. Jamie. I sure will." Garik hopped down, grabbed his shirt from the back of a chair, and began slipping it on as he backed out of the room. "Next week?"

The doctor glanced at him, Garik already forgotten. "Sure, sure. Check with Leah."

"Right-o, Dr. Jamie." Garik turned, let the door close behind him, and rubbed his left shoulder. The man was a monster. He had twisted his shoulder just to make it hurt.

Still, this was about Christian, and for that, there was *almost* no pain that Garik wouldn't endure.

Now, however, Devon was waiting at the climbing wall. The man didn't care about the bandage on his arm. He just wanted to climb.

Well, that was perfect to Garik, because that's exactly what he wanted, too.

JOHN CARTER and Paolo Leveen showed up at the climbing wall

while Garik and Devon Maye, the recreation and activities director, were in harnesses overhead.

John, blond and fitter, if possible, than Devon, was wearing a climbing harness, and he called, "Devon, hey! Can anyone use this wall?"

"Anyone who's good enough." Devon was alongside Garik. Garik was in a harness with a safety line attached. Devon held a remote control to the safety line's overhead winch.

Garik, despite his bandaged arm and shoulder, hadn't needed it even one time.

"That's me, then." John dropped an equipment bag from over his shoulder, letting it fall heavily to the floor. Far overhead, in the three windows that broached the next level up, giving a view to the military personnel housed on Level 1, several bored Airmen leaned on handrails that ran the length of the windows. One pointed, John waved, and the Airman waved back.

"Friends, John?"

"With everyone." John called for Paolo to grab a safety, that he was going up first.

Devon held out his remote, adjusted the winch to take up some of Garik's slack, and moved to a new purchase on the wall. He called for the young man to try a new grip, perhaps one of the orange.

"Orange?" Garik called. "You trust me, now?"

"I trust the safety line." Devon held out his hand, touched the remote, and the winch whined, pulling the safety line tight until Garik's harness bit into his backside.

"Okay, okay. I'm going." Garik reached for an orange, and when he moved, the pressure on his harness eased.

"You'll make it, kiddo. You've got this."

"Right-o, Devon-o." Garik grinned and gave him a thumbs up. That was a mistake, as his left hand began to slip, and only the safety line was there to break his fall.

"I told you," Devon scolded him. "No fancy moves with that injured shoulder. Now, hold on while I move you back to the wall."

The winch began to whine, and when he was close enough, Garik reached for a blue grip, only to have Devon call, "No, not the blue. I told you, that's for when you get good."

Garik grinned and reached for orange.

GARIK STOOD under the shower head in the changing rooms located near the climbing wall. He was glad to have his bandages off, and they sat on the seat just outside the shower beside his limited-access passkey.

John and Paolo were in their own showers, the reason they had "happened" to show up at the climbing wall at the same time as Devon and Garik. No one could be allowed to hear their plans to break Christian out of the research facility, and this was the only place they could be together without raising suspicion.

John was already out when Garik emerged into the common area around the sinks. He carried his bandages, wanting to wait as long as possible before reattaching them.

"A real fall?" John adjusted his belt with a grin, looking up just long enough to wink.

"It kept Devon's attention, didn't it?" Garik slipped his shirt on and kicked his towel near the used towel bin. He sat on a bench to put on his shoes.

They both looked up to see Paolo watching them, already in the room without them noticing.

"You, there, and you, Garik. So, what are our plans to get Christian out? It's been a month. We're running out of time."

Garik looked from Paolo to John and back to Paolo. He was still in training, and Christian was his trainer. They had plenty of time to plan a way out for Christian, didn't they?

Or was there something he didn't know?

— 3 —

BEFORE THEY could work out a rescue plan for Christian, Garik was summoned to the research center's main office block on Level 1. Van Hermoso accompanied him, not quite a guard, but never letting Garik out of his sight. The office block was tucked out of the way behind the main elevator shaft connecting the underground complex of dungeon-like spaces directly to the mall, the lobby, and the upper floors of Corona Tower—and off-limits to program participants of the hybridized sort.

So, the reason behind Garik's visit? He knew it must be big—meaning bad for him—if they wanted him here. He had only visited once, and that was with Jantzen Hefferly, the number two man on campus. Van pulled out his passkey when they reached the office block, inserted it by a door, and it required his hand, also. He pressed it to the panel, a red light scanned the vein patterns under his skin, and the panel turned green, saying, "Accepted, Van Hermoso. Please retrieve your passkey and enter within thirty seconds."

Garik hesitated to follow.

Van jerked his head to suggest they continue moving, asking, "What is it? Shoot, I'm listening."

"What have I done wrong?" There was no sense in asking *if* he had done anything wrong. There was always another rule to break, one they hadn't shared with him yet.

"Maybe nothing." Van chuckled, not in a mean way, but not being friendly, either. "Then, maybe something. They don't tell me everything, and I don't want them to."

"So, you're glad I'm me and you're you."

"I didn't say that." Van stopped before one door out of many. "We're here. I'm told I won't be escorting you back, but I will see you later. I am your occupational therapist. You are still working on an occupation, I trust."

"Sure, Van, just waiting to see what I can do." He tried to be pleasant, but the sign on the door had dropped a rock in his stomach. IT Oversight and Security Specialist. Computers, information, Internet searches, remote cameras, and . . . listening in to secret conversations, like those that involved getting Christian out of Corona Tower while still alive.

Why had he ever thought the changing rooms were any different than any other thing about this place? Everything was suspect. Everyone and everything. Van likely wouldn't see him later, unless he decided to visit Level 5 and search the cages of mewling and pathetic creatures that were no longer of any use in the human-hybrid project's DNA-enhancement program.

"If you need me, I'm here for you."

"I appreciate that, Van. Maybe I should go in." And get this over with. He imagined how it might go: *What? You thought we were helping Christian escape? No sirs, I am a good wolf, er, boy, and the worst thing I do when you guys aren't watching over my shoulder is howl at the moon. Am I making fun of you? No sirs, I would never do that* . . . sheesh, it was as bad as lying to Dr. Jimenez and watching the man eat up every word.

"That's a good attitude." Van opened the door, and when Garik stepped through, he moved back and let the door close.

The room was disorganized, the space of someone who couldn't

158

focus enough to finish one thing before moving on to another. From a side door, a man, as thin as the tie he wore, stepped inside, bumped an open filing cabinet drawer, and barely kept from spilling the coffee in his hands.

"Oh, hot," he said, touching a dripping finger to his mouth to suck off the excess. "Sorry. Welcome, Mr. Shayk. Come in, come in. Our first time to meet, yes, our very first."

"Okay," Garik said, confused. The man didn't sound like he was being accused of espionage and collusion to aid and abet the escape of one of the Tower's hybridized subjects. Three large computer screens hung from the wall, each one with multiple views, eyes overseeing everything that happened in the room and likely anywhere else the man wanted to look. "So, why am I here?"

"We will get to that. Let me introduce myself. Jeffrey Howard. You may have noticed the sign on the door." Jeffrey looked for a place to set his coffee, moved a book to make room, and offered Garik his hand.

Garik sighed. *If I must.* All the hand shaking. They had *kidnapped* him, but he took the hand. He squeezed harder than he should, causing Jeffrey to massage his hand afterward. *For you, Marisa*, Garik thought, her absence a hollow space in his chest.

"Do you know Andrew?" Jeffrey asked, lifting a pair of glasses from the disarray on his desk.

"Should I?"

"No, no, I don't suppose so. I just thought I would ask. Oh, his last name is Miner. Any bells, now?" Howard lifted his eyebrows hopefully.

"Still nothing." Garik shrugged. Uncertainty and frustration were eating at his patience and manners. Another minute, and he would have no polite responses left. "You sent for me. Is there something I should know?"

"Oh, yes, yes, yes. A seat, yes—" The man looked around and realized there was nowhere for Garik to sit. "—how about we use the conference room? Andrew will be arriving shortly, yes, shortly. Do you mind waiting?"

He didn't see that he had a choice.

ANDREW MINER was a barrel of a man coming down the corridor. Jeffrey and Garik turned a corner, startling him, and a box in his hand nearly went to the floor. A stack of papers did.

"Safe!" Andrew held the box up, and it seemed Jeffrey breathed a sigh of relief as he scrambled to gather up the papers. Inside the conference room, the box went on the table as though in a place of honor. Andrew introduced himself. "Andrew Miner, Financial Analyst and Fund Coordinator. You give me your funds and I coordinate them." He smiled broadly as though he enjoyed the tagline.

"I don't have any funds, sorry," Garik said, now convinced they were having a stupid contest.

Andrew smiled, "That's a good one," and he announced, "You, young man, are receiving an upgrade."

Garik looked from man to man. Upgrade, like, from wolf boy to werewolf boy? Level up! Open the box to receive your reward. Upgrade your brain and receive amazing gifts. Infinite lives. Super strength . . . none of this made sense.

"You did tell him, Jeffrey?" Andrew looked at skinny Jeffrey.

"I, um, did I tell you, Mr. Shayk?"

"Garik." He closed his eyes to focus and keep his anger under control before looking up, thinking, my mind, my way, anger does no good. "My father is Mr. Shayk. And no, you haven't told me anything."

"Yes, I seem to remember, using your given name was in my notes. So sorry. The Director wishes you to have an upgraded passkey."

Garik's world shifted, and he couldn't keep a smile from his face. He was one step closer to Houdini time, seeing Marisa, telling her about her sister, Marina, that he'd found her; and visiting the skate park with Muhammad, Ibn, and Hayat; giving his aunt a hug; and maybe even going up to see Mrs. Waggoner to find out how her plants were doing—

"Your new apartment will have—"

"What? I'm moving, too?" He tried to think how that would affect his escape plans, its distance to the main elevator . . . any changes could be vital to his plans.

"One thing before we let you go. I have," Andrew stood and rummaged through the box, "your new computer and something else you might enjoy." He lifted out a gaming console. "For your very own."

Jeffrey said, almost hesitatingly, "I have written, um, am writing, you see, because it is in beta phase, a new, um—"

160

"Stop, Jeffrey." Andrew leaned in to Garik. "Will you test Jeffrey's new video game? You are, well, more—" and he whispered, "—more *normal* than many of our residents. He would appreciate your *normal* opinion."

And give me a reason to gather with my friends. Garik smiled. "Certainly."

Andrew grinned, nodding his success at Jeffrey. He attempted to button his jacket, but it refused to meet around his waist.

GARIK CARRIED the box with the gaming console. Grunt labor, although he didn't mind being the pack mule today. Now, Christian had a reason to be in Garik's apartment, and no one would be looking for something devious or underhanded in their time together outside the recreation area or training cells.

The elevator doors opened. Straight and right would take them to his old room. They made an immediate left, past the emergency clinic with its darkened windows, away from the break area with its fully stocked kitchen, and the opposite direction from the recreation area. People began to fill the corridors, a few at first, then more. Garik recognized many of the faces, even if he didn't know all the names. Christian had been so busy with his training, there hadn't been time for social introductions. At the new apartment, Joseph Howard and Tyrone Brown were just inside the door.

Tyrone flashed his familiar smile, but it was Joseph who spoke. "Weren't sure where you wanted it, and Ty thought near the door. That okay by you?"

"My ZBoard? I didn't expect that. Thanks!" They had already moved the ZBoard's charging unit for him without him having to ask. Rodheimer must have been really impressed with what he saw during his fight with Justin.

"I 'spected you would want it, so when we moved your things, we brought it along."

Garik's eyes went damp. The people at the top could learn something from the little guys on their team. Be nice to the people under you, and they'll be nice to you. How did Kevin Lee used to say it? Leave it like you found it, cleaner if you can.

Garik gave them a nod and said, "You ever need anything, I'll help if I can."

"Thank you. Have a good day." Joseph nodded and touched his temple as if tipping a hat. Tyrone grinned, and Garik nodded back.

Garik still wanted out, would Houdini at the first window, but until then, this was a pretty slick place to be. He couldn't wait until Christian came for a visit.

GARIK TOOK time to explore once everyone left. The apartment had two real rooms. The kitchen was a tiny unit tucked in a nook, but the place had everything he needed, especially a separate bedroom. A living room held a couch and a chair, even a coffee table with two remote controls. He set the box on the coffee table and pulled out the gaming unit.

"So, they love you more."

Garik looked up. Justin stood just inside the door. "Justin," he said, unsure why he was here. He pictured the man's ferocity in the ring, and his stomach turned over, freezing his heart for several beats. He tried to process his best options for the attack he was sure was coming.

"I got demoted." Justin walked in, his attitude casual, almost as if they had something common between them, something besides being hybrid. He looked inside the bedroom and turned back to Garik, his face hardening. He was a gunslinger, ready to draw and fire.

"I didn't ask for this." Garik wanted that between them.

"Yes, you did. When you humiliated me in front of the Director."

"Why are you here, Justin?" Garik would fight, but he didn't want it to come to that.

"I've seen you and your friends together."

"So?" Garik tried to follow the man's intimations, to place what he might be talking about. There was nothing to connect them to anything—

"There." Justin slipped a mini flash drive from his pocket and dropped it on the coffee table. "There's more than one way to listen in on a conversation."

Then he was out the door.

— 4 —

RACQUETBALL. Who would have thought being in a white, windowless room *by yourself* and whacking a tiny ball could be so satisfying?

Garik tossed the ball up, swung his racquet, felt the impact of the racquet against the ball feed down his forearm, followed by the rewarding *whack* of the rubber sphere against the far wall. The sound in the contained, hard space reverberated in his ears.

He leaped, caught the ball on the return, and *whack*.

Over and over as sweat ran down his face, and his shirt and shorts clung to him like wet rags.

Whack! For Marisa. I'm not in Russia, Mari.

Whack! Hayat, skateboarding together off curbs.

Garik's eyes blurred. He pressed his face to his shoulders, a quick move in between leaping for the ball, unable to admit to the emotions.

Whack! Ibn, I miss you, my friend.

Whack! Robbie, my little brother.

Whack! I need a hug, Iri.

Whack! Muhammad, Allah be praised.

Garik grinned when he thought of Muhammad, even as his heart burned.

Whack! Wesji. *Whack!* Wajeha. *Whack!* Vladimir and Giorgio. *Whack!* Mrs. Waggoner. *Whack!* The three shrimps. And Alexi. Regina. Everyone, *whack, whack, whack!*

Whack! For Garik, who's lost and can't find his way back again.

Garik half squatted, his elbows resting on his knees, his emotions ripping air from his throat, and his need to breathe shoving it back in. The blue rubber ball came to rest at his feet, and he watched it roll to a stop.

Justin. *Justin!* Anger tore through him.

Garik had played the mini flash drive. His voice, Paolo's and John's had all been there. There was no mistaking the complicity among the three.

Justin! Of all people!

Garik adjusted the legs of his shorts, unsticking the fabric from his skin, and giving himself room to flex and move. He leaned toward the ball and grasped it in his hand, compressing the hollow sphere, flattening it before tossing it into the air.

A thing few people could easily do.

Whack! Garik watched as the ball passed the service line, slammed into the front wall, returned to him and impacted him right between the eyes. His legs gave out under him, knocking him hard on the short line. His racquet skittered across the floor.

Clapping echoed into the hard-walled space, and Garik looked behind him. Through the glass back wall, Joanie McDonald raised an arm, yelled, "Hoot, hoot!" and slammed a palm against the glass. Sandwiched between her hand and the glass was a package of mints. "Mint, barker boy?"

"Not my name," he called, his face heating with shame. "And no."

"Your way." She yanked open the door and shrugged in the same motion, and she paused before entering. "Your permission?"

"Yeah, Joanie. Come in."

Garik drew his knees up, wrapped his arms around them, and watched the ball. It was still rolling, and it hit the wall, skittered off, and came to a stop.

"Angry game." She dropped beside him, her legs crossed.

"Angry game," he confirmed. He lifted his shirt, pressed it to his face, and dropped it. "Do you need something?"

She reached into her pocket and opened her hand to reveal a mini flash drive.

"Justin." Garik's shoulders sagged. He'd thought he was already as miserable as he could be, but he realized there were always more depths to plumb. The man would be their undoing.

"Ideas?" Joanie popped two of the mints in her mouth and crunched one.

"You play?" He motioned around the court.

"Yeah. Not this. You stink." She pointed a finger at him and grinned. "Shower." She thumbed toward the door and stood.

Garik unraveled himself and joined her, gathering the ball and the racquet on the way. Who else had received a flash drive? He could kick himself. No place was private, no matter what they said. Any word anywhere could be recorded.

He'd do well to remember that.

GARIK ENTERED the changing rooms for the recreation area, the one where he had injured his hand on the broken mirror. A posse of runners, likely off-duty researchers, were pulling on sleeveless jerseys and joking with one another and laughing. One man was seated and tying the laces on a pair of purple and white running shoes. He pushed his tall socks to his ankles before standing and tossed a towel over one shoulder. Street clothes hung on hooks and spilled out of bags, with some scattered on the floor.

The men's glances told Garik that he was different, unwelcome, although they didn't say it. He made his way through them to the showers, grabbed a towel and soap on the way, and tried to block out the sounds of friends enjoying one another's company.

By the time he was out, they were gone, although their things were not. He looked around, certain Justin's recording device was likely still in place. He had maybe an hour before they returned. He began running his fingers under the edges of the benches, moving the men's shoes and clothing, and occasionally scrunching his nose at an item with an especially strong odor.

He was on the third bench when he heard the familiar, "Hey, kiddo, there you are."

"Yeah, Devon." He trusted the activities director, and he continued to search.

"Looking for you. I saw Joanie in the break area, and she pointed me here."

"You found me." He returned two satchels under the bench and stood to move toward the next one.

"You're okay? I mean, you and Christian. He's doing you right?" Devon glanced around the room, taking in the disarray. "Have you taken on some sort of cleanup duty?"

"Yeah, cleanup duty. Devon, I don't have time to chat. Anything specific?" Garik heard Joanie coming out in him. Then, patience wasn't his thing at the moment.

"It's the next mall event. A new group, the Ace Holes." He chuckled and winked. "Really, Ace of Holes, but—" He shrugged like it was a really good joke.

"Okay." Garik dropped and leaned under the bench. He didn't care much about the Ace of Holes. He needed Justin's recording device.

"So, do you want to go?"

"Go?" Garik pulled out from under the bench and looked at him. "To an event?"

"Yes." Devon pushed a bag out of the way and sat on a bench.

"I don't have permission. Last time, I was there only because Jantzen had me on a leash. Sorry, Devon." He dropped back under the bench and satisfied himself that it was recording device free before reemerging.

"What *are* you looking for?"

"Not stinky socks." Garik wrinkled his nose. "Everyone of these guys has his own stinky smell, and I'm going to choke."

"About the event." Devon leaned forward, his elbows on his knees. He grinned. "Jantzen's already said you can go."

"Why?" Garik could hardly focus on Devon's invitation. He had a recording device on his mind, and he didn't know how long he had until the running posse returned. He knelt and began to feel under the sinks.

"Party, kiddo. I need to teach you how. Hey, whatever, let me help you look." Devon crossed the room, chose the next sink, knelt to see what was underneath.

"Okay, Devon, I'm looking for a microphone or something that can record a conversation."

"Oh, easy. Done." Devon stood and slammed the cabinet door.

"You have it?" Garik sat with his knees on the floor, surprised the man found it so quickly.

"Not with me. It's in my office."

Not Devon! Garik could hardly believe the rec director was complicit with Justin in recording private conversations in the changing rooms. He felt his trust in the man bleeding away.

"Are you with Justin, then?" Of course, he was.

"Justin, you mean, Kurtew? I don't get the connection."

"But you have the microphone."

"I sa—*id* that." Devon rocked his head to the side, drawing out the word. "You, my friend, need a distraction, like a party." He grinned. "On the mall!"

"Okay, I'll go, but first, tell me how you have the microphone I'm looking for." Sheesh! Yes, this was proof. Every single person in this place was a total and complete idiot, perhaps even him!

"What you people don't clean, I have to police. This mess?" He motioned around the room. "I can report the people here if I know who leaves it, but if they don't clean it, it's up to me. So, Garik, my friend, clean up after yourself!" He laughed.

"Leave it like you found it, cleaner if you can." Kevin Lee's philosophy. In the moment, Garik missed the martial arts teacher, even if he had barely known him. He was from outside, his life before this place, from Bay City, from a connection that had been broken and was now more desirable than ever.

"Perfect! You, kiddo, understand perfectly. So, we're on? Friday?" Devon with his blond cowlick grinned expectantly.

"Right-o, Devon." Garik lifted a hand, calling, "Bam, done."

"Ha, ha!" Devon laughed and disappeared out the door.

Garik took in a deep breath. Devon. Trees and water. He was surprised he could find the man in all the surrounding stink, and it did stink, all nine of the researchers, each one as individual as the parts of a machine.

Then he realized he'd been able to smell Devon through the rank stable of odors all along. If he met these men again, he'd know each of them by their smell. And it wasn't something he would likely ever forget.

GARIK ARRIVED on the mall.

He hadn't expected his passkey to work one of the main elevators, but finding out it did wouldn't help him out of the basement research complex. At least he understood how the hybrids like him could join the events on the mall without chaperones. Once the wall went up, enclosing the mall, the elevators accepted the passkeys given to the research subjects.

Be home by midnight, Cinderella. Or no pumpkins for you!

More likely, they would turn into pumpkins if they weren't underground when the walls were banished back into the sidewalks by their fairy godmothers.

No lost glass shoes for you! Back, back underground where you live!

Garik could run his fingers through his hair, now. It was enough to show some curl, although not to tie back into a bun. The thought of Marisa, her hands at his neck that day they visited the Tower with Kevin Lee. And now, here he was, living in the Tower.

Well, the *basements,* like a *thing,* a deformed uncle you were afraid to show to the world.

The wind whipped past him when he stepped outside, thrusting chilled fingers down his jacket. He touched the flash drive he carried in his pocket, afraid to leave it anywhere. Devon had invited Annie Vanschooneveld to join them. Annie had dark eyes, and her red lipstick accentuated her big teeth when she smiled. Her hair was pulled back, and her face was softened by long bangs that covered her eyebrows.

Annie was the reason for Garik's jacket.

"Garik, Annie." They had shown up at Garik's door dressed warmly. "Annie's the foreign affairs attaché."

"Hello, Garik." She held out a slender hand to shake.

"Foreign, like other countries?"

"Yes, I'm away more than I'm here. This is my first time to get to attend an event. Devon insisted I come. You've been before?" She smiled.

"Once." He shook her hand, noticing how Devon looked at her when she was talking. He wondered if that was how he'd watched Marisa, and in the image in his head, he also recalled her words to him to *pay attention.*

The memory made him smile.

"You enjoyed it, then." She turned to Devon. "You said it didn't go well."

Devon shrugged and looked down, his Nordic skin flaming with streaks of red under his cheekbones. Annie asked Garik if he was planning on a coat. Garik looked at Devon for clarification, and Devon agreed he should.

Yea, Annie!

Outside, the night wasn't yet fully dark, and around him, Bay City stretched south, rising in elevation toward Stanwick Hill. In the distance, he could just see the Ransom Communications Building with its rack of antennae thrust skyward and illuminated. To its right was his home, except for the other buildings in the way.

Home. Marisa. His friends. He blinked his eyes to clear them and put on a smile. He was at a party, and it was his night to have a good time.

The Ace of Holes was here! Yea!

He stepped into the food court and past the tables he and his friends used to gather around. Out from under the building, the wall surrounding the mall blocked the view of anything at eye level.

He was at the ball. He had gotten his wish, and it wasn't what he thought it would be.

— 5 —

THE ACE of Holes logo spilled across the marquee on the mall's large sign. The image of a card wearing a giant ace of spades twirled, and a gun sent a bullet flying through the center, punching clean through the black ace and stopping the card's spin. The words "Ace of Holes" spilled out, accompanied by streamers and fireworks until they filled up the massive screen.

"Have fun, you two! I'm going to search for my friends." Garik waved to Devon and Annie, certain they wanted to be alone.

"Have fun!" Annie waved, and she tucked her arm in Devon's, the way Garik wished Marisa had tucked hers in his. They had forgotten him before he turned away.

As he searched the crowd, it crossed his mind that if Annie were allowed to attend, so could people like Jeffrey Howard and Andrew Miner. He tried to picture the thin man with his glasses, together with the balding barrel of a man. He couldn't do it.

He did find Airman Wu Han. As with last time, military types were scattered across the mall, likely to ensure that the hybrids attending the event kept their sometimes burgeoning and rampant killer instincts under control. Thank you, Justin, for teaching me that, Garik thought sourly. He headed Wu's direction, hoping to renew a connection with someone he had enjoyed and looked up to.

He was waylaid by Airman Vang.

"Ah, Mr. Shayk. I see you are once more with us for one of our shows."

"Yes. I'm sorry, Mr. Vang. I'm hoping to catch someone. Do you mind?" Garik tried to keep Wu in sight, but he couldn't maintain a conversation with the short Vang and look out across the mall at the same time.

"I will not keep you long. I wish to congratulate you on your performance against Mr. Kurtew. I understand the Director has upgraded your accommodations. Well earned. Enjoy your evening, Mr. Shayk."

"Thank you, Airman." Garik stepped away, now unable to find Airman Han. He took a deep breath and quieted his emotions. Even when he was being nice, Airman Vang was a wrecking ball battering the best things about Garik's day.

"Garik!"

A hand clapped him on the shoulder. Garik turned to a familiar face.

"Jantzen, hi. I haven't seen Christian today."

"No." He didn't offer an explanation. "Perhaps he can make it tonight. I see you're back on good terms with the Airman."

"Speaking, anyway. He speaks, and I don't." Garik heard the criticism, and he knew Jantzen understood. A month ago, he'd have not dared say that. Maybe in anger, but then he'd be forced to apologize and accept the consequences.

"Sometimes best. They are our overlords. He who controls the purse strings, and that they do."

"Feel for me. I'm the peon." That's the way he felt, too. On the raised area where the Ace of Holes would perform, the action was getting under way. The Ace of Holes was a magic venue, and they had a live elephant on the stage with three men attempting to control it. "I need to find my friends."

"Go north. I suggested they meet you there. That's the one spot you'll be able to see some of the Tower's light show."

"It's not real, Jantzen. You made that clear."

"Suit yourself. I must mingle. Maybe we will bump into each other later. If not, lunch tomorrow?"

Garik hesitated. Did the man know about Justin's recording? Is that why he wanted to have lunch with him?

"Or not?" Jantzen glanced around, his eyes already taking in the people he intended to connect with. If there was an ulterior motive, Garik couldn't find it.

"Okay. Sure, why not. I'll see you then."

Jantzen clenched a fist at chest level, shook it and grinned. "Enjoy the show, my friend." He turned, calling to a woman with long, black bangs that did a poor job of covering a scar on her forehead. "Angelica, do you have a minute?"

CHOW DOWN in the actual food court might be shuttered for the night's event, but tonight's magic show was a very different performance than the Howling Pterodactyl's energy-infused assault on people's senses. Numerous Chow Down food kiosks were set up across the mall, with "street-friendly" fare: hot links, burgers, and cheese-covered nachos. Garik was several blocks in when Giselle placed a hand on his arm.

"There you are, Garik. Come. I've been sent to reel you in." She winked at him, smiling.

"You like Paolo. Why do you smile at everyone like that?"

"Oh, poo." She blew out her cheeks. "How do you see through me so easily?" Still, she wrapped one arm in his, and she walked right up against him.

"No one can miss it." Garik felt the pressure of her arm. She wasn't Marisa, so it meant nothing to him.

"Except Paolo."

"I know."

"Oh, you! Why I volunteered to come find you, I'll never

know." She pulled her arm away, and she made a pouty face.

He shrugged. "I could have found you guys. I didn't need someone to find me. I always know just where I am. Besides, I would have expected Julia."

"Right. Heat-sensing. Too many people to single you out."

"I didn't think of that."

They walked for a bit together. This far out, the crowds were thinner, and the night sky was growing darker. Behind Corona Tower, the two-story parking garage seemed truncated next to the glass skyscraper. Headlights flashed inside, someone exiting, likely, and he remembered the family that was arriving for a visit at Stamford Suites the day Marisa and he fell down the elevator into the lair that had trapped him. Likely, whoever was in that vehicle was a Stamford Suites guest, in the tower for a night or two, and out to freedom whenever they pleased.

At some point, Giselle had encircled her arm around his again, and when they reached the table where the others were, she patted his arm, looked up at him, and purred, only stopping when it was clear that Paolo was paying no attention.

Alyna was seated next to Paolo, and she was showing him something. Garik couldn't see what.

Joanie called to him, "Gari! Made it! Whoop, Devon! Convinced you!"

"Yah, twisted my arm."

"Glad he did. Fun show, tonight." Joanie's mohawk seemed to be painted brighter than ever, or maybe it was catching the light of the setting sun over the distant water in the harbor. She looked down, pulled out a fresh package of mints, opened them and popped one before looking away.

Leigh and Laura waved. They were deep in a discussion, and Garik didn't pay much mind. John was returning from a food kiosk, bare-armed in the chill, and he walked up behind Garik, bumping his elbow to Garik's shoulder.

"We've been waiting on you." He nodded at the others, several of them intent on something or the other. "Have you heard—"

He was interrupted by Joanie, who called, "Nachos! Here, John. You! The very, very best."

"I'll be right back, Garik. What I've got to discuss is important."

Marco, with his lemur's tail showing more distinct stripes than when Garik had first met him, sidled up to a table, seeming to appear out of nowhere, and he reached for the food John held.

Joanie was standing by then, and she had John by the elbow, pulling him out of Marco's reach. She tugged him to her table, farther from Garik and the answer to the question in his mind.

Important? What do you mean important? And ... and ... you're going to leave me hanging out there?

Sheesh, John! What have I ever done to you?

JULIA CANTOS was the final person Garik noticed.

"Julia, I didn't see you there." He remembered: not moving and not being seen were part of Julia's camouflage.

"I could sense you from a block away." She pointed the direction of the Tower. "Look. The world's seen nothing like it. A miracle. A giant structure of glass and steel, and there it is. Bam, blowing up right before our eyes. THE BUILDING." She said her final two words like capital letters, and she laughed, ending in a rasping cough. "Sorry, I'll need some gum on that note."

Garik followed her arm. Close to the base, the Tower looked normal, as always, but as he raised his eyes, he could see the familiar silicon glitter flash in the sky, as the Tower shattered into a million pieces and fell, flashing in brilliance to the ground, only to lift back into the sky and reform the Tower into a whole once again.

Except that the effect didn't extend all the way to the ground. The angle of the projectors, perhaps, or some other way that the image refracted from this angle; whatever, the shattering tower was incomplete. And, from here, it was just possible to see the dim imprint of the Tower impressed into the black velvet of the night sky even as the glitter showered the street, thereby ruining the effect.

"Not as pretty as when seen from the city." He shrugged, not impressed, and turned away, taking the seat next to Julia and falling into it.

"Got that right. Most things are prettier from the outside. What I see is best of all." She slipped a stick of gum in her mouth, and she chewed it twice before she began to pop it.

"What do you see that's best?" Garik needed a better way to see everything about his situation.

"I see the inside you." She cupped her hands in the air, framing him.

"Ah. Body heat."

"And you have a lot going on in there. I predict you're about to

172

evolve. We all do once we take the drug."

"The modified DNA serum." He wasn't sure he was ready.

"Julia." John slipped in beside them. "Garik, has anyone talked to you?"

"Yah, Julia's said a mouthful." He grinned, and John laughed.

"I imagine. No, about this." He pulled out a flash drive identical to the one Justin had dropped on Garik's coffee table.

"I'm not getting left out of this little party." Julia worked a cord from around her neck. She also had one of the drives.

As did every person in the group.

"JANTZEN ACTED like there might be a problem with Christian earlier." Garik had a rash of pitted prunes in his stomach—the pits not the prunes. "Is it possible that Justin's that big a fool?"

"What benefit could he get from it?" Giselle pushed her lips into a pouty shape, and she wilted into her chair.

"Revenge. He wants to get even with me." Garik knew it could be the only answer. He'd heard the man's words, that he had been *demoted.*

"It's more than just you besting him in the ring." Paolo tapped his claw-like nails on the tabletop. "He's been, maybe not bested, but restrained many times. If he wanted revenge, there's almost every-one on the campus he'd have to take revenge on."

"Does he have a conflict with Christian? Maybe that's the differ-ence."

Leigh cleared her throat. Tonight, she wore a full sharkskin coat, with a tight collar and large, oversized pockets. When she had their attention, she half stood, then dropped back down. Laura placed her hand on her arm, and Leigh brushed it off and stood.

"Christian has a conflict with nobody, except those fools." She pointed, and sure enough Rodheimer and Sunchaser were coming their way.

Alyna's claws flexed, giving off a rubbing sound each time they slipped in or out.

Marco dropped to the floor of the mall, and his voice hissed from under the table, "Maybe backing out is the thing to do."

Laura leaned under the table and hissed, "No, you little weasel, you."

"I'm not a weasel, you, you, worm, you. I'm a *lemur.*"

"And John's a wood frog, and he doesn't hide under the tables.

Get up here, you weasel." Laura reached under the table, grabbed the nape of his neck, and forced him to sit in a chair.

Hands throughout the group wrapped around mini flash drives, making them disappear as one.

Weston Rodheimer appeared out of the darkness, occluding the better part of the night, while dragging behind him a dark raincloud of muted shadow. Halo Sunchaser basked in his wake, tall and spare to his immense proportions.

"Joanie," Rodheimer began, recognizing the accepted leader of the group. He nodded at Garik. "I see you've claimed the boy."

"He needed claiming." Joanie gave a complete sentence, clearly to appease the man.

"See, Halo, she can construct a complete sentence."

"As you say, Weston." Sunchaser nodded, but her eyes were soaking up the boy, like he had something she would like to possess if only given the opportunity.

Garik felt the drive in his hand press into his skin. He prayed to himself, *Not now. They can't know. Please don't let Justin have told.*

"Okay," Rodheimer announced. "The party is there. Break this up and act like you're enjoying it."

The man held his position until the group on the edge of the mall began to shift position and move away.

Garik found himself with Marco, as the others broke off to go different directions. He double-checked his pocket, wishing now he'd left the little memory device anywhere else. That had been so close.

"Are we giving up?" Marco tugged at his sleeve. "Huh, Garik? You've been spending the most time with him. Are we giving up?"

"I'm not." He glared at the little lemur man. He had *jumped* under the *table*. Who does that?

He knew the real question should be *what* does that?

"And good heavens, Marco, what is that smell?"

"I was nervous." Marco's tail flicked back and forth. "I do that when I get nervous. Sorry."

"Do what, wet yourself?" It was much worse than that.

"I marked your leg." Marco shrugged. "It happens. I try to stop, but sometimes it's hard."

Garik lifted his leg, took a whiff, and nearly lost his nachos. And his leg was four feet from his nose.

"It doesn't smell too bad." Marco smiled. "Now if it gets wet—"

he snickered "—that's a different story."

"And I'm supposed to wear this all night. Sheesh, Marco!"

The night sky had grown darker, and Garik realized he could no longer see the stars. Any light other than from the mall lighting came from buildings that overlooked the mall, and none of them were close.

A rumble started on the horizon, then spidery lightning crawled across the sky. Dark circles appeared on the pavement, then more and more, until their pant legs were ringed with streaks of moisture.

And the smell. Garik knew that if he were hunted, no one would have any trouble locating him. Just take a whiff, locate the stinkiest thing around, and shoot him dead.

He might even welcome it if he had to wear these clothes much longer.

— 6 —

THE RAIN battered the mall for a few minutes, a torrent of cold running off tables and sending the food kiosks into panic, covering their wares with giant tarps.

Then it was gone. The sky cleared, and the stars erupted in a cacophony of brilliant diamonds filling the cosmos overhead.

The marquee on the mall continued to blaze with the Ace of Holes logo. The water dripping from the sign gave it a futuristic look, sparkly, fracturing the lights into multiple tiny rainbows.

Alyna and John had found Garik and Marco. They stood under the building, wet but not soaked. Others on the mall dripped, some twirling in the melee, their arms out, the release of a week's pent-up emotions bleeding out and running down the pavement like the water from the skies.

The elephant from the magic trick lifted its trunk, tossed its ears side to side, trumpeted.

"Looks like he's having fun." John pointed.

"*She's* having fun," Alyna suggested, giving him a jab in the elbow.

"How is it you're not cold?" The tall man's arms were uncovered, and Garik shivered.

"He's a walking heat pump." Alyna tittered. "It's the frog in his veins."

"Enough, Alyna," John cautioned.

"I never found Christian." Garik wanted to see him. He clenched his fists inside his coat pockets, creating bulbous half circles, and he wondered where Jantzen might be. Under the Tower had become standing room only when the sky was really falling, but the press of people was thinning. If the man was around, now would be the time to locate him, before everyone spread over the sixty-four blocks that made up the mall once again.

As Garik scanned the crowd, he caught Airman Vang a dozen tables over watching him. Airman Vang. As soon as Garik caught his eye, the Airman turned, lifted his nose, and began to speak to someone at his side.

Garik clenched his jaw. What am I to you, Airman Vang? A stone in your shoe? Someone who's achieved something you want to destroy? Whatever, it can't be good.

Jantzen was with Joseph Howard. Garik excused himself, saying he needed to speak with Jantzen, and he left them to brave the dripping skies or not, their choice. It became clear that Joseph wasn't there to enjoy the magic show. He held a long push broom with tight bristles. The end was wet, and an area behind him showed drying brush marks where a puddle of water had been worked into a drain.

Some peons are lower than other peons, Garik considered, feeling a swell of emotion for someone farther down the totem pole than him. He didn't get to think more on it, because a ruckus out on the open mall caught everyone's attention. The noise escalated, and swathes of people like waves of cloth billowed that direction, hiding whatever was going on. Jantzen was talking into his watch, and even with the distance and the noise, Garik heard him bark, "Now! Start the fireworks. Or people are going to notice the real show."

Jantzen looked up, saw Garik watching him, and shrugged. He mouthed, "Here we go again," or did Garik just imagine that's what he might have said? In either case, Jantzen's eyes turned a rich purple, deeper than Garik had seen before, and his clothes fell to the pavement, with only wisps of purple smoke coming out of the sleeves by the time Garik got there.

"He's done it again." Joseph grinned. "Likely will do it again, sometime."

"He'll want these." Garik gathered up his clothes. Fireworks on the mall began exploding, sending colored shadows dancing across the food court.

"Yep. Good seeing you." Joseph nodded, lowered his broom

handle, and began pushing the next puddle of color-dappled water to the drain.

POOR MARCO.

Garik lay in bed with the darkness swirling around him, and he pictured the little lemur-enhanced man as he was wheeled off to the elevator to spend the night in the hospital, the reason the military presence was so strong on the mall during events.

Tonight, Marco had seen Justin arrive, and Garik guessed, with the memory of their discussion about Justin's spying and intimidation, the little guy hadn't been able to resist. He'd run up behind Justin, turned around, and scented him before running off.

John and Alyna were laughing, not expecting much of it, but Justin knew the aroma at first whiff. Marco was prone to marking locations all around the facility, and when he did, people knew exactly what they were smelling.

The bigger issue was that Marco could run between people, sometimes through their legs, or under their arms if they were holding hands, and certainly underneath tables and chairs.

Justin could do none of that, and he was blinded to everything except catching the little man and making him pay. What did not move out of his way was forced out of the way, and that included normal humans, hybridized humans, furniture, anything.

The people Justin slammed through often didn't see him coming, and he was gone by the time they picked themselves up. The person nearest got the blame, so Marco's little trick with Justin soon had a dozen fights spreading across the mall.

Justin had disappeared, but Marco hadn't been able to walk once Justin finished with him. Garik never did find Jantzen and left his clothing on the lobby desk on Level 1.

So, what were Justin's strong points? Why was he hybridized from a praying mantis? Garik wasn't sure he'd understand even if anyone told him.

What a night!

He turned, settled in, and listened to the gentle hum of the air from the overhead vent. Often it lulled him to sleep, especially when his thoughts ran away with his mind, causing him to toss and turn.

Tonight, he heard and smelled something that didn't belong. The odor was green and plantlike, the wild outdoors, an aroma he recognized from the gaming center.

Justin!

Garik sat up, working to pinpoint the smells and the sound, wishing he could see at night like a timber wolf. Then he would likely have eyeshine, and everyone else would know where *he* was!

The sounds had gone quiet, but the aroma remained.

"Justin?" he tested.

"Guilty." The voice was gritty in the darkness.

"Why are you in my bedroom?"

"Why did that little creep pee on me?" A big sigh. "Did I kill him?"

"They took him to the hospital, so I don't think so."

Garik rubbed his arms, his fingers gliding over prickles of fear. This conversation *in the dark* was totally surreal. He listened for an impending attack, the slightest movement of the mantis-adapted man.

"Can I turn the light on?" Garik wanted to see the attack when it came.

"Perhaps not." Justin breathed harder, almost a pant. "I'm roasted after this. You win, I lose."

The noise level from across the room increased tenfold, and Garik leaned over as quick as he could and slammed his hand on the light switch on his bedside table. The room erupted into a level of brilliance that assaulted his fear-laced sanity.

No Justin. Garik got out of bed slowly, his eyes searching for anyplace the man might be. In the next room, the front door stood ajar. Garik turned around, pressed his hand to the chair at his desk, and it was warm.

He lifted his hand and smelled of it. Green and soil. Chlorophyll and bacteria.

He wondered how Justin had gotten into his room, and even more, he puzzled how he had gotten out so quickly.

It was frightening what that man could do.

GARIK STUDIED the bearded man across from him in the break area. Half-finished sandwiches and individual bags of chips tumbled across the low table between them like a rocky beach after a storm, with paper napkin seafoam decorating the lot. After the situation on the mall the previous evening, Garik had expected their lunch to be postponed. Jantzen had asked if they could do a light meal in the break room, and he readily agreed.

Now he wrestled with whether to mention Justin being in his bedroom during the night.

Garik took a sip from a canned soda. Several of the tables had been filled earlier, people catching a late snack instead of breakfast, not unusual on the morning after a mall event, but like a wave on the shore, most had washed away when Jantzen arrived.

It seemed to Garik that the purple mist vanishing act set Jantzen apart from the crowd as much as Justin's combative anger drove people from him.

"I checked on Marco this morning." Garik wanted to break the ice into last night.

"And?" Jantzen leaned back.

"You always want me to evaluate things, don't you?" Answer a question with a question. Don't give away everything you know. I'm learning, Jantzen.

"Yes." The dark-haired man studied him, his purple-flecked eyes pulling Garik inside.

"Okay." Garik looked away. He still wasn't strong enough to play games with the man. "Marco will be okay. Maybe," and he glanced at Jantzen with a grin, "Justin should have done more. Marco might have learned a lesson."

"Oh?" A smile cracked one side of Jantzen's face.

"Marco said that as soon as he's out of that bed they have him tied up in, he's going to mark Justin's other leg."

Jantzen laughed. "And you see what I deal with every day."

"What about Justin?" The question just came out. Last night Justin had sounded almost contrite. *"I'm roasted after this. You win, I lose."* Didn't he understand? This wasn't about winning or losing. This was about making the best of the hand they were dealt.

Even if they hadn't chosen to play the game and had been drafted in anyway.

"Is that sympathy I hear?" Jantzen leaned forward, lifted his can, took a sip, and replaced it before leaning back again, likely to give himself time to think. "Justin and I were once . . . good friends. I had my, um, alterations done first, and I didn't expect Justin—"

Garik watched Jantzen's face, his eyes. Not the purple, but the way he held them, looking off to something that was gone and couldn't be called back again.

"He did this without telling you, didn't he?"

"Yes." Jantzen's eyes cut to Garik. "I would have told him no, but then, recovery was longer for those of us who served as the early templates, and I didn't know until after it was done."

"And you feel sorry for him."

"I feel sorry for you—"

"Don't say that." Garik felt something hard rise up. He didn't like what they'd done, but he didn't want sympathy, not ever.

"I apologize. That sounded like pity, and that's not what I meant. For what you lost, for the things you can never have again."

"Why not? Why can't I have them back?" Garik sank into his seat in frustration, his throat raw with emotion. "I haven't changed. I'm still me. What's different? Nothing. Even this is coming back." He grabbed a handful of his hair, and he pulled at it. It was grown enough that he could do that.

"Yes, it is." Jantzen smiled and stood. "Have you been back to Level 5 since that first night?"

"You know I haven't. It still gives me nightmares."

"Do it. Today. I'll be spending some time with Christian this afternoon."

"Christian?" Garik sat up, interested. "Last night, he didn't show. Then with the fighting, everything went sideways. Can I go with you?"

"Visit Level 5 first. Will you do that? Christian and I have some things we need to cover. You will understand better if you do as I ask."

Garik stood, his face growing hot. "What? You do this all the time, not tell me stuff. You don't trust me? I thought we were friends." Garik fought the emotions about to flood his face and shame him.

"Just visit Level 5. You won't regret it." Jantzen glanced at the table and sighed. "I'll send someone to clear this away."

"I'll do it," Garik grumbled after the man was gone.

He wasn't sure if his answer meant he would visit Level 5 or clear the table, but if he cleared the table, he could postpone his visit to Level 5, so that was where he started.

— 7 —

GARIK SMASHED the Level 5 on the elevator's control panel and watched the doors close him in.

What was he doing? He closed his eyes, leaned his head back

180

against the wall, and let his thoughts fall into themselves, pulling him into a black hole of memories.

Marisa. Halo Sunchaser's passkey in her hand. She couldn't have known what would happen. He couldn't either. Would he have run to join her if he had?

Yes. Friends don't let friends go into danger, even of their own making, without standing by their side.

The doors opened, and the clean, bright light of the bottom level of the Tower's basements washed into the tight, steel box. The memory of standing in this spot with Marisa and wondering if Gunther Diehl would walk up, tell them they were in the wrong location, and politely escort them to a suitable exit wiped away the months he had been trapped in the maw of the Corona Tower.

A rising surge of longing washed over him for Marisa's face, for sitting with her on the roof of their apartment building, visiting her at the flower shop, her laughter when his thoughts carried him away, and her reminding him that she was talking to him.

The sounds of the creatures in the cages on Level 5 filtered into the elevator. The door dinged as if to say, "Going up! I'm headed up!" and he moved forward, stepping in its way. He tried not to look into the cages, rather checking right and left while deciding where to go. He gripped his passkey. It now took him anywhere but to the food court, except during events. It was his lifeline back upstairs. He didn't want to be trapped here.

A worker in a white smock appeared from the end of a bank of cages pushing a cart. Garik froze, hearing those words from so many weeks ago. *"Hey, you!"* He expected to hear, "What are you doing here?"

Instead, the man raised a hand, called out, "Hello. We're expecting you," and began to walk his direction.

"I'm Garik." Fear gripped him, despite the man's greeting. The BolaWrap hitting his legs, the feeling of falling, his head smashing into the floor. "Jantzen said—"

"We know. This way." He reached out a hand. He was already moving, Garik's guide through the basement. "Avery Isken. Normally I'm in the labs up on Two, but we all rotate to Five to help with the animals at least twice a month. I didn't make it to the event last night. I was down here covering for Nataly Jago. Have you met her?"

Garik shook his head.

"No reason why you should. I hear something happened during the event—that's why Justin's here. It's a shame, but he would have made it down here sooner or later. It happens with his kind."

His kind? Garik didn't know how to respond.

"Hey, you've arrived at feeding time. I've got the rest of that cart and one more to go. If you're still around, there'll be dinner tonight. You can stay and watch if you want."

"Stay and watch if I want," Garik repeated, repulsed. Was that what Christian would become, an animal to these people? Visited at feeding time, then locked away until the next feeding?

"We have a fresh shipment in, rhesus monkeys. Really cute." Avery glanced at him expectantly, then he shrugged. "Find me when you leave if you think you might. This is it. Take the third door on the right."

They stopped at a dividing wall with double glass doors separating the cages from a softly lighted corridor on the other side. The doors whooshed aside, and fresh-smelling air tumbled over them.

"Third on the right." Garik wasn't sure if he was asking for confirmation or putting off the inevitable. In either case, this was more Level 2 than the experimental operating theater he'd expected.

"Yes. Once people make it here, they don't get many visitors. I wasn't aware you two were friends. Shows you never know." Avery turned and his feet were loud on the hard floor.

Friends? Visitors? What about Christian? Garik had been under the impression he would be sliced up and offered to the latest participant in the human-hybrid program.

He stepped inside and felt the air change as the doors closed behind him. He remembered the way the air had tumbled over them. He turned to look and knew the doors were hermetically sealed. Positive air pressure prevented anything out there from getting in here. It made sense.

He knocked at the third door, mystified. Justin would make it down here sooner or later? What did they want to harvest from Justin? An extra set of joints? He shivered and knocked again.

"I've eaten. Go away." Justin, yelling.

"Good. Then you won't eat me," Garik yelled back.

"What are you doing here?" The door cracked slightly, revealing a darkened room.

"To see you, I think. Jantzen sent me." Garik looked back at the glass doors, wishing more than ever he hadn't come.

"Idiot." Justin slammed the door.

"Do you want me to go?" Garik closed his eyes and leaned his forehead against the door. It was cold.

"No." The sound of a chain being undone, and the door released. "Come in."

Garik pushed the door wide, forcing it into the gloom, and saw Justin disappearing into the depths.

At least he thought it was Justin. It was *something*. If it was Justin . . . Garik's picture of his own future turned upside down.

"SO, WHAT did you expect when you came down here?" Justin growled, a seething cauldron of animosity. Within the growl, a new clicking noise that Garik didn't recognize.

"Not you." The space was living quarters of a sort, though of a temporary kind. The darkness gave it a forbidding cast. "Why no lights?"

"You can't see, can you?" A rough laugh. "Ask Christian. You will soon enough."

"I don't get it. See what soon enough?" *Jantzen, why did you send me down here?* Garik would walk out, but the man had wanted him to discover something.

"Me, this room, you, everything. You don't think who you are right now is all you'll become, do you?"

"I don't know what to think. No one tells me anything." Jantzen had, though, perhaps without meaning to. *I don't know which changes are accelerating initially.*

"I'm part mantis, bred for my lack of fear. I'll tackle any opponent, no matter the size."

"That, I know." Garik had fought him.

"They haven't found anyone better, but I'm not their super soldier."

"Super soldier." Garik heard himself repeating Justin, and he didn't care. Jantzen had said something similar.

"Yeah. I'm too obvious, and I'm still changing."

"Still changing." That could explain what Garik had seen when he followed Justin into the room.

"You like to repeat people, don't you?" Justin laughed, adding a click at the end. "I used to do that when I was coming to grips with a new concept, especially one I didn't want to accept. I guess you need to see so you can get your head around this. By the way, I'm glad the little shrimp will be okay."

"Lemur." Garik wasn't certain he wanted to see.

"Lemur, schlemur. He was a foot taller when he started. Has anyone told you that?"

They hadn't. Julia flashed into Garik's head. She was tall, and she was part boa constrictor. They grew to massive lengths. How tall would she be eventually?

He pictured himself as wolf boy. Hairy ears, bushy eyebrows, and mitts like Christian's. It was too much to take in.

Just when he was ready to curl up and wish it all away, Justin said, "Surprise," and turned on the lights.

It was worse than Garik had imagined.

JUSTIN WAS bare from the waist up. His head wasn't much different, perhaps larger eyes. It was his torso that no one could miss.

"It's better when I have on my coat." Justin shifted position, and he stood. "It irritates my back." He turned. His back was more elongated, but the real difference was in the bulges running down his spine.

"What's happening?"

"Well, it seems mantises can fly." Justin smirked. "And that's becoming me. Not what I wanted to be able to do."

"So, wings in there. They are still growing, right?"

"My arms, too. Did you notice? Popeye." He held them in front of him. The sections between his human elbows and his shorter forearms had thickened, like the massive front legs of the insect he was modeled on. "I don't know . . . I'll take that back. *They* don't know how much longer I'll be able to stay here."

"This happened all of a sudden?" Garik thought of himself. How much warning would he have?

"No. I've been hiding it as best I can. You've seen my duster."

"I thought as much, but not that it was getting worse." Would John one day hop everywhere he went, Joanie require a saltwater pool, or Marco . . . it dawned on him. "Marco will continue to become more lemur-like, won't he?"

"And end up here eventually."

"And?" Like, what would happen? Would Marco also be "harvested" for his DNA-enhanced attributes?

Justin shrugged, but whether he didn't know or didn't want to say wasn't clear.

"Christian—" Now it was clear that the man had begun to shed more heavily, and his hands—all of him—had become more hound-like than ever. "Does it happen to everyone?"

"They've made progress. Your chances, perhaps, are better, if they were careful."

Garik understood why Jantzen had insisted he visit down here. Jantzen could have explained, but that wouldn't have satisfied Garik. Now, he understood at least the tip of what Christian might have to face and why he was being reassigned to the lowest level in the research facility.

"Will they let you continue to live here?"

Justin moved to the small kitchenette in the corner, and he rummaged in the fridge before pulling out a cardboard container. It was unlabeled. He stabbed a straw into the top. It was blood-red when he took a sip.

"Why do you think I gave all of you those recordings?" Neutral, not attacking.

"We didn't know. You planned to turn us in, we thought, but I don't think you did."

"I was angry." Justin nestled into the couch, avoiding pressing his back against anything hard. "But I wouldn't have turned you in."

"We weren't planning anything to do with you. Why would you be angry?"

"Now you're getting it." Justin's voice grew thick, laced with emotion. "You *didn't* include me."

"Why is that a problem?" Say it, man, or bug, or whatever you are!

"Are you stupid, too?" Justin lashed out. "I'm surrounded by idiots."

"No, I'm not stupid. I'm seventeen, I should be in high school right now, and I've been kidnapped to be a part of whatever you people are doing down here. I don't understand any of this." Garik felt the room jump ten degrees.

"You didn't volunteer?"

"Don't *you* listen? Or are *you* stupid? I fell into all this—" literally "—and I want to go home. I'm told that's impossible. The best I can do is try to help Christian escape."

"And I want to be part of that." Justin flexed his arms, revealing more strength in them than his thin torso might suggest. "I can help. Is it a deal?"

"I have to ask everyone else." Garik was sure Joanie and her friends would be grateful for all the help Justin could provide.

"I can appreciate that. Don't wait too long. We may not have much time."

Garik left the way he came. He kept his eyes averted from the cages, still unclear if Christian or Justin would someday be living in one of them. He kept his hand wrapped around his passkey, refusing to think about not being able to board the elevator and leave this place.

When the elevator doors closed, he felt his chest relax for the first time since the doors had opened.

Christian. Now Justin, and maybe Marco before long. Who else? He had started with wanting to save one man, and now it seemed like it was everyone who needed saved.

He was just a teenager. He hadn't even become a wolf yet, not that he could really tell. He was only now regrowing his hair.

What did they expect of him, to save everyone? He didn't even know how to save himself.

Sheesh!

— 8 —

THE WATER in the pool swallowed Garik. He sank to the bottom, turned, looked up, let the rippling ceiling of the natatorium soak into his tortured thoughts. Legs and feet were icepicks across the surface, jabbing through the water, hands splashing, occasionally someone becoming a dolphin, flashing through the water, or a penguin, leaving trails of bubbles to mark their passage.

Workouts were better with Christian, the man tracking his progress with a timer, egging him on, calling, "Don't be a baby. You can do one more."

They had started this to give Christian more time, and Garik hadn't seen what was occurring right before his eyes. The very thing that was Christian's conveyer belt down to Level 5 was still running, inexorably tugging him along, even as the man set out Garik's towel, added another weight to his weight machine, or helped him work out the kinks in sore muscles.

Whoever had programed Christian hadn't set an off switch in Christian's DNA, in his biobricks, in his sequence promoters. In the cellular primer that told his body how to absorb the characteristics of the wolfhound genes they wanted him to take on, they forgot that nature finds a way to bring survival characteristics to the forefront. Cherry picking this or that, precognition or intelligence, kindness or premediated focus that precluded an emotional connection with a perceived enemy was riding the knife edge of a blade, and it was easy to fall off. When you did, people got hurt. The good-hearted often died.

A team of researchers was running tests in the natatorium on aquatically adapted humans, most of whom didn't look especially aquatic, unlike Marina, Marisa's sister. Then, that was the point, to bring out the hybrid side without losing the human side.

It was a circus, a juggling act that could so easily go wrong. Justin's hands, whiplash quick, but one of his props had fallen out of the rotation, skittering to the side, and Justin was scrambling to survive.

Marina, with her vestigial gills, and one side of her body displaying scales and webbed fingers.

Marco, able to climb anything but clearly becoming more lemur than human. At least his intelligence was intact, if scenting people and getting beat up for it was a sign of intelligence.

Was Hector, adapted with a rat, a sign of what Garik would become? Would Garik begin howling at the moon, maybe even gnaw on meat scraps and bones?

Repeated splashing at the side of the pool drew his attention. It stopped, the surface cleared, and Giselle appeared, wavering through the water. She motioned for him to come to the surface. He nodded and waved, and he pushed off from the bottom.

"Yes?" he said, as he broke the surface, shaking the water from his hair. He drew in fresh air, and glancing around, he noticed that the team of researchers from earlier was gone.

"That's my thing, you know." She knelt on the rubberized surface surrounding the pool. "I'm the water woman, able to devolve and reconstitute myself."

"Oh?" Garik was several feet from the edge, and he moved his arms back and forth. The water was deeper than he was tall, and he didn't want to touch the coping. It was a connection with the real world, the one battering his life. In the pool, he was insulated, apart, just Garik for however long he could remain under.

It was motivation to remain submerged for a very long time.

"It sounds wonderful, like a comic character that can liquify herself at any time and become solid again." She touched the water, pushing her hand through the surface, and running her fingers back and forth. She sighed and laughed, a sad sound. "Not exactly."

"So?" Garik moved closer, curious, only now willing to touch the side of the pool with one hand, still separated, still aloof from the world, but making that tenuous connection for as long as the corrosive world around him maintained his interest. "What is it like, exactly?"

"You do know how a sea cucumber liquifies itself?" She pursed her lips playfully, clearly enjoying the question.

"I suppose it squirts out water."

"And all its organs." She grinned. "It has to regrow them later."

"You can do that?" He grimaced.

"You are so funny." She laughed. "The look on your face. I am half human, so no, I don't expel all my organs. I do have to rehydrate everything I expel. It's something better done in a body of water."

"The ocean, maybe a bathtub?" He grinned, enjoying her frankness for a change. "Or a pool?"

"That, too. Come out. Joanie got your message about Justin's offer. She's planned a meeting." She shifted her position as if to stand.

"Wait." Garik wrapped his hand around her wrist. "Can you answer me a question?"

"If you ask the right one. First, my arm." The lower part of Giselle's arm suddenly bled water, shimmering with distorted light, and Garik's hand washed off, sending him backwards into the water. She smiled, jammed the arm into the water for a moment before lifting it and shaking it dry. "Good as new. Your question?"

"Are you still changing? You know, like—" It was important to Garik. Wolf boy, that sort of thing.

"Like Christian? No. Why?" She paused and said, "Oh, I get it. Let me see how to describe this. I'm second-generation hybrid. Christian is first—"

"Like Jantzen, and I think Justin, too." The realization hit Garik. What would Jantzen become? What was he hybridized with? Where had his accessory DNA been sourced? What could allow him to disappear into a cloud of purple mist?

"Yes, but every case is different, especially from the first generation. Trial and error in the initial modifications. Jantzen's was stable, or it has been so far."

"And Marco? What generation is he?" The man had changed just since Garik had known him.

188

"Marco is special. Intentional. Ask him about it, sometime. He loves to discuss it. Okay, I've answered your questions. Out." She stood.

"Wait. Me. What am I?" Second? Third? Or something else, intended to become a bizarre parody of a human being, only recognizable as human by what he once was? He had one hand on the side of the pool, and he floated with the water around his shoulders. The depths of the pool called to him. Her answer was important.

"We all want to know the answer to that question." She shrugged, gave him a teasing pucker and a wiggle of her fingers with one hand, and walked toward the door.

Garik pushed away and let the water swallow him once again. The answer was worse than not knowing. He looked around, noticing the lack of activity in the water. He swam upward, breaking the surface, and realized he was alone.

How long had he been down? Chill bumps erupted over him, tiny volcanoes of dread. He pushed toward the ladder, the water swirling behind him, a trail of bubbles telling where he was, where he wasn't, and that he soon would be no more.

Then what? Garik pulled himself from the water into the air, imagining himself as a sea creature taking its first steps on land, not having a clue that one day it would become elephants and birds and people and this place called Corona Tower.

That was just it. Garik had no clue. And now, it seemed, no one else did, either.

"NO, NO, NO. Justin is not welcome!" Marco Lopez flicked his tail, and he grimaced. "Ow, that still hurts."

"Then don't do it." Julia cracked open a package of gum, pulled out a square, and offered it around before shrugging and returning it to a pocket.

"It's instinctive," Marco moaned, holding a part of his tail that had been shaved, a victim of Justin's aggressive response to his impulsive scenting trick on the mall. "You tell yourself to quit blinking and see how that works."

"Okay. I'm part boa, and constrictors don't have eyelids." She smacked her gum and grinned.

Alyna flexed her claws, chuckling, the soft sound of the knife-like keratin unsheathing and sheathing enough to run a chill down someone's back.

"What?" Marco glared at her. He was still bandaged in several places, and in others, his hair was only now beginning to regrow. "You see me, don't you?" He pointed to his injuries. "Justin did this. Totally uncalled for. Fry him, that's what I say."

"Enough." Joanie stood, her mohawk towering over her. "No trust. Prove otherwise." She pointed to the pile of mini flash drives on the table between them, one for each person present, and she pointed to Garik.

Garik considered his response. Jantzen had started this, used him as a messenger boy. He had sent him on a mission to understand Justin, and now Garik was championing a man who had once been his opponent, if not his enemy. In Justin's plea to help was an old connection between the two men. Garik didn't see it, but he could see how it affected his mentor. For that alone, he was willing to do this.

"Justin's changing—"

The room exploded. "Tell us something new." "Like everyone." "As if we aren't." "He knew what he signed on for." "Deal with it."

Garik gave it a moment to settle. "This is different. I don't think he will mind me telling, but you do realize mantises can fly?"

"I can shoot boiling water." Paolo held up one hand, showing his fingertips. "Any takers?"

Garik restarted. "Justin has boil-like places on his back. He tells me they are developing into wings. And his arms, if you haven't noticed, no longer look human."

When eyes turned toward Marco, he held up his hands and said, "What? I'm human where it counts." He made a fist and hit it twice on his chest.

Garik continued, "I'm learning each of us has been hybridized for a specific characteristic. I learned Justin's when I visited him. Before, I thought, mantis? What's that got that anyone would want? Sure, his arms are lightning fast, but people can see that coming. Justin said they really wanted him for his lack of fear at a bigger opponent. Nothing frightens him."

"He frightens me," Leigh whispered.

"And me," chimed in Giselle.

"See? Justin knows he's on the way out, and Christian—" everyone nodded in agreement "—and you, Marco—" bringing a frown from the man "—and who knows who else? Justin knows his anger issues, the changes he's been trying to hide the past months. That's why he made the recordings. He wants to be included, and that's the only way he knew to tell us."

"Appreciated." Joanie nodded at Garik, thanking him. "Anyone else?"

"If he's already on Level 5, how can he help?" Laura.

"Understood—" Joanie started, when Julia pointed her head at the door and froze. "Julia? A problem?"

"The door. Someone with bad news."

"Bad news?" Garik whispered to Paolo. "She can tell that?"

"Infrared. Stress elevates the body temperature."

The door shuddered, the knob rattled, and then it swung wide. John Carter fell into the room, with Amy Howe behind him. Panic painted his face.

"John?" Joanie invited him to share.

"It's Christian." John crumpled. Amy patted the side of his face.

"Your blood, John. Chill yourself down. You've allowed yourself to overheat." Looking around, she shrugged. "You didn't expect me, did you?"

"Obviously." Alyna's claws were out. "What do you know?"

"More than I've told. I want in, too."

"First, Christian." The one word was all Joanie needed to say.

"They've moved him—"

"Where?" Garik's mind skipped to every possibility. Level 5? He wasn't there when Garik was.

"Jantzen's had a big showdown with Halo. It's still going on—"

"I knew Halo was competitive, but this?" Laura's expression darkened, and she shivered. "Who next, us?"

"Where's Christian?" Garik said it louder than he intended, but it got the attention he wanted.

"Disappeared." John pulled himself to his feet. "He's no longer in the facility. That's what Jantzen and I have been doing, looking for him. When Jantzen discovered he was gone, he exploded all over Halo. Now, Weston's in it. There's no telling—" He took a deep breath and looked pale.

"Suck it up, frog boy," Amy said, patting his arm.

Garik was stunned. This news was as bad as it could get.

At least he hoped so.

— 9 —

"I HAVE told you what I require."

Garik caught the words, the superior lilt that could only come from one person, Halo Sunchaser.

They weren't directed at him, and he couldn't see who she was speaking to, but the steel in her voice was of the tempered kind, beaten and honed to a knife-edge sharpness.

An electrified sword-cutting edge sharpness.

Garik shivered, glad he wasn't in the room. He stood outside the ajar door of the facilities management offices on Basement Level 2, where he had once waited while Jantzen had cleared the calendar with Rachel Prager for Garik to spend the day with him. The long rows of closed-off windows lining the corridor suggested a warren of rooms and no telling how many employees. There was no way to know who was receiving Sunchaser's tongue-lashing ultimatum.

After making his escape from Joanie's—*Christian, lost!*—Garik's head had spun. The corridors had been vast, blurred transitions from non-real space to the infinity of a failure where he had stumbled while guarding someone he had committed his life to protect.

Despair and despondency had transitioned to anger, though it was currently anger with no focus. Who did he blame? Halo Sunchaser? Marisa had worshipped her, or at least her electrified sword, and the woman had been kind enough to escort them on the beginnings of their much-anticipated tour of Corona Tower. Kevin Lee seemed to regard her as a near friend, or as much of a friend as someone as mysterious and powerful as Sunchaser could be. Garik had felt sorry for her when she had dropped everything—literally—when Weston Rodheimer had appeared at the beginning of the tour.

Who wanted to live in that kind of fear? Garik had Arik, his aunt's boyfriend, to contend with, so he understood.

"Halo," Garik recognized Rachel Prager's bright, efficient voice, "I am certain Jantzen wishes to cooperate with you fully and without reserve. He has not been in this office today. When I hear from him, I will pass on your message."

"I will follow through on this, Rachel. What happened this morning was unconscionable and highly inappropriate to a person in my position. I will not have my authority undermined for the sake of a failed project participant."

"Halo," another familiar voice, Weston Rodheimer, "Jantzen is not proven guilty of insubordination. He is technically your superior, so he has the right to question. We must resolve this with care."

"Don't lecture me, Weston. When my parents were killed in the South Africa race riots, they died as the result of cumulative disrespect that began as a disregard for authority. Bongani hasn't spoken to me since I left, but I accepted that insult from my brother rather than live with the racial inequities that took my parents from me. This is important to me."

"I understand, Halo." Rodheimer, again. "The situation today is far different. As a senator, Bongani must keep himself separate from his sister in North America. To do otherwise is political suicide. It is why we let no one know you are a successful part of our genetic modification program. You will have a chance to prove yourself to Bongani when we are allowed to publicize our success. Jantzen's situation is completely different. He supported Christian throughout his transition and was unprepared for the unexpected departure of his longtime friend—"

"Friend?" Sunchaser laughed bitterly. "Are you sure? I hear the tales. I suspect it was once more."

"It doesn't matter. Jantzen has supported our program and been key in most of our advances. He is second-in-command. I will not have him undermined without just cause."

The door clicked, closing completely, and Garik jumped at the metallic noise, thump, thump, that told of the locking mechanism falling into place. This was not a door his passkey would open, even though he wouldn't try it even if it did.

His disappointment not to hear more of the conversation was put aside by his confusion. He remembered how Rachel had "arranged" for Jantzen to keep him out of harm's way after the broken mirror incident involving Devon, and he suspected she had been guarding her words with Sunchaser. She knew more than she was sharing. She had told Sunchaser that Jantzen hadn't been in *this* office today, not that she didn't know *which* office he might be in.

Garik considered where his mentor might be. Facilities management wasn't his only home base. He was a researcher and maintained offices in the research labs, and he was certain Jantzen frequented the research hospital, also, and likely had space set aside for his current projects there. Space was not at a premium in the five-story basement research complex, from what Garik could tell.

Garik hit the heel of his palm to his forehead, whispering, "Stupid, stupid Garik. Of course."

He glanced down the corridor, placing the locations of the underground elevators on his mental map. The floors got smaller the farther down they went, and not every elevator accessed where he needed to be. The main elevator was five city blocks away, if he followed the contours of the city above, and he didn't have his ZBoard with him. His apartment in Corona City was farther, and he wasn't sure where the closest access to additional motorized transportation was located.

He really should have spent more time memorizing the layout of the facility, or at least Level 2 where he lived. He felt so stupid, sometimes.

He could likely sprint to the elevator faster, anyway, as lately, since his track time with Christian, he was rarely out of breath, even after his most intense sessions. Long-distance runs were no longer a blip on his radar of things that seemed impractical or inconvenient.

Two people crossed the corridor at an intersection, one a dark-haired woman wearing normal street attire and carrying a sheaf of paperwork in the crook of her arm. She was talking to a man, slightly taller, who was on a handheld phone. He wore glasses and touted dark hair pulled back severely from his face. The man glanced at Garik, nodded, and looked away. The woman didn't seem to register Garik's presence at all.

Garik knew he would intersect people on his way, and he didn't want to raise questions. Sunchaser. She had been furious, and he didn't want it aimed at him. And Rodheimer? He was frightening, both in his size and his grip on power in the Tower.

At the first intersection of corridors, Garik slowed, looking carefully as he walked across, and only increasing his speed when he was sure he couldn't be seen. Two corridors had groups of people outside, one likely a meeting on a break, with the people wearing their names on lanyards around their necks, and the other workers in paint-spattered coveralls, obviously completing a remodeling project. The name plaque beside the door had been removed, leaving discolored paint and two screw holes.

By the time Garik reached the main elevator, he was running by instinct. He heard the voices before he saw the people, could tell by scent if it was one, two or more—only once surprised by a posse of eight, his sense of smell overwhelmed by sheer numbers—and found himself noting nooks and crannies for hiding and alternate routes he could take even though he wasn't required to use them.

It was the speed that was important, his surroundings blurring into a rainbow haze, using uncanny, wolf-like senses, although to Garik, he was just in a hurry, things sounded and smelled like they were supposed to, and he was making astounding progress.

He arrived at the elevator, grateful to find one of the two unoccupied, and he inserted his passkey. When the panel lit up, giving him permission to select Basement Levels 1-5—but not the food court or the upper levels of Corona Tower—Garik balled a fist and, with his knuckles, smashed the icon for Level 5.

There was only one place Jantzen could be that Sunchaser wouldn't think to look. He was certain he would find him there.

GARIK TWISTED the knob and fell with his shoulder against the door, trusting, hoping, but surprised to find it unlocked and sending it wide into Justin's temporary quarters. He was surprised to find it fully lighted.

"Jantzen? Justin?" He listened, his heart alight with anticipation, willing it to slow its pounding beat.

"Here, Garik." Jantzen, calling from deeper within.

"I knew you'd be here." Garik pushed into the space, to discover Justin face down and stretched along the floor. He wore only shorts, leaving his legs exposed. His shins . . . spurs?

"Forgive me if I don't look up." Jantzen knelt over Justin, with his back to Garik, working on the prone man's torso.

"Garik." Justin's arms were under his head, and he turned to look at Garik. He grimaced, and Jantzen paused, sat up, apologized, and leaned forward again.

Garik hadn't expected this, what appeared to be surgery. Shouldn't this be happening in the hospital, Dr. Jamie or another of the trained staff?

"The best I can do," Jantzen said, pulling a towel from beside him and wiping his hands. "Perhaps the pain won't be so bad."

"What are you doing?"

"What I can." Jantzen turned to him. "You look like you're in a rush."

"It's Sunchaser." Garik could now see Justin's back. The swellings were larger and redder than before. A towel marked with yellow and red looked like Jantzen had been draining fluid from the wing nodules. Justin moved to sit up, placing one hand on the floor, bending his second arm joint backwards, and navigating to a sitting position.

"I'm okay," Justin said, shifting position to try to get comfortable. He called to Garik, "What about her?"

"She's—" He looked between the two men, sensing the moment as a slippery stone, and leaped. "She was in Rachel's office, and Rachel wouldn't tell her where you were."

Justin looked to Garik, smiled, and turned to Jantzen. "Rachel hasn't changed."

"No. What did you overhear?" Jantzen seemed pleased, but his eyes were tired.

"Everything, well, until the door closed. I don't think it's good. And Christian, what happened to Christian? No one knows."

Jantzen seemed to deflate. "I was too late. He's no longer here."

"That's what John said, but where? Can we rescue him?"

"Patience, Garik. Perhaps. I'm working on that."

"There's no time, Jantzen. Now. I promised—" Garik felt his chest tighten, and he fought his face. "I can't let him down. He's a part of us."

"See?" Jantzen turned to Justin, nodding, speaking quietly as though confirming something. "Protect the pack above all else."

"Finally, success?" Justin, in a whisper.

"It's too early to tell. Perhaps."

"I'm right here," Garik barked. "Sheesh, you'd think I'm deaf."

"Maybe not too early." Justin chuckled, and he shifted position and groaned.

"Still painful? There's not much more I can do."

"I'm fine. Talk to the boy."

Boy. Garik had bested the man in the ring, the same way Jantzen had bested him in his fight with Alyna. He tempered his irritation with his old mantra, *my hands, my mind*, convinced that Sunchaser's backstabbing needed to be shared.

"Yes, Garik. What did you find out?" Jantzen made his way to the sofa and dropped.

"She's looking for you. She was talking about her brother in South Africa—"

"That again." Jantzen leaned his head back and closed his eyes. "Halo is jealous, but she has no foundation for it. I hope this doesn't go over your head, Garik, but she once thought we could be together, and that wasn't going to happen. Now, anyone I get close to, she tries to undermine, part of the reason I've kept my distance from you."

"I don't get it. What do I have to do with you and her?" Garik respected Jantzen. Wasn't that a good thing? He was so confused his head spun.

"I'm sure there's more to it—"

"She wants in Weston's favor. That's the more," Justin interrupted. "If Weston can bring her sick grandmother into the country—"

"Our DNA therapy can't . . . isn't designed for repair of cellular organisms. Halo knows that. It only modifies them." Jantzen shook his head.

"Try to convince a desperate granddaughter of that."

"Okay," Garik wailed, no longer caring about Sunchaser's grandmother. "Us, what are we going to do about us? If Christian's gone, we have to get Justin out. How can we do that?"

"He's your proof, your success. I'm telling you." Justin stretched one foot and pushed on Jantzen's leg.

"I can't be a success if you two don't help me!"

Jantzen shook his head and groaned.

— 10 —

"I REMEMBER that Ms. Sunchaser was planning on a trip to South Africa for a martial arts competition." Garik looked up at the mirror spanning the top of the elevator, his face looking back at him, next to him the top of Jantzen's head, and the man's shoulders hiding the rest of his slender shape. Jantzen's arm reached to insert his passkey to engage the control panel.

Garik's shoulders had widened from his time in the gym with Christian. He now went alone. He moved his arms, certain his chest in the reflection had filled out. His lower body? That, he couldn't find in the mirror.

"And she returned, her carved tribal mask in one hand and a trophy in the other." Jantzen pushed the up button, and the doors closed. "Why?"

"She seemed so normal. When I first met her, I thought she was about to eat me alive, like a bird of prey. Then, she seemed concerned that she wouldn't do well in the competition, and she became human."

"Yes, she can do that. I fell for it once, but don't trust it. The human part. She will eat you."

Garik shivered, a cold chill feeding on his self-confidence and bravado. Soon, he would have neither.

"What will you do if—" If she finds you, Garik was about to ask, but as he was speaking, the elevator stopped, the filtered and perfumed air flowing from the vents failed, the lights surrounding the top of the compartment went dark, and the backlight panel around the controls clicked on.

"Not now, Hector." Jantzen looked up at the lights and sighed. "Focus, man."

Jantzen's watch dinged, and he slipped an earbud into one ear. "I'm in the elevator. I told you to wait on my signal. Focus, Hector. I told you I would let you know when to cut the power."

Cut the power? Garik had imagined Jantzen as a team player, even if today had suggested he might be in the process of being voted off the team. Was he planning an insurrection? If so, Garik was totally for it. Maybe this was his chance to make a difference, to save someone, to stand up with the big boys and be counted.

"What's happening on the main level?" Jantzen, again, at the panel, pushing buttons, and he inserted his passkey. The backlight panel became a viewscreen, and Jantzen scrolled through several images with a control Garik couldn't see. They showed the area just outside the elevator on the various basement levels, into the food court, and the Tower's main lobby. Mostly it looked normal, suggesting only the elevator they were on was compromised and not the building, itself.

"What do you mean, when can I get Justin there?" Jantzen frowned. "I'm on the elevator, Hector. Can you give me power just to the main car? Yes, the big breaker. It may be black."

The lights overhead flickered and came on. The air remained silent. Jantzen shrugged at Garik.

"You were supposed to be off before Hector cut the power. Now, we're against the clock. I've got override control of this elevator, and I've cut access from the outside. The second one is still operational, but as soon as it becomes obvious I have an override on this one, an alarm will sound, and this goes belly up."

"Okay, what goes belly up?" Rescue for Justin? Garik wanted to help, but how could Justin get away? He'd never pass for human. He was growing *wings*, for heaven's sake.

"I'm meeting with Kevin Lee—"

"To help Justin escape?" The elevator car swirled with possibilities. Garik had no idea the martial arts instructor knew about the go-ings-on in the basements of the Corona Tower.

"We hope. Our planning isn't that far along, yet. Our first step is to see if we can get him away from the building. Every vehicle Co-rona Corporation has is tagged, logged, and inspected entering and exiting. We need a car no one will suspect."

"Kevin's." Garik pictured the man showing up for private les-sons with Halo Sunchaser, or maybe for his visits to the different recreational activities in the Tower. Perhaps he had received special permission to park in the garage.

If Kevin's car came in or out, no one would see a need to inspect it. He was there to instruct Halo Sunchaser. What could be more in-nocent than that?

"I was meeting him after I dropped you off. Now, you're with me." The car began to move, heading up.

"That might be problematic. Kevin knows me. I'm supposed to be back in Russia." Even as he offered the warning, Garik was calcu-lating how he could get a message back to Marisa and one to his aunt. If they knew, if they came looking for him, he was certain he could be rescued. They would have to let him go.

"That is a problem, I agree." Jantzen lifted his arm, placed his hand on his forehead, thinking, and he worked his jaw. "It can't be helped now. Can I count on you?"

Garik wanted escape, not to work with Jantzen. Yet, the man had become a mentor, a friend of sorts, if in a limited way. He didn't want to abandon what he'd agreed to help him do, but he also didn't want to abandon this opportunity for escape. His mind raced, search-ing for a way to do both, to begin his escape, and to not let down the people he'd come to share his life with.

He couldn't come up with a plan to do both.

"I need an answer, Garik, before I open this door."

"You're helping Justin?" A thousand needles shredded Garik's stomach.

"Yes." Jantzen held his hand over the door's controls.

"And Marco, too?"

Jantzen raised his eyebrows. "If he asks, certainly."

"What do you need me to do?" His eyes burned. He was in the cell, closing the door, and locking it after him. Why, why, why?

"Nothing. Just let me talk." Jantzen hit the open button, left his passkey in the door, and stepped through when it slipped sideways.

"Follow me."

Garik stared at the passkey. Two feet away, and he had his freedom. *Two feet away!* His mind churned with images of the past months, and one kept coming to him, lying in his bed in the darkness listening to Justin say, *"I'm roasted after this. You win, I lose."*

"I'm sorry, Marisa." Garik's eyes burned as he stepped outside of the elevator to find himself in the polished foyer leading to the pool. Through the glass door, a woman in a green suit sat to the side reading a magazine in a woven rush chair, and a man with slender legs and a round belly lowered himself into the water.

"Kofi!" Jantzen greeted the pool boy, Kofi Mandela, with a raised hand. "I believe Kevin Lee is scheduled for the pool today."

"Yes, Mr. Hefferly. After his session with Ms. Sunchaser. He hasn't yet arrived."

"Have you heard why?" Jantzen seemed surprised.

"Ms. Sunchaser had business this morning, and she scheduled Kevin a half-hour late. Garik? Is that you?" Kofi smiled broadly. "We were told you had returned to Russia. I'm glad to see you back. If you wish to use the pool with Kevin, I can offer you a suit. You have filled out. Perhaps a larger size than last time?"

Garik didn't know how to answer, and he turned to Jantzen for help.

"Yes," Jantzen said. "For both of us, if you don't mind, Kofi. Thank you, and yes, a larger size for my friend."

"Give me a moment while I retrieve them." Kofi stepped through a narrow door and it closed after him.

"We're swimming?" Garik's thoughts were entangled in running away, finally free; and following through on his responsibilities to those in the research program. And swimming? What had happened to urgent?

"Kofi needs to think so. He's returning. Quiet."

"These should work." Kofi offered Jantzen two towels and two suits.

"Thank you." The couple still lounged by the pool, and Jantzen said, "We will wait on Kevin in the changing room, and Kofi?"

"Mr. Hefferly, yes?"

"I'm leaving that elevator locked open. I know that's unusual, but this is special. Please see that it's undisturbed."

"Certainly, Mr. Hefferly."

Jantzen nodded for Garik to follow, and they entered the changing rooms. The space smelled comfortably clean, with the odor of mangos filtering through the air. When the door closed, he set the suits and towels on a counter and dropped to a bench. He leaned his head back and closed his eyes.

"So? What now?" Garik's muscles told him to run. His head said the elevators had him trapped on this floor. Perhaps with Jantzen's . . . then he remembered Gunther Diehl resetting the passkeys with Marisa's thumb on Halo Sunchaser's. Jantzen's wouldn't work for him even if he could get to it before Jantzen could catch him. He also remembered the night of the fight between Justin and Alyna. When Justin had gone for blood, Jantzen had evaporated and been across the games room before Garik could blink.

It wasn't likely that Garik could outrun the DNA-enhanced man.

"Kevin's cooperation is key. Maybe this is good, you being here. He knows me, but even more importantly, he knows you from outside, and—"

"You haven't talked with him?" Garik was appalled. He was trading his freedom for a possibility? "I thought you had this sorted out with Kevin, whatever it is you're planning."

"Nothing is ever sorted out, my young friend, and this?" He looked around the inside of the changing rooms. "Opportunity, that's all. I didn't intend to involve you, not until after I spoke to Kevin, and perhaps not then. I might be creating more trouble for myself than I expect, and I expect a lot. Weston will be furious."

The door flew open, startling the two men, and Kevin called out, "Garik? You in here?"

"Yah!" Garik grinned, surprised at the warmth in the words. He expected to be a nonentity to the man. He'd only known him a short time before he had disappeared.

"Hey, you moron. I just get to know you, and you vanish for months. How's Russia?" He grinned. "Mr. Hefferly, did you know this guy refused my invitation to train at Ai Kee!?"

"That's nice, Kevin."

"Have you seen Marisa since you've been back? She must be thrilled. Man, you leaving took it out of her. I hope you're back for good."

"Yeah, about that, um, Kevin," Garik started, looking to Jantzen. The mention of Marisa was a knife.

"Kevin, before you and Garik get too touchy-feely, I need to ask you a very big favor. Are you parked in the garage?"

"Sure, Mr. Hefferly. Ms. Sunchaser validates my parking. Is that okay? I was assured it would be fine on the days I give her lessons here at the Tower."

"Will you rent me your car for the night?" Jantzen pulled out his wallet. "Any amount."

"Rent you my car . . ." Kevin frowned. "Why?"

"My reasons, and if you're worried about damages, I'll guarantee it's returned in perfect condition. If any damage occurs, and you can be the judge, I'll have it repaired to your satisfaction."

"I, um, don't have any plans to use it tonight. What time can I pick it up tomorrow?"

"Will the afternoon do?" Jantzen had pulled out several large bills, and as he talked, he kept adding to them.

"Before you give me all that, I didn't drive my car today."

Jantzen hesitated. "Can you bring it in and leave it later?"

"No, that's not it. I'm in the Center's truck, well, transport van. If you need a car . . ." Kevin shrugged.

Jantzen held out the wad of cash, and Kevin grinned. A knock at the door startled them.

"Yes?" Jantzen called.

"I'm sorry, Mr. Hefferly. I know you said not to let the elevator be disturbed, but Mr. Rodheimer and Ms. Sunchaser are here. They are demanding to see you."

"Thank you, Kofi." He held out his hand to Kevin. "Keys?"

"Oh, of course." Kevin placed them in his hand. "Good to see you, Garik, and thanks, Mr. Hefferly. I know you'll take good care of the van."

"Of course, Kevin. I appreciate your cooperation." On the way out, Jantzen's face lost its luster.

"Is this your big trouble?" Garik didn't need big trouble.

"We'll see, but likely."

"Should I let you do all the talking?"

"Halo may do it for us. Just hope that Weston takes my side. That's our best bet."

Garik had his own opinion there. He intended to keep his mouth shut and look as small as he could.

— 11 —

WHEN THEY stepped into the pool's lobby, Sunchaser was pacing, and seeing them, she seemed to grow four inches, anger swirled around her like windblown debris, and she erupted in a violent assault. Her wrap encircling her hair vibrated with pent-up energy.

"Finally, I put it together. This is the boy that helped that girl steal my passkey, Weston, and here he is, with Jantzen, roaming the tower unsupervised. The lost passkey was not my fault, and this proves it. Something has to be done."

Rodheimer, massive even next to the towering Sunchaser, darkened, his thoughts tumbling across his face like a storm cloud, and he growled, "Jantzen, are you aware of this?"

Jantzen sighed and cut his eyes to Garik. His shoulders drooped. "It's likely. The timeframe fits."

"He admits it." Sunchaser's words seemed to boil as they hit the air. "If I had not been pulled away to South Africa, I would have made this connection before. Jantzen, once more you use your position to undermine mine, working behind my back when I am away. Did you arrange for that girl to abscond with my passkey? And to think, it was your suggestion that we not retain her, also. What are you planning now? I was right to fast-track Christian's removal. I can see it now, this boy. Weston, your number two has plans afoot, and they will not bode well for the project. You must act now."

"I admit I was furious this morning. Christian's removal was unexpected. I can only apologize." Jantzen glanced to Kofi, who had faded into the equipment room with the door cracked. It slipped shut. Kevin had not appeared, likely avoiding the confrontation.

"The boy?" Rodheimer's voice was the rumble of a train track in the night. "What explanation do you offer for his presence?"

"Coincidence, only. We were in the elevator at the same time—"

"And he locked it out, for a quick escape, I'm certain. His passkey is the inescapable evidence. Keep that in mind, Weston." The air around Sunchaser vibrated with energy.

"Is Halo wrong?" Rodheimer, for a moment, seemed hopeful.

"Not wrong, just that my actions have been misconstrued. Let's meet tomorrow, you and me. Invite Halo if you wish. We can work this out, Weston."

Garik recognized what Jantzen was doing, playing for time to get Justin out of the research facility. He offered a prayer, but he also looked to the elevators, wondering if he could get to one and whether his own passkey would operate it from here.

Rodheimer turned to Sunchaser. "What do you suggest, Halo?"

"Restrict him to levels two and four, for a start. He has demonstrated his disregard for your position and mine. He thinks more of those that fail to perform satisfactorily than he does the success of this program. He has made a mockery of my authority and yours. Today is a perfect example, bringing one of his pets up here with him."

"Jantzen, are you taking this in? I have overlooked much for the sake of our history together and your contributions to the program. I forgive people when they fail me, but I expect them to make it right. This is not making things right. You are a brilliant researcher, but I cannot overlook this. I agree with Halo."

"I am fully supporting our research, Weston. My results speak for me. I can hardly work efficiently if you restrict my mobility about the facility. If we can't meet tomorrow, perhaps Rachel can schedule a better time." He smiled hopefully.

"Weston, I expect results, not for this to be put off again. I will not have this man continuing to flaunt my authority, and yours, too. You must support me in this." Sunchaser's voice had gone ragged with fury.

"Understood. Jantzen," Rodheimer turned to him, "I'll expect you to restrict yourself to your apartment until we get this resolved. I will retain your passkey for the foreseeable future."

Jantzen's eyes narrowed and his shoulders stiffened. His pupils glowed purple, and Garik tensed, waiting for the man to evaporate into purple mist. Nothing could hold him. He would be gone. It was an exciting moment, until the impact of his own situation left him flash-frozen in despair. Jantzen's escape would mean leaving him behind. He tried to catch the man's attention, and he shook his head, pleading. *Don't leave me, Jantzen.*

"I will do as you ask." Jantzen relaxed, giving in. Garik's head swam with relief.

"Also, the boy." Sunchaser turned her eyes to him, fire flying. "He is complicit and uncooperative, and for that, a failure. He must be restricted. Better, reassign him to Level 5."

Garik's knees nearly gave way. He was certain he would vomit if he had anything to expel.

Rodheimer looked from Jantzen to Garik, as if evaluating the success Garik had exhibited in contrast to the insubordination of being discovered in the Tower with Jantzen. He seemed to come to a decision.

"I will arrange it in the morning. Airman Vang will escort you both to your quarters."

Airman Vang moved forward from the shadows with hand restraints ready. He slapped them together noisily. Garik was certain the man grinned.

And he thought things were as bad as they could get. Never, never think that, he reminded himself. You will be disappointed every time.

Then the restraints were pulled tight, and he was yanked forward, with what little freedom he'd earned once more stolen from him.

GARIK LAY in the darkness, his head a vice, his brain squeezed, and his thoughts erupting in clumps of misery that spattered the walls with despair.

Locked! His door, his passkey useless!

He wondered why they hadn't taken it away, had tried it in his door, only to understand. They wanted him to be crushed with false hope. Well, it was working.

The sound of metal shearing, of voices whispering furtive things, drew him up and pulled him to the living room. Light leaked from around the lock on the door.

Hope? Did he dare? Or was this his end, Sunchaser sending someone to collect him, banishing him to Level 5 in the dark of the night, or worse, eliminating him altogether? Was that a possibility? He suspected it was.

The thump of metal separating from metal, and the door released. Garik slapped a switch, flooding the room with brilliance, and he backed away, prepared to fight, whatever they might come at him with. When the door swung back, Alyna Lindberg stood, held her hand in front of her, blew on her claws, and retracted them with a grin.

"Like a hot knife through butter." She winked at Garik.

"Or through molten steel." Julia Cantos leaned in behind her. "Inside, Alyna. I can sense someone coming."

They moved inside, and Julia fell against the door, holding it to. She shrugged and explained, "You don't have a latching mechanism any longer, thanks to Alyna. Sorry."

"I, um, what's—" Garik stumbled out the words. "You can cut metal?"

"Not the important question," Alyna suggested, "but yes. The important thing is what to do with you. Did Weston or Halo find out about the car?"

"Kevin's?" He shook his head. "Jantzen already had the keys, and it didn't come up. And it's not a car. It's a transport van."

She looked at Julia and nodded. "Even better. Did Jantzen give you the keys?"

"No."

"Then we hope they didn't search him and take them away. We'll leave that to Leigh and Paolo. If they did, perhaps Giselle can help. We'll have to have water, though. She'll need it if she's going to get inside the van."

"Justin is getting rescued?" Garik felt hope return.

"Yes." Alyna sighed, stretched her neck, and looked up and down Garik's pajamas. "You, young man, need clothes. How quickly can you dress?"

"What sort?" He grinned. He was being offered the chance to help. He was certain.

"Outside clothes, the warmest you have. Now."

He turned, excitement racing through him, and caught the doorway with his shoulder. He called back, "I'm okay," and he leaped for his closet.

As he dressed, he overheard the women talking.

"Has everyone been notified?"

"Marco thought he could do it by the time we got Jantzen out."

"And Justin?"

"He's mine, if Paolo can't manage." Garik overheard the swish of Alyna's claws extending and retracting. "If that kid in there will get the rocks out and get back in here."

"I heard that," Garik called. "I'm not deaf!"

He heard Julia chuckle and say, "Jantzen said he could do that."

Then their voices fell too low for him to overhear.

JULIA LED them, a passkey in her hands. Her ability to sense metabolic heat by infrared—the adaptation she had received from her constrictor DNA—kept them from being surprised by people along the way to the parking garage.

Garik was the one they were concerned about, although no one outside of Rodheimer, Sunchaser, and Airman Vang would likely think anything of him roaming the facility. Still, when someone approached, Garik pulled a hood over his head and kept his face averted. He wore a backpack filled with water bottles. Even with the extra weight, he could have done the journey faster and with less fuss if he knew the details of what was happening, but that was wishful thinking.

They worked their way to the research labs, and Alyna pulled out a second passkey. She held it up and whispered, "Let's hope this works. If not," and she flexed her claws and grinned. She inserted it into the panel by the door, and after a moment, it turned green. The locking mechanism thumped twice, and Alyna placed her hand on the latch. A twist, and it swung open.

"This is off limits," Garik pointed out. The off limits didn't concern him. How Alyna was able to access it did.

"This isn't a spur-of-the-moment plan." Julia entered and pulled Garik after her.

"We're just being forced to move tonight." Alyna followed and closed the door after her.

"What's in here that we need?"

"An elevator directly to the parking garage. The labs have two."

"Oh." That was new information to Garik. The aboveground parking garage was where Kevin would have parked. He tried to picture the layout of the basement facility and place the parking garage outside the Tower over where he thought the research lab was located. It didn't fit. "I don't see how any elevators here could connect to the parking garage. It's behind the Tower. That's six blocks that way." He pointed behind them.

"We're headed to the underground garage."

"Okay." The two women didn't seem inclined to elaborate, and Garik let it go.

The research lab was massive, nearly a quarter of the size of the aboveground mall, and the corridor narrowed in the distance. A red exit light glowed in the distance. "That's us," Julia said.

Garik focused on the red light. He had no reason not to trust them, and a ton to do so.

At the elevator, Alyna inserted the passkey that had granted them entrance into the labs. "One floor up. That's all we need. Come on, elevator."

The controls lit up, the door opened, and they stepped inside.

WHEN THE doors released them into the parking garage, Garik was the last one out. The vastness of the space confronting him contained as many parking spaces as he had ever seen in any one location, even more than Waldorf's Department Store, and their lot went for blocks. This was perhaps not larger, but it also didn't have a department store sitting in the middle of it.

Vehicles of different types filled about a third of the space, mostly small cars, several trucks, and some minivans. They were concentrated around the lab elevators and the main access that Garik reckoned sat directly under the tower. Numerous military vehicles filled the area to the left—the north wall, if Garik had his directions down. From his early tours of the facility, he pictured the military housing block just to the west on the other side of the adjoining wall.

John, Laura, and Joanie stood to the right, with John wearing a backpack, and the two women sorting through several items at their feet. Farther away, Amy and Giselle walked side by side, Giselle rolling a large case, and Amy wearing a backpack. Marco scampered on four limbs beside them. John waved and called, "About time. This way! Paolo and Leigh are on their way."

"And Justin?" Alyna yelled. Garik remembered her claws. He was certain she would return to the elevator if the news wasn't what she wanted.

"With Paolo and Leigh, we hope. They volunteered."

Garik didn't see Jantzen. What about the keys to Kevin's van? And if these people were all here, was this a mass exit, an escape of unimaginable proportions? He hadn't located Kevin's van, probably because there weren't any vans down here. If it was in the above-ground parking garage, how were they going to reach it?

And . . . and . . . when were they going to tell him *anything!*

Sheesh! It was as if he didn't count. He wanted to shout, "Hey! What's going on?" Instead, he picked up the pace and followed the others, wherever that might lead.

— 12 —

AT FIRST it seemed absurdly simple, that they might just walk out. Signs all along the ceiling directed them to the exit. How could they miss it?

It was the massive gate in the way that presented a problem. The passkey was their solution, or it should have been. Alyna pressed her thumb to the small screen on the side and slipped it into the access control panel. The panel turned on, telling her to validate the passkey with her palmprint.

It wasn't an option the hybrid escapees dared try.

Each person carrying one of the illegal passkeys gave it a try, only to be kicked out like an unwanted child.

"Ideas?" Joanie sat on the floor, her back to the gate, and she pulled out a pack of mints. She popped two into her mouth before putting it away and didn't ask if anyone else was interested, a sure sign of her level of anxiety.

"If Leigh were here—" Giselle started.

"She's not." Joanie pulled out her pack of mints, shook it as if considering whether she should conserve, and decided to wait, putting the package away. Leigh could find invisible flaws, even accelerate chemical processes with her ultrasound, but she wasn't here, was she? "Alyna?"

The team knew the question exactly. Was Alyna prepared to slice through the locks, allowing them access to the parking garage above? They also understood the ramifications. As soon as the lock was severed, an alarm would sound, and their escape would be in dire peril.

Catch 22, no good way to find success through either option.

"I will, but we should exhaust our other choices, first. We will be pursued soon enough. No sense in starting the chase now."

John had the top of his backpack unzipped. He pulled out a watch with a blank, black face. He used his thumb to polish the glass surface.

"Tell me that works," Amy pleaded.

"Not in here." He looked up and around the room. "This place is a faraday cage. Only the project's electronics work underground, and only on their frequency. Once past this gate, I should have full-spectrum access to everything out there."

"Listen," Garik called out.

"What?" John's question was fair. It was the middle of the night. There had been no one coming or going out of the underground garage, and the sky they could just glimpse through the metal fretwork of the gate was black velvet littered with stars.

"You can't hear it?" Garik shook his head at the old people around him, their ears already gone.

"Garik's right." Amy stood, and she held perfectly still.

"At least Amy has ears," Garik muttered.

"She's not using her ears." Marco settled beside him, curling his tail into his lap and tugging on Garik's sleeve with a hand that had elongated, pawlike nails. "She's likely feeling the air pressure. Better than ears, sometimes."

"People moving this way," Amy said. "Julia, can you tell more?"

"No, not from this distance. Anyway, the concrete walls are difficult to work though." She had turned to face the direction of the elevators. They were a good three blocks away, if measured by the city above them.

"The other direction." Amy pointed through the gate.

Joanie turned, wrapped her fingers through the gate's openwork surface and pulled herself to her feet.

"Leigh?" she called, hissing the word.

"Joanie? Why isn't the gate open? We've located the van and are locked out. No keys."

"We hoped Jantzen would have them. Garik said—"

"Stop, Julia." Joanie held up a hand. "Unimportant. Software update. Locked in."

"Or out," Leigh said. "I can guide someone manually if anyone is willing to try to pick it."

"Or slice it," Alyna muttered, her claws on one hand already out and ready.

"Or pick it," Joanie reiterated, and she motioned with a hand for Alyna to be patient. "No alarm. Jantzen and Justin?"

"With us? Sort of, well, yes." Leigh wasn't saying everything.

"Okay. Understood. Marco, lock." Joanie's words were fully detailed to the people around her. Marco—part lemur adapted—had the smallest fingers in the group, and Leigh's ultrasound adaptation, allowing her to see what others couldn't, including the inner gearing of the gate's locking mechanism, were needed to get through the locked gate.

"Heh, heh, finally! Something I'm good at!" Marco scrambled over, wrapped his hands around the locking mechanism, sniffed of it, and smacked his lips. "Ready."

"Let me focus—"

As Leigh and Marco worked their magic, Joanie directed the others to gather their things. She pulled Garik aside, "Water?"

"In the backpack, sure. Do you need it?"

"Unsure. Be prepared." Joanie patted him on the shoulder and turned to see how the progress was going on the lock.

"It's hanging, Leigh. I am pulling. Can you get Paolo here? Hot water might work to expand parts of the metal." Marco growled at the lock.

"I can lubricate it, if you think that will help." Giselle offered her hand, her fingers already dripping.

"Try it," Leigh called. "It's almost there." The lock attached to a rotating assembly that interlocked in the center. It wasn't releasing enough to allow the gate to move.

Garik scanned the interlinked rods and the way they twisted together. He pictured his Street Strider and the gearing inside. He had rebuilt it on the side of the road enough times that he understood how to relieve the pressure on troublesome gears that liked to jump restrictive linkages.

"Here," he said. "Keep pulling that, Marco. I'll lift this here, and you, John, when I tell you, pull this rod towards you."

"That will help how?"

"Just do it!" Garik groaned in frustration. This was something he understood. They explained nothing to him. Then they expected him to explain everything to them. Sometimes things just needed done.

"Okay." John stepped to the gate, grabbed the rod, and said, "Ready."

Garik pulled, the rotating assembly moved, and he hissed, "Now, John."

With a snapping rotation that threw Marco backwards and startled Leigh, the locking mechanism released.

"We're through." Laura hefted a pack onto her shoulder just as alarms sounded, and strobe lights across the parking area flooded the space with midday brilliance.

Alyna groaned, "I could have done that," as she wrapped her arms around a box to carry to the other side.

"Now. Move." Joanie tugged on one gate, creating enough room for them to squeeze through. They were almost there. Just a little way to go.

JOHN SLIPPED through with a backpack on his shoulders, leading Laura. She held a zippered bag by the straps, and once through the gate, she took off running.

Marco squeezed past John, now in full run. He was on two feet this time, using his tail to balance the speed of his feet.

Leigh stood on the opposite side of the gate, helping people work their things through the tight opening. Amy, tiny Amy, had a backpack nearly her size. Her strength seemed inordinate to her stature, but she seemed to have no trouble.

Alyna had taken Garik's backpack of water bottles while he was helping with the gate, and she carried it and the box from earlier. He followed her through, both cutting into a run at the first opportunity.

Giselle's rolling case hung for a moment on the gate's tracks. Julia had one of Laura's bags in one hand, and she worked Giselle's case free with the other, helping her to get it rolling before they disappeared into the upper level.

Joanie was last, as any good leader should be, waiting on Leigh before putting her hand on the strap holding her backpack over one shoulder and making her way skyward.

At the van, they found Paolo hunched over Justin, who seemed a pale imitation of himself. Paolo looked overhead at the red lights flashing on the ceiling, running his eyes back and forth. Outside the garage, the night was black.

"Did anyone bring a key?"

"Where's Jantzen?" Joanie forced out two words, a good semblance of a complete sentence, revealing her desperation and determination to be understood.

"That's my sort of." Leigh knelt by the two men, and she asked Justin, "Can you hold on?"

"To you? Of course." He chuckled, laughed, and coughed blood.

Garik saw the complete picture. They were here. Jantzen was not. Whatever had happened to Justin, he needed to be someplace besides here. Alarms were going off, and there was no way they weren't going to be surrounded by the military in about two minutes. He was surprised they weren't already here.

They needed in the van, and he could get it started, even without a key.

Garik took Giselle's rolling case, and he said, "Excuse me, Giselle. Thank you." Lifting it, he smashed the bottom against the side glass. One wheel flew off, but when it came away, it left a crack. He smashed it again and again. "I'm sorry, Kevin," he said, as he hit it the fourth time, shattering the glass and sending the case tumbling inside. He reached through the door, felt for the lock, and slid the door open. He stood back and motioned for everyone to climb in.

"We still don't have the key," Paolo reminded him, as he stood and helped Justin stand.

"Leave that to me." As everyone began climbing into the van, Garik went around and opened the driver's door. He leaned under the dash and grabbed underneath the plastic housing enclosing the steering wheel and pulled until it broke free. "Sorry, again, Kevin," he said, and he tossed the plastic to the side. It clattered on the concrete floor of the garage. He began feeling for wires, certain he could bypass the ignition switch. He knew machines, had seen this done over and over in movies. How hard could it be?

"How long, Garik?" From Paolo. "We might need to make our exit."

"It should have an ignition lock switch I can bypass. I can't find it."

Something hit the outside of the van beside Garik's door, and he looked up to see Jantzen, bare-chested, standing over him, panting with exhaustion.

"What are you doing?"

"Hotwiring it, of course." Garik thought that was obvious. No key!

"And you broke the window for what reason?" Jantzen shook his head. "Giselle, I need some clothes out of that case."

She clicked it open, to the complaints of several others crowded in with her, and she handed him a set.

He began pulling on a pair of pants, and he called, "Giselle, the keys are in there, also. Hand them to me."

They appeared over the seat, and she dropped them into Jantzen's hand. He pulled his shirt on and motioned for Garik to get out of the way. He climbed in, started the van, and shifted it into gear.

"I told Kevin we wouldn't damage the van. He's not going to be happy. You should have used the key."

"I did."

Jantzen looked at him skeptically as he pulled the loaded van out of the parking garage and turned right onto Stamford. To the left, the serene residential lighting of the upscale properties in Overlook Estates seemed incongruous with the desperate escape happening in the van. Cold air poured in through the broken window.

"I did, I did," Garik insisted, turning to look at the faces behind him catching the lights along the street, flashing them into alternating patterns of light and dark. He grinned. "They just happened to

213

still be in the case when I unlocked it."

They were barely more than a block away from Corona Mall, having just turned west on Corona and south on McKinley, when Corona Tower erupted with military vehicles streaming into the streets.

"I thought I could hold them longer." Jantzen put his foot to the floor, the engine in the transport van downshifted and began to roar, and it picked up speed. The passengers held on as Jantzen turned left on Paintbrush, then right on Park Avenue. With his foot planted, the van's speed soon surpassed anything the speed limit signs suggested as safe and legal.

Garik looked to the right as they passed the police station, lighted against the dark of night, and then it was gone.

Jantzen thought he could hold them longer. Garik was sure he understood. The man had escaped his captors by evaporating into purple mist, and he had spent his time before arriving at the van jimmying all the exits to the building. He had bought them time for their escape.

They were on the run, and Garik didn't know exactly what that might involve, but if Jantzen was leading them, he had no doubts they would survive just fine.

"Jantzen, can we risk Bay City Medical?" Paolo's laidback voice filtered over the seat, only now, not so laid back.

"We are being pursued, Paolo." Very matter-of-fact.

"Just so you know, we're losing Justin."

Garik turned. Paolo held his hand on the man's chest. Blood seeped from between his fingers.

"John has a watch." Giselle pulled several items of cloth from the rolling bag, and she handed them to Paolo, saying, "Here, this should help temporarily."

"I've a better idea." Jantzen slammed the brakes and forced the van west, taking a hard right on Summit Court West. At the entrance to the Ransom Communications Building, he took a sudden left, skidding the tires just in front of a metal roll-up door.

"I'll be right back. Garik, can you pull us inside?"

"I can drive."

"Better than you can unlock a car?"

"Jantzen!" Garik wilted. "I didn't know the keys were inside."

"I'll need my clothes." Jantzen grinned, balled a fist, and punched Garik on the arm. Then, he evaporated, leaving his clothes floating down to land on the seat.

"Move, boy," Joanie said, giving him a push on the shoulder.

As Garik shifted behind the wheel, purple smoke gathered around the roll-up door and disappeared through the gaps and cracks around the edges. Ten seconds later, the massive door began to roll upward.

Garik shifted into gear, and he eased the van forward.

He had no idea what he would find inside.

— Book 4 —

Яeflections
Silverback
of the

— 1 —

GARIK SHAYK pressed his foot to the brake and located the shift mechanism. The burble of the transport van's engine took on a deeper tone and, hardly noticeable among the steady midnight hum of the city's power transformers, heat-exchange fans, and occasional sirens, the transport van with its twelve fugitives vanished through the roll-up door leading into the darkened bowels of the Ransom Communications Building.

One side of the van proclaimed it the property of The Martial Arts Center, and the other was marred by a shattered window. Inside lay Justin Kurtew, oozing blood and dead if he didn't get immediate assistance.

Two round circles of light revealed thick cables running up a corrugated surface. Racks of tools and metal lockers stretched into the darkness. Several doors with reinforced glass inserts and a cargo elevator emphasized the functional nature of the space.

Garik, who at 17 should be a senior at Bay City High, listened as the metal door rattled on its tracks, closing behind him, sealing them in. For months, he had been trapped in the basements of the Corona Tower, an unwilling participant in their secretive human-hybrid project. He now lived with timber wolf DNA in his veins. What he might evolve into frightened him.

He pictured Marisa, his girlfriend, his last words to her. *Run!* She believed he had been deported back to Russia, and there was Irina, his aunt, and his friends, Muhammad, Ibn, and Hayat, all jerked from his life, leaving him floundering.

"Garik, clothes?" A hand appeared at his window.

"Oh, right, Jantzen. Here, somewhere." Marisa became dash lights, a steering wheel, and the arm of a shirt on the stubby console. Jantzen had morphed—sublimated was more accurate, a closer technical term—into purple mist in order to enter the locked building and gain access to the underground parking garage.

Each time he did, he left his clothing behind.

Garik pulled a shirt and a pair of pants from underneath him and held them through the window.

"Thanks for the creases, my young friend." The hand wrapped the clothes in long fingers and disappeared.

"Anytime." Garik looked back into the van. The reflections of the headlights on the wall made his passengers into shadowed ghosts. "How's Justin?"

"Not better." Paolo Leveen, his hands dark with blood, held several fabric items against Justin's chest. He spread his fingers over the cloth to ensure even pressure, but it continued to ooze red.

"Lights." That was Joanie McDonald, vitreous-colored hair in a mohawk style, and tacit leader of the group. She could evaluate a situation and make a decision, earning her the position by rights. Her swagger was a visual reminder to anyone who forgot.

"Jantzen? Can we get lights?" Garik called through the window as he fiddled with the dash, searching. Jantzen had been driving before vanishing into smoke and leaving him to take the wheel. He had only ever driven his Street Strider, and the layout of the van's controls in the darkness was lost to him.

Jantzen must have been listening. The metal-on-metal thump of an industrial-size breaker reverberated, and smaller noises told of the overhead lights powering on, each one buzzing for a moment, then glowing deep red before beginning to brighten.

"The engine." Justin coughed, choking on blood and spitting. "Don't want to die ... carbon monoxide ... sorry." He coughed again.

"He's right. Kill it, though it's not his biggest worry." Jantzen appeared at the door with the broken window, now fully clothed, and he triggered the handle and slipped it aside. "We need to get him out."

Garik located the key and silenced the machine.

"Can we try a medical facility?" Paolo, who held the man's life in his hands—literally—looked out the windows at the industrial nature of the room. "The man's bleeding out."

"Bleeding yes, but not out," Jantzen reassured him, as the van began to clear.

John Carter, larger-than-life blond god, exited first, strapping a black-faced watch on his wrist. Now that they were away from the research center in the basement of the Corona Tower, he was certain he would have full access to the web.

Laura Lassere, wearing goth black, and Leigh Jose, in a second skin of leather, tumbled out after him. The relief of freedom was all over them.

Petite Amy Howe, oversized Julia Cantos, and lemur-like Marco Lopez exited together. Marco had a shine in his eyes. The room was a haven of climbable spaces, and he noted each one.

Alyna Lindberg, wearing retractable claws bequeathed by her Komodo dragon DNA, stayed to help with Justin, and she motioned for Giselle Harmon and Joanie to give them some space. The beautiful Giselle stopped beside Justin, made sure he was looking at her, and pursed her lips into a seductive kiss. She touched her fingertips to them and blew the kiss his way.

"Don't make him laugh," Alyna chided Giselle.

"I want Paolo to notice," Giselle hissed, and she softened it with a wink.

"How's he not, um, bleeding out?" Garik was still in the driver's seat, and he called to Jantzen, now leaning in and instructing Paolo and Alyna how best to move the man. He had thought *dying* but hadn't wanted to say it. Justin, DNA-bonded with a praying mantis, had taken on many of the mantis' extreme proportions, including thick forearms and extra joints. Now it seemed his skin was separating from his body.

What could cause that? An allergic reaction to your own skin? Garik cringed, wondering what his wolf DNA would eventually do to him. He'd watched werewolf movies, the horror of bones and sinews reshaping themselves under the full moon, the devastating conversion into full wolf form, becoming a monster that subsisted on other living creatures in the dark of the night.

Well, it was dark, and he *was* hungry. He ran his tongue along his teeth, relieved they hadn't changed while they were fleeing Corona Tower. Then, he remembered. There was no moon tonight. Arrgh! He might yet gnaw on the ankles of all his friends.

"Garik, are you with us?"

"Um, yeah?" He brushed his werewolf worries aside to find Justin already out of the van. Paolo and Alyna were helping him maneuver across the floor. The swelling of Justin's incipient wing structures bulged at his back.

"Are you planning to stay? The rest of us are headed inside." Jantzen had one hand on the upper part of the door opening, and the other on the handle ready to slide it closed.

"Sure, but what did you mean, Justin's not bleeding out? He's bleeding everywhere."

"Some of that is unavoidable. You saw the wings?"

"Sure." He'd watched Jantzen trying to make Justin more comfortable back in the basements. He'd been draining fluid from the bulging wing sacs.

"That's why Justin had to be rescued tonight. He's started to molt." Jantzen motioned with one hand, inviting Garik to join them. The others were disappearing into a door in the far wall.

"Molt?" Garik pictured a snake or a cicada. "Justin molts?"

"All good mantises do. Feel free to stay, but I'm turning out the lights when I reach the door." Jantzen closed the van's door, peered in through the broken window, and said, "Kevin's not going to be happy about this. I'm telling him I didn't break it."

"Jantzen, not fair!" Garik wailed as he threw back his door and fell out. "You didn't give me the key!"

"I gave it to Giselle. Did you ask?" Jantzen was grinning.

Garik broke into a run just as Jantzen reached the door. True to his word, he flipped out the light. Trapped in the dark, Garik leaped and caught the door just before it closed.

Like a wolf would do, covering nearly twelve feet in a single arc of determination.

JUSTIN WAS wrapped in several roughly woven blankets with the Ransom logo stitched onto the fabric, likely designed for wrapping equipment while in transit. Leigh, the most altruistic of the group, knelt at his side with a bowl of water and a stained cloth. She sponged at the rips in his skin where they oozed red and yellow.

219

Paolo, after helping the man inside, struggled for focus, like he needed to be busy, but there was nothing he could do.

"Paolo, can I get you to help Giselle bring in my case? I've brought some things to help with Justin."

"Of course. I just, you know, would like to know if you have anything—"

"Have anything?" Jantzen's response said this was an old question.

Garik looked from Justin, shivering and breathing heavily, to Paolo, who was beginning to look almost as bad, to Jantzen, who seemed irritated at Paolo's question. Nothing about this made sense—well, the escape, perhaps, and he was happy about that, but he was now a fugitive, and that wasn't what he had imagined. The rest of this? There was a small kitchen and Alyna was heating water for coffee, Joanie had located a box of crackers, now opened, and John had inserted an earbud. He was off in a corner, peering out a blind and speaking into his watch.

Garik focused on Paolo, still pleading his case with Jantzen.

"So I can, you know, be there for Justin. In case, he, you know . . ." His words died away, and he fidgeted his hands.

"You're fine, and so will be Justin. With Giselle, please?"

"Sure, but anything for me?" He smiled hopefully.

"Alyna's doing coffee. That's a start. Don't fall off the wagon now, my friend."

"Sure, sure. Sugar, that works. Sugar, Alyna?" Paolo called, nearly pleading. "Lots, if you find any."

She called, "Feed the addiction, but yeah, I found some." She didn't look up, and she measured grounds and dumped them into the pot.

Giselle wriggled her fingers seductively at Paolo, pulling him forward with pursed lips, and she clicked on a large, black flashlight. "Pao, I really need your help. Now?"

Paolo sighed and headed her direction.

Jantzen stepped to Justin and knelt. "How long, do you think?"

"It's never been this bad before." He let out a bark of a laugh. "So, like, until I'm finished, okay?"

"Fair enough." Jantzen looked around at the others. "This is temporary. It belongs to the corporation, and they will eventually think to search here."

"I'm sorry I pulled you into this." Justin grimaced, and he

tensed. The cracks in his skin became more pronounced, and new places began to seep. After a minute, he relaxed. "That one hurt. How do real mantises stand it?"

"You tell me. You're as real as they come. Leigh, keep him comfortable. Maybe he won't die."

"Maybe?" Justin lifted an arm, exposing an extra joint between his elbow and his wrist, balled his hand, and hit Jantzen on the knee. "So encouraging."

"Well, you didn't last time, so I'm holding out hope now." Jantzen stood, walked over to John and spoke to him a moment, before returning to Garik. "An adventure, hey."

"We're not really free, are we?" Garik had wanted out, his old life back. Riding his Street Strider, time on the roof with Marisa, wrapped in blankets against the cold of the night, and the skate park with his friends. "What will we do if they think to look for us here?"

"This isn't the only bolt hole in Bay City."

"Is it safe to stay here?" Bay City, he meant. Garik thought of Christian. His precognition from his wolfhound DNA-infusion hadn't protected him. He was shipped off, and no one had told him where. Weston Rodheimer and Halo Sunchaser, teamed up against all of them, seemed to have the power to root them out no matter where they hid. Garik didn't feel safe.

"Jantzen," Leigh called. "Something's happening. Get over here."

Justin let out a yell, and up and down his arms and legs, his skin began to bleed profusely. Garik pictured a mantis crawling out of its skin. When Justin crawled out of his, would Garik still recognize him?

He had seen the wings.

Garik looked at his own hands, once more reminded. He was no longer human, at least not a hundred percent. He wondered how long until it was his turn.

Then Justin yelled again, and his skin began to peel away.

— 2 —

JANTZEN SEEMED the only one not in full panic.

Leigh pulled away the blankets and ripped one of them to staunch the flow of blood. Paolo and Giselle were just returning, and she called, "Giselle, do you have more cloth in that case?"

Paolo ran to them, removing his top and tearing the shirt in strips. He began helping Leigh wrap the uneven strips around the bloodiest parts of Justin's torso.

"We're here for you, buddy," he said, comforting Justin.

John had turned from the window. Even against the physical deformities each of them had witnessed as participants in the human-hybrid research project, Justin's calamity was a gut-wrenching wound in a life that had begun to tank from the moment of his infusion with DNA from his praying mantis cousin.

Leigh called, "He's burning up, John. Can you help cool him down?"

"Maybe." John could freeze his own blood, but could he transfer that to someone else? Practice in the basements of the Corona Tower had been theoretical, at best.

"Idea." Joanie, good at evaluating a situation and making decisions—the qualities that had elevated her into a position of leadership—stepped into the small kitchen and began searching for something to hold water. Under the counter, a bucket appeared, and she tossed it into the sink and began to fill it. She called to John, "Hands inside."

John nodded, slipped his sleeves up as he crossed the room, and thrust his hands inside as it was filling.

The bucket began to crackle with a surface layer of ice, and Joanie lifted it and placed it beside Justin. Leigh dropped in a folded cloth, cracked the ice, made a face when she touched the water, but squeezed the cloth to press out most of the liquid and placed it across Justin's forehead.

John shook the water off his hands. They were bright red, and he wiped them against his pants to dry them.

"Now that the drama's played out, I need everyone to move back." Jantzen, with his slender face, dark hair and closely cropped beard, walked through the crowded space, motioning for everyone to give Justin room. "We can't stay here long, and Justin needs to get this over with."

What?!? Justin looked like he'd been pulverized by a meat grinder, and he was clearly in pain.

Garik had seen Justin as distant and critical and had fought him in an enforced challenge, barely beating the crazed hybrid in a show of cunning and force. Justin had also peeled back his raging bravado to reveal his damaged inner self, and how could Garik not under-

222

stand that? He didn't consider him a *friend*, but he didn't look like he was going to survive whatever was happening to him, and to want him to *get this over with* just because his deteriorating condition was inconvenient?

Despite Jantzen's earlier assurances to Paolo, Garik's dismay overbalanced his self-control, and he blurted, "You want him to die faster?"

"Hardly, my young friend." Jantzen lifted his eyebrows. "Molt, remember? Or has your sense of adventure shocked your memory into senility?"

"Senility?" Garik heard himself repeat the word, appalled at how stupid it made him sound and embarrassed at his old habit. He reminded himself that getting angry would earn him nothing, even as he felt flayed inside. Still, senility was for old people, and it hurt that Jantzen used the word.

"He gets like that." Amy, with her hyper-fine down shimmering across her skin, leaned in and whispered to Garik. "But I think we should do as he asks."

"But Justin needs our help." Garik saw the others were doing as Jantzen had instructed, and he couldn't understand them not taking up Justin's case. Well, except Leigh, and she refused to move. She dipped another cloth into the bucket and squeezed it out before laying it on Justin's skin.

Jantzen squatted at Leigh's side, lifted one of Justin's arms, inspected the damage, and asked the bleeding man, "Is it bad?"

Justin grimaced, nodding his head.

"It will be over in a moment. Leigh, the cloths aren't necessary, but if you want to continue, they can't hurt. Just be prepared to move away quickly." Jantzen stood, took a deep breath, and explained the situation to the room. "As soon as the Tower registers the energy draw we're putting on this place, the puzzle will begin to fall in place for them—"

"Leave?" Joanie asked it like a question, but she nodded like it was a fact.

Alyna's hands flexed, and her razor claws gleamed for a moment before disappearing.

An odor arose from lemur-like Marco, and he raised one pawlike hand and whispered, "Sorry."

"Not again, little man!" Laura stood and moved away. "Do you have to scent every single place you wave your obnoxious tail?"

"I said I'm sorry," Marco repeated, but he fought a grin.

Justin jerked, and he cried out, not a word, but a call that shredded the soul. The guttural eruption was less human than animal, and all attention centered on the quivering form on the floor.

"Now, Leigh." Jantzen motioned to her that it was time. The cracked skin along Justin's arms and legs began to spit and shrivel, becoming a series of active volcanic fissures sending out red and yellow magma that instead of hardening, popped, burst, and splattered over everything within reach.

"Ew, Justin!" John was rolling down his sleeves. "That's nasty."

"Jantzen?" Paolo moved forward, as if to help, and only stopped when the bearded man motioned him back.

"Not now, Paolo. He only needs space." He looked around the room as though he wished he had more of it.

Giselle called to Paolo, simpering, "Pao? Hold me?"

He didn't seem to notice, or if he did, he intentionally ignored her.

Joanie was taking the bucket from Leigh when Julia cried, "Fire in the hole!"

Garik's head swam. They were all crazy! Sure, Julia was part constrictor, and she had the snake's ability to seek heat in the infrared spectrum, but fire in the hole? Did she see something funny in Justin's impending death?

Then Justin thrashed, his body cracked with a snapping sound, and he began to come apart, literally, like splitting a lobster shell to release the tender meat inside.

Only this time, the tender meat was Justin. Pus and blood, like molten volcanic excreta, flew everywhere.

"JUSTIN, NOT again!" Jantzen jumped backwards, as stringy goo flung itself over half the room and onto his clothes.

Again? Garik thought. How often had this happened?

Garik didn't get to ask his question, as Amy cried out, "Ooh!" and Giselle began liquifying in her chair. Marco leaped to the top of the upper cabinets above the kitchen sink, and John dove behind Giselle's chair.

Justin began to arise from his gooey sarcophagus of flesh, pulling out one arm at a time, and then his legs. He worked his head back and forth, until it snapped forward with a sucking sound. His torso lifted, thinner than ever, and stretching into something longer and bonier than Garik had ever seen. Even Julia was no longer tall by comparison.

His arms, with his extra joints and Popeye forearms, flexed, more armored flesh than skin. He snapped his jaws, clicking, before running a red tongue along his teeth. He growled, spat red to clear his mouth, and lifted himself to a standing position. His knees were bent, his arms held in front, and he turned his head back and forth to reveal large, glittering eyes.

Justin, yes, but not Justin, either.

Then he tensed, shivered, and wet, iridescent wings erupted from behind him. He knelt with one hand on the floor to steady himself as his wings extended to dry.

"Done, yet?" Jantzen had an edge to his question.

"About." Justin's voice came out a gravelly rasp, the sound of teeth grinding against teeth. He was breathing heavily, and he looked up and around the room.

Garik shivered at the predatory expression.

"Let me know when you can travel." Jantzen paused, perhaps waiting on Justin's acknowledgment. When the changeling didn't respond, Jantzen turned to the others. "The van is off limits. By now, they know it, and the damage would draw attention, anyway. Decide what's necessary, and that's what you bring. Only what you can wear or carry. Understood?"

The team nodded. Most had backpacks still in the van, with the bags carried by Julia and Leigh the exceptions. Gieselle's rolling case had provided room for Jantzen's things—and Gieselle's backpack. It sat on the floor, along with two other small packs for the men.

Garik still had his backpack of bottled water. After soaking the chair, Giselle was at the sink, diminished in appearance and throwing back glassful after glassful. Garik weighed the necessity of lugging the liquid around. Carrying it wasn't a problem. Whether he could replace it with something more important was a real concern.

"I have water in my pack in the van," he called out.

"Water?" Marco dropped from the overhead cabinet and scrambled over to Garik. "Giselle likes water. See? Thirsty!"

"It's good for washing off Marco's stink, too." Laura glared at him.

"I said I was sorry." Marco grabbed the end of his tail, worried it for a moment, then dropped it to scamper Justin's way. "Water,

Justin? I can get you some."

"Sure, little guy. Go kill yourself." Grinding pops, bone moving in new and unusual ways, punctuated his words.

"Go kill myself. Funny, Justin." Marco rose onto two legs and moved with a remarkably normal gait to the small kitchen. He dickered with Giselle for a glass and water, and he returned it to Justin.

The wings had begun to shimmer, sheer sheets of mica, obscuring the wall behind, but barely. The air buzzed as Justin fluttered them. They looked completely inflated and mostly dry.

Jantzen sorted through the remaining things in the rolling case, and he carried a stack of clothing to Justin. At the bottom was a leather duster. It was the bulkiest of the items.

"We'll see if we allowed enough room for the wings." Jantzen shook out the duster.

Garik understood. It was full through the torso, much too much for Justin's thin frame. However, when Justin folded his wings—which Garik was certain he could—the duster would fill out perfectly, giving him a normal, perhaps even muscular look.

Blending in with the natives, so to speak.

Amy and John had returned to the van. The door was open, and the lights from the garage laid a skewed rectangle of light on the floor. Laura and Joanie followed them, Joanie's voice offering clipped suggestions that weren't really suggestions. Leigh was helping Justin clean away the remains of the mucus and other goo, while Paolo helped Justin work his newly long body into his fresh clothes.

Garik shrugged. His water comment had seemed to disappear into the busyness in the room, and he moved to the garage, searching for a way to help. Under the bright lights, the van was surrounded by the things everyone had carried. His backpack of water held up a concrete post, the box Alyna had carried was now emptied, and Joanie was working the items into two nearly full backpacks. The escape hadn't gone exactly how he'd expected, and he hadn't been a successful participant. Breaking the van's window. He wanted to hit himself in the head. *Ask, Garik. That's all you had to do.* It had felt he was doing something brilliant in the moment. Now, they could no longer use the van, and it was his fault. He heard feet on the concrete at his side, and he smelled Marco without looking.

"That was something in there, wasn't it? Nobody else does that, molting, not me, anyway. I change sl-*oo*-wly. What do you think you'll do? Quick or slow?"

Garik didn't want to think about it, and he kept his focus on the activity in the underground garage.

"Lemur got your tongue?" Marco snapped two slender, lemur-like fingers in front of Garik's face.

"That's stupid." Garik pushed the hand away.

"Oh, wolf boy is in a bad mood." Marco fell to all fours, darted to Garik's other side, and stood, his long snout barely above Garik's shoulder. "Let me tell you a bad mood. Wait until you're compelled to scent every flowerpot in the room. That'll give you a reason for a really bad mood—"

A siren and flashing overhead lights cut off Marco's whining tirade. Faces glanced up, and the final members of their squad burst through the door into the underground garage. Justin wore a knit beanie in black pulled low over his head, on one hand deemphasizing his outsized cranium and on the other setting off his wide eyes and elongated jaw. In his duster, at a glance, he seemed mostly human. His hands were covered by black mittens—not gloves, Garik noted. What had his hands looked like after he molted? Garik wasn't sure, but not five fingers.

"Booby trap." Marco grinned as Joanie yelled for each person in the game to shoulder a bag.

Forget trading out what was in his pack. He was taking *something*. Garik wasn't making another mistake, and the pack filled with water was the only thing he knew for certain to be his.

Then the door began to rumble with the repetitive metallic clack of a chain-driven opener. The controls beside the door were ominously unattended. It was being manipulated from outside.

Garik's stomach twisted. Personal failure or not, they had escaped the Tower. To be recaptured skewered him.

Marisa! He was so close to home. Not again!

— 3 —

ALYNA YELLED, "Bushwhackers, all! Let 'em come. I'll take 'em all out."

Her claws were fully extended, and they gleamed like silver knives, chromed carbon, nightmares that whispered death in the dark.

"Something better," Leigh said, her voice cracking with pain. She frowned, her face twisted, and she turned to each wall in the room, pausing as though searching. She rubbed her temples. "Julia," she called, "my ultrasound says there are hollow spaces in the wall, deep ones that lead away from here."

"Tell us where." Julia had her pack ready, and she stood with it already across one shoulder.

"I, I can't focus. Too much is happening. My head hurts." Leigh's face crumpled. She was right about the "too much." The large room now struggled to contain more action than a kindergarten classroom on a party day.

Laura wrapped an arm across her shoulders, consoling her with, "Quit trying so hard. Let us help you."

Garik wasn't sure how he heard that. With the noise of the rising door, and people scrambling to gather what they could cram into backpacks that suddenly seemed too small, the hard-walled space echoed with ear-splitting noise. At least it was unimaginably loud to Garik. No one else seemed to mind.

Air moved, warmth feeding from the back wall. He realized it was cold outside—as he was reminded by the wall of frozen darkness sweeping under the rising door—but the large space had been warm when they had returned to gather their things. He listened carefully. He could hear the air moving, a repeated clicking that could be a loose grille. He glanced at the door, now revealing headlights slowly sweeping across the sill plate, ready to rush in and haul them back as one and lock them up on Basement Level 5 with the disappointing rejects from the human-hybrid project's latest discarded has-beens.

Garik didn't want to be a has-been. He wanted his freedom back. They had stolen that from him, and it was no longer theirs to have and to hold. He would fight for his and for the freedom of those with him. They were a kind of family, now, and he would battle for them at risk of his own life.

He hoped they felt the same about him.

The first man that leaned in to look underneath the door got a spray of aromatic scent from Marco. He screamed and ducked away.

"They should know better." Marco grinned.

"Least it's good for something," Laura called out. She yelled over the noise, "Ideas? I can kill a few, but that's not going to look good on our record."

Jantzen stood beside Amy, a neatly groomed statue. He looked as if he'd changed clothes after Justin's volcano. He said, "Are you tracking them?"

"Each one," Amy said, without moving. The hairs on her skin rippled, a windswept continent of knowledge. Her eyes blazed with a hundred images, each of someone or something different.

"How long?" Before they breached the door, he meant.

"I don't think they mean to hurt us. None have weapons ready." The incoming night whipped at her clothing. She shivered.

"So, how long?"

"Not long enough," she said. "And there's nowhere to run."

"Yeah. Stopping here was maybe not brilliant."

Garik was appalled. Jantzen, giving up? No! They had to protect each other, fight, do *something!* He called to Julia, "Behind the van, there's heat. Can you locate the source?"

"A vent?" She was tightening the straps on Leigh's pack, and she gave a strap a yank and moved to the end of the van. "I found it. Leigh, can you tell how big it is?"

"Let me get closer."

Justin blocked her way, and his eyes glittered. His head turned to survey the panic overtaking the room, a swivel for a neck, his head tilting at angles no human neck could manage. His jaw released and snapped shut, the battle-ready response of a warrior-bred fighter.

"Justin, move!" Leigh put her hand on his arm and stepped underneath. He jerked away, stood taller, and clacked his teeth.

"You just had to ask." A clattering growl.

Leigh knelt at the wall, and she and Julia began pushing things aside. Paolo understood and joined them, muttering, "I'm here to help, if you want it."

"Of course, you lug." Julia handed him a bulky roll of insulated wiring, and he tossed it to the side. It hit a good distance away, bounced once, and rolled to beside the van before falling over.

Taunts from the darkness were garbled locks and keys, an onslaught of bravado about to wash in under the door, and yet, even in their indistinct threats, they still managed to say, "We've trapped you! Boo-ya! No sense in running now!"

Clearer, Garik caught an undercurrent of voices, one he remembered from his first moment of awareness in the research hospital. *"You were deported right back to Russia where you could no longer cause our good country additional problems. No one will come looking for you."* He shivered at the memory of Weston Rodheimer's mocking tone. The man had no heart, no compassion, no leniency.

229

Either you joined his team, or he cast you aside.

Garik didn't want on his team. Maybe no one had come looking for him, and maybe they had. He'd never know if he didn't escape this basement parking garage. He pictured Marisa, and his eyes watered with the wasted months he'd been imprisoned in the Corona Tower basements.

Then he focused on what Rodheimer was saying.

"Yes, there's a service tunnel under the street. It runs under Park to the powerline right-of-way. Get men over there now. If Jantzen discovers it first, we may have a real chase on our hands."

"Jantzen," Garik called, wishing he hadn't distracted Julia and Leigh with the heating vent. Leigh's ultrasound ability was crucial to sorting out the missing escape route. "There's an underground service tunnel."

Joanie called, "John, Giselle, our plan. Get the others. Where?" She aimed her final word at Garik.

Jantzen still stood by Amy, and he called to Garik, "You know this how?"

What!? He had time to ask that? "Rodhemier's outside. He's sending someone to guard it. It runs under Park."

Jantzen looked toward the east wall of the garage. Three doors gave them three options. He seemed to hesitate.

Amy called, "Time's up. They're coming in."

"I've got this," Alyna yelled. "Everyone, after me."

Her claws glistened, shadows of obsidian at the tips of her fingers. At the first door, she pressed her hand to the door, leaned into it, and her claws buried themselves. She twisted her arm, pulled back, and a third of the door tumbled to her feet. Inside, a porcelain sink and a toilet gleamed.

"Again," Joanie called. She wore two packs, one on each shoulder, and pulled Justin along beside her.

The second door proved a better option. Alyna used both hands, sinking them into the metal like butter, and the door dropped away like a day-old waffle, bent and battered, and about as useless. A corridor disappeared into the darkness.

"Inside," Joanie yelled. She didn't care about the third door. She had evaluated the situation and made her decision.

She was right to hurry everyone along. The overhead mechanical door, rolling up into its metal cage, although slow, now allowed a full view of the Tower pursuit team. Military vehicles from the Tower's basement parking garage filled the street. Spotlights leaped into action, liquid swords of light piercing the inside of the Ransom Building's underground garage, prepared to slice and dice anyone they found.

Garik didn't want to be found. He didn't want to be sliced and diced, either. He'd had enough of that.

Alyna ducked inside the newly opened doorway, her claws sheathed, and a pack in her hands. John was on the way with Giselle, and they disappeared into the darkness after her. Marco scampered in on their heels, leaving a trail of fear behind him. Amy and Jantzen held their position, Amy pointing out the location of each of their pursuers. Leigh pulled down on Justin's shoulder, suggesting his new height might be a problem in the dark passageway. It was something she could *see*, her dolphin ability to navigate the unknown.

Garik knew he was fast, faster perhaps than anyone else in the room, and he calculated the various bags and packs left behind. His water by the concrete post, he didn't how soon they would have access to more, even in the city, and he remembered Alyna's words: Giselle might need some if she had to squeeze through a tight space. Rehydration afterward would be vital.

More laser pulse than boy, more live electricity than runner, more lightning strike than any human ought to be, Garik was a tornado, snatching up the items, checking off one at a time as he slipped his arms into straps or grabbed waiting handles. He noticed how everyone else seemed to slow down, mired in a psychedelic glow as he ran, but his focus was on escape, not the blurred sense of time dilation that seemed to fog the corners of the room with the remnants of pale rainbows.

The items didn't even seem heavy in the exhilaration of his whirlwind flight across the space. He owed that to his practice in the pool, the repeated laps and breathing exercises overseen by Christian. He felt he could run from Argyle Station on one side of the city to the other and never slow down.

Julia, with her dark demeanor and her stealthy way of moving without seeming to move, paused before entering the passageway to give Joanie access. Garik thought, *Move. We're out of time.* He had seen the teams heading in, the BolaWraps at their waists. He'd had one used on him, and he didn't recommend the experience.

A blast of sound rattled the lights overhead. Amy grabbed her ears, and in the concussion, Jantzen evaporated into purple mist. The two windows in the van closest to Paolo cracked, then they shattered inward. The military team entering the building dropped their weapons like molten metal, and they fell to their knees, pushing their helmets off to yank out earpieces and clutch their ears.

Amy looked dazed when the noise faded. Paolo stood wide-eyed, with surprise on his face. The remains of Jantzen were no more than wisps of purple fading into the night.

"Not again," Amy said, as she shook her head clear and knelt to pick up his clothes. "He'll want these. Out, Paolo. That way." She pointed to Joanie beside the damaged door.

Garik waited, still unsure what had just happened. Joanie stopped Paolo at the door.

"You?"

He nodded, shrugged and managed to look embarrassed.

"How?" Joanie blocked his way, expecting more of an answer. On the other side of Paolo, the men in camo had started to stir.

"Not now," Amy said. "He's given us the time we need," and she pushed past with Jantzen's clothes in her hands.

"I didn't know I could," Paolo said, almost to himself, and he slipped through the door, hot on Amy's heels.

"Didn't know he could." Joanie shook her mohawk in dismay. Then she looked at Garik. "You, get along. Leaving this place behind."

It was a near sentence, so Garik figured she meant it. He hitched up his bags, and he lit off into the darkness, wondering what mysterious skill he would suddenly discover he could do.

And would he like it? Or would it be something he'd wish away for the rest of his life?

He let the thought fade. Somewhere ahead was their hope of escape. He just prayed they found friends on the other side.

THE PASSAGE seemed a black hole of endless night, but they tumbled through the door on the far end after only a few hundred feet.

They stood near the top of Stanwick Hill. The door they'd exited left them in the middle of the powerline right-of-way under a star-studded sky. The industrial park entrance and the Bay City Medical parking lot glowed ten blocks to the east. Kang's Garage was only blocks away on Meyers, if Garik could find the sign. It wasn't lighted this time of night, and he knew better than to waste time looking.

The grassy right-of-way—with thick ropes of powerlines running overhead—cut through town for over twenty blocks, ending at First, where the lines dove underground, spreading their electrical roots to nourish the city's hungry buildings. Garik recognized Powerline Drive just past the right-of-way, although it was an asphalt wasteland at this hour. He and his friends had often taken the long way from City View Apartments—catching the light to cross at Sycamore and taking the Avenue G bridge at Park over the right-of-way—just to jump the curbs all the way to The Martial Arts Center, Central Park, and Corona Tower beyond.

The wind in his face, the thump of his trucks as his board ground along the concrete curbing, the speed of flight—even if it was mostly on wheels. He could taste it, and he wanted it back again.

The Avenue G bridge from Park to Powerline Drive was only two blocks to the south. The other way, the nearest bridge over the wide expanse of the right-of-way was six blocks north at Avenue C. He remembered Rodheimer's words. *"Service tunnel ... runs under Park to the powerline right-of-way ... get men over there now."* It was clear over which bridge they would first see the threat of capture.

"This way," Garik called, raising a hand he was certain no one could see in the darkness. "I know this city, and we need to get away from that bridge."

He pointed to the Avenue G bridge where the street turned into Buda Road, and as he spoke, headlights pooled on the bridge, forming frozen lakes of white. Slamming doors told of dark-suited men on the prowl.

"Garik?" A familiar voice rang crystal clear through the stillness of the cold night air from the direction of Powerline Drive.

"Muhammad?" The familiar voice offered a lifeline to Garik, reaching in to massage his heart and emotions. At that moment, he needed Muhammad—all his friends, but especially the one he could hear right then—more than life or escape.

"Hey, you dundersap! You back to stay?"

"I never went anywhere. Hold up! We're coming your way."

Garik was aware of the cautions being thrown at his back. Jantzen hadn't appeared yet, Marco was scrambling around in the grass, joyous just to be outside, and Leigh was painting a picture of three people she clearly sensed and for Garik to use caution, but he didn't care. Muhammad Saud was his friend, and he wouldn't be with anyone who would bring him harm. His friendships—every one—had been stolen from him, and he intended to make this his night to throw an arm across someone's back, crack an old familiar joke, and learn if Marisa had missed him as much as he still missed her.

He hiked his packs, hailed his escapees with a "Follow me," and tore across the grass, certain this was the start of his journey home.

— 4 —

"MY BEST brother! Allah be praised!" Muhammad clapped his arms around Garik in a quick but firm hug. He backed up, looked into his friend's face, and blurted, "Dundersaps, don't do that again."

"What? Do what?" With his friend's ribbing, Garik's clock wound backwards, and the months underneath the Corona Tower had never happened. *Muhammad!* They were together again, something he didn't know how much he'd missed.

"Go off and leave us. You broke Marisa's heart, you goof." Muhammad pulled off his ever-present skullcap with its skull stitched into the fabric and hit Garik in the chest with it before slipping it back onto his head. "You out to see what's going on at the Tower? News is all over the city!"

"Yah, about that—" Garik barely got the words out before yet another familiar voice accosted him.

"Nyet, my disappearing friend. It is my turn to say welcome back to my Russian comrade." Out of the dark, Ibn Hariri's face appeared, and he held up a hand. Garik threw his up also, and they clasped fists forearm to forearm before releasing hold.

"Your beard, Ibn. It's not so scraggly as it was." Garik laughed. "Someday, perhaps, you'll make a man."

"My dreads say more. I am fully a man. No one can say otherwise."

"Except his girlfriend." A third face, fresh to the group, leaned in, ribbing Ibn. He held a skateboard with a Baker Brand logo, shifted it to one side and extended a hand. "Dieter. So, this is the most, how do you say, infamous friend. You found the basement. Amazing! No one else we know can do that. Ha, ha. You are a good friend to have around."

"Deet," Ibn elbowed him, "no one can know."

"Can know what?" Justin emerged behind Garik, recognizable in the dark by his height and his black leather duster. His question

234

snapped at the end like oversized teeth being clacked together, or the beak of an insect, ready to rend its supper into more manageable tidbits.

"These are my friends, Justin. That's Muhammed with the skull, and the dreads is Ibn. The new one is Dieter."

"Ah, all are new to me." Clack, clack. "We have friends following us. Perhaps *your* friends could help us make our way to safety."

Dotting the powerline corridor, small circles of light bobbed in the darkness, revealing the remains of summer's long dead and dissected grass. The Avenue G overpass where it turned into Buda just to the south revealed a spotlight warming up on the back of a military transport, and six blocks to the north towards Corona Tower, lights flickered on the Cowden Street overpass. The pincher action of the Tower's long arms was about to close them in.

"Move. Now." Joanie shouldered Garik and Justin aside and zeroed in on the three city youths. "Willing to help?"

"Um, sure. How?" Muhammad took charge, wrapping his friends into the excitement, as teen boys will do.

"Someplace to hide." John appeared out of the darkness, his hair and Nordic coloring highlighting him with a wintry brush. "Garik seems to trust you. We must, also. But it happens now, or *they* win." He used his long arms to indicate the two bridges.

From the looks on Ibn's and Dieter's faces, the thrill of something exciting in Bay City was enough. Garik relaxed as a purple shadow painted Jantzen's outline in the darkness.

"Amy!" Garik called. "We need clothes!"

She pressed them into his hand, and Garik held them out to the mist. He shook his head at how often this was happening as they vanished from his hand.

"I appreciate these." The purple mist winced with pain as Jantzen coalesced into something real. "You think this would be fun, if it didn't hurt so much. I've left misdirection for our pursuers, but we must be gone. Justin, can you fly, yet? We need reconnaissance."

"I can try." The tall man awkwardly slipped off his duster and tossed it Jantzen's direction. His skin glowed in the darkness, the sheen from the distant lights glinting on his too-bony flesh. He straightened, and his torso elongated. Against the starry sky, he became more mantis than man. His teeth clacked, the extra joints in his forearms snapped menacingly, and with a shake of his shoulders, his wings swelled against the night. They began to buzz with action, disappearing except for the sound, and within moments, he was aloft.

"Dundersaps," Muhammad whispered.

"Holy moly," hissed Ibn. "Better than Jezebel and the Sticks."

"Is very cool, yes?" Dieter seemed to be having the time of his life. "Wait till Papa hears about this."

"Nein." Garik looked at the three new members of their fleeing group of refugees, deciding he had to take charge of this before it got out of hand. "Got that, Dieter?"

"These are your friends, I trust?" Jantzen was buttoning his shirt.

"If they can keep their mouths shut."

"Good. You, with the skull, we need to hide. What are our options?"

"I'm Muhammad," he grinned, "and Dieter and I have a really good idea. Follow us."

And now they were sixteen.

"TELL ME about Marisa." Garik's arms wrapped his backpack, and his body vibrated to Ibn and Dieter's boards up and down a wood halfpipe. The back of Muhammad's head tapped the boards with each run of the skaters' wheels up and down the pipe.

"Missing you. Like, the lights went off when you left. Man, I never expected you to just up and disappear."

"Me either, Mo." Garik let his eyes rove the warehouse rising like a shell around them, shielding them from the darkness and their pursuers. It belonged to Dieter, well, not exactly Dieter, but it was for Dieter's use.

Dieter lived in the Tower, *in the Tower!* with his father. The reason why, though, was like biting into an apple and finding half a worm after you swallowed. His father was under supervision at the Corona Cancer Center, and he had wanted a place for his son to chill on the days he was taking treatments. At Dieter's encouragement, he had rented the warehouse at Coolidge and Royal and had the ramps and other things built for his son.

Dieter's father hadn't known about the Connel Street Skate Park, Muhammad whispered with a gleeful grin. Otherwise, they wouldn't have this place to play in. Muhammad leaned his skateboard into his lap and spun one set of wheels. "Outside, I might not'a known ya' if it hadn't been dark."

"What!?" Garik laughed and stuck his hand into his hair, working his fingers in. It was long enough to do that now. "You couldn't see me no matter, so how could being dark help?"

Alyna sat across the room. Garik bet she could recognize people in the dark. Her eyes were closed, but he bet she knew everything going on around her. Justin had crashed beside her. He had returned—after an hour—exhausted, revealing that the Tower's search was centered on the powerline right-of-way, and Dieter had found him a box of trail bars to chew on. The wrappers scattered the floor around him.

"Still wondering why you cut off your hair."

"That." Garik pulled his hand away and looked at it. "I didn't—"

"It didn't cut itself, dunderdude." Muhammad punched him on the shoulder.

"Yeah, I know. You should have seen it at first. It was nearly shaved. It's just now feeling real again." He remembered it bristling against his pillow and his dismay that they had *cut his hair!*

"Mostly it's your eyes." Muhammad pressed his palm against the spinning wheel, and it stopped. Even hearing the repeated and loud reverberations from the skateboards, the sound of that one wheel stopping seemed to silence the world.

At least for Garik.

"What about my eyes?" How many months had it been? Last summer, at least, and now it was cold outside. His hair had grown inches. Yet, he'd stood in front of the mirror that first day he'd been awake, and he'd studied his reflection. His eyes, how had they looked? Like always, he recalled. No difference, he wanted Muhammad to say. Ah, Garik, they look just the same. I'm just pushing your buttons.

Garik had just seen Justin *molt* and change into something different than he was before. He knew *he* wasn't the same, either. Timber wolf DNA. What made timber wolves special? Strength enough to break open bones to eat the marrow inside. He'd learned that on the nature channel. They were survivors that could live almost anywhere, survive in almost any conditions. Speed, able to cover fifteen or more miles at a time, at up to thirty miles-per-hour. Endurance. Cooperation with the pack. Oh, and they morphed into werewolves when they shared a human half.

Just pushing your buttons, Muhammad. That's what I want you to say.

"Aw, nothing." Muhammad grinned and pulled his cap off to inspect the skull before slipping it back on again. "Deet keeps extra boards under the pipe. Been on yours much?"

"Some." Garik didn't want to say it had been an electric one. Electrics were for posers. Real skaters powered their own.

"Here. Borrow mine. I'll use one of Deet's."

Garik took the board in his hand, rubbing his fingers over the familiar blood splatters covering the top and the skull on the bottom, and he felt the world was right again. Like it should have been all along.

He still wanted to know about Marisa—and his eyes. What was Muhammad not saying about his eyes?

Then he shrugged. He had a skateboard in his hands, and he had a halfpipe at his back. It was time to have some fun.

GARIK LAY awake, his eyes following the structural supports forming the ceiling of the old warehouse. Long strings of lights ran down the center, now off so people could sleep.

After an hour of skating fun, Dieter had claimed his father as an excuse to leave, saying his papa would be "unpleased" if he was out until daybreak. It was no problem for them to stay in the warehouse, however, as his papa rarely made an appearance. The code to the door was their invitation to come or go as they pleased.

Garik had given Muhammad a slap on the back and Ibn a fist bump, and they had headed back to their homes, Muhammad at his grandmother's and Ibn with his parents. The warehouse had an old breakroom with a small kitchen and a half bath, with both in their original condition. Beggars couldn't be choosers, and the escapees from the Tower had cleaned up and found corners to wrestle make-shift bedding out of backpacks and several builder's tarps left over from the construction of the indoor skate park.

Now, morning light tried to sneak in under the door to the small office that held the only windows in the vast building. The office was boxed out of one corner, only reaching halfway to the ceiling. Dieter's father had pushed the halfpipe next to it, added a loft at each end that covered the office at one side and housed the kitchen and half bath at the other, and a tight stair gave access to the loft. Wooden rails, steel benches, and drop-ins with a bowl off to one side filled in the rest. They now served as nests for the individuals on the run.

Garik was awake because of his dreams. *Nightmares.* His eyes. He kept seeing Weston Rodheimer's face, the man's strangely unusual eyes boring into him. White, white eyes, covered by contacts

238

that kept slipping sideways to reveal nothing there except blank white orbs. Then Rodheimer's skin began to crack and fall away—*molting!*—and his broad shoulders turned into the hairy shoulders of a gorilla, one bigger than Garik had ever seen.

"You," Rodheimer had said in his dream, "are like me, a changeling. What will you become, my young friend? I need you back before your molting begins. I will find you, and I will help you discover what your future can be."

Garik didn't want to molt. He wanted what his life used to be—except Arik, perhaps. If he could have his old life back without his aunt's boyfriend, that would be perfect, but he'd take Arik if Rodheimer would let him go.

Then the gorilla man had put his thumbs to his face, forced his eyes from their sockets and held them out to Garik, saying, "With these, you will see what you can truly become."

Garik had covered his face to protect his eyes, and that's when he had jerked awake, his heart pounding in fear and unable to settle back into sleep.

His eyes. What had Muhammad seen there? Garik felt sorry for Justin, and he wondered if Justin felt sorry for himself—or if the changes sat well on his shoulders, what was left of them, anyway.

Rodheimer, what DNA combination had given him those shoulders and eyes? Some dogs had really white eyes. Surely not—

The despair of the possibilities drenched Garik with emotion, and he fought to keep his body under control. He didn't want to become what Rodheimer had suggested. What if they had been mistaken, if Dr. Jimenez and Nurse Ratchett had given him gorilla DNA by mistake, and that was the reason he had never acquired Christian's precognitive abilities?

Maybe his eyes were gorilla eyes, and that's what Muhammad had seen.

He sat up, listened to the sound of the rousing city just beyond the walls, and he navigated his way to the small restroom, stepping inside and closing the door before turning on the light. The exhaust fan roared, and he was glad. He let himself sink into his despair, attempting to choke back a sob before it overtook him.

When it was done, he wiped his face, looked into the mirror, and tried to see what Muhammad had seen. He couldn't tell. Maybe he'd forgotten what his eyes used to look like. What had Muhammad said? He wouldn't have known him if it hadn't been dark.

At least his voice hadn't changed. What did a gorilla sound like? How about a timber wolf? Could he pretend to be either one, and could he convince anyone if he did?

After his first few attempts, someone banged on the door. "That you, Peach Fuzz? Howling at the moon? Restroom's for all of us."

"Out in a minute, Joanie."

Garik grinned. At least he could guess which he was better at, even if his dream had made one seem more real than the other. And he remembered Joanie's remark the first time they had spoken. *Too human.* It had felt like a putdown then, but he was glad for it now.

No thanks, Mr. Rodheimer, you can keep your gorilla. I don't want any part of it.

Still, he investigated his reflection in the mirror and checked the set of his shoulders. Wider? Not that he could tell. His jaw, chunkier? Not yet. He also didn't have extended canines, but those could come from a gorilla or a wolf.

The door pounded again, and Garik sighed, turned from the mirror, opened the door, and called, "Next!"

— 5 —

A SECOND reconnaissance flight by Justin was out of the question, and Muhammad, Ibn, and Dieter had classes at Bay City High. They wouldn't be of any help until later that afternoon.

The bigger issue for the moment was food and supplies. The warehouse—a boon!—gave them anonymity from the city's prying eyes, but it wasn't equipped to house thirteen people for an extended time. Going outside was possible, but if they were spotted by cameras or, heaven forbid, drones, the Tower would be on them like ants on a drop of honey.

Marco volunteered before anyone even asked.

"I need snacks. I assign myself as the getter of supplies. Money? Anyone? I didn't bring any." He sat up, his tail flicked, and he worked his mouth back and forth in a manner that made him seem more lemur than little man.

"And how are you planning to manage that?" Jantzen, somehow impeccably dressed with his hair and beard flawless, dropped down the distance from the loft to the floor, landing lightly, and becoming bigger with his question than his physical body suggested.

"Just *go*. No one cares, Jantzen. I'm out, then back, so quick.

Who is there to see?" Marco waggled his fingers and grinned. "Maybe a little five-finger discount."

"I'll do it." Laura had been sorting her things from a backpack. She stood and looked over the group. "I'm pretty normal—"

"For a goth queen." Marco snickered.

"You, you—" She darted his direction with her hands prepared to grab his neck.

"Enough of that." Jantzen tried to hold back a sigh, not entirely successful. "John, Giselle, how about you?"

"Sure—" John began when he was interrupted.

"Better idea, Jantz." Giselle smiled impishly, and she raked her eyes up and down John. "Such a tall boy, and so *Nordic*. The man stands out like a lighthouse. Send Leigh with me. We can be two silly schoolgirls out skipping classes for the day. No one will think anything of that."

Jantzen seemed to consider it, waiting on John for input. John gave way with a, "Fine, then," and he glared at Giselle, "if you think anyone will believe you're still in high school."

"Leigh, no leather." Clearly, Jantzen expected an argument. "Doable?"

Leigh glared at Jantzen, then blew out her cheeks, giving in. "At least I'm good with math. Someone needs to keep track of what Giselle spends. Okay," she called to the rest of the room, "who's got something I can wear?"

Items appeared, several flying through the air her direction, a number of them little better than the leather straps and leggings she preferred.

Joanie called, "Peach Fuzz! All too human. Should go, too."

"What? People out there know me, and I don't do silly very well." Despite his protest, Garik anticipated what he might find. It had been dark when they arrived, but he knew the area where the warehouse was located at Coolidge and Royal. Kang's Garage was a few blocks northwest, and from there, Garik could find his way anywhere in Bay City.

"Jantz," Giselle began to whine.

"Joanie's right. He *is* high school, and he'll make you two more believable. Garik, are you good with that?"

He shrugged. "Sure." Secretly, he was elated. The kids from school would be in class, so he wasn't too worried about being recognized. As long as they stayed away from Old Town where he had lived with his aunt, no harm done.

A new wardrobe for Garik's adventure was assembled from what they could find, some of it from what others had worn in their escape from the Tower. Garik stood in front of the small mirror in the tiny half bath with a black beanie pulled half down over his ears, a black turtleneck from Jantzen, a weathered brown leather jacket, and chunky shoes, Leigh's, he thought. Jantzen had rummaged about for sunglasses to hide his eyes, assuring Garik that the upper half of his face was eighty percent of recognition. The beanie and glasses would hide him from anyone who didn't know him well.

Irina and Arik, Garik imagined, but they would be at the apartment. Everyone else he knew would be at work or at school. He felt reasonably safe.

Giselle and Leigh were into their "silly schoolgirl" act before they stepped outside the door. They had canvassed Julia's things for a supply of gum, and they both popped it continually as they walked. Garik felt his face warm as they pulled the door wide, and the two women hemmed him in and each one took an arm, wrapping theirs in his and immediately fawning over him, touching his shoulders and leaning their heads in against him before pointing to nothing in the distance and giggling.

"Are you serious?" Garik groaned. He'd rather be back in the ring fighting Justin. At least then, he'd known how the match was going to end.

"We're silly schoolgirls," Giselle said, vamping, and she popped her gum.

"Yeah, boyfriend." Leigh grinned, more mocking than infatuated. "Pretend you're having a good time. It's not so hard." She stroked his forearm and pursed her lips into a kiss. She released it his direction and leaned forward to say something to Giselle before laughing like it was funny.

"Supplies," Garik reminded them, knowing better than to try to shake them off. He might as well play along, at least for as long as he could stand it. "Who has the money?"

Giselle pulled out a folded stack of bills from a pocket, and she flashed it with a grin before making it vanish. "Now, this way, or that?" She pointed with a bent wrist south along Coolidge, then north along the same street. South, the building fronts sported furious graffiti, but heading north, the streets became cleaner.

"Kang's Garage is on Meyers." Garik pointed slightly northwest.

Leigh pulled his arm down and waggled her finger in his face, whispering, "Silly, silly boy," with an outsized giggle.

"Okay, don't think I know silly, but that way." He pointed with his head. "Coupla blocks past Meyers is a station with vending machines. I think also one of those glass cases with food inside. That's the closest thing."

They tugged him along that way, stepping off the curb onto Center, then heading toward Summit. There were no stoplights this far south, just four-ways. At Norfleet Street, they paused at their first pedestrian crossing light and waited for the walk sign to grant them passage. Two cars and a delivery truck passed. Neither seemed to pay any attention to the three "teens" absconding from classes at Bay City High.

"Nearly there?" Leigh popped her gum and grinned. "I'm getting tired of silly."

"Columbine and Calloway, and the next one is Cowden. I think the station's on Cowden, a block or two west."

"Left, right?" Giselle giggled at her play on words.

"Oh, girl, you are a funny one." Leigh leaned into Garik, put her hand on his chest, and tapped it twice before straightening up, looking around at the buildings as if taking in something she'd never seen before, and chewing her gum with her mouth open.

Garik hadn't considered, but she probably never had. He wondered who else in the Corona Tower project had never been out in the city. Likely, most of them, if they were part of the human-hybrid experiments.

By Cowden, they were walking down the left side of the street. Garik tried to be light and bright, a high schooler out on the town during the day, skipping classes for a lark, but he'd looked left as they crossed Meyers and had seen the sign for Kang's Garage two blocks down. It wasn't lighted, so he doubted anyone was there, but the alley behind the shop was where he'd hit the jackpot with his Street Strider. It had been a wreck, but it was his, and he'd fixed it up on a thread. Now, it was likely Arik's—or sold so the man could fuel whatever habits kept him away from the apartment more days than not.

At Cowden, the sign for LUCKY! Station flashed to the left but five blocks away. Smaller and just readable, underneath it exclaimed, *Get Your Power on Powerline*.

Giselle muttered, "More time to be found out."

"Yeah, I didn't remember it being that far down." Garik was distracted by the aromas of the city, ones he'd never felt enmesh him so fully, and they throbbed in his senses. Unburnt gasoline from the tailpipes of cars, coffee from an open door, cinnamon rolls somewhere making him hungry. The overwhelming wash of perfume as one woman walked by.

And the sounds. He guessed he'd never paid attention before, not really. Notes in car engines that suggested worn rings, the purr of the expensive models, and stones in the treads of tires that clipped along the pavement in a repetitive pattern. He forced the sounds away, tamping them down until they came out of only one small speaker in the sound system in his head.

He realized he could tune them out if he tried, mostly.

Along Powerline Drive, the fresh hiss of morning traffic percolated like coffee in a kettle. A yellow car hit its brakes, and it ducked out of the flow to pull into the station like cream into coffee. Its brake lights disappeared as the station obscured it.

He caught his reflection in a plate glass window across Cowden, bright against the shadow of the building behind him. The creak of a sign overhead—metal against glass—clawed at his ears. His image twisted in the glass, a nightmare Garik, with his forehead low and his arms past his knees. He jerked his eyes away.

"What? Did you see something?" In the question, Leigh morphed into the fighter the military had hoped to breed into their human-hybrid program, alert and aware. She frowned as she looked around, an indication she was probing the surrounding area. "No one here, boyfriend."

"Except the gorilla in the reflection."

"Gorilla?" Giselle looked at him sharply. "Leigh, you sure no one's following us? If Weston's tracking us, well, we can't take that risk."

"Hey!" Garik laughed roughly, surprised they were panicking over his silly response to a reflection. "Just a noisy sign and seeing me in the glass. Just there." He nodded across the street, and sure enough, he was still hunched over. He didn't really look that much like a gorilla. He supposed he was spending too much time thinking about Marisa and the images she'd drawn for him that last night together on the roof, Halo Sunchaser attacking a silverback gorilla with her electrified sword. He guessed he would see silverbacks and swords everywhere until he was with her again.

Gieselle had her hand on his shoulder, and she leaned against him like a teen girl would intertwine with her first boy crush. She snapped her gum and popped it, grinning. "I didn't hear any noisy sign, but you can be my gorilla anytime, so long's you stay in that window. Here, you be Garik, all-too-human boy, out for the day and skipping school. Yo-kay?" She grinned prettily at him.

"Yo-kay, Mother," he said, but he felt lighter, and he did a little skip with his feet.

"Yeah, Giselle, the boy's gettin' it. Whoo-hoo! LUCKY!'s, here we come."

THE YELLOW car had exchanged places with a white delivery van by the time they reached the station, but the three "teens" thought nothing of it. It was likely filling up at the pumps, though they were on the other side. The tinted windows kept the occupants secreted away, but then who cares who's driving a delivery van?

The cashier gave them little more than a second glance when they entered, but as they browsed the refrigerated food cases, he kept looking at a sheet of paper on the wall, then their direction. As they paid their bill, Garik followed his eyes to the paper.

BE ON THE LOOKOUT—ESCAPEES . . .

Three rows of pictures jostled for space underneath, and he jerked his eyes away, running them along Powerline, searching, his heart pounding.

"Let's go," he hissed, grabbing two sacks and slamming into the door with his shoulder. The cold air hit his face like truth in a field of lies. They weren't teens—well, he was, but not like that—and they weren't skipping school, and they weren't free to wander Bay City.

They were on the run.

He focused on the white delivery van. Was it a real delivery van, or was it a mobile Secret Service covert operation on wheels? Nothing seemed safe. Nothing!

"And that was for?" Leigh had gotten a Twizzlers and she was biting off one end, just as a teen girl would do.

"Didn't you see it? That man was checking to see if we were on that wanted poster."

"Wanted poster?" Giselle giggled and turned. "I want to see."

"No! Have you people never been in the real world? Do you even know about wanted posters? The Tower can find us because people will turn us in." He felt the panic from his first night in the

245

Tower's basements burning in him. "That van, what if they are in there watching us right now?"

"Not likely." Leigh licked her lips. "These are good. Besides, boyfriend, I watched the driver go into the restroom. He didn't even look my direction. Probably doesn't like high school girls."

"He would if he'd seen me," Giselle teased.

They were to the street, waiting on the light to cross Cowden. Garik felt, no, *heard* something from behind them. He was already turning to look when the back doors of the van opened, and out jumped two men in one-piece drab green coveralls. "Hey, you three," one called.

"How did I miss them?" Leigh turned pale.

"Sorry, we're late for school," Giselle called loudly, while frantically waving a hand and laughing. "We're not skipping, promise." She held up three fingers in a Girl Scout promise. Then she hissed, "Run!"

Run! The same word Garik had called to Marisa that night in the basement of Corona Tower. She had run—and gotten away—and he had been brought down by BolaWraps around his legs.

He didn't want to be brought down again.

To the left—back the way they had come—a military transport paused between two buildings as if searching. To the right was the right-of-way and the Cowden Street Overpass. Garik wondered what had distracted him. He had heard something, should have *known* it was from inside the van. Then the walk light changed, pointing the way, and they took off deeper into the city.

Even the wrong way was better than no way when the bad guys were coming to haul you away.

— 6 —

THEY MIGHT be on the run, but Garik's heart pounded at the possibility of visiting the skate park only three blocks ahead. It was an interwoven thread to a life that had once been his—and one he wanted back, if he could have it.

The park's convoluted surface consumed the entire block between Connel Street and Forest Avenue and ran from Avenue C (which they were on) north to Avenue B. They could dart in there if they were still being followed. He knew it like the inside of his shoe, and he was already thinking of places they could disappear from view of the street.

Calloway, one block south of Cowden, was one of the few streets that continued west past the grassy right-of-way without a name change, though there was no overpass, and to get from one portion of the street to the other meant hooking north to either Cowden or Avenue C, depending on which side you were on, and taking the Cowden Street Bridge over the right-of-way, then around and back onto Calloway. Calloway to the west continued for seven blocks before making a dead end at Birch.

Between Avenue C and Calloway, a laser strike of an alleyway cut between the buildings and offered service access to the bowels of each business. It also offered protection from prying eyes for three fugitives from the Tower's nefarious human-hybrid DNA recombination program.

Once over the bridge and across Park Avenue, Garik guided them south at Douglas and into the alley, pulling several metal trash cans into the path of anyone that might follow them. Overhead, a powerline rubbed against the brick, swish, swish. Garik looked up, found it, and dismissed it as nothing. Leigh kept reporting what she was finding, but even Garik could see that using her ultrasonic ability distracted her. Once, she nearly tripped over a trash can, and Giselle barely caught her arm before she stumbled. Halfway down the alley, a narrow passage between two buildings gave him a partial view of the skate park. A mother wrapped in a heavy coat and a scarf held a dog on a leash while her son ran around the park bouncing a ball and screaming in joy when it careened over the canted surfaces.

"The skate park's out." Garik sighed. He didn't have a board, but he had such good memories there, and they were almost close enough to touch. Then the white van pulled past, blocking his view of the skate park for a moment, and Garik jerked away from the opening.

"What did you see?" Giselle tried to lean past him, and he put out an arm to block her.

"The van. They might be looking for us." He smelled the odor of its engine, the same as it had been in the parking lot. It was etched in his brain.

"And maybe they just wanted directions, but yeah, maybe they were." Leigh leaned her head against the wall, her face strained.

"Headache, again?" Giselle paused to see if Leigh was okay.

Leigh nodded. "The reason I don't use it often."

"Did you see the military transport?" Giselle questioned Garik. "That's what the Tower would send in."

"Yes." He kept his attention on Leigh. She looked like she was in pain. "How can we help you, Leigh?"

"Someplace quiet for a while. I'll be okay."

"We came north to get here. Can we go south to get back? Then cut across?" Giselle looked upward, perhaps trying to read the city by the way the sky fell against the tops of the buildings.

"If we want to circle the Ransom to get to the Avenue G Bridge. Otherwise, no." Garik had always liked the right-of-way cutting a deep green swathe into the city. Now, it was a barrier that fought them for freedom. "I can get us back."

"Okay," Leigh said, holding one hand over her eyes. "Which direction?"

"West." The direction of The Flower Shop and his aunt's apartment building. He didn't expect to find help in either of those locations, but they were who he was. That connection was stronger than caution or safety.

And besides, Giselle and Leigh didn't seem to know Bay City well. What could a little detour hurt?

Garik's heart pounded as he led the women out of the alley, north to Avenue C, and left towards Sycamore. Just on the other side were the flower-filled shop and the one place in Bay City that had been his home.

All he really wanted was to see the flower shop, to have that small connection with Marisa, just a glimpse of something to remind him of the one girl he'd always loved. He missed her. He missed her more than anything else the Tower had taken from him.

TRAFFIC CRAWLED over the intersections when the lights changed, some with blinkers turning left or right, others offering up flashing brake lights at empty parking spaces. Backup lights flickered on, promising an extended lane blockage and sending oncoming cars into the adjoining lane.

Garik glanced inside several of the cars as the doors opened, revealing the sheen of leather or matte finish of worn cloth, the winter overshoes kicked aside, along in case of snow or rain. He could smell the differences, leather, wood, vinyl, ordinary people, ordinary lives, disappearing into offices or stores to continue their ordinary days.

At one intersection, a car turning right paused to let them pass, sending chills down Garik's back. Like they were evaluating if they had seen him on a missing persons poster. The feeling down his back had him picturing the hackles on a dog or a wolf, and despite himself, he wondered if gorillas had hackles.

Likely not. They were primates. One check for wolf DNA. One X for the gorilla in the reflection.

Garik tried to see the humor in the situation and was derailed when the white van from earlier idled past as they waited at Strickland. People crowded around, and the van didn't stop or seem to notice them. Garik glanced back down Avenue C, concerned about the military vehicle. Search and recovery. Wasn't that what the military was good at? Traffic was heavier—likely because of the hour and being closer to Sycamore—and he couldn't locate it.

At Mayberry—still two blocks away from the flower shop— Garik caught his first glimpse of the store's sign on the west side of Sycamore. It flickered on, meaning it was nine o'clock. Opening time. Mr. Bruni would unlock the front door, step outside, and set out several containers of the store's brightest blooms, in winter, usually pansies or poinsettias. They were an advertisement to step in and browse for brighter, better blooms.

Garik was so focused on the flower shop that he stepped in front of a turning car, igniting a small windstorm of near calamity. Tires screeched, a horn honked, Giselle yanked his arm.

"Whoa, boy. Didn't you hear that? What's got you distracted?" She smiled and waved at the driver, popping her gum, and circled her ear with one finger. *Looney boy*, she seemed to say. The driver waved and drove on, slowing halfway along the block at an empty parking space.

"Just—" he started to explain, then choked back his words. It was seeing the Bruni's flower shop and remembering the hours he'd spent there with Marisa poking his nose in the cases, smelling the flowers, imagining the ones he'd give her on all the special occasions of her life, if only he had the money to do so. It was his distorted reflection in the plate glass window and Giselle making a thing of it like maybe it was true, he really was a gorilla, and his arms just hadn't grown out yet.

The thought would fry anyone's brain, especially after watching Justin *molt*. Just *shed his skin and come out different*. Well, not completely different. He was still Justin, but he certainly wasn't the *same.*

And his dream during the night. He hadn't been able to shake it off. Rodheimer, with his massive shoulders, saying Garik was *just like him.*

No. He didn't think he could say any of that.

"Just careless." Garik shrugged. "Don't want Leigh to feel like she's the only one with a clumsy foot."

"At least she didn't almost get run over!" Giselle hissed the words, even as she smiled and popped her gum.

Then they were at Sycamore, and the flower shop was just across the road. Garik stood, longing—for what, he didn't know, since Marisa would be at school—when the door began to open, and Marisa stepped into the sunshine, set two plants on either side of the door, hugged her shop smock tighter against the cool air, placed an envelope in the mailbox beside the door, glanced up and down the street, and stepped back inside.

It was like a breath of mountain air and a screwdriver in the gut at the same time. To see her and have her disappear. How could he not go to her, and how could he explain that he'd not been in Russia all this time?

How could he risk her parents' shop, revealing the secret of the Tower's basements? How could he risk that she might see through the boy he still wanted to be and find the monster the Tower hoped to bring out in him?

"Your eyes," Muhammad had said. "I wouldn't have known you."

Marisa was too important to him. How could he risk that he wasn't the same person, that she wouldn't know him, that she might turn away, say, "You abandoned me. Russia is where you belong," and close the door on him?

None of that mattered, not then, not there. He looked both ways along Sycamore, saw a break in the morning rush, and decided the risk was worth it.

"Peach Fuzz, I see your brain working. What's happening in there?" Giselle had her arm wrapped in his and held him in place.

"I've got to see someone. Wait right here." Garik worked his arm free, darted into the street before they could respond, and ignored their calls to *not do this.*

It was Marisa. How could he not?

LEAPING OVER the curb and onto the sidewalk along Sycamore in front of the store, Garik let his fingers touch the blooms just beside the shop's door, flowers Marisa might have tended, blooms she might have caressed as they opened in the warmth of the store's back room. The sharp aroma of the flowers arrested his attention. He'd never realized they smelled so bright and summery. He leaned into the tinted glass, the reflection of his face, his hair, his hands shading his eyes, the only things he could see.

Of course, Marisa wasn't in the showroom. She would be in the stock room at the back of the building. He would use the familiar rear entrance he always used.

He looked to Giselle and Leigh across Sycamore, and he waved and grinned, skipping and jumping to the corner and down the side of the building along Avenue C to reach the vendor's entrance on Elm. How could he not skip? Marisa was just inside. He was ecstatic, and he wanted to laugh out loud. The air, the city, the sunlight. Seeing Marisa. It was life returned to him, like his time in the Corona Tower basements had never even happened.

Opening the door, he heard the familiar ding, and there she was, her back to him, her hands working dirt into the roots of a plant she was putting into a decorative pot.

"Mr. Bruni's not in today. Leave the shipment on the table by the door. If you need me to sign, I'll be a bit." Marisa, preoccupied, her no-nonsense, ordinary self.

"Mari?" Garik's throat caught, and conflicting emotions welled up inside him. Hearing her, listening to her voice, he was consumed with anticipation and angry at the same time, angry that this had been stolen from him, and there had been nothing he could do.

She turned, her enormous eyes taking him in. A dirt-covered hand pushed back her hair over one ear, leaving a smudge at her temple.

"It's you. They said you were back. I'm sorry, Gari. You shouldn't have come. There was nothing I could do." Her eyes filled up and she returned to her plant.

"I don't understand." Garik pulled his cap from his head, yanked his sunglasses off his face, and walked to her side. "Mari, it's me. I've missed you."

"And me, you." She kept her hands in the dirt, packing the roots carefully. "Do you know how lonely the rooftop is when I'm the only one there?"

251

"Isn't today school?" An acrid smell—deodorant or sweat—seemed out of place in this world of pleasant smells and quiet, familiar memories and jarred the unexpected question from him. "Why are you not in class? Muhammad and Ibn—"

"Okay." She pushed the partially completed planting back, took a damp towel, and wiped her hands. She sniffled, pressed the towel to her nose, then tossed it into a basket on the floor to join other used towels. "Breaking the law isn't okay, Garik. I'm disappointed in you."

"Breaking the law?" What!? He had done nothing wrong. He had been *kidnapped!*

"We were wrong, Garik, to break into the Tower's basements, and I was sad you were sent back to Russia, but that's the way it is. You can't sneak back into the country illegally."

"I never left. I've been imprisoned in the Tower since that night—"

"That's what they said you would say." She looked behind him, sighed, and pulled a clean towel from a stack, pressing it to her eyes. "My parents, this shop. They haven't let me forget. They will close us down. I had to let them do what they wanted."

"What? What did you let them do?" Garik turned to see a surveillance camera, one that hadn't been there when he was last here. Emblazoned on the side, the Tower's logo mocked him. He heard the door handle turn before he saw it, and from behind him, booted feet rubbed against the hard floor.

Before he could react to the unbelievable betrayal, the back door burst open, and in rushed two fully suited and weaponized warriors. From the front room, the plastic sheeting separated, and a gloved hand closed in a hard fist, calling out to someone Garik couldn't see.

"It's the boy. We're not letting him get away this time."

— 7 —

A CYCLONE of sensations swirled around Garik, shrouding him in a sandstorm of data.

Sounds battered him, the ding of the overhead bell attached to the door, slower and lower in tone than he expected, and more from the front room, the additional scuffling of feet, someone not yet in his view.

Smells eddied in the air, the adrenalin wash of success coming from the direction of the gloved fist, and Marisa, regret tinged with something he couldn't define.

Emotions bared his heart with surprise, anger, the knife thrust of why, why, why. Dismay and disbelief at the precarious situation that had come out of nowhere to yank him back to reality twisted into him, cutting at him. The wind-driven rush of past and present, the purity of what his life had been and the black morass it had become was a hammer shattering his brief hope for happiness.

The Tower was his enemy, and he had no way to fight them, not alone, not without the hybridized humans who had escaped alongside him. Even Marisa . . . *no!* The tide of anger rising inside consumed everything else.

With unprecedented clarity, in a way he had never seen anything before, he envisioned the person attached to the gloved fist—a woman!—in her riot mask, carrying a BolaWrap at her waist with tear gas and a slug-based weapon ready for her use. The person she called to was a man, tall and muscular—how did Garik know that?!—and he was on the radio to a backup team.

The white van. Garik knew it! They were scouts for the military vehicle that had been canvassing the city streets. Within minutes, the flower shop would be swarmed with pursuers. Giselle and Leigh, he had to warn them.

His path out of the mess he'd duped himself into was obvious. He could see it play itself out like it had already happened. Duck, push the small table of flowers aside as he went down, and send the blooms skittering across the floor. The men at the back door would be distracted just enough for Garik to shoulder one in the stomach, kick the other beside one knee, and be out the back door with one of their weapons in his hands.

That wasn't the play he intended to make. He could save himself, but that wouldn't save Giselle and Leigh. That path would place them inside the back of the white van, their hands cuffed and their mouths taped shut. Garik's only option was to exit through the front door.

He brought one leg up, swung it around, and felt his chunky boot impact one man's wrist. He was certain by the sound he left it broken. The man with the broken wrist fell into his companion, disorienting him just enough for Garik to fling himself to the floor, sliding toward the plastic-covered doorway leading into the shop's front room. He glanced at Marisa as he passed, her face still glued to where he used to be, so beautiful, just as he remembered her. *"I had to let them do what they wanted."* How bad had the Tower made life for her that it had come to this? Then she was out of sight and he was in the main room surrounded by the cases of flowers on display. The tall man was just walking through the front entrance, and Garik dove past, smashing into the glass door with his shoulder, and feeling it shatter as he fell into the sunlight. The radio the man held in one hand flew into the air, remaining there, poised in flight. Garik stopped just at the curb. The man still held his hand where the door used to be, unaware for the moment that it was no longer there.

Giselle and Leigh were statues across the street, frozen, waiting, Leigh looking like she was about to yell a warning. The sun cast a strange set of shadows, off in their colors, with refracted rainbows around everything. Even the cars on the street seemed frozen in their little pools of rainbows. Garik felt cold, so cold, as if the day had gone from one season to the next in a matter of moments.

Then he slowed, and the sound of the world around him crashed into him like an ocean wave. Three cars flashed past down Sycamore, their horns blaring at the young man standing nearly in the street. Behind him, the tall man let out a loud exclamation and tumbled outward, carried by the momentum of the door he had been holding. He stumbled and fell, knocking over one of Marisa's pots, and he landed heavily beside Garik. His radio hit the sidewalk beside him, shattering as it landed.

Garik looked down at him, took in the weapon and the Bola-Wrap at his waist, and a Taser—something the woman inside hadn't carried. Garik felt his new future open up before him. The man was military-trained, and he would recover quickly. He intended to roll over, wrap Garik's ankle in the crook of his arm, and in one singular motion, slam the Taser against Garik's leg. The woman would rush out with her gun extended, see the confrontation, and decide to protect her partner at any cost. She would fire at Garik, but with his quickness and hearing, he would pivot his body to avoid the impact, and the bullet would ricochet off the metal curb edge and impale a car already heading down Sycamore, causing a crash involving multiple vehicles.

A localized disaster that would spread, taking innocent victims in its wake, something Garik could not allow. He yelled across the street, "Run!" and relaxed when the two women only hesitated for a moment before turning and disappearing into the background of the

254

city. They could warn the rest of the team if he could lead their abductors away. The scene that had played itself out in his mind might happen exactly as he had seen it, but he was equally certain he intended to do everything he could to change it.

No one dies today, and he meant it.

The man beside Garik stirred. Garik caught the sound of the woman inside drawing her weapon—even though he couldn't see her!—and he began to move, shifting the world into rainbow shadows once again. Just before the world faded completely away, he heard a voice—Marisa's—calling his name.

By then, it was too late. To those watching, Garik might have blurred and vanished, but to him, silence reigned as his speed ripped at his muscles and consumed his available energy. He collapsed three blocks down Sycamore, having made it into the park-like grounds surrounding the Old City Hall. Fire consumed him, his muscles cramping all over his body, and he could barely catch his breath.

He wondered if this was how Jantzen felt each time he evaporated into purple fog.

Before he could come up with an answer, tires screeched from back the way he had come, metal tore into metal, and with an explosive concussion, black smoke boiled into the sky.

Maybe, Garik thought, this was why Christian didn't fight what he knew was about to happen. If he tried to avoid it, something worse took its place.

Then sirens flooded the sky, and all Garik could do was say a prayer that everyone involved was all right. Around him, tables were set up for an event, with chairs, a speaker's platform, and bunting. Sodas sat atop a red ice chest under a sign proclaiming Bay City Fitness Run. Already people were gathering, several in fitness gear stomping their feet to stay warm. He couldn't stay here. He had to get to safety—and back to help the others, if he could.

He stood, his body fighting him in electrified jerks and uncoordinated twitches. And he *hurt!* He hoped this wasn't his future as a hybridized human. He watched two military-style vehicles roar south, likely heading from Corona Tower along Sycamore to either the crash or the incident at The Flower Shop. The street curved just enough that they were out of sight before they slowed.

He hoped—*he wanted!*—Marisa to be okay. He had to know. He lifted one arm to find his black cap still clenched in his fist. His sunglasses were lost, but he slipped the cap over his head, forced himself to concentrate on his coordination, and worked his way through the paths wending through the Old City Hall grounds before heading west on First. By the time he reached Oak, he could walk normally, though he wasn't sure he could run again if he wanted. His mind, his cunning, his planning would have to be his path to survival. Whatever he had done at the Bruni's store was like being jerked through a worm hole—deadly to everyone involved.

He veered south on Elm, and crossing Avenue B, he began working his way from storefront to storefront. The flower store was only a block away, and about halfway down the row of businesses, he had a partial view of both the north entrance that faced Avenue C and the vendor's entrance on Elm.

Old Town started west of Sycamore, and several of the buildings Garik moved along exposed vacant painted-over windows. For Rent signs had become the blood of Old Town bleeding out. The lack of traffic left Garik feeling exposed. Without his sunglasses, he was certain every person in Bay City knew exactly where he was. The "afterglow" of running at top speed had him convinced not to try that again.

His connection with Marisa assured him it was worth whatever it cost.

Garik adjusted his position for a better view and located two military vehicles parked along Avenue C. One had two doors open, and several people in camo kept glancing left and right. Garik sank into a doorway, hoping to become part of the scenery. The door to the shop opened, and he involuntarily tried to disappear.

"It was what you wanted."

Garik's ears perked up. Marisa! He warmed to her voice and tried to see her, but he was blocked by a group of signs on the corner of Elm and Avenue C.

"I didn't warn him or sabotage anything. Check your video."

"He's gone, isn't he?" The woman's voice with the fist. "We had our best here. How could he know—"

"How should I know? You people are in control, at least that's what you say. You made me the bait, and he got away, and now it's my fault?"

"Don't forget, young lady. Your parents' business is only operational as long as we allow it to be. Work with us. We're warning you."

"If he *were* in Russia, how could he have gotten back into the country so easily—"

"Just do as you're told. If he comes back again, we want to know."

The voices stopped, the vehicle doors slammed, and with a roar, they pulled away. They turned north on Elm, drove right past him, and their brakes flashed at Avenue B and Avenue A before turning east on First. Overhead, a powerline swayed in the wind, rubbing insulation to insulation. The sound came to him as a whisper, suggesting, "There are things you still don't know, wolf boy. Be careful, be careful, be careful." A bird landed, one of the few Garik had seen in, well, since forever. There weren't any birds in the Tower's expansive basements.

Somewhere in the distance, he picked up the activity resulting from the car crash. A firetruck had arrived, and one of the cars was being dismembered to get at what or who was inside.

Garik looked toward the shop, leaning forward enough to see the door, now closed, with Marisa still inside. He had no way of knowing if everyone had left, but it made sense that they had. Likely, the wreck was welcomed, a distraction from the devastation they were deploying on Marisa and her family.

Was that why Mr. Bruni wasn't at the shop? Why Marisa was missing school today? They told her to be the only one there just in case he came to find her? Garik's face burned with the injustice of it all. They had no *right* to do that to her and her family.

He touched his wrist, wishing for his watch. Being back in the city reminded him of how useful it was, to just call, ask how people were doing, what was going on. If he could call John, let them know where he was, find out if they were still safe in the converted warehouse . . . then, the Tower could likely trace his call. Pinpoint his location. Send their goons to chase him down, and he didn't think he would get away this time.

Movement at the shop focused him back to his surroundings. The door on Avenue C now boasted a closed sign. Marisa stepped from the back door, her coat wrapped around her slender frame, and she pressed a key into the lock. She lifted her sunglasses and wiped her eyes—*his sunglasses!* She was wearing the ones he had taken off and forgotten.

He wanted to step out and call to her. "I'm here, Mari! I didn't leave. I would never leave. Don't go!"

Yet, *"Your parents' business is only operational as long as we allow it to be."* And Marisa's words. *"You shouldn't have come."*

He had to, he wanted to say. He couldn't have stayed away if he'd wanted. Yet, when he stepped forward to tell her, she was already gone, and despite his despair, he knew his choices weren't his own.

He needed to get back to the warehouse. He needed to know that everyone he'd helped escape was warned.

He had to step up and be what the situation required him to be, even if he had no clear idea exactly what that was.

— 8 —

GARIK DREW in a deep lungful of air, taking time to winnow the smells into things he must deal with immediately, those that were merely interesting, and others that made up the background of the moment and could be set aside.

The city had never smelled so alive before, so vital, so filled with life. The sterile exhaust of a window air conditioner just across the street. It was likely pumping heat into an office. Something delicious from a block over, possibly streaming from a partially open car window, eggs-and-fries-to-go from Chow Down, an aroma Garik would recognize anywhere.

He also caught the acrid exhaust of the white van, revealing that it had driven down Elm, although not since he'd set foot on the street. Fainter, the rotting odor of something dead, likely a rat in the sewer or a trash bin from the alley behind him.

Teasing him, a wafting cloud of odor called, "Here's something interesting. Explore me," and Garik's attention was pulled to the corner to see a red-attired pizza delivery girl appear on a moped with a stack of pizzas strapped behind her.

Entombed within the smell were the burned odor of the oil in the engine, the leather polish she'd used on her shoes that morning, and her shampoo, something with coconut in it.

No judgement, just information, and he soaked it all in. He tried to find Marisa in the inrush of data, but she had been outside and gone, and inside the flower shop, the blooms and the gloved woman had added so many layers of smells that he hadn't had time to sort them into their respective slots in his brain.

Now, the burning of hydrocarbons drifted over the buildings, mixed with the organic proteins of fire-fighting foam. Fear drifted in and out, sharp and acrid, the thorny prick of pheromones released by people possibly injured. The aromatic wash of flour and cheese and oregano from the pizza girl had begun to fade, and he realized how hungry he was. What had happened to the bag of food he had carried? Somewhere in the flower shop, he figured—gone—and he had no money to buy more.

Aunt Irina? City View Apartments was three blocks west. Surely she would be glad to feed him. The possibility flashed in front him, a lightbulb of hope, and was as quickly dismissed. He didn't know the day of the month, and her kitchen cabinets might be as sparse as the businesses around him displaying open signs.

St. Anne's, his church of choice, maintained a food pantry, but it was located on Spruce, twelve blocks away. Every block he walked the streets—or even the alleyways—was another chance to be discovered by the Tower. A shift in the wind returned the smell of flour, cheese, and oregano, and he pictured the girl on the moped. Old City Hall. The Fitness Run. He caught an announcement over a loudspeaker filtering between the buildings welcoming participants to the day's events. The pizzas would be out on the tables, runners standing around chatting, a mixture of faces from across the city. Black, white, brown, and an amalgam of everything in between. Did he dare try to blend in, even for pizza?

He was starving. He pulled his knit cap down, worked it over his ears, and kept his head low. Turning east on Avenue A brought him to the south side of the Old City Hall. Cars lined the sidewalks. People were still gathering, most in some sort of running gear, with brightly colored shoes, snug pants, and bulky layers from the waist up. Knit caps dominated the headwear—thank goodness—and Garik fell in with a pride of runners in puffy winter coats. They broke off to collect their identification lanyards, and he continued to the food table where he could see the pizzas stacked in their boxes. Paper plates and napkins were laid out, ready to use.

"Too cold for you today?"

Garik looked up from the pizzas to discover a petite woman in a thick coat and gloves. Earmuffs buried her ears amidst a cloud of blonde hair.

"A little," he said, hoping she didn't expect him to carry on a conversation.

"For me, too. I usually participate to prepare for the Bay City Marathon—my daughter, Regina, attends Bay City High, and I can't let her show me up—but the forecast was for a chilly day, so I volunteered to oversee the food tables. I can train for the marathon another time." She laughed like it was an inside joke. "Can I get you a slice of pizza to warm you up? Observers are certainly welcome to enjoy the food. We have another delivery coming at noon, and this won't stay warm for long."

"Yes, please." He watched hungrily as she opened the top box, showed him hamburger for his permission, and handed him a slice when he nodded. "Thank you."

"We have drinks if you want one," she offered.

He nodded and bit in, inhaling the pizza as quickly as he could chew. She already had a second slice ready, laughing that he was already done. Others were wandering over, and when she began to lay out pizza for them, Garik stepped to the next table for a can of soda. He popped the tab and worked his way under a tree to hide himself as much as possible. Regina, he thought. The lady must be Mrs. Kournikova, Regina Kournikova's mother. He had recognized Regina in the woman's eyes, and when she had handed him the pizza, he smelled cherry blossoms. Regina had once said her mother liked cherry blossom air freshener.

He tried to think if he had ever smelled cherry blossoms on Regina, but being out of circulation since summer defeated that line of mental investigation, and he let it go. He had other things to think about: Marisa; the group who had escaped with him from the Tower; and how to stay out of the Tower's clutches. He was working on that, but it was beyond him at the moment.

He popped the final bite of crust in his mouth, the buttery, salty, yeasty flavor filling up his brain. He had no idea pizza could smell so good—and taste even better. How had he missed that all his years?

He visited the trash receptacle to toss his things, wiping his hands thoroughly before dropping them in. Before he could step away, Regina's mother joined him to deposit several empty plates.

"The award ceremony is at two. Good luck to you and yours. Maybe I will see you there."

"Thank you, Mrs. Kournikova."

"You must be one of Regina's friends. Be sure to check our giveaway table. It's all branded, but free sunglasses!" She laughed. "I see you didn't bring any."

"I will. I appreciate the offer."

"Corona Tower's offer. They sponsor us." She handed him a water bottle. The side said, Bay City Fitness Run, and underneath was the Corona Tower logo.

Garik smiled, took the bottle, and tucked it into a pocket. At the giveaway table, he selected the least garish glasses—black frames with Bay City Fitness Run in neon pink down the earpieces—and a bottle band that he could hook over his water bottle and to his belt. He slipped the bottle band in the pocket with the water bottle to put on later.

He also picked up a map of the Fitness Run course and was relieved that it stayed on the West Side, following Second west to The Cliffs, then north before twisting through the Shady Ridge Acres residential area, then on to circle Waldorf's before weaving east to Birch and south along Birch to the finish line back at the Old City Hall. Several shorter routes were marked for different age groups or fitness levels. The run along Birch would be uphill, and being at the end of the run, it would likely defeat all but those in the best shape.

Now that he had pizza in his stomach, Garik considered the people he had seen prepping for the run. He could beat them all, and the competitor in him wanted to shed his coat and toss off the full run. It would be a breeze for him, but it would also draw attention to his presence out and about in the city. He sighed, returned the map to the table, set his new sunglasses on his face, and pressed the button to trigger the light across Sycamore. The breeze coming off the bay carried fish and seaweed and diesel, stronger than he previously remembered. He also smelled Chow Down, the eatery at the Corona Mall, reminding him of his fugitive status.

He pulled his knit lower on his face, and when the light changed, he made his way across, walking as casually as he could to try to blend in.

GARIK HAD passed the cross-tipped spire of First United Congregation three blocks to the north on Thomas and the Bay City Transportation Department two blocks later, also to the north and bordered by McKinley, Second, Douglas, and Third, when he noticed the buzzing sound of a drone navigating the streets in a grid-like pattern.

He backed under an awning between Douglas and Eisenhower, hunching his shoulders in his leather jacket, even as he was aware it didn't make him less prominent against the gray of the concrete sweeping him along towards the First Street and Powerline overpass.

"If only I had my Street Strider," he muttered. Riding the jet-assisted bike would hardly be less obvious, but faster was the key, and it would bring less attention than running full out. Running, people would think him a thief or some other hooligan-type character, and they would report him for sure.

He checked his knit cap, ensured it covered as much of him as possible, secured his new Fitness Run glasses on his face, and listened over the low rumble of background noise—the lifeblood of the city—for the drone. The overpass was two blocks away with a light he had to navigate at Park on the near side and another at Powerline once he crossed. He could see the sign for Kerre's Dive at Garfield and First. If he could reach there, he could navigate south and bypass the gridwork of lighted crosswalks through alleys and courtyards.

A second drone caught his attention, this time creating a high-fidelity symphony of stereophonic dread. The music crashed in his ears, turning his stomach over, while assuring him his window of safety was about to end in a cymbal clash of reverberating disaster. He watched the intersection at Park, judging the timing of the walk light. Giving himself half a minute before it changed, he stepped from under the awning and strode confidently toward his destination.

The whine of the drones changed. Garik cringed and walked faster. They both screamed at him from directly overhead, and he began to run. Forget the lights. He was going across.

Events reached a crescendo when the roar of approaching military vehicles began to reverberate against the walls of the concrete canyons.

"No, no, no," Garik breathed, muttered, and prayed, all at the same time. The sun flashed against his face as he crossed the bridge, hot on his skin, leaving the morning chill to prickle any part of him in shadow. The winter-dead grass along the right-of-way filled the air with a dusty and wasted chlorophyll fog, an acrid aroma trapped in the grassy wasteland and escaping into the air directly above.

Escape. Garik reached the far side of the bridge, desperate. He dodged a delivery truck emblazoned with the name and logo for Howie's Hoagies and aimed for the drive-thru portico at Kerre's Dive.

He would have made it, he was certain. He almost did. Then, the sound of the drones grew sharp and angry. He heard tires skidding to a stop and voices began to yell. Then, his body was hit, and he knew exactly what it was.

A BolaWrap encircled him, its octopus arms wrapping his torso, his legs, and his upper limbs in a loving embrace. On the way down, his Fitness Run sunglasses flew from his face, and the brilliance of the sun blinded him for a moment.

"Two pairs of sunglasses in one day," was his last thought as he hit the concrete. With a jarring impact, the sun went out, and night was all he could see.

GARIK CAME to strapped to a gurney, his eyes blurry. He rocked back and forth in a medical transport. A white-suited technician talked into a laptop.

Weston Rodheimer was on the other side.

"Just the boy, then?" Rodheimer filled the screen, his heavy brows and jaw sitting on his too-broad shoulders.

"We were lucky the mother recognized this one. Otherwise, we would have missed him, too. She only remembered his face when he called her by name."

The mother. *Mrs. Kournikova.* Garik wanted to pound himself in the head. If only he hadn't said her name.

"No luck involved. He planned this. Bring him in."

Planned this? Who, him? That was a laugh. Then the computer screen began to blur, Rodheimer faded away, and the technician, well, Garik hadn't seen his face and wouldn't mind if he never did.

Somewhere, he thought he might have pleaded, "This time, please don't cut my hair."

Before he could decide if he had only thought the words, darkness overtook him a second time, stealing even that from him.

— 9 —

OUTSIDE THE big window, snow had started to fall.

Bay City was like a lightly frosted cake, pretty, or it would be if Garik wasn't seeing it from atop the Corona Tower in the penthouse suite.

His image shimmered faintly in the heavily tinted glass, revealing his outline crowned by bushy hair—*they hadn't cut it!*—and the whites in his eyes that seemed crisper than he'd ever seen them.

Was that what Muhammad had meant, he wondered? Or maybe the difference was in the broadness of his shoulders or the thickness of his legs. He adjusted his position slightly, searching for differences in his reflection. He still felt like Garik, but he was also pretty sure Justin still felt like Justin, even if his molting had changed him into something almost unrecognizable.

Would Garik recognize the differences when they happened? Or would he look at his reflection and see what he wanted to see, a high school senior, a werewolf, *no matter how humanoid*, or, and this continued to play with his mind, a lumbering gorilla with a meaty fist that could smash through tables and walls?

The nightmare hadn't gone away, and after all, Christian with his wolfhound DNA had acquired precognition, and Garik hadn't experienced a moment of that, well, except for those few seconds in The Flower Shop, sensing that there were two attackers in the front room, not just one. He admitted that he might have deduced that through his hearing. None of them had been exactly stealthy in their actions.

He certainly hadn't seen the BolaWrap that had taken him down. If he had, he'd have run the other direction.

Behind him, Weston Rodheimer cleared his throat. It vibrated the floor in a low-pitched rumble, almost a growl.

"I'm almost through," Garik called. Almost through being patient. Almost through with what you've done to me. Almost through with answering your questions, with trying to regain my freedom, with having my girlfriend harassed by your Tower goons.

Outside, it was growing dark in the late fall evening. In the distance, the Ransom Communications Building glowed, and left, he found Bay City Medical and the entrance to the industrial park. His friends were right there, in the warehouse Dieter's father had converted into a skate park, that was if they hadn't been compromised by his clumsy efforts to reconnect with Marisa.

Would Justin be in the air searching for him? Would Garik see him if he were? And how would he signal to him that he was in the Tower and behind the glass on the top floor? Or was he lost once again, with all his Houdini loopholes now sealed away forever?

He looked past his reflection to the room around him mirrored in the glass, everything sharpening up with the darkening sky. Rodheimer reclined in a chair that two people would be comfortable in at a desk nearly as spacious as Garik's bedroom back in Irina's apartment, waiting on Garik to give him the answer he wanted to hear. A fireplace filled with crackling flames warded off the perception of cold through the sealed glass windows.

Garik tightened up one arm, flexing without seeming to flex, comparing his biceps to Rodheimer's and struggling to find the similarities between them. Rodheimer wasn't even flexing, and his arms were still twice the size, and Garik had been working out for months. Sheesh! There was no way he could win against this guy.

Not physically, anyway, but there were other ways to win against a bully, and Rodheimer was that, no denials possible.

Sighing, he turned. "Why should I believe you?"

"Why would I lie to you?" Rodheimer's deep voice rumbled, and Garik thought he caught the images in the glass trembling in respect.

"The same reason you have all along, I don't know. You enjoy kidnapping teenagers and shooting them up with monkey DNA—"

"Timber wolf." Rodheimer almost smiled. "That was a personal choice of mine. I hoped to appeal to a wild city boy like you. And how have you suffered? How are you worse off than before?"

"No freedom." No friends. His girlfriend lied to. And his aunt, what had they told her? Had they gone all the way to Russia to tell his parents his airplane had crashed on the way? If Irina contacted them, they might tell her that their precious son had never arrived. What about that, Director Rodheimer?

"That." Rodheimer stood, becoming bigger than it was possible for any man to be as he rose from his chair. He shrugged. "Our people beg to come for our treatments. How could I know you would be the one person to not appreciate all we could give you? My apologies. Come. Sit in front of the fire."

The big man stepped easily towards the fire, shifted two wingbacks to face it, leaving a small marble-topped table in between. He motioned to Garik to take one of the chairs.

The chair swallowed the teen. He sat up as straight as possible, his feet barely touching the floor. Next to him, Rodheimer filled the chair perfectly, as if it were designed for him. Garik realized it probably was.

"This." Rodheimer opened a drawer in the table and lifted out the black sunglasses from the Fitness Run. "Brilliant, all of it. Jantzen couldn't have done better."

"At what?" Getting caught? he wanted to ask, because Jantzen had been helping him *not* to do that very thing.

"Come now. Modesty is not your friend, not with me. The glasses thing." Rodheimer held up the glasses and looked at the words scrawled down the earpiece. "Quite a clue, and telling that mother

her name. Perfect. Planning I didn't expect from you. Rid the compound of your competition, and you would excel."

"Rid the—" Garik clamped down on his response. Did this man actually think he'd let himself be captured on purpose? Even be BolaWrapped, just to abandon his friends without them suspecting? Sheesh!

"I like the way you think. Using your old girlfriend to ditch your two guards . . . bet that caught them by surprise. Good disguise by the way. Without these glasses, my team wouldn't have known it was you. Whoever sorted that out for you is to be commended. Wouldn't surprise me if Jantzen had a hand in it. He always said the eyes are a person's most recognizable feature. Hide the eyes and you hide the person. The reason he wears black beanies. Like the one you wore."

"Yeah, he said that to me, too." Garik sank into his chair, deflated. He'd pictured the Director as a mental goof, the Hulk in a gorilla suit. Now it seemed he had a brain, too.

"So, back in the fold, more like me than you may want to admit." Rodheimer grinned. "My own special additive to your new DNA serum—"

"What?" Garik interrupted. "You said timber—"

"Ha! You amuse me. Like the son I never had. You are third generation. Has Jantzen told you that? Or did he continue to string you along, give you tidbits of lies, just enough to gain your confidence? Well?"

Garik sat, stunned at the words. That was exactly how he'd felt at times, the dark-haired man befriending him, then stepping back as though Garik were an experiment to be evaluated, used if possible, and—he had never dared think it—discarded if he failed to live up to the man's expectations.

"How am I third . . . . your own special DNA . . . I'm confused." Like a salmon fighting a fish ladder and not making good progress.

"See? I do know Jantzen, and very well. He has shared what he wants you to know. I will tell you the truth." Rodheimer offered Garik the glasses, and he shook his head. The big man placed them in the table and closed the drawer. "If you ever want them, a memento of sorts. I am first generation. We had to start somewhere, and I knew it must be me. Jantzen, also, first generation. You've seen the smoke thing? Of course, you have." Rodheimer lifted his hand, and out of nowhere, a man appeared with a tray of drinks and a large cigar. He held it out to Garik after Rodheimer took a glass of amber liquid.

"These are all . . . alcohol. I'm only seventeen. At least I think. I'm not sure of the date."

"November, late. So, still seventeen. Take what you like. Now that you are, um, modified, your body will slough off all attempts to doctor it with stimulants or depressants. It's a shame, but I like the taste."

Rodheimer threw back one glass, and after Garik took a glass of darker liquid, the servant offered Rodheimer another. He set his second on the table and motioned the man away. Garik sipped the liquid and choked as it burned down his throat.

Rodheimer held out the cigar, admiring it. "This, too, is useless, but I enjoy holding it. Not to light, but just to hold, mind you. Now, to business. That fight with Justin. I watched how you moved. Like you knew where he would be before he knew. Tell me how you did that."

"I, um—" This was a time to choose his words carefully. *Don't reveal everything.* Jantzen had taught him that, and whether the man turned out to be on his side or not, he considered it good advice. "Jantzen had fought him earlier. I watched and copied his technique."

"Copied his technique. Okay, let me tell you what it means to be first generation. We must work harder at keeping our human genes dominate. It doesn't work for all of us."

"Christian."

Rodheimer raised his eyebrows. "Yes, Christian was one. Jantzen and his ability to morph into blue smoke is another. Let me show you something." He held the cigar in his left hand, brought his right to the end, and snapped his fingers. Electricity leaped from his fingertips to the end of the cigar *and stayed there.* The big man bit off the end of the cigar, sucked on it, and it flared into life. He moved his hand away, and when he spread his fingers, the electricity evaporated into the air, leaving a smell of ozone.

"What has DNA like that? Electric eel?"

"Ha, ha! You are the first to suggest that. No, just a side effect, unexpected. You could say I've had the DNA of an electric current melded with my DNA, along with other stuff, and now, this is something I can do. It isn't always pleasurable. My clothing? Specially designed to reduce static charge. My body absorbs it, and I can release it at will. Accidentally at times, which can be deadly to other people."

"I bet. If I'm third generation, how am I different?" That was what Garik wanted to know. What would happen to him when he molted, if that was what happened to him? Would he have Rodheimer's giant shoulders, Justin's extra joints and wings, or would he become a lemur-like person like Marco?

Was it his lot to become a werewolf? He used to love werewolf movies. Now, he couldn't keep them out of his dreams. That and crazy gorillas about to be decapitated with an electrified sword, thanks, Marisa.

"We are striving for balance, bonus capabilities, but not so many that we lose the human connection. To be able to jump long distances, but with recognizably human legs. To think faster, evaluate quicker, but retain a normal cranium size. To develop extended smell but not a rat-like face shape."

"You want us to be like secret agents."

"Exactly!" Rodheimer's level of excitement said he was extraordinarily pleased with Garik's evaluation. "If you become the success we hope to create in you, then your success is everyone's success. You choosing to return to us of your own volition, and so creatively, tells me we are on the right track."

"What about the extraordinary things the people I've trained with can do? Aren't those things useful, also?" Alyna with her razor claws. Julia, able to sense heat with her infrared ability. Laura, able to breathe out hydrogen cyanide, even though Garik had never seen her use the skill, and more . . . Marco, Justin, Leigh, Amy, able to track a hundred enemies at once. Even Paulo, with his fingers able to shoot boiling water. How useful must that be in certain circumstances, and Garik had watched John cool water nearly to freezing just by inserting his hands.

Garik was useless in comparison, and in fact had been less than useless, even a hindrance. Breaking the van window. Nearly getting Leigh and Laura captured. Now, here he was in the Tower *with the big bad guy himself.* Trapped once again, and this time, he was certain they intended to throw away the passkey.

"In context, but not in the general world. If your enemy can see your offensive weapons, they can combat them. If you, however, come to them as a teenage boy, they will welcome you inside, and when you gain their confidence, wham! They are at our mercy!"

Rodheimer slammed his hand down on the table to emphasize the word *wham*, and the marble top cracked in two, leaving the legs canted sideways. Garik reached for the glasses, the room creating rainbow swirls around everything for that singular instance, and he held them in his hands with no spillage at all.

"That's it, boy. You just did it again. Just what I wanted to see. You and me, just alike. Do you see it?"

Garik grinned weakly. What had he done now?

— 10 —

THEY WERE soon aboard the elevator and headed to the basement levels.

Rodheimer inserted his passkey, and the unit prompted him for a palm scan. The panel became a Christmas tree, with options from the 40th floor down to Level 5 in the basement. The mall. That's the one Garik wanted to reach out and touch, but such wasn't to be the case. The big man tapped Basement Level 4.

"That's the hospital." Garik grimaced. Still saying the obvious. Like a kid.

"Correct." Rodheimer watched the display as it flashed numbers almost too quickly to follow.

"I don't have a cold." Making light of it might earn him some information. "Unless you think I brought the outside pandemic in, you know, the one that gives everyone else the urge to try their hand at getting out into the real world."

"Which is why we're headed to Level 4. We intend to lock that possibility away for good."

The final light flashed, the door dinged, and it swung wide. The corridor was a ribbon of candy, with blue stripes along each edge. The air, clean, with no odor of its own, not really, giving it a distinctive aroma that was unique even in the research center.

Scrubbed, purified, and likely kept separate from the air pumping in and out of the other basement levels. No diseases in. No diseases out. What every good hospital should strive for.

Garik was surprised not to see Nurse Ratchett waiting for them at the door. The woman had been pleasant enough, but it was clear that she enjoyed the process better than she enjoyed the people. If you wanted to be a cooperative patient and get your DNA modified to a dragonfly, a woolly mammoth, or whatever, that was perfectly okay to her. Suggest that something else is in your plans, and she'd as soon slap you with her needle, regardless.

"I expected someone to meet us." Garik waited on Rodheimer before exiting. The man seemed to be making a point with his silence.

"I asked them to clear the floor. Shall we?" Rodheimer moved forward, a ghost walker inside that massive body of his.

Garik understood. Rodheimer had established their relative hierarchy in the Tower. The Director had the power to order everyone off the hospital floor, and Garik had none at all, not even the power to push the elevator button to choose their destination.

Halfway down the corridor, a utility door to the right opened a short distance in front of them. The latch clicked, metal on metal, thump thump, and the door opened a few inches and clicked shut again, echoing hollowly in the unadorned corridor. Rodheimer paused, his eyes hardening, and his forehead becoming a trough of irritation. The door clicked again, and a man backed out, blocking their way, while pulling a wheeled bucket with a mop handle that chattered along every surface it could reach like a wooden drumstick.

Garik recognized Tyrone Brown with his wide smile and white teeth. He and his boss, Joseph Howard, had installed the charger for Garik's ZBoard, the electric skateboard he had used to get around when he and Jantzen had prowled the vast corridors in the 64-square-block underground research facility.

"Mr. Brown." Rodheimer rumbled the man's name, and Tyrone looked around and turned pale, or as pale as his coffee skin could.

"My apologies, Mr. Rodheimer. So sorry." Tyrone tried to catch the door before it closed behind him, and his hand slipped, and it clicked shut. He fumbled out his passkey and dropped it. He stared at it as though devastated by its betrayal.

"Pick it up, Mr. Brown."

The maintenance man did, carefully, and reinserted it into the door, releasing the lock, thump thump. Swinging the door past, he banged the bucket, sloshing water onto the floor. By then, he was visibly shattered.

Garik blanched at the interplay. The Director had played nice up in the penthouse *clearly wanting something Garik had to offer.* There was nothing he wanted or needed from Tyrone, so there was no reason for him to be kind.

Rodheimer's words were a jackhammer in Garik's head. *"We intend to lock that possibility away for good."* How did he plan that? How did the Tower's research program de-Houdini its participants? Leg bracelets? Handcuffs chained to the wall? Tracking devices inserted in the brain that couldn't be removed?

The Nazis had tattooed the prisoners in their gulag system so they could be tracked if they ever escaped. Was that what Garik could expect, a bar code on his forehead that could be read by lasers in every doorway he stepped through? These people could already fiddle with people's DNA. There was no telling what else they could pull off.

Only when Tyrone had disappeared back into the darkness of wherever the door led, Rodheimer cleared his throat and continued walking. At a door marked Experimental Hybridization, he inserted his passkey and stood back, waiting on Garik to enter before following him inside.

At least it didn't say Tattoo Parlor. Garik didn't know if that was better or not. Experimental didn't sound so good.

Inside offered a small anteroom with a desk and more doors just behind. A cage to capture the unwary. Once you get in, you are trapped with no way out except deeper into the dream. A lobster cage, or a psychedelic rabbit hole, falling deeper and deeper as things get weirder and weirder. Garik looked around for signs of magic mushrooms and only saw the candy stripes still hugging the floor. No Alice, not yet.

He wished he'd studied more on Harry Houdini's techniques at escaping in every possible situation. He could use a little escape magic just about now.

A woman stepped through a private door behind the desk, with large earrings and stringy blonde hair.

"My apologies, Director. We're got a situation in experimental surgery and cleanup hasn't arrived."

Her nametag on her smock said Kim. She popped her gum twice before pulling out the chair and sitting down. She was so thin she seemed to disappear into the chair's fabric. She set a computer keyboard on her desk and typed in a query before looking up and smiling.

"All ready, Director."

"Thank you, Ms. Sanchez."

Kim reached under her desk, did something to trigger the second set of doors, and they began to open, releasing a cacophony of tympanic noises that could have raised the dead.

Garik wished for clean underwear. He was certain he would need them before the night was over.

"MEET CHAD."

Rodheimer towered over a disfigured man on an operating gurney. He was in a hospital gown covered with a sheet from the chest down. To the side was a motorized wheelchair. Noises of whining saws and metallic banging filled the background. The room to the door closed, and the sounds muted.

"How are you doing today, Chad? Any fresh escape attempts lately? How are those legs working? Too bad you couldn't keep your originals, but these will be so much better, and they will allow us to see if it is really possible to transpose adaptations from one participant to another."

Chad, from the cafeteria. Garik remembered him. Keep his original legs? Fresh escape attempts? He was cold with the implications.

"Garik, this is Chad Sherwin. You may have seen him around. We've provided him top-notch transportation, an Invacare Storm Series chair. High torque and brushless motors. Top notch. Chad is very appreciative of our kindness and willingness to provide him the very best. Isn't that so, Chad?"

Chad rolled his eyes. One eye tracked differently, and Chad moved his lips as though answering, but Garik heard nothing.

"I'm sorry, Chad? A little lower, perhaps?" Rodheimer leaned down, putting one ear closer to Chad's face. Chad screwed his face up and closed his eyes, refusing to respond.

"I almost met you once, Chad." Garik took the initiative to ease the situation. "You were with someone named Heath. I was with Jantzen."

Chad pointed to a side table and a small device. Garik handed it to him, and he pressed a switch. When he opened his mouth to speak, the device spoke for him.

"Yes, in the cafeteria several months ago. Your hair looks better now." He smiled, a crooked expression in his lumpy face.

"You have bat DNA, don't you?" It was the only answer. The voice he couldn't hear, the box to speak for him. The unusual facial bone structure. "Your skill is echolocation. I bet you're great to have around in the dark."

"Hear that, Director?" The box spoke, and Chad glared at Rodheimer. "I'm great to have around in the dark."

"Maybe if our little experiment pans out." Rodheimer grasped one of Chad's legs with a massive hand and squeezed it. Chad grimaced but didn't respond.

"Why are we here?" Again, the question was to diffuse an uncomfortable situation. Garik wanted this over with.

"Ah, back to that. We are having a lesson in what happens to people who are not satisfied with our program and our accommodations." Through the door, the sound of someone screaming brought a sigh from the Director. He looked at the door and waited on it to stop. "How is your back, Chad? I'm sorry your bone structure doesn't allow you to sit erect. If we get your leg bones functioning, maybe you can walk where you need to go. With a torso brace, of course."

"I don't understand." Legs, bone structure, the man's back. Put it together for me, Garik pleaded.

"Bat." Chad's box speaking. "I'm designed to fly, sleep upside down, use my wings like arms. My echolocation is unaffected, but the good Director decided to remove my ability to fly, and now I'm restricted to that." His eyes locked on the chair.

"It was too bad, Chad, but necessary. Your adaptations are invaluable for research, and we can't let them get away. The prosthetic arms, though, seem to function well. And your leg donor was glad to gift them to you. He had no use, otherwise."

No other use for the legs—or for him? Basement Level 5, Garik remembered. Christian, sent there to be recycled into whatever useful parts he could supply.

The door opened, allowing the whine of an electric drill inside. Kim Sanchez leaned in. "My apologies for the noise, Director. We're fitting new prosthetics for several people today, and it can't be helped. Ms. Sunchaser is on the line. Do you wish to speak with her?"

"Wait here." He bored his eyes into Garik, and as he left, the door snapped shut with a metallic click and the thump thump of the locks that trapped them inside.

"IS IT TRUE?" Chad's box asked the evenly modulated question as the man's unusual mouth moved silently.

"I don't know. What?" Garik was searching the room for options

273

to Houdini out of there, even if he did realize they were on the fourth basement level. Still, he had gotten out once. He could do it again.

"You're not escaping a second time."

"What makes you say that?" Garik hadn't said anything about escape although it was everywhere in his mind.

"I escaped. They brought me back. Now look at me. Half of who I was. The Director won't hesitate to do the same to you. You don't seem to have anything to take away, so they will likely add to you, DNA testers to trigger specific mods, ones that will make you so odd you don't dare show yourself outside of this facility."

Garik pictured Justin. Had he escaped before? Was that Garik's future? Was that what Rodheimer was showing him? He was being offered two choices, prison or more mods—and then likely still prison.

"So, Jantzen's out?" The question seemed important to Chad.

"Yes." Garik didn't say more. Was this a trap, a set-up so that he would disclose the man's location? If so, he wasn't falling for it. "I'm catching overtones of your voice. Is that possible?"

"You're timber wolf, so possible. Good about Jantzen, and for whoever else got out. If they're captured again—" Chad stopped and closed his eyes, his chest shuddering. When he calmed, he said, "Don't give anything away. Rodheimer still wants them back. He will chase them and do to them what he's done to me."

"Jantzen will protect—"

"He can't. Rodheimer will modify them all. Jantzen, that's a different story. He's hard to hold and hard to modify." Chad chuckled. "We all wish to be Jantzen."

Jantzen, bad guy or good? Garik was so confused. He didn't know right from wrong anymore. And was Chad sure he was part timber wolf? What Garik didn't know could fill a basement, even the one under Corona Tower, as big as it was.

— 11 —

"SO, YOU may get your wish after all."

Rodheimer slammed the door back, yanking his passkey from its interface. His presence swept into the room, a tidal wave of gigantean proportions. He dominated, overshadowed, blocked out all light. His fingertips sparkled with fireworks. Anger rolled from him like a summer storm.

Garik was truly frightened. The man had said he absorbed static electricity, but he was pulling all the electricity from the room. It was coming out his fingertips. Who would die today? He hoped it wasn't him.

"Whose wish?" Garik managed to squeak out.

"Fool, boy! Is that what you wish me to believe? Don't play me the idiot. You are as transparent as glass."

Following him, a whimper of a woman trailed in. Her black bangs didn't quite hide the scar on her forehead. Garik remembered her from the event on the mall, Angelica. Jantzen had stopped to speak with her.

"That one. I want him with us." Rodheimer thrust an arm Chad's direction.

"He is under treatment, Director." She said the words but without conviction, almost as if she realized she had no authority in the Director's presence.

"Under *my care*. This whole facility is under my care. I authorize his treatment, and I am *unauthorizing his treatment*. Bring him. Everyone is to gather in the Lobby." Rodheimer was a black cloud of storm-thrashed weather threatening to inundate the research facility with his fury as he forced his way through the door and disappeared.

The lights in the room buzzed and came up to full strength. Chad caught Garik's eye and raised his deformed eyebrows.

Garik felt he had been yanked by Weston Rodheimer's leash and now had reason to doubt that even Houdini could find his way out of the basement complex of the Corona Tower. They had only managed before with Jantzen's help. Now, he was somewhere in the city, his freedom guaranteed.

What call did he have to help Garik now? And if Weston Rodheimer could be believed, he wouldn't want to. He had used Garik for his escape, and now that he was free, the man would disappear like smoke in the wind.

Purple smoke in the wind, but smoke nonetheless.

Garik's head spun, and he knew if he didn't find some answers soon, it might spin right off, and he'd never find himself again.

CHAD WAS being prepped for additional surgeries. Rodheimer's announcement changed that. His IVs were disconnected, and when Angelica helped him get dressed, his legs were marked with sharpie lines to guide the surgeon.

Clear the floor. If the surgery had been in progress, would they have left the scalpels sticking out, the blood flowing, even as Rodheimer dragged Garik in for his object lesson? Behave, or this is what I'll do to you?

Or had the leader of the project simply known the timing, and he'd organized their visit at the opportune moment? A power play. That seemed more like him.

Hunched into the powered chair and covered with blankets, the merged bat-man became an adroit driver, navigating obstacles like he had them mapped out in his head, nearly clipping corners and barely missing people, but never making a mistake.

Stupid me, Garik realized. Echolocation. Of course, he never collided with anything. The world *was* mapped out for him in his head. No wonder Rodheimer wanted what he had to offer. A spy or soldier who knew within millimeters the exact location of every person and every object that could be a weapon? Even in the dark? Brilliant!

Human hybrids were flooding the main lobby by the time they arrived. Angelica hadn't joined them, and most if not all the participants exhibited some sort of genetic abnormality. Ears, cranium, nose, limb size, coloring, or hair. Many could pass for human, given the correct clothes, but even more would never pass in a face-to-face encounter. Not with wings, true fangs, or skins of scales.

Garik located Marina Bruni, Marisa's older sister. She reminded him of Marisa, until she turned. One half of her was aquatically adapted. On the other side of the room, Hector Mascari scampered in. Garik hated to admit it, but scampered was the only term that described how the man, er, mouse entered the room.

Okay, not a mouse, but more rat than man. He had changed since Garik first met him. Now, he was more rat-like than ever.

The others—well, he didn't know many. The group he'd helped escape, Jantzen had organized his life around them, and there'd been little place for breaking the ice with anyone else.

Now he began to think that maybe he should have. Whatever was going on, nothing like this had occurred since he'd been part of the research facility's team, albeit after being kidnapped and forced to be on the team.

He searched for Van Hermoso, T'Wana Dolalas, Devon Maye, even Leah Fortinier, aka Nurse Ratchett, and Doctor Jimenez. Nowhere. The attendees were a select crew, only those initiated into the human-hybrid program.

Garik suspected this was bigger than he'd bargained for. He didn't want big. He wanted one floor up, the elevator doors opening to the Corona Mall, and he wanted to run as fast as he could, turn the world to rainbows if that's what it took. See ya' lata' Miz Kournikova, I'm outta he-ah.

With the last of the hybrids exiting from the elevators from the lower floors, thick blast shields erupted from the floor, shooting up before every door, effectively sealing them in the lobby. Steel shutters rumbled over the skylights. From the sound, they were blast-proof, also. A stage rose from the center of the room, and from it appeared a metal room etched with designs. The door was sealed with a circular steel handle four feet across, like the hatch on a submarine. It began to unscrew. A door perhaps a meter thick broke free, and out of the darkened space emerged Halo Sunchaser, gleaming in ivory and leather. Her hair was bound at the crown but erupted into a wild cacophony of midnight fireworks, tossing wildly at every move.

The mood of the hybrids fell quiet, a spaceship landing on a foreign world, no one quite sure what was going to happen.

Or maybe they were, Garik allowed, and that was the reason for their silence.

Either way, Rodheimer stepped out, his demeanor blacker than before, as if his anger might erupt into a downdraft that would destroy anyone within range.

They were all within range.

A glass case floated out after them, suspended by some force Garik couldn't see. Magnetics. Wires. Trickery or magic, it didn't matter. The people around him seemed to know exactly what it was. Rodheimer reached a hand, lightning shot forth striking the case, and the lid opened. Sunchaser stepped to it as if performing a ritual, and she lifted a sword by the hilt. The heel of one hand was wedged against the pommel, and the other against the guard. It flashed and gleamed under the lights.

"The sword!" Rodheimer let the words rumble from him, and they flowed across the crowd with a visible ripple, a holy object they all recognized and understood. "Who dares the sword?"

This time, his voice sandblasted his listeners, and all around Garik, eyes fell to look at the ground. Garik wanted to belt out, Marisa, I've seen it! The sword, it's real. You were right all along.

I'm looking at it now!

"Yes, hear it from me. I want there to be no mistake nor misunderstanding. We are minus twelve of our kind. Look around you. See who they are. None are worth your consideration, for all were failures with no opportunity for advancement in our plans. Does anyone not understand?"

"I understand," the hybrids said as one.

It's a cult, Garik muttered, his heart pounding. Are these people brainwashed? Rodheimer had said the participants in the program joined willingly, but this was freaky. Who would behave like this?

"Say it again," Rodheimer demanded.

"I understand." The words came louder.

"Even my second has betrayed us. The outside world will never give us freedom until we force them to bend their knees. The time is coming. Our time is coming. One day, just not yet. The redemption in today's events is that one has returned to us."

Garik looked around for the one of his friends who had escaped with them and returned. Paolo? Joanie? He couldn't see either of them. Before he could cover the rest of the list, he heard his name.

"Garik Shayk, an example for us all."

Garik wanted to sink into himself. He dreamed of Houdini, not being an example for these people. He wanted his freedom, not praise. His goal was to reunite with Marisa, not be separated from her. He was jerked out of his self-examination by an eye-watering flash from the stage and a thunderclap of lightning-laced air.

Electricity—lightning, if you will—linked Rodheimer with the sword Sunchaser held aloft, and it began to glow with a fierce light. Then Rodheimer broke the connection, leaving the sword aglow with energy and power.

"Who else dares to attempt to undermine me? I am the authority over all of this, over all of you. If you think you are different, that you can flee, rethink your plans."

Rodheimer seemed to swell in the brilliance of the sword, one side of his body pulsing with light, and the other bathed in darkness. He reached behind his head, wadded the collar and yoke of his shirt and coat in his fist, and tore them from his body, slinging them to the side. His eyes blazed white and his shoulders and chest were covered with masses of silver-black fur.

"I am the Silverback. This is my domain. Cross me, and the electrified sword will find you!"

Halo Sunchaser let out a yell of triumph, and electricity leaped from the end of the sword and splayed out over the ceiling. It seemed it would never end.

— 12 —

RODHEIMER'S MANIC display of white-eyed and silver-encrusted power was only the outer crust of the deep-fried ball of anger that splattered the hybrids before he was done.

The sword was awesome. Garik admitted that. He admired the pulsing rivulets of power that sprinted across the ceiling, even as the spectacle of the theater playing out around him shocked his grasp of what he thought he knew.

The Silverback. He had been fixated on it, certain it might be him. Perhaps it still was, or would be at some point in the future. Rodheimer's words to him had suggested as much initially. *"You and me, just alike."* Yet Garik didn't think so. At least not yet. There was no way he could shoot electricity from his fingertips, so surely Rodheimer hadn't meant it literally. *"Third generation . . . recognizably human . . . gain their confidence."* That meant intent, desire for power, the love of being different and walking over people because of it. That was how he saw them the same. Yet how had Garik dreamed himself as the silverback? What had sucked him into that black hole and shot him out the silverback wormhole on the other side?

Garik's fog of harsh self-appraisal cleared enough for him to pay attention to several hybrid goons organizing themselves around the outside perimeter of the room. Small groups had begun to clump together, cliques of likeminded individuals, those who had skills or modifications to give them common ground, or maybe they shared goals, like escaping the basement complex, and they wanted the perceived strength that could only come from numbers. Only the outer individuals would get eaten, er, lashed by Sunchaser's sword when things got serious.

True enough, people were cut from the herd, peeled away a person at a time. Sunchaser and Rodheimer flowed from the raised platform into the surrounding sea of people, and the nearest mutant hybrids gave them room, like schooling sardines avoiding a larger, predator species. The smaller group of guilty individuals was banished to the platform, hemmed in by two of the goons.

The sword continued to shimmer and pulse in Sunchaser's hand, although its deadly power no longer crawled along the ceiling. The threat was clear. Hide, and you will be found. Lie, and you will be punished. Plot, and you will be plundered and divvied up to the most deserving recipient.

Chad was the proof of that.

Garik imagined his legs, and he cupped one hand around each thigh. He wanted to keep them. Now was his time to decide the best way to do that. Escape? Both Rodheimer and Chad had sliced that coconut in half, and all the milk inside had drained away with the electrical bath washed over the ceiling by Sunchaser's sword. Cooperation? The very idea curdled in Garik's stomach like eating soured custard on rotted meat.

"Which one will get it?" Chad's voice through his modulated box interrupted Garik's fractured thoughts.

Garik jumped. "Oh, it's you. I thought you would be back in surgery by now."

"No one's leaving till the Director gets his revenge."

"Revenge? What have they done?"

"Plotted, perhaps. Maybe nothing. If he feels crossed, however, someone has to pay."

Oops, Garik thought. I plotted. Hey, I'm still plotting. Can they read minds, too? If so, I'm in for it.

"You worried?" If Chad's electronic voice could chuckle, it would have.

"I did leave and was BolaWrapped." *A second time.* "If he makes anyone pay, it's likely me."

"Nah, that's not Weston. You cross him, or simply don't measure up, and he writes you off. Come back repentant, and he forgives all. I suspect he sees you as repentant. After all, you are back. Good on ya', mate, for finding a way to survive this nightmare without having your legs and arms cut off."

"Yeah, sorry about that. And good on ya'? What does that mean?"

"Aussie. Well done. And you had nothing to do with my punishment, so don't worry about it. Just keep yourself in one piece, whatever price you have to pay. Like the Director says, now's not the time. You wait for it. You'll know when it's time."

"Time for what?" Half-speak. Garik wished people in this facility would spit out what they meant.

"You'll know when the time comes." Chad looked at him hard for a minute before his wheelchair whirred, and he moved away.

On the platform, a tribunal of sorts was in play. A kangaroo court. A mock trial, determined to winnow out a guilty party, even if there wasn't one. That's what Chad had seemed to suggest. Garik tried to hear what was going on, but the volume in the room had gradually increased to an uproar. People were now yelling, some defending, and others accusing. One person was finally separated from the rest, leaving five people huddled together and the other standing alone. Accusations flew, and she didn't try to defend herself. Those in the group of five pleaded, two crying, and one fell to his knees.

Rodheimer and Sunchaser ignored them all. The Director nodded as if a decision had been made, and he turned his back on the lone individual, crossed his arms, and looked over the crowd. At one point, his eyes settled on Garik as if to say, "Watch this, boy. This will happen to you if you don't mind yourself. I'm the Silverback, and in this place my word is law. I carry the power of life and death, and that includes you." Then his eyes moved on.

Garik shivered.

The scene was made worse when Sunchaser let out a yell, aimed the sword at the accused individual, and let its power fly. Electricity leaped from the end, surrounded the unfortunate victim, and seemed to disassemble the person molecule by molecule, atom by atom, until only the light from the sword filled the space. The sword winked off. Finally, the room was silent, with everyone too overwhelmed to speak.

"Payment has been accepted." Rodheimer's words rumbled from him. "The Silverback has spoken."

Sunchaser returned the sword to its glass case, and they returned to the vault-like metal chamber, which began to sink into the floor. The five people remaining on the platform fell at the spot their friend had vanished and wailed in despair.

Around the room, the doors revealed themselves, and the skylights with their views of the black sky overhead blossomed from the ceiling. The human hybrids throughout the room milled around for a time before drifting away through doors and into elevator shafts. The mood had been pancaked by the removal of one of their number, dropping a cloud of blackness over the room.

Garik hadn't known her, but he felt it the same.

"AH, MR. SHAYK."

Garik turned and his world grew blacker. Not Airman Vang. He grimaced and forced politeness from his throat. "Airman Vang."

"I'm looking forward to spending time with you, Mr. Shayk. I am to be your escort to your quarters."

"My quarters . . . and where would that be?" He hadn't considered where he would stay. After spending the afternoon in the Director's penthouse and splitting the evening between the hospital and this gruesome sideshow in the lobby, Garik had expected to be locked into a cell on Level 5, if he was given any leniency at all.

"And where would that be." Vang turned the question into a sneer, more a statement than a simple response to the teen's inquiry. "You tell me, Mr. Shayk. It has only been a day, and you couldn't stay away. You, ahem, *chose* to return of your, ahem, *own volition.* Did you think you would suddenly move to the penthouse with the Director?"

Garik watched the man's mixed message of a face, his eyes more Cambodian than Caucasian, his skin more freckled than fierce, and wondered what the Airman had in for him. His height? Garik now saw that he was an easy half a foot or more taller than the neatly turned-out Airman.

"My old quarters, sure, if you would like." Garik wondered how that had escaped him. If they hadn't cleaned out all his stuff, at least he would have fresh clothes. Still, all that effort to escape, damaging Kevin's van, the disastrous meeting with Marisa, and now a woman dead. And he was back right where he started. "I don't have my passkey any longer."

"You will not need it. I recall the door's locking mechanism has been sliced away. A terrorist act by your fellow terrorist. Pardon, you have been absolved by the Director. Alyna is the likely culprit. If your door won't lock, you won't need a passkey, will you, Mr. Shayk? You can wander in and out at will."

Garik wanted to say, *You can stop calling me Mr. Shayk. That's my father's name.* But he didn't dare. The man was making a point. Garik might have returned, but he had bucked the system, or at least had chosen to flee with those who had, and Vang wasn't giving Garik the benefit of the doubt that he hadn't intended to stay out of the Tower's clutches.

He was a runaway who had gotten caught and was playing to the

Director's soft spot, however Garik had managed to reveal one. Guilty in intent was guilty in fact, even if the Director had praised him before everyone present.

That got Garik thinking. How did Airman Vang know what the Director had said or done with the blast doors in place? There had been no one present except the participants in the human-hybrid program. Someone was revealing his hand, and that someone was Airman Shan Vang.

They used Vang's passkey to take the elevator down a floor. Garik's quarters were a short walk through somber and oppressive spaces that only days before had seemed generous and inviting. After his taste of freedom, Garik wasn't sure he could ever think of the underground research facility as inviting. Prison, no matter how luxurious, was still a prison.

At Garik's quarters, the door was closed but clearly not sealed. One side reflected the claws on Alyna's hands. Garik expected the Airman to accompany him inside, perhaps assign him a guard or, heaven forbid, remain to guard him himself. The thought was worse than mortifying. Instead, the Airman stepped aside and said, "Good night, Mr. Shayk. I will wait until you are inside, so if you don't mind." He motioned with his hand.

Garik pushed through the door and pressed it closed, sealing off Vang and refusing to turn on the lights with the Airman watching. He hit the switch and got a surprise.

"Hey, hey. Lights, please." Someone stretched out on his sofa yanked a blanket over a blond head of hair.

"Devon?" What? Why would the facility's rec planner and coordinator be sleeping on his sofa?

"Yeah. Lights, if you don't mind."

"Of course." Garik hit the switch. "What are you doing here?"

"I'm assigned to be your conjoined twin. I hope you like recreation." Garik heard the man shifting on the sofa, and he was surprised that he could see him sitting up, even in the dark. "So, what went on at the meeting?"

"At the meeting?" Garik groaned. Would he ever stop repeating other people's questions to him?

"You and the weir—er, the program participants. You know, you special people. What do you people do on the main lobby when the walls seal all you off?"

"We weirdos do weird stuff, like play with swords and things.

You know, fireworks. You know what those are?" Garik felt the trauma of the evening boiling over into anger, and he struggled to contain it. Devon wasn't the enemy, and if anything, he considered him a friend. It wasn't fair to take his frustrations out on him.

"I'm sorry. I forget how you hear things, pick up on stuff others can't. Can you see me in the dark, too?"

"Yeah. Start wearing pajamas to bed if you're sleeping on my couch."

"Right-o, kiddo. That's funny." Devon laughed.

"I mean it." Garik's eyes had fully adjusted, and the man had bed hair and wore brightly patterned boxers covered with Christmas trees. "And Christmas isn't for another month. Turkeys are for Thanksgiving."

"For real? They are passing out night vision now? Finally, something useful." Devon fell back onto the couch and kicked the blanket up and over him. "I'll think about it, okay, kiddo? Just leave the lights off when you come through, and we'll get along fine."

That left Garik to question his place in the scheme of this facility that the Director should value his return so highly. He certainly wasn't the next silverback. Rodheimer had clarified that.

That led him to his big question. If Garik wasn't the silverback, then what was he? He didn't have that answer, but as long as he was trapped here, he might as well cooperate long enough to find out. Once he did, Houdini time!

If he could find a way to escape the Tower's clutches once again.

— Book 5 —

TheGlass Siege

— 1 —

GARIK SHAYK opened his eyes, unsure what had awakened him. The soft murmur of air moving through the grille high in the wall overhead lulled him into a pleasant memory: his girlfriend, Marisa Bruni, and sitting together under the stars on the rooftop of their apartment building; the drawing she had created for him on her Micro-Art tablet of an electrified sword; the mesmerizing hold her face had on him.

The memory was shattered by the percussive sounds of the Howling Pterodactyls, the eponymous Rez band of all Rez bands, in concert at the Corona Mall. The driving beat grew louder, and he looked around the room. A glow from under a closed door revealed various pieces of furniture and several additional openings, one showing the brighter gleam of porcelain fixtures. Another one, open and dark, likely a closet.

The driving beat of the Dactyls became a hammer on metal.

"Ah, Arik!" Garik came fully awake with a rush of anger. Arik Oblonsky was his aunt Irina's deadbeat boyfriend, and it was like him to intentionally get on Garik's nerves. He tossed his bedding aside and forced himself to restrain his rising irritation, reminding himself, "Anger gets me nothing. Arik wins if I react. My hands, my mind, the only way." He must be in control of his feelings, or his world would quickly spiral out of his control.

He laid back the door, only to be reminded he wasn't in his aunt's apartment in Bay City any longer. Devon Maye, the activities coordinator for the underground and very secretive human-hybrid project, stood in the small kitchen, *Garik's small kitchen*, in the underground research center under Corona Mall WHERE GARIK HAD BEEN HIJACKED AND IMPRISONED. Joseph Howard and Tyrone Brown, Tower workers he recognized, were head-to-head at the front door, deep in conversation. Garik's memories of Marisa and their time under the stars evaporated, no more than a teasing soap bubble, bright and shiny, and effervescently temporary.

"Right-o, kiddo, about time to wake those sleepy eyes." Devon, physically fit with blond hair and a trademark cowlick at his temple, opened a cupboard door and lifted out two plates. "I've got work today, and you're with me."

"With you?" Garik rubbed his face. "Remind me why you're in my apartment."

"Still doing that, are you? Repeating people?" Devon spooned a pile of eggs onto each plate. From the toaster oven, he pulled out four buttered muffins and nearly dropped one when it was hotter than he expected. "Ouch, ouch. Get it while it's hot."

"Okay." Garik took one of the plates and a fork and found the couch. "I remember you here last night. Refresh my memory."

"I am officially your babysitter." Devon joined him at the opposite end of the couch with a plate of his own. Folded bedding served as his end table. He began to fork in his breakfast.

"Oh, yeah." With the word *babysitter*, Garik's one night of freedom from the secretive basement research complex underneath the forty-story Corona Tower glass skyscraper unfolded before him. Months before, his life had been usurped when he was forcibly inducted into the human-hybrid project and injected with timber wolf DNA in the hope that he would mutate into a military tool with precog abilities. Jantzen Hefferly, able to morph into a cloud of purple mist, had enabled Garik and twelve other human hybrids to escape the Tower's clutches. Foolishly—although he hadn't thought so at the time—Garik had tried to reconnect with his girlfriend, Marisa, and had gotten himself recaptured. Now, weeks of planning were lost, and as a final insult, the previous evening, he had watched a woman be sucked into a bolt of supercharged lightning discharged by the tip of Halo Sunchaser's electrified sword. Weston Rodheimer bleeding electricity from his fingertips to charge the sword with crackling energy, then the glowing weapon eating the woman molecule by molecule, atom by atom, electron by electron, sucked away Garik's appetite like a whirlpool in a bottomless pit, and he set his plate on the floor, no longer interested.

"Eat up, kiddo. We've got a busy day." Devon had polished his plate, and he called to the workers at the door, "Joseph, Tyrone, I've got more if you're hungry."

Garik glanced their direction. Joseph and Tyrone were with maintenance and had installed Garik's ZBoard motorized skateboard charging station in his original quarters and later moved it to this one. It was still there, off to one side, blinking, telling him it was fully charged and ready to ride.

"Already eaten, but thanks. This door, don't think it's getting fixed today or tomorrow, likely. Custom build, need to order in panels to skin the damage. We'll be taking it away."

"How will we have any privacy?" Devon lifted one eyebrow.

We? Garik sagged. The truth of his situation hit him like a jackhammer. Devon's bed was Garik's couch. Devon had said babysitter but jailer was closer to the truth. And the damaged door, something else that was Garik's responsibility, a knife into his morning. Alyna Lindberg, DNA-enhanced with a Komodo dragon, had used her retractable claws to override the locking mechanism by slicing the door to shreds.

Devon stood, his plate empty, and took in Garik's uneaten food. He tapped the plate with the toe of one shoe. "Eat up, kiddo. Gonna be mighty hungry by lunch."

"Yah," Garik muttered, trying to push away the image of the girl that had gotten eaten by the electrified sword. His stomach was upside down.

"Seriously, you're mine, now, and I need to get out of here. Scoot, scoot."

"Yah, yah."

"And some clothes, kiddo. You chewed on me last night. I'm chewing on you, now." Devon was in the small kitchen, and he dropped his plate in the sink and flipped on the water.

Garik snorted, but the man was right. He needed to dress, and he stood, set the plate uneaten on the counter, and made his way to the bathroom. He leaned into the mirror, looking into his eyes. His friend, Muhammad Saud, had said his eyes were different. How? He couldn't find it. And the rest of him. No extra-long canines. No fur sprouting along his backbone. Even his hair. It was starting to curl again, and he had missed that. He was becoming the old Garik, lean and tight, if a bit bulkier from his training. That was a good thing, and he didn't mind that at all.

He yelled to Devon, "What are we doing this morning? I need to know what to wear."

"Training. It's what I do. Have you forgotten?"

"I don't follow you around all day." Sheesh! What did the man expect, for him to memorize his daily schedule?

"You are today." Devon leaned around the door frame from the living room, and he shook his head. He turned away, muttering, "It must be a teen thing."

"What?" How had he screwed up this time?

"You weren't supposed to hear that." Devon had his wrist up, his watch exposed, and he was prepared to tap the face with one finger.

"I can't help it you talk so loud. What's a teen thing? And what's wrong with being a teen? Am I supposed to act like an old man like you?"

"Hey!" Devon stepped into the bedroom. "That's unfair. You admiring yourself in the mirror all the time. Put on a shirt and comfortable shoes. I'm trying to get you new quarters, someplace with a real door. I want you ready when I'm off the phone."

Devon tapped his watch as he disappeared back to the main part of the apartment. "Lt. Shoate, please."

"Why not your place, then," Garik began to rant to himself, as he entered the closet and began pulling clothes off the racks and yanking them on. "Yah, Mr. Recreation Coordinator, or is your place too good for the hybrid wolf boy? You can come here, but I can't go there. Is that how it is? I've lived that life, don't like it, don't want to do it anymore. Sheesh! Quit treating me like a little boy—"

Garik dropped onto his bed to put on his shoes and looked up to Devon standing in the door with his arms crossed.

"I'll quit treating you like a boy when you quit acting like one."

"Yah, blame your life on me." Garik's anger boiled.

Still, the man's words hit home, and equally fast, remorse washed over him. He looked away and blinked his eyes to clear them. Yesterday morning he had been free, wandering the city, looking forward to meeting Marisa, telling her how much he had missed

288

her. And now, now, this!

"Wasn't trying to."

Garik looked up and studied the man's face, trying to find some-one he could trust in his eyes.

"My apologies for pushing you. Remember last night? Me on your couch? Not fun. Now, no door. Less fun. That's what I was on the phone about."

"The door's getting fixed?"

"Better, kiddo." Devon grinned. "We normal people can hear, too. Lt. Shoate better than most, and she liked your idea."

"My idea?" My idea? Yikes, doing it again, repeating other peo-ple's words, but Devon didn't seem to notice, for which he was grateful.

"Let me grab my things—" The blond-haired man with the odd cowlick was already moving. "—cause time is tight to do this. And I want to do it."

Garik had his shoes on, and he followed Devon into the other room. Joseph and Tyrone were gone—and the door with them—leaving a gaping wound in one wall. Outside, life was beginning to stir, people heading to the cafeteria via one of the elevators, or others carrying training equipment, readying for a morning of honing their skills in the hope of not being designated as "Level 5" material. The whine of a floor polisher bled in, and for some reason it caught Garik's attention. He'd not considered that, that regular cleaning crews had to do regular cleaning on a regular basis.

Life goes on for some people, even when his didn't. The realiza-tion fed his frustration. His earlier remorse evaporated, and he burst out, "Stop it, stop it, stop it!"

Devon had been loading a leather gym bag, and he dropped a pair of socks inside and stood. He cocked his head and fought a smile. "Okay, go on, kiddo."

"It's just that—" Garik felt himself getting louder, and outside the door, he could see the floor polisher. It was finally silent, and the man running it was winding the power cord. He looked Garik's di-rection, and they locked eyes before the man glanced away and turned his back. Garik fought to control the volume of his emotions as they began to erupt from him into more than he had meant to say. "Nobody tells me anything. I'm right here. A person, not an experi-ment. You can't just lock me away and expect me to follow along on your leash like a good puppy. If you don't want me, give me to someone who does. Airman Han, what happened to him? He's the only one in this whole place who's even nice to me, and you people stick me with Shan Vang. The man hates me. I'm done with you people."

"Hey, hey, I'm not you people. I can't do anything about the leash, but I don't expect you to be a good puppy. A big bad wolf is more like it. Huff, puff, blow the house down?"

Garik smiled despite his irritation.

"Better, kiddo. You're right. Here's the deal. I've got an extra room in my place in Corona City—well, my office, but it's got a door. Shoate says we can bunk there since your door is toast. I want to get moved. She might change her mind." He winked. "I appreciate your couch, but face it. It's not my dream digs. And I'll try to keep you part of the conversation. Deal?"

"Okay. Do I get a bed?" An office . . . it didn't sound like it.

"If you're a good puppy."

Garik frowned and saw Devon break into a smile.

"Gotcha! Already done. Shoate's having a bed delivered some-time today. You get to set it up, though."

"Can I take my ZBoard?" It was the only thing he owned, even if it really belonged to the Tower.

Devon looked at the unit, as if seeing it for the first time. He nodded. "You ride it, and I'll call Joseph to get the charger delivered. But we've got to move. Now."

Finally! Garik slipped it from the charging station, turned it on, and dropped it to the floor. Devon already had his bag over his shoulder, and Garik followed him out the door.

To discover what, he wasn't entirely sure.

— 2 —

THE SCHEDULE for the morning fell apart two turns in.

Passing the emergency clinic and swinging by the recreation ar-ea for Devon to access the latest updates on his morning assign-ments, they were accosted by two human hybrids making their way to the clinic. The first was Stephen Klandermans, a man with wide shoulders, kinky blond hair in wiry dreads, and amused gray eyes. His clothes were a tumble of well-worn fabrics with frayed edges. He was helping Ineke Van Stekelenburg, a tall, slender woman with dark hair and small eyes, who held one arm cradled in the other. She wore an aloof expression creased with pain.

Stephen flashed a bright smile, easy and natural, and he called, "Hey, Dev. See you've got the little jail-breaker along for a ride."

"Party-hardy, Stephen," Devon returned. "What's with Ineke?"

Jail-breaker? Garik swelled up. And what was with the woman? She looked as though she could burn a hole in his brain. Perhaps she could. He'd seen weirder things in Corona Tower's basement research complex.

"The thing wrong with Ineke is Stephen." Ineke overenunciated, as though making a point with her speaking style. As though no one else would understand if she didn't explain it in the simplest terms.

"Me, yah!" Stephen laughed and waved one hand in the air. "I did a somersault, showing off, and, um, well, I didn't know—"

"He hit my arm and we must visit the clinic for a splint. I will likely not attend my session tomorrow, Devon. I apologize in advance." Ineke nodded to him.

"Not my fault, not really. You were in my way, Ineke. Promise, Dev." His face said he found this amusing, and he turned to Garik. "And I want to hear all about your time outside, little guy. Last night, the big man had good things to say about you. And I like the skaterboard." He nodded to Garik with a grin before making soothing sounds to Ineke and continuing past them towards the emergency clinic.

"Jail-breaker?" That and skaterboard. Garik stepped from the ZBoard, lifted the end and balanced it at his side. The word reminded him of Arik, rancid in his memory.

"Come on, kiddo. I don't know what was said in the meeting, 'cause us ordinary people aren't allowed, but do you really think no one tracked you and your cadre of late-night escapees all day yesterday? Me, I'm not allowed an opinion. I'm not one of you, but for everyone else, you were the entertainment of the day."

"Sheesh." Garik had to stop himself from lashing out in frustration. If he had been the entertainment of the day, that changed his relationship to everyone he saw in the corridors. He might not know them, but they likely knew him and everything that had happened to him—and was likely the reason Rodheimer hadn't felt it necessary to explain who Garik was last night when he praised him. He also expected they all had an opinion of him they would love to share. Great! He was looking forward to that!

"Okay, since we're good on that, let me pull my updates to see what hasn't been uploaded to the Tower's net." Devon pulled several sheets of paper from a message box and laid them on a counter. He began entering the changes into his watch.

Garik observed him without really seeing what he was doing, instead picturing John Carter's black-faced watch the night they were escaping. *The night they were escaping*—it was only the night before last. It seemed days and weeks, and Garik immensely missed those he had bonded with during his bid for freedom. His concern for them battled with his dismay that he was back in the basement complex and had a jailer assigned to him full time, and he forced himself to shake off the feeling. It didn't benefit him now, and he refocused on how anyone down here could know about his time outside. John Carter's watch had only accessed the real Internet once they were outside the basement complex. The Tower wouldn't post updates, not on the Tower's internal net, at least not until they were sure he had been recaptured, and even then, what about the twelve people still on the outside? That wasn't something the Tower would want widely known. It would come across as a failure, and who wants people tagging and following their failures?

So, how was it possible that people had followed his escape, and more depressingly, his recapture?

Devon had returned the papers and picked up his bag. Two people with similar facial structures came running toward them.

"Jacquelien, Bert." Devon greeted them, as if he expected them to continue by.

Instead, they stopped, glanced at Garik and nodded as if they knew him, and the woman placed a hand on Devon's arm. She boasted a red line tattooed from her widow's peak down her nose, past her lips, along her chin and neck, and disappearing into her shirt. When she opened her mouth to speak, the red line broke for the first time.

"Devon, it's—"

"—Ineke." The man finished her sentence. He wore his hair shaved over his right ear, and it tumbled into a bristly waterfall on the left. Black tatts across his upper torso moved underneath a long-sleeved black shirt made mostly of netting. His chocolate jaw sported a darker shadow of bristly black.

"I just spoke with her and Stephen."

"And we all know—"

"—Stephen."

292

Garik looked from one to the other and tried to figure out the pair. They talked over one another, finishing one another's sentences, as though it were natural to them. They couldn't be twins. She was blonde as Devon, and he was breakfast cocoa. Yet, they looked similar. Same DNA source? What other possibility was there? Did the looniness in this place never end?

"And we want you—"

"—to come with us."

"An injury report. You can—"

"—shortcut the red tape."

"If you have—"

"—the time, of course."

Garik's head spun. Did they have their brains linked? Was this a DNA-hybrid experiment in telepathy or something? A voice from around the corner called, "Bert? Ineke with you?"

Bert called, "Nah, Veronika! At the clinic. But the amazing escape artist is here! Let everyone know!" He grinned at Garik.

"As for going with you, I'm baby—" Devon cut off his word and glanced at Garik. "I have Garik with me today. I can't leave him. Sorry."

Babysitting! How could Devon say that? It might be true, but it sounded so childish! Jailer was more accurate, though he supposed it would be equally irritating. And, who was Veronika? She remained a voice only.

"Bring him—" Bert winked.

"—with you. Lansana is—" Jacquelien added.

"—meeting us there." Bert nodded in collusion.

Devon glanced at his watch, tapped it, and took a deep breath, thinking, and released it. "I've got Paul on my schedule. I can come, but I won't have long."

"As long as you need." A new voice, deeper, and a man—a woman?—appeared out of the wall next to Jacquelien and Bert, almost as if his/her skin had taken on the texture and color of the background surface and then had decided to look human once more. Large lips and dusky skin seemed eminently feminine, but the voice said otherwise. After a moment, beaded clothes in bright South African colors and patterns flickered into substance around him.

"How did you, um," Garik shivered, "do that?"

"You must be Garik." The man laughed, revealing gold letters inset into his front two teeth. "Paul Gberie. You didn't see me last night at the meeting. Obviously." He winked at his joke. "How did you escape from the Tower's dungeon?"

"Um, but you, you weren't here a few moments ago!"

"Of course I was here. You should be asking why you couldn't see me. And Devon, consider this my session with you. I also want to know Ineke's tale. Or is it tail?"

Paul began to laugh uproariously, and the other three rolled their eyes and shook their heads.

Garik had missed something. The man, invisible or not . . . he should have been able to hear him approach. Even invisible people made noise when they moved. He wondered how long before Paul disappeared again. And if he would be able to track him by listening when he did.

STEPHEN WAS taping Ineke's arm into a splint when Garik and Devon entered the emergency clinic. Stephen was cracking a joke about Humpty Dumpty, and Ineke tried to silence him with a bored expression and her eyes on a light fixture on the ceiling.

"Not working, Ineke?" Devon chuckled.

"Don't start," she growled, her face pale with pain.

As Stephen finished up the job, an infusion of new people was a tidal wave sweeping Garik along with each introduction, whether formal or contextual.

Lansana was Lansana Opoku-Mensa, wearing patterned scarification on her face in a double line circling each eye and running up her forehead. Her head was shaved and balanced on a neck too long to seem real. She stepped in, nodded to each person present— including Garik—but didn't speak. She seemed to be evaluating the situation, a smart move, in Garik's eyes.

Jacquelien and Bert were Jacquelien Van Kessel and Bert Ellis. They were so interwoven that even their actions seemed coordinated. One would move, and the other completed the motion, just as when they had been talking earlier in the corridor.

Veronika Abbink entranced Garik. Not like love, but like a beautiful sunset that was too astounding to comprehend. Oversized earrings draped from her ears, and her teeth commanded her face when she smiled, but that wasn't what fascinated him. Nor were her messenger bag and the bright, neon colors she covered herself with. Her skin seemed to reflect the hue of whatever she was near, at one point changing before Garik's eyes so subtly he might not have noticed if he wasn't looking.

Benjamin Fuest was quite ordinary, and Garik doubted he was modified. A scraggly beard enclosing a small mouth, large forehead, and heavy eyebrows . . . but his face lit up when he smiled, changing him completely.

The final person to join them introduced himself to Garik with a precise offering of his hand. Zekeria Salem. He looked fourteen, with bowl-cut hair and brown eyes. At first glance, Garik thought he saw through what looked like posturing. Then Zekeria turned his head to reveal a crisp profile, and he smiled to bring the picture to photographic perfection. Immediately, Garik understood. Zekeria knew how to present himself for the best impression. A learned skill or DNA-based, he had no idea, but it worked. Zekeria sealed the connection by saying, "I am Zekeria. I'm sorry that we all know you and you know none of us. Please be patient. We're not as weird as we seem."

You may not be, Garik thought. The rest? He had them pinned perfectly. Weird was the word. He hadn't felt inclined to give them any leeway, but Zekeria's words worked their magic on him, and he smiled back.

"Thank you. There's one thing I'd like to know. How was everyone able to follow my escape—"

Garik didn't get to finish his question. Ineke slumped in her chair, and before Stephen could stop her, she slipped through his hands and tumbled to the floor, hitting her head and spraying blood across the tile.

"I said this was a bad idea. Hospital, I said. No one listens to me." Benjamin twisted his hands and looked out the door.

Paul shrugged, and as if by magic, took on the texture and color of the wall behind him. A moment later, his beaded outfit seemed to twinkle, and it shimmered into nothingness.

"Oh, Ineke. Everyone, we need to coordinate, get Ineke to the hospital. Can someone get a gurney to carry her?" Veronika knelt by Ineke, and soon others joined her, and the injured woman vanished from view. "Girlfriend, we've got you covered. We're with you."

Zekeria puffed out his cheeks. "Let me think. Ineke down. This might not look good for Stephen. Bert and Jacquelien, you have your passkeys back?"

Back. Garik understood. They had been punished for something. Still, the woman was just lying there. He could carry her. Before he could offer, the situation changed.

"Ah, my little South African team." Weston Rodheimer, surprisingly quiet for such a large man, startled Garik. "There you are, Devon. How is your new companion behaving? I hear you are transferring quarters."

Garik swallowed hard. Transferring to Devon's place, and in a rush so no one would stop them. Was Rodheimer angry or pleased? Was it his time to face the electrified sword?

His tried to steady his nerves, but they were running down his back in cold rivulets of tingling sweat, and it was too late to recall them.

— 3 —

DEVON PALMED his door. When it unlocked, he removed his passkey and stepped through.

Watching, Garik recalled Marisa using Halo Sunchaser's passkey the night before Garik was forced into the human-hybrid project. They had learned that a fresh palm scanner update was required every three hours. Garik's passkey—*the one he used to have*—hadn't required him to use the palm scanners. It also hadn't allowed him access to the elevators that would take him up into the daylight of the real world, so that explained that.

During their interaction with the Director, he had been certain that the big man would confiscate all their passkeys, but Rodheimer, surprisingly, had been less brutal than expected. Near to friendly, at least toward Garik, asking about the reasons they were moving to Devon's quarters and offering to speak to Joseph Howard to see if the repairs to Garik's door could be optimized in any way. Devon had mentioned Lt. Shoate's connection, and the Director had paused and asked, "Lt. June Shoate?" At Devon's nod, he said, "I will make a point to offer my appreciation for her initiative in handling this," before he ran his eyes over each person crowded into the emergency clinic and vanished.

Garik was certain each of the people with him had felt the big man looking into their souls to see if they qualified for continued existence in the human-hybrid project, or if he should sic Halo Sunchaser on them now and end their paltry lives before they sank any lower into banal and useless debasement.

Devon dropped his bag onto a nubby textured couch, and he

dropped beside it, his legs splayed and his head back. "Whew, thought I was gonna be toast there."

"You should have been at the party last night." Garik's back still crawled with wet, and his heart hadn't settled yet. "My room?"

"There." Devon pointed to the back of the kitchen. A door revealed a darkened cavern. "There's no bed, yet, and I'll need to make space for you, but it's yours. Check it out if you want."

Garik wanted. After Bert and Jacquelien had returned with a gurney and Ineke was trundled off to the elevator to head two floors down to the hospital, Devon had excused the two of them, and they had worked their way through the various corridors leading to Corona City. Windows mocked the illusion of inside and out, a pretense that was as near to aboveground as the underground facility offered, with two parks, a pool that looked like it was outside, and wide streets planted with shrubs and flowers. The closer they got, the more ordinary the people looked, office workers, scientists who had come from abroad to work in the research program, and people like Devon who weren't hybridized but were necessary to work with those who were. Garik stood his ZBoard just inside the door to the apartment and stepped past the small kitchen.

"You live here all the time?"

"Free lodgings, so sure. Why?"

"No reason, just that not everyone does, right?" The underground parking garage. It was huge. Someone had to be parking in all those spaces. There were the people who lived in the Tower, but they had the parking garage above ground.

"Not everyone." Devon's eyes were still closed.

"Okay. You can leave when you want, though, right?"

"If I want."

"Okay," Garik repeated. He hit the switch and light filled the room. A chair, a small desk, and a computer. A bookshelf with a few pictures, one of a pretty blonde woman in ski gear, and Garik remembered Devon telling him about his mother. Another photo of her revealed a ski slope in the background with an Olympic logo to the side. "Your mother was pretty."

"Thanks. I'll put all that away for you. You can set out what you want." Devon had come up behind him and tapped him on the shoulder to let him around.

"Sure." Garik moved aside as Devon stepped inside, and the blond man opened a box and took out a medal. He held it out for

Garik to take.

"Silver for ski jumping. I was just a kid, but I remember how proud she was of that."

"You can leave it out. Everything, actually. I don't have anything to bring with me." Garik stroked the raised image with his fingers before handing it back. "How long till your next session? I'm hungry."

"I said you should have eaten, kiddo." Devon grasped the back of Garik's neck, ran his hand up to tousle his hair, and grinned. "But yeah, raid the fridge. There's likely something in there."

Devon disappeared, and soon, Garik could hear a shower running. He turned back to the kitchen and the living room. Devon had carried his bag into wherever he was, although with the running water, that was obvious. A door across the entry revealed a bed—Devon's room—and a closed door leaking the sound of the water. Was there a second bathroom? Unlikely. He could wait.

Passing the entry door, he tried the handle to see if it would open. Locked. He should have known. At the window, he lifted a blind. At least it was real. Outside, a woman in a nurse's smock walked confidently by, and after a moment, two men, one laughing at something the other one said.

Garik dropped onto the couch, at the opposite end from where Devon had been, and he looked around. A television and a gaming unit. He leaned his head back and closed his eyes.

What was happening *out there*? That's what he wanted to know. What about his friends, Jantzen and Paolo and Joanie and all the rest? How was Marisa? She had said she missed him, too. She wouldn't have betrayed him without a good reason. No way. And Leigh, Laura, and John. Justin, with his new wings, out and flying over the city. Garik would like wings about now, to fly away from this place. He would wait until an event on the mall, then rip off his shirt and fly away, all the way away till no one knew where he was.

He couldn't, and his eyes burned. He was part wolf, and what could a wolf do? He wasn't even turning into anything special. Jantzen, purple mist. Paolo, steaming jets of water from his fingertips. Joanie, well, no one could prove she could come back to life, but still, better than nothing.

Thanks, Director. I'm a dud and it's all your fault.

Something dinged, and Garik felt between the cushions. He pulled out a MicroArt tablet. It had a message on the screen.

"Hey, Dev. My dad's in for an emergency treatment. I need a ride to the hospital at lunch. See you out front. Have you logged into your social media? Check out this link."

Garik immediately knew. This device had full access to the outside world. He looked toward Devon's room and could still hear the shower. He had to do this now. He stood, moved toward his new room, and inside, he closed the door. He clicked and enlarged the image playing on the screen and his heart began to pound.

There he was, running along Avenue C, with the Cowden Street overpass just in front of him. The light changed, and he was off. The image jittered and changed perspective, likely drone footage, then zeroed in on Garik just as a uniformed man fired a BolaWrap his direction, and down Garik went, hard on the pavement. His newly acquired sunglasses skittered sideways, and his head hit the pavement once, then twice, and he lay still.

Garik felt jittery, his movements jerky, a puppet of his nerves as he returned to the couch and replaced the device where he found it. He had to get control so Devon didn't suspect what he knew. Of course, there was a link to the outside. Just that not everyone could access it, meaning not Garik, except . . . he had, even if he wasn't supposed to. It made sense now that he thought about it. Devon wasn't part of the program, not one of the hybridized humans being experimented on to force them to be something no human was designed to be. Devon could come and go when he wanted. Of course, he could link to information beyond the concrete and steel walls that kept the hybrids safely imprisoned in their subterranean depths.

Who else, he wondered? If only he could contact Airman Han. They had a connection, his Street Strider. He was certain the man would help him if he could.

Devon appeared, his blond hair wet and glistening, his cowlick as energetic as ever, and a towel wrapped around his waist.

"Did you eat, kiddo?" He pulled a juice box from the fridge, poked it with a straw and sucked on it.

"About to." The Internet, he wanted to say. What's happening out there? His heart pounded at the thought he might lose the meager access he'd just viewed. He hoped Devon didn't remember the device, say, "Oh, I forgot to put this away," and lock him out.

Garik moved in front of the couch and willed Devon not to look.

"A banana. I eat healthy, so I always have fruit. Have one." Devon broke one off and held it out.

"Thanks." Garik took it and began to peel it, all the time hiding the device in the couch, pleading with Devon to not remember it was there. The fruit was a hard lump in his throat, and it felt it wanted to come back up.

"You feeling okay?" He tossed his empty box in the trash.

"I'm fine." Garik forced a smile and dropped onto the couch. The MicroArt tablet cut into his back, and he forced himself to relax. "Just wanting to get out there and see what we're doing today. I'm excited to see what you teach some of the other participants."

"That's the attitude." Devon winked and made a quick fist and released it. "I knew you'd come around. Okay, kiddo, you wait right there, and I'll toss on some clothes. Got so much planned today, your eyes'll be spinning by the time we get back."

"Leave me energy enough to put my bed together!" Garik scrunched one side of his face into a return wink and held out a hand with his thumb raised. "Don't want to sleep on your couch tonight."

"Right-o, kiddo. I got'cha there." Devon grinned and disappeared into the bedroom, this time closing off the room from view.

Garik reached behind him and pulled out the tablet. He didn't power on the screen, just looked at it longingly and stroked it along one edge. *Marisa,* he thought. Everyone else he knew, too, but Marisa was most on his mind. He heard the door across the room, and he slipped the tablet under the couch and stood.

"Riding the board?" Devon was gathering his things and slipping them in various pockets. His fanny pack was bulging and off to the side. He nodded at the ZBoard.

"Sure." Garik shrugged. The board connected him to who he used to be, even if he would have laughed at it before his induction into the Tower's basement world.

"Will it need a charge? Joseph and Tyrone can't get the charger here before the afternoon." The fanny pack was going on, and Devon glanced around the room as he adjusted it.

"Not unless we're going more than twenty miles. Are we?"

"No. Downstairs to the training cells." Devon unzipped his fanny pack and began looking through it.

"Leave someone's shoes out?" Garik threw it out like a joke, remembering the first time they'd met, and Devon had pulled out a pair of climbing shoes for him to use.

"I have a tablet. I was using it before I was sent to your place . . . anyway, it's gone missing. It has an app for messaging that I use.

300

Have you seen it?"

"Let me look." Garik turned in a full circle, making a show of taking in every surface, and shrugged. "What does it look like?"

"The size of my hand." He spread his fingers wide to approximate the MicroArt tablet now under the couch. "Not to worry. I can survive without it. I have my watch, after all." Devon held up one arm, stretched his hand until his watch appeared out of his sleeve, and grinned.

"Then I'm not worrying. Here, I've got the door. You look like your hands are full." Garik could hardly keep his eyes from the couch. He wanted to look so badly, just to reassure himself the tablet couldn't be seen.

"Not too full for this." Devon worked out his passkey from a small pocket and held it out. "Insert that for me, and I'll take care of the scanner."

Garik slipped it in the panel and stepped aside. Devon pressed his hand to the sensor, and an internal light traveled from top to bottom and back again. The door unlocked, thump, thump, a sound Garik had grown familiar with, and he removed the key and offered it back to Devon, who nodded in thanks and made it disappear.

Three hours. Three hours before Devon's key would require his palm to be scanned again. Garik wondered if that applied to any door the key worked. When Marisa had used Halo Sunchaser's stolen key, it had given them three hours of freedom to explore every door they wished, including the one in the main elevator that led from Corona Tower directly into the forbidden basements. If the passkeys would lead them down, it likely would allow them back up again.

As they exited the apartment onto the brightly normal street that was really a spacious corridor, Garik's attention was focused a hundred percent on Devon's pocket, hoping, just hoping that the key would fall out, he could scoop it up, and he could Houdini this place once more. Then the wheel of his ZBoard caught a small curb encircling a border of planted and well-tended zinnias, and Garik nearly went down. Devon glanced at him, but he was preoccupied with checking his watch, and when he saw Garik had recovered, he nodded his approval and returned to his watch.

Outside, outside, outside. Garik could hardly think of anything else, even to pay attention to where he was riding. He separated his thoughts into now and wish. Devon's passkey would be best, even as he accepted the unlikely possibility of it falling from the man's pocket. The tablet, however, that was real. He had watched drone footage of his capture. He was out there, on the net, and that meant someone knew he was here, or at least that he had been in the city, and now he was vanished. Not had vanished, but was vanished, as in wiped from the city clean as a whistle.

It's all lies, he wanted to shout. I didn't go anywhere. I should be in class at Bay City High with my friends, getting fries on the mall, visiting with Marisa under the stars on the roof of our apartment building. Weston Rodheimer and his goons had stolen that from him, and he'd received nothing in return.

Except a shaved head, now thankfully regrown. And he'd met some new friends, but that didn't change things.

He sent a silent message to everyone in the city, "I'm here! Under your feet! Look hard enough, and you'll find me!"

Then Devon inserted his passkey into the main elevator, the door dinged, and it opened wide.

"You, first." Devon smiled as if Garik had a choice.

"Thank you." Garik stepped inside. *Play by the book, part of the pack. It's the only way to escape the game.*

The door dinged and closed, crushing Garik's hopes, and the car began to move downward.

Garik gave himself up to what he couldn't control, and despair drained the light from around him.

— 4 —

THE CRYPTIC text on the MicroArt tablet was forgotten in the onslaught of Devon's first training session.

The door to the training cell began to swing shut as Devon dropped his things—including his fanny pack—on a sturdy metal table and took quick steps across the room to a row of lockers. The door latched with the metallic double thump of steel locking steel, and a green light just above it winked on.

Silence numbed every auditory sensation.

"What's with the—" Garik cut himself off, perplexed. He could barely hear himself speak. He yelled to Devon, "What's with the sound?"

"Active sound absorption. The sessions can get loud." Devon yelled back, and still, he sounded two blocks away. "Wait right there. We can talk in a minute."

Garik became aware of the textured surfaces of the walls. Part of the active sound absorption. Devon returned and set a case on the table. Inside gleamed several weapons, including two knives, two air pistols, and the glinting steel of a finely honed sword.

"Swordplay?" Garik's voice had a dull, closed-in sound, like his words were trapped and unable to escape more than a few inches from his face.

"Of a sort." Devon's voice was equally flat, caged to the space just around his head.

The door vibrated, thunk, thunk, and opened. The ambient sounds around them brightened, became real again. The green light above the door turned red. Garik got it. With the door open, the active sound absorption stopped. Closed, it was on. Lansana Opoku-Mensah with her shaved head and scarification around her eyes stepped through. She swiveled her head left, then right, evaluating the room, even though she had likely been here multiple times.

She tilted her head on her long neck. "Garik. Are we ready to start, Devon?"

Devon didn't answer. Instead, he lifted one of the knives, flipped it in his hand to grasp the blade, and flung it hard at Lansana. She ducked just before the blade of the knife buried itself in the wall.

"What—" Garik sputtered, but before he could say more, Lansana interrupted him with a grin.

"Faster. I'm better than that."

"Dodge this, kiddo!" Devon had the other knife and flipped it across the room. Lansana had already started to move before the knife left his hand, and he aimed where she was heading, not where she was. The knife lunged for her as if seeking her flesh with a mind of its own.

Garik instinctively moved—to do what, he didn't know—and rainbows began to shimmer around each item in the room. Lansana and the knife slowed to a crawl, and Devon held aloft a frozen hand to stop Garik from interfering. Garik leaped across the training cell, covering nearly twelve feet in a single burst. Twisting his body, he hit the hilt of the knife with his elbow, sending it skewing to the side and spinning through the air.

Garik landed in a heap on the far side of the room. The rainbows disappeared, the knife clattered to a stop on the floor, Lansana looked from Garik to the knife, and Devon still held out his hand to prevent Garik from interfering.

"Whoa!" Devon's eyes went wide. "What was that, kiddo?"

"I'm cold." Garik burned with the ice surrounding him. The muted sound in the room made him feel even colder. He was surprised to see his skin wasn't frosted with crystals. "I think I should have eaten more than a banana for breakfast."

"Timber wolf. Very fast. My turn. Devon? The guns, next?" Lansana had evaluated the situation, determined that everyone was okay, and was ready to resume her session.

"Why are you trying to kill her?" Garik tried to stand, and he made it to his knees, breathing hard.

"Can't." Devon lifted one of the guns and, before Garik could react, released a pellet that caught Lansana directly in the shoulder. She twisted, hitting the wall with the impacted shoulder, only to straighten and say, "Again."

"How—" No blood! How could that be?

"Lansana's armored." Devon grinned like a schoolboy, the cowlick at his temple adding to the image. "Pangolin DNA. Armored anteater. Watch."

Lansana leaped, and Devon chased her with his pellets, impacting about a quarter of the time. She seemed to brush off each impact as if it were an insect bite.

Garik's eyes followed the interplay, and when they were finished showing off, he called, "The knife. You can't tell me that wouldn't have done damage."

Lansana looked hard at Devon, and the man dove for the knife on the floor and flung it her direction. She didn't try to dodge this time. She hit the incoming blade with her fist, sending it clattering Garik's direction. When it stopped spinning on the floor, he looked at it to see the blade crumpled along the cutting edge.

Then Devon's watch chimed, a tiny *chink* with the active sound dampening, and he said, "Excuse me while I take this." He slipped an earbud into one ear and tapped the watch before turning away to take the call.

Lansana offered Garik a hand to stand. It was the one she had used to bat away the knife. There was no damage to her skin at all.

Garik smiled in thanks and let her pull him to his feet. At least he could finally stand, even if he didn't understand everything. He guessed it was time to accept that likely he never would.

MOMENTS LATER, Devon grabbed his fanny pack, made a beeline

to the door, inserted his passkey, and released the seal. The light above the door turned red, and real sound returned.

"Apologies, Lansana. I've got to be somewhere. We can re-schedule. Garik, kiddo, tuck in and follow me."

Garik found he could barely wobble. He wasn't sure about the rainbow thing, but each time it happened, it walloped his stamina. He waved to Lansana and focused on keeping up. Devon seemed in an unaccountable rush.

"I knew I should have searched harder for my tablet," the rec director called from down the corridor.

Garik dropped his skateboard to the floor and pictured the tablet on the floor under the couch. He remembered the message. *I need a ride to the hospital at lunch.* Maybe he should have revealed it, but he needed it to access the Internet. The tablet had shown him the unexpected bonus of the video footage. Outside! How could he give up that possibility?

"So, where are we going?" Garik had caught up, thanks to the ZBoard, and he slowed to match Devon's rapid pace.

"An acquaintance from the Tower. Do you know Gunther Diehl?"

"Sure, the concierge. We've met."

"I thought so. He matched me up with a resident—"

"From Stamford Suites, right?"

"Right-o, kiddo." Devon looked surprised. "This resident needs coverage sometimes, and being from out of town . . ." Devon shrugged, and he inserted his passkey in the elevator access panel. "The extra cash money doesn't hurt."

"Yeah. I've done that." Garik had grown up poor—and still was, as he had no money at all, now—and he understood taking on extra jobs when they were available. "What do you have to do for him?"

The elevator doors closed, and Devon seemed to see Garik for the first time since leaving the training cell. He hit his forehead with the heel of his hand. "Oh, man, how did I not think of this?"

"What?"

"You." Devon let out a hard breath.

It clicked for Garik. *Ride to the hospital. See you out front.* This was perfect.

"I can stay in your apartment. I won't mess with any of your things, and I can't get in any trouble." The tablet. Locked in, he would have all the time he wanted to explore.

305

"I thought of that. No time." Devon checked his watch and pulled out a key fob. "Already late, so you're with me. Be good. I'm not supposed to have you off campus." The elevator dinged and the doors opened to the main lobby. He sighed. "Why do they do this to me? Act natural and stay close to my side so there are no questions. Got it?" Devon gave him a firm look.

"Got it."

"Okay, kiddo, let's go." Devon moved forward, and he called and waved to several people. They passed the main cafeteria, the one Garik normally visited at mealtimes, and headed down an unfamiliar corridor—to Garik, at least. Devon paused at a door with a wire-reinforced glass window, inserted his passkey, and the door prompted him for his hand. He looked at Garik. "They don't let just anyone outside. Sorry, kiddo. Stick close." He pressed his hand, the door unlatched, thump, thump, and Garik kicked his ZBoard up to grab the end. He followed Devon into the bowels of the very familiar underground parking garage where he and his friends had been only two nights earlier as they had made their escape from Corona Tower.

Overhead lights flooded the space. Vast rows of cars stretched into the distance, tightly packed closer to the elevator. Farther away, they thinned, but Garik estimated hundreds, at least. Worker bees, working for the money, serving the Tower to do what needed to be done. He hated to group Devon with those people, but then . . . and he let go of that thought. Devon wasn't bad, not like some people he'd met in the Tower's dungeon.

Devon's car was an older Merc hatch, with the tristar proudly displayed in the fake grille. Devon beeped it to unlock it, unplugged the power cord, stashed it in the hatch with Garik's board, and leaned the seat forward for Garik to climb into the back. The rear windows were deeply tinted. He shrugged. "Sorry."

As the car moved away, emanating the faint whine of electric motors, the light from the ramp leading to the outside world grew closer. This time, the gates opened for Devon pretty as you please, unlike Garik's previous journey up the ramp two days before. They entered the street, turning right on Stamford, the same direction Garik had driven in Kevin Lee's van. A normal world, two days gone, and a million lightyears away.

"Where are we headed?"

"The high school. Then Bay City Medical." Devon drummed the steering wheel as he waited at the light to go left on Corona. "Sorry

306

if I'm jittery. This is way outside my pay grade. If that tablet hadn't gotten lost . . . but I can't fix that, so here we are. Just keep your head low. You being out here is my job if you're seen." The light changed, and Devon made his left, heading towards Park Avenue.

"So, I can't just jump out and you say you don't know where I went?" Garik teased, even though it was exactly what he'd been thinking. He suspected that was why he was in the back seat.

Devon slammed the brakes. Another car honked, and Devon ignored it as he turned to glare at Garik. "I've been good to you, kiddo. How can you suggest that? I wouldn't just get fired. I'd be blacklisted from every job Rodheimer had any control over me getting with any company in the world."

"Sorry."

"Okay. I apologize for biting your head off. Like I said, I'm jittery with you out here, so head down, and let's do this. Okay?"

"Sure, kiddo." Garik kicked underneath Devon's seat. When the man looked in the mirror, Garik grinned and gave him a thumb's up.

"I'm never having kids, ever," Devon muttered.

I can hear you, Garik thought. Still, in the cause of not getting his head bitten off again, he didn't say it. Even a seventeen-year-old knows how to use wisdom occasionally.

GARIK'S BIG surprise came when Devon pulled up in front of the school and his passenger climbed in the car. The high schooler fell inside, pulled off a knit cap, and said, "Thank you. I texted you this morning, but you surely missed it. I am happy I found your number stored in my watch." He lifted a hand to his thick shock of tousled hair to sort it out, then brushed his palms along the sides where it was cut short.

"Dieter?" Garik leaned forward and smashed the familiar youth on his shoulder with a fist.

"Ah, my friend." Dieter's face lit up when he saw Garik. "You were disappeared when I returned from school. You, my friend, are blowing up the social media. Boom!" He put his palms together and exploded them apart.

"You two know each other?" Devon seemed to melt, and his face turned paler than arctic ice.

"We are the best of friends!" Dieter held up a fist for Garik to bump. "No one can argue otherwise. Is that not so?"

Garik bumped the fist. What else could he do but agree?

DEVON TOOK Fourth south from the high school, bypassing Central Park and coming up alongside The Martial Arts Center. The two teens talked skateboards while Devon drove white-lipped and refused to look to either side. Instead of taking Ninth east along the front of the Center, when the light changed, he accelerated toward the next intersection at Lilac.

"Should you not turn here? Ninth is less slow. My father does not enjoy traffic lights." The street sign for Ninth faded behind them.

"Less slow but obvious," Devon muttered, as he reached Lilac, turned left, and accelerated.

Garik would have preferred taking Ninth along the front of the Center, although Devon was correct. The Center's parking lot was filled with people squeezing in a practice session on their lunch hour. Lilac would require stops at each street along the way, but the streets would likely be clear of pedestrians.

"Sure. I am not the one driving." Dieter shrugged and gave Garik his attention. "This, let me show you this small movie, a drone shot, I think it is called." He pulled off his watch and held it out to Garik with a grin.

"A drone shot," Garik repeated, and he took the watch. He imagined the video clip from that morning, and a razor shard of guilt twisted in his gut for not telling Devon he had hidden his tablet.

"I did send it to Devon, but since he did not receive the text, I am confident you did not view it. The play arrow, smash it to enjoy your movie."

"Thanks." Garik fell back into the seat and tapped the watch's face, uncomfortable for not being transparent, and the video from that morning began to play. He studied it intently, hoping to see something new. After it finished, he offered the watch back to Dieter, too overwhelmed by the memory of the events to speak.

"So many views." Excitement sparkled in Dieter's eyes. "Did you see? Many thousands. I did not know I was a friend to someone so popular. All over school, everyone sending your video to everyone else. In one class, the teacher stopped teaching and asked what we were doing. He said it was a current event and allowed it to play on the wall screen. You are a hit, my friend. What do you think of that?"

"On the wall screen, like a projector?" Devon was pulling up to make a right on Industrial, which would lead them directly to the Medical Center, and he blew out his cheeks in a huge sigh. He glanced in the rear-view mirror and studied Garik. "What else? Your picture on a billboard? There's no way I'm getting you back to the Tower without being seen."

"You are going back?" Dieter leaned over the seat and smashed Garik's knee with a fist. "You are here. Stay. Muhammad and Ibn will be filled with happiness that you have not disappeared once again. I am excited to tell them."

"No, Dieter, you absolutely cannot. I'm in big trouble if you do." Red streaks painted Devon's neck, and they were crawling into his cheeks. "This can't get any worse."

He drove blindingly fast, covering the next three blocks from Lilac before getting caught at the light at Pansy. He slammed the brakes, skidding the tires. A car pulled up on the right. Devon ducked into his seat, but the car turned and pulled away as though nothing was the matter.

One block ahead, the main entrance to the Bay City Medical complex on the left framed the group of medical buildings and their tall, elaborately landscaped masonry backdrop of a wall. The wall separated the hospital from the industrial park two blocks farther down.

The shifting colors of a large television in a display window to the left caught their eye. They couldn't hear the newscaster, but across the top it said Bay City Noon News. The words scrolling across the bottom of the screen said more.

Bay City police, where are you? Yesterday, a local youth was forcefully abducted by armed assailants and whisked away in an unmarked vehicle as seen in this drone footage taken by a local blogger. The video clip from Dieter's watch filled the screen. Garik's face was clearly visible. During the abduction, a superimposed circle appeared around Garik with his name to the side.

"You are on the TV, my friend." Dieter lifted a fist in the air. "Maybe Hollywood, someday. This would never happen in my country. I am filled with more excitement than I thought possible. You must see your friends to tell them you are okay. Your girlfriend, Marisa, surely she would want to know you have not disappeared from her once more."

"I would like that." Garik looked in the mirror. Devon refused to acknowledge him, and the man's face tightened.

Dieter's watch dinged. He touched it and began to read, and he grinned. "Too bad I must leave school, although my father will not think so. Something exciting is being planned, and I would enjoy being part of it."

"I give. What?" Garik leaned forward to read the watch as the light changed, and Devon surged the little Mercedes forward. The electric motors whined in protest.

"A march to the police station with banners and more." Dieter looked up, his eyes shining with anticipation, and when Devon didn't respond, he shifted his enthusiasm to Garik. "Perhaps you can be there, my friend, to show them you are okay—"

"No, he can't." Devon cut him off. "I'm dropping you off at the hospital as requested, and Garik and I are returning to the Tower, which we never should have left." He stomped the brakes at the entrance to the complex with his blinker on, waiting for an especially slow minivan to pass.

"But, that is unfair." Dieter's eyes reflected his astonishment.

Garik agreed. It was very unfair, but Dieter didn't seem to realize that Garik was in the back seat for a reason. He was a prisoner. If he scrambled from the vehicle, where would he run? Devon's life would be ruined, the Tower now knew its weaknesses, and Garik wasn't sure he hadn't been given an implant just for the purpose of tracking him.

Even Garik's friends in the city would be punished if the Tower thought it would aid their chances in retrieving him, and they wouldn't care who got hurt. The surveillance cameras in The Flower Shop were evidence of that.

Then Devon's phone dinged.

"Now what? Is the Tower planning a protest, too?" He sighed, pulled into a parking space, and placed an earbud in one ear. "Devon speaking."

Dieter had pulled a small phone from his pocket and was typing away. Every few words, he glanced at his watch. He paused, looked at Devon and Garik, grinned, and returned to typing.

"What?" Garik asked. He leaned over the seat, looked at the words Dieter was inputting, and absorbed the impact.

Everyone. See the abducted boy. Lol. We must find a way to rescue him.

Dieter held the phone up, aimed it at Garik, clicked the camera icon, snapped a photo, and asked, "I shall send it?"

Yes, Dieter, send it! Still, it felt cruel to betray Devon. The man had been good to him. But to return to captivity? How could he allow that? There were no good choices. Freedom was so close, but to take it and risk losing it again—

Dieter took the choice from him. He winked, clicked send on his phone, and slipped it in his pocket. His watch chimed, he held it to let Garik see that the message had gone out, and he grinned.

"Thank you, Devon." Dieter released the door with excitement and pushed it open. "My father will be pleased at your help. I will see you later."

Devon, still in conversation, held up a hand for the teen to wait.

"My father will be expecting me. I must go." Dieter threw himself from the car, closed the door, gave Garik a thumbs-up, and took off running for the building.

Devon rolled down the window and called, "Dieter!" When the youth looked back, waved and laughed, then vanished into the caverns of the hospital's interior, he rolled the window back up.

"Can I at least sit up front?" And run away while I'm at it? Garik stuck one shoulder between the seats and reached for the gearshift, popping it with his fingertips.

"The Director is looking for us." Devon took Garik's wrist and returned his arm to the back seat. "That was Airman Vang. The Director has also seen the drone footage. No lunch for you, kiddo."

"Why? I hardly had breakfast."

"I told Vang we were in the cafeteria for lunch. So was he, so I had to lie and say we were in the hospital cafeteria."

"Well, we are at the hospital."

"Yeah, right-o, kiddo, like that's going to fly." Devon had already pulled forward, and he took a right on Industrial. "Van, you remember him? He has direct hospital access, to he's meeting us in the garage so we can take the hospital-only elevator to Level 4. How sick can you pretend to be?"

"I don't know. Why can't you be the sick one?" But Garik understood the man's plan. He wanted to save his skin—understandably—and it might work, if no one tried to match up all the details.

"Do you notice anything here? I'm driving. How sick can I really be?" Devon had the little hatch screaming down First, and with hardly a pause, he hit his blinker, took a right on Park, and pushed the upper limits he could squeeze out of the small car's electric power plant.

"I know how to drive." Garik fell back in his seat. He had driven his Street Strider and Kevin Lee's van. "You don't trust me," he muttered.

Devon didn't answer. He simply shook his head, barely slowed at Ninth, and aimed the nose of the car for Rock Island and the back entrance to Corona Tower.

Garik hardly had time to begin an internal tirade of accusations against the Tower, Weston Rodheimer, and his unwilling induction into the secretive human-hybrid project changing people into military monsters in the Tower's basements when the screech of tires caused him to look up. Daytime running lights filled the window, Devon's little hatchback became an origami project, and the metal skin of the car crumpled around them.

THE GOOD news was that they did make it to the hospital, and the one on Basement Level 4 in the Corona Tower, although by accident. A happy one as far as Devon's future with the Tower was concerned.

The daytime running lights belonged to a large military vehicle driven by Airman Wu Han. Devon had shaved the light at Rock Island a bit too close, and he had charged through the intersection just as the bigger truck rumbled across. The little Mercedes may have crumpled beyond recognition, but the massive bumper on the Airman's truck-like transport was barely scratched.

Airman Han immediately recognized Devon's car. When he saw Garik inside, he made a call to alert the Bay City Police that there had been an accident, but it was a military training exercise, and there was no infrastructure damage. He apologized for not filing permits ahead of time but that they had slipped through the cracks. He had his team attend to the injured passengers, moved the damaged car to a vacant alley for later retrieval, and delivered Devon and Garik to Corona Tower.

Arriving in the parking garage, Airman Han brought the vehicle to a hard stop. Van Hermoso seemed surprised to find Devon severely injured. Garik's clothes looked as bad, but he was sitting up and asking where they were.

"You've been in a car accident. You're injured, so lie still." Airman Han had been driving, and several other people in similar dress were with him.

"I'm fine." Garik saw he was in the back of the vehicle. Devon beside him didn't look so good. A bandage around his head was a red lollipop, and a leg was a pretzel. His own clothes were painted dark crimson, especially one leg of his pants. The pant leg was sliced open, and his leg was wrapped with bandaging. "Can I take this bandage off?"

"Not a good idea." A woman with dark hair and dark eyes and riding in the back seat cautioned him. "Lt. Trenessa Miyoshi." She smiled. "We barely stopped the bleeding."

"I'm fine." Garik hit the bandage with the flat of his hand. "It doesn't even hurt. What about Devon?"

He didn't get an answer. After Van Hermoso realized the extent of Devon's injuries, he paled and called for a backup emergency team from three floors below.

Garik climbed out of the truck, looked back toward the ramp leading outside, and watched the gates to freedom close. He couldn't deal with both that and Devon, and he let it go. The backup medical team arrived, and everyone fell into the elevator with one thought in mind.

Devon had to be saved . . . if he could.

— 6 —

EMERGENCY SURGERY swallowed Devon far into the night. The bigger questions hovering over Garik were how, why, and *what were you doing off-campus with one of the Tower's employees?*

He expected everyone he met to bombard him, to grill him for duplicity, to implode Devon's thinly veiled attempt to cover the broken rules he'd left scattered over the city streets. Instead, he was caged in an examination theater, zapped with high-powered machines, and prodded like a wild animal. *Does this hurt? That? There? How about here?*

During a break in the interrogation, with the room quiet and no one else around, he listened to the forest of voices from through the door. He was certain they were unaware he could hear them, but mostly they weren't saying anything interesting, so he didn't care, until he caught the timbre of Airman Han's voice.

"Yes, we were careful to check for injuries. The young man was unconscious—they both were—and we were unsure of the extent of

313

the injuries—"

"I was certain there was severe damage to the leg." Lt. Trenessa Miyoshi. Garik recognized her voice when she interrupted. She had seemed kind in the transport. "I suppose it could have been the amount of blood. The pant leg was soaked, but clearly, the X-ray proves otherwise." The shrug in her voice was unmistakable.

Garik pressed his fingers into the bronze skin covering his leg. They had cut off the pant leg, leaving him a sort of one-legged pogo boy. He pictured his time in the ring with Justin. The man had opened Garik's arm from the wrist nearly to his elbow, and minutes later, he was completely healed. Jantzen had once said to him, "Don't give away everything you can do." Now he wondered if they were about to discover more than he wanted them to know.

His hearing. He had come to accept that since his infusion with timber wolf DNA, he could hear things no one else could. He was now quicker than he used to be, though he still struggled with understanding the rainbows when he moved too fast. And healing quickly. Devon was in surgery still. How could Garik not have suffered almost as badly?

He suspected he had, only there was nothing now to prove it. Rodheimer might want to convince him that Jantzen was using him for his own purposes, but he trusted one piece of his advice. *Don't give away everything you can do.* He'd already seen the wisdom in that.

The door opened, and Dr. Jimenez stepped through. He smiled and stepped aside as Nurse Ratchett followed him inside and handed him a tablet.

"I'm sure you remember Nurse Fortinier."

"Yes." Not that he wanted to, although she hadn't done anything specific to anger him, more what she hadn't done, like not give him repeated shots of sleepy juice when she didn't want to answer his questions. She was a walking needle in Garik's eyes.

"And who am I?"

"Are you serious?" True, he hadn't seen the man in months, but to ask such a stupid question?

"Just answer the question."

"Dr. Jimenez. How could I forget?"

"Ah." The doctor smiled, perhaps too brightly. "We can confirm your attitude was not damaged in the accident. I wish to talk about the results of your X-rays. First let's discuss bone density and muscle composition . . ."

Garik's mind wandered as the man went on about calcium absorption, fast twitch muscles, and unusual glucose reserves. His attention perked up when the doctor asked whether recent intense activities had tired him out unusually.

"What sort of intense activities?" In the training cell with Lansana just that morning, he'd dived for the knife, and he'd felt wiped out afterward.

"Sprinting. Jumping. Anything that requires a high level of agility."

Like rescuing the drinks when Rodheimer broke the table, or at the flower shop when evading the Tower goons. Garik processed the memories, and he overlaid them with Jantzen's warning: *Don't give away everything . . .*

"No more than usual." Garik smiled. Say what the man wanted. Anything to be released from this hamster cage. "Can I go now? I think the Director wants to see me."

"I'm sure he does. Your on-line presence is quite the talk about the place."

"Okay, then, I have a question." If the guy was talking, maybe Garik could get something clarified.

"And that is?" Jimenez handed the tablet back to Nurse Fortinier and crossed his arms in front of him, indicating the consultation was nearing its end.

"How come you guys know everything happening out there? Sheesh. I'm always locked out." The doctor frowned, and Garik thought, oops, that didn't come out well.

"That should be obvious. We are not subject to the restrictions of the program participants. As for you, we wish to observe you overnight. Leah will see you to a room." The doctor dismissed Garik and exited.

"Now, my young friend. We need you in the proper clothing for an overnight stay." Leah lifted a sealed pack from a cabinet. "Change into these while I get your room assignment. Leave your old things on the examining table. Don't be slow. I'll be right back." She winked and was gone.

Garik groaned as he pulled his shirt over his head. Inside the package he found a hospital gown and cloth booties with elastic tops. No underwear. No way was he doing that. He would leave them his tattered pants. They were already destroyed. But that was as far

315

down as he was willing to disrobe.

Oh, his socks. They could have them, too. He had no idea what had happened to his shoes.

Changed, he sat on the examining table, and he looked around the neutral and vapid space. Nothing to give it personality or make it memorable. He swung his feet, right, left, bored. Then he heard footsteps outside the door, and he jumped down. When the door opened, he preempted whatever Nurse Ratchett might intend to say.

"What about Devon?"

"What would you like to know?" Nurse Ratchett, polite but noncommittal.

"Do I get to know how he's doing, or do you people plan to leave me in the dark?" Like, is he still alive?

"His injuries were severe. We're doing what we can. Now, if you'll follow me."

Garik sighed. This was the Nurse Ratchett he recalled. The only thing she hadn't done was give him a shot to put him to sleep. He'd better play nice, or he was certain she would enjoy doing that, too.

LT. TRENESSA Miyoshi appeared the next day to escort Garik to his delayed meeting with Director Weston Rodheimer. On the elevator, he was surprised to see her press the icon for the main lobby of the Tower aboveground.

"I thought I was restricted to the basement." He said it sourly. He had not had a good night, and he still didn't know about Devon.

"Perhaps. That's not my area. We're busy today, and since I helped bring you in yesterday, they assigned me to escort you."

"Too busy for Airman Han?" That's the person Garik wanted to be here. He'd bonded with him over shared Street Strider experiences, and besides, the man had been kind to Garik and his friends, once even offering them breakfast at the food court.

"The Airman is helping in other areas. I'm sorry I can't tell you more. As soon as I drop you off, I'm to join him."

The elevator car dinged, and the doors opened to the vast and sunlit main lobby of the Corona Tower. Miyoshi walked Garik to the Front Desk. Charity Cellers, today in spangly earrings and throwback peach and teal, looked up.

"Mr. Shayk. Lt. Miyoshi. The Director is waiting. You may step through to his office."

"Can I leave the young man with you? I'm assigned to help with the riots—"

Riots? Garik glanced at the display Charity had been watching. People were marching along the waterfront holding placards. *What are they hiding?* Then, *Freedom is a right.* And, *Boycott Chow Down!* There were more, but to boycott Chow Down? Everyone loved Chow Down, the restaurant on the Corona Mall. Outside the expansive wall of windows across the lobby, he could just see the top of the flagpole that normally flew the Bay City High school standard, one of three thrusting skyward for the national, state, and school flags. The wind caught the flag, only it wasn't the one he expected.

A senior prank? It must be. Likely one of his friends, Ibn or Muhammad. The flag popped and shifted in the breeze, but it was without doubt Garik's face from back when his hair was long. Well, longer, as he was working to grow it out again.

His attention returned to the Front Desk as Charity hung up a phone and said, "Ms. Sunchaser will be right out. You may leave Mr. Shayk with us. Thank you, Lt. Miyoshi."

The lieutenant nodded to Garik, turned, and strode purposefully toward the elevator. The bellhop Choi Bok stepped off, in his standard Corona Towers cream top and tan trousers with a microfiber cloth dangling from his back pocket. He pushed a polished brass cart, now empty, toward the entrance of Stamford Suites, the Tower residence block extending five floors above them. He greeted Gunther Diehl, the concierge, with a respectful nod, before exiting out the double glass doors toward the parking garage.

Halo Sunchaser appeared, saying, "Mr. Shayk, this way. The Director is ready to see you."

Garik's throat was dry. The last time he had seen Sunchaser, she had been wielding her electrified sword, and she had used it to dismember a recalcitrant hybrid mutant one singular atom at a time, until there was nothing at all left.

He tried to calculate, with all serious consideration, just how much longer he had to live.

GARIK EXPECTED Rodheimer to be waiting just off the lobby area. Not so. Sunchaser led him to the elevator, inserted her passkey, and placed her hand on the palm scanner. She chose the penthouse suite, and the door dinged and closed.

"I didn't expect to be invited back to the top." Garik had been there just days earlier. He watched the numbers change, blurring with their speed.

"And you wouldn't be, if not for Mr. Maye's accident." Sunchaser, in her towering headscarf, nearly brushed the mirrored ceiling.

"Yeah, that." Garik heard the rebuke in her words. He had a hard time picturing this elegant, statuesque woman the same as the one two nights ago that had terrorized the hybrids. Yet her tone told the truth of it.

She turned to him, looking down her nose. "Yeah, that," in a mocking lilt. She looked forward once again.

In the penthouse, Rodheimer stood facing outward at the bank of windows wrapping the southeast corner of the building. Sunchaser cleared her throat and said, "The boy, Director."

"Yes, the boy." He didn't turn or otherwise acknowledge Garik's presence.

"Thank you, Director. I'll leave you two." Sunchaser backed away without a word to Garik.

"This way, boy."

Garik moved forward. He noticed that the table Rodheimer had broken last time had been replaced by one in a similar, though not identical style. Unlike the last time Garik was here, the city was washed by the sun, and closer, he could see the roof of Bay City High directly east and the Ransom Building distantly to the south.

"That." Rodheimer didn't have to say what. The flag with Garik's image buffeted in the breeze. "Your doing?"

"Hardly. Remember, you people have me in a straitjacket."

"A straitjacket." The man glanced at him for the first time. A glint of amusement? It was hard to tell. "Tell me about the training exercise."

"Sure. What training exercise?"

"You, my boy, are wiser than you appear. Never give anything away. I like that about you. Mr. Maye has been an outstanding asset to this facility. I was not aware he was participating in military triage exercises, especially ones that could so easily go awry. One point in his favor. It will be a shame if we lose him."

"Oh, that training exercise." Here it comes.

"And he kept you at his side—and somehow protected you at risk of his own safety. Uninjured as you stand here. Is that how it went?"

Garik's mind raced. Devon. Dieter. Bay City Medical Center. Marisa, Ibn, Muhammad, Wu Han . . . until it all ran together, and the Director's tale became the fact that the Director needed it to be.

"Devon always watches over me. He's the best there is." Protect the family, protect the pack, take care of those under his care. Say whatever the man wanted to hear.

"Is that how it went?"

Garik heard the threat in the repeated question. He answered, "Yes, Director Rodheimer. That's exactly how it went."

"That's what I thought. I'll advise Colonel Brace to ease up on Airman Han. Now, we will need to see who else we can arrange to serve as your companion. That, however, can wait for a time, as this has come to my attention. Observe."

Rodheimer lifted a remote and dropped a screen from the ceiling. Light darkening shades around the room hummed as they fell from their hidden recesses, and a projector began to whir. Multiple images appeared on the screen, one of the drone clip Garik had seen earlier, but there were more. The waterfront placards, a large protest march at Central Park, and at each, black-suited enforcement officers with smoked face shields with three glinting metal reinforcement bars running from left to right on the lower half.

"Wow," Garik breathed. "Someone's not happy."

"We—" the Tower, it was clear Rodheimer meant "—like to stay below the radar. Our research facility is off the records. No one, even the city planning department, knows it is there. You are an unknown immigrant who has been successfully deported back to his native Russia. And yet, each of these protests is about you."

"I can't deny the face on the flag, but then I have stupid friends." Thank you, Ibn and Muhammad! I love you! "The rest, what does that have to do with me?"

"That." Rodheimer clicked the remote, and the drone footage grew to eclipse the other three. It looped back to the beginning, and once more, Garik was running at full speed across the bridge to reach the parking lot at Kerre's Dive.

"Not my drone." Garik shrugged.

"Not your drone, not your friends, not about you. I can't prove otherwise, but I do know this." The man's voice darkened as the images on the screen changed, post after post, many with pictures of Tower security, military vehicles going in or out of the parking garage, and others more tightly connected to Garik. He recognized his name in some of them, and others called for an end to the Tower's secrecy. Even Dieter's photograph from yesterday of Garik in Devon's car was there.

"Most of those say nothing about me." Please don't ask about Dieter's picture.

"You think not? If I could, I'd shut down social media across the city. We are the future of this country, and nothing must be allowed to get in the way."

Garik shivered as the burn of the electrified sword crawled across his skin. He hoped it didn't come next for him.

— 7 —

GARIK'S DISMISSAL from Rodheimer's penthouse retreat was a welcome relief.

The man who appeared to accompany him wasn't.

"Mr. Shayk." The elevator doors slipped aside, revealing Senior Airman Shan Vang. He lifted his head slightly and spoke down his nose. "I see we meet again."

"It seems so, Airman." Garik should be accustomed to the man by now, but his stomach clenched. The Airman had repeatedly disparaged him when he thought he couldn't hear. *Useless. Runt. Mongrel.* That last one might have been from a Lt. Wilder. He and Airman Vang had joined Garik and Jantzen in the Tower's elevator to share the ride. They had belittled him in whispers, thinking he couldn't hear. Perhaps a normal human wouldn't have been able to, but then, that wasn't Garik, was it? Now, the words danced through Garik's head anytime Vang was around.

Garik stepped inside and saw a second Airman, a woman with light freckles, reddish-blonde hair, and a tinier waist than Vang's. He nodded at her, wondering what descriptive words they had used about him in the privacy of the elevator.

"Airman," Garik said in greeting, unsure if he should trust her or not.

"Close." She smiled. She glanced at Vang and unmistakably winked before saying to Garik, "Master Sergeant Megan Valladao. One small notch above Airman."

"I suppose I should apologize." Garik was out of apologies. These people should be apologizing to him.

"Your call." She shrugged. "I'd like to observe Airman Vang's interactions with you. It is my duty to support the welfare of the unit assigned to the Tower, and I can't report what I don't observe. I'd welcome your input into how you feel you are being treated. Will that earn me my apology?"

Garik saw her differently. He glanced at Vang, who stood with his arms behind his back, his face blank and watching the wall above Garik's shoulder. It stood out to him that both Vang and Valladao were equally freckled, Vang with his light complexion and Cambodian eyes, and Valladao so clearly not Cambodian yet with similar coloring. It was an odd thing to notice, but it was none of his business.

"Master Sergeant," Garik offered, nodding once more.

"Now that's rude." She smiled, though. "Ma'am, or my name, if you don't mind. Or Sergeant Valladao. I prefer Megan unless commissioned officers are present."

"Thank you, Megan." Garik relaxed his guard. "I prefer Garik, and I apologize for thinking you were an Airman."

"An unintended slight, perfectly understandable from a civilian, and thank you. Shan tells me he's assigned to escort you to your quarters. Your supervisor is out of commission for a time—"

"Jailer," Garik muttered, glancing at Vang before looking to the floor. He was aware that he should shut up, but everyone always wanted him to shut up, and he was tired of shutting up. "That's his real job, and no one's bothered to tell me if he's still alive."

"Let's not say jailer. Or guard or bouncer or anything like that. It disrespects the man. I know Devon, and he likes working with the people here in the facility." She smiled briefly. "Do you have any complaints about him?"

"None, just that he needs to wear pajamas at night."

"Pajamas." Her eyes twinkled. "Noted. Anything else?"

"Can I see him? Another thing, I'm staying in his apartment, and I don't have a passkey."

"Shan?" She directed the question at the Airman.

"I have one here, ma'am." Vang pulled a passkey from inside a pocket, and he held it out. "It will allow *Garik* entry and egress to the apartment and permission to ride the elevator to the Level 1 cafeteria and the Level 4 hospital."

"And Level 3 for training," Valladao elaborated, revealing that she had known about the passkey and was allowing Vang a level of control and responsibility over Garik as his new jailer. "You will need to validate your thumbprint before using it. Shan will help you with that. Okay, we're here, and I'm good. Garik, feel free to contact me if you need anything. I'm sure Shan can accompany you to check on Devon, or if he feels you can be trusted . . ." She looked at Vang. The elevator dinged and the door opened as she finished speaking.

"Yes, ma'am. I've got this covered." Vang gave her a salute.

"Garik, I'm sure we'll speak again." She nodded and exited the elevator.

"Okay, to the hospital. Is that what you wish?" Vang held his thumb over the Basement 4 icon.

"Please." Garik noticed the change in the man. A thicker veneer of respect. He hoped it lasted, although it would be weird if Vang started calling him by his first name. Garik absolutely didn't want to address the Airman by Shan.

He shivered at the thought of that.

THE VISIT to the hospital was informative but not as much as Garik had hoped. They learned Devon was indeed alive and out of surgery. His leg had required the most work and he would likely wear a cast for months. To visit? Not possible, not today, as he was fully saturated with painkillers. Inquire in a day or two, hopefully calling before visiting a second time.

Airman Vang returned with Garik to the main lobby in the tower to validate Garik's passkey. Charity Cellers wasn't at her desk, but Gunther Diehl was at the concierge's desk for Stamford Suites.

"Good morning, Airman Vang. And Garik, how nice to see you again. What can I do for the two of you today?" The concierge was cheerful and helpful, as always.

Vang explained the unvalidated passkey, and Gunther assured him he could help. He entered a code, Garik pressed his thumb to the passkey, and Gunther hit accept to link the passkey to Garik's identity. Garik mentioned to Vang that he hadn't eaten, so he accompanied Garik back to the elevator and to Level 1, and he continued on in the elevator, leaving Garik to find his way where he needed to go.

Garik headed to the cafeteria and was especially surprised to see Kevin Lee from Ai Kee! sitting at a table enjoying a meal with Bert Ellis and Jacquelien Van Kessel. Kevin's van was sandpaper in his memory. Garik had broken the window, and who knew what other damage it had taken when the Tower had stormed the parking garage under the Ransom Communications Building where Garik had parked it. And that was after Jantzen had assured the man he would take good care of it. Garik's enthusiasm for lunch soured, and he looked for an easy exit, but Bert had seen him and called to him, waving his hand.

Garik approached awkwardly, unsure of how to handle the van thing. It had been, what, only three days that Kevin had offered the use of his van? It seemed longer.

"Hello Bert, Jacquelien, Kevin." Garik ran a hand through his hair, unwilling to look Kevin in the eyes. "I'm sorry about your van."

"Yeah, about the van. You and Mr. Hefferly said, and I quote me, 'I know you'll take good care of the van, Mr. Hefferly,' and now I quote him, 'Of course, Kevin,' and now I don't have a job at the Center anymore. They didn't like their van coming back trashed."

"I'm so sorry." He really was. He hadn't meant for Kevin to take the brunt of his poor decision to shatter the window when all he had to do was ask Giselle for the key. Now the Center had fired him. It was another black mark against everything he had become.

Kevin shrugged. "After the Hollywood shoot, I was too hot for them to handle. People coming by, getting in the way, all to see the movie star. Mr. Mandering said he wasn't running a celebrity show."

"But your autograph session at Chow Down. He was making money right and left." Garik slipped into a seat, his concerns about the van forgotten.

"He liked that." Kevin grinned. "He didn't like me giving them away for free at the Center. That's why I was giving Ms. Sunchaser private lessons here at the Tower. Hoping to go it on my own. Now, I am."

"But how did you get permission—" Garik cut off his question, unsure if he was allowed to even ask it. He looked to Jacquelien and Bert, searching for a lifeline. Jacquelien shrugged, and Bert grinned. "What? You guys, well, you look normal, but you know what happens down here. And they don't tell anyone. Much less city people."

"Hey, my man," Bert shifted position, and his black tattoos flexed under his net shirt like they were dancing, "this falls into my skill set. We all knew Kevin was teaching Halo, and when Devon took a fall, I matched up two and two, and Kevin made four." His eyes sparkled, and he looked at Jacquelien like it meant something special just between them.

"See," Kevin filled in, "I brought you up with Ms. Sunchaser after seeing you with Mr. Hefferly. Thought she might know something, you being deported back to Russia, then appearing in the Tower. Even I know that's not the way things happen. When someone's deported, they can't get back into the country, not without special reason. I think she wanted to buy me off with this job."

"Keep you close to keep an eye on you, more like it." The electrified sword in action. Garik tingled all over.

"Okay, fine, as long as I get a paycheck. She said I would be working with some enhanced people, and I would need to sign a confidentiality agreement. I said sure. So, my friend, are you enhanced, too?" He balled a fist and punched Garik on the shoulder. "If so, how?"

"Maybe. What about Callie? You were hot after her, as I remember." Callie Fornya worked at Ai Kee! and was the ex-Olympian poster girl for the franchise. Kevin had worshipped her, although she didn't seem to know he existed. Garik didn't want to talk about his "enhancements," and he was certain she would distract the man.

"Yah, it's been a while since you were around. Callie got married a few months back. Gonna have a baby. Not my thing."

"Who else have you met?" Garik glanced around the cafeteria, which was mostly empty. "Do you have an apartment, yet? I mean, everyone down here has to, don't they?"

"Just us." Bert pointed to Jacquelien, Garik, and himself. "Not them." His hand shifted to Kevin.

"But Devon—" Garik hesitated. Surely they wouldn't give Kevin Devon's apartment. He liked Kevin and wouldn't mind him as a roommate, but the tablet under the couch. That was vital, and Kevin might ask questions Garik couldn't answer, not truthfully, anyway.

"Devon's choice." The red stripe on Jacquelien's face split when she opened her mouth to speak. "He could have lived in the Tower or anywhere in Bay City. He didn't have a reason to so stayed with the people he worked with. He liked us."

"Likes us, Jacke. He's not gone."

"Okay. Likes us. Bert wanted to be a welcoming committee, and I said, 'I'm open to anything.'" She laughed. "You can join us if you wish."

"Yes, please. Can I get something to eat, first? Breakfast was yesterday, and I haven't eaten since."

"I remember you and my nachos at Chow Down. You chowed

down." Kevin teased. "I know where the food is. My first require-ment when I accepted this job. I'll be right back."

Kevin stood and walked away, lithe and confident as a martial arts trainer should be. Garik whispered, "I know what you guys said, but Kevin being here shouldn't be possible. I'm glad and all, but what's the real reason?"

Bert glanced at Jacquelien. She nodded, and Bert leaned in. "You know why Devon was assigned you, don't you?"

"My jailer." He remembered Sergeant Valladao's remark about respecting the activities director and he took a deep breath. "Sorry, that was mean—"

"We understand." Jacquelien reached her hand as if to reassure Garik, then withdrew it before doing so.

"Since Kevin knows you—remember, he made the connection with Halo first—plus he promised to keep you, um, safe."

"Safe. Like, from what? And he doesn't live down here? How's he supposed to manage that?"

"That is the million-dollar question."

And it didn't get answered, because Kevin arrived with a steam-ing plate of nachos.

"Something I knew you would like," and he slipped the plate be-fore Garik. He dropped several napkins and set a drink beside it.

Garik grinned and dug in, pleased for the moment, and willing to push his problems aside for a few minutes of taste-filled happiness.

— 8 —

"EVERYONE KNOWS there's a secret. Especially among the richies in the Tower. They just don't know what it is."

Bert and Jacquelien's tour was long over, and the idea of a game of racquetball had piqued Kevin's attention. Non-contact, the blood-line of the game, and a great way to get a workout, heh? Now, Kev-in's hair was damp, and he gleamed with sweat.

"And you do?" Garik now did, and he wished he didn't. He swung, *whack*, and the ball hit the front wall, echoing with frustra-tion and anger. Kevin leaped forward in response, missing the ball.

"Some of it, I guess, but likely not all. I know you. That was enough to get me interested." Kevin grinned. He pressed one shoul-der to his face to clear perspiration from an eye. "You're quick. Don't you get tired?"

Tired of what, this? It was nothing compared to the secret. His girlfriend, Marisa, had been determined to ferret it out after her sister vanished into the Corona Tower cauldron of disappearing people, and it had swallowed him, toes, fingers, and ears.

And now, Kevin, stepping into it willingly. What was he thinking?

Kevin retrieved the ball and tossed it to Garik. He put his hands on his knees, his legs bent, breathing hard. Garik tossed the ball up, and *whack*, into the front wall. Kevin danced, returned the ball, and the game was in play.

Enough of an answer? Huh? Yet Garik was careful of one thing. Playing too well. When the rainbows shadowed the ball, his racquet, and Kevin; and the ball began to slow to easy speeds; he knew he was moving too fast. He also knew the consequences: exhaustion, complete and debilitating. He could go and go and go at a human level of endurance, but upping his play to that level of skill, whether it was competition or unfair DNA-enhanced mutant performance, took everything from him.

Better to play the game Kevin expected from him than the one he knew he could win.

"I'LL MAKE you a deal." Kevin stood before the mirror in the changing room, freshly showered and wearing street clothes. He put a comb through his hair, adjusting it to perfection.

"Hollywood style?" Garik was on a bench across the room, also freshly laundered, and tying his shoes. He looked up and watched in the mirror as the man grinned. Even from across the room, Garik's keen sense of smell revealed Kevin's tangy, fresh bodywash.

"You got me." Kevin flipped his comb to the counter and joined Garik on the bench, all energy and excitement. He put his elbows on his knees and leaned in like an old friend sharing a familiar story. "That was just for kicks. Boris wanted me to do that audition, but I knew it wasn't what I really wanted. I like the excitement, not the glamor."

"Boris with Lindemann Airways." Garik remembered him as a twenty-something richie with blue-tipped blond hair from one of the exclusive apartments in the Stamford Suites section of Corona Tower. His girlfriend was Kirsten Kaudlitz, an heir of the Kaudlitz hotel chain.

"Sure. He founded it, you know, the reason he has so many

buckets of cash." Kevin rubbed his fingertips together like shuffling greenbacks. "I told you I had to sign a confidentiality agreement to work here. Right? I didn't tell you the rest."

"Okay." Garik didn't like this. Handcuffs, anyone? Locked doors? Was he about to lose his new passkey? What had Kevin agreed to that Garik wouldn't appreciate?

"It's like this." Kevin looked at the ceiling, pausing and tracing it with his eyes. "Is it private in here, I mean really private?"

"Probably." Garik recalled the microphone Devon had retrieved, the one secreted under a counter by Justin Kurtew. It wasn't likely the Tower had one. They promised privacy, or as much as possible, and Garik trusted them in that.

"Okay, then, all those demonstrations, that's me." Kevin sat back, and the electricity evaporated from him. He laughed a short bark of a sound. "Can you believe it? And Sunchaser hired me anyway."

"No handcuffs?" Garik held out his wrists, able to tease, finally.

"I don't get it."

"Jailer." The unintended word slipped out, breaking the crust of Garik's self-control, and his inner torment boiled out. "Isn't that why they hired you? You're the heavy, and I'm the mark? I was born in Russia. The police work for the politicians, not for the people. Don't tell me you weren't hired to rough me up if I don't follow the rules." *Shut up, Garik! My mind, my thoughts. Don't let out your anger. It never brings good things to you.*

"Hey, it's not like that. Well, I guess I did agree to some of that, but not like handcuffs or anything. I didn't agree to tie you to your bed at night, rather to, um, hang out with you. Yeah, that's right. How's that, hang-out buddy?" Kevin held up a fist, and he grinned. "Fist bump, buddy?"

"Okay, I give." Garik returned the fist bump. "Isn't hang-out old-person? My aunt says that, but I never do."

"Nah, I've always said it. Back to my story. I told you I asked Ms. Sunchaser about you, but here's what I didn't say, not with those guys out there." Kevin leaned in again. "Marisa knows something, that I've been sure of all along. About you, I mean. See, I asked her, and she acted like she didn't, like you had really been deported, but a guy can tell. Her eyes, her voice when I asked about you. I didn't believe any of it. Then when you showed up with Mr. Hefferly, well, what could that mean except that you were with Mr. Hefferly!"

"That doesn't make sense." Garik took to his feet, forced to move, thinking about Marisa, and remembering the last time he saw her, and how she had said she had missed him, too. It ripped him apart.

"But it does. Everyone knows Mr. Hefferly. His face is all over the adverts, the man who turns into purple mist. With a magic trick like that, how can you miss him?"

Magic trick. Kevin didn't know what he had signed up for. At least Garik still had real ears, no tail, and hadn't begun howling at people yet. Maybe Kevin could continue in sublime ignorance a while longer. Wait until he met Justin, with wings and extra joints, more hybrid mutant than human hybrid. "So, what about Marisa?"

"She was the trigger. Like bang, when I saw you, I said, this is fishy. Boris' theories about something weird in the basements? Yah, something weird, so I decided to do something about it. The excitement overrode my good sense, and there you go."

"I'm still not with you. Marisa and seeing me? How did that turn into weird things in the basement and demonstrations across Bay City?"

"No, no, not just that. I thought you knew about the footage on the news. You, on camera. Have you seen it?"

"Me falling on my face. I've seen it." Garik had made his way to the sink, and he looked at his face in the mirror. "Yeah. My friend showed it to me."

"Bam! You have lots of friends in the city. I should have so many." He looked sheepish. "Well, I guess I do, otherwise there wouldn't be such excellent crowds for all those demonstrations. Anyway, the next video was the big cannon."

"Next video?" Garik shifted his attention to Kevin's reflection, then he turned around. "What next video?"

"Them trying to silence you. Take you out. Prevent you from ever talking about what's down here. It's part of me taking this job, except I need the money. That was important, too."

"Silence me?" And take him out? Was Kevin now also part of the looney toons? And Garik thought everyone in the Tower's basements had lost their minds. It had now spread everywhere.

"Here. You can't tell anyone I have this. It's all over social media." He pulled out a watch. "I recorded it before they took it down, and I sent it to everyone I know. I think it's from a surveillance camera from one of the fancy places along Park. Several people also uploaded footage, but this is the only one that shows the actual attempt on your life."

Garik tapped the image. The video title was *Merc vs. Truck, Truck Wins*. It played out in low-resolution black and white. Devon's little electric Mercedes appeared from one side of the picture, and then the massive military transport rumbled in from the other direction and dominated the image. He winced as the I-beam of a bumper attached to the military truck rolled over the small car like a can opener. He didn't see how anyone survived. He now understood why Devon was marinating in feel-good medicines and the confusion when Garik had shown no injuries at all at the hospital.

"You can access the Internet on this?" The video continued with people exiting the big truck and moving the small car off view before loading the victims into the large truck and continuing on as if nothing had happened. When it was played out, he offered the watch back to Kevin.

"Nah, locked up tight when I'm in here. But outside, sure. Why?"

"I want to know what's happening. Bert said you don't have to move down here full time. You can leave when you want."

"I can't take you, though, or tell anyone about you. Or anything else from down here. I did sign that agreement."

"Okay, let me think, then." He'd hoped he could get a message to his friends, but that didn't seem possible.

"They didn't say I couldn't tell you what I learn from out there, though." Kevin grinned.

"That's something." Garik sat beside Kevin, and he leaned back, his head against the wall, his eyes closed, trying to decide where to go. "You said you set up demonstrations. I watched a couple from the penthouse on the top floor. They've got Weston Rodheimer like a tornado looking for damage to do." Garik had never lived through a tornado, but he had seen Rodheimer threaten and cajole the human hybrids. The comparison was apt. "Tell me about them. And my face on that flag at the school. What do you know about that?"

Kevin laughed. "That's my favorite. But later. Here's what you can expect across the city. Sure, I can't participate now—"

"The agreement you signed." Garik waved off his disclaimer.

"Right, so you know I'm out of it. Hear that, microphones?"

"There aren't any." Garik kicked the side of Kevin's shoe with his.

"So you say, but I want the record clear, just in case. Here's what I did."

As Garik listened, he hoped his assurances about no microphones were accurate. If not, Kevin was likely to be strung up to dry. He'd scheduled repeated media posts, though that wasn't a real problem. Then he'd contacted several controversial fringe groups that liked to buck authority, a few of which had recently been embroiled with race issues and immigration policies.

"Race issues!" Garik snorted. "What race issues?"

"You're Russian, aren't you? That's a race, and that's the reason they said they deported you. Now we know they didn't, so that means they were lying. Why? And people already suspect something with so many people 'disappearing' into the Tower's workforce. Transferred overseas. No one believes that."

Garik had paid attention to the news before his induction. Current events had been a part of his high school classes. Fringe groups, especially radical ones, did bad things when they found a cause they could jump on. He wondered what bad things would happen to Bay City now that Kevin had them riled up.

He hoped Marisa wasn't involved.

And that flag with his face! That's what he wanted to know. Who had done that? C'mon, Kevin, get to the good stuff!

— 9 —

KEVIN FELL easily into his new position as the underground research center's recreation coordinator and activities director.

The human hybrids on the five floors of the basement complex needed direction in their training, schedules needed organized, and supplies and material had to be ordered and maintained in an accessible manner.

When Garik described Devon Maye's penchant for wearing an oversized fanny pack, Kevin at first thought he was teasing. When Garik brought out one and showed him how much it held, Kevin laughed and insisted he could come up with a less embarrassing solution. The less embarrassing solution was Garik, which was fine with him. He got to trail along with the championship-winning martial arts expert, and along the way, he discovered that martial arts was a much broader discipline than he expected.

"Of course, I don't just sit around and kick box all day." Kevin laughed. "I box, the real kind, and wrestle, and you played me at racquet ball. I nearly smashed you into the wall."

"Because I let you." Seriously, Garik thought. I had to slow down to keep from beating you too badly.

"T'shush. Even American football, the only kind, in my eyes. A football player is better if they wrestle or train in martial arts. I even swim. I was a diver in high school."

"Did you compete?"

"Not good enough. My strength was elsewhere, but I enjoyed it. Here, I get to do it all."

ONE AT a time, they met with the various people Kevin would begin training. Among them, Stephen Klandermans, narwhal bonded, was focused on gymnastic skills. His super-dense bone structure allowed him to endure bone-jarring landings that would shatter other people. Kevin's job was to keep Stephen from shattering himself. The man didn't see his own limits and didn't like being told.

Ineke Van Stekelenburg, vastly strong from her ant DNA infusion, faced an uphill battle from her recent injury. Kevin suggested fencing. It would give her time to heal while learning control and developing lightness on her feet.

Jacquelien Van Kessel and Bert Ellis trained together. They were in the natatorium most days. Kevin and Garik joined them at the start of their sessions, but they were capable and motivated, and they didn't require supervision.

Garik described the training session he'd attended with Lansana Opoku-Mensah, and Kevin was intrigued. After a day's consultation with Lansana, they agreed that she didn't require speed to survive, but she would build a better disguise with finesse. So, she began ballet training. Small movements to create the impression of what she wanted others to see. Lansana took to it like second nature.

Paul Gberie needed group skills, interactive cooperation, to not stand on his own but to achieve a goal as part of a group. He needed team sports, and Kevin challenged him to choose between basketball and soccer. "Ah, sokker," Paul laughed. "True football. I have made my choice."

Benjamin Fuest had a recently injured femur and he said he must rest before he could even think of training. He would be glad to produce a medical exemption if Kevin wished. Kevin said he could revisit his training options later.

Veronika Abbink and Zekeria Salem wanted to combine a mix of speaking, presentation, acting, and standup comedy.

"That's training?" Kevin was surprised at the non-sports selections.

"They are our strengths." The two seemed pleased to have made their own choices.

"I have to show you're doing something, um, physical. Do you use the climbing wall, like, ever?"

"Do we, Veronika?" Zekeria raised his eyebrows at the woman.

"I'm sure we will now, Zekeria."

They laughed and turned to walk away. Kevin called after them, "Document your time on the wall. I'll look for it."

They waved over their shoulders and continued walking.

"People," Kevin moaned.

In between training sessions, preparing for training sessions, and stowing gear after training sessions, Garik learned bits and pieces of what was happening outside.

"So, what's happening today?" Often Garik's first question when Kevin arrived at breakfast.

"What happened last night, you mean. Today, I'm as clueless as you are." He tapped his watch. "No Internet means no news. I know what you know."

"Not true. You know way more than I do."

"What? Say that again."

"I said, you know way more . . . oh, I get it." Garik grinned, caught out.

"It's about time you admitted it." Kevin cut into pancakes with syrup and butter and forked a large slab into his mouth. "Who was your babysitter last night?"

"They locked me in my room."

Garik was still in Devon's apartment. His bed had been delivered Kevin's first day, and the new activities director had helped him rearrange the space and set it up. His ZBoard charger had already been moved, and even after his door was repaired, no one asked him to change back. His biggest disappointment was the tablet under the couch. He discovered it would allow him to preview incoming messages but remained locked to Devon's ID. With Devon in the hospital . . . well, it was as good as useless to Garik. At night, either one of the staff stayed in the apartment, or Garik was forced to stay with them. They could disengage his key function remotely, so he had no choice. Tag along or be stranded on his own. He felt like a stepchild being shunted between parents, none of whom wanted him.

"Humiliating, I know," Kevin commiserated.

"You could come live down here. You'd have your own room." Garik pleaded.

"I've seen where you live. No thanks. I like sun and sky. Besides, how else would I be able to keep you up on the outside news?"

Kevin was right. But for Garik, being watched over like an unwanted stepchild was demeaning, and he was ready for something to change.

"So, what happened last night?" Garik looked forward to the answer each morning. The stories were his version of knights in armor or of castles and dragons, and the audaciousness of the events Kevin relayed was every bit as exciting.

"A car was set on fire last night." Kevin seemed unconcerned as he licked one finger.

"In Bay City? Nah." Still, Garik lapped up the possibility. It was what he had left Russia to escape during the ethnic hostility his family had tried to shield him from. It was as exotic to him as the memory of his former home.

"I drove by it. I took a picture for you." He unclipped his watch, held it out, and there it was, red flames and black smoke. Wooden sticks and crumpled placards littered the ground, and people were cheering. Several were waving flags, one U.S. and another matching the one that had hung at the school.

"There's a flag of me!" The car no longer seemed the central theme of the image. Why was he on a flag in a picture of a burning car?

"Yikes!" Kevin took the watch, tapped it, and let out a hard sigh. "Wrong picture. I took a second one without that person. Here. Enjoy this version."

"No." Garik pushed the watch away. "You don't get off that easily. Why am I on that flag?"

"Because you started this." Kevin pushed his plate back. "Rather, it all started *with* you. My apologies. *You* didn't start anything."

"Why were you trying to hide it? You've got to tell me." Garik rapped the table, his frustration close to boiling over.

"Not so loud." Kevin held up his hand and pressed the anger away. "It's getting bad in the city, more than I intended. The high school—"

"What about the high school?" Muhammad, Ibn, Hayat . . . and Marisa and Maria and Alexi. All the people he knew from school. Surely Alexi was out of detention. Then there were Giorgio and Robbie . . . and Wajeha, all of them. He wanted to hear everything.

"The school has been closed for three days. How do you like that? Everybody you know, placard carrying do-gooders all."

"How . . . why?"

"You really don't get this, do you?" Kevin took a deep breath. "The school is closed due to bomb threats. The police are guarding the water towers, and I've been bringing a change of clothes in case I can't get home at night."

"Yikes." Garik sat back, stunned. "I didn't know."

"Exactly the way the Tower wants it. I'm on your side, my friend, but I'm playing two games here. You can't share any of this down here. It would all come back to me."

"Got it." Garik lifted a hand to draw a finger across his lips to zip them closed when the lights overhead flickered once, then dimmed, then went out altogether, leaving them sitting in the gloom of near darkness. Small amounts of light filtered from the main lobby where skylights let in the outside world.

"O—kay." Kevin moved his chair, and in the darkness, the sound of the metal feet on the hard floor reverberated.

"It's never done this before." Garik pictured the elevators, poking in the passkeys and punching the buttons, and the elevators refusing to release them to the outside. On the floors below them, it would be worse. They had no skylights, except in Corona City, where the pool ceiling cut through Level 1 to a windowed skylight to mimic an outside environment. Everything else would be blacker than black, except for battery powered devices.

Then, Devon! If he were awake, he would be terrified. And it was all Garik's fault. If only he'd told him about the message from Dieter instead of hiding that he knew where the tablet was.

"Kevin, I want to check on Devon. Can we get to the hospital, do you think?"

"There's a power generator down here, right? I was told that, I think. How long before it kicks on?"

"I don't know. Can we?" The air began to move, and with a flicker and a buzzing sound, the lights came on with an audible click. They were dimmer than before. "Now, can we?"

"Yeah, kid. Let's go get trapped on a lower floor. That's what you want, we'll do it."

"What's wrong?" Even Garik could see the man's color washed out.

"I told you. I need the sun. You said it's never done this before, right?"

"Not since I've been here." He watched the lights. Two minutes were about right for the backup generators, and they had to build to full power, meaning they weren't on city power.

"Okay, let's go get lost in the dark. I don't know if we're on city power or Tower power. Get it, kid? City power or Tower power? Either way, it's this way. Elevator, ho!"

Garik watched Kevin's eyes. They had never seemed so large. He didn't know adults could be as scared as he was. He wanted Kevin to be in control. If adults weren't, well, he didn't want to even think of that.

THE ELEVATOR worked fine. It was backed up with others who had arrived before them, and they had to wait for several minutes. However, Kevin's assigned passkey got them to the hospital level without incident. As they exited, the car filled up with people headed the other way, several with nursing staff in attendance.

"Okay, that was strange." Garik looked back. "They should be coming to the hospital, not leaving."

"Not the only strange thing." Kevin's mouth was tight. "Being down here is another."

The lights brightened as they moved along the ribbon candy walkway toward the hospital entrance. The people they met seemed preoccupied, and many of them kept glancing at the lights, as if unsure how long they would remain on.

At the main desk, confusion reigned. After a minute they got someone's attention and requested, "Devon Maye, please. Visitors."

"Maye, Maye, yes. He's not with us any longer."

"He died?" No! They had been in to see him only days before. Garik couldn't imagine it!

"Oh, no. No, of course not. You likely just missed him. We're moving non-emergencies. He's on his way to his apartment. Do you know where that is?"

"Yes," Garik said. "I live there."

"Then you don't need directions." The nurse turned and busied herself at other tasks.

Garik pictured Devon's cast and wondered how he could walk. Then, he realized he wasn't a stepchild any longer. His babysitter was back.

The ride on the elevator was all uphill to him.

— 10 —

"HEY, DEVON, it's good to have you back." Garik burst into the apartment, pleased to see his friend on the couch and sitting up.

"Thanks." Devon attempted to stand, but one leg was wrapped in a full cast and propped up on the coffee table. "Hey, Kevin," he called, as he struggled to get up.

"Nah, I don't think so." Kevin stepped forward and pushed his shoulder. Devon sank back into the cushions. "No need to prove anything with us."

"So, if you're not well, why did they kick you out of the hospital?" Garik dropped next to him, surprised at how much it meant to have him back.

"I hardly think I was kicked out." Devon knuckled Garik's knee and chuckled. "I suspect they expect I could get better care from you than from them."

"Have you lived with this guy?" Kevin snorted. "He barely knows how to change his own socks."

"Yeah, I know. Typical teen. Still, I've missed you, kiddo. Good to be together again, right-o?" Devon winked at him.

"Right-o, Devon-o." Garik grinned. "What can I get for you?"

"News. What's going on up there?" He thumbed toward the ceiling. "I know nothing, except that the power went down, and the hospital said they would be short-staffed for the day. If we were ambulatory, we were out of there. Do I look ambulatory to you?"

"I hope looks are deceiving," Kevin said.

"Look what I found." Garik reached under the couch and brought out the MicroArt tablet. Revealing it was a pit in his stomach. "I'm sorry you didn't have it and missed Dieter's text."

"Not your fault, kiddo, but I'm glad to have it back." He took it and fell into it, immediately typing inquiries and notifications. Moments later, he spoke to Kevin. "You changed everyone's schedule. How's that working out for you?"

"For me? Busy. For everyone I'm working with, great, I think. The kid's been with me every day. Incredibly useful. Couldn't have done it without him."

"You, the pride of the team." Devon wrapped a hand around Garik's knee and dug in with his fingers. Then he punched him on the shoulder. "If you want to be useful this morning, how about you get me some coffee. You know how to make that?"

"Sure. Kevin's taught me." The dread of revealing Devon's missing tablet dissipated with the request.

"Right-o. He's a good man. So, go."

GARIK HAD *watched* Kevin make coffee, so his assurance to Devon was more hopeful than accurate. He did know what the coffee maker looked like and where it was located.

He enjoyed listening to his two mentors talking—no longer jailers, not with Devon back—sharing the traits of each person on the training schedule and discussing the possible repercussions of the power failure. The location of the coffee threw him off, until Kevin caught his eye and pointed up. He located it in an upper cupboard, relieved. He opened the package and pulled out a scoop and panicked. He looked back to Kevin who held up two fingers, and Garik dipped them out and poured them inside. He added water and turned it on before returning to the board meeting in the living room.

Devon had been accessing his tablet, looking up from time to time, laughing, or asking questions of Kevin, when something on the tablet seemed to grab his attention.

"Kevin, um, you're still in your apartment in the city, right?"

"Absolutely. Why?"

"Then you are keeping track of what's going on up there. The, um, stuff that's happening?"

"Let me see that." He took the tablet and scrolled through several images. "Some of this I haven't seen, but yes. There's the one I showed you this morning."

He handed it to Garik, and Devon intercepted it before Garik could take it. Still, Garik had seen it, and he moaned, "That flag. People, what's with the flag?"

"He's seen this?" Devon seemed surprised. "Tell me you didn't show him."

"Well," and Kevin shrugged. "If you want the truth . . ."

"Aren't you, I mean, you did sign the agreement, didn't you?" almost like it was a secret Garik couldn't be told.

"Oh, that." Kevin grinned. "I took it like this: I can't give out

337

any information about the research facility, but there was nothing in there that said I had to shield this place from the outside. Besides, your boy pumps me every morning for information. How can I resist?"

"So, what has Kevin told you?" Devon glanced at his tablet, studying the screen.

"Everything, I think." He looked at Kevin, who nodded. "I don't know why the power went out, but Kevin can't access the Net in here, so he won't be able to tell me until in the morning. Other stuff, yeah, like the bomb threats at the high school. They haven't had classes for three days."

"So, Kevin's our leak." Devon seemed to come to a decision. "I have more current information, thanks to my tablet. It links to my router which can access the outside Net directly. Look at this."

He held out the tablet, and on the screen, a current news article boasted, "Social Media Fuels Continued Blackout in Bay City."

"The Director said he wanted to eliminate all social media in Bay City, but he can't." Garik reached for the device to read more.

"One more thing." Before he handed it over, Devon turned it around and scrolled. This time, a video played, melting Garik's morning.

"That's . . . not possible." A crowd gathered around a large power company circuit breaker the size of a tractor-trailer rig. A large military truck, likely stolen, had been turned loose to crash into it. The front of the truck was blackened and foamed with flame retardant. The cheering crowd held a mix of flags and placards, some of which showed Garik's picture, and others saying, "Free the Boy," or, "Where's Garik?" Among them were people Garik recognized from Bay City High, although none of his closest friends. Words scrolled across the bottom of the screen. *Will the shipping docks be next? Corona Tower needs to respond before more damage occurs.*

"Respond to what?" Garik fought his face for self-control. He didn't want to be the catalyst for revolution in Bay City. He would sure enough be deported.

"It's happening again." Kevin twirled one finger in a circle at his temple. "Sheesh, to use Garik's word."

"What? What's happening again?" *Tell me*, Garik thought.

"Always. I've seen it numerous times." Devon retrieved the tablet and nodded with a grin.

"What? Just tell me!" Garik wailed. He wanted to strike out. He wasn't a kid, and he deserved to know.

"Chill, kiddo. We're on your side. You, repeating the obvious." Devon looked to Kevin. "Should I clue him in, or do you want to?"

"I will. That car that burned. Remember?"

"Sure." Garik clinched and unclenched his fists.

"And those videos of you?"

"Just tell me."

"I am telling you. People know you're here, more than I've let on. Someone out there is on your side, and they are getting the word out. You, my friend, are stirring up Bay City, and the muck is going everywhere."

"I'll be deported." Garik fell into a chair, consumed with the news. "I just want to be left alone."

"Well, for one, I think the excitement is fantastic. It's the reason I skipped Hollywood. This is the best thing that's happened to me since I won nationals." Kevin grinned.

"Better than Callie?" Garik was glad he could at least tease.

"Oh, much better, especially since she's having a kid now. Not mine, by the way."

"Callie?" Devon frowned. "Okay, kiddo, what have you guys been keeping from me? I want to know all about Callie."

"Sure." Kevin dropped into the chair across from Devon and leaned forward, sharing the story of the failed Olympic competitor.

Garik watched them talk, his own world closing in on him. *Getting the word out.* Who? Muhammad? Ibn? Or maybe Dieter with the rich father and an apartment in Stamford Suites?

He wanted Marisa on his side, but the last time he'd contacted her, the Tower had slammed him back into their basement dungeon. He glanced at Devon's tablet, once more wishing he could contact his friends. He wanted to know more, and he suspected he wasn't hearing everything.

Especially about the people he cared about. That was what he needed most.

THE COFFEE pot dinged, and Garik was startled back to the present. He stood, and the two men barely registered his movement. The aroma of the coffee permeated the room, either that or it seemed that way to Garik because his sense of smell was so acute.

As he poured the coffee into two cups, the lights flickered and brightened. Garik watched to see if they remained on.

"City power." Devon studied the lights in the ceiling. "It's done this before, just not in a while. This is definitely city power. Let me see what I can uncover."

He fell back into the tablet, and Kevin moved toward the kitchen for his coffee. His watch dinged.

"Hm. That's strange. Why is this notifying me now?" He looked at it like a foreign object he'd never seen. He tapped it and nodded. "My morning session with Paul. We're assigning volunteers for possible soccer teams, and I need to be there. Devon, are you okay with Garik staying here? There's nothing for him to do except watch us talk. No game time today."

"More, I *need* him to stay. I've got this." He tapped the cast that had him tied to one spot on the sofa. "You good with that, kiddo?"

"Right-o." Garik found it easy to fall back into the familiar teasing banter.

Kevin left at a run, and Garik carried one of the cups of coffee to Devon. "Anything in it?"

"I'm a black man. You want Kevin's cup?" He nodded toward the counter.

"I can try it, if you think I should."

Devon shrugged. "Your call. You can add sugar to sweeten it or pour it back. It'll keep in the pot."

"Don't think there is any sugar." He didn't move to empty the cup. "It's good to have you back."

"You told me." Devon chuckled. "But thanks."

"I'm sorry about the tablet."

"Why? You found it. What's there to be sorry about?"

"The wreck. You were in a hurry. That was my fault."

"Okay, explain." Devon laid the tablet beside him, just about where it had been when Garik had first found it.

"I knew where it was that first day. It received a message, and I thought I could access the outside Internet with it, and I didn't want you to take it away." Garik's voice choked, and his eyes burned. "I really messed up, didn't I?"

"Maybe, but heh, kiddo, I was driving. You didn't have that accident. I did. But since you brought it up, about my car. I didn't hear how badly it was damaged. Have you seen it since the accident?"

"Yeah. I don't guess you saw the clip." Garik sniffled and wiped at his eyes before moving to sit beside Devon. "Kevin showed me. The Tower tried to take it down, but Kevin saved it before they did

340

and sent it to everyone he knows. Search for *Merc vs. Truck*. I bet you'll find it."

It was in there a few layers deep but not difficult for Devon. He watched the entire thing and pointed to the driver that exited the big truck.

"You know who that is, don't you? Your favorite person."

"Airman Han. I talked to him that night."

"You talked to him?" Devon clicked to replay the video, stopping and stepping it forward when the little car began to roll under the big truck's bumper. Looking closely, they could see the occupants flailing around as the car was crushed, at one point setting off several airbags. "And how are you not in the same condition as me?"

"I heal pretty fast."

"Oh, you do?" Devon grabbed his neck and, with the other hand, ground his knuckles into Garik's scalp.

"Sorry." Garik laughed. "I'll try to heal slower next time."

"You didn't tell, did you?" Devon rubbed harder.

"No, no, stop!" Garik pulled away, panting with laughter. "Jantzen says never give everything away. I said it was your blood."

"Good. He's a smart man. Now, kiddo, another cup of coffee, please."

"Sure, big kiddo. Anything you want." And Garik meant it.

— 11 —

OCCASIONALLY, Garik stayed with Devon on the days when his leg bothered him too much to maneuver on his own. Most days, however, the dark-haired teen was with Kevin in the recreation area or locked in one of the soundproof training cells, quizzing the various hybrids for any information he could get from them.

He was desperate to know that his own induction into the human-hybrid project was, if not a total success, not a failure. He had traded his city life, his friends, and possibly his future for what had amounted to little of nothing. Better hearing, he could run fast, and he healed quickly. Worth it? He had yet to think so.

Outside news filtered in through Devon's tablet and from Kevin's evenings and weekends. The tablet forecasted the anger seething in the city. Kevin revealed the individual downdrafts that buffeted the Tower's authority and power at every turn.

The first citywide power disruption had only lasted several

hours, the first harbinger of the coming storm. Several others were longer, with Old Town going dark at one point for nearly two days. The Tower was unaffected, likely because they now kept their in-house power plant online and fully operational at a moment's notice. The lights would flicker, and things would go on as normal, if at a slightly reduced level of brightness.

Devon hadn't offered Garik his outside access password to his computer, telling him he was willing to share what he learned on his tablet, but only because Garik would learn it all from Kevin anyway. To let the teen explore the real-world Net on his own? Not if he had control over it.

Kevin's arrival each day was a boon for Garik.

"Good morning, people." Kevin had taken to showing up at Devon's apartment in Corona City. Today, he seemed more harried than usual.

"Who are we training today?" Garik had come to enjoy Kevin's sessions with the modified humans in the secretive basement complex. Learning what they could do and seeing them in action was better than any video game he had ever played.

"Soccer game." Kevin mimed kicking a pass with the inside of his foot.

"I knew today would be Paul!" And lots of people Garik didn't know, including non-hybrids from other departments in the research complex: medical, staffing, and office workers, all signed up in the new soccer league. Even Tyrone had joined them in their last game.

"Before you two head off to kick balls with Paul and whoever else joins the game, let's have breakfast." Devon had crutches leaning against the arm of the couch, with foam swim noodles—provided by Kevin—cut and fastened to the top part of each crutch. He shifted his cast off its cushion on the top of the coffee table and leaned for the crutches.

"I can prepare breakfast." Kevin dropped his things on the table, to be stopped by Devon.

"No. I need the exercise. I'm turning into jello. Me getting up is good for everyone, me especially. I might go berserker on you guys."

"Can't have that." Kevin grinned at Garik.

"And Annie is in town and stopping by to see me." Annie was Annie Vanschooneveld, the Tower's foreign affairs attaché. She traveled most of the month, but she had a thing for Devon and hadn't been in town since his accident. Devon seemed pleased.

"Ah, the truth. You need to shave and put on clean clothes."

"That, too." Devon tugged on his crutches to get up, and he hobbled to the kitchen. On the way, he dropped his tablet in front of Kevin. "Tell me what you know about that."

"Can I look?" Garik leaned forward, doing his best to catch a glimpse.

The tablet showed a section of streets between First and Ninth. Garik recognized Stanners Tower at Eighth and Elm in the background. Cars barricaded intersections, tents were set up in the streets, and people gathered in layers of clothing around makeshift fires.

"That's near my house," Garik exclaimed. His aunt's house, actually, six blocks away, but close enough. "What are they doing?"

"It's called Take the City. They've named it the Tower Free Zone. Birch to Cherrywood, the entire section between First and Ninth. You can see the barricades they've set up. Electric fences in some places. You have to sign a document that you are a free person and don't owe allegiance to Corona Tower or Bay City before they'll let you enter."

"First and Ninth blocked off?" Devon leaned hard on his crutches and rubbed his head. The injuries to his temple were scabbed over, and he scratched at one before dropping his hand.

"You can still drive First and Ninth, just nowhere in between."

"I used to go to We Got Junk." Garik studied the image, remembering. "Do you know Wesji there?"

"Sorry," Kevin said. "I do know they've posted signs at the barricades. I've driven by. You can see them easily along First and Ninth."

"Let me see it." Devon held out his hand, and he scrolled to see more. "That's Central Park. Are those homeless people?" Tents and accumulated trash gave a ragtag appearance to the once pristine grounds.

"There's been a call out on social media for people to join in the revolt—"

"We're revolting, now?" Devon shook his head. "What next, military intervention?"

Garik recalled the video posted about his recapture by the Tower's security forces. The military was already involved.

"According to social media, it is a revolt. People are being bussed in from Nevada and Oregon to join the cause." Kevin rubbed his neck. "I wasn't sure I could get here today with the crowds. And everything that happens, someone snaps a picture and uploads it. Then it's shared over and over."

"Can I search?" Garik was never given the tablet, and the computer in the apartment had him locked out of the outside world.

"Sorry, kiddo." Devon glared at Kevin. "Tell me what you want, and I'll do the searching."

Kevin encouraged him. "You'll find pics of my car entering the parking garage."

"I've seen them." Devon was to the kitchen, and he pulled milk from the fridge with eggs and cereal. He was working one-handed, and it looked precarious, but he hadn't dropped anything yet.

"Messages. Are you looking at any of that? And not just pictures." Perhaps Garik's friends—

"Accounts? If you know any logins, I'll be happy to see if they are saying anything." Kevin held a hand over the tablet, ready to type.

"Careful what you offer," Devon warned. He dropped butter in a pan, and it sizzled.

"It's okay. Go, kid. I'm ready."

Garik threw out his favorite social media sites, several of which he knew didn't need logins, not unless you wanted to post. He had to specify accounts, and he named places, businesses, and people he knew. It surprised him that the Tower had accounts, also. He was fascinated to find what they had to say.

CORONA TOWER'S social media accounts painted blue skies and good weather, including two-night specials at Stamford Suites and a discount code for Chow Down. They also offered parking garage vouchers with receipts from The Luncheon Lady. Even the movie schedule at the Tower's 10-Plex was online for everyone to see.

"What?" Garik was crushed. "They have discount codes for Chow Down? Why hasn't anyone told me before?"

"Do you visit their website or their social media pages?"

"Well, no." Still, he thought, he'd paid more than he had to, and that wasn't fair.

"Okay, then, don't complain." From the kitchen, Devon grinned.

Kevin continued to explore, and sometimes, posts let them link to accounts of places and people Garik didn't know. They followed the links, gathering information. The images of signs posted around

344

the city and graffiti on city buildings were telling, but Garik wanted to see texts from people. Marisa, Muhammad, and Ibn, to name a few. Irina, his aunt, didn't have a mobile phone, so he would have been surprised to see anything from her, but the others? They were online all the time.

Devon had managed breakfast passably well, with one leg, two crutches, and a cast that ran from his thigh to his foot. He called to the other two, set out plates and the food, and asked them to take what they wanted. He wasn't serving, so they needed to come and get it. He wanted to lie down before Annie arrived, so he would let them get on with their day. Leaning hard into the crutches, he lurched toward his bedroom, and once inside, he fell onto the bed, calling out, "I'm fine, if anyone asks. Just don't ask right now, cause I'm not willing to be polite if I have to answer."

"Okay, we won't ask," Kevin called with a laugh. He pulled off his watch and held it in his hands. "I don't know if you should see this, and I don't want Devon to know."

"What?" If he couldn't tell Devon, then he wanted for sure to see it.

"Are you certain you want to? Once you see it, you can't take it back."

"That's not fair." Garik threw himself back in his chair and crossed his arms. "That makes me want to see it, and you know it. And you're telling me I might wish I hadn't. How can I know until I've seen it?"

"Just giving you the chance, you know, to back out. Now you can't say I didn't warn you. I found this series of pics on one of my feeds. I think you know some of the people."

The images were from a party. He looked at Kevin, "This is in the Tower, isn't it? Stamford Suites. We were there—"

"The day you disappeared. I thought you might recognize it. Flip through the pictures. You might recognize more than just the location."

He swiped, and there were three people laughing, and one was looking up, almost at the camera. Garik grinned. "That's Ibn." His familiar beard, almost full along his jawline, and a shirt that shouted out, Jezebel and the Sticks. His hair was in long dreads, gathered around him like a wreathing mass of snakes.

"Go on. You'll see more."

Garik did, and in another picture, in a kitchen this time, he recognized Dieter, the new boy whose father had built him the indoor skatepark. This had to be Dieter's apartment. He looked up at Kevin, who nodded and motioned with his hand for him to continue.

He was certain he saw the back of Hayat al-Haber's head, a headscarf tied with a rope. Who else would wear that in Bay City? It had to be his friend. He smiled at his friend's habit of saying, "What, what?"

There were people he didn't know, but Vladimir with his wrestler's shoulders and Giorgio wearing shoes that could only be in the current fashion were sitting knee to knee, deep in each other's eyes. Vladimir was grinning, and Garik could almost hear the joke.

"Why wouldn't I want to see this?" Garik had fallen into the images, and he didn't want to come back out. It was like he was there. He knew each person, and he could imagine exactly what they were saying and how they felt about each other. Even Robbie Icardi, but not with Wajeha. Robbie held a bowl of chips and seemed to have claimed them as his private fiefdom. Then, Robbie was fifteen—or had been fifteen when Garik was inducted—and had no business with a serious girlfriend, anyway.

"You must have missed one." Kevin took the watch and scrolled back. "There. I saved it somewhere else. Here." He handed the watch back.

Garik's heart was gutted. In happiness, in pain, in longing, he couldn't say. It was Marisa, it had to be, though he couldn't clearly see her face. Still, her hand was at her temple, obscuring her cheek, and shifting her dark hair away from her face, just the way Marisa would do. She was alone, looking out an expansive window, and she seemed filled with longing for something outside. Garik followed her view, and like an arrow, he took in the drone aircraft trailed by a long banner filled with words.

THEY ARE FEEDING US LIES. TAKE BACK BAY CITY TODAY.

"Notice her shirt."

Garik realized it was the picture of him he had seen on the school flagpole. He flipped through the images, faster and faster, occasionally stopping to study one. He looked up. "Except for Ibn's, they're all of me."

"You think they know?" Kevin grinned. "Okay, I have a session, and you're with me. Now. Hustle."

Garik did. No more did they step outside, than they ran dead smack into the biggest man in Corona Tower.

"Mr. Lee. I see you have your protégé with you. Good. And you, Garik, are just the person I was looking for. Come with me."

Garik sagged. His good day, foiled once again.

— 12 —

"YOUR SUPERVISION is unnecessary today, Mr. Lee. I am responsible for Mr. Shayk for the time being. I will either return him to Mr. Maye or notify you of my need for your continued assistance." Weston Rodheimer smiled, but his use of last names spoke more than his measured manner and even tone suggested. Two uniforms behind him didn't bother to smile.

"Thank you, Mr. Rodheimer." Kevin nodded. "Is everything okay?"

"In good time. I believe you are due to oversee a soccer game. Halo has been monitoring your work with us. She approves, and so do I. I am surprised to see you were able to get through this morning. Commendable. Now, if you will excuse us." With a nod, the Director dismissed the smaller man.

Garik watched Kevin walk away, trying to read the undercurrents between them. Whatever wasn't being said was out of his depth, and he knew he might as well let it go. As a woman at the next junction in the corridor walked past, paying them no mind, the Director's expression darkened, and his shoulders shifted under his clothing. The transformation was that of a fighter in a ring dominating an opponent.

Garik felt dominated, and he wondered what game they were about to play. He doubted he would understand the rules or that Rodheimer would choose to share them with him if he asked.

"Now, boy, we have matters to attend to. Follow me." Rodheimer turned, surprisingly light on his feet for his massive girth, and headed toward the elevators. The two heavies fell in behind Garik, and there was nothing to do except try to keep up.

"TELL ME what you see, Mr. Shayk."

They had entered a security monitoring station unfamiliar to Garik, an amphitheater lined with massive screens stacked five high and thirty or more side to side. About half showed corridors, likely somewhere in the research facility, and in several, people walked past, about their business. He found Kevin's soccer game in progress just as the ball was put into play. Another showed a hospital operating theater, although Garik didn't know enough to tell the procedure being done.

A handful of the screens were dark, and one winked out as they watched. The rest revealed chaotic views of the city. He recognized the mall, the interior of the parking garage looking out towards Stamford Drive, and a view overlooking Central Park. The tents and littered grounds were the same as on Devon's tablet, just from a different angle. Other views revealed people running, wrecked cars, and suited goons in black riot helmets. One of the black goons threw something, and smoke billowed out.

"Is that tear gas?" In Bay City? Even Garik knew this was bad if they were using tear gas. That only happened in third world countries, and well, his native Russia when people didn't behave as the government wanted.

"Likely. We are under siege. Do you understand that word?"

"Like a castle." He might be a teenager, but he wasn't stupid—or uneducated. Sheesh!

"Without a moat, but to use your example, yes, like a castle."

"Raise the wall." Garik had been on the outside so many times when the twelve-foot-tall wall was raised during mall events to separate the city riffraff from the Tower richies. He guessed Rodheimer had never been forced to stand outside and wish he were inside.

The Director chuckled. "Each time I begin to doubt you, you renew my faith in what you might become. This is bigger than the wall. Your influence has spread to the entire city. I have twice seen you act in a way that suggests you can help us now, if you wish."

"How can I help with this?" Garik felt the anger. His influence? Like he had started this? He was the victim.

"You play your cards close to your chest, as always." Rodheimer motioned, and a tablet appeared. He took it and held it to Garik. "Remember this?"

The video recording of his battle with Justin Kurtew. Justin was fast, spinning his knives into a blur, at one point striking Garik's arm. Blood spurted, then Garik was no longer there; rather, he was across the ring, and he held his arms around Justin, restraining him. Garik remembered Justin's slicing strike down his right arm, getting angry, and standing in shock for a moment before moving against his opponent. Yet, in the video, he was one place and then the next with no movement in between.

"And the table. You rescued the glasses. As if you could see what was about to happen before it took place."

The table. Rodheimer had smashed his hand down, splitting the tabletop, and Garik had stepped up his speed to keep their drinks from crashing onto the floor. He now wished he had let them shatter and bleed their contents out.

"Precognition. You know the term." Rodheimer retrieved the tablet and handed it off to an aide. "I am sure we've achieved our goal in you. Tell me, what about the destruction you see all around us? How have you brought this about? What else are you able to do that we don't know about?"

"I—" Garik had no words. He had known some of this through Devon's searches and Kevin's stories, but seeing it all at once over-whelmed him. But, he had done this? How? What skills had he developed that would allow him to turn Bay City upside down? Jantzen Hefferly could turn into purple smoke. Justin, with his newly developed wings, able to fly. Alyna Lindberg with her razor-sharp claws. They were out there, escaped, free to wreak all the havoc they wanted on the city. The one person that couldn't was him, Garik, the only human hybrid they had recaptured. They couldn't lay the blame for everything on those screens on him.

"Come, now. You can surely give us more than one word. Bay City is your home. I'm sure you want to preserve all the places you love. And the people. Your aunt, your girlfriend." He called out to no one in particular, "Avenue C and Sycamore," and one of the screens shifted to show The Flower Shop. Traffic still flowed along Sycamore, unobstructed, with no sign of the destruction from the other video feeds swirling across the mass of screens. White flecks floated in the air—snow, Garik realized—and the lights in the shop showed through the windows.

"What do you want?" Garik knew what the image was. A threat. He didn't know if Rodheimer would jettison the Bruni's flower shop with a military-sourced missile, shut it down with invented city code violations, or plow it under by widening the intersection and claiming it by right of eminent domain. Likely a missile, as the rest would be too slow to make an impact on Garik's participation today.

"This to stop. You are key."

"How am I key?" Garik's frustration spewed from him. He wanted to strike out, and he watched the room take on a rainbow-hued tint before backing down and regaining self-control.

Before Rodheimer could answer, the door burst open, and Colonel William Brace, with his firm step and straight back, strode in. He was followed by Major Alfred Lipstitch and Lieutenant Colonel Marjorie Fair.

"Colonel." Rodheimer frowned, but he acknowledged the man civilly. "Your presence is not necessary. We have this situation under control."

"As I see, Director." Brace let his eyes rove over the screens. "Absolutely under control, each atrocity on those screens."

"Yes," Rodheimer replied. "We have mobilized security, and soon—"

"Are you a horse's behind, Director, or just so blind you wish to see only what you wish to see?" Lipstitch and Fair glanced away, pointedly giving Brace plenty of room to run. "The U.S. government has given you loose reins, and you have assured us our investment would yield the results we desired. Now, you are allowing bedlam to risk everything."

"Not allowing, Colonel." Rodheimer's words were tighter, and his eyes narrowed.

On one of the screens, a protester under a flag with Garik's picture on it tossed a glass bottle at a parked car. The bottle burst, and flames erupted over the vehicle, sending black smoke barreling skyward. In the scene, a youth with dreadlocks cheered, and Garik thought of Ibn. He wanted to know that his friends were safe, not if the Tower was under attack, or if the military's investments were "yielding the results we desired."

Another screen showed a protester hefting a broken brick. He looked into the camera feeding the image into the Tower's basement security room, and giving the camera an insulting hand sign, he lobbed the brick. It grew larger and larger, then the image on the screen became static and died.

The lights overhead flickered, the screens on the wall blanked for a moment before the images returned, and a second later, the room shivered.

"That was?" Lipstitch voiced the question.

The screen with the view of the aboveground parking garage looking out to Stamford Drive gave them the answer. Dirt and grit floated in the air, the brick and mortar making up the walls of the parking garage began to collapse inward, and as dust filled the air and occluded the camera's view, the screen went dark.

"Lockdown," Rodheimer barked. "Full alert. Walls up. Mobilize everything to clear that garage." He turned to Garik. "Okay, Mr. Shayk. The moat's in place. Tell me that you didn't see this coming, because I believe you did. You could have helped us avoid this disaster."

Rodheimer spun on his heels, walked past the military higher-ups without recognizing their presence, and exited just as red lights in the ceiling began flashing and an alarm wailed.

Garik watched the screens. He knew castles and moats and sieges. He knew how the wars were won. The people inside starved to death, either that or they began cooking and eating one another to stay alive. He didn't want to be eaten, not in stew or any other way.

He had to find a way to fix this, whatever that might take. Except, he had no idea where to begin.

Book 6

Taking the Tower

— 1 —

ALARMS BATTERED the Corona Tower security center.

Garik Shayk scanned the viewscreens covering the enormous wall in front of him. They towered five high and thirty or more wide, a kaleidoscope of moving shapes and repeating images that monitored the basement complex, the 40-story Tower aboveground, and anywhere in Bay City that cameras could be accessed.

Six months earlier, Corona Tower had been a fascinating draw to 17-year-old Garik, an object of desire for the rich lifestyle and the exclusivity that oozed from the shimmering glass building. It cut into the skyline, a black fist that dominated Bay City.

Then, he had fallen into the Tower's highly restricted basement research center and been forcibly inducted into the complex's military-funded human-hybrid research project. His girlfriend Marisa had managed to escape, but the trap had ensnared Garik, his DNA combined with that of a timber wolf and fed back into his veins.

Now, across many of the screens, people carried placards in the streets and smoke billowed from burning cars. Farther from the Tower, traffic moved along First or Sycamore, blissful drivers unaware of the gathering storm in Uptown. Inside the Tower, diners in the upscale Stamford Suites Grill were insulated from the mayhem more than five stories below. Were they aware that the haze now filling the air wasn't rush-hour pollution but the bomb-strewn remains of the Corona Tower Parking Garage on the back side of the building? Would they care if they did?

A handful of the screens were blank, revealing camera feeds already lost. Garik had watched a protestor fling a brick at one, killing the image feed, and another had broadcast the bomb destruction in the parking garage before that camera, too, had winked out.

"We have a situation at Stamford and Avocet."

Garik searched for the speaker to his left. The words had been whispered into a microphone, but his hearing was sharper than most, one bonus of his timber wolf DNA. He caught the acrid odor of restrained panic—again a byproduct of his enhanced DNA—and he located the speaker. She watched the wall of monitors, and he followed her eyes to a rough-looking crowd cheering and rejoicing. He cringed to see his face on a flag one of the revelers carried. Another turned to grab a brick—hefting it to check its throwing distance—and Garik's face rippled across the back of the man's shirt.

Not my fault, he thought, wishing the images away. He didn't want to be blamed for this, and Weston Rodheimer, the Director over the human-hybrid project, had already aimed a massive finger at him.

In the display, a military vehicle pulled up, and several suited individuals rolled out wearing masked riot gear with weapons in hand and began shouting instructions at the group. Trash and rocks flew, the man's brick hit the vehicle's windshield, people ducked, and the situation devolved into bedlam. Someone on the other side of the room overrode a third of the screens, calling out, "Eyes up. We have a runner." A handful of screens changed at once, revealing a drone view.

Garik followed the runner. Several goons gave chase, clumsy in comparison to the slim, female figure. The images on the screens shifted from drone to stationary cameras as buildings or trees obstructed the view. In the background, the duck pond in Central Park reflected the sky. The park was littered with tents and debris from protesters bused in from Oregon and Nevada. Tracking down Park Avenue for several blocks, with the runner and her pursuers leaping over tumbled trash cans and once dodging a car at an intersection, they passed the monument in the small park across from the police department.

Garik cheered the runner on, despite his frustration at the damage in the city being blamed on him. The runner dodged into an alley between Second and Third Streets, confusing her pursuers. The cameras searched for a moment before locating her on Eisenhower. The view shifted as the feed reset, and at the last moment, the runner turned and lobbed something at the goons, creating a flash-bang that washed out the video image. When the screens came back up, the goons held their arms over their face masks, and the runner was gone.

Garik had seen, though. The face, the lithe body, the running style. The runner was Marisa, his girlfriend before he was drafted into the DNA-enhanced human-hybrid shapeshifting project. An avalanche of memories swept away the room, and he was watching the stars with her on the roof of their apartment building, offering her a ride on his Street Strider, enjoying a snack with her on the Corona Mall and listening to her dreams of wanting to be this, do that, make something of her life.

He turned and ran from the maelstrom on the viewscreens. He thought he heard Lt. Col. Fair call his name, but he didn't slow down. Someone must have answers, and he wasn't finding them in that room.

LIFE at the main elevator block sucked the urgency from Garik's frantic run with soft lighting, scented air, and a cleaning lady whose name he didn't know running a floor buffer in a side corridor. He had expected a torrent of military types racing to reach the mall level and miraculously rebuild the entrance to the parking garage. A military contingent was assigned a large section of Basement Level 1, and they claimed a section of the underground parking garage for military only. Their entrance and exit? The bombed garage on Stamford.

Two researchers exited the elevator when the doors opened, pushing a cart loaded with computer equipment. They had to steady a loose monitor twice. They apologized, and irritated, Garik stepped through the door and inserted his passkey. Basement Levels 2 through 4 lighted, the only floors his key allowed him to visit. Not the mall, not the Tower's main lobby, and certainly not the upper floors of the 40-story Tower. He was just lowly Garik, peon research subject, too unimportant and too human to be trusted.

He touched Basement Level 2 for home. Kevin Lee, the acting activities director and Garik's "handler" was in a training session with Paul Gberie, who had been DNA merged with an octopus, giving him the ability to morph his skin color and texture to become essentially invisible. Paul's training was intended to teach him group cooperation and teamwork, and that meant Kevin was overseeing a soccer game.

Devon Maye, Garik's backup handler, should be in the apartment he and Garik shared. Devon had been injured in a car accident, and one leg sported a cast from thigh to foot, the reason Kevin had taken over the position of activities director.

The elevator dinged, and the door opened. Exiting, Garik caught his reflection in the mirrored ceiling. He had ridden this elevator with Marisa to the bottom floor of the basement using Halo Sunchaser's stolen passkey. Marisa had escaped. At least he could take some comfort in that. In the reflection, his hair now curled at his temples, and he looked very much like himself, unlike his shaved scalp from six months ago. The door dinged again, telling him it intended to close, and he retrieved his passkey and stepped into the corridor. He turned left toward Corona City and inserted the passkey that opened the door to the apartment.

"Hey, kiddo. Back already?" Devon had his leg propped on the coffee table with his tablet in his lap. Beside him, Annie Vanschooneveld, wearing red lipstick and her face softened by long bangs, leaned against him.

"I, um—" Garik hesitated. He'd wanted advice, someone to listen to him, to be able to vent his anger and frustration. Now, here, the normalcy of the room mired him in indecision. "I . . . there's a thing happening. I don't know what to do."

"That's odd." Devon, boyish with a blond cowlick at his temple, turned to Annie and winked. "He's never admitted that before. He always has all the answers."

Annie sat up. "What's wrong? Anything we can help you with?"

"The, um—" He looked behind him, realized he hadn't released the door to close, and he turned it loose, waiting until it latched. "You have Internet on that." The tablet, he meant.

"Of course."

Garik wasn't officially allowed access, but Kevin had made it clear his job confidentiality agreement only precluded him revealing what went on in the basement research center and not the other way around. Devon had resigned himself to going along and sharing what Garik wanted to know.

"Devon," Annie cautioned. "I hope you don't intend to do what I think he's asking of you."

Devon shrugged. "Too late. Kevin started it while I was still in the hospital and what was I to do? Anyway, I never let him touch it. I'm not that ready to lose my job." He nodded to Garik. "What is it you want to know?"

"Not me. I know all about it. You're the one who needs to know—"

"Wait a minute." Devon cut in with a puzzled look. "You are supposed to be with Kevin at Paul's soccer game. He sent you back on your own?"

"Just check the tablet. On the way to the game, Rodheimer and two goons commandeered me. Now everything's blown up. Literally. Use that and see if you don't believe me."

"Devon?" Annie reached for the tablet. "Let me see that. I knew things in the city were tense when I arrived this morning. There might be something to what he's saying."

Might be? Garik would have laughed if he weren't so stressed. Marisa! Running from the Tower's goons! Nobody down here concerned! And the parking garage collapsed, possibly all of it!

Then there was Rodheimer's threat against The Flower Shop, Colonel Brace intimating he would take control, and Rodheimer blaming it all on him. He would throw up, if it would help, but he suspected his stomach would still be an iron cable tied in knots.

Annie handed Devon the tablet as she glanced at Garik and back to Devon. Devon studied the screen, stroked the tablet several times, read something, then stroked it again. Without looking up, he motioned to Garik and patted the arm of the couch.

Garik found Annie had pulled up more than the Tower's security cameras had shown. Bay City's news outlets were out in force, and they were having a heyday with the tsunami of violence sweeping across the city.

"Wow, kiddo." Devon shook his head. "The Director likes things to be as low-key as possible, and this isn't it."

"Not the Tower. That he likes to show off." Annie smiled and patted his arm. "I've seen the light show, and so has the city. Every night." Visual effects made it appear the obsidian glass tower repeatedly shattered into black glitter and showered the surrounding mall before reforming to do it all over again. It was the Tower's calling card.

"Right-o, but this is more. This involves the research down here in the basements, and the city doesn't know anything about that." He enlarged an image to reveal Garik's picture on clothing and banners. Several placards mentioned him by name, pleading with the Tower to relinquish the stolen child of the city. "I bet the Director will pull out all stops to get this under control. Not to worry."

"He can't. No one can get out, not any vehicles, anyway. The exit through the parking garage has been bombed."

Devon and Annie looked at each other, and Devon blew out his cheeks and released the air.

"Likely that's not going to be a problem," Devon said, shifting uncomfortably on the couch and restricted in his efforts by his leg.

"Are you sure you should do this, Devon?" Annie's fingers fumbled with a button on her shirt, a clear sign she didn't think he should.

"What?" Garik wanted to say, *Just tell me!*

"There's something no one's shared with you . . ."

— 2 —

GARIK DIDN'T get an immediate answer. Annie's watch chimed at her, and she glanced at it, sat up straighter, and apologized. "Excuse me. I must take this. Do you mind?"

"If you need privacy." Devon pointed to his bedroom.

"Oh, no. Not the bedroom." She laughed and winked at Garik, patted Devon on his good leg, stood, and walked past the front door into the darkened room. She left the door open, letting the murmur of her voice as she answered the call filter back in.

Garik waited a moment for the promised revelation about the "something" that no one had told him, but the moment with the parking garage was broken, and Devon held out his hand.

"Help me stand, okay, kiddo?" He grinned awkwardly, as though he was intentionally shifting the conversation a new direction.

"Sure, Dev-o, change the topic. Leave me hanging." Garik grasped his hand and pulled, surprised at how light the tall man seemed. "Your crutches are right there."

"Hand them to me, please." Devon balanced easily using his good leg and his "mummy" one, but to walk was another matter.

Annie returned, slipping her sleeve down to cover her watch, and she hung a leather satchel over her shoulder. "My exit point. Sorry."

"You just got here." Devon's face fell. "Can't they give you even one morning off?"

"Not with what's going on upstairs. We've got partners across the globe calling in. News travels, and this more than some. I've got fires to put out and funding to save." She stepped to Garik and placed her hand on his forearm. "Devon thinks highly of you. If he gets crotchety, ignore him. The love is still there. I'm telling you this, because I don't think any of this is your fault. However, your name is at the center of the protesters' demands. That's not fair to you, and I know it. I don't know that I can insulate you, so prepare yourself. This isn't likely to be pretty."

She turned to Devon, blew him a kiss, and said, "Maybe next month, if this is all still here. What'cha say?"

"Right-o. What else can I say?" His shoulders sagged.

Annie laughed. She tossed her head slightly to one side to shift her bangs, stepped to the door and was surprised to find it locked. She dug in her purse and inserted her passkey. When the door unlocked, thump, thump, she questioned Devon, "Why is the door locked from the inside?"

Garik raised a hand.

"Oh, right. The jailbreak." She winked at Garik, slipped outside, and let the door close after her.

"SO, WHAT has no one bothered to tell me?" Garik followed Devon through his bedroom and into his bathroom.

"I shouldn't have mentioned that." In the bathroom, the blond man rested the crutches against the wall and stared at his face in the mirror. "You know I'm just an employee here, and right now, I'm not even a functional one, an amputee, almost." He pulled a washcloth from under the sink, flipped on the water, and soaked it. He squeezed out some of the water, pressed the cloth to his face, and ran it over the back of his neck before dropping it in the sink. He pulled the towel from the wall and shook it out.

"Now," and Devon rubbed his face vigorously, leaving his shirt ringed with wet around the collar, "maybe I can think. You need an answer. In situations like this, I ask myself what Kevin would do."

"What's Kevin got to do with this?" Garik was out of patience, and he growled as he abandoned Devon for the living room. *Like always, don't tell Garik anything. Keep him in the dark.*

"I told you I was coming up with an answer. You don't have to be irritated." Devon followed on his crutches in his awkward three-legged gait.

"What gave it away? My hackles on end? Or maybe my howl of despair?" Garik stood at the real window opening into the corridor. The blinds were cracked, and outside, life continued as usual, busy in this part of Corona City. A man rode by on a Segway, a cloth backpack over his shoulders, and his hair in a bun. A pair of women shared a two-seater bike, the first one Garik had seen in the basement complex.

"Well, you did growl." Devon made it a joke. "Hey, kiddo, give me a break. I'm trying to think like Kevin. I can't just *tell* you, so, how can I tell you without actually telling you?"

"By just telling me?" Duh. How simple was it?

"Sorry. I'm not good at bending the rules like him. When I do, this happens." He tapped his plaster-encased leg. "Okay, I have an idea."

"Finally? The city is on fire, and it takes you this long?" Garik was surprised steam wasn't rising from his ears.

"Easy, kiddo. I'm not your enemy." Devon gathered the tablet, made his way to the table, and motioned for the teen to join him. "Let's have a geography lesson," and he tapped the screen to bring up a maps app.

"You do know stuff is blowing up in the city?"

"Back to the geography lesson. Humor me, okay? I'm trying to tell you what people haven't told you, and I'm trying to find a way to do it. Can we do this?"

"Why not?" No Dev-o this time. No teasing. No thump on the shoulder. Garik churned with impatience and irritation, and he wished Kevin were here. He at least told him stuff or said he couldn't, plain as that.

"This is Bay City from space." The water and the land split the image in two. Devon touched the screen, and the coastline expanded to reveal streets and buildings. None were identifiable, but Corona Mall, surrounding the Tower and covering 64 city blocks, was obvious, even from a distance.

"I know all this. What's your point?" Even irritated, Garik was curious if this was a live view and if he would see the smoke rising from the bomb blast that had taken down part of the Corona Tower

Parking Garage.

"The buildings." Devon shifted the image to a three-dimensional view, and as he zoomed in closer, it was clear it was still summer. Trees were in leaf, and yards popped with green.

"That's Overlook Estates. I can see the marsh, so that must be Scenic Drive. I don't see the Tower, but that's the north side of the mall. I've never been on some of these streets. That, though, is Lowell, and maybe that's Beeker Street next to it." Garik pointed to a street that took a sharp right for no good reason. "There Stamford Drive becomes Stamford Lane."

"I need you to look at the buildings."

Garik studied the image. From an overhead view, it had been difficult to see how the ground dropped off as it fell towards The Docks and Harbor Shipyards. In 3-D mode, it was easier. Corona Mall, while level across its surface, formed a cliff face of decorative stone and landscaping on the edge abutting Lowell. Past Lowell and Beeker, the app labeled the streets, Highclere, Castle, Ridgeway, all the way to Shorefront six blocks farther down. Each one dropped off, terraced and shadowed in the app's image.

After a short time, one building stood out. "That one." He pointed to a nondescript building fronting Lowell. It didn't reach the height of the mall's decorative cliff face so had a landlocked view, and tall landscaping crowded it on both sides.

"That one. Okay." Devon zoomed in closer. "What about it?"

"Can I?" He reached toward the tablet.

"Sure. Just no searches."

"Dev-o, I'm not stupid-o."

"I didn't say you were, just no searches." Devon set the tablet in front of Garik and released it.

Garik expanded the image again, shifted it so he could view the sides of the building, and noticed that parts of the building wouldn't come into focus, especially one end. The concrete parking lot in the front was also unusual. It was striped as if for parking, yet it was empty and looked as if it had never been used. Also, the lot simply blended into the street, except for a bold paint stripe where the curb should be, as if to allow access to larger-than-normal vehicles.

Two final things: The windows looked flat, like they were painted, and he couldn't find any air conditioning units to service the building.

"That's not a real building." Garik pushed the tablet away.

Devon studied the image. "Interesting. Now, tell me why there would be a building right there that's not a real building."

"So, you admit it? It's not real?"

"I'm not admitting anything. You said it, not me. I want you to tell me why there would be a fake building next to the mall."

"It's not tall enough to see in the mall—"

Devon nodded in approval.

"—and you can't see it from the mall."

Another nod, and a hand motion to continue.

"Landscaping hides most of it, and someone's gone to a lot of trouble to blur part of the picture. They want to hide something."

"Anything else?" Devon seemed pleased.

"No windows . . . a dead giveaway—" causing Devon to pull the tablet to him to study it closer, "—and it doesn't have any air conditioners on the roof. It would be unusable in summer."

"I never noticed the windows. That's good. So, draw a conclusion."

"You're as bad as Jantzen." Garik rapped the table hard and looked away. "I always have to figure things out. Sometimes I can't."

"Okay, let me show you this." Devon tapped on the tablet, and he pulled up images of military vehicles all over parts of Bay City. There was no shortage. "These are current and dated from this morning. You can see the protesters. Even there, The Docks. How can they be there if the parking garage access is damaged? That's what I'm asking you to figure out." He said figure out with an emphasis to get Garik's attention.

An epiphany like bricks falling from the sky tumbled over Garik. The restricted underground parking garage, the vast number of military vehicles located there, the ramp leading up to the real world . . . most of those vehicles wouldn't be able to navigate the exit ramp, anyway. It was obvious. There had to be a back entrance.

"That building's the second entrance, isn't it?"

"I never said that." Devon smirked, pleased.

"Rodheimer said the city doesn't know about this research facility. There had to be a second entrance. It's the only way to move equipment in and out without anyone knowing." Garik imagined how it might work. The blurred end of the building as a massive garage door? Use the exposed parking lot as a lift, raising and lowering vehicles directly underground? He was certain there was a passage running underneath Lowell connecting directly with the parking garage underneath Corona Mall. How had he not already thought this possible?

"You shouldn't tell anyone you've figured this out.'

"I figured it out?" Garik barked a laugh. "You showed me."

"I will never admit to that." Devon held up one hand in a pledge. "I always suspected the entrance was on Lowell but wasn't sure. I mean, it had to be, didn't it? And that building? Now that I see it, of course."

"You didn't know?" Garik laughed, this time real. "All that, and you had no idea?"

"I just hadn't determined which building. I'm an employee. They don't tell us anything."

"Clearly."

"How could they make that building work as an exit? I've been up and down Lowell. It looks pretty normal."

"Maybe the exit's on the back side. I'm pretty sure the bushes on the side drop into the ground, like the entrance to Batman's lair," Garik teased.

"Could be." Devon tapped the tablet, bringing back the map. "Let me see if I can tell . . ."

Garik was more concerned about the images he'd seen on the screens upstairs. Marisa, running from the Tower's goons in their helmeted riot gear. What had she done for them to make such a fuss?

And that thing she threw, a flashbang grenade. Where had she gotten that? The questions kept coming, and none of the answers wanted to fall into place.

— 3 —

EVEN DURING the city-wide protests, the planned Friday-night events on the mall had taken place as scheduled. The perennial crowd favorite, the Dactyls, had performed two weekends in one month. A martial arts showcase—more martial than arts by the time it wound down long after midnight—had filled another weekend and decorated the pavers with copious amounts of Friday-night blood. Finally, Stephen Klandermans had volunteered to take on all comers in a wrestling competition, the challenge being that losers had to take a hit from another hybrid of their choice. Crowd participation was over the top.

That changed with the explosion that brought down a sizable portion of the aboveground two-story parking garage on Stamford. An announcement went out over the inhouse net that the week's entertainment would be postponed. The Tower's sign posted the news to Bay City as "necessary upgrades to prepare for the best spring season of new performance acts ever seen in Bay City history!"

The human hybrids that depended on their nights on the mall to let loose their inner fires and burn through their pent-up angst simmered. The first of the burning coals lobbed by the frustrated hybrids slammed into Garik and Devon the next morning as they made their way to the Level 1 cafeteria for breakfast.

Devon, still on his crutches, was determined to make a show of being able to get around, and entering the elevator, they were joined by three hybrids whom Garik recognized from his time in the recreation area and the gaming center. Fabiola Bello, a thick-bodied girl with a muscular stance and spiky blonde hair, took her place at the rear, flipping her thumbs back and forth with one foot against the wall. Raphaël Giannotti seemed planted to the floor, with tree-trunk legs and a gray cast to his skin. His nose required more real estate than his face seemed anxious to give. Finally, Mike Lamonte, with tousled hair and large eyes that looked as though he could see everything around him without turning his head.

"Fabi, Raphaël, Mike." Devon greeted each one.

Garik nodded at the three. They weren't on Kevin's training schedule, so he hadn't interacted with them. He jotted their names on an internal list for future reference, picturing Fabi as a fighter, Raphaël as one of God's angels, and Mike saying, "Take a hike!" certain he would remember them.

"Let me." Fabiola reached past Devon to insert her passkey and tap the Level 1 on the panel. She leaned into his shoulder and nearly forced him off balance.

"You good with that, Devon?" Raphaël chuckled, and not in a friendly way. His voice was deep and his laughter deeper, filled with an ominous growl.

"What's with you, Raphaël? And you, Fabi? Be more careful." Devon readjusted his crutches for better balance.

"What's with you, Raphaël?" Mike "the hike" repeated. "Devon must not know they've cancelled the event this week, and that makes me wonder who got the Director riled up." He leaned in and sniffed of Devon's shoulder. "And is that *Annie* I smell on you? I didn't know Annie played so rough. But, like they say, break a leg. It's worth it every time."

Fabiola snickered.

Mike continued, "Do you need Fabi to help you off the elevator, or can you manage that on your own?"

"His pet wolf will take care of him." Raphaël's deep voice ground the words in like sandpaper.

Garik drew in a sharp breath, and the changing colors in the elevator echoed his rising anger. He chanted to himself, *my anger, my control, I am better than that.*

"Keep calm. Don't do it."

Garik focused on Devon's subvocalized directive. He had known Garik would pick it up, but that no one else could.

"Don't do what?" Mike, with his big eyes, taunted Devon.

"Forgot he can hear super-low frequencies," Devon muttered.

"Pet wolf" hadn't bothered Garik as much as them making fun of Devon. What had the man done except help in any way he could, even spending an extended time in the hospital to cover for Garik's foul-up about the tablet? The colors in the elevator grew stronger, ever more vibrant, as Garik's anger shattered the light in the car into a rainbow cacophony. Before the number on the elevator door could fully light up to indicate their destination, Garik was in motion. The people around him froze as technicolor rainbows encased each person. Garik took Fabiola's hand and worked her fingers into Mike's hair. He felt in Raphaël's pocket for his passkey, yanked Fabiola's from the control panel and inserted Raphaël's. He tucked the filched passkey into his pocket and pushed the icon for Basement Level 5, as far away from the Level 1 cafeteria as the elevator could take them with a hybrid's passkey. He was back at Devon's side before the Level 1 light reached full brightness, and he let the rainbows fade. The familiar exhaustion made him shaky, but the satisfaction from his revenge gave him a jolt of excitement.

The doors opened halfway, but before they completed their race to the sides, an alarm began to sound, and the doors stopped.

"Hey, woman." Mike. "Get your hand out of my hair!"

"Eu-wee, gross!" Fabiola gave a screech of disgust.

Garik glanced at Devon and grinned. He noted the red light blinking around the passkey, and a voice began, "Incorrect passkey. Please insert correct passkey now. Contacting security in five." A countdown began.

"Hey," Raphaël exclaimed. "Where's my passkey?"

"Let's go, Garik." Devon nodded.

Garik tried not to let them see his grin. He touched the doors, triggering them to fully retract, and he let Devon out ahead of him. Before he stepped away, he leaned over, pressed the close door icon, and released the doors before joining Devon.

"Hey, wait," Fabiola called as the door sealed her in.

"That was you, wasn't it?" Devon watched as the indicator changed to Level 2, Level 3, Level 4, then Level 5. "They'll be right back, and we still have to eat breakfast with them."

"Maybe not that fast." Garik's synapses crackled with pleasurable energy. "Here's the passkey they need. I traded it for Raphaël's."

Devon began to smile. "I shouldn't find this funny. So, how fast *can* you move?"

"You saw. It does take it out of me." His head had begun to spin.

"No, I didn't see, only the results."

"I think I need food soon. You might want to get rid of the key."

He thought Devon took the passkey, but his power plant switched off about then, the lights went out, and he had no idea if Devon took it or not.

THANK GOODNESS for Ineke Van Steckelenburg. By the time Devon and Garik reached Level 1, Kevin Lee and several of the hybrids on his training schedule were gathered for breakfast. Ineke might seem aloof to those who didn't know her well, but she understood the importance of order, form, and presentation. Even from a distance, she saw Garik collapse at Devon's feet. That was out of order, and the crutches meant Devon was the plucky underdog in this story, the valiant underachiever who would try his best but never quite reach his goals.

Ineke commandeered Zekeria Salem, with his bowl-cut hair and youthful looks, to rescue the situation. Devon assured them he was certain the cure for what ailed the boy was food. He hadn't had breakfast, so?

By the time they had him at a table with food in front of him, Garik had his eyes open and the story was unfolding. Lansana Opoku-Mensah, with her patterned scarification decorating her face, tilted her head and grumbled a personal embarrassment. "That man, sharing my elephant DNA and making me a humiliation unto myself."

"Is not your fault, girlfriend," Veronika Abbink consoled her. "You got the best of the genes, beauty and the ability to think. That man got his big nose from his elephant forebears, and he likes to trumpet his arrogance to everyone who will listen."

The round of laughter made things a little better, but Garik was uncomfortably aware of the mood across the cafeteria. Patches of hybrids congregated here and there, and storm clouds of frustration hovered darkly over them. They remained separated from the military personnel, scientists, and office workers, those people in the non-hybrid sector of the campus needed to keep the project running, even if they didn't have to endure the changes that kept their jobs secure.

Matches in a powder keg of tinder, ready to strike a flame and see how fast it burns.

Garik was reminded of the reason for the events on the mall and why the public never acquired tickets to attend. It was also the reason for the Tower's iconic lightshow, shattering the 40-story tower into a million shards of black glitter before reforming into the Tower to do it all over again. The human hybrids needed a place to let off steam, to be themselves, and to have no restrictions on being the person they had been modified to become. The events were wild because the hybrids were wilder. With the upcoming event cancelled, he hated to think where all these people would let out their steam. They would want someone to blame, and his picture was all over the protesters, literally. In every scene, they wore his face on their clothing, their placards, and likely their lips. If people wanted someone to blame, all fingers would point at him.

Garik didn't especially want to be himself right then, at least not in this place. And he was locked in, with hundreds of people who had little reason to like him.

Death at the hands of a fellow hybrid . . . not a fun way to go.

THE SPARKS Garik imagined speeding along the detonating cord were snuffed out by the appearance of Weston Rodheimer and Halo Sunchaser. The presence of the broad-shouldered Director and his tall, hawk-like second-in-command had a way of smothering every other activity. Rodheimer's face darkened at the sight of Garik beside Devon, although he didn't call him out.

"We need muscle to complete the clean up to the parking garage. Melanie, Chris." He pointed to two people, who stood. He looked across the breakfast crowd, called out, "Joachim, you, Lansana, Ineke and Stephen. Come with me. Where are Raphaël and Mike?"

Raphaël, Fabiola, and Mike appeared, escorted by a security guard.

"What's happened here?" Sunchaser. "Security? Why is that necessary?"

From a distance, another security guard near the elevator held up something too small to see, unless you had a hawk's telescopic vision, and yelled, "Found it!"

"Oh," Sunchaser said with thinly veiled bitterness. "A passkey. I wonder how that got lost."

Garik looked up to see her eyes boring into him. He wanted to melt into his seat. Her intent was clear. He had been with Marisa when she had "borrowed" Sunchaser's key the first time they visited the Tower. Using it was what had gotten him inducted into the human-hybrid program—and, he suspected, earned Sunchaser a reprimand for losing a highly sensitive and important piece of electronic wizardry.

When Rodheimer and Sunchaser left with their team of workers, Devon leaned in, "I'm glad I disposed of that key. I'd hate for them to have found it on you."

His words didn't make Garik feel much better. When Devon had messed up and wrecked his car, he'd wound up in the hospital and now wore a full leg cast. If Garik messed up, he might well find himself facing Halo Sunchaser's electrified sword. He pictured Rodheimer—the Silverback!—with his fingers discharging bolts of electricity into the sword, charging it up, and the sword flashing out and dissolving someone atom by atom until they were nothing.

It had happened. Garik had been forced to watch. He didn't want it to be him next.

Houdini time, anyone? He needed to get out of this place, if only he could figure a way. The Tower's exits were locked tight, but surely there was a crack in the façade somewhere.

The laughter resumed around him, but the darkness in Garik's head was hard to drive away.

— 4 —

EVENTS UNDER Corona Tower continued their downhill slide. As it went across Bay City aboveground, so the dusty depths followed.

Of course, no bombs exploded in the underground research center. Nor did open fights or demonstrations erupt among the human-hybrid participants in the program.

The tension, however, was something you could feel. The awareness of who walked the corridors with you; the group members sitting at the next table; locking your door to your quarters where at other times it wouldn't have occurred to you.

Devon was going nuts in the apartment, and Garik convinced him to try a Segway, determined to stay out and about with the people he had befriended.

"Look, Dev-o, it's easy-o." Garik stepped up on the personal transport device and back off. It remained perfectly still and level the entire time, not tilting once.

"Easy for you to say. I'm guessing I've been driving you bonkers with the kiddo stuff, huh?" Devon held one side of the handle, giving the computerized machine a doubtful glare.

"Why?" The unit didn't have a custom wall charger. It had to be plugged in each night, and Garik dropped to his back to work the cord between a chair and a small table. The wall next to his ZBoard charging station didn't quite hold the larger Segway, and Devon had refused to consider parking it in his bedroom.

"Oh, Dev-o. Easy-o. That type of stuff." Devon drew in a deep breath and released it, a tired sound.

"Hey, no." Garik plugged the unit into the wall and jumped to his feet. He brushed his hands off and then the sleeve of his shirt. He smiled at the morose expression devouring Devon's face. "You're my friend-o, Dev-o," and he clapped him on the upper arm, then balled his hand and punched his shoulder.

"That's kind, but it's not fair to you. I'm in a position of power as your activity director, and that makes us not even. You have to be friends with me."

"That's a good one. Make me laugh at something else. Now get on the Segway."

"Seriously. You don't have to be friends with me. I know how this works."

"What's with you? You're not activity anything right now. Broken leg, remember? Full cast? Kevin Lee? He took your job, at least until you get better, and with you refusing to get on this freedom machine, that might be forever. I'm friends with you because I want to try to save your sorry attitude from getting me equally depressed.

Let's go do something, the pool, watch people train, cheer them on. Quit moping, and let's get out of this hamster cage."

"Hamster cage." Devon looked around. "Didn't know I lived in a hamster cage. You could go with Kevin. He could use your help."

"Kevin has enough enthusiasm for two people. You sit on the couch all day, and when I go with Kevin, I find you in the exact same spot when I get back. Do you even get up at all?"

"Um, yeah. The bathroom is in there." He pointed through his bedroom.

"And then you come right back to the couch."

"Okay, yeah." Devon shrugged.

"I'm saving you from that, friend-o. Now get on-o."

Devon took a deep breath and decided his good leg needed to go on first, but he leaned too hard into the steering arm and it twisted, toppled forward, and he tumbled straight down.

"I told you!" Devon balled a hand and smashed the floor.

"And I told you. It's easy-o." Garik reached for his hand to help him to his feet to start over.

"And enough with the 'o' after all your words. I get it."

"Right-o, Devon-o." Garik continued to hold out his hand.

"Sheesh. Why I ever agreed for you to share my apartment—"

"I got you doing it!" Garik hooted. Devon frowned as Garik grasped his hand and pulled him to his feet, light as a feather. "You're using my words. Excellent!"

"God help me, I'm becoming you."

"Only if you can bark." Garik caught his eye and grinned. "See, I can find it funny, too. I don't like being here, but it's not all bad. I miss my friends outside, and I wish I hadn't been recaptured, but every now and then, I like a little bit of it."

"That day we first met, remember?" Devon's eyes had gone shiny.

"The climbing wall? How could I forget? I was mortified."

"Remember what I told you?"

"That I couldn't climb? No, I remember. You said even Amy could climb the red route."

"Sorry for that. No, I said I might even like you if you stuck around." He shrugged. "Well, you stuck around."

"And?" Garik teased as Devon focused on the personal mobility device.

"And what?" He rocked the steering arm, letting it resettle each time, and taking a deep breath.

"Do you like me now?"

"I'm not on this mobile death trap, yet. We'll see." But he grinned.

"I should push you over just to see you fall. Here, bootie on first, then your real foot. I'll hold it till you balance. There, got it?"

Devon looked dubious but he was standing and balanced on the Segway. He said, "Now what?"

"We go and say hi to the world." Garik took his ZBoard from its station, dropped it to the floor, and hopped on. He motioned for Devon to follow, and they headed out the door.

THEY STAYED in Corona City to start. Devon was familiar with the area, and there wouldn't be any surprises, especially with most people at their places of employment or training on one of the lower floors.

Several times, Garik had to encourage the older man. "Lean into it to go faster." Or, "It's just a curb, Devon. It'll go right over. Trust your machine."

Garik convinced him to practice in both of Corona City's parks. Across grass, up and over walkways, and in one place, over a curved footbridge that crossed an artificial stream. On the way down, the Segway built some speed, and Garik called, "Just lean back."

The second park held the Corona City pool surrounded with plantings and small trees. "I've not been here before. Very pretty," he called to Devon, and he stepped off his skateboard to explore. A skylight the size of the pool jutted two stories upwards. He remembered this from the outside, a big service block of a structure. Before living underground, Garik had never dreamed it topped an indoor pool in an underground park.

"Okay, I'm still over here. Broken leg. Yoo-hoo."

"Segway." Garik motioned with his hand.

"Curb."

"Lean into it." Garik pantomimed. "I'll rescue you if you fall."

"I'll expect you to follow through."

When Garik heard the wheels crunch beside him, he pointed up. "That should be clear, right?" He had expected to see blue, and the sky through the glass roiled with gray.

"Should be." Devon followed his hand, and the Segway began rolling backwards.

Garik took the handle and steadied it. "Smoke, maybe?" With what was happening in the city, that worried him.

"Burning leaves, perhaps. People do rake and burn them." A crashing sound beyond the glass two stories overhead said otherwise.

"Not leaves. Be quiet for a moment." Garik listened to see if he could pick up on anything to help determine the cause.

"A car crash?" Devon smiled helpfully.

Black smoke began to billow over half of the glassed expanse. "I didn't hear any breaking glass, and the smoke wouldn't look like that."

"That makes sense."

"Where's the nearest Internet access?" Garik berated himself. The blank corridors and basement "streets," mostly empty. He had been so focused on Devon's riding skills that he had eclipsed everything else from his awareness. Now, somehow, they had missed out on something vital happening outside. With everything else that had taken place, there was no way it didn't involve him, and the only way outside was through Devon's non-hybrid Net access.

"My place. Or anywhere with a hardwired computer. I would need to log in."

"What's closest? The gaming center?" Garik had begun to run toward his ZBoard, calling, "Keep up if you can."

He tried not to outpace the half-crippled man too badly, but Garik wasn't so far gone from Russia that he didn't remember what burning buildings sounded like, and Kevin had kept them abreast of the increasing tension throughout Bay City. He felt it in the marrow of his bones.

They were barely started when Kevin appeared. He was in his soccer clothes, a white tee, black shorts, and tall white socks, with athletic shoes. Paul Gberie matched him, and as he ran, he kept morphing his skin color and texture to the surrounding walls, a clear sign of his urgency. The third person Kevin breathlessly introduced as Joachim Warakaulle, a man with a South Pacific vibe, with skin color and hair to match. Kevin took time to explain that he and Paul had been putting in extra time in a soundproof training cell, and Joachim had been sent to find them to get them to the lobby. Everyone was there. That's when Kevin knew he had to search for Garik and Devon, and *what are you guys doing way out here, anyway? Didn't you notice everyone gone?*

"Practice," Garik answered, "on the Segway," as they headed

371

toward the elevator.

NOT EVERYONE was upstairs, but Garik understood what Kevin meant. All the human hybrids and many of their instructors, aides, and medical facilitators, anyone, basically, not from Level 5, the hospital, or the research labs. Even a scattering of military types and clerical office personnel were present.

Televisions had been rolled out, with large screens, revealing just why so few uniforms were on the floor with them. The different screens showed various snapshots of Bay City, but they all revealed the same story. People were running, some holding placards aloft, and others attempting to get out of the way. A number carried flaming Molotov cocktails, and occasionally someone would throw one, and it would smash through a storefront. Firetrucks pumped water on burning buildings, but there were so many aflame that how could they put them all out?

It was impossible to make out individual people. Some of the buildings, yes. The Luncheon Lady, aflame. The City Transportation Depot was blackened on one side, as if a fire had started but hadn't taken hold before being extinguished. One of the big old houses on Pill Hill, the roof crashed in. A tornado of sparks spun skyward. It would soon be consumed by the flames.

What had Garik heard burning near the pool's skylight in Corona City? It was mostly residential, except for the area to the north where the supposed back entrance to the underground research center was located. Even that wasn't likely noticeable from the pool, as it would be blocks away.

Then there it was, a giant effigy of the Tower, right there in the middle of Stamford, beams and logs and crates piled into a towering bonfire, blazing away.

"Look at that," Garik whispered. "Someone wanted to send someone a warning."

"*We* burned it." The rumble of Rodheimer's voice broke Garik's focus on the television screen.

"Why? The rioters are the ones causing the damage. Why would you make it worse?"

"Look again, my boy. A rescue attempt, I believe. A scaffolding, perhaps for a crane. Tell me, boy, who would they wish to rescue?"

"I don't know." Garik was truly frightened.

"The deeper we go, the more difficult I find it to believe a word you say."

When Garik unearthed the courage to look around, the Director was gone. The carnage on the screens still ruled. Bay City was coming apart. Who knew when it would end?

— 5 —

THE TALK rose and fell as people pointed to new atrocities, letting themselves be pulled from screen to screen like puppets on a string. Eventually, the shock faded, and a few people wandered off to sit in the cafeteria—set off from the main lobby by a large, arched doorway some hundred feet wide and nearly to the ceiling—or make their way to an elevator or drop to the floor in groups of two or three.

Garik, Devon, Kevin, and Joachim wandered into the cafeteria where the blare of the rioting in the city was muted. The televisions continued to shift from atrocity to atrocity, revealing the slashing destruction being torn into Bay City's skin like a samurai's sword cutting to the bone, but it was easier to not look.

Garik found it harder not to listen, and the yelling and sounds of destruction were a mallet banging his skull. He found it easier to stare into space, his eyes seeing the tables, the serving lines, the cleanup areas, and the kitchens that opened to the rest of the room.

The only way to truly avoid the screens was to keep them to his back. Joachim sat in a chair across from Garik, studying him, while the two "normals" discussed life outside the basement complex, with Devon pressing Kevin for what he knew.

"What?" Garik grew irritated at Joachim's attention.

"Nothing." The man grinned and looked away.

"No, what? You're not looking at me like that for nothing."

"I'm not looking at you, man. Out there, that's where I'm looking." He tilted his head toward the screens in the lobby.

"Not a minute ago, you weren't." Garik had first seen the man with his skin and hair and felt a kinship. Different ethnicity but different in the same way Garik's bronze skin and curly mop of hair made him, ostracized by people who didn't like things that were "different" to intrude on their safe little lives.

"You sitting so wrapped up in all this." Joachim waved his hand around him, indicating the two activity directors and the screens blaring the news from the outside.

"I am wrapped up in all this." Garik narrowed his eyes, his anger

373

overcoming his dismay at the images he'd seen of Bay City's undoing. "Did you pay attention to any of that? Those people are protest-
ing because of me. That's my name on those placards, my picture on
their shirts and signs."

"Yeah, man, I noticed." Joachim leaned forward, and he looked
side to side as if checking for people who might overhear. "I've seen
all this before. The overlords." His eyes moved to take in what he
could see of the upper floor of the basement that stretched around
them for acres and acres. "Us, the peons, here just because they say
we can be here. Then, there's those guys—" he pointed to where the
screens still let the outside leak in, "—who think they can right every
wrong and save us. They don't even think that maybe we don't want
to be saved. What do you think about that?"

"Sounds like nonsense to me. I want to be saved."

"That right, huh, man?" Joachim leaned back, and he stretched
one arm over the back of an adjacent chair. "Then why aren't you
out there cheering them on? I don't see that from anybody here.
Nope." He swiveled his head and looked around. He leaned in again.
"And you know why? All those people don't want to rescue you.
Nope, not in a heartbeat."

"But—" Garik tried to work out the man's logic. They were
torching the city in his name. "Of course—"

"I see you're working on it up there. It just hasn't become pud-
ding yet." Joachim reached and tapped Garik's forehead with his
knuckles. "Now, let me tell you how this goes. One, those people out
there get what they want. This place turns throat up, gives in, and
they get to walk in and take what they want. You, me, even, and
maybe a lot of people in here. Not all, mind you, because some of us
come from far away just to get done to us what was done to you.
Maybe we don't want rescued, and maybe they don't want to rescue
us, but supposing they do. What do they get, tell me that, man?"

"I get to go home." Just talking about it made Garik want it more
than ever.

"But do you? That's the hundred-dollar question. I was there
when Rodheimer gave you that pat on the back."

Pat on the back. Garik forced his gears to shift. What pat on the
back?

"Not as bright as we thought, is he?" Joachim grinned, asking no
one and, in the same breath, asking everyone.

"What pat?"

"Your welcome home. 'One of our own has returned to us,' that type of welcome."

"That." He remembered the first night after his recapture. All the hybrids had been required to gather in the lobby. That was the night when Sunchaser and her electrified sword had sucked up a condemned hybrid and melted her into the nothingness of atomic dissolution. "I'm on the outs with him now."

"Sure, you would be, all that nonsense outside. Tell me, when you were out, did you get the welcome you wanted?"

Seeing Marisa in the shop washed over him, and he studied the floor. His dismay at her rejection, the chase, and his recapture.

"Don't answer. I can see it. Man, you've got to know that they don't want you. They want what you used to be, and you can never be that again. This place gave you a new life, well, for you, maybe stole your old one to do it, but that doesn't change that you can't go back. You're one of us now, man."

"What's way number two?"

"Okay, you're sharper than I give you credit. Power doesn't give up power without a fight. Way number two is Rodheimer or whoever is in control—"

"Whoever?" Garik jerked his head up. "He's the Director."

"Yah, man, but he don't fund the place. Get what I mean? *Whoever* is in control opens the taps, and out flood the guns, the troops, whatever they need to get back control. That's way number two. Don't think they won't do it."

"They're already out there. Those people are military, Air Force, likely, even in those black suits—" Garik cut off his tirade. He didn't *know*, but it made sense. Who else could they send out?

"There's always more." Joachim nodded his head several times.

"You guys?" Garik crossed his arms on the table and rested his chin on them. He glanced at several groups doing the same as they were, trying to work though the events pounding at Bay City's infrastructure.

"Ha! That's wishful thinking." Joachim seemed to find Garik's suggestion a good joke.

"Isn't that what this is for, training people for military exercises?"

"Hey, man, everyone knows the people you left out there. Hefferly can pretend to fit in, but you think that Justin dude can even be around people without them wanting to know what Rodheimer is doing to people down here? Even down here. You can pass, and maybe me, but Mike with those eyes? Jacquelien? No, no, maybe Paul. Get Paul up there, and no one's going to look at him twice, is that it? We're not superheroes. We're freaks, at least to them. That's why the events, so we can pretend to dress up, but really it's just us, normal in one way, but bizarre freaks of nature to anyone on the outside."

Garik kept his eyes on Devon for a moment, still tight in conversation with Kevin, attempting to get his head around the man considering him a freak of nature. Then, Kevin. If Garik grew a tail and howled at the moon, would he still claim him as a friend? Marisa didn't even know, and she'd dropped him right into the Tower's clutches. With her arm twisted, he was convinced, but still. Here he was back in the Tower's grasp.

"Then why bring everyone up here if they aren't going to be part of the plan? I don't get that. If they're planning to keep us sealed in here like microbes in a laboratory, why bother? Let us train, and that's the end of it. We don't know, and we're better off for it."

"Support, I think, and mental conditioning. The idea that if anyone gets a notion that out there's better, that's what the reality is. We're better off here." He shrugged. "Maybe. It looks the way you want depending on where you're standing."

Noise in the main lobby caught their attention, and they saw several black-suited men show up and begin rolling the televisions to the side. They were still broadcasting the events on ground level, so they weren't being disconnected, more as if they were in the way.

"What now?" Paul appeared at a neighboring table, literally appeared, as if shifting from one light spectrum to another.

"Oh, it's you." Joachim looked annoyed. "Rude boy, that's you, man. You hiding in plain sight? Not cool."

Paul was once again in his beaded tunic. It shifted from imitating a table and chair a fraction of a second after Paul appeared. He laughed, causing Devon and Kevin to look his direction.

"I must practice my skills. I am getting better. What is happening?" He pointed to the commotion in the lobby.

"I'm guessing you overheard. Do you need me to repeat it?" Joachim drummed his fingers on the table.

"Predict, not restate." Paul smiled, revealing the gold letters inset into his front teeth. He winked at Garik and called to Kevin. "As a *teammate*, may I inquire what my *teammate* predicts is about to happen?"

"No idea." Kevin shrugged. He stood and joined the dozen others from across the room who were headed to the door for a closer look. "Bet it's good. Come see."

"I will wait for you to discover and share." He shifted his attention to Garik and Joachim. "I have a joke I wish to share with you. You will find this very funny. Two chickens come upon an egg in the middle of the road—"

Before he could go further, booted feet began to echo in the hard-walled space. The sleek furniture, bright colors, and modern art that gave the area a museum-like hush receded with the press of black-suited men in full riot control gear. The entire area darkened, although the lights didn't change brightness. Each one wore a face shield with three metal bands across the smoked surface, a black helmet, and an active response shooter vest over a multi-threat body armor vest. A tactical backpack with entry tools dotted the shoulders of a quarter of the men, and many wore Damascus-style hard shell armor, including knee and shin guards, or carried some portion of it in one hand. Among them were various weapons, including pneumatic blaster guns and several spooling guns. Two men shouldered detonation cannons, normally used to dispel flocks of birds, but the prospects were endless when the flocks were of the human type.

A tall man, bulkier with muscle than his companions, took a position at the front. "Ready?" he called.

"Ready, sir," the team replied as one.

The leader turned, and they began to run in step towards the military housing section of the Level 1 portion of the basement, only to turn at the last minute and disappear into the corridor leading to the underground parking garage where the military-style and tactical vehicles were parked.

Garik had two thoughts when he saw the last man vanish into the distance. One, that was a lot of force for a security team already dispersed throughout Bay City. Where had they come from? With their helmets and gear, it was impossible to identify them.

Two, access from the parking garage to the military quarters was direct and did not route through the lobby. The chances of the men being military were unlikely.

Three, he remembered Devon's observation. Most of the tactical vehicles in the garage couldn't navigate the parking garage egress up and through the aboveground parking garage. These men were taking a different way out.

He wanted to follow, to be with them, to Houdini out the parking garage using the secret exit. But that was possible only if he had a riot-control suit to wear.

And just like everything else down here, he had no idea where he would find one of those.

Life as Garik, a looming disaster in every way.

— 6 —

SEVERAL OF the screens could be seen from inside the cafeteria, revealing reporters talking to viewers, their neatly coiffed hair belying the grime and blackened disease of disruption invading the city behind them.

Garik's attention was drawn to a drone shot of the mayhem. The camera hovered over the city, focused on Central Park and the garbage and broken tents left by the protesters. Fires had stained the playground equipment with blackened soot, in several places still trailing smoke into the air; and plastic bags, one in purple clearly stamped Fasst Market, floated at the edge of the duck pond. A lone duck prodded it, perhaps hoping for a tasty snack.

The image shifted—a different drone, likely—to the blocked-off area between First and Ninth, the "Take the City" Tower Free Zone. The camera panned south, and Garik could just see the roof of City View Apartments. His heart skipped a beat, and his back tingled. He imagined he might find Marisa on the roof looking out over the disruption, perhaps even observing the very drone looking back at her, a link of a sort between him and her. A connection. A renewal of what once was, not Joachim's acerbic accusation that she would have no interest in him as he was, only in what he had been.

He saw the truth in it, however. There was no Marisa on the roof of City View Apartments. From City View's vantage point, most of Bay City was hidden. Taller structures dominated the apartment building, blocking the light, the air, the life from it. Garik quickly pushed his last encounter with Marisa to the deepest part of his mind, shut it away as if it had never happened. It was a betrayal of them, of their time together, of the dreams he had once had—still had!—of their possible future together.

Then the camera rocked downward as the drone began a flyover of the barricaded area. Flattop buildings were drizzled with ocher and gray, weather-stained; and in the shadows of roof parapets and air conditioning units, remnants of snow hunkered for safety against the sun. Bare tree branches cast spidery shadows on concrete sidewalks. Open-top barrels stood in the center of several streets. One was ablaze as people huddled around, warming themselves with gloves, mufflers, and toboggans. They seemed oblivious to what was happening elsewhere in the city.

Crossing Ninth to the north, the luxurious cul-de-sacs of Shady Ridge Acres were business as usual, the tennis courts and swimming pools, several covered, and as many open and glittering with reflected sky. The divide between rich and poor. The haves and have-nots. The peons and the overlords . . . the power brokers, the Weston Rodheimers of the city.

The view slipped down the hillside past West Corona, over Starnes and Richardson and the parking lots at Waldorf's Department Store, filled as if protests weren't happening elsewhere in the city. Richies unite! Let nothing get in the way of shopping for more luxury goods to pack our over-filled homes!

Then Waldorf's was gone, and Garik tried to imagine where the drone was headed. The riot control troops that had just left the Tower . . . the drone traveling north . . . the only thing that direction was the waterfront. The Docks. Harbor Shipyards. Then there was Argyle Station to the west, with Interstate Transport nearby. Both were vital to The Docks and the Shipyards, and The Docks and the Shipyards to them. They were the life of Bay City, its reason to exist, or at least the reason a hundred years ago. Now the city had Corona Tower, Bay City Medical, Ransom Communications, Ai Kee! and a hundred other businesses, but the waterfront remained essential to all the rest.

The drone's camera fell into the sweeping bend of Shorefront Boulevard on its way to the four massive piers of The Docks, crowded with overhead cranes and warehouses. Garik knew the area, one of the places he and Maria had liked to explore. Why show this to the world if things were normal, under control and operational?

Soon, the monitor revealed a warehouse in flames and a tractor-trailer rig twisted awkwardly, spilling boxes of electronic goods. People were looting, even as the drone's camera panned them, zooming in to reveal two men wedging a large, flat television box into the back of an open-top Jeep. Without strapping it down, they jumped inside and sped away. One of the men held the box against the wind.

Along the bottom of the screen, a banner scrolled: "Hundreds descend on The Docks, disrupting commerce in and out of the city. Harbor Shipyards closed after bomb threat. Interstate Transport officials say the economic impact could soon be felt across the western half of the United States."

"Still want to be out there?"

Like waking from a nightmare, the question jerked Garik's attention back into the pandemonium of the lobby. Paul Gberie was beside him; and more people, most he was unfamiliar with, watched the video feed with them.

"It's bad." It was worse than bad, but his comprehension was eclipsed. He never expected Bay City—his home!—to ever experience what he had run from in his Russian homeland.

"Did you miss the shock troops?" Paul cocked an eye Garik's direction. "Bet they show up on those cameras if we wait on them."

"The ones headed to the—" He almost said secret exit, and he clamped his words off. "The ones we just saw?"

"Getting smarter by the minute." Paul laughed, and he gave Garik's shoulder a good slap, causing him to nearly stumble. "Come. Some friends and I have a theory. Since you're key—by your own description—we want you part of our discussion."

As Garik turned to follow Paul, the scene on the screen zoomed out, and black suits began to tumble from military-type transports. They spread out in hopes of containing the virus invading the waterfront.

Garik was no longer certain it could be done.

"YOU KNOW Jacquelien and Bert," Paul threw out casually before they reached the group sitting around one of the clean and modern "conversation" groupings in the bright, museum-like lobby.

"Like I could forget." He pictured them, Jacqueline with a red line tattooed down her face and Bert with hair even a punk rocker would enjoy rocking.

"And the reason they aren't with the shock troops fighting the war." Paul pricked Garik with his reminder.

Garik felt the prick and accepted it as justified. Still, war. The implication was ominous. As they approached their destination, Garik was distracted by six striking hybrids he had never met, all no less forgettable than the two he already knew.

He had begun to realize that the friends he'd helped escape the

Tower were normal by comparison, well, with the possibility of Justin, and Justin with his praying mantis wings was outrageous by even a hybrid's broad measure.

"What's your beauty mark, sweetie?"

Garik located the speaker, a woman with emerald hair and bright, iridescent patches over her skin. She studied him through emerald-green eyes. Body suit? He suspected that down here, no one would bother, not unless they were attending an event, and this weekend's had been cancelled.

"Forgive Charlotte." Paul apologized for the woman, but his skin morphed into an angry, mottled red. He called to her, "Chill, pill. You're not a beauty, yourself."

"Yah, just ribbing. You're okay, sweetie. Come meet the bunch of us. We're nicer than that loser you're with."

Two lookalikes, tall, dark-haired brothers, with pale skin and full features, likely twins, smiled at the tease. One, with a hair-free break in his right eyebrow, touched his brother. The other, with a small mole by his left eye, seemed more reserved. He nodded and removed his brother's hand from his arm.

"Anatoli and Andrey, meet Garik. Garik, the twins."

"*Garik, the twins.*" Anatoli with the eyebrow repeated Paul's words, an exact mimicry.

"And we are *Anatoli and Andrey.*" Andrey mirrored his brother when he recited their names, and he also could have been Paul speaking.

"That's good." Garik laughed. "Parrots?"

"They. Can. Parrot." A pretty woman with coffee skin, a dark halo of hair, and long legs looked down at them. They were tall. She was taller. She clipped her words as if each was a sentence all on its own. "Melanie. Hatherill. If. Paul. Doesn't. See. Fit. To. Tell. You."

"Garik, meet Melanie Hatherill. She runs really well." Paul's skin now rippled blue with laughter.

"I've. Heard. You. Are. Faster."

"Maybe. Glad to meet you, Melanie." Then and there, Garik decided. These people had a status quo among them, a pecking order, and he didn't plan to be at the bottom of it. He would be if he didn't assert himself. He put a little attitude into his bark, calling, "Anatoli and Andrey," to get their attention.

"*Anatoli and Andrey.*" Anatoli could have been Garik speaking.

"Funny how you can do that, but I didn't get your last names. Do you have one?"

"Anati?" Andrey nudged his brother. "Do we?"

"If you can pronounce it, *sweetie*," he barbed.

When the man said sweetie, Garik heard the shift in his voice. He mimicked Charlotte. The woman frowned.

"My last name is Shayk. I'm pretty sure I can handle whatever you throw at me. Shoot, I'm listening." Van Hermoso, his occupational therapist, had used that phrase.

"Bur-gor-ski—" Anatoli drew it out like he was sure Garik couldn't handle it, or he wanted to mock him. Garik wasn't sure, and he cut him off.

"Burgorski. My mother's sister's married name. Simple. For the rest of you, if you want to meet me, last name, please. I've got a good memory and I won't forget." At the same time, he etched the Burgorski twins in his mind, picturing his grandmother's twin dolls Annie and Andy skiing down a booger of a mountain. He was certain he would remember.

Charlotte raised a chartreuse finger, and she offered, "Mnich," with a grin.

"Got it, Charlotte Mnich." Garik said three times to himself, Charlotte Mean Witch. He grinned at the image.

Louise King wore flowing robes, likely a coverup, Garik decided, though for what he couldn't imagine. Her face's patterned colors gave her a royal presence, and he pictured her on a throne. Louise King was stamped in his memory.

The final hybrid was Chris Beer, a man whose long, coarse hair and thick-soled boots gave him a workman's stance. He prefaced his introduction with, "Oh-h-h-h," almost like a horse's neigh, and then gave his name. Garik pictured the man at an old-fashioned western bar ordering a beer, meaning the man would forever be Chris Beer in Garik's mind.

THE GROUP'S theory didn't fall too far from Garik's own. He didn't reveal Kevin's part in jumpstarting the protesters, but they knew Jantzen Hefferly, the one-time second-in-command of the human-hybrid research complex, was on the outside. The man had a reputation as a Loki-type prankster, someone who liked to prod the system to get the results he wanted.

They also asked about Joanie McDonald, with her mohawk and swaggering half-phrases. Likely, she would do all this, right? And

Alyna Lindberg, with her vicious Komodo dragon claws . . . they described damage they had seen that could only be Alyna.

Each of Garik's fellow escapees got thrown into the discussion's volatile blender. Julia Cantos, Giselle Harmon, Amy Howe and more.

Louise was especially interested in John Carter, a larger-than-life blond god, even fitter than Devon Maye had been before his confinement in his one-legged cast. Garik heard her emotions when she spoke his name, literally heard them. Her heart pounded faster, her pores opened to expel excess warmth, and she gave off the faintest papery rustle when she put her hands to her face to pat her flushed cheeks.

Garik hadn't imagined John with an admirer. He wondered if the man knew. He grinned. It would be a good thing to store away. He could tease him when they next met.

And they would soon, he was certain of that.

— 7 —

THE NIGHTMARE taking over Bay City didn't remain in Bay City.

A security team all in black entered the austere and modern lobby with its displays of cutting-edge sculptures and widely spaced seating areas. Closer to the cafeteria entrance, the television displays still hawked the outside disruptions, hoping to sell the horror to anyone they could draw in, but nearer Garik and his new acquaintances, quiet and organization ruled. That made the four black goons stand out like black beans in a sea of white. Weapons dangling from their belts shifted with an ominous sound, suggesting heavily armored protection they couldn't see.

The four goons drew up sharply, and Garik could hear their joints lock into place, prepared for resistance, and determined not to let it deter them from their mission.

The lead goon spoke.

"Major Judy Kennedy. And this is Captain Ryan Lee." The captain didn't nod or give any indication he had been introduced. His shirt said Lee, the only way to tell which of the three people accompanying the major was the captain, unless they wanted to look for rank insignia. She didn't see fit to introduce the final two, so likely they were far down the totem pole. "Garik Shayk, will you please stand? Director Rodheimer requires your attendance."

"For?" Garik wasn't military, and he understood the Director held all the power, but he wasn't sure it was military power.

"Not mine to say. If you will." She took one step back, as if allowing Garik the room to join her.

Garik looked at the people around him, inquiring with his eyes if they had anything to offer to explain this. In the distance, the cafeteria held its arms around Devon and Kevin, the two people he knew and trusted best. They were too far to offer him any help.

"Paul?" Garik stood, and he turned his full attention to the colorful man. He noted his adaptation enabling him to blend into any background scenario was now tuned to mimic the security team. It wasn't exact but not far off, either. Garik understood the pointed joke, the mimicry that made fun of the people who dared to step into the hybrid's world to make them dance to a tune they didn't hear or care about.

"Ship to, my young'un," Paul said with a mocking tone as his face shifted into a bearded pirate. "Else they'll have you walking the plank soon's the sharks snap their shiny teeth." He laughed, bowed as if accepting adulations for a stage performance, and offered his hand. "Watch for that sword," he whispered, and he winked. "I hear it has quite a kick."

"Thanks." Garik wanted to roll his eyes, and he fought the impulse. Then he turned to face Kennedy. "Ma'am."

It seemed ominous, a black cloud, when Kennedy and Lee took his left and right flank, and the other two fell in behind. The feeling was old coffee, staining the moment, hard to swallow. Like he might try to get away, perhaps run for the hills, make this his opportunity to Houdini once again and be gone from here.

He would if the opportunity presented itself. He let his eyes scan the area as they walked, hoping, yet nothing appeared to him. He was a blind person being led into the darkness. Even his quickness was no good to him when he had nowhere to run.

He couldn't get one thing out of his thoughts. What could the military want with him? The last time he had seen Colonel Brace and the Director in the same room, they had been at one another's throats.

Blackened grounds of dread swirled at the bottom of Garik's cup, and he expected it to be bitter when he was finally forced to drink it down.

"ABOUT TIME." Rodheimer's growled greeting grated across the room.

"Sir." Major Kennedy nodded, and she turned to Colonel Brace, also in the room. "Colonel, is that all?"

"Thank you, Major. Please wait outside with your team. I may need your services again."

"Yessir." She saluted and backed out of the room, leaving Garik with the two men. The tension was a brewing thunderstorm, and electricity crackled in the air. Brace broke the tightly tuned silence first.

"Mr. Shayk, tell me your predictions. Why are you here?" His tone said this was a test.

"Um, your person out there said to come?" Garik had been cowed when walking with the four goons, but Brace was sandpaper on his nerves. He felt his attitude growing spikes, and he wasn't sure he cared. What good had these two ever done him? And what could they do *to* him? Besides the electrified sword, and if they wanted that, he suspected Sunchaser would be here, also.

"Understand, Mr. Shayk," Brace said, his feathers clearly ruffled, "you have been a promise unfulfilled since your arrival. I have been convinced not to terminate your line of research only because I have been assured your development would indeed be worth the investment. Convince me."

Garik looked to Rodheimer, saw a dark cloud hanging over him, and knew he would have no help there. Something had happened between the two men before he arrived, and Garik was to be the tiebreaker. Or they would break him, whichever made them happy. He suspected Brace would rather break him, even if it meant losing whatever unfinished battle was taking place between them.

He recalled an earlier conversation between the two men. Rodheimer had insisted the situation in Bay City was under control, and Brace had mocked his assurances. They had only ended the escalating confrontation when the Tower had come under attack and the parking garage on Stamford Drive had gone down in a haze of broken bricks and powdered concrete, the victim of a protestor's well-placed bomb.

The situation between the two men took on a clarity that Garik should have seen then. Rodheimer was fighting for control of the project, and Brace was determined to wrest it from him. Opportunity was his only roadblock, and the events in the city were eroding that

385

roadblock as surely as a torrent of water rushing from behind a shattered dam.

Garik had to tread carefully. He was on the knife edge, with Rodheimer on the left and Brace on the right. To slip down the wrong way was to cut himself to the bone. These men wouldn't care, not about him.

He decided not to hold back.

"So, Colonel Brace, about your backup plans to take over once the protesters do enough damage—" That was all he needed to say to crack the man's stone face, and Brace exploded.

"How dare you, Director! Our dealings are a matter of the utmost confidentiality. You would ply this boy against me, use one of your *experiments* to embarrass me?" Brace's composure had broken, and his cheeks turned red.

"You are a fool, Brace." Rodheimer's shoulders seemed to broaden, as if his muscles were tightening for a fight. He crackled with electricity. "What could I have said to him? Your people retrieved him. It seems you required prescience of him. Perhaps his foresight told him what you've attempted to hide from me."

"It is impossible. The boy is guessing."

"As Christian did?"

Garik's attention lit up at the mention of the man's name. Christian had also been melded with canine DNA, although from a wolf-hound rather than a timber wolf. He had developed precognition skills—prescience—and been deemed a failure. Christian had no drive to use his far-seeing skills to further military intervention in world affairs, and he had been shipped off to *somewhere* to be further used in research.

"Christian was a false hope." Brace had regained much of his composure. "This one, I fear, is no better."

The man had been assured Garik's development would provide what the military needed, a successful precog with the tractability to be amenable to the military's rigorous demands. Or, in other words, to do the dirty work of guiding the killers that would keep Brace and his cohorts firmly embedded in the halls of military power.

"He knows about your backup plan."

It was interesting to Garik that the Director didn't seem especially concerned about whatever Brace was planning. Perhaps the Director had an ace up his sleeve, his own backup plan, on the off chance that the military did step into the quagmire of conquest over the human-hybrid program.

"There is no backup plan." Brace's face was expressionless. "I want what is best for the Air Force's investment, and not only the Air Force, but every division of the nation's military forces."

Garik heard the lie, in the man's breathing, his heartbeat, and the way he exhaled a sharp breath at the end of each sentence. He was, however, out of his familiar territory, and he didn't know how to step on only the stones that would keep him from falling into the quicksand. He also wasn't convinced Rodheimer was the good guy in this situation, so why should he help him?

Rodheimer made his choice for him with his next sentence.

"The boy is the cause of all this." Rodheimer pressed something on his desk, and one wall exploded into a giant image of the events outside the basement research center. He touched the desk again, and different parts of the image zoomed in, revealing Garik's name and image blasted across the scenes of protest. "Somehow, he has fostered people's natural sympathies, and this is the result. I had hoped his alleged deportation to Russia would eliminate any possibility of this, but then Jantzen aided the boy in escape, and my carefully orchestrated plan evaporated. This boy is the one to blame, not me."

Rodheimer turned to a side table, leaving the image playing out on the wall, and he turned back with a series of photographs. He spread them on the desk.

Garik's aunt, Irina, and her boyfriend, Arik, coming out of Fasst Market, hand in hand, with Arik holding a plastic Fasst Market bag. Irina was smiling and she looked happy.

Another showed The Flower Shop, the back door, Marisa inserting a key. It seemed to be early morning with the long shadows, and Marisa wore a coat, gloves, and a bright scarf around her neck. Her cheeks were red with the cold.

Another of Hayat al-Haber in his headscarf and robe in the skate park on his sister's unicorn board.

And Muhammad, Ibn, even Mrs. Waggoner at City View Apartments, his upstairs neighbor.

"What's this?" Brace touched the photos, shifted them around.

"A way to get control. Give me time, Colonel. This worked once." Rodheimer tapped Marisa's image. "The boy will crack when we use what's important to him."

"We hardly have time." He lifted the picture of Marisa, studied it, then looked at Garik. "Pretty girl. You care about her? If so, we can see that she is happy, or—"

"Not yet, Colonel." Rodheimer slipped the paper from the man's hand and returned it to the table.

"The waterfront. We've yet to discuss that. We require access for our ships." Brace cut a hard eye to Garik, making it clear he would slice him like a tomato if he could, before returning his attention to Rodheimer.

Rodheimer touched his desk. The wall switched to show the events at the waterfront. "I have dispersed security to clean it up."

True enough, the men Garik had seen in the lobby—or ones very much the same—were doing what they could to get the chaos under control. It was hard to say if they would be successful. There were a lot of them, but there were more rioters, and the rioters didn't care what they damaged. Rodheimer seemed to treat it as manageable.

"I can offer more, if you need my help." Brace's statement was less an offer than a suggestion that he knew it was needed.

"This is my fight, Colonel." Rodheimer stacked up the photos, tapped them straight, and returned them to the side table.

"And my funds."

Garik didn't suppose the Colonel expected him to overhear that. He didn't think the man knew exactly what he was dealing with when it came to the hybrids in the Corona Tower basements.

And Garik knew one thing with an overwhelming confidence. He wasn't planning to be the one to tell him.

— 8 —

GARIK, RELEASED from Rodheimer's office under a raging storm cloud that had yet to discharge the torrent he still expected to flood the research center at any moment, was escorted back to the cafeteria through a lobby now devoid of humans, hybrids, and anyone who could claim anything resembling mutant fame.

The roving televisions were also gone, except for one that had been somehow shuffled into the cafeteria and overlooked. He found Devon and Kevin, to his amazement, still sitting at the same table with glasses of clear drinks and waiting on him. He threw himself into a third seat hard enough that he shifted the chair, bumped the table, and sloshed one of the glasses. Devon caught it just in time.

"Where's everyone?" He glanced around. Only one other person was present on the other side of the room with a plate of food, and she didn't look up.

"Back on schedule. Sunchaser came through and said we were wasting hours that could be put to better use. No one dared argue with her."

"You guys are here."

"Sunchaser instructed us to wait on you. We were under no account to let you out of our sight until Bay City was calm again."

"I bet. You think there's a war up there. I just got back from—"

"Not here." Devon leaned down as if to push a finger inside the top of his cast to scratch, and he hissed the words at him. When he raised up, he smiled. "Okay, kiddo, Kevin and I have decided you need to let off some steam. You've been babysitting me so well, you need some fun. We've cleared Kevin's schedule just for you. How does that sound? Pool, or something with a little more smash and bang?"

"I can smash and bang pretty well." Kevin grinned. "That's my specialty."

Garik looked from one man to the other. He understood. He was being hushed up, but down two floors, there were places they could talk freely without being overheard. And they wanted to know exactly what had happened while he was gone.

"Yeah, that would be fun, sure. I bet you can't touch me, Kevin-o."

"Watch it, Kev, the kid'll be doing that from now on if you don't stop him." Devon laughed, stood, and looked for his Segway. It was just inside the door by the lobby. "Garik, can you fetch my wheels, please?"

Garik also retrieved his ZBoard. Kevin walked. Devon had his passkey out, and they used it to get to Level 3. Garik needed time to process the meeting, so their plan was exercise first, then time in the pool. Heat up then cool off. Garik could reveal the details of his detention in the privacy of the changing rooms. To allow Devon to participate, they chose racquetball. Devon could serve, and the other two would continue the game. It gave them a valid reason to be on the training floor and together.

Garik found he was more worked up over the accusations lobbed at him by Rodheimer and Brace than he thought. He felt he had his emotions under control, not moving too fast, allowing Kevin plenty of good hits, and careful not to impact Devon, who didn't have the agility to avoid wild balls. But as the game went on, he found himself hitting harder, the ball blurring faster, and his companions more out of breath with each round. Finally, one ball left his racquet, impacted the front wall, and exploded with a loud pop, leaving a powdery stain where it had hit.

"Maybe it's time for the pool, kiddo. How about that?" Devon hobbled to him and grabbed his neck. He called to Kevin, who was panting with his hands on his knees, "See, Kev, I told you he was faster than he let on."

"But I won last time." Kevin stood, his face red, and sucking in air. "How did you manage to get so good today?"

Garik shrugged.

"I'm telling you, the kid's good at not giving away what he can do. Isn't that right, kiddo?" Devon slapped him on the back and called to Kevin, "My ride, James."

"Psst! Let Garik get it. I'm headed to the pool." Kevin dropped his racquet and grabbed the handle to the door.

"Leave it like you found it, huh?" Garik called after him. "Better if you can. Seems I heard that before."

"Grr. I should have tackled you before you reached that elevator. At least Marisa escaped. Now I have you to babysit." He did return to gather up his racket, and he also picked up two used towels from the floor.

"Lucky you." Garik grinned. When Kevin threw one of the towels at him, he caught it and threw it back. Then he ran to the front wall, picked up the remains of the burst ball, and pulled off his shirt to clean the wall. By the time he returned, Devon was on the Segway, but Kevin had absconded with Garik's ZBoard. He shrugged, glad he was feeling better. He jogged to the natatorium, selected a suit and towel from the supply room, and disappeared under the water.

Several others were using the facility, but they were diving, and the lanes were uncrowded. Garik's practice sessions with Christian returned to him as soon as he hit the water, and he began holding his breath for longer and longer stretches. At one point, both Devon and Kevin were slapping the water to get his attention.

He broke the surface in the middle of the pool and called, "What?"

"Time!" Devon pointed to his watch. He was still clothed, but Kevin knelt on the side in his suit.

"You guys ready to go already?" Garik treaded water easily.

"No, come up for air once in a while. We thought you'd drowned."

"You mean I'm that good?" Garik laughed, dropped back under, and swam three more lengths before making his way to the side.

Devon had a waterproof board, and he marked a time on it. "I heard you were good underwater. No normal person can hold their breath that long."

"Am I missing something?" Garik grasped the side of the pool and swung himself up, landing on his feet, his skin a waterfall of wet. "Or are you? I'm not normal any longer. This place made sure of that."

Kevin shook his head and stood. "Are you blaming them for the sass, too? Bust a nickel. Let's get changed."

In the changing rooms, with their towels tossed to the side and fresh clothes on, Garik confirmed, "No microphones, right, Dev-o?"

"Shouldn't be. Except for the training cells, this is about as private as it gets down here."

"As long as Justin's not around, right?" Justin Kurtew had rigged one months before. Devon had removed it and monitored the place regularly.

"Right-o, kiddo. So, what happened with the Director?"

Revealing the accusations cut him. Colonel Brace enjoyed twisting the Director's accusations just to make them bleed. Anger surged in him, but it wasn't Devon or Kevin at fault, and more than once, he had to pause and repeat his old internal mantra: *Anger gets me nothing. I must use my hands, my mind, my desire to achieve.*

They were exiting the elevator on Level 2 when red lights on the wall began to flash. The corridor leading to Corona City was a bric-a-brac shambles of spooked people. Stephen Klandermans and Paul Gberie ran toward them.

"What's with the excitement?" Devon waved and pulled them in.

"You people been hiding in a closet?" Stephen with his kinky blond dreadlocks and tattered clothes yelled to them as he slowed.

"You people been on the elevator." Paul's laugh revealed his gold-inset teeth. His skin flickered in random pulses of orange, revealing his high level of excitement. "Up into the real world, and welcome!"

"Have they cancelled the training sessions?" Kevin checked his watch. "I have several scheduled for later."

"Then you haven't heard. The Air Force is being booted out. If they're outside now, they can't return, and Rodheimer has security forcing those inside to pack their things and leave. He's already set up guards at the gate to the parking garage to keep them out."

"He can't keep them out," Garik blurted. "They'll come in—"

Devon elbowed him in the ribs, shutting him up and rewording his sentence. "They'll come in using the main elevator."

"He's put guards there, too. Everyone's trying to find out what's going on. You, Kevin, they're locking down the underground garage. If you're parked there, you'd better move your car while you can."

"I'm not. Besides, this is exciting! I'm the luckiest person in the world to be down here."

Garik thought of Lt. Miyoshi, part of the Air Force. She had been nice to him, and Airman Han, who had bonded with him over his Street Strider. Others he didn't mind being kicked out, but not everyone deserved to be booted onto the street. He also wondered if this meant the back exit through the parking garage was sealed off. It was his only hope, even if he wasn't sure how he could access it.

The red lights flashed several times, visible at intervals along the corridors, with a short burp of a siren in between. A voice announced, "All military personnel must exit the facility. Things left behind will be inaccessible until further notice." The lights flashed once more.

It was a mystery that no one was bothering to explain.

LANSANA Opoku-Mensah, Veronika Abbink, and Zekeria Salem joined Stephen, Paul, Devon, Kevin, and Garik in Devon's apartment. Armor, color-changing skin, night vision, bone regeneration, a cloak of invisibility, a broken leg, a martial arts expert, and a teen who didn't know yet what he might become.

The big surprise came when Anatoli Burgorski and his brother Andrey knocked on the door. They brought in a white box about a meter square. Louise King followed with a small package in her hand.

"Garik," Devon began, pulling him to the center of the living room, while Anatoli, Andrey, and Louise gathered out of sight in the kitchen, "I wonder if you remember what day this is."

"Not really." He'd been knocked out for weeks, put through strenuous tests, not allowed access to the Internet, hospitalized more than once, and generally kept away from anything connected with the outside world. Even Christmas had slipped by unnoticed in this underground world without seasons or holidays.

"This is not possible, and we will not allow it." Veronika, with her large earrings, reached for her messenger bag, pulled out a giant envelope, and with a smile showing off her oversized teeth, turned it to reveal Garik's name.

"What's that for?" Garik's heart raced. There was only one thing this could be. How had he not remembered? Could he be eighteen *today*?

"What do you think Kevin and I talked about in the cafeteria for so long? Your good looks?" Devon laughed. "Not on your life. I do have access to your records with all kinds of good stuff." Devon motioned, and everyone turned to see a birthday cake on the counter with eighteen blazing candles. "I've wanted to tell you all day."

As everyone began singing, Garik's eyes filled with tears. He didn't even bother trying to wipe them away.

— 9 —

GOOD TIMES are meant to be enjoyed, especially when there's every likelihood they can't last.

The people offering Garik best wishes on his eighteenth knew how to enjoy themselves. Stimulants did nothing for them, except bring back memories of good times from the past—a byproduct of their updated DNA—but that didn't keep them from being creative about other ways to have fun. Prankstering, good jokes, the unexpected application of their hybridized skills that were unique to them and them alone.

Armored coating? "Come on," Lansana taunted. "All knives welcome." If she was hit, it didn't matter. However, she was certain she wouldn't be.

Dancing skin? Paul pranced to a throbbing musical number, and his skin pulsed with designs to make a kaleidoscope slink away in shame.

Pranks in the dark? Zekeria proved he was the master, slipping in and out of shadows and startling everyone.

Kevin slammed Stephen to the floor over and over in martial arts moves that might kill other men. Stephen stood each time, unbroken and inviting more.

Even Garik got into it, blurring the world around him into a bevy of rainbows. He rearranged shirts on the men, shoes on the women, and if they had food to eat, switched out their plates and beverages. He was back in his chair, his muscles quivering, before the first person exclaimed, "What happened to my shirt?"

Kevin took the couch that night. Of course, Devon was in his bed, and Garik tumbled under the covers in his own room, not even closing the door, and only slightly wishing his old friends—Ibn, Muhammad, Marisa, and the others—could have been at his party. He then could have eaten a salty biscuit, jumped over a bonfire, and danced with a girl. It was what he had looked forward to in his early years in Russia. He wondered what his aunt might have given him for turning from a boy to a man. That's what the evening had been, a celebration of putting off his short pants and slipping on trousers for the first time.

He pulled his blanket to his chest and traced the corners of his ceiling. It no longer seemed strange to be able to easily follow the lines in the dark, or to count the recessed fixtures, or to make out every item of furniture in the otherwise darkened space.

He closed his eyes, content in the moment. Houdini time could wait until morning. For one night, he had good dreams to keep him company.

GARIK'S DREAMS were barely an hour old—not even adolescent status when you compared the eight hours a person dreamed to the eighty years of a person's life—when pounding at the apartment door jerked him awake.

"Open up!" The pounding started again, more insistent this time.

"Coming!" Kevin's voice.

Something fell off a table and shattered, then light from the living room tumbled through Garik's door. He pushed himself up on his elbows. His eyes burned at the searing brightness.

The door unlocked, thump, thump, a familiar sound, and a gruff voice stated, "Take this. List everyone inside. Your door is being manually disengaged. If you try to exit, you will be shot. Keep the list by the door. We'll be by in the morning to retrieve it."

The door slammed and locked, thump, thump, and Garik swung his legs to the floor and called, "Kevin?"

The man wandered in, disheveled, and held out a sheet of paper. "Here, they left this. Let me get the light." Kevin stumbled on Garik's shoe and said, "Ow, are you trying to kill me?"

"I can see fine."

"You have better eyes than I do. Have it your way. I don't mind the dark."

Garik took the paper and recognized it as a type of census. The top said NONCOMBATANTS, and there were lines for names and other information, some of it in small print.

"So, who gave you this?"

"Some guy in black."

"Riot control?" Garik pictured the people from the lobby earlier. They had been headed out to the city to squash the rabble and bring them under control.

"Nah, different. Their helmets had gas mask things, and there were these symbols on their sleeves, like an eagle in a circle. Do what you want with that. I'm back to bed. Nite."

Kevin left, leaving Garik with the form. When the light in the other room went out, it really was too dark to read, so Garik set it on the side table and slipped back under the covers. The form might say noncombatant, but it wasn't protection. It was tabulation. People added to it wouldn't be excused from the fighting if it came to that.

Devon hobbled in some time later, his cast only partially covered by one pajama leg that had been sliced open. "Hey, kiddo, do you have that form?"

"Sure." He was awake instantly. He'd been caught up in a battle between Weston Rodheimer and Colonel Brace, and Halo Sunchaser had just appeared with her blazing sword sending lightning everywhere. He was ready to be done with that. He reached to the bedside for the form and held it out.

"Garik, the form?" Devon remained at the door.

"Right. You normal people need light to see." He meant it as a joke, not realizing how true it was. He hit the switch, and the lamp beside the bed clicked on.

"Thanks. Sorry for not waking up. I took something for the leg and didn't hear anything." He made his way to the end of the bed and sat. He didn't have his crutches, and he braced his fall with his hands. He straightened the form and read it over. "So, the Colonel wins."

"What?"

Devon handed him the form, and this time, Garik absorbed it, even the small print. It even provided scheduled times for each apartment for each meal of the day. They would have a military escort every time they left the apartment.

A rising tide of dismay in Garik yelled, "No, no, no!" He was supposed to escape. The secret exit was his plan. If the Tower and the basement research campus were now the military's domain, what good was Houdini? He could be locked in a trunk and cast adrift, for all the good he was, and he would likely drown.

He wished for his birthday celebration back again. For one night he had held something good, and now, it was taken away again. They couldn't let him have eighteen, not even for a full day. How crummy was that?

BREAKFAST REVEALED the true scale of the disaster.

Two unfamiliar goons in new and different attire showed up at their door, their faces covered, and their voices filtered through circular masks elongating their chins. They could have been the true mutants, for all the humanity they revealed through their black chiton shells. They took the form, looked at the three names, and passed it from one to the other.

"Two normals and one half-human. Who's the half?"

Garik raised his hand.

"Okay. You look normal enough that we need to mark you. Hold out your left hand."

Garik looked to Kevin and Devon, but he knew they had no say in this situation, and he gritted his teeth and did as the man asked. He watched him clip on a bright orange band and tug it tight. The man tested it, satisfied it wouldn't come off, and motioned the three of them to follow.

Sentries stood at every corner with weapons strapped over their shoulders or at their side. Equipment belts, heavy boots, helmets, with the white on black logo stamped everywhere. Not regular military, Garik stored away, after they passed the fifth one. There was no cafeteria on Level 2, so it was no surprise to have the masked strangers press Level 1 in the elevator.

There was evidence of a struggle during the night. Scorched places littered the floor like scattered clumps of windblown paper. From the outside, one of the elevator doors on Level 1 didn't match the other. One of the exotic modern sculptures had been reworked with a hail of gunfire, and it was more hole than sculpture. Garik wondered who had been hiding there, and if they had made their escape.

Other residents were also being escorted to the cafeteria, but all were being kept apart. Even inside, no two occupied tables were next to each other. Food was brought to them by one of the kitchen staff. They weren't asked what they wanted, so clearly, there was no point in requesting something special.

Those eating had either one or two guards at their side. One for a single person, two for groups of two or three. No table had more than two guards, so it was a bit of a surprise when a third goon guard walked up, gave an awkward salute, and spoke to the two who had escorted them from Devon's apartment.

"The hybrid needs to come with me." Like the two earlier, his voice had a filtered sound, odd but not unlike a real person's.

"The half-human, you mean." The guard pulled his gun from his shoulder and tapped the bracelet at Garik's wrist, as if to touch him was to "get" his hybrid disease.

"Just him. He needs to come with me. The Colonel needs to see him."

"Good enough. You're welcome to it."

It? Garik felt his blood heat up. He was a *him*. A *person*. Captured and *forced* to become what he was. No one had asked him, no one said if you please, and he didn't appreciate being called an *it*.

Before he could go off on the man, the new guard rapped the table with his knuckles and said, "Garik, if you please."

That got Garik's attention, the way the man said his name, as if he knew him. That gravelly voice, even through the suit, seemed . . . no, and Garik shook his head. Wishful thinking got him nowhere, and he stood.

"Devon, Kevin, if I don't return, you, Devon, can have all my pajamas. Put them on, please. And Kevin, I want you to have my ZBoard. Ride it with spirit." He grinned, then wiped it from his face and turned to the guard. He held out his wrists. "Handcuffs?"

"Not likely," the man's voice growled. "Let's move it. No time like now."

They moved toward the corridor leading to the underground parking garage. The damage was greater, leading Garik to think this was where the research complex had been compromised. An opening where there used to be a door; shattered glass; blackened places where things had burned.

Once they were completely out of view of everyone else, his guard said, "Whew! This is exhausting." Then, he melted into a more familiar shape, or at least his head and hands did. His beaded

clothing took a second longer to change from eagle soldier to rescuing friend, making Paul whole.

"Paul?" Garik wanted to whoop. "What's the plan?"

"Wondering if you want to go for a ride." Colors rippled over
the man's face, riddled with yellow for humor and interspersed with
orange for excitement. He pulled out a key fob from his beaded robe
and held it for Garik to see.

At voices from just ahead, Paul grabbed Garik's wrist to cover
the bright orange band and held a finger to his lips. "Shush," and his
color and shape transformed into the military goon from minutes
before. His clothing took a bit longer and made the change just before the men rounded the corner.

"Sirs," Paul said in his filtered, gravelly voice, as he pushed
Garik to the wall and out of their way. He offered a salute as the men
passed.

"Take care, soldier. At ease." The men nodded but didn't salute
back.

When they burst into the garage, to the right, the access from the
old parking garage on Stamford was brilliantly lighted. The aboveground garage was gone, and the ramp now led to open air.

What was better was far in the distance. A portion of the north
wall of the garage—the back entrance!—was no longer secret. To
judge by the damage, that was how the military had gained access.
Olive-drab trucks and other transports filled the underground, and
black-suited men were everywhere. Several vehicles waited to head
out, as one rumbled in.

Paul pushed the fob, and an ordinary black SUV with tinted
windows flashed its lights and beeped.

"They won't let us out in that." They needed to pretend to be
military if they intended to escape.

"Trust me. They'll let us through."

Garik turned to argue, only to find he was standing at Colonel
Brace's side.

— 10 —

"COLONEL, SIR."

A big man in a black suit with the eagle logo on his upper arm
stepped to them and saluted. He carried his helmet, as though he had
just removed it and might have need to put it on again. The air in the

garage was warm near the elevator but colder near the two exposed exits. Neither Paul nor Garik was dressed for the cold.

"Yes, um, Rodrigo." Paul cleared his throat, not sounding very much like the colonel but giving it his best "military" voice. He glanced up from the man's name on his uniform. "I need to take the, um, hybrid with me. We have, um, business to take care of. Thank you."

If Garik weren't so nervous that they would be exposed as imposters—rather that Paul would be exposed, as it was clear who he was—he would have found Paul's attempts to mimic Colonel Brace as a good game, but not a very successful one. Apparently, to their good luck, Rodrigo accepted Paul's stuttered impersonation without much thought.

"I saw your truck unlock, sir. Let me get you a driver." The man was already looking across the garage for an available man. Paul as Brace stopped him.

"Thank you, Rodrigo. I need to do this on my own. It can be our little secret." Paul winked.

Garik's heart dropped when he saw the wink, prepared for the soldier to sound the alarm and for the handcuffs to come out. Winking was something Brace would not do in a million years.

"If you're sure, sir. Understand that things have gotten much worse since we broke through last night." He pulled a paper map of Bay City from a back pocket and a thick-tipped marker from another. He walked to Brace's SUV and spread the paper map on the hood. "These streets are a no-go, sir." He placed bold X marks on them. "To get out, you need to take a right on Lowell. Left is obstructed. At Scenic, you can go either direction. If you can give me a destination, I can radio ahead to ensure your safety." He traced the short route to Scenic Drive in a bold stroke.

"Um," and Paul glanced at Garik, who mouthed, Argyle Station, and said, "The Argyle, um, Station? Yes, that's where we need to go. I'm, um, meeting someone."

"Are you sure, sir?" Rodrigo frowned. "The trains haven't run all night. Whoever you're meeting isn't likely to be there now."

"No, I mean, yes, I understand, er, know that. How could I not know that? I am the Colonel, after all." He nodded awkwardly. "I expect he, er, they will still be there. From the last train, I mean, before things were, shall we say, interrupted."

"Are you sure you don't want me to get you a driver, sir?" Rodrigo looked from Paul, whom he had been studying intently, to Garik and the orange band on his arm. Then he relaxed. "Ah, this is the boy from the protests. I understand. Negotiations. If anyone asks, you weren't here."

"Thank you, Rodrigo. We'll be off, now."

"The map, sir?" Rodrigo folded it twice and held it out.

"Of course. Wouldn't want to run into a roadblock and get stopped."

"No, sir." The man glared at Garik, as if he were the reason for all this nonsense that was happening to Bay City.

Perhaps he was, Garik considered, as he walked around the truck to the passenger's side. Even so, that didn't mean it was his *fault.* Blame Dr. Jimenez. Put the onus on Weston Rodheimer. Take aim at Halo Sunchaser with your blame machine. When you fire, you might also lob your accusations onto Colonel Brace, and maybe a few others who liked to stand too close.

Paul, as Colonel Brace, started the black truck, and he shifted into gear. The darkened windows gave them a sense of separation from the military anthill around them, but they weren't out yet. The gauntlet had just begun.

RODRIGO UNWITTINGLY made their escape easier than pie. He rapped the hood of the big vehicle once they were inside, lifted his left arm, and stretched it toward the ragged hole where the back entrance used to hide. He motioned Paul forward and walked with him as he instructed others to move out of the way.

Closer to the exit, the man held his hand up for them to hold, and he navigated the line waiting to exit the garage. As one big truck shifted into reverse and forced another truck to pull out of the way, Rodrigo reached in his helmet, placed a clear breathing mask on an extendable tube to his face and drew in a deep breath. He returned the mask to his helmet and motioned Paul and Garik forward. Approaching the exit, the massive automotive elevator that would have dropped vehicles below the street level to access the dummy office building across the street dropped down ten feet beside them, exposing part of the concrete tunnel running under the street. A blackened troop transport, crushed, rested half on and half off the elevator and suggested it might not be operational again anytime soon. Garik hoped no one had died, but the transport had clearly been allowed to burn itself out. That explained the new hole in the wall opening directly to Lowell.

Rodrigo saluted, and Paul eased the vehicle into the morning sunshine. A slight haze filled the air, adding a subtle otherworldliness to the scene, and the sun glinted off scattered patches of snow. The dummy building across the street with the painted windows and false bushes jumped out at Garik. Whoever had constructed it had done well. Without knowing what he knew now, there was nothing to differentiate it from any normal building in Bay City. No wonder no one knew its real use.

Left, as Rodrigo had suggested, no one was getting through. A large panel truck was overturned with goods scattered across the roadway. Intentional? Garik couldn't tell. A team of black suits was in the process of clearing one lane, and a crane was setting up to put the panel truck back on its wheels.

They were almost to Scenic Drive when Paul resolved back into himself. His skin rippled, pulsing with finding his original shape once again and finally settled into his true features. He grinned, flashing his gold-inlaid teeth.

"Well, that went better than I expected. That was a long time to be an evil man. Better me than him."

Garik scanned the marshlands past Scenic. To the left, ten blocks away, Harbor Shipyards dominated the horizon. Normally, he would expect to see gantry cranes and giant trucks moving about, with sparks flying as welders attached this to that to build the biggest and best ships on the West Coast. Smoke rose ominously from the end of one of the giant warehouses, and the whole end was collapsed and blackened. Everywhere else, the Shipyards was devoid of life. The Docks wasn't visible from this end of Lowell, but he had seen the television screens. It was unlikely anything was getting in or out from there.

Garik glanced at Paul, taking in his large lips and dusky skin, noting the feminine cast of his profile but thinking nothing of it. He was trying to overlay the colonel's features, and even the soldier goon's from before that on the jokster's face.

"Aren't you afraid your teeth will give you away?"

"Me?" Paul laughed. "How many times did you see me smile?"

"None, I guess."

"No guess. I am pretty smart up here." He tapped his forehead. The big SUV pulled up to the light at Lowell and Scenic Drive, and Paul asked, "To Argyle Station, correct? Right or left?"

"You're asking me? I thought you had a plan."

"No plan. The keys, that's what I brought to our little escape. They came available, and I said to myself, Paul, that boy needs your help. He will be chopped into tiny pieces. How can you allow that? So, I borrowed them, and here we are. You, my friend, must have a plan, otherwise—" He shrugged broadly.

"We're not going to Argyle Station. I'm not empty-headed, either. That was a distraction."

"Ah, smart boy." Paul laughed hard for a moment. "Now, I can only say *man* because you blew out all the candles on the cake. No more do I have a little boy sitting in the car with me, true?"

"Turn right." Garik turned his head, irritated, and looked out his window. He hadn't been a *boy* since before getting entangled with the Tower, and he certainly wasn't one now.

"Is all in good fun, heh?" Paul reached over and pushed on Garik's shoulder.

"Stop it," Garik said, tucking in against the door.

"Stop it," Paul repeated.

"Hey," Garik threw out, turning to find himself riding with Charlotte Mnich. "Stop. Be yourself. I don't like not knowing who I'm with."

"So be it." Paul's voice was as gravelly as ever, telling the truth of who he was, and he let his body shift to match his true form. "We must go somewhere, and we must get there soon. The keys, someone will miss them, and we do not want to be discovered."

"Right, right." Garik tried to process. Right on Scenic would eventually take them out of town, but the forested area to the east of Bay City was undeveloped, and he didn't know the lay of the land, except what he'd seen on maps. He had friends in the city, though he had no easy way to contact them. Jantzen and the team that had escaped with him before might still be in Bay City. They would help him hide.

And now he had Paul to consider. Would he fit neatly into that group of friends? Or would their shared experiences exclude Paul except as an unwelcome and abrasive sticker in their side? He seemed to find satisfaction in turning over rocks to see what crawled out.

The light changed, and Garik motioned to the right. Paul turned and accelerated. Here, there was little to suggest Bay City was in an uproar and the military was stepping in to quell unrest and exert control over the rioters. The marshy floodlands to the left and glimpses through the bare trees of the large estates to the right revealed a normal scene untouched by the protesters.

At Park Avenue, Garik again pointed right. He didn't have a destination, but south was what he knew. The high school, Central Park, the police headquarters, the skate park, and even the Ransom Building, although that wasn't even remotely on his options list. They had erased that place the first night he and Jantzen Hefferly had escaped using Kevin Lee's van. It could never be used as a safe house again.

His sense of right and wrong was shifted off its foundation when they passed Bay City High. A banner covered the name on the front of the building and proclaimed it BCA Tactical Staging. The parking lot was filled with military trucks, and the sports fields revealed soldiers involved in training exercises. An unfamiliar flag fluttered on the flagpole, one with a stylized eagle superimposed against a black background.

"That's not Air Force." The knowledge was a flood in Garik's mind. "They're not real military at all."

"Para," Paul stated, his word empty of inflection. "You saw the emblem. The eagle in the circle."

"Yes, but—" Garik considered his "but." He had seen it and considered it another level of military, not paramilitary. They were no more than hired thugs. At least that's the way he pictured them. "They are working with our military."

"That's what paramilitary does, least if they're on our side, and I hope these are. I don't think Colonel Brace liked losing, so he took whatever steps were needed to make sure he didn't."

Passing Central Park, the black-faced goons were working the park side-by-side with the real military's camouflage green. The goons held the weapons, and the camouflage green walked along, seeing that the people who had decimated the park policed their own trash and other garbage. Even the tents were mostly gone. Garik was sure they would be by dark.

The duck pond was still lined with trash, likely carried in by the wind. He watched a duck land, oblivious, and dip its head underwater as if searching for food.

Now that he was paying attention, he had no trouble seeing the difference between the Tower's black goons and Brace's equally black goons. These goons were bigger, wider, and more ominous than the Tower security forces had ever been. If that wasn't a giveaway, the masks they wore painted them as mean as they looked.

Except for seeing Rodrigo's face, Garik could easily believe they weren't human at all.

That's when the light came on. Perhaps they were like him, half human, only designed to be bigger, better, and more powerful than any normal man could be . . . only their kind had received a hybrid-induced flaw. That would explain the masks.

"Pull over, now," he insisted. Before Paul could stop the truck, Garik had the door open, and he let his breakfast fly.

— 11 —

THE STATUE in the small park across from police headquarters was toppled over. Where it lay in the grass, it was decorated with spray-painted words that extended onto the base. Garik read aloud, "Let the—" and his eyes skipped from the toppled statue for the rest, "—boy go."

"And now they have." Paul laughed and popped him lightly in the chest with the back of his hand. "Bet Brace never saw me coming, you think?"

They continued to navigate destruction, including parked cars with windows punched in or graffiti on the sides, and one with its nose jammed through a storefront. People wrapped against the cold turned and watched as they passed, a few dropping to hide, and others remaining blatantly in the open, as if daring the black SUV to challenge them in their fight to reclaim Bay City for the people.

Garbage bins overflowed, revealing the lack of trash pickup, and there was more scattered along the curbs and sidewalks, giving this part of Park an abandoned, apocalyptic feel. Where the black-suited goons with the paramilitary eagles hadn't intervened, violent-looking crowds swarmed, lemmings all, and off the cliff we go.

Even the police station had graffiti scrawled on one wall, a message that blasted, "Tower Owned and Operated." One window was covered with plywood, and the brickwork just underneath was blackened as though an explosive cocktail had tried to burn the building down.

Garik wondered if he would recognize anyone he knew. Coats, scarves, the sheer volume of protesters. They could be hidden behind any number of things, even abandoned cars, mounds of garbage, or simply a passing street sign. He would have no idea.

At Third Street, something high in the sky caught his attention. He followed it and grinned. "Paul, turn right on the next street."

"Oka-ay. Whatever you say, boss." He hit the brakes and turned at a faster clip than the big SUV appreciated. The backend skipped and slid before falling in line. Away from Park, the damage from the rioting was left behind. Within the first block, the residue remaining from the riots was mostly windblown trash, and of course, the garbage bins that waited to be emptied. Paul asked, "Now where?"

"Hold on. I'm tracking it." Garik leaned forward, watching out the windshield. "Slow down. I don't want to lose it."

He was about to, anyway, and he rolled down his window and pulled himself out to sit on the window ledge. He braced himself using the mirror and the top of the door. The air was cold, but he needed to be sure before giving Paul additional instructions.

"There, Paul. Right on Douglas. Now, this street."

The truck jerked Garik against the doorframe, smashing the edge into his chest. He held on until the vehicle righted itself. The City Transportation Department covered the entire city block to their left. It didn't look like any city transportation stuff was happening today, probably closed with the rest of the city over the ensuing riots. Through a substantial fence, backhoes, a dump truck, and several snowplows nestled in the remains of a snowstorm that had come and gone without Garik getting to enjoy it. Several smaller vehicles were covered, the edges of gray tarps held down with large concrete blocks peeking out of their snowy grave. Garik began waving with both arms, and Paul hit him on the leg.

"We're trying to hide, not give ourselves away."

"I see someone I know." He yelled, "Justin!"

"Kurtew?" Paul hit the brakes hard, sending the map into the floor and Garik nearly to the ground. "Where?"

"In the sky." Garik had to make sure Justin saw him. He forced himself through the window and dropped to the pavement. He ran in front of the truck and jumped up and down and waved his arms.

Far overhead, a winged shape hovered for a minute, then began to drop. The wings were there because Garik knew they must be, but they were more blurred sky than visible wings. Justin, however, was unmistakable, with his long torso, the extra joints in his arms, and his head that was more insect-like than ever. Garik called again, and Justin waved and fell like a stone to gingerly alight on the street a short distance away. His wings slowed, became visible, but continued to flutter, as if he were ready to return aloft at the first opportunity.

"Justin!" Garik started his direction when the man's wings blurred, and he lifted from the ground. He called, "Wait!"

"Why is Brace here?" Justin clacked his teeth, his jaw more beak than mouth.

"He's not. I escaped. I hoped to find someone—"

"That's Brace's truck." Justin's hands whirred, and he held two knives, from where, who knew? He still hovered just above the roadway tarmac. "Brace must know, we won't go back."

"Hey, loser!" The SUV's door opened, and Paul stepped out, his hands in the air, only it was Jantzen Hefferly, with his dark hair and beard, and his piercing, purple-flecked eyes.

"I don't think so." One of Justin's hands blurred, and a knife blade was buried in the metal of the door. "Another lie and I won't miss."

"Have it your way." Paul shifted into his true shape, and he walked forward, exposing himself to whatever Justin wanted to do. "Haven't seen the wings. Impressive, you loser, you. Come on down and give me a hug."

"Paul Gberie." Justin's feet settled on the pavement. "So, you become Brace, and you drive away with no repercussions. And you secret out Garik at the same time."

"Well, some repercussions." He leaned over and touched the blade of the knife where it pierced the door. "And they know Garik's with me. We're on an errand for a secret meeting to negotiate with the protesters to make all this go away."

"What?" Justin's wings blurred, and he was once more aloft. His second knife hovered in an outstretched hand, and it was clear someone might die.

"No, Justin! Don't throw it." Garik turned to Paul. "Be serious for one minute. Sheesh!"

"Explain," Justin commanded.

Garik took charge. "That's what the soldier thought, that we were going to Argyle Station to negotiate with me as the prize. They get me, and Colonel Brace gets the city back."

"No one is at Argyle Station. No trains have run for days." Justin's hand hadn't wavered.

"I know, Justin, and so does Paul." Garik wanted to yank the man from the sky. He could beat him at whatever he wanted to try.

He'd proved that, but what he needed was Justin's cooperation . . . and for Paul to quit poking the anthill just to see the ants run. "It was a ruse, a secret negotiation that he couldn't reveal. We hoped it would give us more time."

"I see." Justin touched down again. "If true, only partly success-ful. I have been tracking this truck, assuming it was Brace. There are others on the way."

"We thought as much." Paul's face rippled with laughter. "We need to hide. Can you help?"

"Agreed. Hiding is paramount. You are already being tracked by Brace's men. We know about the reinforcements from Canada. They appear to be as fearsome as suggested."

As suggested? Garik's ears perked up. So, Justin knew about the upgraded men. He wondered what else the man knew.

"Is anyone else with you?"

"Just us chickens."

Garik turned to glare at Paul only to see a man-sized chicken standing in the street. "Stop it, Paul," he demanded. "Sheesh! You're worse than a twelve-year-old. No, Justin," he called. "No one else is with us. Check if you want."

"Thank you." His wings stilled, and he folded them at his back. With a rocking gait, he moved toward the truck, peered inside, and nodded. With a flash of his wrist, the knife disappeared. "We will move the truck into the lot and cover it. There it will be safe."

A wide gate began to roll sideways, the wheels rumbling on their tracks, the chain-driven sound of welcome already gathering them in.

TWO PEOPLE appeared from behind the rolling gate. Joanie McDonald, once sporting a bold mohawk, now had a knit beanie pulled tightly over her ears. She was wrapped against the cold in a thick, quilted coat.

"Peach Fuzz," she called with a wave.

"Joanie!" Garik grinned.

The second was John Carter. His larger-than-life torso was cov-ered only with a thin tee. Once the gate got rolling, he took over and shooed Joanie away.

John called, "Paul, pull that truck in before we get drones over-head searching for it."

"Johnnie boy," Paul called. "Missed you, friend."

John snorted. "Just pull in the lot. We'll talk about the friend part later."

Paul grinned and climbed in. He rolled down the window, reached out, worked the knife back and forth until it came loose, and he tossed it Justin's direction. The man's hand blurred, and he held it. It blurred again, and the knife disappeared.

Once inside, John pulled a tarp off one of the city vehicles, and he, Paul, and Garik worked it over the SUV and secured it with four of the concrete blocks.

"Are we safe here?" This was a city building, and Garik remembered how quickly the Tower had found them at the Ransom Communications Building. They had triggered sensors, and the Tower had sent forces to retrieve them within hours.

"Not to worry," Justin assured him. "This way."

Once inside, Garik saw what he meant. The side of the building facing Douglas was undamaged. They hadn't driven past the McKinley Street side. They found the front of a commercial truck buried in the façade, and the hood and one axle protruded into the room.

"It shorted the power to the entire building. We have a generator for lights but use propane for heat." John nodded at Garik and Paul. "Bet you're glad for that."

"Sure. Where's everyone else?" Paolo Leveen, Alyna Lindberg, the others.

"Just the three of us," Joanie answered. "Come." They entered a machine shop, also set up as a makeshift living space. She pulled off her cap to reveal little more than fuzz on her head.

"They cut your hair?" Garik was used to her towering mohawk, and he remembered the first time he woke in the Tower's basements and learned that they had shorn his completely off. He had been devastated. It was only now growing out to what it used to be.

"Better that than this." She dropped into a chair and didn't elaborate.

"Part of the reason we're here and not out there," John said. "Can I tell him, Joanie?"

"Knock yourself out." She waved a hand to brush away the question.

"Joanie has had to regenerate—"

"It works?" Garik lit up with excitement. He knew exactly what he meant. That was Joanie's supposed skill from her jellyfish DNA. It had never been tested. She would have to be killed—or nearly—to check it, and not even the Tower had wanted to risk that. Then the

408

other side of what must have happened dropped him to a chair. "Then you were—" He couldn't say it.

"Yah, about," she said. "You got it, Peach Fuzz," and she drew one finger across her throat.

"I'm sorry." Garik had seen Justin's transformation when he had molted to get his wings. He tried to imagine what regenerating from death might be like, and he couldn't.

"Hey, got something you might be interested in." John pulled up a chair to a desk and slipped a keyboard from a drawer. He turned it on, and on the wall above the desk, a large screen flickered on. John typed in some instructions, and a room appeared on the other side. They could see the back of someone's head and that there were other people present but not who. John called, "Amy. Turn around."

Amy Howe shifted her position, and the petite woman smiled. "John! What do you need?"

"Look who's with me." He motioned Garik over.

"Garik!" Amy's face lit up. Then someone pushed her aside.

"Garik? Move over, Amy. Garik, is that really you?" Marisa's face filled the screen.

It was the happiest moment of Garik's day, and he couldn't wipe the smile from his face.

— 12 —

"MY APOLOGIES, Garik, but we don't dare keep the line open." John turned from the darkened screen, and he slipped the keyboard back into the drawer. "I was certain you would want to know she is okay, and for her to see you, well, you saw her face light up. Knowing you're free did that for her."

"Still, we barely got to speak." They had said hello and I've missed you, and little more when Amy broke in and said she had to sever the connection.

"This bolt hole is only safe as long as we keep it safe. The Tower hasn't let go of us so easily. Joanie's the truth of that."

"Can we go where they are? That's safe, surely. If they're there, we can be there, or she can come here." To have seen Marisa, to be out of the Tower, to have all his nights dreaming of her so close he could touch, how could he not? It was so simple.

"Not so simple." Joanie rapped the table with her knuckles.

Garik looked at her as if she had read his mind. Maybe she had.

409

Had anyone ever studied if jellyfish could do that? Maybe they could, and people had never thought of it, and it took Joanie's DNA being combined with jellyfish DNA to find out.

"It *is* simple. Paul and I got here. We can get to where Marisa's at as easily. Paul has a good disguise, better than maybe any of us, and I can move really fast. We won't get caught."

"Seriously," Justin confirmed. His eyes seemed clouded by something dark, but then, had Garik ever seen him happy or cheerful? "Not so simple. We divided into four teams, and we haven't shared the locations."

"But, you must need to talk to one another, plan—"

"That." He pointed to the large monitor.

"For more than two minutes, I hope." It reminded him of the research center's rules. Do it this way or that way because that's what the rules said. Well, he was tired of the rules.

"Not even for two minutes." John glanced at the dark screen. "It's why we couldn't let you and Marisa say much to one another. If the line happens to be tapped, too many verbal clues might lead them to us. No, we use it to set up drop-offs. In code, of course. No one wants to show up at a drop off and discover a team of Tower bullies there to apprehend us."

"You go out to the drop offs? How is that better? You are just as exposed." This sounded like another convoluted way to keep him and Marisa apart.

"Only Justin for us. He flies. Each team has someone who's especially suited for reconnaissance and retrieval."

Julia Cantos came to mind. DNA merged with a boa constrictor meant she could sense body heat with uncanny accuracy. When people were too far away to sense her, she already knew they were there and likely their body weight and gender.

Of course, Amy. Her leafcutter bee DNA had given her hyperfine hair all over her body, and the simple shifting of air pressure or temperature was enough that she could avoid all but dead people, and she could usually find them, too. She would have no trouble out and across the city.

The final piece of the puzzle had to be Marco Lopez. He looked less human than the others, but with his lemur DNA's climbing ability and his tail for balance, he could travel routes that would shatter the confidence of parkour enthusiasts.

"You, Justin," Garik said, noting the names he'd come up with, "and Julia, Amy, and Marco, right?'

"Well, yes. How did you—"

"They are the only ones who could. The rest have useful fighting skills, but to navigate without being caught? It's obvious who you'd pick." Anyone could see it. "And Jantzen, no one's said anything about him. I would have put him as reconnaissance, but we know Jantzen."

John looked at Joanie and grinned. Justin's face grew even darker than it already was. Garik wondered what hold Jantzen had over Justin and why the other two were amused by him.

He also had a splinter of doubt, firmly driven in by Weston Rodheimer, that Jantzen had his own agenda in helping Garik and the other hybrids to escape. Where was he now?

Or was Jantzen being excluded because he might double-cross everyone?

It was something he couldn't resolve, and he didn't want to create tension by bringing it up now. Instead, he said, "How much do you know about what's happened in the Tower since yesterday?"

They wanted to know it all.

GARIK WAS astonished to learn that the new hybrids he'd befriended were all known to them. It shouldn't have surprised him. When he and Paul first encountered Justin in the street, Paul had barbed Justin, and Justin had replied in kind, if with a barb that was a bit more pointed and deadly than Paul's verbal jabs.

They just hadn't run together in the research center. They were divided by skills or backgrounds or potential usefulness to the program, or as in the case of those who had escaped with Jantzen, their lack of potential in the program. Tractability, or willingness to work with the military authority in power over the program, was a vital requirement in defining a candidate's potential. No matter the skills, if you weren't willing to bend your morals and goals to Colonel Brace's, you were shuffled down and down and finally out.

Garik wondered at a few of the hybrids he'd met, why they were still in the program. Paul, even, while Garik was glad he had disregarded Brace's authority to help him escape, had a distinct flair for carelessness with people and a disregard for authority. Maybe the difference was in how Paul disregarded authority. He didn't disregard authority for personal satisfaction. Rather, he saw a problem, and he disregarded everything that kept him from resolving it.

411

Benjamin Fuest had been a puzzle to Garik from their first meeting. The man had no clear skills, not any that were DNA enhanced. He would have expected him to have been assigned to Level 5 early on, but then Garik also had no overt and quantifiable skills, not like Jantzen, Justin, or Paolo, and he wasn't on Level 5.

Yet.

Fabiola Bella, while Garik hadn't known her long, she had a clear lack of interest in anyone who wasn't Fabiola. At least, that's the way Garik saw it, and he didn't think he was wrong.

He hadn't sorted out the Burgorski twins. Their ability to endlessly mimic any person or sound seemed like a useful trait, but both Anatoli and Andrey had used it to mock others. How could that be beneficial in a military sense?

When filling them in on what had happened since they'd been gone, Garik mentioned the power outage that had shut down the entire underground research center for two minutes, which brought grins, but most of all from Joanie. Garik asked why the happy faces and learned that was how Joanie had come so close to death. She and Alyna had stolen a military vehicle, and Tower security had pursued them. They'd driven it into the power transformer. It had blown, nearly killing Joanie but giving them the chance to escape. Her jellyfish DNA had triggered her body to revert to a younger self and begin regenerating. It was weeks before she woke and was able to function again. She still didn't have her full capabilities back, but she was getting stronger each day.

He also regaled them of some embarrassing things, such as Devon's daring dash to deliver Dieter to his dad at the hospital, and how he'd wound up in a crash and was now on crutches. John said he'd wondered about that. They had seen the video uploads showing the accident before they were taken down. They had no idea Garik was involved. Garik admitted it was his fault, and they wheedled him until he came clean. He'd wanted to keep Devon's tablet to search out what was happening in the city, but as it was, he was locked out anyway, so Devon had gotten injured for no reason, except to let Garik—who had been injured just as badly—know that he healed fast.

That got them onto Garik, asking what he had learned about himself, and had he developed any marked DNA-related skills, which set Garik to thinking. Some he shared, his hearing and sense of smell, and of course, healing amazingly fast, and he thought of his super speed and decided not to mention it. It was mostly useless, anyway, because it exhausted him, left him with quivering muscles and made him desperately hungry.

Precognition, they asked, like Christian? Garik said Rodheimer thought so, but he didn't see it. He just evaluated things cleanly, could anticipate, and didn't hesitate when in a tight situation. That wasn't precognition, just quick thinking.

Finally, Garik got around to Marisa, the one thing he'd wanted to discuss more than anything else. He'd seen her one time, he'd thought, in a video in the Tower. His old friends were there, and a girl had been at the window wearing a shirt with his face on it.

They didn't know about that, but she had been instrumental in the shirts. After learning Garik wasn't deported, she'd contacted them through Garik's old friends, saying she wanted to fight the "system" and had gotten the students from Bay City High involved. That was much of what they'd been doing the past weeks, preparing the placards, setting up protest marches.

Garik pictured the destruction that had torn the city apart. "Surely there was an easier way. You've crippled Bay City."

"Not us," Justin growled. Once again, he didn't look up. He hadn't interacted much, just sat assembling an electronic kit, occasionally soldering and clicking switches to see if it worked yet.

"We were as surprised as anyone. People started showing up that we didn't know. We knew about the high school students, but the rest? They walked off buses from all over, taking up residence in the park and along street fronts. That's when the trouble started."

Garik thought of Kevin and his calls to get several fringe groups involved. What he said was, "So, the truck that took out the power station? An accident?"

"My idea." Joanie held up her hand hesitantly, but she seemed proud. She said, "Hit 'em where it hurts."

"Alyna helped her steal the armored truck." John pantomimed her razorlike Komodo dragon claws. "Just," he went on, "copycats started stealing cars and running into everything. You must have driven past some of it. Which way did you come in?"

"Down Park," Justin growled. "I told you, John, I was overhead, tracking them, thinking it was Brace."

"Right." John snapped his fingers. "The Brace path. That's how he usually goes. I think he likes to see the destruction, part of the reason Justin was certain it was him, even though there were no support vehicles. You saw some of it then, cars left to burn out."

"And the one in the front of this building," Garik reminded them.

"That was me," Justin volunteered, still without looking up.

Paul had been dozing, and he sat up and said, "Did I get that right? You, Justin, have my utmost respect. You needed a hideout, and this was as good as any, but only if you could take out the surveillance systems first."

Justin didn't answer, but he did smile.

Garik took a deep breath and said, "Back to Marisa—"

Everyone stopped and looked at him, even Justin.

"No, my bushy-haired friend." John stood from the desk, and he walked across the room. "You cannot go see her." A small fridge served as the support underneath one end of a workstation. He pulled out a canned drink and popped the top. "I don't know why I don't save these for you people. I can cool my own."

"You're trying to distract me. Just stop it." Garik blew out his cheeks, and he tried to push his growing irritation to the back of his mind.

"Sure, let's talk about your girl," Justin said, his voice grating, the smile gone, his eyes down. "You like her so much, but does she feel the same? That's the question you must answer. Same as me and Jantzen, 'cept I know how Jantzen feels. He chose you."

Garik's face burned with anger then embarrassment. How could Justin say that about Marisa, and what he said about Jantzen? Too many things clicked in place, and that sent his thoughts reeling. He wanted to hit Justin, make him take his words back, but he knew it wouldn't be a fair fight. Marisa did care for him. She always had. They were best friends, always. No one could say different. And Jantzen had been a friend when he had no one else. He stood, paced in barely contained fury, then slammed his fist into a wall.

"You're a liar, Justin!" he spat.

Anger gets me nothing, he recited to himself, but it didn't help. In his fury, he had nothing but white hot in his head, and he was blinded to everything else. He hit the wall again, and fire encased his arm. He realized he'd smashed it so hard the first time, he must have broken bones in his hand. He staggered back and fell to his knees, clutching his hand to his chest.

"Hey, kid."

He looked up, his eyes leaking pain, with Justin over him. John

414

and Joanie were in the background, and to the side, Paul flickered with amusement. He was enjoying this.

"I only asked if she felt the same. Must have hit a nerve, huh? I heard that hand crack the first time you hit the wall. The second time must have been murder. Stand up and let's see how fast you really heal."

The man pulled him to his feet, and he forced him to hold out his curled-up hand. Without warning, he opened the fist and pressed Garik's fingers flat.

"How's that?"

Garik couldn't answer. The expectation that it should hurt had scared him, and no words came out.

"Already healed, am I right? When we fought, I thought as much. We all heal fast, but not even they could have planned for you."

"You're an idiot." Garik jerked his hand away. "You goaded me just so I would do that."

"Goaded, yes. You hit the wall. I'd watch out if I were you." Justin returned to his electronic puzzle and took up the next piece.

"Watch out for what?" Garik looked to John and Joanie and to Paul. Paul shrugged.

"What, Justin?" He pushed on the man's shoulder, determined he would look at him. Justin whipped his hands around and pinned Garik's arms.

"For what gets you angry. I've watched you. Those people in the Tower are smart. They've watched you, too. You've remained the same as when you first joined—"

"Kidnapped!"

"—and I expect that's about to change. Will the real Garik please stand up?" He released Garik and waved his arms in the air, making sure Garik took in the multiple joints. "I was the golden boy. I was *Jantzen's* golden boy, and then this happened. Something's going to be your trigger, and I think I know what it is. Chances, they do, too."

"Enough, Justin. Give the boy some space." John took Garik's shoulder and walked him away.

Trigger? What trigger? Garik sat, let his eyes find the hole in the wall, and asked himself, *What should I watch for? What makes me angry? And why should that make any difference?*

It would come to him. He was tired and hungry. Food would fix

415

him for now, and tomorrow, he could figure out the rest.

And if he was still angry, maybe smash Justin in the face to remind him who was boss. That would sure feel good, and he suspected he wouldn't regret his decision afterwards.

— Book 7 —

The
Rage

1

NO ONE KNEW better than Garik Shayk what the 40-story steel-and-glass Corona Tower had stolen from him with their military funded human-hybrid project. His friends. His girl. His senior year at Bay City High.

His life.

He had been forcibly inducted into the project—*unwillingly modified with timber wolf DNA*—and now he was on the run. He had escaped as the military had overrun the Tower, reclaiming what they had funded and considered theirs.

Now he was in hiding in a warehouse portion of the damaged City Transportation Department building on McKinley Street. Justin Kurtew was across the room, hunched over a worktable filled with machined and printed parts, assembling what he hoped would become an unregistered drone for overflying Bay City's riot-devastated streets. His stick-thin torso and multi-jointed arms suggested his praying mantis DNA connection. The wings folded at his back were definitive proof.

John Carter, curled on a couch and asleep, seemed perfectly

normal, if a blond example of perfection could be considered normal. He was the most human appearing of Garik's companions. It was what he could do that made him unusual. His wood frog DNA gave him the power to freeze his own blood, allowing him to function at extremes, both hot and cold, that would kill other men.

Joanie McDonald sat in front of the computer, appearing little more than a girl, with a substantial screen covering much of the wall in front of her, where she had pulled up a list of city news reports, and she was organizing information she felt pertinent to the Tower's interest in them. Despite her apparent efficiency, she was still recovering from her death. Yes, her death, or coming so close she might as well have died. Her jellyfish DNA had regenerated her to a younger version of herself. She was determined to regain the person she used to be.

Paul Gberie was the most unusual of Garik's companions, even more so than Justin. His octopus DNA enabled him to reconfigure his body texture and color to mimic any background or person and blend in anywhere. Now, he was preparing lunch, and he wore his normal face with its feminine cast, with large lips and dusky skin. His beaded clothing was inset with LEDs that could mimic his body's changes, allowing them to transform with him.

Additional escapees were scattered across three other bolt holes, or safe houses, places they could stage their struggle against the Tower—and keep from being recaptured and locked away in the massive basement research complex under Corona Tower. They kept safe by not revealing their locations, even to each other, and only communicating by coded messages through designated drop-off locations throughout the city.

Paolo Leveen, Giselle Harmon, and Julia Cantos were part of Team 2. Julia, with her boa constrictor's infrared heat-sensing ability, was Team 2's outside person, able to safely move about the city without fear of being caught.

Team 3 contained Alyna Lindberg, Leigh Jose, and Amy Howe. Amy was modified with a leafcutter bee, giving her hyper-awareness of the world around her through air pressure and temperature. No one worried when she was out and about, so she was the assigned reconnaissance member of her team. Garik's girlfriend Marisa was aligned with Team 3. She had joined to "fight the system" and reclaim Bay City, although her methods were her own, and she came and went.

Team 4 made do with only two people, Laura Lassere and Marco Lopez. Marco's lemur DNA made him perfect for leaping through the city like a parkour's dream, but his long tail and pointed face forced him to keep away from people when he could. Still, of the two, he was the choice for safely maneuvering about the city. Jantzen Hefferly, able to morph into purple mist, was nominally part of this team, although he hadn't been seen in some time. Laura and Marco hadn't heard from him since everyone vacated the indoor skate park located at Coolidge and Royal.

"Paul?" Garik ventured, calling to the man standing at the makeshift kitchen. He was scrubbing vegetables under a faucet over a utility sink. A double hot plate sat to one side. A rolling cart to the other side held neatly organized crockery, and a lower shelf boasted a very basic collection of pans. Nothing for baking, but no oven, so that was of no account.

"Yes, young sir." Paul turned and carried the vegetables to a cleared space on a broad counter in the center of the room. It served as a preparation area and a dining table. He separated the vegetables and began cutting a pile of carrots into smaller pieces and adding them to a pan he had set out earlier.

"We have plenty of room here—"

"Before you finish your question," Paul interrupted, cutting Garik off, "I could use your help. I need these chopped." He put his hand beside the second pile and pushed it Garik's direction. "There's a knife on the cart."

"Sure." Garik grinned, and he raised his metabolism, moving faster than needed, just to where he could see the faintest whir of rainbows around the objects in the warehouse. It was slow enough that Paul would still be able to see him but Garik's blurred speed would impress him, and Garik shouldn't be too exhausted when he was finished. He stood, walked around the counter, selected a knife, moved to stand at the counter, chopped all the vegetables, even took Paul's carrots from his hand and chopped them, too. Then he rinsed his knife, returned it to the cart and stepped back to stand by Paul. He slowed down, determined not to let his quivering muscles betray his exhaustion—the price he paid for stepping up his speed to such extremes—and let the world catch up with him. He asked, "Do you want me to put them in the pan, too?"

"You little showoff." Paul looked at his empty hands, his knife in the process of chopping, and nothing to chop, and he called to

Joanie, "Think of things for this boy to do. And lots of them. We need to slow him down."

"That's funny." Garik's head was starting to swim, and he took a deep breath. "I'd better sit down."

"Dizzy again? Expect you'd learn by now." Joanie hadn't looked, but she *had* warned him before.

"I suppose." It had become a bit of a game. And it *was* fun. He didn't feel like he was moving fast, rather like the world was moving slow. And he never felt tired, not until he slowed down afterward. "I know it's a silly thing to do—"

"Ache, not silly, boy." Justin turned to face him, abandoning his electronic jigsaw for a moment. His beak-like jaw snapped as he spoke, a side-effect of his mantis DNA and his latest molting. "None of this is silly. You must find a way to *use* it. Discover how it can be successful to you. Seems like your friend Paul already knows. Ask him."

Justin had said his piece, and he turned back to the pieces of his drone, dismissing the discussion like he'd never participated.

"Okay, Paul, what's the secret?" There was a package of fruit bars in a plastic bag, and Garik tore one open and began chewing. Even that little bit helped.

"Justin's got a big mouth. What were you saying about plenty of room?" Paul was adding spices, and he watched his hands and specifically not Garik's face.

"You're distracting me on purpose with the spices. That's doesn't work anymore."

"That you know of." The tall man glanced at him and gave him a sharp look.

"Okay, that I know of. Still, how can I make my speed useful?"

"The better question is what all our space has to do with anything. What do you need it for?" He kept his eyes on Garik, and subtly, he began to shift his features. They took on Marisa's big-eyed expression. Even his hair began to mimic her dark locks.

"Stop it and good guess." Garik was to his second fruit snack. "You never get shorter, though, do you, when you imitate other people? You can't change your height, even if you can everything else."

"The boy be smart." Paul chuckled. "We all have drawbacks to our skills. None of them are perfect, not even yours. It's the ones with the fewest drawbacks that the military wants."

"Like the Colonel's goons." Garik blew out his cheeks at the memory of them barging into his life.

"The Colonel's goons?" Paul poured water in the pot, frowning before saying, "Ah, the paramilitary."

"They're big and strong, but I think there's something wrong with their respiratory system. It's the reason they wear the masks. Am I right?"

"Likely." He lifted the pot to carry it to the hotplate, and he paused for a moment to study Garik's face. He turned to set the pan down and turn on the heat. "How about you? Your shortfalls. Can you list them?"

"Getting tired when I move too fast. And I startle people sometimes when I heal so quickly—"

"Not a shortfall."

"Okay, then, my hearing. Sometimes I can't get to sleep because of all the background noise." He considered his answer. "No, I can tune that out. It's sudden noises, and sometimes conversations. My mind can't let them go."

"And your sense of smell? I hear that's pretty good, too."

"I guess. I don't notice it much unless I think about it, so I don't think that's a shortfall."

"Unless you tune out important smells that might give you vital information. What spices are in the stew?" Paul had turned the labels so they couldn't be seen.

"Spices?" Garik laughed. "Those," and he pointed to the bottles.

"A test, a test, by any name a test," Justin muttered.

"Oh." Garik thought, took in a deep breath, then asked, "Can I smell the stew?"

"From there. What did I use? Name each of these bottles." He covered them with a cloth just in case part of any of the labels might be visible.

"Um, ginger. That one's easy. Onion—"

"I don't consider that a spice, but I'll take it."

"And garlic. My aunt uses that as a spice."

"Sure. Others?" Paul held up the towel and separated the containers Garik had already named.

"Cinnamon!" Garik smiled. "Only a bit, though. I can barely smell it."

"Right, right." By this time, Joanie and Justin were paying attention. John still slept, even snoring slightly from time to time.

"Some spices I'm not really familiar with. My aunt didn't cook

421

often except at the first of the month when we had plenty of food. But I know I've had them at school, and probably at the food court." The food court was the Chow Down eatery on the Corona Tower mall. They served every sort of food there. "One is something my mother used to use in Russia, um, cumin, maybe?" He was right, he was certain. When Paul smiled, he called out another one he remembered from his childhood. "You also put in turmeric."

"And?" Paul glanced under the towel, scanned the spice containers, and looked at Garik expectantly.

"There isn't anything else, except the vegetables."

"Are you certain?" Paul raised his eyebrows like he was disappointed.

"Salt, maybe pepper? Only because people use those all the time, but I can't smell them."

"Because they are not there." Paul pulled away the towel and turned the spices so Garik could see. "See? You can do it when you want. I suggest you practice."

"It might be a useful skill, I agree. Now, about all this room—"

"No," Justin interrupted. "Your girlfriend cannot come stay. No sleepovers."

"How do you know—" Garik was startled that the man had guessed. He never seemed like he was listening, then he would come out with something like that.

"It's what you always ask. And why? Ask Joanie. She knows. Maybe she'll tell you if you ask nicely."

"She can have the back room. I'll keep in this part of the warehouse." He looked to Joanie hopefully.

"Nice try." She turned from the computer to Garik. "Message. From Justin's favorite person."

"Not mine." Justin growled the words.

"Used to be." She smirked, keeping her eyes on Garik. "Jantzen. Here, later. To see you."

"Jantzen's back?" Garik knew he should be cautious. Everyone had tried to ring alarm bells about him, but he had been Garik's only friend during his early, hard days after first being forcibly inducted into the human-hybrid program. Just the idea of the dark-haired man showing up downshifted his anticipation like a Street Strider in jet-assist mode. Weston Rodheimer searching for them, Halo Sunchaser and her electrified sword, even the destruction that had bombarded Bay City were moved to the back burner.

Jantzen here. To see him.

How exciting was that?

2

"OKAY, PAUL. Joanie said you could tell me how to keep from becoming so exhausted when I move fast."

"Doesn't pay attention, does he?" Justin mumbled.

"I heard that." Garik eyed the loaf of French bread on the table, deciding where to slice it. Four long chunks, or more manageable slices that would be easier to eat? He decided on small wedges.

"Justin's right, and you're right, too. The sliced bread goes beside the butter." Paul had out four plates, and he dashed up a mountain of stew on each one.

"That's not an answer, and you know it." Garik piled his *wedges* of bread on a platter, and he set it out.

"I also need glasses." Paul's pot of tea on the hotplate began to whistle. With the glasses out, he poured the steaming liquid. He set one beside each plate. "Now wake John."

"Sure, but that tea's gonna be too hot to drink."

"John's gotta have something to do. He'll take care of it."

"If you say so." Garik shrugged. "John," he called. "Stew's ready."

John, sprawled on the couch with his feet off the end and one arm behind his head, didn't respond. The couch barely held him.

"Joanie?" Paul called. "It's ready."

"Headed that way." Joanie moved to the utility sink and began washing her hands.

Justin cut his eyes from Garik to John. "John won't move if you don't make him. Try kicking his foot."

"Sheesh, why not let him sleep?" Garik scraped his chair back, stood, touched John's arm, and called his name again. He looked back at the others. "He's freezing."

"And the reason we don't need ice for the tea. Justin's right. Kick his foot." Paul grinned. "Or shake his shoulder. He won't wake just for anything, so make it a good one. He'll be grouchy if he misses a meal."

"Get to it, and sooner than later. The rest of us are hungry." Justin now seemed more interested in Garik waking John than in joining Paul for stew.

As soon as Garik grasped the man's shoulder, he found himself face down on the couch with his arms behind his back, with John fully awake and leaning into him, trapping him and putting pressure on his arms.

"Ouch," Garik groused, not quite sure what had happened. "Not so tight, you big hulk. Dinner's ready."

"Oh. Sorry." John released his hold on Garik and stood. "I *am* hungry. Thanks for not leaving me out."

Garik twisted around, glared at Paul, pulled himself to his feet, and straightened his clothes. He had noticed one thing. John's arm had been ice cubes, but when the man was on top of him, he was a toaster.

He thought he had figured out some of it when John, without being asked, wrapped a hand around each of the glasses, and frost crackled around his fingers, spreading over the glass until the tea inside just began to freeze. Then he released his grip and moved on.

"Unfair. You tricked me." Garik tucked in at the table in front of a plate of stew. He took two wedges of bread and spread them roughly with butter.

"And you fell for it." Paul was already into his stew, and yellow laughter mottled his skin.

"And you need to quit pranking people." Garik set a spoonful of stew on his bread and bit into it. "John, how did you move so fast? I blinked and you were on top of me."

John flushed. "It's my, um—"

"Talent." Joanie said it with emphasis.

"Quit being ashamed of who you are." Justin was eating, but it looked odd with the extra joint in each forearm and his mantis-like beak. He stopped and held out his arms. "At least you don't have these."

"And I'm enjoying my ice-cold tea." Paul held up his glass, took a deep drink, and set it back down. "Ahh!"

"I'd prefer to have a real power, like Paolo." John scrunched his shoulders and hunched over his stew. Paolo Laveen could shoot boiling water from his fingertips, his DNA adaptation from the pistol shrimp he had been mated with.

"Or Justin, who can fly," Paul suggested, as if that were perfectly reasonable.

John looked at Justin, and Justin glared at Paul.

Garik attempted to diffuse the rising tension. "How did you disarm me so fast? I'm quick, but not that quick."

"You noticed?" John warmed to the question.

"Yah!" Garik laughed. "I was suddenly face down on the couch." Likely how people felt when he ramped up his own speed.

"Fast twitch." Joanie, using two words where five would do.

"Fast twitch." Garik repeated her words, something he often berated himself for doing, but this time there was no easy way to define what she meant. "That was more than a twitch."

"It's my, um, DNA from, well—"

"From a wood frog. We all know." Justin pushed back from the table. "I'd trade for wood frog to look like you and not like this." He held up his arms again. "Or this." He shifted his shoulders, and iridescent wings, reminiscent of thin sheets of mica, unfolded behind him. He fluttered them for emphasis.

John said, "I have elastic tendons, not fast twitch muscles. Sorry, Joanie, I know you like to say that, but it's not true."

"Works the same." She grinned.

Garik saw her enjoyment in goading him, though it seemed a friendly thing. He asked, "Then that's a skill you have, like Justin or Joanie or Paul." He looked around. "Am I right?"

Paul chuckled, and his face rippled, changing, and taking on Justin's features. Paul's voice spoke from Justin's face, "What do you think?" then Joanie's, then John's, but never really locking into any of them. He finished by mimicking Garik, holding his the longest, even to his bush of curly hair. "Maybe not like this skill." He held Garik's face until Garik frowned at him.

"That's freaky, Paul. Please stop."

"He's right. Enough, Paul," John said. "What I did isn't like what Paul can do, or any of you. I can't control it. It's instinctive, like a frog jumping. I can only move fast when startled. So, it's useless."

"Not useless," Joanie snorted, this too-young version of her unlike the forceful adult Garik remembered.

"Practice is what you need. Even I have to practice." Justin lifted his flatware and began to spin the items around until they blurred. When he stopped, the tip of the knife was embedded in the tabletop and the fork beside it.

Paul reached across the table, pulled the utensils from the wood, and laid them flat. "Enough showing off. You, Garik, have you figured out how to resolve your exhaustion when you go hyper on us?"

"Practice?" He caught John's eye. John smiled.

Justin stood with a disgusted huff. He folded his wings and stepped around the table. He lifted the bag from earlier, the one where Garik had snitched the fruit bar, and he pushed Garik's plate back and set it in front of him.

"Well," Paul said, chuckling. "Can't get any more obvious than that."

"I don't get it." Garik pulled a fanny pack from amid the fruit bars. "And this?"

Paul lifted the bottom of the sack and let the fruit snacks tumble over the table.

Garik pictured Devon Maye, the Tower's activities director, carrying whatever he needed in his oversized fanny pack. He unzipped it and began inserting the fruit snacks. "I eat these while I'm *hyper* even if I'm not hungry."

"Finally," Joanie barked a laugh, "Peach Fuzz."

Joanie turned her attention to her stew, but Garik heard the laugh. He didn't have long to think about it, because behind her, a purple haze began to coalesce in the air, just obscuring the monitor hanging on the wall. As soon as he saw it, Garik knew who it was, and in his excitement, he felt the world around him begin to crawl as he shifted into his maximum "hyper" speed.

THE PURPLE was all over the room, very near frozen, at least from Garik's stepped-up perspective. It was his first time to see Jantzen, who had been DNA-hybridized with a squid, materialize from nothingness while Garik was moving fast enough that he could observe every detail of the amazing event.

The purple discoloration in the air twisted and fought with itself, a slow-motion dance of violent proportions as Jantzen's dematerialized body rejoined and abruptly shattered over and over, ever so slowly rebuilding into the framework of a man. The pain on the bearded face was intense as he began to pull himself together. Garik began to understand Jantzen's exhaustion after returning to his solid form.

Then Garik remembered one of the most important things of all: clothes!

Jantzen never carried clothing with him when he morphed into his DNA-enhanced form. That meant, of course, the same thing when he returned to his solid form. Jantzen would appreciate the throw John had been sleeping on. Garik stood—casually to his way of thinking but likely in a blur so intense he would seem to vanish to the people at the table—and stepped to the couch, crumpled the edge of the throw in one hand, and moved to where Jantzen silently screamed in pain. He held out the throw to allow the man his dignity in mixed company and looked away as the final shimmers of purple in the air settled onto Jantzen's shoulders.

"Wow," Jantzen spat, as his hand grasped the throw and he doubled over. "That was one of the worst yet."

"How long since you last materialized?" Justin took in the man's narrow face, black hair, and tight beard, and his eyes brightened as if glad to see him. "The longer you stay atomized, the worse it hurts when you pull yourself together. I thought you'd learned that."

"Too long. Thanks for your concern." Jantzen guzzled the air in the room in deep, sucking gasps.

"Anytime." Justin seemed to enjoy the biting exchange, and Garik wondered if that's what he missed about not being Jantzen's "favorite" any longer.

Paul stood and said, "Jantz, here's a chair." He glanced to Garik's empty chair and reminded him, "Garik, fruit bars."

"I would like some real clothes," Jantzen said as he took the chair. "And a plate. This smells good."

"Right," Justin said. "Not eating, either."

"You know I can't eat when atomized. I have to wait until I can, as you say, pull myself together again. I had to travel across the city to get here, and that taxes even my abilities." He didn't wait on the plate but pulled the remains of Paul's to him and began to eat. He took a slice of bread, scooped up a mound of vegetables, and shoved it in his mouth. "Perfectly sliced bread," he said through his mouthful of food.

Garik glowed inside, though he knew the compliment was minor and only obliquely his. Still, it was something he'd done the way he'd chosen, and Jantzen had called it perfect.

"Garik, join us." Jantzen motioned him over with a smile, pointing to the chair he had just vacated. "The fruit must be yours. No one else here snacks."

Garik slipped into the chair, took one of the fruit bars, and opened it. He glanced at Justin to see him glare at Jantzen, then at him, his eyes flashing daggers. Garik bit into the bar, already feeling his muscles twitching from his shift into hyper speed.

427

"I'm glad you're back," Garik offered, unsure how else to navigate Justin's mood.

"Thank you. I'm here about Marisa."

"Marisa?" Garik grinned, Justin forgotten. "What about her?"

"Still repeating people, heh?" Jantzen looked at him several moments before shifting his attention and saying to the others, "Seriously, this time she's gone too far. If we can't stop her, she might get herself hurt. Garik, we need your help. You're the only one who might get through to her."

Garik nodded his head. He would do anything for Marisa. All they had to do was ask.

— 3 —

CONVERSATION STOPPED as deep, double sonic booms flexed the metal walls of the warehouse. Dust shifted from between the suspended ceiling tiles high overhead, creating a smoky haze of nervous anticipation.

"I told that girl if she prodded the anthill, they were going to swarm." Jantzen shoveled more stew into his mouth, picked up a second wedge of bread, stood, bit into it, and talked as he chewed. "I need to fix this. Garik, talk to Marisa," and he evaporated into tendrils of purple haze that paused for a moment then fled for the exit.

Left behind, the blanket and wedge of bread began to fall. John leaned forward, caught the bread in midair, and let the blanket tumble into a pile on the floor.

"Practice," he grinned, dropping the wedge of bread on the table.

"Anybody? Anybody?" Garik was totally lost. Jantzen had appeared, something had created a blast big enough to shake the building, and now his old mentor from his days in the Tower's catacomb research center had abandoned them. "What did he mean, anthill, and how am I supposed to talk to Marisa if I'm not allowed to *talk* to her?" He shook his hand at the screen where he'd barely had time to tell her he'd missed her.

Paul joined him. "I also would like to know." He had covered the stew, and he watched the ceiling to see when it was safe to remove the lid.

"We know when we know." Justin, with a clacking snap to his words. He brushed away a few larger specks of dust in his stew and spooned a bite into his mouth.

"We don't have to know when we know." Garik, with his penchant for repeating what others said. He heard it and didn't care. He stood, stepped to the computer, and pulled out the keyboard. "Turn on the computer and get in touch with the other groups. That could have been a bomb."

"It wasn't, though." John talked around a mouthful of stew. "The last few days, lots of those. You likely didn't hear them underground. The Air Force is doing it. Sonic booms."

"That's illegal over populated areas."

"From the one who's been kidnapped and changed into part wolf." Justin sniggered. "Do you think Corona Corporation cares about legalities? They own it all. Even us, they think."

"Actually." Joanie shrugged but didn't elaborate.

"So." Garik tried to decide whose button to push to get information. Joanie, a leader in her previous life but now still on the rise from a rebirth that had sapped much of her dominance over the situation around her; or John, who seemed unaware of his physical presence and how his skills as a hybrid might benefit the people around him; or Justin, who was amazing by any standard but struggled with his confrontational attitude.

Then there was Paul, who could, perhaps, offer the greatest advantage of anyone in this group, but who enjoyed the conflict he stirred as much as the resolutions they needed.

And Marisa. He thought he understood. When the Tower had threatened her parents' business if she revealed what she and Garik had uncovered in the basements of the 40-story behemoth, she had given in to protect her parents. Yet, she had seemed broken by it when Garik had managed to contact her the first time he escaped from the basement warrens beneath the Tower.

That hadn't been the Marisa he knew. She never wore authority well and was always a champion of the underdog. The "system" was no more than a synonym for "authoritarian overlords" who needed to be brought down. He recalled the first time she met Halo Sunchaser. She immediately questioned her about her sister, Marina, who had disappeared into the Tower's clutches two years before. Of course, Sunchaser had denied any knowledge of Marina, only to be caught in her lie when Garik found himself trapped in the Tower's malevolent clutches. Marisa's eyes had sparkled with glee when she had stolen Sunchaser's passkey so she could prowl the Tower at will in her search for her missing sister. Marisa would stop at nothing to achieve her goal if she felt she was in the right.

What goal was she chasing now? Him? He wished so. Still, he tried to remember a time she had . . . no! He pushed that thought aside. He and Marisa were meant to be together, and she felt that way as strongly as he did.

Didn't she? Justin's question dug at him. *"You like her so much, but does she feel the same? That's the question you must answer."*

He focused on Joanie's response.

"They don't own me." Not a bit. They had stolen him, and he intended to take his life back. His friends, his bedroom in Irina's apartment, his Street Strider that he had rebuilt from a broken heap and ridden around the city.

Yet, could he have any of that back? In six months, he had become someone much different than the boy that had followed Marisa heedlessly into the depths of the Tower's basement without regard to the outcome, happy to share her adventure simply because he was at her side.

"The rest of us." Justin stood, his arms and extra forearms moving in a manner that was more unnerving than normal. He paused before walking away from the table. "We. Signed. That. Contract."

"He's right." Paul pulled out Jantzen's chair, draped the blanket Jantzen had left behind over the back, and sat. Overhead, the sound of a jet overflying the city vibrated the building, or perhaps they just imagined the ceiling tiles shaking because of the sonic boom that had blasted Jantzen back into the nether world. Paul studied the ceiling until it was quiet enough for him to continue. "Legally, we are their property, half of us, anyway. We believed the promises and took the risk."

"Marisa didn't. I didn't." Garik could hardly believe their apathy. He wanted to, *needed* to fight back. "Doesn't it make you angry?"

Paul didn't answer. Rather, his face began to shift colors, his features elongated, giving him dark hair, a familiar tight beard, and piercing purple eyes.

Garik felt a dam inside about to break. His emotions were walled up, his need for his aunt, his papa and mama, the friends who had filled their place before the Tower had yanked all that from him. The man Paul imitated had become a surrogate, the mentor Garik looked up to, and his face in Paul's chair when he wasn't there at all threatened to crack his façade.

430

"Stop it, Paul. Why are you doing that?" Garik turned away, his fingernails biting into his palms.

"For me, the risk has been worth it. I don't like the direction the Director is taking the project, but I enjoy what I can do. I have no regrets."

Garik turned, his eyes brimming, to find Paul back in the chair. He turned to Joanie, too young to be his Joanie, and she said, "Alive. No regrets." She shrugged, in agreement with Paul.

John mumbled, "Only wish it wasn't with a wood frog. Embarrassing."

"Justin, you understand, don't you?" He was the one person who seemed to hate his DNA-enhanced existence as much as Garik did.

The man was at his drone, and his hands were busy attaching the cover. He held a small, powered screwdriver, and it whirred. "Jantzen abandoned me. That's the only thing I regret."

"For me." Garik let the words tumble into the room, not intending to say them, but not wishing to reclaim them once they were gone. What did that mean, if Jantzen had chosen Justin then cast him aside? Was Garik already on the way out? Did Jantzen care as much about him as Garik cared about his mentor?

Would Garik one day be in Justin's place, replying, *"Jantzen abandoned me. That's the only thing I regret,"* angry with the world and wrapped up in his own head?

Justin announced, "Done," and his chair scraped the floor as he stood, holding the assembled drone in one hand. He lifted a controller, and he tossed it towards John, who caught it easily. "Test flight. Send it up."

The computer monitor came on, and the image was blacked out with halos of light at the edges, then the light balance adjusted, and Justin's legs were on the screen. They shifted position as he reached to the machine to tweak something.

"Ready?" John watched the smaller screen on his controller.

Justin held it overhead and said, "Send it."

The blades whirred, the machine lifted from Justin's hand, and the large screen showed Justin looking up, his arm raised, his face insectile. He was more mantis than man at that point, and he receded into the larger room. His worktable appeared, and then the computer monitor showing a duplicate of what was on the smaller screen, and finally, the table, the makeshift kitchen, and the rest of the human hybrids watching the demonstration.

"Bring it down." Justin moved bits and pieces aside to give John room to land. "I need to upgrade the battery pack, and we can go see what the wolf boy's girlfriend has gotten up to. That okay with you, wolf boy?"

Wolf boy. A day earlier, Garik would have bristled. Now, it almost felt like Justin was offering him an invitation to become part of an elite club, no longer a token outsider tolerated because he must be, but someone who might fit in someday, even have something to contribute, perhaps even participate in their success, if they could find a way to achieve it.

"Is that my new call sign?" Garik noticed the others had stopped talking to look his and Justin's way, as though this was important. A test. A rite of passage. The air buzzed, ready for the storm to break.

"It can be." The drone had landed on the worktable, and without looking at Garik, Justin plucked it up and turned it upside down, undoing a connection and removing the battery pack. The offer hung in the room, carrying the bitter tang of ozone and as potentially destructive.

"Wolf boy on board."

The tension evaporated, the conversations resumed, and Justin pointed to a far shelf. "Batteries, wolf boy. There. Bring me a pack."

JOHN FLEW the drone. He needed to be outside with the remote. He was in his tee shirt, his arms bare, indifferent to the snow still nestled in the nooks and crannies of the equipment lot.

Joanie was in front of the computer. She might still be struggling to become the bravura she had once been, but her skills were no less honed for being younger than she used to be.

Justin remained inside, fretting that his handiwork might prove inadequate. Any adjustments would be made through Joanie's computer, and he paced the floor just behind her.

Paul observed it all, more amused than anything else. It was more recreation than retaliation, more game than game-changer.

Garik joined John. Unlike John, he was bundled in a heavy coat and gloves, with two pairs of pants. It was winter, and even wrapped up, he shivered.

"I envy you." Garik worked to keep his teeth from chattering.

"Oh?" John hit the power switch, and the propellers on the drone spun, small whirlwinds in the chilly air.

"You're not cold at all, are you?"

"Nope. Watch this." He moved his thumb, and the little drone leapt skyward.

"What are we looking for?" In the distance, the top of Corona Tower broke through the buildings. It looked normal as always, even if at ground level, Garik doubted things were anything near normal.

"Whatever Marisa's planning. Too bad Jantz didn't give us more clues. You know the parking garage was Marisa." John glanced at him with a raised eyebrow before turning back to the drone. "And the bomb threats that closed down the Shipyards."

"The high school, too?" What was Marisa up to? How far would she go?

"Nah, that was the Tower. Brace, more specifically. You drove by if you came down Park, saw it. BCA Tactical. He wanted the place vacant when he brought in his paramilitary forces."

"What next?" Garik didn't mean it as a real question, but it got answered, anyway.

"We're prime on Brace's agenda. We've been lucky here, but Marco's group has had to move twice, the second time just before a bomb took out their hideout. We're not sure if Brace waited until they were out or didn't care. We're only as safe as we make ourselves."

And risking everyone else in the city, Garik thought.

"There. Found her." John held the control so Garik could just see. Marisa was running south along Powerline full out. Others ran with her. Behind them, smoke broiled from an armored transport. "Don't get this. No way that transport was unguarded. Sometimes I think Sunchaser is baiting her, hoping she'll trip up."

Garik remembered the stolen passkey. Marisa had taken Sunchaser's, and Sunchaser was reprimanded. Surely she wasn't getting even?

It was more likely that she was.

— 4 —

FROM THE drone's viewpoint, the world was in John's hands. The image grew to encompass the Uptown area east of Sycamore, revealing the damage left behind by the protesters camping in Central Park, the shattered remains of the two-story Corona Tower parking garage, and the new City Hall, now surrounded by enforcement officers hoping to ward off the inevitable rising tide of destruction brought on by the Tower's lies and the residents' virulent clamor to regain control of a city they had built and learned to love.

Farther out, the Shipyards smoldered, the shorefront along The Docks looked like a war zone, and nearly eight city blocks to the west of Sycamore between First and Ninth bore the unmistakable signature of prepper readiness, with barricades and burn barrels to keep warm.

That was in sharp contrast to the affluent areas of Bay City that the tsunami of destruction seemed to simply flow around, leaving their pools shimmering and the shopping events well attended, as if those areas were off limits to anything that might disturb their idea of country club propriety and order. Waldorf's Department Store parking lot, only six blocks from Shorefront and three from the Tower, gleamed with high-end automobiles, as if nothing except sunny skies dared unroll over Bay City each morning. SUVs moved along the streets in Shady Ridge Acres, occasionally catching the sun on polished chrome and winking at the sky.

Garik recognized the steeple of St. Anne's Church, even Fasst Market, but only by its location on First. Across Sycamore, he saw First United Congregation, not three blocks from where they were. All the way east, The Martial Arts Center parking lot showed the residue of the rousing rallies that had galvanized the city's citizens to rise up against Corona Tower. Now, military vehicles dotted the lot, and black suits and green shirts worked to clear the area.

The City Transportation Department where they were located, very near the center of it all, covered a city block, half being building and the rest open to the sky. Two small specks in the equipment lot were the two people hovering over the controls to the overhead drone spinning somewhere out of sight.

Garik noticed the first tendrils of smoke from along Sycamore, only a few blocks east of his aunt's apartment on Maple. He located the familiar shape of the apartment complex's roof where he and Marisa had sat under the stars on cool nights, wrapped in blankets and sharing their dreams for the future. His eyes jumped eastward across Laurel, Ash, Beech, and Elm, tracing the sharp angle of Sycamore where it cut the small block at Elm and Avenue C in half, a pizza slice tract, with barely enough room to run a business and keep your family fed.

The Flower Shop, the establishment owned and operated by Marisa's parents, coughed black blood into the sky.

"There," Garik pointed, shifting John's hand to get a better view of the small image on the controls. "The Flower Shop. Marisa's parents own it." He pointed to the small wedge of a building.

"It looks to be on fire, and black smoke is the worst there is."

"Why?"

"It suggests accelerant. And that's as black as it gets. I hope Marisa has the sense to stay away."

"She won't." Staying away was the one thing Garik was certain she wouldn't do.

"Look." John shifted his fingers, and the image zoomed in towards Sycamore and The Flower Shop. As the picture in the display swept across Bay City, the Connel Street Skate Park to the east expanded off one side of the screen, revealing white snow glaring against the banked areas and lining the halfpipe, until the park slipped out of sight of the drone's camera. The smoke pouring from The Flower Shop's front windows soon centered the screen.

Along Oak Street and Elm, and farther south along Beech, military vehicles hunkered under tree branches, in the shade of buildings and mixed in among parked cars. One was cocked behind a city dumpster, not hidden from the drone but in a position not to be easily seen from the burning building. Several had doors open. Black figures with weapons stepped out, and they pulled their firearms free. They positioned themselves against the vehicles pointing toward the flower shop.

John's statement, *Sometimes I think Sunchaser is baiting her.* This was a trap.

The back door to the Transportation Department burst open, and Paul and Justin erupted at speed, already yelling, "Locate Marisa. She has no idea what's about to happen."

John was already shifting the view, tracking east to Park Avenue, then heading north, looking for the burning transport she had been fleeing. They found her crossing the powerline right-of-way at the Cowden Street overpass. She was knees down, searching through a pack, waiting, apparently. The others from earlier began to gather. She offered them something, small packages, and they dispersed along the length of the bridge while attaching them.

"She's going to blow up the bridge." Garik was both proud and mortified, proud that she could do this, and mortified that she would do something so dangerous, so incredibly destructive. What was the damage this would do to Corona Tower? He couldn't see it, unless she planned to blow up additional bridges along Park and Powerline Drive, and it came to him. She was isolating the Ransom Communication Building from the Lower East Side, the industrial park, and Bay City Medical.

"She doesn't see the fire," Paul said, the colors on his skin rippling from the blue of loyalty to a worried red. "They're drawing her in. Brace must be desperate to capture her if he's willing to do this."

"Likely Sunchaser. Brace has regained the Tower, and his paramilitary team is centered east. This looks like Tower forces." Sure enough, a closer look at their helmets told the truth of it. Sunchaser's hand was all over this.

In the image, something caught Marisa's attention, taking it away from the bridge. She looked around, seemed to test the air, then she lifted her head and looked to the sky, eventually tracking west. She stood, calling out something to her team, pointing west. Leaving everything, she took off running.

"She sees it now." Justin took his eyes from the small screen and looked to the sky. Even they could now see the black volcano spewing forth the flower shop's life into the winter sky.

The words fell into Garik's head: *Likely Sunchaser*, and more: *driven; guided; herded.* Halo Sunchaser or someone had set the trap, and if Marisa continued along Avenue C, she would run directly into it.

He looked to John's wrist, searching for the watch the man had worn when they first escaped the Tower. He could contact Marisa if he had a watch. She always wore hers, and she would answer if he called.

If he called from his watch, and that had been taken from him long ago.

"I have to warn her," he said, working the first button of his coat. He couldn't get it off fast enough, but he couldn't run with it. He felt the colors around him begin to shift, when a hand wrapped around his arm, hard enough to cause pain. He gasped and the colors faded.

"Don't do this. They will trap you, too."

"I can catch her before she gets even close to Sycamore, convince her, get her to understand what they are doing."

"While you're exhausted? Perhaps collapsed on the street?" Paul still held his arm.

"You don't understand. I've got to go." Garik wrenched free with more strength than he realized he possessed, leaving Paul with a stunned expression on his face.

"Jantzen's with her!" John zoomed the drone's camera, and the final purple wisps of the man's ephemeral mist cleared around him. He materialized with his arm in an open dumpster, and he withdrew a pizza box for modesty. He leapt toward Marisa to block her.

She clearly recognized him, paused, started an arm-waving argument, pointed to the sky, behind her, then toward Sycamore. She tried repeatedly to go around him, and when he wouldn't let her pass, she shoved him to the side and continued running. Jantzen evaporated, leaving the pizza box to drop to the sidewalk, only to reappear half a block down, this time half hidden by the trunk of a leafless tree.

"He won't be able to stop her. Jantzen said I have to do it." Garik worked the last of the buttons on his coat loose, and he dropped it to the ground.

"We can all go—" Justin tried to intervene.

"I can get there faster alone." Garik had taken on the Tower's goons in the flower shop, danced around them. And in the Director's penthouse, he had rescued the glasses before they could hit the floor. Chopping the vegetables for the meal had been so easy as to be fun. He could reach any distance, do anything, achieve any goal. Time became meaningless. For that short space, it no longer applied to him.

And Garik unleashed the rainbows. The human hybrids in the parking lot became statues out of time, the cold that had burned his skin earlier was nothing, and he was off like the wind.

GARIK SOON found that even the wind can only blow so fast. His experiences had him convinced that when he ran at top speed, he truly stopped the world around him, and he could warn Marisa with little effort, take all the time he needed to explain the situation, apprise her of the waiting military vehicles ready to take her into custody. As the old saying goes, if wishes were fishes, but they are not, and no net can catch fish that aren't there.

He first noticed a small bird as he crossed Second Street, a finch, he thought. The world was frozen, but he startled the bird, and he could see the wings begin to ruffle and lift. *Run faster*, he said to himself.

Crossing First Street, the four-lane thoroughfare overflowed with drivers who likely weren't aware of the battle going on for control of the Tower and Bay City, or who didn't care. People still roamed the sidewalks, though not as many as in better times. Garik took them in, planned his path, and started across the street. To the left, the flash of a brake light caught his eye. It hadn't been on, and it was.

I'm not fast enough!

McKinley was an easy run, until he reached Avenue B. A large delivery truck filled the intersection, taking a left and heading his way. He couldn't see to the other side. Yet, he dared the risk, and he dropped in a skater's move, slid under the truck, his shoulders pressed low, barely aware of the truck's frame as it brushed along his back. Yet, the back wheel was closer to him than he expected when he came out the other side, and he was relieved when he realized he was in the clear.

West on Avenue C took him past Forest, alongside the Connel Street Skate Park—closed for the winter—and then across Connel. Five blocks, could he make it?

Far ahead, a figure pummeled the sidewalk, one leg lifted and the other against the ground. Marisa! He could catch her. He would! Yet, as he pushed himself harder and harder, he noted two things. One, her legs shifted position. She was no longer frozen. She was running! How could that be? He was giving it everything! He could see the front of The Flower Shop, already beginning to bow outward with the internal pressures of the flames. And the smoke. The cremated remains of a life's work, reaching for the heavens. It seemed to hold, then slowly curl, then billow faster and faster.

Understanding swept over him. He hadn't touched his meal, only eaten a couple of fruit snacks, and his internal battery was nearing depletion. Recharge, recharge, his body was telling him.

He was only a block behind Marisa when his muscles shut down, and he fell to his knees, his body aflame with exhaustion, and his lungs begging for air. He yelled, "Marisa!" She turned and looked just as she leaped the curb at Avenue C and Sycamore.

Two devastations became real before she reached the far curb, changing everything from that point forward. Two unforgiving swords lanced deep into Garik's soul. Two bear-like claws ripped his heart right out and consumed it in front of his eyes.

A skidding car with the Corona Tower logo on the side clipped Marisa, sending her spinning into the air. Before she came to rest, the front of The Flower Shop erupted into the street, a burning wall of glass and brick and mortar, falling in a flaming conflagration that encased the spot Marisa had landed, sending sparks and burning debris into the sky as it sheathed her in its fiery embrace.

— 5 —

DISBELIEF WRENCHED Garik from his moorings.

The heat of the collapsing building roiled the air, rolling toward him, filling the street, and pushing past him in a billowing cascade of impossibility. The wave of death sucked at him, pulling his breath from his lungs, burning burning burning his eyes; the air acrid with scorched wiring, charred roofing; the remnants of flowers and dirt and other worse things pummeling him as it tumbled past him to dissipate in the cold, winter air.

Car horns sounded, distant to his ears, coming from a different world, a different planet, a different life. Somewhere, tires screeched, and the reverberating impact of metal against metal ricocheted through the brick and glass canyons of the city. The higher tinkle of shattering glass followed, then an unending horn singing a plaintive wail of death, destruction, and woe is me.

Louder sirens soon washed out the horn's song, the alternating pattern of firetrucks and first responders. Shop doors around Garik flew open, and workers and customers, most poorly dressed for the cold, spilled out to see what had torn the city apart. Had the riots moved as far west as Sycamore? This was the secure part of Bay City, an area where the working people could still work, and it was safe to move about, drive a car, leave it parked on the side of the street.

More people, these bundled against the cold, pedestrians who had seen Marisa running and heard Garik call her name, tried to press forward towards the disaster. The heat fought them closer to the flames, pushed back, forced them into retreat.

A man knelt at Garik's side, placed his hand on his shoulder, questioned him, got no response, and called for someone to join him. "Shock," he said. "He's burning up. He may be ill. He was running after her, called to her. I think they were together."

"Marisa," someone else said. "I heard him call that name."

"What happened?" A shop owner in a white apron with dustings of flour on her forehead burst from her shop, turned from Garik to take in the burning building.

"The façade fell on someone. Smoke was coming out, and then it just tumbled into the street. The fire department hasn't even arrived."

"Terrible." The woman with the white apron.

"The Bruni's daughter, we think."

"No!" the apron said. "I recognize this young man. He spent time at the shop, Marisa's friend. He rode past the front of my shop sometimes on a skateboard."

The firetrucks grew louder, hoses soon tumbled over the scene firing off waterfalls of relief and turning the smoke from black to gray to the white of steam.

It was terrible, everyone agreed. No one thought anything when a tall blond man, a forceful young woman in a knit cap, and a helpful woman who looked very much like a Bay City Medical nurse knelt at Garik's side. The onlookers allowed them room, even thanked the nurse for her kindness, and took time to explain that the youth was a friend of a girl thought to have been caught when the front of the building fell.

That they helped Garik into an SUV and not an ambulance didn't strike anyone as especially odd. The real oddity was an exploding building in Bay City—the Bruni's flower shop! They had been there since Marisa was a child. They were such sweet people. They hoped Mr. and Mrs. Bruni were okay. How would they manage if the worst proved true? Then, maybe it hadn't been Marisa. All in all, it was terrible, terrible, they repeated over and over.

BEFORE GARIK'S body had collapsed to the sidewalk in exhausted defeat, his mind was already adrift in a black sea of bottomless despair. The red wall reaching out to eat Marisa, the belch of flames, the rising sparks dancing in the air.

He heard the man's questions, felt the touch on his shoulder, and they meant nothing. Marisa couldn't be *gone*. John at his side. Joanie barking instructions. A nurse with Paul's voice. He moved at their touch, stepped into the SUV at their prompting, was locked onto the scene of destruction that had eaten Sycamore and Marisa.

No! He wanted to yell, hit something, someone, anything. He had run, done all he could, been close enough to call her name, and she had looked at him. She had looked at him, *seen him*, and she hadn't slowed, had run into the destruction anyway.

"Why?" he managed to whisper. He was too weak to do more. The running. The rainbows. It stole everything from him. What use was his timber wolf DNA-enhanced ability to *run* if it took everything from him, and he couldn't even save Marisa? It was useless. *He* was useless.

"Easy," Joanie said, her tone and voice from the old Joanie, her kindness from the reborn one. "Not your fault."

Then whose, Garik thought. Marisa's parents, for building The Flower Shop on that tiny wedge of land fronting Sycamore? Marisa's, for wanting to uncover what had happened to her sister after she disappeared into the Tower's clutches? Kevin Lee's for introducing them to Halo Sunchaser? Or Jantzen's, maybe Justin's or Alyna's or Amy's. Yes, Amy's for not being forceful enough to tell Marisa to *go home. Stay out of it. Let us handle the Tower and the destruction happening to Bay City.*

"I brought these." Paul, once again Paul, the nurse relegated to the memories of the bystanders watching The Flower Shop burn, held out several of the fruit bars. "I didn't have time to grab anything else. I'm sorry. Oh," and he hefted a bottle of energy drink with a screw-off lid, "this, too."

"But why," Garik said again. "I was nearly there. I called to her. She didn't listen."

"She couldn't listen." John from the front seat. "She had to protect what she loved no matter the risk."

What she loved, and she ran from him when he called her name. The scene was etched in his thoughts on continual repeat, playing itself out over and over.

Garik took one of the fruit bars, grateful that Paul had unwrapped it. The drink, too, the lid already gone. He sipped, then took a bite, feeling the surge of strength as it went down his throat.

"I don't like having this vehicle in the open." Paul's skin rippled with yellow, intuitively attempting to repel his growing anxiety.

"Agreed," Joanie replied.

"I can ditch it when I let you guys out." John, at the wheel. "Hey, kiddo back there, will you be able to walk by the time we get there?" The Flower Shop was twelve blocks, give or take, from the Transportation Department building. They would be there soon.

"Maybe." Garik took another bite of the fruit bar and another drink. "Sure, yeah, whatever you need me to do." Why should he care? No point, no point, no reason to stay in the car, to get out, to run from Sunchaser, to eat, to go to bed tonight, to get up tomorrow. So, sure, whatever. He was game for anything providing he didn't have to choose.

"Maybe we shouldn't drive it all the way back to the lair." Paul said *lair* like it was an underground hideout instead of a city building sitting out under an open sky. "This is the Colonel's car. If it's seen . . ." He didn't need to finish the sentence.

"Done," John agreed. "How about I let you out at First United? That leaves you two-and-a-half blocks. Kiddo, are you good with that?"

"Wolf boy ready to rumble." He muttered his reply. Outside, they were passing the skate park. He tried to fathom his interest in it, remembered Marisa showing up to watch him skate and her lack of interest in the heart-racing sport. She had been content to let him ride his board while she drew on her MicroArt tablet. That was still real to him and could never happen again.

John took a left on Forest, then another left on Avenue B, following the skate park with each turn. Garik let his eyes trail along the ramps and drop-offs, unsure why it had meant so much to him. With Marisa gone . . . then they crossed Connel and left the skate park behind. The SUV took the next right on Thomas Road, trying to be as inconspicuous as possible for the next five blocks to First United. Traffic as they waited at the light to cross First Street was steady but light. Red changed to green, and John accelerated slowly, not wishing to draw attention to the truck. At the church, he pulled into the lot on the south side of the building. They would only need to walk a couple blocks to the Transportation Building, three exposed blocks. Security cameras if there were any could pick them up, something they didn't need.

"Joanie," Paul said, taking his knit scarf from beside him and handing it to her. "Wrap this around your face. Leave just your eyes exposed."

"And you?" She took the scarf as she questioned him.

"I need to be uncovered. That's my protection. You, Garik, take my coat."

"No, thank you." Warmth . . . what was warmth when everything was gone?

"It has a hood. Your face needs to be covered."

"A couple blocks. No one cares. I'll be fine." Garik still hadn't looked at the man. His eyes were out the window, but he had no idea what was there. His brain was on Sycamore reliving something that never should have happened.

"Garik." John reached over the seat and took his knee. When

Garik didn't respond, he shook it. "Kiddo, I care. Paul does, too, and Joanie. Why do you think we're here? What just happened? Wrong, wrong wrong wrong. You didn't deserve that. What am I saying, Marisa didn't deserve that, but we can't undo it except to keep ourselves safe. You, me, all of us. The coat, please?"

Garik lifted his eyes to the scene above the buildings bordering Thomas, the remnants of smoke that were now more puffy cloud than churning disaster, the white of redemption rather than the color of destruction. He pulled his eyes back into the car, for the first time taking in John leaning over the driver's seat, Joanie next to him, her face already covered, and beside him, Paul, his skin mottled, changing into something or someone that would be invisible to anyone watching and holding out a coat with a faux fur-lined hood unzipped and lying flat across the back.

"Sure." He reached his hand, accepting the offering.

"It's big—" sized to fit Paul, he suggested, "—so the sleeves are likely long for you. The hood you may have to keep pulled down. Your eyes. Keep your eyes covered. That's what will give you away."

Garik remembered Jantzen once saying that the upper half of the face was eighty percent of recognition. He wondered how true that was. He'd seen Marisa standing before a window in the Tower looking outside. Her face had been turned from him, and he'd known it was her. No doubts, just that it was her. And running on the street towards her family's business, the building aflame, he'd known it was Marisa. No one could have told him different and expected him to believe it. It was in her height, her legs, the way she carried herself. He hadn't needed to see her face to *know*.

"Cover my eyes," he repeated. "Why not?"

He moved forward in the seat, worked the coat around him and his arms into the sleeves. He turned his back to Paul to let him zip the hood closed and pulled it over his head. Fur surrounded his face, and he felt claustrophobia closing him in.

"Ready?" John's voice was bright and encouraging.

"Been ready to get out of this hamster cage since last summer. I'm gone." Garik threw open the door, stepped out, and felt the cold bite into his face. In that moment, he was glad for the coat, though he would have done fine without it. He didn't *need* it, even with its warmth.

He didn't wait on the others. He closed the door and walked

away with a strong stride, determined, angry, and disgusted with everyone that had anything to do with the Tower. This was *his* city. Bay City belonged to *him*. He knew the streets, had lived them, walked them, ridden them on his skateboard, and covered most of them on his Street Strider. He didn't need directions or companions or guards or protectors. He could see the Transportation Department from where he stood, just there, three blocks. The others? They could follow or not. He had listened to people tell him what to do, and now Marisa was beyond reach. He should have listened to himself, shucked off everything they told him, and Houdinied out of that Tower long ago. Then Marisa would still be alive, still with him, still creating storyboards on her MicroArt tablet, still watching the stars with him from the roof of City View Apartments.

The tears . . . his tears . . . he felt them, but they weren't tears at all. They were his soul, his humanity, every soft spot he'd once known inside leaking down his face. Who cared who saw when he didn't care anymore?

His life was his, and he was determined that someone would pay.

— 6 —

GARIK FELT different inside.

The cold winter air reached deeper into his lungs. The smell of asphalt from the road told him it was more recently laid on Forest than on Connel. His heart, pumping with determination, preparing him for . . . what? Flight? He wanted to flee but to where? There was nowhere to go. He had learned he could run only so far at top speed. Half a minute, then exhaustion. His future: he could see two possibilities, both real, both available for him to choose. One, he would enter the Transportation Department on McKinley, join Justin, wait on the others, do as he was told. That was the safe choice, though he admitted there were no safe choices. Marisa was proof of that. He should have . . . and he choked back his emotions, attempted to swallow his longings, felt them come back up anyway. He should have told her how he felt, had tried to, was always afraid he would lose her if he did.

Then he lost her, anyway.

His heart punched at the walls of his chest; the coat enveloping him was hot, too insulating, too claustrophobic, and he wanted it off.

The second possibility overlaid the first. He would shed his coat, toss it to the side, take his freedom, and make his world his. Grasp it, claim it, refuse to let anyone else have any say in who he was or what he did. That outcome was certain. Drones overhead—he could already hear them, different than Justin's, tuned to the buzzing cadence of the Tower's military-styled mantra—were already searching. Whining. Screaming. Looking for him and likely for the other hybrids loosed upon Bay City, but for him, mostly.

Two options, two outcomes, his choice. Bolt hole or bolt for freedom. The outcomes were inescapable, as if written in stone. One, he would retain his freedom from the Tower's clutches, even if it wasn't the freedom he desired. Two, he would be recognized on a drone's footage, and a team of paramilitary soldiers would arrive before he could exit the city. He could picture, no, *knew* they would have BolaWraps, and he would be bound and in their custody within fifteen minutes.

After that? Events became less distinct, but the questioning, drugs, Rodheimer looming over him expressing his disappointment, Sunchaser withdrawing her sword, the double thump of the lock as they ensured he couldn't escape yet again. All were there, part of that choice, if he took it.

Where was Brace? He tried to find him in the probabilities but couldn't. Likely, Garik was already dismissed from his awareness, a failure, something to be cast aside as failed and worthless.

He pulled the hood's fur tighter against his ears. The sirens at Sycamore were a reminder he didn't need. The varying tones told him the ambulances had departed with no one inside. The firetrucks knew the building was a loss. The police were settled in to guard the scene until they could assess the cause. He could hear each distinctly as it happened. And the smell. Overlying the difference in asphalt from Forest to Connel, the aroma of the bakery where he had last seen Marisa hinted at bread and rolls and yeasty donuts. He frowned at being able to smell the bakery from this distance, yet it was there. Mixed in was the burnt smell of wiring and charred masonry, a dry, chalky smell, dead and unpleasant, breathed in with every breath.

He shook the grim reminder from his thoughts as he approached the Transportation Department building. Justin stood outside, his hands on the drone's remote. Garik couldn't see him, but he would be there in the equipment yard. Either choice, to return or run, Justin was there, as certain as the man's confrontational attitude and his willingness to help when the need arose. What would his reaction be when Garik shucked his coat and ran for his freedom? As soon as Garik made that choice, in Garik's mind, Justin disappeared from his vision, erased from the choices, left behind as part of another world.

Garik paused his feet, looked around at the sky and the buildings and everything that was the same as when he had run to warn Marisa an hour before, and he considered whether this was what Christian had seen, his prescience, his use of precognition to determine future events. All Garik saw were possibilities, not certainties, nothing clearly more than fifteen minutes out, and half a day? Beyond that, there were only uncertainties.

He glanced at the building, the structure's street side façade injured by the vehicle Justin had crashed through the front wall, and pictured Justin on the far side, unseen but unquestionably there, and he turned to look down Third, his avenue of escape and, yes, capture by the Tower. There was no choice. None at all.

He waited for a car, turning his head away as it passed, and stepped off the curb. No pedestrians were out on this back street, none except him and his two hangers-on coming up behind. He heard their footsteps, certain which were Paul's, fluid but heavy against the concrete sidewalk, and Joanie's, lighter but determined, and at a faster clip than Paul's fluid ones. Her smaller size required her to expend more steps. Somewhere in the distance, east, he thought, a car's door slammed. He recognized the sound, one he was certain only the most sensitive instruments in the Tower's arsenal would be able to pick up. John had found somewhere to abandon Brace's SUV after wiping away any evidence they were there, he was sure. No, not sure. He *saw* it. When he entered the door to the Transportation Department building, that knowledge would become indisputable fact, even if he had no way of confirming it until John returned.

Garik continued across the street and to the equipment yard facing Douglas without looking back, made his way to the gate, still unlatched from the SUV's exit onto the city streets, and pulled it wide.

"Welcome back, Garik." Justin didn't look up. "How do I know it's you?" He raised the control just enough to indicate that he was watching everything from far above.

"Okay. I'm inside." Garik didn't slow. Let Justin watch him. Let anyone watch him. Option one. He'd chosen it, but he didn't like it.

Inside, he would be trapped just as surely as he had been trapped in the Tower's basements. Dread filled his throat as he pushed through the door and into the building. The ceiling rising over him pressed in. The vehicle leaping through the front wall threatened to reach out and grab him, eat him, consume him. He looked away, moved toward the more familiar warehouse where the team spent their time.

He had made his choice. The tower's drones, the drugs, Rodheimer, the sword, all vanished with his entry into the equipment yard. Now, as he walked into the high-ceilinged warehouse, new possibilities erupted in his head, a volcano of timelines. In each one, Jantzen waited. Choose this, choose that, get this outcome, get that, always with the purple man affecting his decisions. How was he to choose?

He tossed off the coat, fell onto the couch, pressed his hands to his eyes, and tried to force them away. The trouble, he found, was that the choices rising like an incoming tide along The Docks weren't in his eyes. They were in his head, and that he couldn't do anything about.

He was adrift and about to drown, and there was no one there to help him to the shore.

GARIK HEARD, he *heard* the shifting of the air, the brushing aside of molecules, and something, no, *someone* entering the room, yet the doors hadn't opened. A popping, bubbling, fizzing sound like a soda can being opened tickled Garik's ears, not loud, just there, and he opened his eyes to see Jantzen change from translucent to solid as the effervescent purple mist congealed into a man. He stood behind the table, and as he firmed up, he pulled the blanket from the back of the chair and wrapped himself.

"How can anything hurt so much?" Jantzen twisted his face in dismay.

"Hello, Jantzen." Garik wanted his presence known. "I'm surprised you don't know why rematerializing hurts you so much. I've seen it. But then, you have your pain, I have mine. What's new?"

"I'm sorry I couldn't stop Marisa."

The purple man sounded repentant, but then, that was just how he sounded. How he *felt* was what Garik wanted to know. He listened to Jantzen's breathing, took in the sharp tang of his physical presence, knew what he would say next, preempted him.

"You don't know how I feel, will never know how I feel. So

don't tell me you do."

Garik wanted to shift blame on the man, accuse him of Marisa's death, but he could smell his sincerity. Jantzen had truly not wanted Marisa to end the way she had. The man's grief, while far less than what Garik wanted him to feel, was there in his heartbeat, the pheromones cast into the room by his skin, the heat that emanated from him.

"Okay," Jantzen agreed. "I will never tell you that, but I truly tried—"

"Just that she couldn't turn around because she had to protect what she loved." And it wasn't me, at least not enough to stop running toward her death.

"I didn't say that." Jantzen walked across the room, searching, and finding a pair of pants, slipped them on under the blanket then tossed it aside. "A shirt, is there one?"

"Yes." Garik pulled his over his head and tossed it at him before throwing an arm back over his eyes. "There."

"I can tell you're upset." Jantzen slipped on the shirt.

"Yah! You got that, huh?" Garik pulled his arm from his face, and he was on his feet before he could express the desire to stand. "What told you I might be upset, Jantzen? Maybe a war in my city? My life stolen? My girlfriend pulled into a trap, then killed, and for what? Why would they do that? It was me they wanted, not her. They want you and John and all the rest. Why didn't they just leave her alone?" The words poured out hot, hot and bitter, aimed at Jantzen and intended to hurt.

"Just you, I'm afraid." Jantzen, calm and unaffected by Garik's tirade. "The rest of us, destroyed, perhaps, but not back. We were already on the way out. You are their ultimate goal, what they've worked to achieve. They will pay any price."

"They might get their wish." Garik meant the words hard but felt the despair crawl back over him.

He fell back to the couch, his head back and staring at the ceiling. For a moment, his anger had made him feel good, powerful, but now, it was fading. He didn't want it to fade. He wanted to push the grief away. He mustn't, *couldn't* allow it to swallow him whole. Marisa would have expected more than that of him.

"There's something I want you to see."

"Don't distract me. I deserve to be left alone in my misery. Or can't you even do that?"

"I do push people." Jantzen slapped him on the side of the leg. "This will interest you. Up, young man."

Garik sighed, leaned forward, and with great effort, pulled himself to his feet. Jantzen held out a hand, motioned to Garik in a familiar way, with his palm up and crooking his fingers, and Garik relaxed into a small grin. Jantzen could always manipulate him, and he let himself be pulled along.

Jantzen turned on the light in the small bathroom, and he pulled Garik inside. He took his shoulders and placed him directly in front of the mirror. Garik could see the top half of his bare chest supporting his head.

"Notice anything?" Jantzen behind him squeezed his shoulders.

"You behind me. Otherwise, no." As he said the words, he studied his chest. It was leaner, the musculature more pronounced. He remembered jerking free from Paul's hand and the surprise on his face. That was all, though.

"Look at your face. Keep your eyes fixed. Don't blink." Jantzen released his shoulders and he turned out the light, leaving the two of them just visible from the light streaming in from the room outside.

Garik's eyes immediately adjusted, as if the light were still on, the bathroom nearly as bright as before, with Jantzen still fully visible behind him. He wasn't sure what Jantzen intended him to see.

"I don't see it."

"Okay, let's try again." Jantzen fumbled for the switch, missing it twice, although it was easily visible to Garik. It came on, Garik felt his pupils readjust, and that's when he saw it.

Eyeshine. Something he'd never had before.

"Turn it off again," he instructed, this time staring at his eyes. When the lights went out, as his pupils expanded wider than he had ever seen them, the light from the door glittered in his eyes.

Like a cat. *Like a wolf,* washed over him, able to see in the dark.

"It's starting," Jantzen said, clapping his hands on Garik's shoulders before exiting back into the room and leaving him alone.

Starting, Garik thought. No, Jantzen, it's already here.

— 7 —

GARIK HEARD the distant sound of feet on the rough concrete floor, the rustle of cloth, felt the way the air swirled through the building and around him, knew each person who entered the warehouse before a word was spoken.

And the order of their entrance.

Paul first, hurriedly, as though searching. The searching meant concern, worry, building dismay. Of course, it did. It could mean nothing else.

Next, Justin, although he had expected Joanie. Then, fifteen minutes was all he could be sure of, and the *knowing* of a matter changed the *happening* of a matter. It was inescapable. He could not *know* a series of events was about to occur without *acting* on those events. Even if he did nothing at all, the events were altered by his awareness of them.

The reason Justin had broken Garik's predicted pattern swept over him, a gestalt of understanding as he played out his memory of the last few minutes. Garik had brushed by him while walking through the equipment yard, creating concern in the man, providing the temptation to pull him inside when he had previously held no intent of doing so. The very fact of Garik *knowing* Justin would remain at the controls of the drone had precipitated an *action* by Garik—his terse greeting—giving Justin a *reason* to change his behavior.

Inescapable.

Justin would be looking for him, but he wouldn't call to him. The scene was laid out in Garik's mind, a stage fully set out with the players walking through their parts, the lines scripted, and no one allowed to change a word. Jantzen would be there, a surprise to Justin, and would shift Justin's attention from Garik's terse answer to why Jantzen had returned.

"Jantzen! You're back!"

Garik smiled at his reflection in the mirror, though it was not a pleasant expression. The new hardness in his eyes, perhaps the way the smile stayed on the lower part of his face while the muscles around his eyes tightened. Like Jantzen had said, eighty percent of who a person was could be seen in the eyes.

This was the new Garik, he said to himself.

The third set of feet, the rasp of knit cap on recently shorn hair, the careless toss of that cap as it swirled the air on its way to a chair. The sound, the feel, the brush of air molecule pushing against air molecule then moving against his skin told him it was Joanie.

He wouldn't hear John enter. John was already lost. A moment of regret brushed the old Garik now buried deep inside, and he closed it off. That was no longer who he was. John had made his choice, he had chosen the location to abandon Brace's SUV, he would have to survive on his own. Could he be helped? Twelve hours, six hours, fifteen minutes. Further than twelve hours out was impossible to see. Anyone claiming otherwise was a fool. Six hours, well, at six hours, the paths of possibilities spread out like the branches on a tree, the main path lush with likelihood, then paths veering off, still high with probability, then more choices branching from them, harder to define.

Fifteen minutes? Garik could *see* it. Dead certain. Yet, seeing it meant he changed it, so even that wasn't certain. How had Christian said it to him? *"And here you are telling me this."* Extrapolation and confirmation. Take all the information I can access through every sense I have, sort the probabilities by likelihood, and extrapolate the outcome.

Like the cards during the test he had failed so badly. It hadn't been about the cards, knowing which would be turned over in what order. It was the hand dealing them, the eyes in the face, the way the dealer shuffled them, the pattern of the cards as they interwove with one another, how many cards he pulled off when he cut the deck, the weight of the ink on each card, the smell of his pheromones— anticipation, glee, or disdain—his breathing rate . . . all of it told the next card the dealer would display. Probability, not prescience.

Garik saw it, understood what Christian knew and why he hadn't run from his certain end on Level 5. The man knew what was coming—as much as "precognition" could tell him—but it wasn't enough to change the future. He *heard* the movement, *felt* the brush of the air molecules, *saw* the difference in how heavy each card was, the way the dealer licked his lips, the narrowing of his eyes. The crisp *smell* of his satisfaction—or gloating or condescending sneer or premature triumph—gave him away. The card he would display would be the ace of hearts. Always an ace of hearts, charred to inky black and ripped away in the fiery aftermath of tumbling bricks and stone in the center of the street.

Garik balled his fist and slammed it into the mirror, aiming for the face on the other side, the hair that had finally regrown, the out-sized features telling his Armenian heritage, the bronze skin, the *eye-shine* telling of his hijacked life. The glass shattered, pain arced through his hand, and he pulled his fist away, watching the blood well up from the deep cuts, so distant, so far away, affecting someone else, not Garik, not him, not anyone he knew. Then, the bleeding slowed, the skin began to knit, and that's when the burning started.

"Sheesh!" he hissed, shaking his hand and flinging blood to the mirror. He hit the cold water tap and held his hand underneath. "Colder, please," he pleaded with the handle, wondering why the city couldn't provide ice water through its pipes. It was *winter*.

The heat in his hand as it healed distracted him. He realized he had an audience of three crowded at the door. He looked up, saw a dozen of him in the fractured mirror, each of them splattered with drops of his blood.

A dozen, he considered. Each with a different path to follow, and only one will survive. Which of us will it be? In fifteen minutes, in six hours, half a day from now? Me? One of them? Or another Garik that appears in yet another shattered mirror on a probability path I've yet to see?

He lifted his hand. The water was running clear, the heat in his skin had dissipated, and he knew it was undamaged. He flexed it, turned it over, inspected the flesh. Perfect, as his "prescience" had assured him it would be.

"So," he began, sure of his words, speaking to himself as much as to the three people watching him study his hand. "We need a plan to rescue John. Who wants to suggest one?"

They were free to suggest, but the plan was already in motion. The question was the catalyst, the detonator was him, the outcome . . . well, it was further out than fifteen minutes, so that he couldn't say.

"LIKED THAT mirror," Joanie grumbled, turning away from the bathroom door. She ran a hand over her head, shaved on each side, with an underwhelming mohawk just starting from forehead to crown.

"Not me," Justin said, unbothered by the broken glass. He broke away from the bathroom door when he saw the uninjured hand. "Nothing in them I like to see."

Jantzen was more to the point. "The blood. Yours, I'm guessing." He leaned against the doorframe, still in Garik's shirt, and crossed his arms.

"You should be asking me about John." Garik turned off the water and dried his hand on a towel.

"What do you know? He's proficient at surviving, what he was bred for. Why would we need a rescue plan?"

"Stupidity abounds in this place." Garik pushed past Jantzen, wondering what he would do for a shirt now that Jantzen had his. "Justin, Joanie, I need a shirt."

"Why stupidity?" Jantzen caught his arm.

Garik looked at Jantzen's hand, knew he could pull free. He'd done so with Paul, yet he allowed Jantzen's hand to remain, looked into his face, and said, "I know why it hurts when you morph back into your body."

Jantzen's hand relaxed and fell away, as Garik had known it would. The man had wanted to challenge him, and as soon as Garik showed that he was willing to interact with him, even about a totally different subject, the challenge had fallen away, and with it, his hand.

So much easier.

"Hyper speed. For me, of course, not you. I watched your body come back together." He saw Jantzen's eyes widen. "You've never done that, have you? A high-speed camera was all you needed."

Jantzen berated himself. The widening of the man's eyes, the elevation of his heart, the increased body temperature revealed it. Reading him like a book was now a kindergarten level skill.

As they say, easy as pie.

Garik shrugged, ready to move on. "Your body doesn't want to come back together. It fights itself. I watched it. Now, about John. How about getting on to saving him from wherever they've taken him?"

JUSTIN SWORE at himself for calling in the drone. "I might have seen something, perhaps where they took him," he said. "No one told me John was going off somewhere to ditch the truck."

"You would have lost the drone," Garik told him. He was still shirtless. Nothing was available unless he wanted something of Joanie's. He had declined. "They already had theirs in the air. They saw Brace's SUV before you arrived to pick me up."

"Now you're telling us this place is compromised." Jantzen sat back on the couch, and he motioned around him.

"Three hours, maybe. They will be here." Garik nodded. They would work out the direction of the SUV's travel, eventually recognize the place it had remained covered in the equipment lot, the one that was now empty, and determine what Garik had worked out in

453

about two seconds. The possibilities for their escape or discovery branched out, the likely ones growing broader and the others fading away the more time they took to discuss it.

"And you know this how?" Justin, his confrontational side refusing to abandon their hideout without an explanation.

Garik had tried to explain how he knew John was already in the Tower's hands: the sounds of the drones, their direction and volume level, what they would be able to see, how the Tower would control them, aim the cameras; the slamming of the truck door when John abandoned it, the direction and volume revealing its location even from blocks away; the path John would travel to get back to the Transportation Department warehouse, circuitous, under awnings, designed to disperse any attention, yet in the process attracting exactly the attention he hoped to avoid. The answer for *knowing* had been in the *information*. Yet, what Garik's listeners couldn't sense, they didn't understand, so this time, he skipped the effort.

"The real question is, do you trust me?" Either the man did or didn't. If he didn't, Garik was prepared to move on his own. The Tower had created enough havoc in their lives, and he wasn't willing to give up another person to them. This warehouse? They could find another. Bashing in the Tower's nose and getting John back was the important thing. He would rather have them help him, but he would get John back, one way or another.

Joanie looked around the warehouse, evaluating, and her decision was in her eyes. She nodded at Garik and moved to the computer and began dismantling the connections.

"We can't take the big monitor," Justin called.

"Duh," she said as she dropped to the floor and continued disconnecting cables.

"It's not the first hideaway we've given up. It may not be the last, either." Jantzen studied the ceiling as though thinking. "I'll need to find us a new place."

"I can help," Paul offered. His face shifted, and he was a Bay City policeman. His clothing followed his lead a second later. Then, he slid seamlessly into a businessman, a shopkeeper, a longshoreman, and a too-tall housewife.

"Not the last one, but the others, I can see some benefit. You'll be on your own. My search, well, I'll be here and there, difficult to keep up with."

Paul smiled broadly, revealing his mother's initials inset in his two front teeth. "Yes, massa. I be able to find my own way home." He let out a laugh, enjoying his off-kilter joke.

"I'm sure you will." Jantzen stood, and as he did, he thumped a fist against Garik's knee. "So, my body doesn't like coming back together. I'll have to work out a counseling session for that." He smiled, and in a wisp of purple smoke, he vanished.

Garik caught his shirt on the way down, put it to his nose, decided it was clean enough to wear, and worked his arms into the sleeves. He did note it was tighter on him than it had been on Jantzen. That wouldn't have been true six months before.

Muscle up, he thought. The better for smashing a little bit of Tower face. Bring 'em down to size. Make them pay for what they'd taken from him.

Whatever it took, even if he had to go it alone.

— 8 —

"YOU STILL have this?" Garik found he could be surprised. He laughed sourly as he helped Justin uncover the old Martial Arts Center transport van. The windows broken when they'd first escaped the Tower were boarded up with plywood, and numerous slug holes were filled with translucent filler. Garik touched one. "Silicone?"

"Maybe. It was here when we took over the place. Kevin told us the city compensated the Center with a replacement, and he didn't know what happened to the old one. I told him we found it. The keys are inside." Justin opened the door.

It was as Garik remembered, with the steering column partially disassembled where he had tried to hotwire it before discovering he couldn't bypass the key mechanism. Garik didn't need a prescient revelation to know that the months it had sat under a tarp meant the battery would be toast. That was just common sense. He called out, "What about a battery? Or a charger?"

"I've seen a charger inside." Justin peered at the building, and he seemed to be thinking. "We would need an extension cord, too, one about a hundred feet. They have everything in there. I can look."

So, option one: Use a battery charger and extension cord. The van would start, but the first time it was parked overnight, the battery would fail, and they would be stranded. Unacceptable.

Option two: He saw three seasonal-use trucks and a small city bus that would have batteries out and on tenders. Replace the battery with one from inside the warehouse. He glanced at the building, finding the door.

"Through that door. There's a battery inside we can replace this one with. You'll find tools to remove the leads. Go."

Justin jerked his head sideways as if ready to argue, and Garik cut him off with a look, pushed past him, and dropped in the van and tripped the hood release. When he stood, Justin was moving toward the building and muttering, "Thinks he's the boss of me—"

I am the boss of you, Garik thought, although it was more a dismissal of the words. Garik had given him instructions, the only path forward that offered a positive outcome, and Justin had no choice but to follow through. No argument needed or tolerated. Bam. Done. Bought the farm, just like that.

Joanie had the computer and several boxes of supplies ready, including Justin's drone, when they pulled the van up to the back door. The van had a slight cough, likely from the old fuel, and Justin argued that it needed repairs. Garik dismissed his argument. The fuel filter would do its job and the van would be running properly in another twenty minutes, he said. Logic. Information, evaluation, extrapolation.

Obvious.

As Joanie and Justin loaded the van, Garik closed his eyes and pictured the tree branching out in front of him. The discovery of the City Transportation Building as their base now consumed the entire trunk, meaning within a quarter hour. They needed to move. What happened after, less certain. John was down one branch, splitting off to either a failed attempt to retrieve him from the Tower's clutches or his successful rescue. Further along that path it grew dark, and Garik knew they must wait to make those choices.

The second branch offered a successful hideout provided by Jantzen. Safety. Security, but without John. That path branched into disappointment, lack of trust, and giving in to the Tower and recapture for each of the escaped hybrids. Garik refused to follow that branch any further. The branches grew dark with possibilities he refused to consider.

"Where?" Joanie. Her clipped speech patterns had followed her through her rebirth, but her intent was clear. Where do we go now?

"For John." Garik started the van and put it into gear.

"Are you nuts?" Justin slammed the gear lever back into park, immobilizing the transmission before Garik could apply the gas.

456

"*They* have him. Count us, one, two, three. What can we do against them? We need a plan, and we're not it. I can fly, lot of good that does with all the drones overhead. Joanie is still recovering from being dead. You? Do you want to be recaptured *again*?"

Garik pushed Justin's hand off the gear lever and took a deep breath. Even in this, branches split into smaller branches, paths became convoluted, offered him options he could choose or dismiss. Selecting one meant changing all the others. Seeing them at all, even the ones that appeared certain, meant none of them were.

Stone. He wished at least one option could be written in stone. Even the Tower finding this place. He had seen it, felt its immediacy, and that had caused him to react. They had moved the van, and that meant they had changed the circumstances of the equation. A plus B equals C becomes A plus D equals a completely different outcome.

One element of the equation was non-negotiable. John. Safety was a dead end, already cast aside, even if Justin couldn't see it. Joanie? Garik felt her on his side. Her expression inside the warehouse when she had weighed his words and their situation and immediately begun packing—she hadn't lost her skill of evaluating and moving forward relentlessly with her decision. Dying and coming back to life hadn't changed that.

"Stay in or get out." Garik pulled the lever back into gear.

"Joanie, talk to him. Jantzen said—"

"Joanie, are you with me?" Garik directed the question to the back. In the rearview mirror, she raised a hand clasped in a fist.

"We have no weapons," Justin muttered as Garik pulled ahead.

Garik knew otherwise. Joanie was brilliant. She could read a situation and move forward into the best option possible. Justin, well, Garik had fought him and had barely defeated him. The man's hands were power saws when he spun his blades.

And Garik, what did he have to offer? The Tower had killed Marisa. They had taken her life, stolen her from him, and that he could never set aside.

Garik's weapon? His anger. He intended to make everyone pay. As he pulled away from the Transportation Department building, the safe option of a secure second hideout evaporated, leaving only one path before him.

John. Rescue. And best of all, his fist buried in the Tower's face.

THEY LEFT the van on Lilac, far enough for the battered vehicle to fade into the riot-weary city landscape, and close enough to run to it for quick escape. At least the military wouldn't recognize it, as it had been out of commission so long.

They crouched at the corner of Cleveland and Ninth looking out over the Center in front of them. They wore their coats with their faces wrapped in scarves like pedestrians huddled against the cold. Justin was covered with his leather duster, the winged hump on his back diminished by the duster's broad shoulders. Garik had on the fanny pack filled with fruit bars and high-energy snacks. The sign for Ai Kee! was missing much of the "K" and looked like Ai nee! Several of the military's trucks were in the parking lot, but from this angle, it could have been six months ago, with Bay City an adventure waiting for Garik's attention, and Kevin Lee getting ready for his Hollywood audition.

Justin groused, "They wouldn't bring him here."

"And you know that how?" Garik's heart pounded, feeding extra oxygen into his blood, fueling his fast twitch muscles for quick movement, flooding his brain with oxygen for thinking more quickly. He was ready to move forward. True, there was no sign of John, of Brace's SUV, or of a team that might be interrogating their friend, but the Center was a big place, and they could be forcing John with threats and torture even now. He had seen Basement Level 5. He knew the depths of the Tower's depravity.

"The high school," Justin said. "Or the Tower. This place is nothing."

"Exactly why they would bring him here."

"Agreed," Joanie said, bringing Justin's glare on her. "Following you. Advise?"

What do you advise? Garik understood her completely. At the same time, he was listening intently and drawing in the smells coming from the Center. The breeze was fighting him, forcing the aroma of burned building and firefighting foam to him from Sycamore, and he kept picturing Marisa's last moments, her headlong rush into the flames as they billowed from the falling wall.

"Hold." Garik held up his hand, closed his eyes, and concentrated. "Voices."

"Ai Kee! or elsewhere?" Joanie asked.

"To the left." Garik still had his eyes closed. The location he described was the office section of the building.

"I told you," Justin hissed, triumphant.

458

"Shush!" Joanie jabbed him with her elbow.

"In the offices, I'm sure. I hear, um, office things." What he heard was filing cabinets being slammed one against another, the sound of hanging files and metal drawers shifting violently.

"Office things, sure," Justin started, an edge of arrogance giving his words a mocking tone, before catching Joanie's stern expression. "What do office things mean?" he asked more politely.

"Bad things," Garik said. Paramilitary things, military-bred hybrids with breathing-assisted helmets ready to rumble. With the sound, probability lines had fractured the future. Each one he followed shattered into branches of disasters that might lose John, or even the three of them.

Garik found himself breathing faster and deeper, flooding him with predatory awareness. He slipped his coat off and unwrapped his face, and he reached into his pack, more by instinct than awareness, and removed a fruit bar. Half a minute at a time, no more, before slowing to allow his body to regroup. That's all he had. He peeled back the wrapper, raised it to his lips, and chewed absently, one bite after the next until it was gone.

Then a scream from the building across the road, faint but clear. Joanie stiffened. Justin whispered, "John?" and Garik felt his control melt away. Rainbows filled in the gaps around the world, and he found himself at the Center door, not even registering his run across the street. He grasped the handle, his arm muscles tightened, and the door came free. He flung it aside, no more than a trivial nuisance in his way. The warmth of the building washed outward and swept past him, flooding him with the residual metallic smell of friction on the metal hinges as they had twisted and separated, the acrid body smell of numerous men inside, and the sour undercurrent of gym beneath it all.

Caution for Garik was no longer possible. The scream had stirred his anger into a rage, and his frenzied state whipped his body into a more powerful machine than ever before. It also sapped his reasoning and his ability to evaluate the situation and choose the best path. He knew only that he must follow his senses to a glass door on his left, and with a bare-skinned elbow, he smashed into the translucent surface and felt it shatter as his arm broke through. Fire crawled across his skin, his body healing the fissures the jagged, knife-like glass tore into him as he bounded with an animal-like motion through the opening and into the room.

John was held up by two black-suited masked goons—para-military hybrids—and a third was burying his fist into the man's gut. John's head was wrapped in a black cloth tied around his neck with a cord. He was stripped to the waist, and his feet were bare. One hand was missing two nails. On a desk, laid out haphazardly, power leads, handcuffs, sharp instruments, and other things he didn't recognize, many of them fresh with the shine of wet blood, telling Garik they had been recently used.

They didn't know John was hybrid like them! He had resisted, and being stronger by his hybrid DNA, they had begun to push him beyond the limits a normal human could endure! Blinded by his fury, Garik let out a snarl more hybrid than human as he whipped through the room and punched his elbow through the facemasks of each of the three goons. The one with his fist in John's stomach flew backward, hitting a wall. His arm impacted the side of a desk and fell to his side at an odd angle. The other two fared worse. The head of the man to the right hit the corner of a filing cabinet, the crunch of his helmet revealing the damage done, and the other, not yet realizing Garik was even in the room, became airborne through a window and tumbled outside.

Before the goons could hit the ground, Garik had his arms wrapped around John to keep him from falling and protect him from further injury. Then, his energy spent, the rainbows faded, and with them, his awareness of where he was. Both of them met the floor, oblivious to the destruction Garik's lightning-flash of an entrance into the room had strewn around them.

— 9 —

GARIK CAME to life as Joanie and Justin carried him from the building to the van. His arms thrashed, he grabbed at empty air, and flailing, he impacted the side of someone's head.

"Enough, wolf boy," Justin muttered, grabbing the hand just before it impacted his face and absorbing much of the energy. "You've already taken out the headhunters."

"Long thirty seconds," Joanie grunted. She was under one side, with Justin opposite, and when Justin shifted position to deflect Garik's hand, she took most of his weight. As Justin took part of Garik's weight off her, she said, "Too long."

"What happened?" That single, thrashing blow against Justin

had drained Garik, and he felt he could barely move.

"You don't remember?" Justin shifted Garik's weight as he opened the van door. "Here. Into the van. We'll explain once we've gone. We're about to have real company." In the background, a siren wailed.

John was already inside, one hand wrapped, his upper body bloodied, and bruises already starting to show. He was hardly in better condition than Garik, but he gave a lopsided smile and said, "Thanks."

"For what?" Garik began to weakly search for his fanny pack when Joanie pressed it into his hand before closing the door and climbing into the front seat.

"You truly don't remember?" Justin was in the driver's seat.

"You can't drive, Justin." The half-mantis man behind the wheel of a car? Not possible!

"You'll think can't drive. Watch how fast I shift gears." Justin's hand hit the shifter, the machine jerked into drive, and all four of them were pressed back into their seats.

Garik focused enough to pull out one of the fruit bars, and he took a bite. He felt the energy begin to flood through him. The world took on a brighter tone, and he noted they were passing Central Park. The duck pond appeared through the front window, just visible to the right and cleaner than in the drone shots, before it disappeared behind the plywood at his shoulder. He registered that Brace's military teams had done a good job of clearing the debris away.

"How are you here, John?" Garik took a second bite, and as he chewed, he pulled an open drink from the console and chugged it down.

"You saved me, and you don't remember?"

"I . . ." Garik tried to focus. "We parked the van . . . after that, nothing."

"Not nothing." Joanie. She pointed to Justin to continue west on Ninth.

"Your cap," Garik noticed. Joanie had refused to be without it until her mohawk regrew.

"Lost it," she said.

"Fighting the black suits," Justin called as he ducked into his seat while they passed the police troops standing guard outside City Hall. Then they were past, and he sat up taller.

Anytime, Garik thought. They were talking in riddles, and he no idea what the clues were.

"Let me fill you in." John hardly looked fit to talk, much less fill anyone in, but he had seen much of the aftermath, after the black bag on his face was removed and he extricated himself from Garik's embrace.

Justin and Joanie had realized Garik's intent when he disappeared and the main door flew off the Center, settling some fifty feet away. By the time they reached the building, the other paramilitary hybrids were also aware of his intent and arriving to protect the interrogation team.

In the pressure of the moment, Justin became the weapon Garik had seen in him. His hands blurred, ripping weapons from people's hands, his knives cutting suit atmospheric tubes and bringing down people with a kick to the solar plexus or a slice to the back of the knees.

Joanie did what she did best, observing, evaluating, wiping the floor with those Justin had already sent down. Electrical cords secured men's wrists, closets became prisons, and personal communication devices were brittle bones under her heels.

It was all stopgap, as these men were trained to succeed in exactly this situation. If Justin and Joanie weren't hybrid themselves, with above-average stamina and aggressive healing capabilities, the paramilitary hybrids would have batted them aside like irritating mayflies, bothersome but no more than that.

Garik pondered that, and he asked, "I heard a noise in the office. That must have been you, John. You said I saved you. What about that?"

John smiled. "I was blindfolded. I only saw the aftermath. I doubt the three men interrogating me will be functional anytime soon. One did a superman move through the window. He was still outside when we left. I only have one suggestion."

"What's that?" He was rescued. What more could he want?

Joanie turned in her seat for the answer, and Justin looked in the rearview mirror. Garik gave them a shrug.

John said, "Open the door next time. You pulled one off the hinges, and the glass one you shattered and walked right through."

Garik frowned in disbelief, but Justin's and Joanie's smiles told him it was true. He looked at his hands, flexed them, and turned them over to look up and down his arms. Then he noted his shirt. It was covered with bloodstains. Something caught his side just under his arm, a tear in the fabric. He pulled at something hard in the tear, and a small piece of glass came free.

"Yours?" He held it out to John.

"Not on your life." He shook his head.

Garik studied his arms, searching for the memory John had described. Burning, he would have felt that if he were injured. He reached through his clothing at every torn spot, felt the skin underneath, trying to make the burning real.

Nothing. He got nothing, even as the blood and tattered clothes assured him it had happened.

What have I done? he asked himself. What triggered me to do something I can't remember? And had it happened before? Would he know if it had? Or was it something new, a fresh atrocity inflicted on his life, one more thing to endure on top of all the others?

He was pulled back into the car by a question.

"We need a place to wait on Jantzen. Garik, you're the one who knows this city best. Your suggestion would be appreciated."

"Where are we?" The wood covering his window blocked his view to the side.

"Coming to Sycamore."

Sycamore, Garik thought. Just this morning, Marisa was with me . . . he forced that away, paying attention to what was out the windshield, the shadows on the buildings, making out the time of day.

"Left. My aunt will be home. I'd like to tell her I'm alright." Not Arik. The man was a torment, but Irina, yes. It would be a risk, but surely she would allow them to stay for a while.

"Left it is." Justin hit the blinker as they approached Sycamore.

"Not here. Sheesh!" Garik cringed at passing anywhere near the flower shop. He couldn't bear it, not even to get within sight of it. "Past Sycamore, then the first left you can take. I think the preppers have several streets closed off as a Tower Free Zone, so any that aren't blocked will do."

"Okay. Left *after* Sycamore." The light changed, Justin pulled past Sycamore, and he began to look for a street not blocked by the preppers who were claiming their streets as a Tower Free Zone.

With Brace's paramilitary hybrids roaming Bay City, Garik figured they wouldn't be Tower Free much longer.

GARIK DIRECTED Justin to City View Apartments. The taste of indecisiveness burned his throat. He had claimed his aunt's loyalties long before Arik, and he trusted that she would welcome him, but he also remembered showing up at the flower shop to see Marisa, and she had spurned him. The Tower's goons had appeared as if they were waiting to take him into custody. He had barely escaped with his skin, and still they had managed to BolaWrap him in the end, locking him away in the Tower once more.

There was his Street Strider, parked almost where he had left it, with a For Sale sign taped to the jet assist tube. It looked forlorn, old, and abandoned. Appropriate, because it was all three.

"Joanie, you go. Upstairs, right there." He pointed to Iri's apartment.

"Doesn't know me." She looked to Justin for confirmation, then to John, but he was occupied elsewhere, looking outside, soaking up what he could never again have.

"Her nickname is Iri. She'll know it's me. Show her the van and I'll wave. Then if it's clear . . ." He pictured the flower shop and the camera with the Tower's logo on the side. "Keep your eye out for surveillance cameras. If you see any . . ." He didn't finish that thought, either. It was too obvious for them to not understand.

"Understood." She looked out the windows, took in the courtyard, and nodded, certain of the plan. She opened the door, made her way to the stairs, and began to climb.

Garik felt his shirt grow clammy, a little boy again, doing something he knew was wrong. This wasn't safe. Iri didn't expect them, wouldn't be able to lie to Brace if they questioned her. He wanted to call Joanie back, but he needed to see Iri, let her know he was okay, reassure her that she had done a good job raising him and that he loved her nearly as much as his mama.

A fist pounded on the window. "You can't park here."

The wooden panel blocked Garik's view, but he heard the voice perfectly well. Arik. His stomach turned. So many times he'd been berated by the man, had to take it, couldn't fight back. The last six months were stripped away with the voice from the past, demanding the key to his Street Strider, sending him to his room, forcing him to repair yet something else that *Arik* had broken. The little boy Garik had once been shrank into his seat at the sound of the man's demand.

"Do you know this man, Garik?" Justin, a reasonable question.

"Arik." Garik could barely get it out. "Yes, I do."

"Does he have the right to ask us to move?" He twisted around to look at Garik for an answer.

Garik let out a hard breath and shrugged. Yes, because Arik had always had power over him, and no, not really, because Arik had no power anywhere else. Before he could say any of that, the door opened, and Arik forced his upper body inside.

"I said—" The man caught sight of Garik in the back and laughed. "So, little man, not in Russia after all. I expected you'd be back when you needed something. Go away. Irina doesn't need you around. You're not worth the space you take up."

"I refuse to allow that—" Justin's arms quivered with anticipation, frightful to anyone who had watched him in action.

"It's okay, Justin," Garik pleaded, knowing that a response would only get Arik going, and it would get worse. "Ignore him." He wished he could see the door to Iri's apartment, know if she was there, at least wave to let her know he was here.

"Ignore me, huh?" Arik fell into the empty seat next to Justin. He turned to take in John with his injuries, most on the way to healing, and he twisted around to rake his eyes up and down Garik's ragged, blood-stained clothes. "Introduce me to your friends, little man, or do they embarrass you, too?" His expression gloated, like he'd scored a victory in a battle they were waging.

"Justin and John." He regretted revealing their names, but he was stripped of his power to say no to this man.

"And the little lady?" Arik motioned up the steps. "Your new honey?"

Garik's heart pounded, and he felt his breath coming faster and deeper. *Stop it, Arik. Stop it, stop it*, he pleaded. He balled his hands into fists, and his nails were razors of pain in his palms.

"As always, too weak to fight back. Go away, Russian scum. If they won't have you over there, we don't need you. And take your loser friends with you—"

That was the last thing Garik heard when the years of Arik's abuse boiled out of him, prepared to right the injustices he had endured for far too long. He snarled and leaped from the back seat to the front, twisting his body in a way only a canine killer can, and he attacked with a ferocity even the goons at the Center didn't endure.

The damage to the van was unavoidable. The damage to Arik might someday heal. The damage to Garik . . . in his outburst of fury—a response designed to protect those of his pack—he had failed to send his love to Iri, and for that, his actions, when he was told what he'd done, cut deeper than a knife.

A BURN BARREL at the intersection of Fourth and Laurel blazed, the red of the flames washed out in the sharp clarity of the winter sun. They were in the Tower Free Zone. Generators hummed, creating islands of energy, but most of the area had regressed to the 19th century, with paper messages tacked to door frames and people walking about tugging their things in small wagons or pushing shopping carts.

The van was no longer protection for them, not after City View Apartments. Arik had seen Garik as the boy he once knew, not the hybrid whirlwind that had just overcome three of Colonel Brace's paramilitary super soldiers, and at first, the pressure of Garik's hands on him was little more than an irritation. Then rainbows had painted Arik dead. Justin was already in motion by then, reaching to block Garik's leap. It became a stalemate. Justin, Garik, or Arik. One would surely die.

John made all the difference. What's the value in a wood frog? John's hybridized DNA gave him elastic tendons, and when startled, he reacted instinctively. In the moment Garik leaped for Arik, John reacted, every bit as quick as Garik, even if it was completely out of his control and only for that singular moment.

Justin received a black eye from John's shoulder as he was flung against the driver's door. Arik tumbled free from the open passenger's door, saving his life if not his dignity or his skin. John held Garik as the youth did his best to pursue his prey out the door. In his uncontrolled frenzy state, Garik crumpled the doorframe and collapsed part of the roof as he pulled himself from John's grasp.

Arik was lucky that Garik's energy reserves were still depleted from his run into The Martial Arts Center and his takedown of the paramilitary hybrids battering John. His speed was diminished, allowing Arik just enough time to roll far enough away that Garik missed him and slammed into a curb when he hit the ground, shattering the bone in his upper arm in the impact.

The rainbows around Garik faded and he had no idea why he was on the ground, but the pain in his arm was perfectly clear. Fire lanced through him as electric needles of healing stitched the bone back together.

Then had come the sirens, and Joanie was certain her time at Irina's door was recorded. They were readying to drive away when a police cruiser blocked their exit.

The officer walked to the van, looked inside, and said, "You need to follow me." He turned to those in the courtyard, "All's covered, folks. Your Bay City men in blue at your service. Send your donations to the Bay City Police Department on Park Avenue. Thank you, thank you."

Justin cut his eyes to Garik, a hooded expression of respect in his expression. "I don't think that's the police." He rubbed his reddened eye tenderly, then shifted into gear, backed out, and accelerated after the police cruiser.

Joanie was now in the back with Garik, and she inspected his arm, healed but severely crooked. "Needs rebroken."

Garik groaned. He remembered the fire this time. He liked better what had happened at The Martial Arts Center. If he had to be injured and to heal so rapidly, he at least preferred not to be around when it happened.

He tried to piece together why he had been against the curb instead of inside the van, and he remembered: Arik. What had happened to Arik? Then he asked the question differently. What had he *done* to Arik? He looked inside himself for paths that included Arik, and he couldn't sense one. That meant one of two things: either he would never encounter Arik again or the man was dead.

What was going on in his life? What was triggering this? Was this the fatal flaw in DNA interwoven with that of a timber wolf? His future lay before him, branching paths he could follow, and too many of them took him into darkness, into places no one should be forced to go.

Then the van came to a stop, the police officer returned, and he asked them to move to the cruiser. They would need to ride with him from this point forward. They could secure their things in his trunk if they moved quickly.

Garik climbed onto the hard plastic of the cruiser's back seat, with Joanie and John beside him. Justin couldn't compact himself enough for the back, so he took the front seat. Surprisingly, the officer seemed to accept the man's unusual shape and size as natural.

Then there was Garik's arm. For this, there were no good options, none on any of the paths he saw before him.

ONCE THE cruiser was in motion, the officer's face melted into

Paul's round, full-lipped features, and he let out a laugh. "Did I fool you?"

"Would I have followed you if you did?" Justin cut him a glare.

"Perhaps. The important thing is that you *did* follow. We must abandon this vehicle, also. I only borrowed it, and it will soon be missed. I have located a safe place for you to hide, but there is a bit of a problem. We are resolving it as I speak."

"For *us* to hide," Joanie said, including Paul in their group.

"No, no," Paul replied, with a raised hand and wagging his finger. "I am my own safe place. I can hide anywhere." As he said the words, he became the police officer again.

"Fine," Joanie said. "Garik, about that arm—"

"I can freeze it before we rebreak it," John offered, showing his hands. Already, they sparkled with frost. "It will dull the pain."

Garik took a deep breath. "Sheesh-ola. Why not?"

John took the arm, moved his knee up as a wedge for breaking the bone, and his hands on Garik's arm crackled with cold. "I will have to pull hard to straighten it. Brace yourself when you feel it break." Without waiting, John brought it down sharply and the bone snapped.

Garik gasped, and he pressed his feet to the floorboard to stiffen himself. John yanked his arm, working the bone to keep it from healing while he straightened it. Finally, he hit it with the flat of his hand, something popped, and it was aligned properly.

"Did the cold help?" John smiled.

Garik wanted to answer, but he felt the interior of the car begin to blur. He only had time to hear Joanie say, "Should'a fed him first. Don't die, Peach Fuzz."

Peach fuzz, he thought. I'm already eighteen. Then, he was gone once again.

THE SMELL of food brought Garik around. They were on the street, the boxes from the trunk were stacked alongside a building, and a burn barrel tried to beat back the cold.

"It's freezing," he mumbled.

A tall, willowy blonde handed him a hot dog topped with chili and said in a deep voice, "This will help. Eat up."

"Paul?"

The blonde grinned and put a finger to her lips. "I will be. For now I'm Paulette. We're waiting on a ride."

468

Garik sank his teeth into the hot dog, felt the energy flow into him, and looked for the others. John, well, John was built for the cold. He was easy to recognize, the only person out in just a tee shirt. He seemed to have healed, with just minor bruising to reveal the beating he'd received. His bare feet might have attracted attention elsewhere, but here? Not at all. Joanie had managed to find a cap with the Bay City logo on it, a stitched port scene with BC scrawled across it in cursive script. Justin towered over everyone else, his insectile features offset by a thick knit cap, and his body moving oddly under his leather duster. Still, he was no odder than many of the other Tower Free people, and no one seemed to take any notice of his bulging back or unusually long arms.

A commotion caught their attention, as a number of the Tower Free residents tried to block a large black limousine from making its way down the street. The limo was having none of it, crawling over curbs and threatening to push through groups of people. Eventually, it made it to where they were. The window rolled down and Jantzen appeared.

"Get in," he said. "The chauffeur will load your things." Jantzen reached beside the door, touched a button, and the door gently swung open.

"This way, all tour members," Paul as Paulette called, gathering them in. He had now acquired a nametag that said Paulette and a pillbox cap with PanAmerican Tours on it. "Our flight departs Bay City Airport, Gate 4, in two hours. All souvenirs and packages must be checked. Don't forget to declare your cash and valuables when we reach customs. Inside the car, everyone."

The most surprising person they discovered inside was someone Garik already knew. "Dieter!"

"My friend. You have filled out, grown taller, too."

And punched in a few faces, if I believe what people tell me, but he didn't think Dieter needed to hear about that.

AS THE limousine pulled away, its darkened windows shielding the inside from the outside, Jantzen explained the puzzling mode of transportation for a team that was trying very hard to lay low.

"Paul reminded me that Dieter and Garik know one another." A few puzzled looks, and he explained, "When Devon had his wreck, he and Garik had just delivered Dieter to his father at Bay City Medical. Of course, when the wreck went public, Dieter's father forbade him from riding in other people's cars—"

"The reason for this." Dieter motioned around the big machine.

"—and with the rioting, his father has been requested to stay at the hospital full time—"

"And I'm in our apartment." Dieter grinned.

"Okay, Dieter. How about you tell it?" Jantzen relaxed back into his seat and gave the youth the floor.

"This is so exciting!" Dieter grinned and shook with the enthusiasm of a boy starting an adventure he had never dreamed possible. "You know the school is shut down. The military has taken it over. I am doing, how do you say it here, remote learning, and Papa cannot leave the hospital, and I have plenty of room." His eyes were bright as if that said it all.

"And that means?" Justin didn't seem so sure.

"I get it." Garik had seen the possibilities fan out with Dieter's words. The choices made, the possible outcomes. Learn, evaluate, postulate. "Brace's military teams will search everywhere now that they know we're out there. Especially any that are abandoned, just the places we'd choose. Nowhere is safe, except the very place where they know we won't be."

"Inside the Tower," Joanie breathed.

"Can't get in." Justin extended one arm out of a sleeve, and he articulated his extra joint. "You don't think they'll see this?"

"But you must be aware," Dieter said, all enthusiastic, "the parking garage, it is now gone, and with it, the um—" he glanced upward, searching for the correct word, "—yes, the private entrance to the building. Part of the underground parking is now allotted for the use of the apartments, as well as the service elevator to access whatever floor we're on. We will be like in the movies, secret agents, and no one will know."

"Maybe. Drive underground, but we have to get to the elevator. We'll be exposed once we exit the car." Justin was working it out.

"I'm sure there's a way." Paul's face began to resemble a harlequin's mask. "I asked Jantzen to bring along a few costumes. They are in the trunk."

"The driver?" John brought up something the others had been considering. "How do we know he can be trusted?" He'd already loaded their things in the trunk. He'd seen each of them.

Dieter touched a switch, and the window between the driver's compartment and the back of the car slipped into a recess. "Luka, say hello."

The driver turned his head, and without his cap and sunglasses, he bore a striking resemblance to Dieter, with tighter planes to his cheeks and shorter hair. "Ya, little brother. Hello, everyone. I am playing the kid's babysitter. I will keep him in line for you."

Dieter beamed.

Garik let himself breathe. Maybe, just maybe he could get a break and find out what was making him change so rapidly.

And beat up people.

And not remember what he had done when it was over.

He looked at Jantzen to find his eyes studying him. What do you know, Jantzen? What haven't you told me? What am I becoming that you haven't seen fit to share with me?

It boggled Garik's mind how stupid people could sometimes be.

— 11 —

JANTZEN AND Paul's plan was as good as they came, and it nearly worked. Even Dieter's involvement, and his brother's, too. All magnificent. The tip of the options iceberg.

"Nearly worked," however, is like that old proverb: A miss is as good as a mile. You either come in first place or you don't. No matter what parents tell their kindergarteners, not everyone can be president, star on a professional team, or own their own business. Some of us are the winners, and the rest of us—by default—are the losers, the ones who give life their all and still come up short.

The big limo pulled into the parking garage, leaving Justin on the street. He could fly. He would find his own way in. The blue sky above vanished as the black machine crossed the barrier between the world above, one of freedom and endless choices, and the one that had stolen Garik's life from him.

He felt the weight of the massive Tower pressing down on him. Wrapped in the luxurious car, his ears were useless for telling him anything. Only the softest whisper from the tires betrayed movement. The faintest scent of rubber, oil, and exhaust trapped underground by the mall's massive overhead expanse worked its way through the air conditioning system and past the seals lining the doors.

The prelude to the storm.

Jantzen didn't bother with a costume. He could travel truly in-

471

cognito—so incognito that he would be no more than a mist in the underground cavern, one washed in an effervescent purple shade. Luka was the driver, and his photo and credentials were on file with Stamford Suites; and his brother, Dieter, had been in and out of the tower for nearly half a year. Everyone knew him, even the military teams going in and out of the newly repaired back entrance to the garage. And Paul. When was Paul not in disguise? He could be any person he wished, even Colonel Brace, if he desired.

Garik, John, and Joanie were the ones who needed to worry, but life sometimes lulls our senses just when we should be paying attention most. The costumes had become a way to divert the iceberg for a time, to not have to make hard choices, and to stroll an easier path, even if only for the few minutes it took to make it to the elevator and breathe the freshly scented and purified Tower air.

The new "Stamford Suites" section of the underground garage was divided off with concrete barriers, each one giving enough room to walk between them, but none with enough space to drive a car. A city block deeper into the vast garage, bright yellow tape between columns restricted Tower personnel from parking too close, and in the distance, military trucks idled with a muffled authority; their tires complained against the unforgiving concrete each time one moved; and occasionally one man yelled to another. Half wore the black paramilitary masks with the hockey puck on the front and the eagle, white on black, on the sleeve, visible even from this distance.

Several cars were parked in the Stamford Suites section, and as expected, none were occupied. Dieter had charted them, and that was part of the reason for the wait. They needed to enter the Tower when none of the cars were likely to be in use. What people couldn't see, they couldn't be suspicious of. The military teams arriving in and out of the building were so distant, they weren't a concern. They were toy men, no more than distant echoes as they yelled to one another.

The fault in the planning was failing to consider what the eagle emblem entailed. The paramilitary wasn't just military. Each man was DNA-enhanced to be bigger, tougher, and better in just about every way, including their eyesight.

And those helmets? All sorts of electronic aids were worked into them.

Luka stepped out of the car first, in his smart chauffeur's jacket and cap. He opened the door, and Dieter appeared next. Several of the black suits across the garage noted their egress from the black car, and they paused to watch. They were so far away, no one paid them any mind.

Even Garik, waiting inside with his ribbons of time unrolling before him . . . well, we can't all watch *everything*, not *all the time*, can we?

Jantzen evaporated before exiting. He didn't intend to enter the Tower at all, and he was gone. Paul was back as Paulette, and he vamped as his jokester side teased and prodded to find the fun in the moment. Joanie turned into a boy-man, wearing Jantzen's shirt and a flat driving cap with matching gloves.

John had rolled his eyes at a nun's habit. His height, he complained. Won't they be able to tell? Still, it was long enough, and with his pale skin, his cherubic face was believable from a distance.

Garik was the final one to appear. He was dressed in full Tower livery, cream top and tan trousers, with a cap to cover his hair. He would be shielded among sacks and other goods, the heist from a good day out and about town.

A dozen steps in and one of the black suits in the distance called, "Hey, you there! Hold up! I know you!"

"Hello! It's me, Dieter." The high school youth raised one arm in recognition, and he responded in a loud, bright voice. "We've been asked to park down here, now."

"No, you!" The man moved their direction rapidly, more so than a normal man might travel. He walked hard and quick and pointed towards Garik. "I know you. You don't work here."

The others tried to hurry Garik along, but the suited man now had other black-suited men interested and following. Dieter tried to intervene, and Luka stepped in front of them both. By then, the man was crossing the barrier, and he pushed the two youths aside and grabbed Garik's arm.

"I don't guess you remember me." The man pulled off his helmet. "Rodrigo? You were with fake Brace and drove off with the Colonel's SUV. You have no idea the trouble I've been in."

"He couldn't have been—" Dieter tried to insist.

"Back, boy." He gave Dieter a shove in the chest, hard, knocking him against another car. "I'd know this one if his head was tied in a burlap sack." He tapped his forehead. "They bred us to be bigger and better than all the rest, and that means what I see, I don't forget. There's no mistaking those shoulders and that skin. I'm thinking I might get my stripes back if I produce the filthy little tramp that snuck out from right under our noses *in the Colonel's truck*."

"You broke my brother's hand." Luka stood, his face flaming. "You can't push people around like that—"

"I can't?" Rodrigo's face had darkened, his anger crawling over his skin.

"Rodrigo," one of the men behind him called. "You thinking this is a hostage situation?"

"I think you're right." Rodrigo smiled. "These two we know, and the others, look at what they did, roughed up one of 'em, and now we gotta take them in." He lifted a hand and motioned to the men gathering behind him. Rodrigo was beginning to wheeze by then, and he stepped back and slipped his helmet on, disappearing into the morass of paramilitary supporters behind him.

Farther back, green-suited men stood in groups, none masked, with several on vehicles to get a better view. They called to one another, their words jumbled by echoes as they tumbled across the concrete, but they made no effort to stop what was happening.

Garik was following it all. Tracking Rodrigo was no problem. The man's heart rate thundered angrily through his black suit, and he left a trail of pheromones ramped up by his resentment at his punishment over the stolen SUV. Clearly he had kept an eye out knowing he might someday intercept the guilty party, and when he did, they would pay.

Had he shared his frustration with his fellow hybrids? Likely. In any case, they were fully prepared to support him.

The possibility paths unrolling before Garik shimmered so brightly he could no longer ignore them. This wasn't just an arrest and hold. They had intent—trumped up but plausible—and they knew that in the city's volatile state, abductions were as likely as not. If they claimed hostages were taken to gain entrance into the Tower, that was a capital offense, and deadly force would be justified in Colonel Brace's eyes.

If the hostages suffered as well, a severe injury might mean no one could remember what was said or done.

Fifteen minutes. Sure as gold. Six hours away, the paths before Garik darkened, hidden by what was already in play right before him. These men intended to take what they wanted, and what they wanted was him.

His lungs filled with air, his senses came alive, and he fought what he felt happening. *My way, my mind, I am in control.* He had to be in control. Twice, maybe three times, he'd lost himself, done damage he didn't remember. He would not allow it to happen again.

He looked around him. The elevator, just there. Dieter on his knees, his crushed hand protected against his chest, his face pale with shock. Luka standing in front him, his eyes telling that he knew he was helpless against these men. John's habit leaking white freezer vapor. How much damage could the man do? Garik suspected they were about to find out.

Joanie, where was she? And Paul? Garik felt the barest hint of a rainbow color his vision as he turned to find them, when a surprising voice barked from the far side of the limousine.

"At ease, men. These people are with me. I'll take responsibility now." Colonel Brace stepped into view, and he walked with confidence, his hands carried behind his back. "You, there, Rodrigo, a good man. I'll see that you get something for your trouble."

"Take your cap off, Colonel." The voice came from the one Garik still pegged as Rodrigo.

"I beg your pardon!" Brace snapped erect. "I said this is my responsibility now. That's all, gentlemen."

Somewhere, a weapon lifted, a shot fired, echoing harshly in the hard-surfaced space, and the colonel twisted sideways, catching himself and standing tall again.

"I hit him. That's not Brace!"

"One of the monsters!" From farther back, the green-suited men began cheering. "Don't let 'em escape again!"

Colonel Brace's image shifted, blurred, and then Paul slumped to the floor, his chest torn and bloodied.

"You, Jameson, Hyatt, Simpson, with me! These are some of the misfits from Brace's briefing. Get that nun, Hockney, and you, Rodgers, help him. The small one in the cap and shirt, where did he go? Howard, look between the cars."

Rodgers got a shock when he tried to take John. From the hybrid's hands, frost crackled across Rodger's body, and he stiffened and dropped to the concrete, his body shaking with the extreme cold. The next man in line held back and unhooked a BolaWrap from his belt.

"It's faster this way." Rodrigo, holding a gun that to Garik's sensitive nose smelled recently fired, so recently it had to have been the one that dropped Paul to the ground. The gun fired, and John fell. It fired again, and Garik's body spun out of his control, his shoulder blossoming with fire. He staggered, found his feet again, and lifted himself erect to face the crowd.

"My god, the creature's still standing."

"You heard what happened out at the martial arts building. This is the freak that took out Jenkins, Alberts, and Welling. They never saw him."

"Hit the thing again, Rodrigo. Make sure it's dead."

Garik staggered as another slug slammed into him, this time in his chest. He gasped, heard his opened chest gurgle, and he took a second breath, the burning in his torso telling him it was nearly healed. He forced his heart to slow, his breathing to settle. No rainbows, he vowed. He touched his chest to be certain, relieved to find himself whole.

"Why isn't it dying? Do it again, Rodrigo."

"You, Jameson. Maybe your aim's better."

"I could use a little target practice." One of the men with Rodrigo lifted a weapon twice the size of Rodrigo's. He squeezed, and the bullet spiraled directly at Garik as a burst of flame whipped it from the barrel.

Garik watched the ribbons of choices in front of him wink out. What had been a tree branching into every choice he could possibly make now revealed only one.

This ended here.

Marisa, gone, and now Paul and John. Dead? It looked that way. Luka hovered over his brother, shielding him, but that couldn't last, not with these men out for blood. Joanie was an unknown.

Garik jerked again, taking another hit, drowning in the death around him, and all because of him. Maybe it would be better to walk down the only path remaining open to him. If he ran, death would chase him, destroy all those around him. All the pathways must be brought to an end in this place and at this time before anyone else had to die.

GARIK STAGGERED with hit after hit, holding himself together with his repeated mantra, "My mind, my reasoning, not anger. Anger never wins. Anger always loses." No rainbows allowed.

"I know we're not missing," a voice yelled. "How many hits can this thing take? Not even we can endure this level of abuse."

Through the pain, Garik heard Rodrigo's whisper, "Friendly fire. No witnesses. We need to make this a clean slate. I'll get the one standing, you take the young one."

"No!" The word ripped from Garik's throat, rainbows shot from every surface, and he turned toward the brothers to see a bullet already speeding their direction. Flame decorated the muzzle of Rodrigo's weapon, and ripples of air radiated out from the projectile like shimmers of water across a lake.

He knew he couldn't stop the bullet, but he could take it, deflect it, keep it from hitting either Luka or Dieter. He was at speed, and the rainbows swept him forward. He fell back into real time and staggered as the bullet entered his body, tore through him—impacting dense bone and deflecting just enough to miss Luka—and exited on the back side. He looked for the second weapon, saw it already raised. Rainbows again, and he stood before the gun, the muzzle at his chest.

"Enough," he yelled, and released the rainbows. His chest exploded with pain, and he staggered backward, grasping the man's gun arm, his helmet now splattered with red. The man yanked his helmet off, tried to pull free, and stared at Garik, then to the youth's chest as Garik's injury began to knit blurringly fast.

"Not possible," he gasped.

Garik couldn't reply. There was no air in his lungs to speak, not yet, anyway. As he tried to breathe, the man and the garage and everything around him became mist rising from dark water, slipping from him as he reached for it, flickering from frozen rainbow to reality, and short-circuiting his connection with the life around him. The air between them took on a purple hue just for a moment, the suited man was flung backwards, and the purple was gone. Over and over in the garage, people yelled, some in surprise, others trying to work out what was happening to their companions, their own wrists now wrapped with plastic restraints, and weapons disappearing from their hands and belts.

Garik picked up the weapon that had fallen at his feet and cradled it as a friend. He tried to map out his next steps, even if it was only a quarter hour. Either the path wasn't there, or the choices were too dark to be seen.

Rainbows continued to flicker erratically around him, flashbulb images of death and misery. His eyes burned and his shoulders took on a life of their own, shaking with an unstoppable tide of rising despair.

"GARIK, WE must leave." Jantzen knelt in front of him, with the cacophonous sounds of yelling men surrounding them. "Their disarray won't last long."

"It won't stop, Jantzen." Garik watched his mentor flicker, not really flickering, but shooting with rainbows, frozen, then moving forward once more. Already, if he moved, he left Jantzen looking at where he had been, unaware Garik had already changed position.

"Move, now." He slapped the side of Garik's knee and stood as if he hadn't heard Garik speak.

Garik understood. He hadn't. Garik's world had short-circuited again, fast-forwarding him into the land of rainbows, unable to slow down until the hiccup in the circuits righted itself.

Had he taken too much damage? Had the repeated, rapid healing left some irreparable glitch in his DNA structure? He knew one thing. He was still in overdrive, and he didn't know how he was still functioning. His energy levels should have crashed by now, and they hadn't.

Even that worried him.

To his left, John, crumpled, the white habit soaked with red. To his right, Paul, someone he had begun to depend on, his robes dead, and the man looking equally so. Behind him, Luka with his arms around Dieter, shielding the younger youth with his body.

Garik stood, filled with anger that Rodrigo had tried to *shoot* them, and the world wrinkled with twisting rainbows. He found himself by Luka and Dieter. *No more rainbows*, he pleaded, needing them to stop. He looked behind him, and Jantzen was turning to talk to him where he had been, not where he was. He didn't know Garik had moved.

"We must get you somewhere safe."

"My brother," Luka began.

"I can help." Garik helped Dieter stand, surprised at how light he felt, and in a fresh surge of anger, his head filled with rainbows, and they were outside. The sun sparkled in the cold air, and Dieter shivered. Garik's head spun with the change in location. Even he didn't know how they had gotten there.

"How did . . ." Dieter looked around.

"Short circuit. Will you be okay while I see to your brother?"

He nodded, and as Garik turned to walk inside, the world shifted in a brief blaze of color, and he found himself already there. Jantzen was still turning to speak to where Garik had been, unaware he was no longer in that spot.

"Luka, your brother is outside. Can you join him?"

"How did you . . . I mean, yes. Where?"

Garik started to point toward the ramp leading upward, when he caught sight of Paul, and the colors around him shifted, and he was outside with Luka beside Dieter. Luka let out a deep breath and staggered.

"I'm sor—" The colors shifted before Garik could finish, and he was with Jantzen, who was just realizing he wasn't where he expected him to be.

"Garik, what—"

"I'm short cir—" Movement caught his eye, a burst of color filled his head, and Garik had his arm around the throat of a black-suited paramilitary goon who thought working his way out of his hand restraints was a good idea. The man now had his suit's breathing apparatus dangling in Garik's hand. Several dozen feet away, Jantzen stood, still talking to where Garik had been.

"Jantz, help!" Desperation broke Garik's voice as he dropped the goon, and anger at what was happening to him churned into color at the corners of the void.

Jantzen vanished and reappeared at Garik's side. "My friend, you cannot keep this up."

"I don't want to keep it up." He searched. "Where's Joanie?" He couldn't help Paul or John, and he needed her to be safe.

"She came to warn me. She's safe. Let's get you safe." Jantzen reached for his arm.

"No! I don't want to be safe." The deaths he had endured swept up inside him, and in a flash of color, Garik found himself outside on Stamford Drive, with Luka and Dieter half a block away. The houses in Overlook Estates were visible through the bare trees, and to the north, the roof of a military truck could just be seen on Lowell. It moved rapidly, likely in response to what was happening in the parking garage.

He wanted to offer the two youths help, and as he caught sight of the ragged wound gouged into the back of Corona Tower where the parking garage had once stood, he thought of Marisa setting the explosion that had taken it out, and he raged at the injustice of the

Tower that had sucked him in and destroyed her world for trying to help him. The city around him turned chaotic and red, filled with every color, and he let out a yell he couldn't control.

He was through giving in. It was time for Garik Shayk to win, at least once, whatever he had to do to bring it about.

Rainbows, you're on, and the city around him blurred with color.

JANTZEN WAS correct. It was impossible for even Garik's hyper-enhanced body to maintain its frenetic pace forever. Muscle drain, brain drain, the energy had to come from somewhere, and eventually it had to end.

Garik fizzled out on Sycamore at the burned-out site of The Flower Shop. He didn't know how long he was collapsed in the rubble before he realized he wasn't alone.

"There you are." Jantzen called from the window of a nondescript car, one likely borrowed with or without permission. He set the transmission in park and stepped out.

"Jantzen." Garik watched him walk forward to tower over him, black on black, the mystery man in purple, able to evaporate and reappear at will. He envied him. It was so easy for Jantzen who never had to lie in the rubble of a burned-out building because he could do nothing else. The colors around Jantzen shifted, became a ragged rainbow like a television trying to change channels but unable to draw in a complete signal.

"We were afraid this would happen." Jantzen sat beside him, stirring the ash that had settled from the fire.

"What?" The world flickered again, colors flashing, asking Garik's body to come play, but there were no reserves left. He had nothing to give.

"The switch that's flipped in you. It's why we held off on the timber wolf DNA. Then Rodheimer insisted. He was impatient to move the program forward."

"You couldn't tell me?" Garik relaxed into the odd sensation of being on the edge of reality, his body and brain and abilities caught in its short circuit, trying to shift him into hyper speed, and his body jumping the connection, unable to make the leap. He compared it to holding an electric lead, and every time the energy pulsed through him, his head buzzed with pain. It was starting to feel good. Delirium? Likely. Did he want it to continue? He thought maybe it wasn't a bad idea. He was at least feeling something other than anger.

Or was it the anger that was driving his short circuit? They were jumbled in his head. One was the other, and that seemed okay.

The world buzzed again, the colors shimmering, and he realized he had missed something important from Jantzen.

"Say that again, Jantz." Garik waved one arm awkwardly in the air, trying to put his hand on the man's wrist and unable to control its movements. He grimaced as the electric buzz lanced through his head, but then it stopped and he smiled, feeling pleased with the sensation.

"There's only one place that can help—"

"Did you bring me food, Jantz?" Garik interrupted. He had begun to feel dreamy. "I can't follow the rainbow without food. You know that, don't you? It takes all my energy. Thirty seconds, then I need my fruit bars. You brought me fruit bars, didn't you?"

"No fruit bars, my friend. I need you to stay in one place."

"Then, I guess you never were my friend, were you?" Garik smiled, and he let his head loll sideways to look at Jantzen. "What does a not-friend suggest for a person who doesn't have any friends anymore, at least not any that are alive?"

"I am your friend. Always. However, my suggestion won't sound like it."

"So, tell me." The buzzing overrides in Garik's brain were straining his ability to speak. He skipped in and out of his private rainbow world, his body unable to follow, his voice escaping in a fuzzy whisper.

"Only the Tower can help you now."

"The Tower?" The words blurred on Garik's tongue. "I want you to help me."

"I wish that I could."

"Can you go with me? I don't want to be alone."

They talked for a time under the fading winter sky, Jantzen shivering occasionally, Garik too far gone to feel the cold. Mostly Jantzen did the talking, with Garik occasionally shifting his head or flopping his arm Jantzen's direction. His responses became nearly incoherent.

"This isn't unexpected," Jantzen said.

"We weren't sure what would trigger it, or if it would occur." Again, Jantzen.

"Something similar happened with Weston." Still Jantzen, with Garik listening, distracted, his eyes shifting position occasionally.

481

"I don't want you to go back, but you'll burn yourself out if you don't." Jantzen watched the sky, not demanding, just offering.

"And hurt people." Garik tried to lift a hand, and only his fingers moved.

"That, possibly." Jantzen took Garik's hand and squeezed it.

"And not remember." Garik wondered where his tears had gone. He wanted to be sad, to grieve, and he couldn't. Marisa. Irina. Paul. John. Devon. Dieter. The three shrimps. Muhammad. Ibn, all of them. Everyone who had come into contact with his life and suffered for it. "Don't want to remember."

"Do you want my help?"

"Tower's, you mean."

"Yes."

"Can I forget—" He tried to move his hand, but all he could do was look around at the damage that surrounded him. "—all this?"

"I don't know, but you will live. They can give you that."

"Don't want it." Marisa . . .

"Maybe get your life back."

"Can't. Gone."

"For me?" Jantzen stood, knelt before him, and held out his hand, palm up, and crooked his fingers. "Please?"

"Don't do that." Garik wanted to close his eyes, blot out the man's hand. Jantzen had always been able to manipulate him, and he felt himself wanting to give in. A friend? He was here, wasn't he? Who else had come to find him? No one. *I am your friend. Always.* Garik wanted that more than anything.

"Garik?" Jantzen still held out his hand.

"You're my friend?"

"Always." Jantzen smiled.

"Yo-kay. Can't stand."

"Here." Jantzen produced one of Garik's fruit bars from a pocket. "The reason I had to drive. I needed to bring these."

Garik looked at it, unsure what Jantzen wanted him to do with it. He knew he was fading, but a fruit bar? What good was that?

"Okay, my friend. Let's get you to the Tower. It's the only choice we have. I'm going to help you up. Assist me if you can."

Jantzen pocketed the fruit bar, lifted Garik's arm, and placed it over his shoulder. Wrapping an arm around the youth's torso, he hefted him to his feet.

Garik allowed himself to be dragged along more than he walked, but the touch of a friend, the pressure of the man's skin against his, the human connection to a very real and solid world . . . sometimes that's what a person needed to have the motivation to go on.

Even if his destination was a place he didn't want to go.

Here, puppy. Good puppy . . . the pound is just down the road.

— Book 8 —

Sunchaser's Gambit

— 1 —

CORONA TOWER scowled from its position on the Bay City skyline, a lone, upthrust pillar of steel and glass, an obsidian blot on a city embroiled in protests, riots, and rebellion.

From Sycamore Avenue, looking north toward The Docks and Harbor Shipyards, the setting sun glinted off the massive monolith into the windows of approaching cars across the city.

Garik Shayk, barely eighteen, rode in one of those cars. He had been unwillingly inducted into the Tower's secretive human-hybrid research program. Now part timber wolf and escaped from the Tower's underground warrens and test facilities, he found himself faced with an unbearable decision.

Return to the Tower or risk certain death.

His DNA, irrevocably modified in the Tower's attempts to create the world's perfect super soldier, was glitching, forcing his body into a hyper-enhanced state, short-circuiting his senses and draining energy from him that he could no longer afford to give.

"Hang in there, my friend," Jantzen Hefferly muttered to the nearly unconscious youth. His car dodged through lights daringly, narrowly missing several pedestrians and one car. The urgency was worth the risk. He knew the likelihood of Garik not surviving his ride to the Tower. Jantzen was also modified, although not with something so tame as a wolf. He was half squid, enabling him to sublimate into purple smoke and reform in any location he desired. Purple specks in his eyes were the giveaway, and they increased in number and intensity just before he morphed and disappeared. Jantzen understood the critical nature of Garik's trauma because a man Jantzen had once admired before they became estranged, Weston Rodheimer, had almost been killed by something similar, a glitch in his silverback gorilla DNA modifications. Jantzen had nursed him back to health before becoming part of the project himself.

Now, Weston Rodheimer and his second-in-command, Halo Sunchaser, battled Colonel Brace and his hybrid paramilitary forces for control of the Tower and the military-funded human-hybrid project brewing in the five floors of the building's extensive basement complex. Bay City had been decimated in the conflict, notably the sections of the city nearest the Tower and along the waterfront. Another sizable area of the city had proclaimed itself a "Tower Free Zone" and now refused access to police, the paramilitary, or anyone who refused to disclaim any affiliation to Corona Tower.

Jantzen was driving into the belly of the beast in an effort to save his teen protégé. Military vehicles sat parked on side streets, with green-suited men patrolling next to black-suited paramilitary hybrids. Remaining on Sycamore, Bay City's main north-south thoroughfare, allowed him to bypass the Tower Free Zone and much of the worst decimation on the east side of town near Central Park and The Martial Arts Center. He slowed at the Corona Street exit, wary of showing his face this close to the Tower. On his own, he could escape anywhere but from a hermetically sealed room, but he had Garik in the car with him. He was locked into his bodily form as long as he controlled this car.

Jantzen weighed his options. He had once been second-in-command of the research program, the true genius behind the controversial and forward-thinking DNA-enhancement process, but he and Rodheimer no longer shared the same goals . . . and, well, Rodheimer still had all the power, so that told all there was to say about that. Jantzen had run for his own welfare, and in the process, aided the escape of twelve hybrid rejects due for termination. They were his friends, and he refused to let them be parceled out for research or something worse. His betrayal had separated him from Rodheimer, a fracture that couldn't be breached.

"Garik, we're about there. Can you hold on a minute more?" Jantzen glanced at the youth beside him, taking in his curly, dark hair and his strong features. His bronze skin told of his Armenian heritage. His shoulders, now wider than before, and his height . . . Jantzen saw for the first time the growth the boy had undergone since his wolf-based modifications had truly come into their own. No wonder he had been able to perform at a super-human level against Brace's hybridized soldiers. Except Garik wasn't flawed like the men Brace had sent after him. Jantzen didn't consider Garik's current glitch a flaw, more a hiccup that the Tower could address. They had expected it to show up, had hoped it wouldn't, and then when Garik had escaped the Tower . . . well, that's why they were back. In computer terms, Garik needed an update, and Jantzen couldn't provide it without the Tower's mainframe, and to access that meant Jantzen risking his freedom. This was a balancing act he couldn't afford to get wrong. Off one side was the knife edge of death, and the other side was the razor blade of locks and keys, and Rodheimer would not give him any rope this time, not and risk his escape after the trouble he'd caused the Tower.

Jantzen refused to think of what Colonel Brace would do if he got his hands on either of them. They could kiss their tomorrows goodbye.

Garik moaned, his eyes shifted as though he was trying to look around, and he mumbled an unintelligible response.

"What? I didn't catch that." They were nearly to the back of Corona Tower. The area leading to the underground parking garage seethed with suited and armed troops. The hybridized paramilitary men could be identified by the white eagle logo on black dancing on their sleeves. A better indicator was the black full-face helmets with hockey puck-shaped breathing adaptors at their mouths. In a conflict, take them off, and within minutes, they would be wheezing for breath. It was their fatal flaw, the one which Garik was bred to overcome.

"Trap you, too."

"Not if I can help it." Jantzen pulled up to the curb and waited. The youth was the key to the Tower's newest generation of military fighting men who were bigger, stronger, and more resistant to the rigors of war than humanity had ever seen. He must be protected from becoming a research project that might well end in something worse than death.

"Jantz."

"I'm still here." Jantzen could hear the effort in the teen's words.

He searched the troops moving about, looking for any sign of recognition. The car he had "borrowed" was nondescript and unfamiliar to anyone searching for them, but that would give them minutes, at best. The Tower had eyes out—and drones over-flying Bay City—and they would find them on a camera somewhere, track them to the burned-out hulk of The Flower Shop, and place them together in this car.

Then they would trace it to right here. Minutes only.

If only he had a watch with him, he could call. Rodheimer would pick up, if only to threaten him, to gloat over his success, even if he had already lost control of the Tower to Brace's forces. It was Garik that Rodheimer wanted, not the Tower, even if the two did go together. He brushed off the hope of a watch. Nothing translated with him when he sublimated from a solid into his purple, gaseous form, so he could carry nothing with him. It was an inconvenience he had learned to accept.

He noticed Garik trying to get his attention. "Yes, say it again, my friend."

"Window." It came out as two whispered puffs of sound, but Garik looked toward the windshield, and Jantzen understood.

"Window, yes. What about it?"

"Write." Garik tried to raise his hand, but his energy levels were barely keeping him alive. His body was continually attempting to flip him into hyper mode, allowing him to sense, think, and move at speeds almost too fast to be measured. Each time, his "glitch" sent a throb of electric current though his head, but his body couldn't perform. His brain was asking his body to dance, and his body just flopped away, a rag doll instead of a streak of lightning.

"Write. I get it. A note on the windshield." Jantzen began searching for paper and pen. He found an envelope in the glove box and felt under the seat for a pen.

"Lights," Garik tried to say. "Flashers."

Jantzen didn't understand those words, but he and Garik were thinking alike, so he already knew what to do. Write Garik's name on the envelope, stick it in the windshield, and turn on the lights and flashers. Leave a window slightly open, and Jantzen would have plenty of time to vanish as soon as the men were close enough.

He wrote, "Garik Shayk. NEEDS FOOD. Glitching. THE DIRECTOR HAS BEEN NOTIFIED." Well, not yet, but Jantzen would find a phone immediately and let Rodheimer know his precious cargo was alive and waiting below and to get down here before Brace's paramilitary decided to take matters into their own hands once more.

There was an element of danger, for Garik, especially. Hours before, the paramilitary had tried to eliminate him. How many shots had Garik taken? Too many and likely what had triggered his DNA glitch. No one's body, even the best of hybrids, was designed to heal that deeply and that often, and the speed at which Garik had healed had proven to be astonishing.

If the goons decided to move against him before Jantzen could notify Rodheimer, could they kill him? Even the paramilitary hybrids could be destroyed. Likely, the same was true of Garik, just not without effort.

He eased the car to the corner of Corona and McKinley, giving him a view of the residential parking garage that had been bombed by a terrorist and cleared away for access to the underground, highly restricted garage, leaving the entrance now exposed for everyone to see. Men made an anthill of the former garage, going in and out like black insects, knowing their business without anyone seeming to tell them what to do.

His position also allowed them to easily see him.

He pictured the scene he'd left behind when Garik's glitch had forced him from the building. Paul and John down, their bodies broken, lying crumpled on the concrete. The two youths who had tried to help them, neither one hybridized, whom Garik had spirited to safety. Joanie and Justin, well, at least they had gotten out before the fireworks started. If only Garik could have done the same.

"I'm sorry, my friend, that you must go back inside. I have no other options, and I want you to live." Jantzen took the youth's hand, squeezed it, and when he released it, Garik refused to turn loose. Jantzen knew the effort it was taking him, and he squeezed it back. With his other hand, he slipped the note on the dash, words outward, rolled the window partially down, turned on the lights, then hit the flashers. His last thing was to lay his hand on the horn and wait until the men came running.

It took a moment. The horn blared, and one, then two men looked their way. They were slow to react, likely occupied with communications from inside their solid-faced helmets.

"Why aren't they coming?" Garik's words were little more than grunts. He could no longer control his body. All he wanted to do was sleep, to be rid of this feeling, even if in his delirium the electric jolts in his brain calling him to attend had become pleasurable.

"I have to find a phone. I'll help you if I can. I've promised to be your friend, always. I'm not forgetting that just because I'm leaving you now."

Garik could no longer answer, so he forced his energy into his hand. Jantzen squeezed back and evaporated into a purple haze that whipped out the car window and into the darkening evening sky.

Jantzen's clothes sank into the seat. Garik turned his eyes—he could do nothing else—and saw a fruit bar tumble out of the pocket of the empty shirt.

A fruit bar. He tried to remember the good in a fruit bar. Had Jantzen brought it for him? That was kind of him, though he had no need of a fruit bar. He couldn't eat, could he? He couldn't move. A fruit bar was silly for a person who couldn't chew or eat or think or do anything else.

Garik thought he heard the door open, and he was certain his body fell hard to the side. Hands grabbed him roughly, and a voice called out, "Hey, get Rodrigo. We found the punk, the one we couldn't kill. He's come back for more." Then paper rustled, a short pause, and the same voice said, not as loudly, "That burns my hide."

"What?" Another voice. "What does it say?"

"This one belongs to the Director. He already knows it's here. Target practice has to wait."

"We can still kick it a few times, right?" The second voice laughed.

Garik didn't know the rest. He sank into a rainbow, and it tasted as pretty as it looked.

— 2 —

NO ONE SEEMED to notice Garik's additional scrapes and bruises as he was bundled on a wheeled gurney and navigated down Stamford Drive and through the entrance to the underground parking garage.

Perhaps they pictured how *normal* he looked after observing the devastation precipitated by his arrival in the garage earlier that day. The remains of weapons fire still scarred the concrete, and bloodstains were just being scrubbed away, so a little physical "damage" could be expected on the youth that had been at the center of it all.

Once he got food, his body would heal the injuries inflicted by the paramilitary goons who had retrieved him from the car, but for now, nurses and medical technicians struggled to keep him breathing and his heart pumping. The short-circuiting rainbows in his head? Good luck with that. He needed a full DNA patch. A software upgrade . . . and a reboot in the process.

A limousine with deeply tinted windows pulled down the ramp into the basement parking garage and stopped alongside the team surrounding Garik. The car flashed its lights and honked to get their attention. The driver's door opened, but the back door flung itself wide before the driver could exit the car. Weston Rodheimer emerged, his massive shoulders dominating every other person, including the oversized and intimidating paramilitary goons.

"This is the boy?" Rodheimer's tone said he expected it to be.

"We think so, sir." A male nurse holding a bag of plasma over Garik's arm lifted one of the youth's eyelids. The pupil contracted, but there was little else to indicate he was alive. "We need to get him downstairs."

"You've seen the video feeds?" Rodheimer raked his eyes up and down Garik. "He doesn't seem that . . . different. Where are the changes, the improvements? For him to do the damage he did, move the way he did . . ."

"We are looking into that, sir." The nurse was respectful, but he looked to the elevator door. One of his team was holding it open and waiting.

"I want updates. Anything you find. If he comes to, notify me."

"Yessir."

Rodheimer took another long look at Garik, turned, dropped into his car. His driver closed his door after him, climbed in, and the big automobile moved toward the exit, picking up speed until it started the turn up the ramp to the surface.

COME TO? Garik wanted to laugh, but his body wouldn't respond. He was awake, fully conscious, perhaps too much so. In between the searing jolts of rainbow electricity that sliced through his brain, leaving him woozy and perhaps a bit drunk with endorphins, his senses were soaking in the world around him, the sounds and odors and temperature fluctuations. His awareness was flooded with each person attending him, their heartbeats, their breathing patterns, even the scent on their skins. One had a heart murmur, another suffered with asthma, and the cat lady carried the aroma of newborn kittens about her. Too much information, more than he wanted to know.

When they had pierced his arm with the needle to allow the bag of plasma—oh, so cold!—to flow into him, it had been an ice knife, the sword of an ancient being, a viper's tooth slipping inside to inject him with mind-bending venom and reveal the workings of the world before time and of time to come.

Video feeds, video feeds . . . Garik's brain glitched in rainbow swirls, and he saw what the cameras must have seen. Him, there and gone, flashing in and flashing out. He smiled at the idea of Jantzen flashing in and flashing out, flashing more than he ought. Well, he thought he smiled, but he couldn't be certain.

"The plasma is helping. His facial expression just changed."

Expression, suppression, recession, digression. Mine, yours, hers, theirs? The words flowed around Garik. He heard the ding of the elevator doors—the sound of a cash register, the one-minute bell indicating time to get to class, his watch notifying him he had a message. Hello, Marisa, yes, I can hold your hand, sit under a blanket with you on the roof of our building and watch the stars . . .

His eyes burned. Watch the stars . . . they were all in the sky, and he was riding an elevator into the depths of—an alarm sounded, something outside Garik's head, sharp and insistent. He wanted to push it away. He was sleepy and ready to close his eyes and dream his world the way he wanted it to be.

"Cardiac arrest," the male nurse called, his words even but his voice tense with urgency. The gurney jumped and leaned as if they were running. He seemed out of breath.

"O.R. 3 is ready, Sean."

The gurney turned sharply and came to an abrupt stop. Garik felt hands on his body, he was lifted, abruptly released. He heard a buzzing sound, felt his head tingle, sensed something on his scalp.

"Brain scans indicate he's still conscious."

"During cardiac arrest?" Disbelief.

This time, Garik's chest grew cold. Someone called, "Clear!" Then, lightning jumped into him, his world went white, and he knew what the buzzing sound was.

They had cut his hair, *again!*

GARIK OPENED his eyes, took a deep breath, remembered Sean's name, smell, and the asthma the man battled; and he absorbed the white ceiling overhead. A light burned in the center.

"Awake." The word rumbled rather than flowed.

"Director," Garik acknowledged. He moved his eyes and found the man at his side. He shifted his gaze and was interrupted before he could scan the rest of the room.

"Brace isn't here." Brace was Colonel Brace, the Air Force brass who had wrested control of Corona Tower from Rodheimer by use of DNA-enhanced super soldiers, albeit soldiers with a respiratory flaw requiring them to supplement their bodily requirements for air with breathing masks. They were unable to absorb enough oxygen from the air to fuel their bodies' inefficient furnaces.

Garik hadn't known all that before, but he saw it now. How? Notice. Quantify. Deduce. It had to be, simply because it *was*.

"Where is—" Where is Nurse Ratchett, Garik intended to ask, but Rodheimer cut off the question with an answer.

"Nurse Fortinier is also not here. It is just the two of us. I've asked for some time alone with you."

Alone? Garik was about to ask why when the big man started talking.

"Why, you are about to inquire. There are things that need to be said just between us. And for your next question, how do I know what you're about to ask so accurately? We are too much alike for me not to understand your thoughts."

Understand my thoughts. Garik kept his face clear of emotion, but the man didn't understand his thoughts at all, or he would understand how much Garik wanted to be free from this place, and he would let him go . . . well, as soon as he fixed the glitching rainbows in his head, but let him go, nonetheless.

"You won't want to leave when you realize what we can offer you, my young friend."

Garik shifted his shoulders, felt his head rub on the pillow, anger flared, and without thinking, he spat, "What's with the hair-cutting thing? Are you all idiots?"

"Perhaps." Rodheimer smiled. "This time, however, you did it to yourself."

"Blame me. Yeah, that's right." Garik started to sit up, and his arm was affixed to the bedrail. A tube trailed overhead. "What's this?"

"That. Yes. I know you were with Jantzen. I've seen the videos. He must have informed you what you've been going through." Rod-

492

heimer ran a hand over one of the readouts for Garik's medical devices. "The numbers these machines are returning, they are unbelievable. I now regret not monitoring your development more closely. I assumed—" He shrugged and turned his attention back to Garik. "I want you to be happy here. It would be best for all of us."

"For you, you mean." Garik could smell the man's anticipation. He wanted this badly.

"Yes, for me. Equally for you. I realize now I didn't allow enough time for your, shall we say, enhancements to come to fruition. You've interacted with Brace's private army." He said *private army* with disdain.

"You don't approve."

"Oh, no, the product we provided is outstanding, mostly. Just incomplete. Brace insisted we give him *something*, but we weren't ready. The man doesn't understand how science works."

"How does it work?"

"Inquisitive. That's good. Your mind is working. That's something Brace's men don't have, the ability to think beyond the current situation. It's something we hope to see in you."

"In me." Garik cringed, and he waited on the man to say, *Repeating others, still?*

"I expected you would see this already." Rodheimer raised an eyebrow. "You are the completion to what Brace's men are missing. The next step. The final evolution, we hope."

"And I'm also broken." With his good hand, Garik indicated the hospital room.

"Not broken. Far from it, my boy. This is an expected bump in the road, one we are smoothing out as we speak." He touched a bag hanging above Garik. "The final ingredient. In a short time, we can begin evaluating how far you've come."

"Where I've come is back to where I started," Garik said bitterly.

"To where you started." Rodheimer looked around the room and chuckled. "Your memory is as good as I'm led to believe. I do think this is the same room where we first met. Halo will be surprised to hear about this." His chuckle became a laugh, and he turned, Garik already dismissed, opened the door and stepped outside, leaving the door ajar. "Dr. Jamie, I am finished. Testing perhaps tomorrow?"

"If you wish, Director. An extra day would be better for accurate results."

"If we must. I will expect him fully fixed and that defect in his head gone. If only Jantzen were here. This was his specialty. That's old water, though. Can't be helped, and I'm sure you have Jantzen's records for reference."

"Yes, Director. No mistakes this time."

"Make sure. I don't want to lose this one, too."

LOSE THIS one, too. How many had they lost? The names flashed through Garik's head: Christian, Paolo, Alyna, Joanie, Giselle, Amy, Leigh, Laura, Paul, John, Justin, Marco, and now, Jantzen.

Jantzen was at least alive. Garik couldn't be sure about the rest. He'd seen Paul and John on the floor of the garage, their clothing painted red. Christian, sent away somewhere for research, either whole or in parts.

Nurse Fortinier came in, interrupting his thoughts, and she held a vial and a needle.

"Not the needle." Garik groaned. "I'm awake. I'm fine. I'm not fighting or argumentative. I'm being good."

"You need to heal," she said. "This will help."

"Help put me to sleep?" He remembered the sleepy juice. He'd slept most of the first few weeks here.

"That too. And I'm sorry about your hair. It's a shame it had to be cut again. It was growing out beautifully." She took his good arm and rubbed it with an alcohol swab. She pressed the needle against his skin, it slipped inside, and the cool liquid surged through him.

It was different this time, though. The rainbows in his head, lessened but not gone, might have been the difference, or maybe it was that he was becoming something other than even the Tower's research teams imagined. The drug flowed in, a poison of sorts, though not one that would kill him. He sensed the compounds as they moved into his blood. He felt their composition, the arrangement of the molecules, and he instructed his white blood cells to shift an enzyme, relocate a peptide, and in the doing, change the structure of the poison, mitigating the toxicity of the drug.

He didn't negate it. He turned it into a soporific, something to make the time flow faster, to put his mind in another place, to have back what had been taken from him, if only for a short time.

He closed his eyes and dreamed of Marisa, the way their life should have been.

"That's it. Sleep away." Nurse Fortinier withdrew the needle and exited, leaving Garik alone with his dreams.

— 3 —

"HOW TALL did you say?" Sheesh, Garik thought. Even their machines didn't work down here. No wonder this place had messed up so many of their "super soldier" hybrids.

They couldn't even measure how tall he was!

"Five-eleven. Is that surprising to you?"

"Yes. That can't be right." Five-eight, always and forever. He could prove it. It was on his license. A momentary surge of anger hit him before he choked it off. Right! They had taken that from him, too. Sheesh!

"I can double check." Sean Ito, the nurse who had wheeled him in—and smelled of asthma—stepped away and tapped numbers into a tablet sitting on a counter.

"Please." He had stopped growing when he was fifteen. People didn't just shoot up three inches when they turned eighteen. No one got that as a birthday bonus. Yet, in the elevator with Airman Vang. And Dieter's comment, *"You are taller . . ."*

"Let's use the laser scanner this time." Sean didn't seem put off that Garik doubted his skills, just opened an adjoining door and waited for him to step through.

As he moved past, Garik did notice he was eye to eye with the man, a little over, if anything.

"And you are?" He glanced about, noting the array of high-tech devices, unlike the manual height and weight machine he had been on for his INACCURATE HEIGHT MEASUREMENT.

"Sean Ito. You likely don't remember—"

"I know your name," Garik barked, before he caught himself. Sean had not been unkind, the opposite, in fact. He knew what it was. His anger at being here was bleeding out, affecting how he saw things. Also, they had pumped him full of fresh DNA sauce, and while it might need to marinate in his veins a while, he was ready to come out of the oven. He now saw the world in permanent rainbow shadows, calling to him, whispering, faster, faster, *faster, FASTER.* The repeated jolts of electricity feeding into his brain, stoking his endorphins, were a metronome, an addictive reminder that he was different, changed, and likely deadly to himself if he let the rainbows take control. His brain now bled rainbows, deadly arches that fed on who he was, wanted to suck him dry in exchange for a feeling of endorphin-charged power . . . and speed . . . and forgetting what had been done to him without his permission . . . and could never be undone—

"Garik? Are you with me?"

He shook his head to force the rainbows into the background and let the white, antiseptic room expand to fill his vision. How many times had Marisa said that to him to bring him back from la-la land?

"I'm sorry, Sean. I was—" What? Dreaming of deadly rainbows? He couldn't say that, and he was embarrassed that he had snapped at the man. He tried again. "It was inconsiderate of me to cut you off. Do you mind telling me your height?"

"Not at all and thank you for the apology. Not too many of those come my way down here. Five-nine. Why?" He indicated a square marked on the floor inside a glass-walled structure.

"I was eye level when I walked by you."

"Bit above. I'm pretty good at judging height." He shrugged and grinned. "Practice. I do this frequently. My machine says five-eleven for you. I could judge that even before you got on the scale. This one also gives your shoe size."

"I need that?"

"If you've grown, your feet will have, too. New shoes for you!" Sean stepped to the side of the unit. "Hands to your side. We'll know every inch of you after this. Remain perfectly still. Don't want you to come out with four arms."

"It can do that?" Garik had seen weirder. He didn't want it to be him.

"Only on the results. You want four real arms, you've got to grow them yourself. You might close your eyes. The laser can surprise you."

The lasers flashed, Garik fought his rainbows, and he imagined himself as he used to be. Average size, lean and tight from riding skateboards, with a thick mop of curls he could tie in a bun. Now, he was tall and bald. Well, tightly buzzed. Not a fair exchange, not one he would have made in a million years.

"Done," Sean called. "Come on out."

"It says?"

"What I said, five-eleven, maybe a smidge over. Shoe size eleven—"

"Can't be right." Garik studied the readout. It showed his image in full color, bald head to shoeless feet, with measurements. "That's me?"

"I wasn't in there. Let me print this. It saves to your file automatically, but I can give you a copy."

Garik heard him, but he was focused on the image on the screen. Shoulders, thighs, forearms. It was his face, but the rest of him was not what he remembered from his mirror. Had his hours in the pool, games on the racquetball courts, time on the climbing wall done this? He didn't feel that different, well, except things were easier—running, climbing, laps in the pool—so there was that. Maybe . . . it was too much to think about, too many changes in his life, and he turned when Sean cleared his throat.

"Now, we have some tests to run. The Director has asked to attend, so shipshape! Show him what your ticker can do. He seems to have high hopes for you." Very upbeat and encouraging.

Sean led him out the door, pointed to his shoes, and casually remarked that he'd noticed how quickly he'd healed since wheeling him in from on the street where they'd found him. That puzzled Garik. He'd been with Jantzen in the car, not on the street. Then he remembered the goons, *"We can still kick it a few times, right?"* and the rainbows threatened to take control, pulsing in his head with electrical jolts of precision pain.

He chanted to himself, "Anger gets me nothing. I must use my hands, my mind, my desire to achieve what I want."

"A question?" Sean smiled pleasantly.

"Practicing self-control. Hoping it works."

"Mr. Rodheimer will be pleased, I'm certain."

Garik breathed deeply and let the rainbows fade, becoming a background surge of finger-in-the-socket reminders that they weren't gone. They didn't go away. They never did any longer.

He wondered what the tests would be this time. Sixteen bricks and a bag of sand? Likely. They seemed to expect more of him every time he was tested.

The reality that he could only blame himself was a black cloud. He had Houdinied out of this place twice, and he was back again. Sheesh! He wanted to hit himself in the head. He felt as stupid as they were!

He firmed up his resolve. Where a man can Houdini once, he can Houdini again. *Get these rainbows out of my head, and I'll be gone all over again.*

Bet on it, Mr. Rodheimer. And you can take that to the bank.

AT A SIGNAL, Garik slowed his stationary bike and dropped his forehead to the handlebars. Sweat streamed from him. He was down to shorts, a monitor was strapped to his arms, sticky pads were wired all over his torso, and he breathed into a tube wedged into his mouth.

"Let me take this." Loren Gershon, with red hair and freckles, reached under him and placed her hand around the breathing tube.

Garik raised his head and allowed her to slip it upward as she released the straps around his scalp. One check mark for a good buzz cut, he thought. Nothing to get tangled in the straps. The sticky pads on his body? They had removed all the hair there, too.

Remembering that, he thought, what next? Armpits? Do you really want to go there? Just try it!

Through a glass wall in front of him, in an adjacent observation room, Director Rodheimer lifted a handset wired into the arm of his chair. He was surrounded by a cadre of associates. Halo Sunchaser was missing, and of course, there was no sign of Colonel Brace. He was likely off laying claim to what was left of Bay City, along with all military personnel not currently guarding the entrances and exits to the basement research center.

"Dr. Jamie, well?"

"Yes, Director, I have the results you wish." The man kept his eyes on his monitor as he spoke, his gaze flicking from point to point, indicating he didn't quite "have" it. Then he smiled and relaxed. A printer next to him whirred, and he lifted the printout and stood.

"Well?" Rodheimer's voice, so low the speakers had trouble conveying its timbre precisely, resonated in the room. He still held his handset to his ear.

"Amazing, Director, simply amazing. The readouts—" he held out the paper towards the window with one hand and tapped it with the other, "—are approaching the parameters of Colonel Brace's people, and there are no signs of oxygen deprivation when the body is under full stress."

"So, lung capacity—"

"Never a problem, even with Brace's people. It's the absorption rate, the ability to metabolize the oxygen that's the issue there. Garik, well, his chest size says it all. The numbers show lung capacity more than fifty percent above standard, which means his heart

. . ." Jimenez grinned, studied the printout as though he couldn't believe his good fortune, and drew in a deep, satisfied breath.

"And, Dr. Jamie?"

"Right, right." Jimenez looked toward the window, his eyes bright. "All top athletes, as you surely know, develop enlarged hearts—"

"Enlarged?" Rodheimer frowned. "A disease? Cardio . . . ography? That's not a good thing, doctor."

"No, this isn't cardiomegaly. The muscle walls are not thickened or in any way injured." He laid the paper aside. "An athlete's heart stretches to pump more blood—enlarging the ventricle and thereby allowing a lower resting heart rate. That's a very good thing. Here's what's important. More blood means more oxygen, which means faster muscle response, greater endurance, and a quicker recovery rate."

"And the, um, issue we are attempting to resolve?"

Not *issue*. Brain glitch, Garik thought, wishing people would quit sidestepping the issue. Just say it. We all know it happened . . . was still happening, even if it was better than before. And he was living with it. Who did they think they were hiding it from?

"The treatment seems to have been successful."

Treatment. Garik reminded himself he was in control of his emotions. His hands, his mind, his desire. It was no treatment. They had given him an upgraded DNA infusion. Now he was likely to grow claws and a tail, and he would for sure howl at the next full moon.

Rodheimer seemed to be evaluating Dr. Jimenez's answer, his eyes on Garik, seeing the newly shorn head, the broader shoulders, the extra height on his frame. Then he relaxed slightly, shifted his arms, tilted his head differently, and his face lost its intensity.

"Good news, then, Dr. Jamie. A shower and fresh clothes, then I want to meet with both of you." Rodheimer replaced the handset, carefully for a man of his immense bulk, stood, and made his way out of the observation room. The rest of his cohorts followed him one at a time.

"MR. SHAYK, Garik, come in."

Director Rodheimer personally held the door. His offices in the research center lacked the views from his penthouse suite at the top of Corona Tower, but it was as luxurious in every other way.

"Dr. Jamie, please." The Director invited Jimenez to join them, and he showed them to a group of Le Corbusier chairs in blocky black leather and chrome. From a small refrigerator hidden inside a wall of cabinets, he withdrew three bottles of chilled water, offered one each to Garik and Jimenez and kept the third for himself. He sat and placed his water on a glass table at his side.

"How has your stay with us been, Garik? Have you been well treated?" The Director smiled and seemed truly interested.

Garik looked to the doctor and back to the Director, unsure what game they were playing. He decided to go along and said, "So far, except for the tests—"

"Over." Rodheimer laughed. "Hear that, Dr. Jamie? No more tests for our young friend. There are no reasons for more tests, are there?"

"Um, no, I suppose not, although there are endurance parameters I would like to probe—"

"That's that, then. Garik, we have new quarters for you. How would you like a room with a view? Penthouse level, will that do? Here's your new passkey." He slipped one from inside a pocket and tossed it hard Garik's direction.

Garik caught it, the rainbows swirling, and immediately let them slip away, in control once more.

"That's what I thought," Rodheimer said, smiling. "Good as new."

Penthouse, but with a catch. Garik wondered the price Rodheimer would expect him to pay.

— 4 —

"WHAT IS this?" Halo Sunchaser in a bright pink and jet headwrap appeared in the room. Her hawk-like eyes peered from her ebony face, made more menacing by the round silver earrings that dangled at her jawline.

She took in each member of the cabal: Weston Rodheimer, casually at ease, his expression revealing how pleased he was; Garik, the new passkey held aloft, studying it, attempting to weigh out its value in favors and compromises; Dr. Jimenez as the odd man out, neither friend nor foe, neither Tower royalty nor basement rabble.

"A meeting, Halo." Rodheimer smiled, equal to equal, giving her that. Then he took it away. "You do understand meetings, where deals are worked out, alliances formed, relationships that breed success. It's how a successful business moves forward."

"Business." She dropped her wrap in a vacant chair, exposing a pink paisley suit in a business cut, with black and pink suede flats. She walked along the back of Jimenez's chair. He turned his head to follow her as best he could. "Doctor business, I presume. Checkups, weight regimens, perhaps even the correct *medications* to keep our new subject from escaping once again and embarrassing us all over."

"He is the doctor," Rodheimer remarked, dryly. "That *is* what the good doctor does."

"Then there's this one." She was to Garik, and she took a finger and ran it along his jawline. "What does the good boy do?"

Garik kept silent. He had seen Sunchaser's electrified sword at work, watched it eat a fellow hybrid, dissolving her until there was nothing left but empty space, not even a pile of ash to collect and mourn. The doctor would be quaking in his chair if he had seen what Garik had seen. Then, he supposed it best he hadn't. The bedlam in the parking garage that had left John and Paul crumpled on the floor was nothing in comparison.

"And this." Sunchaser gently lifted the passkey from Garik's palm and balanced it in her own. "A passkey, and in the boy's hand."

"Not much of a boy any longer, Halo. Look at him." Rodheimer came very close to a smirk before letting it fade from his face. "Third generation and very near flaw free. For the second time he has returned to us, of his own accord."

Returned to them, yes, but of his own accord? The first time he saw how Rodheimer might have thought that, and Garik hadn't corrected him. This time, however, he had battled for his freedom and only returned when he accepted that his life was forfeit without the Tower's help. Sheesh! Next, they would be saying he was the savior of the Tower's plans to usurp Brace's newfound and irritating domination of the Tower's operational sector.

"Has he, Weston? I wonder." She sat elegantly on the arm of Garik's Le Corbusier, placed one hand on his scalp, and gently stroked the stubble that was just starting to regrow. "We have been breeding for independent thinking, the ability to outmaneuver an opponent mentally. When we get it, it comes with intractability, the refusal of our subjects to adhere to our plans. If we get cooperation from our subjects, they are no more than mindless machines, such as Brace's men. A pity. They fight so well not to have a thought in their heads. Then there's this one, very near flaw-free, allowing him to

501

think and do all those things we saw on the video feeds. Hmm."

"Get to the point, Halo. I assume there is one." Rodheimer, his tone even, his expression ready to move on.

"Someone once swapped my passkey." She held up Garik's and studied it. "Then, this *boy* allowed himself to be trapped and inserted into our program—"

"Halo." Rodheimer's word held a warning.

"Allowed, Weston. And we didn't see it. He is outmanipulating both of us. He returned, and another of our participants is gone. Now, Paul, one of our best creations, and John, whom I'm sure would have been outstanding, if we could have harnessed his skill, are lost. I'm sure of it. We've DNA matched the blood. I'm told they couldn't have survived."

DNA matched the blood . . . couldn't have survived . . . that meant they also didn't have the bodies. Could there be a chance for Paul and John? All hybrids were hardy, and they healed quickly. A small amount of hope welled up in Garik.

The other things Sunchaser was saying were way off the mark. He had nothing to do with stealing her passkey. That was all Marisa's fault. And returning? What did that have to do with additional hybrids escaping? The first time he returned, they captured him with video feeds and a BolaWrap, both of which were unfair and not part of any plan he had concocted. Just the opposite. The second time? It was their fault he was back, their flaw in him, and he harbored no plan, no intent, and no desire to stay, thank you. Give me my receipt, show me the door, and I'm outta here. Next she would be saying he had caused the whole Rodheimer-Brace debacle, plunging Bay City into a cauldron of riots and terrorist incidences.

"Halo, can we discuss this in private?"

"Certainly. Dr. Jamie, do you mind?"

Jimenez looked at Rodheimer, and when the man nodded, he stood. He motioned to Garik, but when Garik started to stand, Sunchaser touched his shoulder firmly to indicate he wasn't to leave.

"Go, Dr. Jamie. It's okay." When the man exited, Rodheimer asked, "Halo, the empty chair, please? The doctor didn't touch his water. Feel free."

"This," she said, holding out the key. "A penthouse key. What are you thinking, Weston? He's already escaped twice, right under our nose. What makes you think he won't walk out the front door the moment we're not looking?"

"The apartment and the Stamford Suites amenities. That's all it accesses."

"And the research facility?"

"Just the apartment and the amenities available to Stamford Suites. And before you tell me every other way he could exit, you are right on each one, except that I have covered those, too."

She stood, dropped the key into Garik's hand, and moved to the empty chair. She selected the bottle of water from the table, twisted the lid loose, and took a sip. When finished, she said, "Elaborate."

Rodheimer spoke to Garik. "I would have explained later, but now's as good a time as any since my hand is forced." He cut his eyes to Sunchaser before looking back to Garik. "We've installed a tracker. You can remove it, but it will be difficult. I don't suggest you try. You might do, um, other damage you might not find acceptable. It will set off an alarm if you are out of bounds for more than ten minutes."

Garik studied the passkey. This was his price. The gleaming device didn't hold the same appeal. He looked up, a quick glance at Sunchaser to see a smug smile and a longer look at Rodheimer.

"The apartment, the pool, and the gym." He had lost everything once again. He might as well push to see what he could gain. "The restaurant? I might get hungry now and again."

"You will have room service, but I'll see about adding the restaurant to your permissions."

"The hospital, the mall, or have I lost all that?"

"Let me think about it—"

"Weston," Sunchaser snapped, "don't let your hopes cloud your judgment. This boy has already removed your number two man from your employ. Jantzen would still be in the research labs . . ."

She kept talking, but Garik's head was white with confusion. Did she think he held any power at all in this place? Jantzen had organized and aided every move of his first escape. The next one had been Paul's doing, none of his.

Garik was yanked back into the conversation when Rodheimer barked, "Enough, Halo. Leave my wife out of this. I am not looking for a replacement for my unborn son. How dare you say that. The number two spot in this organization remains unfilled as a memorial to my and Jantzen's old friendship, and it will continue to remain so. I will be the one to decide if someone will someday move into that slot."

The air was tense. In the silence, Garik picked up on Rod-heimer's heartbeat. Slow, steady, not missing a tick. Sunchaser's was fiery hot with anger and indignation. This was more than an argument over the position Jantzen had vacated when he left the Tower. Sunchaser felt the rebuff was personal, as if Jantzen leaving the program affected her on a more intimate level than it should. Her accusations sounded closer to retribution than reason.

Once more, he wondered what game Jantzen was playing and who all was involved. Before he could spend any time working it out, Sunchaser was gathering her things and on her way out the door.

"MY APOLOGIES," Rodheimer said, taking a long swig from his water bottle. "You should have been allowed to leave. I meant the key to be a symbol of my trust in you, not of the restrictions you must endure. You must understand, Halo is right about some of what she says, although less diplomatic than I might prefer. The key will allow you a great deal of freedom—"

"And I have been chipped and validated. If I'm lost or wander off . . ." He stared at the bigger man.

"What I understand and not everyone does is the need for independent thinking, for a soldier to find himself in a hostile situation, evaluate the information he is given, and decide on a plan of action. Good soldiers can infiltrate the enemy, pose as one of them, and still get their job done, even return to base to receive a new assignment. You've appeared to master that. My question to you: Are you a good soldier?"

Garik considered the question. He was with the enemy. Could he evaluate the information he was receiving and decide on a plan of action that would allow him to HOUDINI OUT OF HERE?

"Absolutely. Always." He made sure his voice was utterly sincere.

"I saw that in you. People want to join us, but few manage to infiltrate us the way you did. I knew I wanted you on this team the night of your intrusion. It takes guts to embark on such a plan. I was disappointed to lose Jantzen, but he and I were headed opposite directions. He and I were quite close once. Did he tell you that?"

Garik nodded. He'd told him much more than that, even though Garik suspected it hadn't all been intended for his ears.

"Childhood friends. He was the one there for me when I suffered what you've just gone through. Jantzen came up with the cure, if we want to call it that. He never did, but I like the way it sounds. A cure for what ails us, meaning those of us who have been upgraded."

"What does Jantzen call it?"

"Oh, Jantz?" Rodheimer chuckled, using the nickname unexpectedly. "Jantz likes to say we were rebooting the system. I never liked to think of myself as a machine. Cure. That's much better. How does it feel to be cured?"

The colors in the room glitched, Garik controlled it, and the addictive buzz reverberated in his skull, painful in a very pleasurable way.

"It feels good, Director."

"Fine. Let's show you your room."

ROOM? ROOMS. A whole suite of rooms.

A tiny kitchen—at least they didn't expect him to cook—with a dining room, an office, a living room, and a loft. Two bedrooms completed the suite, each with a private bath. The walls, broad expanses of glass with views south and west over the city. Northwest he could just catch glimpses of The Docks and Cassel Dunes along the shore.

The closet revealed the extent of the Tower's involvement in the lives of its citizens. Racks of clothes sized to fit his new shoulders, and shoes. Who could wear so many, and all in his new size eleven? He shook out a pair of pants, held them to his waist, and was pleased to see that they landed just at the tops of his shoes—which he hadn't noticed were too tight for him until he was measured by Sean. He kicked them off and knew he would never wear them again.

One thing he was determined to find: pajamas. In these places, people tended to come in and out like he had a revolving door. If he was sleeping in one of these beds, he wanted to be presentable all hours of the day and night.

Looking out over the city was when he became heartsick. Halfway up Stanwick Hill, Sycamore jogged west, exposing the blackened remains of The Flower Shop. Three blocks west, the rooftop of City View Apartments. The view would be gone in the summer, but now, it was a connection with Marisa.

Then the doorbell chimed, and someone called, "Room service."

Garik was hungry, and he moved away from the window to answer the door.

KOFI MANDELA, the twenty-something attendant at Corona Tower's Stamford Suites pool, rang early on the phone the next morning.

"Garik, good morning. This is Kofi at the pool. How are you this morning?"

"Still in bed." Garik hadn't identified himself. Talk about personal service. He pictured the sunlit pool where he, Marisa, and Kevin Lee had enjoyed part of a summer afternoon. Kofi Mandela had been as charming as every other Corona Tower employee, and friendlier than some.

"Welcome back. We are so glad to be able to offer you our extended Corona Tower experience. Your schedule today indicates lunch with the Director. That gives us several hours free. The workout facilities and the pool are available all morning. What time would you like me to arrive?"

"Arrive." Garik, still in bed, glanced toward the room's glass wall fronting Bay City. Moisture glittered at the edges of the glass, proof that it was cold outside. He understood Kofi's call and the reason Rodheimer hadn't felt it necessary to give his passkey full access to the building. He was to have babysitters, though apparently ones that were less obtrusive than Devon had been in the basement facility. "I haven't had breakfast. After that, maybe?"

"Certainly. If you would like, I can place that order now. Any preferences?"

"Is there anything in my kitchen? I didn't look last night."

"The inventory shows your kitchen has the upgraded package. It should include—"

"Just milk and cereal. Okay? Tell me that."

"Yes, you will have milk and cereal. I'll be there about nine. You will be ready?"

"Nine it is."

"Thank you, Garik, and enjoy your breakfast."

The phone disengaged, and Garik set it down. Kofi had been extremely pleasant and eminently helpful, but Garik understood perfectly well. His passkey and this apartment didn't give him freedom. His days were to be sliced and diced, monitored by Tower personnel and overseen at every moment. Cameras in the apartment? Audio recordings? Who knew—likely in the corridors and the elevators, but he shouldn't have any expectation of privacy even in the apartment, except hopefully in the bathrooms. And those were areas he could easily inspect for intrusive devices.

He threw back the bedding, grateful for his pajamas, and he yawned, felt his back pop, and stepped to the window. He found blinds overhead tucked into a hidden pocket and understood the remote he had found in the bedside table. The city was blanketed by fog, the Tower a fist thrust into the clouds, the home of the gods, according to mythology. Bored, he turned toward the bathroom, taking in the sharp nothingness of the bedroom's overly scrubbed air. Halo Sunchaser had once said the Tower guaranteed the purest and most odor-free environment possible. He believed her. He caught only the musky tang of the night's rumpled bedding and the citrusy residue of the previous evening's shower on his skin.

One thing he did appreciate. Kofi's call, his warning, rather. He hadn't just appeared at nine, wandered in, and expected Garik to muster to, shipshape and all that. Instead, he was getting The Corona Tower Experience.

He closed the bathroom door, looked around for anyplace a camera or microphone could be hidden, and didn't find any. Satisfied, he ran a hand over his bristly scalp, hit the sink faucets, leaned over, and splashed water over his face.

Patting his face dry, he studied himself in the mirror, the water running down his chest, his hands holding the towel. He was different, wasn't he? If he still had any of his old clothes in Irina's apartment, he wouldn't be able to wear a one. His arms had thickened, his shoulders likewise, and his height. Even the light switches forced him to reach lower. Still, his eyes were the same, clear gray speckled with gold, except for the eyeshine, and that was only noticeable when the lights were low.

"Bright lights," he said to the face in the mirror. "That's the solution."

His mood brightening, he tossed open the bathroom door and made his way to the kitchen, flipping on the lights as he entered, wondering what sort of cereal he would find.

"GYM FIRST," Kofi said as he inserted his passkey and the elevator doors closed. He smiled, warmly friendly. "That will allow you to freshen up at the pool before meeting Mr. Rodheimer. Your breakfast, did you find everything satisfactory?"

"Crunchy oats, yes." Garik was in workout gear, trainers and shorts underneath a thin track suit. Kofi had pulled a garment bag from the closet and selected an outfit for after their morning session. *For the Director*, he had said with a smile. Kofi carried it across one arm.

"Did you visit our gym when you were last here?"

"Not this one."

"We only have the one." Kofi chuckled as though Garik's reply was a joke. "Kevin Lee used it on occasion when training Ms. Sunchaser. I believe you were here with Kevin."

"And Marisa." The memory burned itself into Garik's eyes, and he blinked it away.

"Yes. I have heard. You were friends. I'm sorry for your loss. It's the disruption in the city. Perhaps we can get back to normal soon. You and I are likely to be the only ones using the facilities this morning. Not many guests just now."

It came to Garik that Kofi truly had no idea of the basement research facility. For him, the Tower stopped at the mall, and if there were storage facilities beneath that, they were none of his concern. A world existed in the Tower's basements, and it was hidden so well that even the Tower's aboveground employees were unaware of it.

What if Garik let it slip, suggested to Kofi that things weren't as he thought, that there were hybrid mutant not-quite-humans now wandering the city, and they had been crafted right under his feet? Then he let his eyes search the nooks and crannies of the elevator and knew he wouldn't. Too many places for cameras and microphones. The first word and the elevator would freeze, Brace's paramilitary goons would drop in through the ceiling of the car, and bedlam would break out.

Kofi didn't deserve that. He was a good guy, earning a living at an honest job, and Garik felt the need to protect that. He recalled something he'd once thought during a conversation with Rodheimer. *Protect the family, protect the pack, take care of those under his care.*

Was Kofi under his care? He didn't see how, but he didn't want him to suffer because of him. He did notice that the man smelled of sun and water with a faint hint of coconut. A good smell, a pool attendant's smell. He decided he liked Kofi and he wanted to play the game for him, at least for the morning.

"YOU'VE BEEN putting in some gym time." Kofi offered Garik a towel. The man was unruffled in his Corona Tower polo and shorts, with his hair crisply clipped to imitate braided rows. He carried a tablet and tapped on it as Garik progressed through his workout.

"Not as much as I should, apparently." Garik was battered, and he accepted the towel and wiped his face. What had happened to easy? Kofi kept upping his expectations until he saw Garik starting to struggle.

They hadn't been alone in the gym. A blond man Garik recognized, Boris Lindemann, the founder of Lindemann Airways, arrived midway through their session. His hair was no longer blue tipped but his face was the same, and Garik remembered what Kevin had once told him. *"Lindemann likes to tell people that there's something going on in the sub-basement."* Little did the man know how right he was.

Lindemann called, "Hey, Kofi," waved and moved to one of the treadmills.

"Good morning, Mr. Lindemann," Kofi replied, ending the interaction.

Lindemann left at some point without Garik being aware. He was more concerned with the kettlebells and making sure he didn't release one by accident and damage something or kill Kofi. Later, at the pool, Kofi became a drill instructor. Diving was with a resistance belt, foam dumbbells, strap-on weights. The more Garik proved he could do, the more Kofi insisted he do.

"I thought you were the pool boy," Garik panted as he pulled himself from the water to sit on the side of the pool. He realized the difference in this and his training with Christian. Christian had let him train at his own pace. Kofi was setting the pace.

"Competitive college swimming." Kofi grinned. "And I've been told to challenge you. Are you challenged?"

"I shouldn't have tried to impress you." Garik stood, lifted a towel from a chair, and began to dry off.

"Not if you wanted an easy morning. We have an hour before lunch. How much time do you need to shower and dress?"

"I can take time for this." The pool was just them, and Garik tossed his towel to the side, wrapped an arm around Kofi's torso, and vaulted him into the water.

Kofi came up sputtering. "What was that for?"

"Trying to impress you. I'm ready for that shower now." He grinned, retrieved his towel, and headed off to prepare for lunch with the Director.

SCRAWLED ACROSS a faux stone-and-cedar wall in black iron and backlit with a soft white glow, Stamford Suites Grill welcomed Tower guests to an *exceptional dining experience*.

It said so right under the name, An Exceptional Dining Experience.

Ted Charles, the restaurant manager, greeted Garik at the entrance, taking over for Kofi. The transition was so smooth that it would have been seamless had Garik not known what they were doing.

"Good morning, Garik. You were here in the summer, I believe, on a tour with Gunther." Gunther Diehl was the concierge who had given Garik, Marisa, and Kevin a partial tour of the facilities.

"Yes, and you are Mr. Charles. I'm surprised you remember."

"It's my job to remember." He smiled. "This way if you will. The Director is already here."

Their table was nestled in a generous bay fronted by glass and a view towards the waterfront. This side of the building faced just to the northwest and the glass was protected from the sun. The room was warm but the water in the distance was winter gray and whipped by the wind. When Garik listened carefully, he could just hear it wail outside the building's glass walls.

Rodheimer invited him to sit, asked him about his morning, but didn't offer him a menu. Food arrived shortly without any further interaction with the waitstaff. The portions were impressive, with steak, chicken, and cod. On the side, cottage cheese and yogurt. Potatoes, asparagus, and two boiled eggs. Each.

"This is a lot," Garik said, as he leaned sideways for yet another plate to be added to the table.

"Big men require big meals."

Garik had never thought of himself as a big man. But Kofi had worked him hard, and the food was appealing. Still, even he couldn't consume the vast quantity he'd been offered.

Rodheimer ate with gusto, polished his plates, and called for dessert.

"I don't think I can," Garik said, pulling his napkin from his lap and dropping it beside his plate.

"Then neither will I." He called, "Ted, no dessert. We're done here."

Garik caught Charles nodding, and when he raised his head to turn away, he locked eyes with Garik for a moment, and Garik remembered the tic from the previous summer. It was back. It hadn't been there when Garik arrived at the restaurant. But he couldn't decipher the clues and shrugged it off. He turned back to Rodheimer, "What's my schedule for this afternoon?"

"You've worked that out. I knew you were smart. You keep proving me right, and we'll make something of you yet. We're meeting someone. He's useless in his current condition, so I'm putting him to work. Be good to him this time."

Be "good" to him? What did that mean? He hadn't been "bad" to anyone.

Except Justin, and that didn't count. He wasn't in the Tower any longer . . . he hoped.

Absorb, understand, extrapolate. He should be able to predict this, but again, he had to let it go. He needed information to see the future, and that he didn't have.

— 6 —

GARIK FOUND himself handed off to yet another keeper, one that puzzled him.

Kang Song, the Tower's event planner and hospitality head, a person he had *nearly* met on his first visit to the tower BACK WHEN HE WAS AN UNMODIFIED HIGH SCHOOL STUDENT, appeared in the corridor outside the restaurant in a black suit with a white banded collar finished out with diamond bracelets and earrings.

"Good afternoon, Director." She nodded her head to Rodheimer slightly, whether in respect or deference was hard to say. Bypassing Garik slotted him into his order of importance. She continued to the Director, "Thank you for the opportunity to help you."

"I am sure you will handle this assignment beautifully, Miss Kang. Kofi is occupied for the afternoon, and it was inconvenient to alter his schedule. See that Mr. Shayk gets to the lobby with no side trips. If Charity isn't at her desk, I am certain Gunther will step in." He lowered his voice, "At no point is he to be unattended. Is that clear?"

"I will do all as you say." This time, she did bow, a slight bend of the waist, before she turned to Garik. "Good afternoon, Mr.

Shayk. Do you prefer to use your last name or your first?"

"My first." He glanced at Rodheimer. "If that's okay."

The big man nodded. "One warning. I have obligations this afternoon so cannot intercede if there are problems. Colonel Brace isn't your biggest fan just now, so steer clear if you can. Miss Kang, thank you for your time. I know it is valuable to you."

He was gone, surprisingly quiet on his feet for his size. Garik thanked Ted Charles for lunch and was told, "Anytime, Mr. Shayk. Dine in or order up, the choice is yours. Let me know if you wish to dine in and are unaccompanied. I can provide a companion to retrieve you from your apartment."

Garik got it. He could dine in but not travel from the apartment to here without a handler. Very smooth.

"Shall we go, Garik?" Kang motioned with her hand, tinkling each time she moved. "If you wish, my first name is Song. Miss Kang if you prefer."

"Song. I like that. Who are we meeting?" The elevator doors closed them in, and the car barely seemed to move. In the scrubbed air, Miss Kang was vanilla and cherry blossoms, a pleasant aroma.

"I am afraid I do not know him. I am so sorry." She nodded her head in a bow, only slightly involving her shoulders. "Understand, I am event planner, but with the city, we have few events, so my time is free. I know many people here, but not this one." She smiled.

"Surely they told you his name." Someone he needed to be good to. Nothing in his head was coming through on that one.

"Oh, yes, I have him. His first name is De-Voon. I am unsure of his looks, however, so we must trust Charity to make us connected. Charity is Miss Cellers. You know her?"

"We've met." De-Voon. Garik tried to place a De-Voon. His mind was blank.

"Ah, I expected such. Thank you." She did her bow again. "Ah, we are here." The door dinged and opened. Miss Kang retrieved her passkey and they stepped out. Charity was away from her desk and Gunther was nowhere to be seen. "We have a few minutes. I will take you on a short walkabout. We have exceptional facilities, the best in the city."

She led him through a wide doorway into the glass-walled atrium, pointing out the oversized artworks that leaped from the floor to proclaim, "Notice me!" and gave him a short history of the artists and how each one came to be in Corona Tower.

Garik listened but also thought of the Director's whispered, *At no point is he to be left unattended.* The instruction wasn't unexpected. The fact that he whispered it and didn't realize Garik would be able to hear it was.

So, Director, he thought. I might still hold a few surprises. Houdini, anyone? The third time will be the charm. Then his rainbows zapped his head, he missed something Miss Kang said, and she paused and turned to him expectantly.

"I'm very sorry to ask this, but is everything okay? Miss Cellers is waiting."

Garik pulled his head together, brushed aside the lingering endorphin rush the zap of rainbows had left behind, and focused on Miss Kang's words. Charity . . . waiting . . . and that meant De-Voon. He turned to locate De-Voon and was pleasantly surprised to find a one-legged blond man with a pronounced cowlick just visible at his left temple.

"De-Voon," Garik called, raising one arm to wave.

Devon Maye looked around, puzzled at the unusual pronunciation of his name, and paused when he caught Garik. He looked him up and down, as if evaluating whether this was the same person he'd spent time with only recently. He decided it was, shifted his crutches, and grinned.

"Get over here, kiddo. I'm your babysitter for the afternoon. How's that sound?"

"Like peaches and cream." Like a big brother, an old friend, someone he could trust. Yes, Mr. Rodheimer, I can be good to De-Voon.

Especially as the broken leg was one hundred percent Garik's fault.

WHILE THE city might be in disarray, the Tower's 10-Plex was fully operational and showing the latest films. Devon didn't have permission to allow Garik into the basement research center, so they decided on an alien shoot-'em up taking place on a distant planet.

"This might make the people I work with seem normal, eh, kiddo?" Devon chuckled as he hobbled to his seat. He could stand without his crutches, but the cast was heavy, and he couldn't bend his knee. The crutches were a convenience, and he left them at the door and chose a handicapped seat with extra space to stretch his leg.

"Makes me seem normal." Garik glanced at the empty theater.

Only three other people, and they were way at the back.

"Seriously? Have you looked in the mirror? And I don't mean just the new haircut."

"Several times." They were seated, and Garik placed two drinks between them. He also had a bucket of popcorn for snacking. He set it on an extra seat for later.

"I was taller than you the last time I saw you. Not any longer. I've been the activities director for a long time—" He started to say something else, paused, and sat up and looked around. The lights were dimming, and he relaxed into his seat.

"What?" Garik asked.

"Being careful. Up here, we have to watch our words."

"The confidentiality agreement. Kevin mentioned it once."

"Any new abilities?" Devon seemed amused. "Like being able to climb the wall all the way up? Heh, kiddo?"

"Maybe a few." Rainbows. Lots of rainbows. The film was rolling the intros by then, and he asked, "How are things down there?" Not in the "research center" but "down there." Devon would understand.

Devon shared that while the upper part of the Tower seemed normal, downstairs was a cauldron of distrust between the researchers, the hybrids, and the military. Garik expected that. He'd only left the hospital shortly before. He learned the hospital on Level 4 hadn't experienced the worst of it. Brace had an iron fist on everything.

"Here's something you'll want to know, that is, I think you will." On the screen, an alien with claws for hands was ripping through the ship's hull to get at the beautiful captain who wasn't yet in her spacesuit.

"Sure. What?" Garik was enjoying the events in the movie, people in a worse situation than his. He tried to put aside that they could take off the makeup and go home to their families when the cameras stopped rolling.

"Kevin attended Marisa's funeral. It was held at St. Anne's. Her parents told the crowd that Marisa had been visiting and drawing pictures of the paintings on the ceilings, and they knew she loved the old building."

Marisa. Garik squeezed his eyes shut, trying to dam the moisture about to spill over. Even with his eyes closed, color ricocheted in his head, his heart raced, and his lungs swelled with air. The anger at what had happened wrestled with him, tried to take from him what he refused to give.

"Garik, dude!" Devon hit him hard on the knee with a fist. "What are you doing?"

"Doing?" Garik fought his lungs, his heart, the rainbows. He forced his anger inside, sealing it away, repeating to himself, *Anger gets me nothing. My mind. My desire. My way.*

"The arm of the chair. Look at it."

Garik opened his eyes, looked down, and found he held the arm of the chair, but it was no longer attached to the floor or to the side of his seat. The handle revealed the imprint of his grip on the wood.

And his seat was canted, completely unattached on one side.

"The seat on your other side is free. Maybe I should move there." Garik leaned the arm against his seat, collected the popcorn, and shifted to the new location.

Devon leaned in, "How much *have* you grown?"

Garik tried to focus on the film, the aliens slicing up the ship section by section, but Devon wanted to know everything . . . about him . . . about what had happened to him . . . where he'd been after disappearing from breakfast. Part of it Garik didn't mind sharing. Some of it was too horrible. And the worst he could only hope wasn't true, like Paul and John lying crumpled on the parking garage floor, unmoving and lifeless.

Then the aliens began to eat the remaining crew members, and for a short time, Garik's problems faded into the background, and not even Devon had any questions for him. The aliens were truly nasty, almost as bad as some of what the Tower's research center had unleashed on Bay City and the world.

GARIK FINALLY worked up the courage to ask about Dieter and his brother, Luka. They were his biggest fear. The brothers were innocents in a battlefield of committed assailants, and he was afraid for them. He'd experienced the terror and despair of the worst that life could throw at him, and he wouldn't wish that on anyone else.

"Well, I lost the opportunity to drive Dieter anywhere—"

"As if you could." Garik tapped the cast with his shoe.

"Right-o, kiddo, but even if I could. His dad hired a car to drive him—"

"His brother, Luka, the chauffeur. I met him."

"You know more than I do, then." The movie was at the end, with loud music and ending bloopers popping up to keep people in their seats for the final credits. Devon took a last sip of his drink before handing it to Garik to drop in the trash bin.

"Hardly. Are they okay?"

"Your guess." The lights were coming up, and Devon shrugged. "I visited the apartment, and it was vacant. Gunther said something about their father's treatment taking them to Galveston."

"Texas." Garik tried to picture what he knew about Galveston.

"I think they have a big cancer hospital there, likely a better treatment facility. At least we won't forget Dieter." Devon tapped his cast-covered leg and grinned.

"Right." Garik dropped the empty drink containers in the bin and retrieved Devon's crutches. He knew why the brothers had left, and it was nothing to do with a better treatment facility. Dieter's broken hand at Rodrigo's forceful push. Garik's unexpected rainbows forcing them into the cold. The limousine destroyed by Brace's hybrid goons. They had run for safety, their father willing to trade his health for his sons' protection. His sons were safe, no matter if he gave up every other thing that was important to him, even his life.

Where did Garik fit in that formula? Was he the son that needed protecting or the protector willing to sacrifice everything for those under his care?

Information. Evaluation. Extrapolation.

He didn't want to extrapolate. He wanted to wipe every path from his future, have just today, enjoy the moment without seeing it change the options branching out in front of him in a spaghetti tangle of impossible "what ifs."

"I'm ready," Devon said, pulling himself to his feet. "Good movie, by the way."

"The best," Garik chimed in. And no werewolves involved. He would take what he could get, and for no werewolves, it had been more than worth his time.

— 7 —

GARIK RAN ON a treadmill. In front of him, the glass wall. Beyond that, a series of names he had come to know and either respect or dread.

Colonel Brace, the de facto person now in charge of the human-hybrid project, even if his power was due to the force of his paramilitary hybrid forces and the money wielded by the U.S. and Canadian coalition of Armed Forces that funded the project.

Airman First Class Wu Han, whom Garik knew and had formed a bond with even before he knew about the Tower's secretive DNA-melding experiments. He sat just behind Colonel Brace and next to Second Lieutenant Ron Wilder, whose arms looked like they could break bricks.

Senior Airman Shan Vang sat on the other side of Wu Han, wearing a strawberry face and Cambodian eyes. He presented a mannerly, polite demeanor, but Garik knew otherwise.

Master Sergeant Megan Valladao, whom Garik had found supportive. She backed Brace and his policies, but she was mostly unknown to Garik. He had interacted politely with Valladao, but he didn't yet trust her.

Garik knew Major Judy Kennedy and Captain Ryan Lee from their escort service when Director Rodheimer and Colonel Brace had demanded to see him. At the time Rodheimer and Brace were still nominally on the same team, but the lines had been drawn that day, Air Force personnel under Rodheimer's oversight or the hybridized soldiers supported by the funds to which Brace held the drawstrings. Brace's hybridized paramilitary goons had won the draw, but for how long? Kennedy and Lee were on Brace's side of the bleachers.

Three more Air Force support personnel lined the back wall, standing. Garik knew them by title but little else. Airman Ronisa Kim, computer specialist; Airman Megan Franke, warfare specialist; and Airman Molly Biggs, senior logistics coordinator.

They had come to see him sweat and outperform in every quantifiable statistic they could come up with. Could he run farther, maintain his endurance longer, be the super soldier they hoped him to be?

The standard was high. Brace's paramilitary goons could do everything they had asked of him. They expected more of Garik.

And yet, and yet . . . Garik understood who he needed to impress, that his true test didn't come from Brace or his covey of tittering birds.

The true evaluators on the other end of the scoreboard held the placards they could raise either giving Garik their approval or condemnation. Approval meant he lived to labor another day. Condemnation was a one-way ticket to Level 5, the basement floor that said you were on the way out, perhaps even to be dismembered for further research purposes.

Director Rodheimer with his massive shoulders took up the

space of two men. Occasionally, he glowered at Brace, but his expertise had kept him in charge of running the program.

Halo Sunchaser had been in attendance early, but she had disappeared with a scowl at Garik's ever-improving scores, especially when Rodheimer had seemed pleased.

Senator Gleeson Arcady was new to the mix. He had arrived after the blowup between Rodheimer and Brace. Large—tall as well as wide—with a polished head, the man carried an unlit cigar and dismissed people by placing it in his mouth. He seemed shady to Garik, and he wondered what the man had over others that kept him in power.

Also from the Tower's retinue, Annie Vanschooneveld, the foreign affairs attaché. It seemed surprising to see her without Devon, but then, Garik had never seen her in her official position. She had winked at him and given him a smile at the beginning of the day.

Last, Michelle Winn, the staff development and personnel coordinator. Garik assumed she was present to fill a chair, more to bolster Rodheimer's numbers than to do anything helpful.

Garik continued to run, his eyes watching the watchers, unconsciously extrapolating what would likely happen next. Brace and Rodheimer had crossed swords earlier. Rodheimer was still convinced Garik had precog tendencies, and Brace had laughed it off, saying his hybridized paramilitary were the direction to go. Why was this one punk worth their time? All Brace required was a genetic fix for oxygen absorption and he would have the soldiers he needed.

Of course, none of that happened in front of Garik, or to be more precise, not *directly* in front of him. They had been out of sight but not out of hearing, not yet clued in to how well he could hear. Now, Garik gave them nine-out-of-ten odds they would come to words over it, and Brace would demand Garik prove himself against his hybrid goons. As if that wasn't what the incident in the underground garage had already done. Garik had bested them all, well, with Jantzen's help, and two of his friends had been taken down, but Garik hadn't known it was a fight to the death until it was already underway AND he was suffering under a DNA-triggered deficiency that was now supposedly repaired.

He ran, not out of breath, not tired. Perspiring, but that was his body adapting to the demands he placed it under. He tracked his predictions for Brace's blowup and knew he was within his fifteen-minute window for accuracy, his "precog" window, and could now even predict the men Brace would choose to battle him. Rodrigo, for sure, and he would likely choose from Jameson, Hyatt, and Simpson. The three goons Garik had taken out in The Martial Arts Center—Jenkins, Alberts, and Welling—were unlikely to be back in fighting trim. The men who had been with Rodrigo in the garage? They would be amped to smash face, likely with upgraded hardware and out for Garik's skin.

Brace finally raised his handset and barked, "Enough of this. We know the subject can run forever. I want to see him best some real men. Suit him up and get him onto a training mat."

The man stood, intentionally not looking at Rodheimer, and turned to exit the room. Garik thought, *real men.* Just on time, Colonel. I have your number down.

"THIS IS what the man doesn't know you can do."

Rodheimer had dismissed everyone from the ready room. He had out a tablet and he tapped play. The garage as seen from a security camera played. Garik was there, Rodrigo fired his weapon, and Garik blurred. Then he was standing in front of Dieter and his brother, and he slumped before blurring again and appearing before another man, this time blocking the view, but he seemed to take a hit before coming to his feet once more.

And that nearly killed me, Garik thought. I didn't have control of it, and it nearly killed me. Now I'm in control, but I don't dare go there again. I don't know what triggered that, and I don't want it to be triggered again. The jolt of electric rainbows eating at me inside, feeding me endorphin highs to convince me to do it again. Rodheimer thought they had resolved that with their upgraded DNA infusion. Yet, it still thrummed in his head, a string plucked over and over, so often it had become his nights and his days and his mealtimes and part of who he was.

Thrum. Surge. Ah, the endorphin high, then after a time, thrum, surge, endorphin high. Over and over, each time with a cymbal crash of electric rainbow, like a puddle of oil-infused water and a dinosaur walking in the distance. The water vibrates with each step, the oil shimmers on the surface, beautiful, but you know something deadly is on the way.

"It looks impressive," Garik admitted. "You people fixed that." Or so they thought.

"You are faster than anything we've managed so far, exactly

what we've strived to achieve. Look at your clothing. You can barely fit, and these were custom made for you on your arrival. We must get your body rescanned, determine the growth rate."

"New clothes would be nice." His had been too snug recently, especially in the thighs and shoulders, and some in the length of his pants. He didn't feel taller or bulkier, but the proof was in the fit.

"You can outthink anything Brace's men throw at you. Keep that in mind. You are better than them." He sounded almost proud.

"His hybrids, you mean."

"Men." Rodheimer took a deep breath, as if making an announcement he had worked on over and over yet never had an opportunity to share. "You and me, we are men, above all else. Improved in many ways, yes, but fully men. Never forget that. You will be fighting hybrids who are men, nothing else. And they have a fatal flaw, one that requires them to wear an oxygen concentrator. Breaking it won't kill them, but they become ineffectual. Keep that in mind. Outthink them in every way. It's the one thing they cannot do. Think."

Think. Garik pictured the fight in the garage. He had achieved dominance by use of his incredible speed. Was it possible to edge just close enough to use it but not give in to it? To stand on the rim of the black hole and not fall inside?

To fly like the gods and not have his wings burn up when he was too close to the sun?

It seemed he had no choice. Rodrigo was good, and if the others were allied against him, it was a fight he might be challenged to win.

GARIK WISHED he weren't so correct all the time, that his evaluation skills, his "precog" talents, weren't so close to infallible.

They were on Basement Level 3 in the recreation area. A large area was cleared and the floor marked off with boundaries. Across from Garik were his opponents, standing shoulder to shoulder with their helmets off and resting in the crook of one arm. Luis Rodrigo stood in the center, an even height with the three men alongside him. Rodrigo was dark with piercing eyes that said, *You've betrayed me twice, little man, but not a third time.*

Samuel Jameson had a scar on his face, with wiry blond hair. Huey Hyatt was more freckle than face, and Wally Simpson held his nose high, an aloof Roman god chiseled from stone.

All were decked out in paramilitary black, with the de rigueur stylized white eagle on their sleeves. Their legs were tree trunks, their arms logs, and their necks thick columns of impenetrable strength.

Garik wasn't so sure this was a good idea. Yet, as his opponents began donning their helmets, their visors hiding their eyes, and their hockey puck breathers taking the place of normal lungs and oxygen infusion through red blood cells pumped by the heart into the chest cavity, Garik felt his own heart triple its blood-transferring capacity, a repeated tympani thump in his chest moving faster and faster. His lungs swelled with more air than the room seemed to contain, and his hearing. *He could hear them speaking into their internal microphones.*

"Hyatt, left, use your knife. He doesn't have one. Cut a tendon, any tendon."

"Understood."

"Jameson, I'll feint after Hyatt, then I'll go right, confuse him. Stunner ready. I want him to die at my hands."

"Ready."

"Simpson, be my backup. Track what I do. If I don't get him, I want you to slice the icing from the cake. Electroknife charged?"

"And safety off."

Garik tracked the four of them. To the side, Brace glowed with confidence. The man knew his goons were cheating. He had selected the men, the weapons, and the charged situation to motivate them. It locked into place how Paul had managed to get the colonel's keys to his SUV so easily. The man had known, planned it all along, and had reprimanded and demoted Rodrigo just for this purpose.

Brace wanted Garik to die, and he wanted it public and with Rodheimer as a witness. Anger burned the rainbows hot, and Garik wanted to give in, give in so badly. The room burned with them, they encircled the para-goons; and even Brace, Rodheimer, and their collection of slimy eels bled vibrant rainbows.

The world in Garik's head vibrated with the need to release the rainbows and smash some goon faces. And yet, he knew that to do so was to reveal more than he wanted Brace or Rodheimer to know. He must skirt the black hole, skim the hurricane, slide down the rainbow to get to the pot of gold at the end. And so, with his grip tightly on the rainbows, he moved quickly, but not so quickly as to freeze time, just blur it a bit, confuse his opponents, remove the knife from Hyatt's sleeve, the stunner from inside Jameson's tunic, and the electroknife from the collar of Simpson's boot. He wasn't sure what weapon Rodrigo carried, and he had to step into his circle three times to find it. A contact stun-stud mounted on the man's wrist, just where he could slam it against Garik's skin at any exposed point, slowing him as he took him out.

Garik lined the weapons along the floor just inside the marked boundaries. His last move was to disable each of the breathing masks. They were sturdy, but with a firm twist, he broke the contacts that enabled the exchange of oxygen-thin air to nearly pure gas and, he hoped, completely cut off the men's airflow through the masks. When finished, he stood beside the confiscated weapons, his arms crossed, and he listened to the men behind him crumple to the floor, forcing their helmets from their heads and leaving them clawing at their throats. Garik had seen this, too. They could breathe fine at normal activity levels, but their bodies were modified to operate at extreme levels closer to what he could achieve. Without their breathing masks, their muscles were starved for oxygen within moments.

Colonel Brace leaped from his chair, clearly not following Garik's moves. He cried, "Not possible! This is . . . Rodrigo, get up! What are you men doing? Jameson, Hyatt, Simpson, say something, men!"

"Can't . . . breathe, sir." Huey Hyatt's freckles had blended into one solid red face, and he was on his knees, pulling at the chest of his clothing, trying to undo it for more air.

"Get your helmet on, Hyatt!"

"Broken, sir." Samuel Jameson could at least speak. He held up his helmet. "The end is twisted nearly off."

Rodrigo and Simpson pawed at their helmets until they found the air transfer devices and discovered that, yes, theirs were the same.

"How—" spluttered Brace, infuriated. He turned to face Rodheimer. "This is you, Director. What tricks have you played to embarrass me like this?"

"Garik," Rodheimer called, clearly pleased with the outcome of things, "what's that at your feet?"

"Hyatt had a knife up his sleeve. Simpson had an electroknife in his boot. The stunner is from Jameson's tunic, and Rodrigo wore a contact stun-stud on his wrist. It's not there any longer."

"I suspect not." He turned to Brace. "I played the one thing that could best your men, even with the surprises you evidently asked them to carry to ensure their victory. Your men are no match for what I can offer the world."

Garik glowed with his success. He even chose to overlook the Director's final words. *For what I can offer the world.* With his anger unleashed, he had felt powerful—and free of the torment of losing Marisa, his family, his friends, and his entire life.

Just for those few moments, he had felt like he was back in control once more.

— 8 —

WARDEN. GUARD. Sentry. Escort. Chaperone.

Handler.

Garik had no misconceptions, wore no blinders, looked through no rose-tinted glasses. For the next few weeks, he was restricted to the few places his passkey would allow him to go or was in the presence of one of his Tower minders.

Yet, his resentment faded. Many of his custodians, such as *De-Voon*, cracked jokes with him, sometimes teased, and felt like real friends. Others—Kofi, Gunther, Song, even Choi Bak on one occasion—were polite and unobtrusive, showing up, fading into the background when necessary, and making the transition from handler to handler seem as fluid as oil flowing across water.

Kevin Lee appeared at his door early one morning. He wore a lightweight track suit with dark banding at the wrists and waist. He grinned and held out a package, folded cloth wrapped in a contrasting cloth belt.

"Good morning, Kevin." Garik yawned and accepted the package. "It's too early for the day to start, but come in."

"Fancy place." It was Kevin's first time alone with Garik since his return, and he hadn't visited the apartment.

"Yeah, boring with no one around." Garik set the package on the counter and opened the fridge. He was just up and still in his nightclothes and barefoot. His torso was uncovered, and the light from the fridge revealed how much he had changed since his return to the Tower. Around his face, his hair now looked like real hair, long enough to begin to curl although not long enough to have any real dimension. It had been trimmed twice around his ears and the nape of his neck.

"Thanks," Kevin snorted, noisily sliding out a chair and sitting at the table.

"What?" Garik pulled out a plate of fruit. He was constantly hungry, something Dr. Jimenez had assured him was normal as his body transitioned from youth to man. Garik had pictured his words differently. In his mind, youth to man became human to wolf-hybrid-thing.

"I'm a no one." He chuckled, tapping the tabletop. "Open that."

"Okay. You hungry?"

"Apparently not as much as you. C'mon, we've got plans, and I'm scheduled for lessons later this morning. Devon's improving but he's still a slacker. I can't depend on him to absorb my caseload."

"So why are you here? I'm not kicking you out, mind you, but it's usually Kofi this early, especially when he can't change his schedule for me."

"Because Kofi can't do this." Kevin stood, threw off the jacket to his track suit to reveal the top of a snug singlet encasing a tight, athletic frame. He crouched, raised one arm, and slashed it down, calling out, "Ai Kee!"

"We're going there?" Out of the Tower, Garik meant, not believing it possible.

"Now who's dreaming?" Kevin pushed the cloth package a few inches closer. "Open it and tell me you like it. It's sized to your latest body scan."

Garik set his apple aside and pulled the package to him. It would be clothing, then. He'd been forced to upgrade his wardrobe two times since being back in the Tower, each time requiring a complete replacement of every item. His height had settled at just under six-four, but his shoulders and shoe size refused to do the same. His neck was now a stovepipe, and he shaved daily. Wolf boy, indeed, forced to shave off his DNA heritage each morning to appear as a human being.

He shook out the package to find a loose, long sleeve jacket and matching pants.

"I'm guessing training this morning?"

"My treat. I invited you to Ai Kee! and then you had to get yourself tied up in all this. I have decided there's no time like the present."

"And they gave you permission—"

"Mr. Rodheimer jumped on it. Best all-around training a soldier can get—" He cut off his words. "Sorry. I know you don't like the soldier thing."

Garik shrugged. He lifted a black item wrapped in clear plastic. "This?"

"Compression shorts in your size. Guaranteed."

"Part of the uniform?" He ripped open the plastic to reveal mid-thigh, shiny fabric banded with white stitching.

"No, but you might appreciate that better than the old-world alternative." Kevin laughed. "Get changed. Let's see how quick you pick up on what I'm already really good at. Like Neo, download into your brain, zap, zap, martial arts expert."

THE REAL training equipment was in the basement, and with Kevin as his monitor, Garik tagged along. The chaperoning was seamless, with Kevin remaining almost within touching distance, whistling under his breath occasionally, mentioning that it had felt like it was still winter outside on the way in that morning.

Still winter outside. There were balconies Garik could access, though with his minders, he rarely did. Looking through his windows, there was a hint of green across the city, and he knew he would soon lose sight of City View Apartments. Then, he had nothing there, nothing except memories. Even Irina, his aunt. Arik had made it clear he was no longer welcome.

It was still early, and in the sunless basement, few people were out. Kevin had allowed that many people did wear tees under the uniform jacket, so Garik had pulled on the black shorts, found a black tee to match, and tied the jacket with the contrasting cloth belt. His shoes were black, lightweight kick trainers that were more slipper than shoe. His heavier shoes were off to the side for when they finished their training.

Partway through their training session, Stephen Klandermans appeared, easily recognizable with his kinky blond dreadlocks. He had shed his tattered clothes and boasted broad shoulders under a fitted, patterned tee and black shorts with Kick It in lime green letters on the front. His socks picked up on the lime, and his shoes were vivid yellow. His workout bag matched the black and green.

"Hey, Garik!" Stephen walked to the edge of the mat. He smiled broadly. "That's your face, but where did you get that body? I want one of those."

"Hey back, Stephen." Garik waved, and Kevin took the opportunity to turn Garik's lack of attention into a lesson and flipped the bigger man onto his back. Garik hit hard and lay panting.

"See?" Kevin knelt at his side. "Never look away. Even for an old friend. Let's take a short break."

"If you want. I know I do." At least until his back stopped hurting.

"Am I an old friend?" Stephen called, walking up, laughter in his words as he looked down at Garik.

"Not anymore." Garik shifted, in one motion came to his feet, and he straightened his sleeves. He was surprised how tall Stephen *wasn't* anymore. And his smell, the crisp aroma of arctic ice. Clear, pure, nothing else.

"I see they finally decided you were good enough to train with Kevin. He's unrelenting. Has he taken you to the wall, yet? He's now timing us. The last one up gets to clean the changing rooms."

"Maybe I should avoid the climbing wall." Garik missed this, people. One at a time was great, but he had lost something without a familiar river of people flowing through his life.

"Ineke is on her way. She's helping me with my gymnastics technique. Will you be here long? She would enjoy seeing you. And if not, well, I will enjoy seeing her see you." Stephen laughed. "See, there's Benjamin. Will he wave? Likely not. Benjamin!"

Ineke Van Stekelenburg was a hybrid modified with an ant for strength. Garik had never seen her spit formic acid—which he had been assured she could—but he knew she was strong. Benjamin Fuest, with caterpillar DNA, had clearly not undergone his metamorphosis stage, as he had demonstrated no skills at all. He hadn't yet been responsive to Garik in a friendly way.

Their attention shifted to a group entering the recreational area. Halo Sunchaser, in a mango headwrap and fresh green wraparound robe, emerged from a sea spray of aides and hangers on, the forefront of an incoming tide headed directly toward Garik in his martial arts uniform. Garik recognized Raymond Layton, the center's special events coordinator. He was surprised to see him on the training floor but supposed there was some cross-knowledge between many of the staff and the research fellows. Rachel Prager, who did clerical and data entry, carried a tablet and was dutifully entering as she walked. A man Garik identified as Jason Teague, although he hadn't met him and didn't know his duties, carried a slim case with a hinge on one end. Michelle Winn, with staff development and, Garik thought, the personnel coordinator, trailed the lot. He tried to make out their purpose here, when his thoughts began to turn like gears in an old-fashioned clock, and it clicked, the alarm going off.

This was about him. Sunchaser, disgruntled with Rodheimer's enthusiasm about Garik's apparent success. Layton, the man who would know that he and Kevin were down here training outside of Garik's regular training regimen. Rachel Prager, one of Jantzen's supporters, recording everything for the record, and Michelle Winn, likely to decide if Kevin had crossed a boundary that would require him to attend "staff development" courses to reacquaint him with Tower procedure.

Garik braced himself. He knew what was coming, could see it, and already grieved for the loss of something he'd only received a taste of: time with Kevin in a world that had been his home for much of the past year.

"Mr. Shayk," Sunchaser began, lifting her hawk-like nose and speaking crisply. "I see you don't feel the need to respect your boundaries."

"What boundaries? Kevin's with me. No alarms, and we have permission. Right, Kevin?"

"Ah, Kevin. This is not about Kevin. Let's not choose to blame him. I'm sure he thought he was doing the right thing. This is about you, Mr. Shayk. About your limits, your boundaries, your intrusion into your assumption of rights you do not possess. I would like to spell this out for you in the clearest way possible. Jason, if you will?"

Stephen had given them some space. Ineke had arrived, and they watched from a distance, trying not to be intrusive, but obviously listening to everything.

Benjamin, stalwart defender of his own interests, had vanished with the appearance of Sunchaser.

Kevin seemed mystified by all of it. He had asked permission, and the Director had enthusiastically approved.

Jason had a marker board unfolded, now sitting erect on its built-in stand. He held two board markers in his hand ready for use.

"A rectangle, Jason. The top for Corona Tower, and the bottom for where we are now."

"Just one?" He uncapped a marker, blue.

"One will do." Sunchaser nodded.

When he had it drawn, four easy strokes, he stepped back. Sunchaser took the second marker from him.

"This, Mr. Shayk, is your boundary, the line between your world and all of this." She stepped to the board and drew a red horizontal line to bisect the slender rectangle. She wrote *mall* on the line in neat, crisp letters. "Do you have a question, Mr. Shayk?"

He did, but he knew the answer already. He wanted to say, *I know who I am. You can quit calling me by my father's name.* However, she was making a point, and he shook his head no.

"Good. This is your world." She circled the top of the tower in red. "This is not." She inserted a large red X on the portion under her line.

"That's it?" Garik could hardly resist laughing. It had hit him. She wanted Rodheimer to know how disgruntled she was. All this to make her point, to have it recorded, all her boxes checked. To discredit Garik in some sort of battle she was having with the Director.

Garik was her chess piece, and she would sacrifice him if necessary, as long as she won the game.

Garik hadn't yet figured out the game, but it would eventually come to him. Gather the information, sort the probabilities, extrapolate the outcome.

He had already sorted out one probability. Someone would suffer, and Sunchaser wanted it to be him.

— 9 —

AFTER HALO Sunchaser's vitriolic tirade, Garik fully expected to have every freedom stripped from him.

His passkey, his access to Stamford Suites Grill, the Tower pool privileges, even the martial arts uniform Kevin had provided him. He would be locked in, escorted from place to place with his hands bound, even his clothes given up for striped prison garb emblazoned on the back with Corona Tower. Danger. Approach at Your Own Risk.

The only risk he proposed was the hole that would be left when he Houdinied out of this place. His run for freedom would generate a sonic boom of unreal proportions.

So, he asked himself. Why hadn't he already done that? He had received the DNA modification. His rainbows were under his control, if only marginally. What was keeping him here?

He understood the reasons even as he hated that he understood them. He was no longer the high school senior that had lost a summer, a fall, and a winter to the Tower. It was more than the months he had been out of circulation. His mirror said as much, reflecting back at him eight inches of height, and arms as thick as his legs used to be.

His old friends wouldn't know the person that hid in Garik's mirror, waiting to come out and mock him each time he brushed his teeth or took his razor to his chin.

And the other changes, the ones he could never talk about, never reveal. Kevin knew, and Devon, plus his hybrid friends, although most of them weren't in the Tower any longer.

The rest? He watched every word he spoke.

Kofi, well, Kofi was a great guy, but he didn't know about the human-hybrid project and what was happening just under his feet, and Garik wasn't the one to tell him. Nor Song, not that he could consider her a friend, but still, he did see her on a regular basis, and they had developed a distant but professional relationship.

Who understood him, could talk with him about what was really happening in his life? Dr. Jimenez? Unlikely. The man went into total meltdown if he wasn't addressed as Dr. Jamie. Nurse Ratchett? She thought of the hybrids as another mote in a petri dish. If it grew well, success! If not, toss it out.

Halo Sunchaser considered him the enemy. Jantzen had abandoned him, by necessity, but it still felt like abandonment. Paul . . . he had grown to like Paul, only to lose him in a gruesome fashion, and John, someone like him, gone, vanished, face-down and unmoving.

The rest of his friends? Even Dieter, someone he knew only through Ibn and Muhammad, vaporized in the heat of battle, cast aside, running to a safer place.

That left one person, Weston Rodheimer, a bear, er, gorilla of a man, someone who frightened everyone he was in contact with.

Except.

Except, except, except.

The Director had stood up for him in front of Colonel Brace. He had bragged on his skills, assured him he would continue to improve, even thought he had skills Garik knew weren't there. It might be a lie, but it was a lie that felt good, to be thought of as better than he was, to have respect, even if it was unearned and undeserved. To have someone whose eyes lit up when he walked in the room, who patted him on the shoulder, and when he penalized or restricted him, sounded as though it was the hardest thing he'd ever done.

A father figure.

Not a father. Garik had one of those, and he would never believe the Director if he said he cared about him. He wasn't sure the Director even liked him or wanted to spend time with him, and Garik knew he often didn't like the Director. Still, a pat on the shoulder, a kind word, someone who believed in him even when it wasn't warranted. Sometimes that was all life offered, and you took what you got.

"COME IN, Garik!" The Director's voice rumbled from inside his penthouse suite.

Garik stepped through the door. There wasn't a bell, and it had opened before he could knock. No one stood to greet him but the Director's massive voice.

He was in his best, grey slacks, polished brogues, a black silk shirt with deeper black woven stripes, a matching belt, and under it a black tee shirt with a label that said it cost more than every item of clothing he had owned back in his aunt's apartment. Gunther Diehl had joined him that afternoon, informing him that he was requested to freshen Garik's haircut, offer him a custom shave (clearly not an offer), and provide him a new outfit appropriate for the evening.

This was to be dinner with Mr. Rodheimer, and Garik needed to be at his best.

"Thank you," he called, the politeness coming by reflex. His nerves were on edge, and his stomach churned. He did note how the entrance seemed smaller than the last time he was here. Tighter, the walls closer, the ceiling lower.

Or he was wider, taller, larger in every sense.

Rodheimer appeared, held out a meaty paw to greet him, and when Garik took his hand, the man uncharacteristically pulled him forward to clap him on the shoulder. Not a hug, but near enough that it startled Garik.

Father figure, he thought. Hardly. Yet, the action relaxed him, drew him in, gave him a sense of oneness with the man, an intimacy that Garik had with no one else. A false sense? Garik didn't look too hard. What one needed—and desperately—one didn't inspect too closely. If it didn't stand up to inspection . . . the letdown might be unbearable.

"Follow me a moment, my boy." Rodheimer released him, tilted his head to indicate the way, and started down a corridor. He led him into a wood-paneled room. A low couch in a nubby, pale green fabric stretched along one wall. A large painting above spoke to energy and color but no design that Garik could define. A wide desk, mostly empty except for a lamp and a writing pad. A wall of shelves packed with books.

"An office." Garik stated it plainly. The label asked why they were there.

"Mine, though used infrequently. Here is what I want you to see." He pulled out what looked like a book from a lower shelf but turned out to hold files. He removed a stack of photos, laid them out on the desk, not all fully visible. In one, a well-groomed man in his late twenties, no longer especially young, but his face still unlined. Garik realized it was the Director before he had undergone his DNA enhancement. Another, a woman by a ski lift. A mountain towered behind her. She looked pregnant. Garik pulled it out from the rest.

"My wife." Rodheimer touched her stomach. "My son. That was taken the day she—" He cut off his story and pulled out another photo, this time with the Director in a hospital bed hooked to lifesaving equipment. "This is what I want you to see."

"You. What was wrong with you?"

"I was first, the original of all of us. We had to begin somewhere, and when I lost Meg . . ." He stumbled on his words for a moment, then he took a deep breath and plunged ahead. "I was in that bed for six months. What happened to you put me there. Jantzen saved me. The man is brilliant if misguided, but that's beside the point. I was under sedation the entire time. I want to know, what was it like?"

Garik was surrounded by the man's aroma, the anticipation. This was why he had been invited this evening. This was something he needed to know, and it had been denied him.

"Intense," he said.

"You move, and it's as though you disappear and reappear. Relive that for me."

"It put me in the hospital. Your people topped me off with new DNA juice, and now it's over." He studied the picture, but the one of the man's wife was on the table, and he couldn't help glancing at it. He remembered Jantzen's story, that Rodheimer had lost his wife and changed. Maybe been driven to become the guinea pig for the program.

"But when it was happening? You must recall something."

"A little." It was still trying to happen. The DNA upgrade only helped him control it, and it would run away from him again if he let it. "You don't remember any of it, do you?"

"An opportunity missed." Rodheimer sorted through the photos, lifting out one occasionally. "But no, and I want to understand how it feels. Such speed!"

One of the photos showed a youth that looked like the Director, maybe fifteen, with a dark-haired boy of about the same age. Garik picked it up. It was outdoors, and a fire burned in the foreground. Rodheimer sat on a log, and behind him, the dark-haired boy had his arms under Rodheimer's, laughing and trying to pull him off the log. In that moment, Garik saw Jantzen with Justin in the ring, holding Justin's arms just like that to keep him from injuring Alyna with his knife-wielding hands.

"You and Jantzen. Why couldn't he tell you how he felt?" It was something Jantzen had said. He laid the photo back down.

"That is a very interesting question. What prompted it?" He lifted the picture Garik had held. "A long time ago. That was our last adventure in my father's old tent, when we knew, or at least I knew we didn't see the world the same."

"Okay, then don't tell." Garik shrugged, not really understanding why they were looking at images of Rodheimer's past life. Maybe to get him to open up, form a bond of intimacy between them. It took two to go there, and the Director didn't want to play. "I remember one thing about moving so fast."

Rodheimer dropped the photo of him and Jantzen, and he focused fully on Garik. "Tell me."

"It hurt really bad, every time I moved. It's not something I'd wish on anyone."

"No, I guess not." The Director didn't sound convinced.

THE TABLE was set for three.

Garik didn't think much of it, although later, he realized the pictures in the Director's office had jarred his brain. To him, Rodheimer had always been a big, broad-shouldered gorilla guy. To think of him as a normal guy with a wife and expecting a child, a son, readjusted everything about the man in Garik's head.

The third guest arrived just before they sat down to eat. The doorbell rang, Rodheimer tapped his watch, and he called, "In here, Halo. Perfect timing, as always."

Garik's stomach dropped. Why was she here? As she walked in, she seemed equally surprised to see him. Yet, her manners were impeccable, and she greeted them both, giving the Director an air kiss and taking Garik's hand and patting it once before releasing it.

The meal arrived in several courses. When Garik had trouble deciding on which utensil to use, Rodheimer chuckled and tapped the one farthest from his plate, saying, "Outside in. Never start next to the plate."

"Weston," Sunchaser said with a smile. "You're treating him like a—"

"Like a child?" Rodheimer snapped. "My apologies, Halo. We were looking through some old photos. My thoughts were still in the other room."

"Quite all right. I was going to say like a son, the way a good parent would do. You would have been a fine father if things had happened differently."

"Let it drop, Halo." The Director sighed, suggesting this was less a compliment than a jab for some unknown reason.

"You've even given the boy Jantzen's apartment. Like a good father would. When one son moves out of favor, the next one takes his place."

Garik remembered something the man had told Sunchaser: *I am not looking for a replacement for my unborn son.* Was that what this was all about?

"I never considered Jantzen my son. Let this rest."

"No, I don't suppose it was a father Jantzen wanted from you."

"Enough, Halo!" Rodheimer's hand hit the table and rocked the flatware. His skin sparked with static electricity. "Let's settle this now. You are not to interfere in my plans for this boy. I had hoped to be able to handle this gracefully, and you've not allowed that."

"And I will not allow him to usurp my place in this endeavor. Don't try to fill Jantzen's spot with this child. He is a child, Weston. Keep that in mind."

The tension eased and the meal continued, but Garik's mind was filled with two things. He was in Jantzen's apartment. Jantzen's! How special was that? And *boy?* Didn't they have eyes? The dining room blurred, the rainbows threatened, and the endorphins surged through his brain. Then, he steadied himself, picked up the next utensil and began the next course.

His head churned, however. Jantzen's apartment! His couch, refrigerator, bed! All Jantzen's! He could hardly eat for how excited he was.

— 10 —

GARIK FELL into his bed, thinking, Jantzen's room.

Unless of course he had used the other bedroom, but still. He pictured evaporating into purple smoke and just *being in the kitchen in the morning*, no more walking across the apartment to get breakfast.

He killed the light, and with his wolfshine eyes, he studied the ceiling Jantzen would have studied. Once, he'd envied him being on the sign on Corona Mall, and now he was living in his apartment.

Better if Jantzen were here, but still exciting.

Garik dozed off, woke enough to turn on his side, kick at the sheets, and feel his breathing slow until he was hardly breathing at all.

Then the darkness in the apartment ate him up, swallowed him down, and welcomed him to the land of Nod where all dreams come true.

Especially the ones with wild wolf-boys, men who could morph into purple smoke, and other things that can only be formed from sealing wax and string.

STEPPING OUT of the apartment the next day, Kofi cautioned Garik that the Tower was under a bit of a strain.

"I needed special approval just to access the gym today." Kofi nodded as if that explained everything as he triggered the elevator, and they began moving downward.

Bit of a strain? Garik shrugged it off, still wrapped in his old mentor's apartment, imagining him watching television in the living room, heating up pizza in the microwave, brushing his teeth at the sink.

He paused. Did Jantzen watch television? He didn't know.

He understood Kofi's remark better when they exited at the gym. Tower security, the regular kind, not the Air Force or paramilitary, littered the building.

"Did anyone say why there are so many of them?" Garik watched them watch him as they walked, and he brushed off the feeling they were hoping to find trouble even if he was doing nothing

534

wrong.

"Got me. Gunther approved our workout session, but we don't dare go anywhere but here. I have to call in now that we're here, then again when we're ready to leave. I'm sorry we can't do lunch or anything. Even the pool is off limits. The good thing is we can extend your workout session."

"Thanks," Garik said sourly. He pulled off his tracksuit jacket and tossed it onto a bench. Kofi picked up a gym phone just inside a small office. Garik dropped his carryall to the floor next to the bench and sat down.

Absently, he kicked off his shoes, slipped out of his tracksuit pants and tossed them after the jacket. He wore a gray tee, tight across the shoulders but loose at the waist, and black outer shorts over red compression shorts which ran almost to his knees. His socks were red against his black shoes. He put his shoes back on and stepped on a treadmill. He inserted the key and triggered the treadmill to elevate the walking deck and set the speed to five.

Garik had moved to the stationary bicycle and on to the rowing machine when Bom So-hye, Kang Song's secretary, with her hair a swirl of pink cotton candy, showed up at the door and motioned to Kofi. Garik continued to row, but he listened. Every word was perfectly clear to him.

"I'm sorry, Kofi. We have to clear the gym."

"I have Gunther's approval."

"I regret that this overrides everything else." She shrugged. "I told Song she should come tell you, because you wouldn't believe me, but you can call her if you wish. It is very quiet about this, so do not tell everyone." She glanced at Garik.

"No one knows we're closing the gym? It will be obvious when the door is locked."

"I just know what I am to say. There is a—" and she tiptoed, leaned in, and whispered, "—manhunt happening, and all security are asked to be on the mall."

"Manhunt!" Kofi glanced Garik's direction, and he turned back to So-hye. "Who are they hunting?"

"Shh." She put her fingers to her lips. "Jantzen Hefferly. Don't tell or I will be in trouble." She turned, waved coquettishly at Kofi, and left the gym.

Garik slowed his rowing for a moment, and when he saw Kofi look his way, he speeded up. His mind began clicking, a clock tick-ing the time, lining up the gears, and coming to a conclusion.

Rodheimer's unqualified approval of Garik and giving him Jantzen's apartment.

Sunchaser, clearly jealous, and ripping into Jantzen for some reason Garik couldn't define. Then there was her obvious anger that her place in the Tower's ruling echelon might be offered to someone else—in this case, him.

Now, they were on a manhunt for Jantzen. Even the word sounded like a tribal thing. Elephant hunt. Tiger hunt. Wolf hunt. Man hunt.

Garik would like to see his old mentor again, show off, let him learn how far he'd come. Jantzen had championed him when he was at his lowest, and he had been a friend to him when no one had seen how much he needed one. Look, he wanted to say, I'm in your old apartment. Look how much we're the same.

But manhunt. Who next, him? If Sunchaser caught Jantzen, would she stop there, or would she remove the next obstacle in her path to power?

Would the next manhunt be for him?

"WE HAVE to end our training session," Kofi called, and he carried Garik's bag to drop it beside the rowing machine.

"You promised extended time." Garik only slowed his workout slightly. He didn't want him to know he'd overheard. The longer he delayed, the more likely he was to find out additional information. Locked away upstairs, he'd learn nothing at all.

"Sorry. We have to get you back."

"I'm just getting warmed up." Garik laughed and gave the oars another strong thrust.

"Can't do. Sorry. This is from the top. Off." He paused before saying, "Now."

"Sure. I can shower though, right? You can't expect me to wear this on the elevator."

Kofi looked toward the door, sighed heavily, and said, "Make it quick. If they do a building lockdown—" He felt of his passkey around his neck. "Just hurry."

Garik stripped his clothes and fell into the shower. Finished, he put on his clean things, stuffed the sweaty ones in the plastic bag in his carryall, and emerged with a bright look on his face.

"Hurry," Kofi said, already moving toward the door. "I don't

536

want to be responsible—"

They were met in the corridor by two security who stopped them.

"Where are you two headed?"

"I'm delivering Garik to his apartment. He's at the top of the tower."

"Jantzen Hefferly's old apartment," Garik tossed in with a grin.

"So, you're the one under 24/7 supervision. Shayk's your last name, right?"

"Yessir, that's me." Garik said, bright and friendly.

"Are we okay to go?" Kofi looked hopeful. He pulled out his passkey to show he had one.

"Those are no longer working."

"I have Gunther Diehl's approval to be here—"

"You can have the Director's approval, and it's not getting you anywhere with that passkey. This building went into lockdown ten minutes ago. Come with us, you two."

The security team's passkeys did work the elevator. They dropped to the lobby to discover Charity Cellers' Front Desk vacated and several military types scattered around. None of Brace's hybrid goons were in place. Portable tables were erected, and everyone seemed to be in planning mode.

A cadre of men erupted from Rodheimer's office, with the Director in the midst of them, like something tasty surrounded by a cloud of hungry gnats.

"Director, if you have a moment," one of their security minders called.

"Yes—ah, Garik! Come with me." He motioned, and when Garik drew close, he placed his hand on the youth's neck and pulled him along, leaving Kofi and the two men who'd brought them to the lobby to fend for themselves.

GARIK FELT confused at first. The Director was organizing what seemed to be a citywide hunt for Jantzen. From their conversation the night before, he had been convinced Sunchaser wanted to punish Jantzen, but the Director was Jantzen's supporter.

Now, the man who had been Jantzen's boyhood friend pursuing him like a criminal? Why didn't they just let him go? He didn't know what to think.

As search teams across the city called in, Garik knew they'd never catch the man. He was purple smoke, able to exit the smallest crack and reform into his physical self in any other location. The reports gave Garik a sense of pleasure.

"Team 6 at Fourth and Rock Island. Subject is headed south. Team 9, be set up and ready."

Subject. They meant Jantzen. They should just say it, but that's likely why they had the Tower in lockdown. They didn't want anyone to know what they were doing. Jantzen was well known, and if they were pursuing him publicly, the bad press could be devastating.

"Team 9 at Waddell and Fourth, ready to spring trap. We see subject now."

Jantzen was moving too quickly for him to be afoot, which meant he was in a car. Even in a car, he wasn't restricted from morphing. That meant he was driving . . . alone? If not, someone else could take over.

Unless they had used dart guns—or something worse—to disable everyone else in the car, forcing Jantzen to retain his solid form. If he were the only one able to man the wheel, he could be pursued until the car was brought to a halt. But even then, he would vanish in front of their eyes. How did they plan to get around that, force him to drive into a hermetically sealed building? That was likely impossible. How silly did they think Jantzen was? He wouldn't fall for any of their ridiculous shenanigans.

The radios lighted up again.

"Team 9, that's a no-go. Repeat, a no-go. Capture failed. Subject turning south on Ninth. Repeat, south on Ninth. Who's south on Ninth?"

"Team 4 arriving on Ninth. Stopping now. Repeat, stopping now. Setting up as I speak. Team 4 out."

Garik moved beside the Director. "What do they mean, setting up? What are they setting up?"

"Something I couldn't talk Halo out of. I know you looked up to Jantzen—"

"Looked up to?" Garik nearly hit panic mode.

"We don't think this will damage him too much—"

"He's your friend." Garik had seen the picture. The last camping trip. "You have to stop them."

"It is in process already. Jantzen could have stopped this before it began. Now, we're finishing what he started."

"What are they going to do to him?" He's your friend! Yet,

Garik remembered what else the Director had said. They no longer saw the world the same. Jantzen had told him something similar. Whatever the reason, the Director was willing to let Sunchaser potentially damage Jantzen in some way to force him back into the Tower.

"We have theorized that we can prevent Jantzen's transformation from a solid to what is essentially a gaseous state through a pressure wave. It should interfere with the sublimation process."

"You'll kill him."

"Hybrids are pretty hardy. We can't be sure it will work, but it shouldn't kill him."

"How will you create the pressure wave?" Garik's heart raced, and he worked to control his breathing. No rainbows, not now. He needed to figure out a way to help Jantzen.

"Sonic boom derived from electrically induced lightning. It's why we've had to shut down Bay City."

"Everything's in lockdown?" They could do that?

"We've put the city under martial law. Colonel Brace has his paramilitary troops out in the city, and the Air Force is in pursuit. Tower security is filling in where necessary. The lightning we're producing is localized but strong. We don't need injury lawsuits."

Garik thought, *Jantzen, run! Evaporate, sublimate, whatever you've got to do.*

Use your rainbows if you have them.

Garik would offer him his, but he didn't see how they could help. He didn't know where Jantzen was headed, and in any case, he couldn't get there in time.

"Dear God, Holy Jesus in Heaven," he whispered. "Whatever you do, don't let Jantzen die."

Then the electronics in the room flickered, came back on full strength, and blinked out.

"Do we have him?" Rodheimer demanded.

In the darkness, no one had an answer to that.

— 11 —

THE BUILDING'S backup power supply jerked to life, indicators glowed, electronic devices clicked, and small machines made noises that said they were alive and breathing.

As screens illuminated and radios began to chirp, watches also began to glow. Somewhere in Bay City, a blown transformer had shifted power to a backup unit, industrial breakers the size of railroad cars had reengaged, and mobile devices and the Internet of all things were connected once more. The lights, now on, brightened, an indicator that city power had absorbed the load, and the Tower's basement power plant had returned to standby status.

A large screen showed multiple images around the city of traffic video feeds, several in color, most not. Some of the squares were blank, suggesting not everything was back online. A man worked a keyboard, searching though images that revealed empty intersections, with traffic lights blinking in neutral patterns, not yet fully operational.

No cars were on the streets, anyway. The larger military-type machines ignored the lights no matter what pattern they flashed.

"Where is he?" Rodheimer muttered.

Garik heard the emotion in the man's question. Concern. Respect. The frustration of a situation that shouldn't have been allowed to happen. Layers of anger washing over it all.

Finally, one scene caught the computer operator's eye, he took control of the camera, and he shifted it to pan the intersection. The image swelled to envelop three others, then it grew again to eat the entire screen.

"Enlarge. I wish to see detail."

The image zoomed past men packing up equipment with thick power leads, to reveal an SUV with the front left side crumpled around a power pole. Garik's mind involuntarily evaluated the possibility that the electrically induced lightning—the reason for the power leads—had created the power failure with its electromagnetic pulse, or whether the power pole strike had been enough to cause the damage. Gears clicked in his head, telling him that only an EMP could have wreaked so much damage. Everything had powered down, including things that should have been able to draw on battery reserves and continue working.

In the scene, now fully magnified, the camera revealed cracked plate glass in buildings. Windows hung limp in their frames. A section of curb was layered with concrete fragments, as though the street had rippled with the blast, and the surface had sheared away into dust.

How much power had they discharged to create a pressure wave that could disable Jantzen's ability to sublimate from solid to gas, to morph from man to mist, to escape any confinement that wasn't hermetically sealed?

How much did Sunchaser hate the man that she would risk the city to bring him home, even as she skirted his death?

In the image, they watched as men armed with weapons surrounded the vehicle. One tapped the cracked glass on the driver's door with the muzzle of his weapon, then he looked closer, took the door handle, pulled it, found it wouldn't open, and motioned to the men with him. One man got on a radio, and a siren began that they could hear even in the Tower. It was mere minutes before the scene began to strobe with the lights from an emergency response unit. During that time, other doors were forced open, and people were pulled from the vehicle. Giselle Harmon, modified with a sea cucumber and able to liquify and resolidify. Julia Cantos, with her boa constrictor heat-seeking ability. Paolo Leveen, pistol shrimp modified and able to shoot boiling water from his fingertips and stun his opponents with sounds up to 200 decibels.

None were moving. What had happened to them? Dead—Garik couldn't think it, refused to let himself consider the possibility—but what else could he think?

Then the Jaws of Life, peeling away the roof of the SUV. The door hinges were cut away, sparks flew, and the door was tossed aside. More sparks from the interior, and they pulled out Jantzen, limp, with blood streaming from his ears and nose.

Garik was furious. How could they have done this? He fought the rainbows, clamped down on them hard, his head resonating with the clamor of their presence, repeating the mantra: my mind, my power, my choice. Anger never brings success.

Yet, that was all he wanted. He hoped beyond hope Sunchaser hadn't killed him. If so, well, he didn't know what he would do, but it wouldn't be kind. She had no right, *no right*. No matter what Jantzen had done, he didn't deserve to die.

The world blurred with color, and Garik struggled to keep it under control. Release the rainbow, his head cried. Yet, his will prevailed as the scene of horror continued to unveil before him.

"IS HE DEAD?" Garik knew he should be asking whether *they* were dead. They were all his friends, had escaped with him the first time he had broken free of the Tower's chains, and had done what he could not: remained in the city to effect change in the Tower's control over Bay City.

Yet, that one image washed out all the others, Jantzen, his ears bleeding, his body limp in the hands of his captors.

"Apparently not." Rodheimer's deep voice seemed amused. "Watch."

On the screen, two men appeared, and they opened a case with four circlets securely wedged into preformed foam inserts. They withdrew each one, keyed it with a remote, and it popped open. One was placed on each of Jantzen's wrists, and the other two found his ankles.

"Capacitors." Rodheimer sounded satisfied. "If the man tries to sublimate, they will sense it and release a charge to stop it."

"Built in pressure wave." Garik pictured it, the ultimate chains for a man that couldn't be chained.

"Not exactly, but it serves the purpose. Come, let's locate Halo. She has been at the forefront of this, and she will wish to be congratulated."

"You approve?" Garik was still in shock at what he'd seen and heard.

"Approve? Hardly, but it had to be done at some point. I understand your connection to the man. I felt the same myself at one time, but he was no longer thinking rationally. To throw away everything we've worked toward when we are on the cusp of success? When we have you as proof? I could forgive his shortcomings, his penchant for softness toward those who couldn't further our ends, when he accepted my authority and bent to my will, but as you see, the man is no longer sane. He had no hope of success, yet he still ran. And for what? That?"

Rodheimer stepped to the screen and gestured to the three people carelessly dumped on the street, their bodies lined up but not in any way cared for. It was Jantzen they were after. The others didn't matter, or so it seemed.

Garik was gutted, his sense of right and wrong spilling from him unchecked and tangled. Rodheimer, for whom he'd developed a grudging admiration, and Jantzen, for whom he didn't exactly admit love, but the feeling was close. A mentor, a friend, a surrogate father who had been his lifeline, both figuratively and literally.

He watched the men give Jantzen a shot, wait a few moments, then slap his face, once, twice, then three times until he stirred. Garik's anger surged, his rainbows surged, and he felt time around him slow as he skirted the black hole just enough to see Jantzen on the screen become translucent, causing a spiderwire film of electricity to emerge from the circlets and encase his body. He went limp again, and the men attending him acted disgusted. Once again, Jantzen received a shot, and this time, he recovered quicker, after only one slap.

Trapped. The ultimate chains. A prison not even Jantzen could wriggle out of.

The humiliation must be crushing. Garik absorbed his pain, wishing to take it all, if he could.

THEY MET Sunchaser on the way to the hospital on Basement 4. Her hair was wrapped in camo green and her matching kaftan broken only by a vine of red flowers that bled down one side. Her eyes narrowed at Garik's presence, but she immediately warmed to Rodheimer. She took his hand and air kissed his cheeks.

"My dear Weston, a step forward. You must be pleased. The wayward prodigal is returned."

"Your doing, Halo. I would have chosen a different method."

"And a more tedious one." She sighed. They walked, their retinue with them, and when they entered the elevator, there were too many people to fit inside.

"We will take this one," the Director announced. The retinue held back as indicated.

When the doors closed, Sunchaser mused, "Now to see the damage."

"We are a hardy bunch, Halo. He will likely recover."

"All the more disappointing. Some things simply need to—"

"Die?" Rodheimer cut in the word harshly, his face going dark.

She looked at him, glanced at Garik, and pursed her lips in thought. "I intended to say step out of the way. No one wishes harm to Jantzen. He has been a stalwart leg of this program, indispensable. It is simply time for him to realize his usefulness is over, and we are ready to move forward without him."

"Yes," Rodheimer said, his face relaxing. "I concur. You, Halo, must also realize *how* we are moving forward."

"The boy." She didn't sound pleased.

"Of course."

"He will not take Jantzen's place. He may be in his apartment, but he does not have his—"

"I have not said he is taking Jantzen's place. We have discussed this. He is using a vacant apartment that Jantzen no longer requires. If Jantzen comes to his senses and makes this right—"

The elevator dinged, Sunchaser's expression hardened, and they moved forward before Rodheimer could finish.

Garik understood perfectly. Jantzen was being given a second chance, one that didn't make Sunchaser happy. The ribbon-floored corridor led them to a discovery that would either reveal that Jantzen had survived, or his capture had damaged him beyond repair.

At least he was alive. For that, Garik thanked God for answering his prayer.

INSIDE THE trauma ward, Garik was relieved to learn that none of those brought in with Jantzen was being dumped directly into Basement 5's holding cells for genetic misfits who hadn't matured to standard in the human-hybrid program's quest for the perfect super soldier.

The corridors bustled with people and equipment, though the melee opened into a cone of free space anywhere the Director and Sunchaser walked. Garik caught sight of Paolo, his eyes closed and his head lolling to one side, on a gurney being rolled into an operating theater. What had happened to him? There was no blood he could see, but then, with the pressure wave from the induced lightning strike . . . it had broken glass and cracked concrete. How much damage could a human body endure, even a hybrid one?

They didn't enter the operating theater where the medical team worked on Jantzen. They viewed the goings on from a glass-fronted observation room much as Garik had been observed during his various tests and challenges. Three times during the procedure, the circlets encased Jantzen's body in a fine-meshed electric web, causing the medical team to jerk away. Each occurrence brought out the needle, and twice they patted his face, once hard, before his eyes opened and they were sure he was alive.

They were kinder, gentler than the team on the street, but still, it was hard to watch. Rodheimer was in observation mode, expressionless, but if Garik had to place an emotion on the man, it would be satisfaction. Sunchaser was more transparent. Hope flared in her with each setback, as though she hoped the man didn't survive.

The others in the room seemed to gravitate to Team Rodheimer or Team Sunchaser, picking their champion and certain they were on the winning side.

Garik was on Team Jantzen. Each time the man glitched, he whispered, "Dear God, Holy Jesus in Heaven . . ."

He needed Jantzen to live, more than anything he knew.

— 12 —

IN THE DAYS that followed, Garik worried the floor in his apartment, kicked his bedding off at night, and pounded whatever happened to be around him. Even Rodheimer kept urging him to be patient. He could visit Jantzen when he was better.

During a Devon visit, as Garik paced, Devon pointed out that he had developed a unique way of walking. Fluid, almost catlike.

"Why not?" smarted Garik. "Since I'm so unique around here, as the Director keeps telling me. A better topic, why won't they let me visit Jantzen?"

"They will. Likely today, remember, but back to my observation. Do something for me. See if you can touch the floor with your palms."

"Sheesh." Garik rolled his eyes, but he did it, bending over to place his hands flat on the floor.

"Six-four and you can do that. Okay, pretty good. How about your legs over your head?"

"This doesn't get me down to see Jantzen. Follow. My. Lead. Devo."

"No, it doesn't help get you to Jantzen, but until we get permission, that's off the table. Your legs over your head. I'm still the activities director, and I direct you to do this for me."

"Yes, Father." Garik sat, pulled his leg over his head, and look at Devon. "Good enough?"

"Does it hurt?"

"Sheesh. All the questions. How about this?" He made a pretzel of himself and walked through it before standing up, an impossible feat even circus performers would find difficult.

"I have some theories about you. I do have training in human physiology. And you are human, even if you claim you are not."

"Says the man with no extra DNA strands coursing through his blood."

"Says your friend. Hear me out."

"Yeah, yeah, Devo. Tell me all about myself. I appreciate that."

Garik fell into a chair across from him and scowled.

"I've been making a list in my head—"

"About me. I'm glad you think about me so much."

"Take it down a notch, kiddo. I feel like I'm your friend, but I'm also over your health and welfare, even if you do live in the clouds now. So, one. We know you're taller. The way you just moved tells me your spine has developed a level of flexibility only seen in cheetahs, some of the fastest animals on the planet."

"Timber wolf. Let's keep to the correct species."

"I'm just giving my observations. Two, your tendons, they have become more elastic, as proven by the pretzel boy."

"Tsh!" Garik was paying attention now. "What else?"

"That enormous chest? Not all muscle. I guarantee that if we ran you though an MRI machine, we'd confirm larger lungs with greater air capacity and a massive heart that pumps two or three times the blood volume as us normal folk. Mind you, I would like some of that, so that isn't a criticism."

"And my headaches?" He had shared the throbbing resonance, just not the rainbows. No one, and that meant no one could know about those.

"I think that has to do with your sense of smell."

"Yeah, right, Devo." Garik laughed. "How does my sense of smell have anything to do with my head?"

"First, your nose is in your head. Second, something in there has to make room to smell all those smells. I don't know about the size of the canine nasal cavity, but there's forty times more olfactory receptors in a dog's nasal cavity than in mine. And I bet there's a forty times greater spot in the brain to process all that information. Your brain is making room for that."

"And giving me headaches in the process."

"And likely using up all the space your common sense used to use. Now, when we get you back to the basement where all the interesting people live, how about we test those new tendons and that flexible spine on the climbing wall? I think it's time to get a new name on the leaderboard."

Garik cocked his head, absorbing the question.

"And that, too. Have you noticed how you tilt your head when you decide you're interested in what you're hearing? Don't give everything away. Hasn't anyone ever told you that?"

And that brought them back to Jantzen, the man who had taught him that lesson. He had to find out how he was doing, and he was through being told no. He stood.

"Now, Devo. Your passkey will take us down there. We have to check on Jantzen."

"Whoa-ho." Devon tapped the cast he had worn for nearly two months. "Just let me remind you that this is your fault. What else do you want me to give up for you? My arm next time? My neck?"

"That cast is about to come off. This is just an elevator ride, and the Director made it clear that Sunchaser has no say on my training in the basement or elsewhere. Say I got hurt on the climbing wall. My carabiner broke and I fell. Everyone knows I'm abysmal at climbing."

"And I know you heal like that." Devon snapped his fingers. "Something else I'd like to have. Okay, what's there to lose? Just my job. Help me to my feet."

Garik took his hand and pulled him erect, only to have Devon lean into him and intentionally catch his ankle with his good foot. Garik, overbalanced, let go of the man and hit the floor hard.

"There, first payment on whatever happens to me because I'm doing this for you. Surprised you didn't see that coming. Now, let's go."

Garik was surprised, too, and attributed it to trust. He'd had no reason to suspect Devon was about to force him down. He grinned, found his feet, and handed the man his crutches.

Jantzen would be fine. He was the best at everything. Nothing could beat the man down. Nothing.

THEY EXPECTED the elevator to carry them all the way to Basement Level 4 where the hospital was located. It stopped on the research center's lobby level on Basement 1. Security were at the door, and they instructed them to exit the car.

"No cars to the lower levels," they said, "and no traffic up. We will let you know when access is reinstated."

"We're stuck here?" Devon asked.

"I'm afraid so, sir. You can help yourself to lobby seating or visit the cafeteria." He pointed to the tables through a wide doorway just past the lobby.

"Sure." Devon glanced at the distance they needed to travel and hefted his crutches. "A wheelchair or a scooter would be nice."

"Certainly. Right here, sir." The man pulled a manual wheelchair from behind a column. He took the crutches, handed them to Garik, and adjusted a support to hold up Devon's cast.

"Thank you." Garik nodded, took pilot's position, and maneuvered Devon towards the cafeteria. Devon sent Garik for a snack, and he returned with a tray of gooey breakfast sweets.

"What's this?" Devon touched one, licked his finger, and nodded approvingly. "Never mind. Good choice."

"Not a choice. It's all they had. Have you noticed the school of fish swimming upstream?" He motioned to just outside the cafeteria. A steady flow of people, some hybridized, even more not, swelled the direction of the underground parking garage. Many looked to be from the center's office staff housed on Level 1, with others garbed in military drab. Voices leaked into Garik's ears.

"She actually has it out."

"I never thought it was real."

"Do you think she'll use it? Wouldn't that be a story to tell."

A hybrid—boasting imposing red eyes and the leathery skin of a crocodile—exposed large, pointed teeth as he called excitedly to a companion, "Someone's breaking Jantzen out!" They were pushing others out of their way as they ran.

Click, click. The gears in Garik's head turned. Information in, compute values, extrapolate an outcome. *She* could only be Sunchaser. *It* . . . the sword. The one time he had seen it in action, she had used it to eliminate a dissenting opponent. The final value was *Jantzen*. With the circlets on Jantzen's wrists and legs, it wouldn't be a fair fight.

"Now, Devon." He stood. "It's time to move. Whatever's going on involves Sunchaser's electrified sword and Jantzen."

"And you know this how?" Devon crammed the last of a sweet bun into his mouth.

"I cocked my head. Now, or I'm leaving you here."

THROUGH THE doors to the parking garage, even with his height, the crush of people blocked Garik's view. The military drab had fists raised and hooted for their choice of champions. Despite the riot-charged atmosphere, Brace's paramilitary, lodged at the high school, had yet to arrive.

The crocodile man yelled, "She has it charged, and the Director's not even around."

Sunchaser. Why would she have the sword out now? A flying

creature with long limbs, thick in the forearms, and legs that bent in an unusual way caught his attention. Massive eyes and a pointed snout told of its insect DNA, and wings at its back thrummed the air. Justin Kurtew! The man had . . . continued to evolve in the time since Garik had seen him. Now, Garik was having a hard time finding the man in the mantis hybrid.

"Devon, stay here." Garik leaped on a concrete barrier for a better view. Beyond the press of the onlookers and their cheers and chants, Halo Sunchaser vibrated with intent in an all-black kaftan with a thick cloth belt in deep red. Her headwrap matched her belt, and with her ebony skin, she was frightening. The electrified sword glittered in her hand, spitting white sparks that kissed the ground with black-painted stars.

Justin hovered over a disoriented and stumbling Jantzen Hefferly. The circlets at his arms and ankles flashed, electricity formed a spiderweb over his body, and he staggered.

Garik looked to an opening in the crowd and found Alyna Lindberg, modified with a Komodo dragon. Her claws of glasslike keratin were more razor blade than bony material, and if she were the one rescuing Jantzen, the reinforced doors in the basements were no match for her. Garik expected she had left some badly damaged infrastructure in her wake for Jantzen to reach this far.

Metal echoed against metal, a door slamming back, and an earthquake of a voice rumbled.

"Halo, you cannot continue to use the sword this way. It is inappropriate and unacceptable." The mass of people parted as Weston Rodheimer strode her way, an angry storm threatening to lash out in roiling waves of destruction.

Cannot continue. The words jumped at Garik. Rodheimer and Sunchaser had worked together when he had last seen the sword in action. *What else had she done with it?*

"Leave it, Weston. I will end this once and for all." Sunchaser tracked Jantzen, Alyna, and Justin. The sword backed up her words with jagged fingers of crackling lightning.

"You have an audience. Have you noticed?"

"And that means?" Her eyes shifted and locked on Jantzen with hawklike intensity. His circlets flashed, and he stumbled once again. Alyna stepped to him to help him.

"He means nothing to you, Halo," Alyna yelled.

"He means everything to me. Step back, Alyna. You and the fly-

549

ing creature can go free. Jantzen is mine."

Halo grasped the hilt in both hands and lifted it over her head, pointing it toward the ceiling. Energy leaped from the tip and splayed across the concrete overhead, and when she let it fall, the full force of its charge surged to envelop Jantzen. Throughout the underground facility, lighting fixtures on the ceiling brightened and shattered as the sword's power coursed through the air.

"No!" Garik yelled, and he unleashed the rainbows swirling in his head. They were his arrows, his lightning bolts, his coin to ride Charon's boat to the other side and back again to retrieve what mustn't be lost. The people around him flashed with brilliantly colored swirls, the ceiling swam with red and blue and purple, and even Justin became a rainbow bridge, a Bifröst arc leaping through the air to grant access to Asgard, the fabled city of the Norse gods. Ragnarök hovered at the edges of Garik's perception in distant echoes of impending cacophony.

Even so, there were a hundred people in Garik's way. He couldn't go through them. He had to go around each one, and electricity can travel faster than even the quickest hybrid, even when melded with the DNA of a timber wolf and given tendons of steel, bellows for lungs, and a heart that could pump an ocean of blood.

He did get to watch the circlets around Jantzen's wrists and ankles tumble to the floor of the garage as Jantzen was eaten by the power of the sword. With Jantzen gone, Garik's rainbows fled, leaving him a dozen feet short of Sunchaser. He collapsed to his knees, exhausted with the energy he had expended. Alyna let out a shriek of frustration, and she turned and began to run. Justin, freak that he was, dipped, adjusted his attitude, and flashed after her.

Sunchaser raised the sword in victory. Many in the crowd—too many—cheered with her.

Rodheimer exploded in anger, electrical sparks of his own burning those who stood too close.

Garik was overcome with dismay, and his anger surged through him. Sunchaser! How could she? He had watched part of himself die as Jantzen was eaten by the sword.

He remembered a quote his priest once shared: Vengeance is mine, sayeth the Lord!

And mine, decided Garik. As soon as I figure out how.

Book 9

The Electrified Sword

— 1 —

HALO SUNCHASER towered over Garik Shayk, and the light of her electrified sword cast fractured shadows around the bronze-skinned teen, creating brittle shards of darkness that reached out to slice anyone who dared draw too close. The rest of Corona Tower's underground parking garage was dark, the lights shattered by the sword as its power had arced through the air to consume Jantzen Hefferly, Garik's mentor and the man he had come to think of as a father figure.

In her black-and-red kaftan, with her ebony skin, Sunchaser looked a vengeful goddess. Pools of spilled ink danced as she exulted in her victory. Second-in-command in the secretive human-hybrid research project and modified with the DNA of a hawk, she had the avian's intense stare and saw herself as homo superior, a class above ordinary people.

Jantzen Hefferly, hybridized with squid DNA and able to sublimate directly from a solid to a purple mist and the second subject to be hybridized in Corona Tower's secretive human-hybrid project, had proved a threat to Sunchaser, and now he was gone.

Garik was also modified, but not by choice. He had been forcibly inducted into the Tower's highly classified human-hybrid program in an effort to create the military's perfect super soldier, but his gene-enhanced quickness from his timber wolf DNA hadn't been enough to save his mentor.

"Halo," a voice roared. "Brace's men are arriving." Weston Rodheimer, the Director of the underground research facility, with his gorilla-like shoulders and rumbling voice, intervened to take control of the situation. With each word, his limbs erupted in sparks of white-hot electricity, a fireworks display to compete with the electrified sword. Colonel Brace had vied with Rodheimer for control of the Tower's super soldier project. He had disbursed his paramilitary team of hybrid soldiers—magnificently powerful but fatally flawed—to step in when rioting had threatened the stability of Bay City and the Tower's military-funded human-hybrid project.

"I am rid of Jantzen. Let them come!" Sunchaser vibrated with her success. The electrified sword flashed in the darkened parking garage, a brilliant beacon casting harsh, otherworldly shadows, the symbol of Sunchaser's fiery triumph over Jantzen in her bid to cement her position in Corona Tower's power structure.

"Halo," Rodheimer stepped close to her, the sparks from his skin fainter only in comparison to the blazing sword, "I will break you if you reveal a working sword to Brace."

"I just won, and people are cheering me, *me*, Weston, not Jantzen. I can take anyone who comes against us."

"Not without me, and I don't intend to play."

"I don't need your permission. The sword is my creation—"

"And it took you how long to charge, twelve hours, fifteen? There will be fifty men here in minutes. Think again before you consider this your best option. We mustn't give away everything we can do."

Garik's attention jerked from his immersion in Jantzen's horrific death to Sunchaser and Rodheimer. *Don't give away everything you can do.* Those had been some of the first words Jantzen had said to him. He watched Sunchaser deflate in the face of the truth. The light from the sword was fading in intensity, telling the reality of her ability to wield it against multiple enemies.

The night had been cold, and with the growing shadows filling the parking facility, people began moving toward the doors of the underground research center for light and warmth. The back wall of the massive parking garage, now bathed in darkness, fronted Lowell Street and provided a secretive back entrance for military access to the outside world. Tires hit the concrete, ripping rubber, as the Lowell Street entrance erupted with five military transports.

Rodheimer turned his attention to Garik. "Get up from there, boy. Where is your chaperone?"

"There." Garik pointed. Devon Maye, the research center's activities director, now confined to a manual wheelchair, sat with one leg propped on a leg extension. Garik had escaped the facility twice. His movements up and down Corona Tower were now tightly controlled, and Devon Maye was his jailer. He was being reined in once more.

"Go. Is that clear?" Rodheimer radiated fury.

"Yes," Garik assented, even as he fought what he wanted to say. *No, Director. Things aren't the least clear. Sunchaser has just killed my friend and mentor. How is that going to be dealt with?* Yet, he didn't want the Director's fury focused on him or on the activities director. That part *was* perfectly clear. Anger at Sunchaser swirled in him, bleeding from him until every object around him vibrated with a rainbow sheen of churning color.

"Now," the Director growled.

Garik felt his control slip. The parking garage bled color, the rainbows surging in a pyroclastic eruption from every crack, and the world slowed around him until he was a blur, a ghost, a whisper in the darkness. A rainbow god who could move at the speed of light. Seemingly without moving, he was beside Devon, the rainbows evaporated into wisps of color, and Garik was once more a youth who should be finishing his senior year at Bay City High.

Except that final year in high school had been stolen when he was inducted forcibly into the Tower's human-hybrid project, and now that he was in, he could never be out.

THE MILITARY vehicles swung around, stopped hard, the doors opened, and paramilitary hybrid soldiers fell out and to attention, wrapped in black with a stylized white eagle flying on each arm and heads encased in helmets with hockey puck-shaped breathing apparatuses for mouthpieces. Colonel William Brace exited more sedately, with the false genial charm of a would-be Southern gentleman. A solid man with a firm way of placing each step, his straight back and white hair made him a visual force to be reckoned with.

Garik wondered if the four hybrid soldiers he had defeated in Brace's rigged contest were among them, Luis Rodrigo, Samuel Jameson, Huey Hyatt, and Wally Simpson. Their cheat weapons—

sanctioned by Colonel Brace—had been a wrist-mounted stun-stud carried by Rodrigo, a full stun gun from Jameson, a steel knife from Hyatt's sleeve, and an electroknife from inside the collar of Simpson's boot. With the helmets, he likely wouldn't be able to tell. The paramilitary troops were identically hybridized, so they displayed a uniform build and height. Their faces or their manner of walking sometimes gave them away, but Garik hunched his shoulders in an effort to be inconspicuous.

Rodheimer called to Brace, "Colonel, what can we do for you?"

"Tell me what's going on in my building." The man held out a hand to tell his men to hold back, and he walked Rodheimer's direction as he spoke.

"Your building?" The Director looked at Sunchaser, took in her expression, and turned to the colonel. "I assume you mean the building you have temporarily and illegally commandeered by sheer force."

"If you must, but mine, nonetheless." The colonel seemed pleased with Rodheimer's admission of his command.

"I wouldn't know, Colonel. This is Corona Tower, home for my research center. Bay City High is three blocks east. If you follow Stamford south to Corona and go east, you will eventually reach the school." He turned with Sunchaser and began to walk away.

By this time, most people had returned to the building. Several dozen Airmen were busy at their equipment, either working on it or pretending to while they listened to what could become a very entertaining headbutt session. A few others were scattered here and there, several of them hybrid. They wanted to be part of the entertainment, also. They weren't usually permitted into the garage, but they hadn't been stopped during the melee with Jantzen Hefferly and his clash with the electrified sword.

It surprised Garik that many of the hybrid program participants had no interest in escaping. Governments from across the world sent their brightest and best to the Tower for a chance to be part of the super soldier human-hybrid program. If it worked, they were one step closer to creating a whole new level of military power. If not, then the secrecy of the program kept the world from being the wiser.

Garik hadn't been chosen by his government. He hadn't volunteered. And each time he'd tried to escape, he had been pursued, hounded, and BolaWrapped ... nearly killed to get him back. He looked to the ramp leading upwards into the open air and to Bay

City. He could do it, run. Leap so fast the world became a rainbow-hued blur and be out that door before anyone in this place knew he was gone. He could. *He could!*

And still, the facts didn't change. He no longer lived in that world. He had been hybridized with timber wolf DNA and now boasted eight extra inches in height, a heart and lung capacity that gave him impossible durability, a newly flexible spine and elasticized tendons that amped up his speed blurringly fast, and ears that could hear a pin drop in the next room.

And then came the mental changes: increased memory, smell recognition, and what came very close to precognition, except Garik's was more like listen, evaluate, and extrapolate. He was rarely wrong.

"Hey, kiddo, think we should go in? This is over with." Devon socked his arm with a fist. He sounded like he wanted it to be over with.

And that was another thing Garik had gotten from his timber wolf DNA, the instinct to protect the pack. His pack outside of the Tower had been stolen from him, his girlfriend killed, his aunt alienated by her scummy boyfriend, his parents in far-off Russia. Every person he could share what had been done to him was here—in the Tower or escaped from it—and he didn't know if they lived or died, except Justin Kurtew, who was hybridized with a praying mantis—giving both awesome and horrifying results—and Alyna Lindberg, hybridized with a Komodo dragon, giving her massive claws that she could extend at will. They had come to rescue Jantzen and had gotten him this far before Sunchaser had chewed him up with her electrified sword.

The three escaped hybrids who had been captured with Jantzen were likely still in the research center's hospital on Basement 4, but Garik didn't know for sure. After surviving the artificial lightning-induced sonic boom that had created a pressure wave so strong that it had prevented Jantzen from sublimating from his solid form directly to a gaseous purple mist, their injuries had to be severe. Hybrids were sturdy and healed quickly, but the blast had shattered windows and pulverized concrete. Paolo Leveen, Giselle Harmon, Julia Cantos, all lost as far as Garik knew.

Who was Garik's pack? Right now it was Devon Maye. A wolf doesn't abandon the pack, not in peacetime, and especially not in a time of crisis.

"Okay, Devo, I agree. Let's head in."

However, several of the black goons with the white eagles on their sleeves had come close enough to recognize an old opponent.

"Hey, there's the thief." One goon pulled off his helmet, which was perfectly safe while he was in low-activity mode. It was when he hiked his metabolism to battle readiness that his body would not be able to metabolize the required oxygen from the air. The oxygen concentrator in its hockey puck shape did that for him. With his helmet gone, he revealed wiry blond hair and a scar running down his face. "Did you enjoy my stunner, scum? You had no right to it. My property, and I want it back."

"Jameson," Brace called, his voice loud and sharp. When the blond man didn't respond, Brace turned to another man. "Rodrigo, control your man or you *will* be in the kitchen tonight peeling potatoes."

"Private Jameson!" The man, Rodrigo, still helmeted, lifted a stone from the floor, let it fly surprisingly hard, and impacted Jameson in the back of the head.

"Hey, I ain't no private." Jameson rubbed his head.

"You will be if you continue down the road you're on. Helmet on, mister. We are here to do a job, not play out your private fantasies."

"You and your crip friend, I don't forget a face." Jameson shoved his helmet on his head, and he turned to walk away, his tree trunk legs pumping in his black suit.

"Hey, kiddo, I can walk if you don't want to push." Devon's voice was barely under control.

"I could take him," Garik growled as he set the wheelchair into motion.

"And I'm in a cast. I couldn't."

And you're my pack. I'd do it for you. He didn't say that. It was understood. It's just the way wolves were.

Timber wolves, especially, and that was Garik, bone and marrow. Human was what he used to be. Now, he was more.

— 2 —

AS GARIK and Devon moved back into the research center, the mood had already taken a celebratory air, especially among the hybrids. The main campus cafeteria, where most of the successful hy-

556

brids were required to dine, was on the lobby level—Basement Level 1—and as Garik and Devon walked by, a jubilant cheerfulness spilled out.

"So, my friend is killed, and they celebrate." Garik growled the words under his breath.

"You're just behind me, kiddo. I can hear you." Devon's voice was calmer but barely steady. "Jantzen's not the issue. The sword is. Let's go in, catch the tone of the crowd. Besides, I haven't seen some of these people since Kevin stepped in to help me out."

Devon would know most of them. As the activities director—and he would be again as soon as his cast was removed—he had planned and overseen most of their training regimens and could call them by name.

A familiar group was off to one side, already in party mode, and Garik headed Devon's wheelchair their direction.

"Devon!" A coffee-colored woman with a dark halo of hair called to them. Melanie Hatherill was modified for speed but with DNA from a hippopotamus. Instead of Garik's tall, lithe shape, with his flexible backbone, she wore long legs and a high waist, a different enhancement for quickness. She spoke in a separated, hard fashion, each word coming across as a complete sentence. "Come. We. Are. Having. A. Discussion."

"Cripple!" Louise King, wearing a flowing robe to disguise the winglike structures under her arms, her nod to her butterfly extraction. She displayed bright and colorful designs undulating across her pale skin. She could retain and release toxins at a touch, a deadly tactic if she wished to deploy it.

"Not much longer, Louise," Devon responded. "I can already walk if my slave will get my crutches."

"Yes, massa." Garik picked up on what Devon had just done: diluted the reason they were together. No one would ask why Garik was with Devon, forcing them to explain that the younger man was under constant supervision by chaperones to keep him from Houdini-ing from the Tower once again. It would appear he was there to help Devon navigate the vast research center, and they would accept him as such. So, he retrieved the crutches from across the room and leaned them against the table.

"Hey, man, you're keeping this loser from stagnating in his own self-pity. Appreciate you." Joachim Warakaulle, modified with a lobster, wore a self-imposed South Pacific vibe, with skin color and hair to match. He had received special enzymes that modified and repaired his DNA when in high need situations. *"They* want us to lose focus, shatter without them constantly over us. The overlords think we peons can't exist without their guiding light. Man, they don't know us at all. But you, Garik, my man, what's with the new tallness? Thought you were all wolf, not part giraffe." He smiled and shot him a thumbs up.

"The better to eat you with, my dear." Garik's words came out sharper than he intended, as Joachim had done nothing to incite his irritation, but Sunchaser sure had, and he felt it seething just under his skin.

"The wolf now has a bite." Mike Lamonte, bovine-enhanced, with tousled hair and large eyes. "I smell anger. Is that anger I smell, anyone, anyone?"

"Was no one besides me out there?" Garik looked hard at them, Melanie, Louise, Joachim, Mike, and several others. He mocked Mike's repeated word. "Anyone, anyone? Did you see what happened? Jantzen just killed? Or am I the only one that noticed?"

"Sweetie, we noticed." Charlotte Mnich, covered by bright iridescent patches from her hummingbird DNA, tried to soothe him.

"Sweetie, we noticed," came from behind Garik in Charlotte's exact tone and modulation.

"Anatoli or Andrey?" Garik didn't need to turn to know it was one of the Burgorski twins. The tall, full-featured men had dark hair and pale skin. Their skill at mimicry came from their mockingbird DNA. Anatoli could be distinguished by a break in his right eyebrow from a childhood injury, and Andrey boasted a small mole by his left eye. Garik turned to find both men now shorter than him.

"We've shrunk." Anatoli laughed, touching his brother on the arm.

"No, Anati, I think not." Andrey looked thoughtful. "You may have shrunk. I am the same size. Garik is now a mountain."

"A mountain." Anatoli laughed again. "I know a mountain man. That's a first."

"Are you idiots done?" Garik was about to punch some faces in. Jantzen was dead. Did no one care?

"No," Anatoli said, grinning, "but what did you need?" He looked around the group to gauge their reactions.

"You people are on a completely different wavelength from me." Garik saw Fabiola Bello standing at the back of the group, a thick-bodied girl with a muscular stance and spiky blonde hair. It had been a while since he'd spoken with her, but he hadn't forgotten her honeybee-infused ability to read a situation. "Fabi, what am I missing?"

And he *was* missing something. His anger, perhaps, was throwing him off. Normally, he was outstanding at reading a situation, evaluating the information, and extrapolating what was coming. Now, he seemed a sheep in wolf's clothing. A beast on the outside and really stupid where it counted.

Fabiola pulled a chair free, whipped her leg over it, and was seated, the picture of agility. She narrowed her eyes at Garik and reminded him, "You left me stranded in an elevator once."

"Sorry about that." She and her group had been mocking Devon unmercifully, and he had taken her passkey from the elevator and inserted Raphaël Giannotti's.

"And took my passkey."

"You got it back, didn't you?" Sheesh, this wasn't about passkeys. A man had been *killed*.

Raphaël, to the side, with tree-trunk legs and a gray cast to his skin, opened his eyes wide, produced a passkey from a pocket, and held it out for everyone to see.

Fabiola took it, said, "Replaced it with Raphaël's. Best trick, ever," and she grinned. "Can you teach me that?"

"It's part of my DNA." The wolf part. "It's not something you can learn. Are you going to help me, or should I just go it alone *again*?"

"Notches, notches," Andrey said, sounding very much like Devon.

"I do say that," Devon admitted, chuckling.

"And you also say to take it down one." Anatoli this time. "But I'm enjoying this. Fabi, tell the man what he's missing, cause I'm missing it, too."

"We all," and she looked around at the others with her, "like Jantzen. Well, liked, after what happened today."

"Yeah."

"He was the best."

"Loved his magic show. Looked like real magic."

"Stood up for us."

"Okay," Fabiola said. "Enough eulogies. See, Jantzen's been gone a long time. When he left, we understood why, but he's made it hard for all of us."

"Lockdowns." Mike, the word harsh.

"And this whole military thing. Brace was looking for an opportunity, and Jantzen handed it to him." Joachim. "Never give the man the power. Always keep it in reserve, that's what I say. It's the class struggle. Jantz let us down on that."

"He was saving those people." Garik had to defend him. And the military thing? That was on him. He was taken aback that they didn't realize it was all about Rodheimer and Brace feuding over him. "They were being sent to Level 5. You know what happens on Level 5."

"Sweetie, that's why it's hard." Charlotte, with her iridescent hummingbird skin. "We loved them, respected them, wanted the best for them. But we all know when we sign up for this what the rules are. Jantzen did what he thought best for them, but it wasn't best for us."

"Jantzen needed to be taken down a notch, even if I think using the sword was too much. That was a harsh way to meet your end." Raphaël shook his head.

"But the sword!" Joachim's eyes glowed with excitement. "To see it like that, in the open, the power! Man, we could make the class struggle a thing of the past with that."

Garik was filled with despair trying to make them understand. Jantzen was dead. Nothing outweighed that.

LIVING AT the top of the forty-story Corona tower in Jantzen's old apartment, and monitored with each outing he took, Garik's thumb on the pulse of the basement research campus was filtered by several screens. Devon, occasionally, though he was mostly with him when no one else was available. He had seen Kevin Lee, the man who was acting as Devon's interim activities director, only a few times, and as he didn't live in the Tower, he sometimes knew less than Garik. The rest of his minders had no connection with the research center and likely didn't know it existed. They were highly efficient but clueless cogs in a giant machine that was there for the sole purpose of hiding the super soldier production facility in the building's enormous five-story basement complex.

Garik admitted he had seen much of what Fabiola and the others had described in his own relationship with Jantzen. He could be manipulative and secretive, and at times, Garik had wanted more from the man than he seemed inclined to give, even stepping away occasionally when Garik had needed him most. Still, when a man you've come to think of as a father figure makes a misstep, it doesn't sever your attachment to him. You forgive and move on. Your relationship is built on the good things between you, and there were plenty of those with Jantzen.

Man, he missed the guy, to use Joachim's expression.

Garik's first real clue that something big was happening came two weeks in while meeting Kevin for an early-morning visit to the climbing wall.

"Okay, my friend. Devon has suggested some climbing wall challenges for you." It was breakfast, and they were in the Stamford Suites Grill. Ted Charles, the manager, had been excited to see them and had welcomed them with fresh croissants steaming in a basket.

"I'm more awake at ten." Garik was awake enough, however, to break open one of the croissants and inhale the steam before biting into it.

"Ten's not good. Seven is."

"I can see." The clock on the wall showed a quarter of. "Who are you seeing at ten?" Kevin was the acting activities director through the end of the week. Devon would be taking over again then.

"No one." Kevin chewed and swallowed a bit of bread, then dripped honey on a fresh roll. "The ceremony. I'm surprised you haven't heard. Everyone will be there."

"Stop the guessing game. What haven't I heard?"

"Ms. Sunchaser is getting a promotion. The lobby will be filled."

"The lobby will be filled." Garik searched his head. Lobby . . . promotion . . . he couldn't put it together.

"Still doing that, huh? How do they say it? You can take the boy out of the country, but you can't take the country out of the boy. Isn't that it?"

"I've never lived in the country. Well, since being here. Back in Russia—"

"See? Can't take the country out of the boy, and you keep repeating what other people say, not that I mind. It reminds me that you're still the little Garik I first invited to Ai Kee! inside that huge body you have now."

"But what's special about Ms. Sunchaser's promotion that the entire research center is attending?"

Kevin hesitated, and he groaned and bumped his forehead with his knuckles. "Ouch. I shouldn't have mentioned it. I didn't even think. There's a reason they kept you in the dark. You likely don't want to know."

"I do want to know."

"Probably not. I shouldn't tell you anything else, not if I value my job—"

"Kevin—" Garik growled the word, and it came out a wolf-like snarl.

"Hey, wolf boy, don't gnaw my leg. I'm just the messenger. It's a reward for the, um, incident in the underground garage."

"The incident." Where she had killed Jantzen with the electrified sword.

"See, that wasn't so bad, and I have my little Garik back."

No, Kevin didn't have his "little Garik" back. To celebrate Sunchaser? For killing the man he looked up to as his father?

The idea was impossible to contain.

— 3 —

GARIK'S FIST flew into the punching bag, sending a cloud of talcum powder flying in the impact. His hand wrap vibrated with the force of the hit. It was nearly ten, and he knew what was happening at ten.

"So, Jantzen is killed, and they give her a promotion." Garik growled the words, and he slammed into the punching bag again.

"Easy, champ," Kofi Mandela called. He was officially the Stamford Suites pool boy, but he also served as gofer and general "fill in the blank" positions. Right now, he was assigned to oversee Garik's time in the Stamford Suites gym for training.

"Easy, champ," Garik repeated as he slammed one fist for each word into the punching bag, his anger a storm cloud that threatened to break at any time.

"Come on, Garik, you can damage the bag. And you're seriously punching it. We don't have a spare."

Garik turned his head to take in Kofi sitting on the corner of a table, one leg hanging and the other on the floor, in his standard Corona Tower polo and shorts with canvas shoes. His tight hair was freshly trimmed in a braided look. He emanated an aroma of sun and water.

"Do you have any real clothes?" Garik wiped his forehead with the back of one arm. "Like these types of clothes?" He punched the bag hard, sending a haze of talcum into the air.

"And do you have to use talcum powder at the punching bag? That's what I want to know." Kofi held a tablet, and he hadn't looked up yet.

"What do you care?" Garik faced the bag and punched it twice more, wham! wham! and looked back to Kofi. "You've yet to join me in a practice session once. You know that? Every day you're with me, and not once have you joined in."

"Not my job." Kofi finally looked up. Kofi had been taller than Garik when they first met, but in the past months, Garik had out-stripped him. Kofi was no wimp, however.

"Let's make it your job. How about that?" Wham, wham!

"Like in the pool? Once was enough for me." On their first training session, Kofi had pushed Garik hard. As a reward, Garik had tossed Kofi in the pool. Kofi hadn't let him forget.

"Not enough for me." Garik punched again and again, faster and faster, not letting up, blanking out everything except the blurring of his fists into the bag.

"Enough," Kofi said, this time at Garik's back, and he touched his shoulder to get his attention.

The connection of hand to skin whirled Garik around, and in a blur of gym and punching bag and treadmills and braided hair and sun and water and Corona colors, Kofi was flat of his back, and Garik knelt over him, his forearm against the man's chest, leaving Kofi's eyes wide with a look of . . . amazement? fear? shock?

"Not enough," Garik said, not even winded. "Not enough, ever, Kofi. C'mon, get changed and challenge me. Show me you're better than me. I'm up for it."

"I don't know if I am. You don't see how fast you move. Off."

Kofi made to push Garik aside, but Garik held against him, not giving, until he saw the man's eyes harden in frustration. Then Garik was up, quick, in one motion, leaving Kofi still flat on the floor.

"You need help?" Garik cocked his head and raised an eyebrow.

"Would you give it?" Kofi went up on his elbows.

"Only if you needed it."

Kofi held out a hand, and Garik effortlessly pulled him to his feet. The pool boy leaned down to retrieve his tablet, checked it to be sure it was still working, and shook his head.

"Did I worry you?" Garik rested a hand on the punching bag, setting it swaying the smallest amount.

"You're too good to worry me. Surprised me, yes, but you have too much control to make me think you don't know exactly what you intend. What's got you so angry?"

Garik wanted to answer. To share. Have someone know his frustration, drain the wound, tell him that Sunchaser had been wrong, wrong, wrong to do what she did. But Kofi was a Tower employee, not privy to the secrets of the classified research center in the Tower's basement. And while Kofi wasn't part of Garik's core pack, not the one he had truly bonded with, he was on the perimeter. Garik felt a measure of protectiveness toward the man. They spent time together nearly every day working in training sessions around the man's real work schedule supervising the pool for Stamford Suites guests, and he had no desire to jeopardize his job with the Director.

Protect the pack. Above all else, protect the pack.

THE AFTERNOON brought a return of Kevin Lee.

"How was the shindig?" Garik sat on a bench in the basement changing rooms, readying for a session doing real boxing, not the nonsense where he pounded a bag and someone sat on the side watching, meaning *watching Garik when he wasn't watching his tablet.*

"I told you this morning that you don't want to know." Kevin was wrapping one of Garik's hands. He would wear gloves this time as he would have a real opponent, and hand wraps in the gloves made it easier on his hands—or so Kevin said.

Garik suspected he wouldn't notice the difference. When he started hitting, his anger dam burst, and he didn't feel his hands. And he healed really quick, so what did it matter?

"Here's what I need you to think about." Kevin worked a glove over one wrapped hand and began tying the laces. "Kofi told me about you and the punching bag this morning—"

"Stupid Kofi." Garik narrowed his eyes and looked away.

"Don't give me that. Kofi's a good guy, and he enjoys working with you. Be nice to him." Kevin patted the first glove, and he tapped Garik's other hand with a balled fist for him to hold it out.

"He's afraid I'll damage the equipment. And maybe I would, but when I start, the anger comes out, and—"

"You have good reason to be angry. Don't let the anger control you."

"Too late for that." The rainbows. They did control him if he wasn't careful, causing him to slip into a frenzy state that he couldn't easily cut off. He could see the connection, just not how to resolve it.

"It's never too late. Hold your arm steady." He had the second hand wrapped, placed the glove over it and shoved hard, forcing it over the hand, then pulled Garik's gloved hand against his stomach and began to lace it.

"Why no talcum?" Garik always did, felt it kept his wraps and gloves fresher.

"I use a dryer when you're finished. No need for talcum. Don't be a wimp. This is the best way. Hold out both your hands." Kevin lined them up, looked at them critically as if one might be different from the other, and satisfied, he clapped them on the outside, knocking them together, and said, "Good to go. You're sparring with Samey Borat today."

"Big guy, hairy?"

"Same Samey."

"He's what, grizzly?" The man was built like one.

"Kodiak, if my sources are correct. I asked Devon to sit in. He loses his cast this week. Don't expect him to be a hundred percent right away, but he really wants back in play."

"We're losing you, then." Garik stood, smashed the gloves together, and shook his arms.

"Like you could arrange that." Kevin laughed. "Buddy, you've got to beat me harder than that to chase me off. Did you miss the 'don't expect him to be a hundred percent' part? I'll be around for a while."

"Good."

"Oh, and why is that?" Kevin was packing things up, and he had his attention on his equipment bag.

"I need someone in my corner."

"Like I said, Devon's coming this afternoon."

"You know what I mean." Garik smashed his gloves together again, frustrated that the man didn't seem to understand.

"No, what do you mean?" Kevin, still in the bag, taking a long time sorting out the equipment.

"You're important to me." Garik's stomach turned at the admission. He had said it, and now it was out there. It frightened him that it could come back and bite him.

"What?" Kevin looked up. "I didn't catch that."

"I said—" irritation caused Garik to growl the words, "you're important to me."

"Yah! I thought that's what I heard!" Kevin leaped to his feet, smashed a fist into Garik's shoulder, and laughed. "Took me long enough to pull it from you. Let's go smash some face. Just not *too* much smash!" He hefted the equipment bag to the bench, grabbed a set of towels, and was out the door.

Garik stared at the closing door, feeling silly. That was something he didn't have figured out. As he moved toward the exit, he caught himself in the mirror. His height, but he had grown used to that. His hair, long enough to actively curl but not long enough to be tempered by length. His eyes, gray with gold flecks and just a hint of eyeshine under the changing room lights. His Armenian features and bronze skin, the most familiar thing about him.

What caught his attention was his shoulders, the definition in his arms, his waist, the way his shorts hung on his hips. Someone he didn't know. A man, not a boy. Someone formed from human and timber wolf DNA to be a super soldier, different than he had been— better, bigger, stronger.

He was bigger. And stronger, too. Better? A super soldier? He didn't see it, yet. He was still Garik, perhaps not quite human, but still wanting to be.

No rainbows today, Garik, he chided himself. *You don't need the rainbows. You're good enough on your own.* He tightened his arm, watched the muscles flex, and felt good.

Yet, as he exited the room, he doubted his own words. He was the rainbows. They were the new Garik, and until he learned to control them, they were more Garik than he was.

SAMEY BORAT took no second-place trophies when he stood in the ring. Bear country faced Garik, and it looked like Samey Borat. The man was every bit the bear's DNA he hailed from. Paws, claws, fur, and torso. Limbs of seasoned oak. Human in shape but clearly extra. Like the strongman at the circus that can lift the elephant, and you wonder if he's wearing a padded suit until the elephant's feet are six inches in the air.

"Garik," Samey called in greeting. He lifted his snout, er, his chin and huffed twice after saying Garik's name. He also had boxing gloves on, but they were twice Garik's size. He crunched them together, and the man's arms flexed with power.

"Samey," Garik returned, unsure that he was the equal of this man. Brace's goons? He *knew* he could take them, and they were big. Samey? The pit in Garik's stomach suggested fear.

He scanned the observers for Devon—there were a surprising number present—and found him standing beside Annie Vanschooneveld. He was propped up with his crutches but had one arm entwined with hers. He nodded, and Devon returned the motion. It seemed the hybrid crowd was making an afternoon of it. Steven Klandermans, Ineke Van Stekelenburg, Jacquelien Van Kessel, Bert Ellis, Lansana Opoku-Mensah, Veronika Abbink, Zekeria Salem. He noted the absence of Paul, but then Paul had been face down in the parking garage the last time he'd seen him, and that told the story of that.

Benjamin Fuest? Garik would have been surprised to see him. He barely had motive to say hello, much less gather to see the show.

Zekeria Salem was off by himself, separate from Raphaël, Fabiola, or any of the others that Garik and Devon had visited with the day of Sunchaser's betrayal.

It was when Weston Rodheimer and a newly glowing Halo Sunchaser entered the viewing area that something shifted inside Garik. In his mind, she held the sword aloft, and the white electricity of its energy blast reached out for Jantzen and absorbed him molecule by molecule, atom by atom, until there was nothing left. Fury rose up in him, filling every limb, every digit, every part of who he was. His skin could not hold it in, and the rainbows filled the room, swirling until there was nothing else.

He let out a snarl, filled with understanding. *Anger.* Emotion strong enough to override his control was key. This time, the fury of what Sunchaser had done served as his trigger. In his rage, nothing else mattered except the rainbows.

Let the frenzy begin!

— 4 —

GARIK SWAM upward through the murky haze. At the top was air and light and . . . and not the boxing ring.

"I've done it again, and I don't know what I've done." Garik moaned and fell back into the haze. He let himself be swallowed up, unwilling to deal with the ramifications of whatever *thing* he had messed up *again*.

"A NEW family is moving in." Irina, Garik's aunt, was just in from work at Fasst Market, and she set several bags on the counter with *Fasst Market* emblazoned across the front. They would be from the reduced aisle but still good, if they were consumed before too long. The breads would keep a few extra days on the top shelf of the fridge.

"That's nice." Garik, a small eleven, and slender, with the bush of brown hair and the gray eyes he knew so well, was on the couch. The coffee table was covered with a radio he'd discovered beside the dumpster, and he was certain he could repair it.

"You could help them carry boxes. They have a girl about your age."

"Why do I care about that?" He visibly shivered. He was more interested in skateboards and gaming and two-wheel, go-fast machines, even if he didn't have any of those.

"She's pretty. Her parents own The Flower Shop on Sycamore. You know the place. They put out flowers by the door every day even in cold weather."

He shrugged, intent on his radio. Doing stuff like repairing things made sense to him, and he liked it when they began to work again.

"And they might give you a dollar if you help them."

"Five dollars," he whispered, focused on a broken connector. He looked at it, considering if it could be fixed. Maybe he could trade his time for someone's help.

"They might give you five dollars."

"A box."

"Maybe not, Gari. Be reasonable." Irina walked to him, took the broken part from his hand, looked at it, and handed it back. "Maybe enough to repair this."

"Okay, I'll go." He wiped his hands and stood.

"I knew you would. You're a good boy, Gari. I'm glad you came to live with me." She tousled his hair and pushed him away. "Off with you before they get finished."

At the door, he stopped and asked, "What's her name?"

"Marisa, I think her mother said. She has an older sister, Marina. Or maybe I have it backwards. You can ask."

"I will. Bye, Iri."

And that was the day he met Marisa.

THIS TIME Garik came a little closer to the surface. He looked for the light in the ceiling, the machines along the wall, even the door with the wire-filled safety glass.

"No, Nurse Ratchett," he mumbled. "I'm being good. I don't need more sleepy juice."

He waited for the prick in his arm, and he waited, and he waited, and eventually the room grew darker, until the light faded completely away.

"I WOULD want a jet-assist bike. Maybe a Street Strider."

It was seventh grade, and they were at lunch sitting across from each other. Marisa had a tray lunch with pizza, tater tots, and applesauce. Garik carried a sandwich in a paper bag. His aunt had gone from Fasst Market to Kerre's Dive. She waited tables now, but with bus fare to get there, the money wasn't better.

And there was no "reduced aisle" to soften their grocery bill. Garik carried a paper bag a lot.

"Not me," Marisa said. "I want to be the captain of a ship."

"Seriously?" Garik was skeptical. "Even the lottery wouldn't buy a ship."

"Not own, Gari. That's silly." She laughed and was beautiful. "I want to tell everyone where to sail and how to get there."

"Oh, a people ship."

"They're all people ships. Mine would have guns on the sides in case pirates tried to attack—"

"Pirates!" He shook his head in disbelief. "That's only in movies."

"Do you ever do anything besides fix stuff?" She leaned forward. "I saw a program that said real pirates still attack ships, and they sometimes fight them off with water cannons."

"Okay, then I want to run your water cannons when you get to be a captain."

"Sure, but first—"

About that time, the bell rang, and they began to gather up their things. Garik never did learn what he had to do to be Marisa's water cannon operator, because the next time they pretended they won the lottery, she had moved on to another dream, one that was bigger and further away than ever before.

GARIK FINALLY reached the surface to a bacon-shrouded mist of delectable aromas. He inhaled, felt good, and opened his eyes to a familiar room, but one that was not his.

"Devon?" He threw back the covers, recognized the pajamas, even if they were small on him. The room was Devon's office. He had stayed here when he lived with him for a time. The bed was familiar, as though Devon had found it useful and never bothered to have it removed. The door was slightly open, and he stepped to it and pulled it wide.

"Good morning, Garik."

"Hello, Annie." Garik felt his face warm. She was in a sleeveless tee and shorts, as if she hadn't yet gotten dressed. She was cooking, and she opened the oven and pulled out a tray of biscuits. Bacon sizzled on the stove.

"Um, where's Devon?" He hung back in the doorway, using it to hide. With his too small pajamas, he felt awkwardly uncomfortable.

"I told Devon those pajamas didn't seem your size, but he assured me you had worn them before." She glanced at him and smiled. "I've set you out some clothes in Devon's bathroom. You go change, and I'll finish this up."

"Okay, thanks." He scooted past her, feeling like a small boy, and dashed for the bathroom. Inside, he closed the door and looked in the mirror, surprised at himself. An unexpectedly thick coating of hair on his jaw and chin, and his eyes. He turned off the light. Then back on and off again. Full eyeshine, and turning the light off hardly made a difference. That was the murky haze he'd navigated. He'd opened his eyes to a dark room, only it wasn't dark to him. He ran a hand through his hair, felt a difference. An inner and outer coat, with a soft underlayer and stiffer guard hairs. He turned, relieved to see it wasn't growing down the center of his back. And his hands, the aroma of his hair. Musky, canine-like. He sniffed his arm, then his armpit. Not . . . terrible, just not Garik.

Well, not Garik before the fight he didn't remember, but certainly Garik now.

He searched for Devon's razor, found shaving gel under the sink, and set it out. With his face clean, he would feel more like himself. With a shower, he was certain he would smell more like himself . . . or at least like the Garik he used to be.

Timber wolf . . . at least he wasn't something swampily aquatic. People liked dogs. There were other things that were much worse.

"CAN I ASK some questions?" Garik was at the table, now appropriately dressed in a black turtleneck—a nice nod to Jantzen, thank you, Annie—and gray slacks with leather tassel loafers. He had needed a belt, as his waist was too small for his hips and legs, and he had rummaged through Devon's closet to find one. He'd been surprised to find women's clothes alongside the men's.

"Certainly. Give me a moment." She had put on a thin sweater over pants but wore sandals without socks. She poured two glasses of juice and set them on the table. "Come help yourself."

"Sure." His face warmed again that he'd expected her to hand him his food. It was something Irina would do, and he remembered his dream of her. That was so long ago that he thought he'd forgotten it. He stood, took a plate, and loaded it with food. After he was seated, she gave herself about half the amount and joined him.

"My apologies for the lightweight clothes earlier. We weren't sure when you would wake. I told Devon this afternoon, but as you see, I was wrong." She wasn't contrite, just explaining. "Your questions?"

"That's one of them but not my first. You, here. How?"

"I should have expected that." She laughed lightly and took a sip of her juice. "Devon wasn't really mobile, so I offered to help. I stayed overnight. Next?"

"Where is Devon? Breakfast—" He motioned to the things on the table. "—he should be here. He's not working, is he? His cast . . . he has . . . had days before it was coming off."

"It's coming off a bit early. I stayed behind in case you woke. So, I get to enjoy breakfast with a handsome young man, and you get breakfast." She smiled. "Any more questions?"

"How bad was the damage if I can't remember anything?" The rainbows . . . how far under did he dive? And why couldn't he control it?

"That's not my answer to give you. Devon should be back shortly. He has all the answers you need. I can say one thing you'll appreciate hearing."

"What's that?"

"Your body has amazing healing properties. No other person I know can do what you can."

No other hybrid, he thought. As much as he liked Annie, he still found cause to be irritated. *Hybrid. Say it, Annie. Wolf man, canine critter, utter freak.*

And likely in big trouble for whatever he did to Samey Borat.

SURPRISINGLY, DEVON arrived back at the apartment still on crutches, delivered by a hospital orderly who exited as soon as he was inside.

"Hey, kiddo," he called when he saw Garik at the table. "Life's looking up."

"Right," Garik said. "I thought the crutches were last week's news."

"The cast was step one." Devon shrugged and laid his crutches aside. He limped to the table and pulled out a chair. "Where's Annie?"

"Getting dressed. She said that since I'm awake, she wants to talk to you about her plans. I told her I didn't mind if she stayed here, and she said it's her job. She postponed her flight to help you out."

"And for that I thank you." He dropped his voice. "She cooks so well I might want her to stay forever."

"I heard that. Makes it a good time for me to make my exit." Annie appeared with her suitcase packed. "And you'll be glad to have your closet back."

"No, I won't." He winked at Garik before pulling himself to his feet to give her a kiss.

"You, sir, sit back down. They'll expect you to stay off that leg and soak it twice a day. I've been in touch with the nurses, so I know, and I'll be checking in with Garik. You're too important to me to not take care of yourself."

"She's never said that before." Devon grinned.

"Devon, Annie said you could tell me why the last day disappeared for me."

"And he wants to know about his too-small pajamas. Tell him that story, too. I'm gone. The airport calls. Bye, guys." Annie clicked out the handle on her suitcase and was gone out the door.

"So, Devo?"

"Get me some food and I'll spill it all."

IT TURNED out that Garik did fight Samey, and Samey gave Garik a good fight. His size and strength were an even match. Garik was faster. Afterward was when it got interesting. Garik leaped the ropes and went after Halo Sunchaser.

"I did that?" He was surprised not to be on Level 5 and packaged up for shipment out of the Tower.

"Rodheimer saved her by zapping you with a bolt of electricity. Even then, you didn't want to go down."

"So why am I here and not on Level 5 or locked up?"

"I don't know." Devon shrugged, pushed a biscuit in his mouth, and talked around it. "But Sunchaser seemed pleased, not angry. She was the one that stood up for you with the Director. When you wouldn't wake, Annie offered to be your nurse, and here you are."

"And the pajamas?"

"That, kiddo, you *really* don't want to know." Devon grinned and shoved another biscuit in his mouth, and he refused to give in no matter how much Garik pleaded.

— 5 —

"THIS IS the real reason I convinced Annie to take you in last night." Devon had a second slice of bacon in his hand, and he bit off the end.

"The real reason?" Garik looked across the table.

"Seriously?" Devon chewed and smirked at him.

"What . . . oh, yes, I still repeat things." Garik stood, carried several empty dishes to the sink, and dropped them in. They clattered as they settled. He ran water over them and turned it off. He was using the time to process. Sunchaser. Rodheimer. Samey. "How bad was Samey hurt?"

"Oh, don't worry about Samey. Here, I have another plate for you." Devon slid it across the table Garik's direction.

"So, he's not hurt." He took the plate.

"Are you kidding? He was out cold, but he got in a few good punches." Devon stood, limped to the counter, held it and paused, then limped the three steps to the couch. He lifted his leg to the coffee table, worked a pillow under it, and leaned back, closing his eyes.

"Enough!" Garik's patience fractured. He slammed the plate on the counter, and it shattered in his hands. "I wake up in a place where I don't remember going to sleep, and no one spells things out. I know I'm good at figuring out most things, but sometimes I need people to tell me stuff."

Devon opened his eyes and glanced at the shattered plate.

"Okay, kiddo. Is this about Samey . . . or?"

"I don't know Samey. I mean, I fought him, I guess, and I care that I didn't hurt him, so it is, but—" He felt his frustration bleed from him to be replaced by a sense of loss. Childhood, innocence, his parents in Russia, his Street Strider, Muhammad, Ibn, visiting the flower shop, the way Marisa's father used to ask him to stay in the back room when Marisa was helping a customer. "I'm sorry about the plate."

"There are more plates."

"I know. I don't have control anymore. I . . . I never did this, break plates before. Never."

"I told you once about my mother. Do you remember that?"

"She died of that baseball player's disease. ALS, I think."

"One day not long before the end, she told me something. 'Deki,' she said, 'here's what I learned from all this.'"

"Deki?" Garik smiled.

"My mom's pet name for me. Get over it, kiddo. The important thing is what she said. She said, 'Before and after are two different things. Before, I was one of the best in the world. I could have won the Olympics. Everyone said so. Now, I can't even win at staying alive. Here's the thing, Deki. I'm still the same person. The before me is completely different than the now me, but I'm still the same. Remember that. Things change. There's always a before and an after, but if you, the you at the heart of you, stays the same, then before and after don't matter. You are always still you.'"

"Am I still me?" Garik wasn't sure.

"How did you feel the first time you woke up after they did the . . . *thing* to you?"

"Not different. Nothing at all." He remembered his first look into the full-length mirror in the bathroom searching for differences. "Only my hair. They shaved it off."

"You didn't feel any different?"

"Angry."

"That's not different. I've seen you angry lots, kiddo. Tell me something I don't know."

"Yeah." Had he always been so angry before? At Arik, maybe, his aunt's boyfriend. Had he ever acted out on it? He'd wanted to sometimes. He remembered being on his Street Strider after dark on Sycamore, seeing the Tower in the distance with its façade shattering into glittering shards of silicon glitter, teasing him with its impossibility. He had wanted to be part of it so badly. Now, he was angry that he *was* part of it.

"And?"

"I had fun with my friends." At the skate park. With the three shrimps at his apartment. With Marisa under the stars. "I lost all that."

"Like my mom said, before and after. That's life. Are you still you? What about new friends? If you had friends then . . ."

"Not the same, Devo."

"So, you don't have friends now. Poor, poor Garik, so unloved."

"You're an idiot." Garik fell into a chair across from him, lost in the before and after of his life. The change for Devon's mom had been her ALS. The change for him had been his induction into the human-hybrid program. But when had he really changed? Become so angry? Started losing part of who he was?

"And you can say that to me, and I'm not upset with you." Devon pushed the coffee table with his good leg and the corner bumped Garik's foot.

"Thank you."

"And Annie postponed her flight to help take care of you."

"Okay." Garik understood what Devon was trying to do.

"And Kofi says—"

"I get it. It's not the same."

"And it never would be, even if you weren't in here. You'd graduate, move on, leave people behind."

"But Marisa—" He stopped, his memories clogging his thoughts with what might have been.

"Change of tactics. Differences then and now. Let's make a list. Number one, uglier." Devon kept his face straight. Leaning his head back, he peered at him through half-closed eyes.

"Shut up. I feel lousy enough already."

"So, you agree, ugly is number one."

"Taller. That's number one." That was the most obvious, but Garik knew the list was a lot longer than just his height.

"Your hair's back, twice, I might add."

"I've always had that." He ran a hand over his head, remembered it long enough to tie into a knot at his neck.

"Forget that, then. Name me something else."

Running. He was fast, even without the rainbows. Endurance. Nothing much tired him. He could hear most anything, even someone's heartbeat—and he could tune it out, thank goodness. And smells, they were like flavor to him, the things he could unwrap from them.

"Eyeshine. I see pretty well in the dark."

"Number two, night vision. Is that so bad?"

"I guess not. I hear better, too."

"And how's that working?"

"I can tune it out mostly, but I hear things I'm not supposed to."

"I remember." Devon laughed. "Do you recall that first day on the climbing wall? You knew everything Vang and Dr. Jamie were saying about you, and they had no idea."

"Yeah." Garik grinned.

"That's three. Go on. Maybe those shoulders. That's different. You've become a beast—"

Garik cut a hard look to him.

"Sorry. Poor choice of words. A machine, how's that? Two other things I've noticed not on your list. The way you walk and hold your head."

"You're trying to make me feel better, right?" Garik looked at him, waiting on an explanation.

"You remember the boxer Muhammad Ali, don't you?"

"Of course. I'm not stupid."

"You said it. Not me." Devon grinned. "Float like a butterfly. He used to say that. That's you, now, the way you walk."

"My head's not a butterfly. No wings, either."

"No. But you never used to cock it to the side when you were listening. You don't even know when you're doing it."

"I can stop." Garik realized he was doing it then, and he straightened his head.

"I saw that, and no, you can't. Before and after. This is after. Figure it out. Accept what you can't change and run with it."

"What did your mom accept?"

"And there's part of the new Garik, able to turn my counseling session back on me. My mom . . . let me take a moment to sort it out." He paused for a time then continued. "She accepted that she could never ski again, that she would never see her grandchildren—"

"You'd better talk to Annie about that." Garik grinned.

"My turn to say shut up. Back to Mom, she focused on protecting me, I think. Making sure I knew she cared about me, and even though she wouldn't always be there, I would always know she loved me."

"You were her pack."

"I don't get that." Devon pulled himself erect.

"Her family, the one she wouldn't abandon ever, that she would take care of no matter what happened to her."

"Yeah, that's it." Devon smiled. "You described her exactly. That's how she was before she got sick, and her sickness didn't take that from her. She was still my mom, even when life was as bad for her as it could get."

Devon seemed caught up in his memories. After a few minutes, Garik asked, "What's the plan for today?"

"This." Devon patted the leg that was now cast-free. "I need a babysitter. Care to apply for the job?"

"AM I KICKED out of Jantzen's apartment?"

"Should you be?" Devon was on his Segway, and Garik had found his ZBoard still on its charging station in Devon's apartment.

"I thought with Rodheimer angry with me . . ." He was unforgiving when people went against his wishes. His anger at Jantzen had proven that.

"That's one of our stops today. You get to apologize." Devon slowed his Segway and turned to focus on Garik. "He has no patience for errors, but if you apologize, he wants to give second chances."

"He said that about Jantzen, only Ms. Sunchaser took away Jantzen's options."

"You and Jantzen must have hit it off. What Halo did was sketchy, but it really hit you hard. Any thoughts on that?"

"None I want to share." *He was like my father!*

"Your call, kiddo. About Annie—"

"You and Annie must have hit it off," Garik teased, to change the subject as much as anything else.

"Enough about that. With her gone, we'll be eating back in the cafeteria. We're on an assigned schedule since Brace's takeover. We'll have to plan around that. We need to get you onto the schedule with me if you stay."

"Sure. If I still have the apartment, you could come there. It has two bedrooms and two bathrooms." He liked the idea of a separate bathroom.

"Who would cook? No Annie, remember."

"Order up from the Grill." All at no charge, too.

"And miss out on cafeteria dining?" Devon chuckled.

At least, Devon pointed out, the military escorts around the research center, especially to and from meals, had been rescinded. Once Brace felt fully in control, he had let the facility return to a semblance of normality.

As if anything in the Corona Tower research facility approached anything resembling normality.

"HMM." The Director's guttural greeting vibrated, a rumbling, jarring noise, and it felt more ominous than a sharp rebuke. He addressed himself to Garik. "You are mobile today. I assumed you would recover."

Devon and Garik had waited in the main lobby. They had not, notably, been invited into Rodheimer's office, a slap of disapproval for Garik's precocious actions the previous day.

"I apologize for my lack of control, Director Rodheimer." Devon had coached Garik on exactly what to say. "I was disrespectful to Ms. Sunchaser, and I appreciate you intervening before I could injure her. Devon has been very kind to look out for me, and he assures me he can teach me coping skills so that it will never happen again."

Devon glared at Garik. The last part Garik had ad libbed.

"Understood. Halo was very forgiving, and for that, I accept your apology. Charity has your passkey to your apartment. Devon, a good deal of effort has been made to keep our young man out of mischief. Are you certain you are up to this?"

Devon, now caught in a catch-22 between Garik's lie and the Director's expectation only had one choice.

"Of course, Director. No more mischief. I promise."

"Then that's done." The Director turned and walked away.

"You promise?" Garik hissed the question.

"Teach you coping skills?" Devon returned the gibe. "Only if I can get you to listen."

"Not likely." Garik grinned and headed to retrieve his passkey.

— 6 —

DEVON'S NEXT planned stop was on Basement Level 3 where the soundproof training cells and the natatorium were located. The elevator from the main lobby in the Corona Tower stopped at Level 2 on the way down. Second Lt. Ron Wilder and Senior Airman Shan Vang joined them.

"Lieutenant. Airman." Devon recognized them and was courteous but not overly friendly.

Garik was even less so. He remembered a time when they hadn't known he could hear them. *Mongrels, every one.* Garik didn't have a high opinion of the two men. He stood behind them, noted how much taller he was now, and framed a retort in his head if they decided to make critical remarks about him.

They remained on as Devon and Garik exited, and just before the door closed, Garik heard Wilder remark to Vang, "Who's the big guy?" Garik thought of his hair—now grown out—and the good clothes he wore. With his new height and larger frame, they hadn't known it was him.

He smiled.

"What are you happy about?"

"Those two guys in the elevator. They didn't know who I was."

"And why does that make you happy?"

"No reason. It just does."

Devon didn't spend time on it and instead headed his Segway past the Level 3 cafeteria, where several pockets of people sat together, a couple with food but most visiting, past the training cells, and to the natatorium.

"Have you met Chad?" Devon hit a switch on the wall, and the door opened electrically.

"That's new," Garik said, "and yes, if his last name is Sherwin."

Chad Sherwin had been hybridized with bat DNA, but his transformation had outpaced the Tower's parameters for a successful hybridization. He could no longer pass for human, with wing-like arms and atrophied legs. His ability to echolocate in the dark was invaluable, so he had received functional prosthetic arms and new grafted-on legs.

Twenty surgeries later, he was still restricted to his electric wheelchair.

Chad's most unusual feature was his speech. He could communicate only in the high-pitched chirps and squeals of a bat. He spoke into a translation device, which always interpreted his words as polite and well-mannered, even when Chad was not.

"Chad's in the pool today. He's one of my most impressive suc-

579

cesses. Follow me in."

The humidity in the room felt good. It softened the air, although it didn't mute the sounds. Various people touting numerous adaptations were about, many in the water, a number not. Several were being coached, by whom, Garik didn't know. The oddest person was a misshapen lump submerging and surfacing about a person's length from the edge. It surfaced, and a box on a small stool spoke.

"So, it's true. You did make a second escape . . . and found your way back again." The words from the box were perfectly enunciated and flawlessly correct, but the thing in the water was clearly laughing at Garik.

"I don't see you flying out the door." Garik jerked his chin up, a reverse nod, letting the water creature know it had his attention.

"Because they stole my wings and gave me those. Look on the chair."

Beside the stool with the box, a pair of prosthetic arms were jumbled into a pile. Off to the side, a top-of-the-line Invacare Storm Series electric chair was charging by an outlet.

"I thought you two knew one another." Devon put his hand on Garik's shoulder to steady himself and leaned down to work his pants off his feet. He had on red trunks underneath. He tossed the pants and his shirt onto Chad's mechanical arms. Devon's Nordic heritage painted both legs lily white, but the one fresh from the cast was thinner and dry. "I have to soak the leg twice a day. This is soak one. Hold on while I drop in." Devon held Garik's arm until he was solidly over the water then let go and hit the surface with a splash.

GARIK REFUSED to change and join them, despite them pressuring him to do so. Instead, he wandered to the door, looked out to the people making their way to the training cells, some people he recognized but didn't know, a few he'd met a couple times, and Stephen Klandermans. He glanced back at Devon to find him floating next to Chad, and he slipped through the door.

"Stephen," he called. "Wait up."

"Hey, Garik!" The man raised a hand and flashed a bright smile. His gray eyes—similar to Garik's, only without the gold flecks—crinkled, and he pushed aside a thick tangle of kinky blond hair in wiry dreads. His tattered clothing—by choice—covered wide shoulders, and medicinal amulets lived in his hair. He carried a crisp ice smell of arctic purity, likely from his narwhal DNA base.

"You work with Kevin, right?"

"Sure as rice on toast. And hey, I'm sorry about Jantzen. Can't believe they let that happen to him. You two were like that." He crossed two fingers and let them slip past one another. "The man didn't deserve his end, even if he was a little off sometimes."

"I appreciate that, Stephen." The condolence tripped up Garik for a second. *A little off*, whatever that meant, but he had another question to ask. "Have you seen him today?"

"Now, like in about ten minutes. Jujitsu-nastics. My creation. Kevin teaches me jujitsu, and I add in gymnastics moves. You want to come watch?"

"I can't. I'm with Devon—"

"How's the man doing?" His expression shifted. "Hey, Dev won't mind. Come on—"

"Really, I can't. He's with Chad right now—"

"I'm there. Little Chad, that's a sad story. What can I help you with about Kevin?"

"I just—" and he didn't know what to say. Hello? I miss you? You knew Marisa and no one else did? "Just tell him I'm looking forward to our next session."

"Okay. I'll tell him just that." Stephen frowned like it didn't make any sense. He threw an arm over Garik's shoulder and pulled him in, looked side to side, then spoke low. "That sword thing? You know that was only the second time the woman has used it in public. And none of us got to see the first time. We don't mean to disrespect Jantzen, but seeing it was top of the radar. So, if we go *cool*, we're not saying cool to what happened to your man, just cool seeing the sword in action. You good with that?" He patted Garik on the chest with the flat of his palm.

"I'm good, Stephen."

"Then I got to go. I'll say your words to Kevin. You're a good man, Garik. Peace out to you." He hit him on the chest with his hand balled into a fist this time and took off.

Garik watched him go, got brushed by several people moving through the corridor, and headed back to the pool. Through the doors, the repeated sound of swimmers stroking the water and the occasional splash reverberating from the ceiling gave the place a melancholy feel.

Devon called, "Get in, kiddo. Extra suits are in the locker room."

Garik sighed, thought of Kevin and Stephen and jujitsu-nastics

581

and Jantzen and Marisa and respect and disrespect and *even if he was a little off sometimes*. What had Stephen meant? And how was Jantzen *his man*? He looked down, crossed his fingers, and shook his head. He wasn't even sure what that meant.

He looked out across the pool. It was big, and whole lanes were unused. At the bottom, no one could hear him think, and he didn't have to listen to what anyone else thought.

"Thanks, Devo. I will."

"Right-o, kiddo!" Devon shot him a thumbs up and splashed water his direction.

"About time, loser," the tin box teased in its polite, well-mannered voice.

UNDERWATER.

Warmth. Quiet. The overhead lights creating ripples of alternating shadow and brightness across the pool floor. The occasional muffled splash of someone breaking the surface. The distant fountain of bubbles dragged along behind the person as they paddled their hands, flippers, or fins to glide through the water to the side.

And none of us got to see the first time.

Everyone saw the sword in use the first time Garik returned to the Tower. Very publicly as a hybrid was punished by being eaten alive by the white-hot surge of the electrified blade. What had they not seen? When had Sunchaser used the sword that no one had been around to view it?

Even Rodheimer had validated Stephen's remarks. Before Sunchaser brought Garik's world crashing down, when Jantzen was still alive, with Justin Kurtew and Alyna Lindberg attempting to rescue him, Rodheimer had insisted, *"Halo, you cannot continue to use the sword this way."*

Cannot continue . . . *what else had she done with it?* What other terrible thing had she done that was so distasteful that even the Director would try to steer her away from it?

Someone appeared in front of him. Devon, blond hair, the quirky cowlick at his left temple frozen even as his hair swirled in the water. Red shorts at his waist sliding against his skin, shifting position, brushing his legs in a different place. A hand, thumb up, jerking. Then Devon shooting upward, hands paddling, one leg kicking, the other hanging.

What had he wanted? Devon . . . Devo . . . his friend, his roomie, the man who listened to him, didn't judge him, yet was no longer like him. Devon was . . . Devon, still ordinary, still human, still . . . Devon.

And Garik, what was he? Human? Hardly. Two legs, yes, and two arms, and a head with a nose, ears, eyes, and a mouth. But then . . . an oversized heart, lungs he could fill with an hour's worth of air, muscles that could run without stopping. And the rainbows changing the world, lifting him out of time, moving faster than the events around him, becoming a shadow in the real world, a mere thought, before releasing the rainbows into the void and becoming Garik once more.

And where was the void that swallowed him when the rainbows took control? It was out there, a black hole of time and experience that was lived by the other Garik, the one he could never know, never contact, never *feel.*

A hand, Garik's view blurred by despair, a blond head of hair swirling in the water in front of him, fingers gripping his arm, tugging, pulling him upward, Garik struggling, not wanting to give up the peacefulness of the water. Desperate not to lose the serenity of the underwater world where he was himself and no one else, and he could be who he was meant to be.

Garik and only Garik.

Not a hybrid mutant thing with incisors and claws and a howl that would chase the full moon month after month.

His face broke the surface of the water, the warmth of the pool streamed from his skin, air scraped down his cheeks, and arms pulled him from the water.

"Garik, breathe, man!"

"Turn him over. What were you thinking, kiddo?"

Garik's chest convulsed, and he felt the water pour from his mouth. He turned on his side, coughed, realized the water had replaced the air in his lungs. He hadn't needed to return to the surface. His lungs had adapted to his environment, exactly what his abductors had bred them to do. It was refilling them with air that hurt each time he coughed.

He rolled to his back, looked around, and found the crumpled man named Chad. Then Devon, his face reflecting his panic. And Stephen.

"Stephen," he called, his voice still harsh from the coughing. When he knelt, Garik grabbed his shirt and pulled him down. "The first time. When was the first time?"

"I don't understand." Stephen frowned, and Garik yanked hard on his shirt.

"The sword. When did she use it the first time?"

"On some shop, a place on Sycamore, I think. The whole place went up in flames."

Garik let go and closed his eyes. To draw him in. That's why Sunchaser had done it. She had used the sword on The Flower Shop knowing Marisa couldn't stay away, and he would be wherever Marisa was found.

Tears or pool water, it didn't matter. Who could tell? They were for Marisa, and he let them flow.

— 7 —

DEVON'S APARTMENT was dark, but determination heightened the eyeshine in Garik's eyes. He lifted the passkey from Devon's bedside table, accepting the offering as the gift it was.

No regrets. Never any regrets, not where Halo Sunchaser, Marisa Bruni, and the devastation that had become Garik's life were concerned.

Now, he intended to break out of the electronic cage the Director had built around him, even if temporarily, and find out what he wasn't being told. John Carter and Paul Gberie, last seen crumpled on the parking garage floor, taken out by Luis Rodrigo's weapon. Jantzen eaten by Sunchaser's electrified sword. Giselle Harmon, Julia Cantos, Paolo Leveen, pulled from Jantzen's wrecked SUV after Sunchaser bombarded it with a sonic blast to prevent Jantzen from sublimating from solid to gas, the only way to capture a man who could escape from anything less than a hermetically sealed room.

The sound wave—a true sonic boom created by artificially induced lightning—had broken windows and peeled away the top layer of nearby sidewalks and done who knew how much damage to the three friends Garik hoped still survived in the research center hospital on Basement Level 4. He intended to find answers to the questions no one would even allow him to ask.

He inserted Devon's passkey into his computer, gifting him wider access to the research center's database than his own limited one would provide, though not much wider. That required Devon's thumbprint on the passkey, and while Garik's eyeshine might allow him to rifle through Devon's bedroom for his passkey while the activities director slept, he couldn't very well bring the man's thumb with him to fully log into the computer.

Now, he scrolled down a list of available computer workstations, part of a closed communication system within the research center's thick, underground walls. He hadn't realized there were so many people, or at least computers. He only needed one. A smaller window popped up, offering him help. He read, *Would you like me to search the database for your contact? Upload the information you have.* A box inside the window appeared with a blinking cursor.

Klandermans, he typed. *Stephen.* Before he pressed enter, he added, *Hybrid*, and *Narwhal.* That was all he knew for sure. He held his finger over the key, cringed at the thought that alarms might ring or security might show up at the door. He was risking Devon's safety, job, and reputation doing this, but it had to be done.

He clicked and nothing happened for a moment. Then, the screen said, *Accessing Stephen Klandermans. Stephen is online and accepting messages. Continue?* Yes and No appeared on the screen, and he clicked on Yes.

Words scrolled across the screen. *Hey, Dev. Late but guess you knew I'd be up. How's the new kid? Talked to him today, but you know that. Did he survive his baptism in the pool? Ha, ha. What can I do for you, man?*

Garik glanced at the passkey—Devon's—and understood why no alarms had gone off. He typed, *New kid here. Want to have an adventure?*

"SO, YOU'VE got a *tracking device* inserted in you?" Stephen grinned. "Inserted, like, *where?*"

"Not anywhere I can easily remove it. The Director made that clear. That's why I have to have Devon's passkey, and that's why we have to be back before he wakes up. I need you because his passkey won't get me anywhere without a way to bypass the palm scanners."

"And I'm your palm scanner friend." Stephen smiled broadly. "Can't waste time, then. You are a sneaky one. I like that."

Stephen was pretty sneaky himself. The research campus ran on an aboveground schedule, with a full night for most people. Cleaning crews and night owls roamed the dimmed corridors but bumping into someone who knew them was unlikely. Still, Stephen had his dreadlocks bundled into a knit cap and wore a gray tracksuit rather than his usual tattered threads. No simple glance would connect the ordinary man walking past with the outrageous Stephen Klandermans.

Garik was dressed in a nod to Jantzen in a black hooded shirt pulled around his face with his hands covered by black gloves. It was the Jantzen from the food court screens from before he had gotten to know him. It was a stretch that they were anything alike, what with Jantzen's beard and Garik's height, but with his dark brown hair a black shadow under the hood, it gave Garik a sense of purpose that they might.

Garik's first goal was to infiltrate the hospital. Find out about Giselle, Julia, and Paolo. They had escaped with Garik the first time he'd managed to get away, certain they were being phased out of the program. That meant Level 5, possibly in cages to allow DNA or body parts to be harvested before being shunted to whatever final destination was planned for those no longer viable for use.

If they were considered beyond use then, why nurse them back to health now? Garik's only conclusion was that the researchers wanted to monitor the recovery rate of a hybridized body when subjected to excess shock waves. Liver pulverized . . . how long until a new one grows? Blood vessels ruptured . . . could the body reroute the blood flow quickly enough? Soft membranes, heart structure, even the eyes? What parts of the damaged body would recover . . . and would they be better or worse afterward? Perhaps sonic shock waves were a new way forward, the trigger to initiate the change from one level of development to the next in a newly hybridized body.

Jantzen had said the Director took six months to achieve his final form. Garik considered himself: no changes at first, then wham! and look at him now. Kevin had called him a beast, then changed it to a machine. Then and now. Before and after. Sonic boom, the shockwave that triggers the new and different hybrid to erupt from the human it had been.

What was his sonic boom? What vital thing had happened to him that vaulted him from a boy to a beast? From ordinary to something more?

Something had triggered him to suddenly accelerate his changes from human to hybrid. He needed to work out what. Information, evaluation, extrapolation. Not precognition or prescience. Rather, he would gather information efficiently, match it all together like a puzzle, and see the possible outcomes like a tree laid out before him. The main trunk revealed what was about to happen, then primary branches, each with equal possibilities, and then smaller branches diverging off those, each possible, but each less probable the further he looked along the tree.

Now, Garik gathered. Stephen was with him because Garik had seen down the path without him, and his search had collapsed into disaster every time.

"Listen." Garik touched Stephen's arm. "Now, into here." A short corridor gave access to three doors, none of which were open, but the recess got them out of the sight path along the main corridor.

"I don't hear—"

"Shh!" Garik placed a hand just in front of Stephen's mouth. *Not a sound*, he mouthed.

"Down this way." A familiar voice, Airman Shan Vang, a man who had little patience with Garik and had at one time suggested he was a failed hybrid and should be disposed of.

Airman Vang, Garik mouthed to Stephen. Stephen frowned doubtfully, then the diminutive Vang stepped briskly down the corridor followed by two of Colonel Brace's hybridized paramilitary goons in full blacked-out gear, including helmets with oxygen concentrators on the faceplates, their one flaw, and what the Tower was trying to overcome to create a more perfect super soldier with no flaws at all.

"They're gone," Garik said softly. "Vang hates me. He'd know something was up for sure."

"And you heard him. Wolf, I know, but you hear that well?"

"And smell even better. I can smell the last thing you ate on your fingers."

"What I ate?" He sniffed his fingers.

"Yeah. Squid, and you like them raw."

"And the rest of me?" Stephen chuckled. "Better or worse?"

"Better. Arctic ice. I like the way you smell." Garik stepped to check the corridor and finding it clear, motioned Stephen forward.

"What's so great about arctic ice?"

"No smell at all, just cold and brisk. Pure. I don't have to think when I smell you, well, except for your fingers." Garik grinned.

"Idiot." Stephen didn't seem particularly irritated. He pulled out his passkey. "Elevator. Hospital, here we come."

He inserted it, palmed the door, and they stepped inside. He reinserted it into the inside panel, pushed the icon for Level 4, and the car began to move.

GARIK WAS surprised to find Level 4 fully lighted and filled with activity.

"I thought the hospital would be shut down at night. Well, the lights turned down, anyway."

"Nah, man. This is their busiest time. All the crazy stuff. The rest of us are in bed, and they don't have to hide anything they do."

"You couldn't tell me?" His three friends. He was this close.

"See, I knew it might take the edge off, and I didn't want to dampen your excitement. I also know that where there's a will, there's a way. I work down here some, and my passkey is cleared. I have a back door in." Stephen took Garik's arm and pulled him along a secondary corridor with minimal activity. Once, they passed an orderly who nodded at them, asked if she could help, and when Stephen shook his head, went about her business with no suggestion they shouldn't be there.

Stephen's back door took them to a storage area. For reference, he explained that it was underneath the research labs two floors above, and that was just under the research center's main lobby where the hybrid family had gathered the time Sunchaser had "demonstrated" her electrified sword.

Garik remembered. He had watched a woman be dismembered by the sword's beam of pure lightning . . . molecule by molecule . . . atom by atom. He shivered at the power it contained to be able to do something so awful. He glanced at the ceiling. "So, the sword is stored in the research labs."

"Why would you think that?" Stephen was navigating racks, bins, and long corridors, many with indecipherable equipment, but also with paper goods and cleaning supplies.

"It dropped into the floor. It makes sense—"

"Nothing around here makes sense, man. It drops all the way down, comes *here*, to *storage*. Deep storage is safe storage. Wanna see the room?"

"Yes." He didn't have to even think about it. The sword. Marisa's sword, the one she had drawn on her MicroArt tablet. It wasn't hers, of course, but it had fascinated her, and she had scoured the Internet to learn everything about it. She had always felt there was something in the schematics the Tower had never released—a missing layer—and if it could be found . . .

Stephen opened a door with his passkey, unmarked except for B4-ES. A light clicked on as they entered. Inside was a small room with shelves along the sides. A heavy-duty door faced them with a wire-infused glass window.

"There," Stephen pointed.

"We can get to it?" Garik looked through the glass, rested his hand on the handle, and gave it a try. It didn't budge. On the other side, in the darkness, the glass case he had seen once before with the sword resting inside, glinting with the light leaking in from the small window. "I don't see the steel vault."

"No one gets in there without the big brass in attendance. The vault stays on Level 2. I'd turn the lights on and let you have a better look, but there's no switch out here."

"That's okay." The shadowed ceiling with a seam down the middle. Scissor arms to open it. The lighting, now dark, recessed into the walls. He didn't tell him he could see inside just fine.

"Come. Let's check in on your three friends. Make sure they are in one piece. Has anyone ever told you we're pretty hard to kill? If they brought them down still alive, they'll likely pull through."

Unless they are blown apart by a bullet or disintegrated by a bolt of lightning spewed out by an electrified sword. Other than that, sure, Stephen. We're pretty hard to kill.

He hoped the man was right. For his friends' sakes. Death was too permanent, and he was tired of it happening to people he knew.

He almost said loved, but Jantzen hadn't hung around long enough for that. And nothing had filled the hollow he'd left behind. He expected nothing could, except perhaps a good dose of revenge.

— 8 —

"I THINK that's Julia," Garik whispered, motioning to a bed with a tall form, although the monitoring equipment and the low lights might make it difficult for anyone else to make out her identity.

"In one piece, it seems," Stephen agreed.

Garik had tagged behind through the unfamiliar corridors once they reemerged in the underbelly of the hospital. It was the middle of the night, and the ward they entered consisted of glass-fronted rooms arranged around a central nurse's station, typical of many ICUs. The lights were down except just at the station.

589

"Can I help you?" The nurse had been reading a paper book, and he turned it upside down to mark his place and stood. The ward was silent, with blinking lights revealing life-monitoring machines in most of the glass-fronted rooms. Two were completely dark, suggesting they were empty.

"We're checking up on some old friends."

"This late?" The nurse wasn't unfriendly, just questioning.

"I can't get out easily during the day. My eyes, understand." Stephen had pulled out a pair of tinted goggles and slipped them over his face despite the dim lights. "I brought my friend to help me navigate the brighter areas. If you think it's best that we come back . . ." He let his enquiry trail away as if the nurse was right to turn him away, but it would be devastating if he did.

"Of course. I should have noted that. And you are?"

"Stephen, and my friend is Kiddo." Stephen glanced at Garik and gave him a wink. "We can offer our passkeys as verification." He held out his and motioned to Garik to do the same.

"Sure. Here." Garik held up one, unsure if it was his or Devon's.

"Let me see—" He reached for Stephen's passkey, paused, looked at his desk, and said, "No, that's okay. You won't be able to visit, anyway. As you can see, everyone's resting. I can give you a verbal review on them. Who are you interested in?"

"Julia, for sure," Stephen said. He pointed to the bed Garik had indicated. "That's her, there."

"You can see that?" The nurse paused, then he smiled. "Right, your eyes. You said friends. Who else?"

Garik leaned in and whispered, "Giselle Harmon and Paulo Leveen. Julia's last name is Cantos."

"Giselle Harmon, Paulo Leveen, and Julia's last name is Cantos."

The nurse frowned at the recited list of names before looking at his screen. "Okay, all here. Let me look at their progress . . . not surgery . . . ah, internal injuries, monitoring only. Hmm, this says . . ." He looked up, impressed. "Readings are off the charts. It seems your friends are making good progress. At this rate, I don't see any apparent cause for concern. Quite the opposite."

"They're okay, then." Garik still held the passkey, by now gripped tightly in one hand.

"I'm just the night nurse, so I haven't personally attended them, but the reports say so." He picked up his book to indicate an end to their visit. "Then, that's hybrids for you. You'll need to know they are in induced comas, so even if you return tomorrow, they won't know you. Call in next time, and that will save you a visit. Have a good night."

"I NEED access to the mainframe."

"You need . . . what?" They were back in the elevator, and Stephen, even with his penchant for boldness, gave Garik a look of amazement.

"Yes." They had passed by door B4-ES on the way out, and while they hadn't stopped, Garik hadn't been able to get the sword and the impact it had made on his and Marisa's lives out of his head. If he could learn more about it, maybe discover the hidden schematics Marisa said were missing, it would be like giving her something back, finishing a dream that had been stolen from her.

"I don't have access to the mainframe, man. How are you planning to do that?"

"I'm working on it." Which meant he didn't have a plan, only hoped to think of one. He pictured the ICU and thought of the nurse's words. The sonic boom, had it been instrumental in *improving* Giselle, Paulo, and Julia? If so, what would Jantzen have vaulted into? If he hadn't been dismembered by Sunchaser's sword, would he have become a super-hybrid, able to morph into anything he wanted, perhaps even with god-like attributes? Maybe walk through walls, X-ray vision, or live on an airless moon? Could the sword be something different, even more than they were led to believe? He asked, "What was your sonic boom?"

Stephen laughed as the elevator door opened. "I have no idea what you mean, but I can come up with some interesting answers."

"I'm sorry." Garik had so much in his head, and he forgot others couldn't follow everything he was thinking. "The thing that caused you to be like you are."

"My mother and my father got married . . ."

"C'mon." Garik smiled. They were in the corridor, and they were forced to keep their voices down. The night was coming to a close, and more people were moving about, some dressed for early training, others using the corridors as a convenient jogging track. The breakfast crowd would emerge in waves in another hour. "Here, when you had the procedure done. You didn't change immediately. No one does. Something must have caused you to change from who you were to who you are now."

"My magic powers, you mean."

"Yes."

"Sorry, I didn't get any. My special power is all about bone density. Space travel, all that. I can't see it or feel it, but the doctors seem to think it's important. The rest of me is how I've been all my life."

"Oh, sorry."

"I'm not sorry. I like me."

"I didn't mean it that way. I, well, I wasn't any different for a long time, then everything became different. My before and my after. I need to find what came in the middle."

"Your catalyst. That's what you're looking for. Man, I know how you feel. Like when I wanted to do gymnastics. Everybody laughed, but I'd seen the Olympics on television, and I knew I could compete and take gold. I was inspired."

"I didn't know you competed." Garik thought of Devon's mom who'd never had the chance for gold.

"Nah, but I could. Well, not now, but I could."

"So, you'll help me?" Garik felt the pressure of needing to get Devon's passkey back, but this was as important. He was risking their friendship, but to not take the risk meant leaving a personal hole in who he was, and that was worse.

Protecting himself. Protecting the pack. Which would win in the end?

"RISKY BUSINESS," Stephen said when he and Garik passed each other in the corridor later that morning. He slipped a folded piece of paper into Garik's hand and leaned in, lips to ear, to say, "Eat it when you're done, sooner than later."

Garik did, memorizing the filched passcode, and now he sat immersed in exploring the Tower's mainframe, searching, searching. Risky business indeed, as he was in Devon's apartment. He was certain his searches could be traced back to here if someone looked. He hoped no one did.

He didn't have access to *everything*, but then he hadn't wanted or needed that. He hoped to find out about the electrified sword, check out the research lab records on hybrid transformation rates, and if possible see what they had on him. What had they recorded that they hadn't shared, the thing that made the Director so willing to give him second chances and for Sunchaser to be pleased that he had leaped from the boxing ring to attack her?

He had pleaded tiredness after lunch—true after his all-nighter—and asked to be left in the apartment. Devon offered to bring something from the emergency clinic, but no, Garik had assured him rest was all he needed. By the time Devon left, he was in his pajamas.

He had, however, no intention of sleeping.

PROPOSALS. Committee meeting reports. Financial documentation. Job openings. Military assignments. The categories of information seemed endless.

Then, case studies, and Garik knew he was moving in the right direction. He clicked to open, and names flooded down the screen. He looked for ones that were familiar, Paolo, Giselle, Julia, and there they were. John Carter—

Garik's emotions hiccupped. John, left face down on the parking garage floor. Pointless.

He scrolled by Stephen Klandermans' file, refusing to open it. Stephen had passed him the code to access this information. Snooping wasn't why he was here, at least not snooping into Stephen's files.

Marina, Marisa's sister. A red X. He opened it. She had been transferred out of the complex, sent away to some distant location. He searched for where, only to see a series of letters and numbers that meant nothing to him.

Then Jantzen Hefferly. The file, still open, unlike Marina's. He clicked it, and Jantzen's life spilled onto the screen. His birthdate, hometown, pictures of him before and after his involvement in the human-hybrid project. Garik found professional credentials telling that the man was not only a participant, but a medical doctor and a celebrated researcher, with mentions in too many prominent research publications to scan in the time Garik had.

One of the pictures was the photo of Jantzen attempting to pull Rodheimer off the log. Garik zoomed the image to fill the screen with the youthful face, like yet very unlike the man who had befriended him. He closed the picture. That wasn't the Jantzen he knew, only an earlier version of him. No purple eyes, no beard, none of the character that had made up Jantzen.

He caught a boldface subheading, Catalyst, the word Stephen had used. He read: *Jantzen Hefferly's hybrid transformation oc-*

curred over two stages, the second of which seems to have been precipitated by a "trigger" event. 1. His initial transformation spanned four months and was thought to be a failure. During this time, he continued his work in the research labs, although he reported increasing headaches. Multiple MRI scans found no evidence of abnormalities. 2. Jacques Ricciardo, hybrid, was reclassified as a failure and excluded from the program, creating the trigger event that enhanced Hefferly's transformation exponentially. Note: the reason for Hefferly's intense reaction to Ricciardo's reclassification is unclear, but the inescapable conclusion is that severe emotional stress can accelerate the change into full hybrid state.

Garik forced himself to consider, could his own emotional trauma have forced him to change? He swelled with missing Marisa, certain the two must be connected. He closed Jantzen's file and reopened Marina's. He scanned for Catalyst and found it. Underneath, it said, None. He looked for Benjamin Fuest, a man who seemed to have no hybrid characteristics. Catalyst: None. Then he went to Justin Kurtew, a man who had made the most extreme change he could imagine, from a person to a creature that was more mantis than man. Under Catalyst, he found something unexpected. *Jantzen Hefferly/severed relationship.*

Severed relationship. Garik had known there was something there, a sore spot, a grudge Justin held against Jantzen, almost envy for Garik's new place in Jantzen's life. What relationship fracture could have been so serious that it would trigger Justin to become what he was now?

And Dr. Jimenez's comment on the mall when he'd seen Garik with Jantzen. Garik had surprised him, but when Jantzen said they were together, the doctor had said, "Then I'm not surprised."

He also thought of Stephen, the crossed fingers, his reference to Jantzen as "his man." And when Justin was molting, Jantzen had been there to help him, caring friends. None of it made any sense.

Then something he was reading clicked. At the bottom of Marina's file had been a code telling where she was transferred. He reopened Jantzen's file, and in parenthesis, as if not official, was the same code. What did that mean?

He thought of the sword, what had happened to Jantzen, other people Sunchaser had hit with the electrified weapon. He searched for his own file, and he scanned it for the dreaded subheading.

Catalyst: Subject's progress has stalled. A trigger event is sug-

594

gested. Strongest probable emotional connection: Marisa Bruni. Suggest severing the connection. See Jantzen Hefferly's file for a successful example.

When poisoning her against him hadn't worked, Sunchaser had upped the ante. She had killed Marisa to bring about his full hybrid transformation.

Garik knew one thing. Somehow, she would pay.

— 9 —

GARIK SEARCHED for one more thing in his file. The odd code. The rest was in there, summarized, of course, but very much reflecting his life since entering the center, even his assignment to Jantzen's apartment in the Tower and the statistics from all his training sessions.

His file had no code, the only thing that seemed to connect Marina and Jantzen. They were both no longer in the Tower. He closed the folder and went to Christian Maguire, a hybrid reject he and Jantzen had tried to save but who was ejected from the program and the Tower before their plan was complete. The blowup between Jantzen and Sunchaser over Christian had created a rift between them, with the result being Jantzen's destruction by the sword.

Christian. Red X. Inside, the mysterious code. Garik looked to his Catalyst, where it said: *No successful triggers found. Subject continues to develop at a progressive and steady rate.*

Down the list, he caught other names: Veronika Abbink; Anatoli and Andrey Burgorski. He opened that one, caught a description that said each had half a butterfly birthmark. He grinned and moved on. Fabiola Bello; Bert Ellis; Amy Howe; Leigh Jose; Laura Lassere; Marco Lopez; Hector Mascari; Jacquelien Van Kessel; and there were others. He opened Jacquelien's file, was surprised to learn that the blonde woman had African ancestry in her blood. He wanted to read more, but Devon might return at any time. Faithful, dependable Devon, out to watch over him, and good-hearted, too. Garik appreciated each of Devon's qualities, and he had come to trust him as a friend; but he needed time in the mainframe, and Devon wouldn't mesh well with that.

He scrolled, clicked when something looked promising, and entered a folder labeled Research Center Electrical Plans. All five basement floors were inside the folder with detailed drawings identifying each room. Several voids were marked Utility Access. After studying them, he closed the folder and thought for a minute. The sword. He tried to think how Marisa had accessed the information all those months ago, back when it was summer, and he was still a high school boy who had liked a high school girl, and he hadn't known the research center in the Tower's basement existed. At the top of the screen, he selected New Window, and in the search bar, he typed Corona Tower, added a slash, put in Halo Sunchaser, another slash, then added ESS. Tapping Enter brought up a list of pages, all of which told something about the electrified sword, from images to plastic toy versions for sale.

One option was labeled Corona Tower Home, and he clicked it. A picture of the sword appeared, and at the top, a series of drop-down menus. One said Schematics, and Garik clicked it. A labeled diagram of the sword appeared, and at the bottom, a tag said 1 of 59.

One of fifty-nine. Not one of sixty—an even number, which would make more sense. He flipped through the pages. Add a cover sheet, maybe a page with credits at the back. Even was complete, and the Tower never did anything in halves. He understood Marisa's declaration that the Tower must have published the schematics—required by law—but left off a page. It was too complicated to easily know if you had all of it, and just one part missing would be enough that anyone trying to build it from this would fail and likely not understand why.

Interestingly, the longer he studied the pages, the more sense it made to him. He had always been able to look at items, especially mechanical or electronic ones, and have a feel for how they worked and how to repair them. And now, hybridized, his memory was nearly photographic. In his head, he began to overlay the pages on the screen one on another, building up the finished sword in his head as he surveyed the images. By the time he was finished, he had a good grasp on what each part of the machine—and it was that, simply a machine with energy reservoirs, controls, and feedback sensors—did to make it operate.

One thing puzzled him. The sword didn't feel destructive. It felt passive, a conduit, not a rail gun for electricity. The design wanted to *channel* something.

He needed page sixty. The design wasn't finished. Thank you, Marisa, he thought, sending his appreciation to wherever she might be. I wouldn't know to keep looking, but thanks to you, now I do.

The front door to the apartment unlocked, thunk, thunk, and Devon called, "Hey, kiddo! How's your afternoon been?"

"Fine, Devo," he called back, as he logged out of his mainframe search. He didn't know if he would be able to get back in, but what he had found so far was invaluable.

"Studying?" Devon was at the door on his crutches. His leg was mostly better, but it would be months before he would walk and run like his old self.

"Yeah. Lots of information out there."

"Don't let it suck you in. Do you feel like a trip to the cafeteria, or should we plan to eat in?"

"Out." Garik pushed away from the computer. He suddenly wanted to be away from it, out of the room, gone from the apartment. He needed to see some faces besides his own.

"I'm on the Segway. I just need a fresh shirt. Are you taking your board?"

"Of course." Garik looked beside the computer to the passkey to Jantzen's apartment that he had yet to use since the incident with Sunchaser. Two bathrooms didn't seem so important anymore. The place was large, with great views, but it didn't have the one thing this place had: Devon. Someone who would walk in the door, ask him if he wanted to go out, and be satisfied no matter how he answered.

In other words, a friend.

He followed Devon into his bedroom, and he found him in the closet, his torso bare, flipping through an assortment of hanging shirts. His old shirt was on the floor and his crutches leaned against the bed. Garik dropped into his boxing stance and threw a couple mock jabs with his fists.

"Ho, ho, watch out, Devo," he said.

"What's that for?"

"Gotta fight'cha while youse is still all cripple up. Utterwise, ain't no contest. I be losin'."

"Gotta get your head screwed on straight before I let you back into civilization. Are you wearing that to eat?" Devon pulled a shirt down, slipped it over his head, and buttoned it at the collar.

"Comfy." Garik grinned.

"Not with me, you're not. Put on some real clothes." He reached for his dirty shirt, and he popped Garik with it. As Garik ducked and ran, Devon chased after him, one footed, popping as he went, finally calling, "Ow, ow! You win."

"Always, Devo." Garik snatched the shirt from him and popped him back, before throwing the shirt at him and heading to his room for real clothes.

IN THE cafeteria, mealtimes were still assigned, so they had a good idea who they might see. Melanie Hatherill and the Burgorski twins, plus Lansana Opuku-Mensah and Jacquelien Van Kessel. Schedules could be rotated, but it took prior approval from Colonel Brace's team, and for most people, it was too much trouble.

There was no restriction about where they sat, even with Brace's men at the door checking off each person who walked in, so they tended to pull together tables for a good time. Anatoli and Andrey had already pulled two tables together, and when Garik and Devon walked in, they waved.

"Spots saved. Join in," Andrey called.

"Got a joke for you," Anatoli shouted, standing to be sure everyone heard. "A cripple and a wolf walked into a diner—"

He was booed into silence by the other attendees, and he sat with a grin on his face.

"Happy, Anatoli?" Devon had his Segway at the table, and he stepped off. He used the edge of the table for support and dropped into his seat.

"Got everyone's attention, right? Of course, I'm happy." He looked to Garik. "Three more chairs, slave. Right over there where we got the tables."

"Massa." Garik left his board with the Segway and headed across the room. From behind him, he heard Anatoli whispering, *"I heard he's wearing a tracking device."* Garik turned, and Anatoli waved, as if he hadn't said anything. He worked his arms under three chairs at once, growling to himself, *Stephen!* He couldn't believe the man would reveal something Garik had told him in what he thought was confidence.

Back at the table, Garik seated himself, and when the three women arrived, he stood beside his chair until they were seated.

"A gentleman," Jacquelien purred. She was blonde, which forced the red tattooed line running from her widow's peak down her face before disappearing into her shirt to stand out. The only thing more distinctive was her blue lips. She was willing to take a risk, and Garik liked her for that.

Lansana, with scarification about her eyes, watched Jacquelien sit before pulling out her own chair.

Melanie had her chair out and was seated before either of the other two.

"Jacquelien," Garik said as an opener, "do you like challenges?"

"Already smells good." She rubbed her hands together. "What it is, and what do I get if I'm successful?"

"What you get is respect." Garik drummed four fingers on the table once for drama.

"Hmm," she said, looking at the other people around the table. "Whose?"

"Someone who knows something only two other people at this table know. Someone who can smash in the face of a paramilitary goon and walk away. Someone who can hear whispers from across the room." Anatoli looked at Garik sharply, and Garik thought, *Process that.* He said, "Mine."

"Ooh, so sweet a reward. I'm in. What's the challenge, and what do I lose if I can't meet it?"

"You help me find—" It came to Garik like inspiration. "—the missing schematics page for the sword."

"Shut up. It's not possible," Anatoli said.

"What schematics?" Devon looked doubtful.

"How did you—" Lansana, her eyes narrowed.

Melanie didn't say anything, but Anatoli elbowed Andrey, and Garik found he had their full attention.

"Deal," Jacquelien said. "The challenge?"

"A butterfly landed, half on one, half on the other. Tell me where it is, the first half and the other, before we finish eating."

"Ooh, a good one." She smiled and rubbed her hands together.

Anatoli and Andrey looked intrigued until they figured out it was them, and the butterflies weren't in a location suitable for public viewing.

"Who wants pizza?" Garik stood. It was the only thing on the menu tonight. Brace hadn't relaxed *that* rule. What one person ate, everyone in the room shared.

As he walked across the room, he thought, *Let them sweat that.*

BY THE end of the meal, the twins were squirming and asking to be dismissed. The women assured them it wasn't happening. Besides, there was a guard on duty that said they were to remain in the cafeteria until their slot for dinner was up. As the brothers grew redder, Jacquelien focused on them. Matching men, half and the other, and she called them on it. When they denied it, her only solution was to ask for proof, which they declined to give.

"I suppose we must help you look for your treasure, since we've hit an impasse on your riddle." She placed her hand on Garik's and released it equally quickly. "Anatoli and Andrey will be glad to join us."

"I can give you a hint, if that's all you want." Andrey. "It won't do you much good."

"I'm good at putting things together. Try me." Garik.

They all knew about the missing schematic. Andrey had seen the room where the only copy was kept locked away. He described the location, telling them it was behind an unmarked door, impossible to access.

Garik listened, placed the room on the electrical plans in his head, and he said, "What if it is possible?"

They rounded up a pen and opened several napkins, and Garik began to draw from his memory. Each floor, crisp and clear, and right behind the room Andrey described was a void labeled Utility Access.

"Get us in there," Garik said, "and we're in the room."

Jacquelien smiled. "I like this part even better."

Melanie joined in, "So. Do. I."

Garik smiled. The quest was on.

— 10 —

"SERIOUSLY," Devon said, taking in the group of hybrids at the table, "you are just going to go in there, prowl around, and poke into what you shouldn't?" He shook his head. "And in the most secure facility in the country. You do know that's off limits."

"Practice." Lansana's eyes carried a look of anticipation. "Trained for this. Classes, the military instructors, all of it. What they have given us. Military-grade skills. No good if not used."

"She's got a good point." Andrey leaned back, frowning, thinking.

"I'm in, Andrey." Anatoli grinned and placed his hand on his brother's arm and removed it. Neither man seemed to notice he'd done it. "A real covert operation. Maybe even under the cover of night. Let's do this."

"Darkness. Anyway." Melanie's speech was separated into clipped sections, each seemingly independent of the other.

"Leave that to me," Garik said. He could smell the eagerness of the chase from each person at the table, all except Devon. Devon emanated hesitancy, concern for the rules of the game, worry that the current status quo, already tenuous, might topple one or all of them into a place that they wouldn't be able to rescue themselves from.

"I promised no shenanigans, kiddo. Remember?" Devon balled his hand and bumped Garik's shoulder. "Aren't you worried that this might be considered a shenanigan?"

"You're worried it might be, that's obvious," Garik said. He looked to the others at the table. "Is this a shenanigan? Devon's worried that it might be."

"I have been challenged." Jacquelien stood, sliding her chair back, and crossing her arms over her chest. "Where is my honor, my identity, if I do not meet the challenge? My grandfather was a tribal leader in my South African homeland, and I dishonor him if I do not hold to my end of any bargain I have entered into."

Lansana smiled. Melanie put her hand under her chin and studied Devon's reaction. Anatoli took one of the napkins Garik had drawn on, wadded it, and tossed it Jacquelien's direction, hitting her before it tumbled back to the table.

"Climb off your pedestal, woman. You don't have a tribal leader in your DNA. You are Dutch seahorse through and through. Look at that blonde hair."

Jacquelien glared, and Garik stepped in. "Airman Vang, anyone know him? Cambodian or Irish? Anyone? Anyone? So, leave it, Anatoli." Garik had seen the file. He knew she was telling the truth.

"Thank you." Jacquelien sat, but she glowered at Anatoli.

Devon said, "I'm not here, and I'm not hearing any of this. We had dinner, then I went to check on the emergency clinic supplies, and after that, well, I'll think of someplace that proves I wasn't with you people. Garik," he rapped the table with the knuckles of his fist, "you need a minder. How are you planning to deal with that?"

"I forgot." Garik's enthusiasm hit a wall.

Devon moved his hand, and his passkey rested on the table. "I'll be back to the apartment by nine. I'd hate to think I misplaced my passkey and couldn't get in. It might be embarrassing when security shows up, and you're nowhere around. I did promise the Director I was up to keeping you in line."

Garik covered the passkey with his hand, grinned, and said, "Lost passkey? What lost passkey?"

As Devon rose and made his way to his Segway, Garik motioned the others to pull in, and he leaned forward. He kept his voice low.

"First, we need to get to Level 4. Who wants to volunteer their passkey?"

Five hands shot into the air.

ACCESSING THE utility corridors seemed impossible at first. They tried several of the entrances Garik recalled from his view of the center's electrical plans, but none allowed them through. Their break came when Joseph Howard came down the hallway pushing a mop bucket with a wooden handle protruding from the top.

"Hey, Joseph, let me help you with that." Anatoli took off at a trot to catch the head of the center's custodial team. "You should have Tyrone doing these sweat jobs. You're his boss, you know."

"Not that Tyrone knows." Joseph Howard chuckled, and he studied Anatoli's face. "I thought that was you, Anatoli. How is that brother of yours?"

"Just down the corridor. There, see him?" He pointed.

"Sure, with the big guy. Looks familiar, that face."

"Likely. Can I hold the door for you while you roll this inside?"

"I bet you can. Let me unlock this."

With the man's passkey, the door swung wide, and Anatoli held it out of the way while the older man pushed the bucket inside.

"You need help pouring that water out?"

"I'm good with it. Thanks. I won't be needing anything else."

"I see an electrical panel behind you. It looks big enough to be a doorway."

"Yessir. Been through it a few times. A whole world behind there nobody sees but me."

"And Tyrone." Anatoli chuckled.

"When I can get him out of his lazy shoes." Joseph had the bucket empty and the mop hung to dry. "Be going now, Anatoli. You tell that brother of yours to be better than you are." He winked.

"Yessir, Joseph. I sure will."

After Joseph exited, Anatoli let the door swing to, and he pushed it firmly closed. He watched Joseph round the corner before he waved to his cohorts.

Andrey called, "C'mon, Anati, we have another location to try."

"No, *you* come on, brother. This is the way in." When they arrived, Anatoli touched the handle and the door swung open with a feather touch. Anatoli gestured to where he had slipped a magnetic plate to keep the latch from engaging. "Alarms, do I hear alarms? No? After all, what is there in a custodian's closet to steal?"

"This. Helps. How?" Melanie, her voice curt with impatience.

"I understand." Garik smiled. He had seen the electric panel, and he had already placed it on the plan in his head. It had to be a door. The path through it was as clear as if it were painted on the floor.

Actually, it was. Two lines, black and red, with voltage symbols inscribed alongside them. The lines stopped at the front of the electrical panel. Garik knew they continued on the other side.

"Jacquelien," he suggested, "check to see how to open that panel. It opens to the utility corridor."

"That's what Joseph said," Anatoli confirmed.

"A. Door." Melanie smiled.

"I told you Anati would be good for something." Andrey smirked.

"You said what?" Anatoli punched him on the shoulder. "I'm always good for something."

"If only we could figure out what it is." The electrical panel was open by then, and Andrey ducked through just before Anatoli slapped the side of his head.

THEY LEFT the electrical panel ajar, as it didn't latch from the back, and wedged the door to the corridor shut. Anyone trying it. . . but then no one would. It was locked, after all.

Garik had no trouble following the path to the room Andrey had described. The lighting was low, but the plan for the building was firmly fixed in his mind. This corridor, that one, turn there, and access that wall to gain entrance.

One thing the building's electrical plan hadn't shown was how large each electrical access was to the various rooms. The one they had entered—a full door. The one they needed to gain access to the backside of the room with the final schematic for the electrified sword? Yet another difficulty to work out in pursuit of their goal.

"This is it." Garik tapped the wall with his knuckles. A cable burrowed through concrete block and gave off a hollow thump of resonance from inside the invisible cavities.

"No. Door." Melanie, stating the obvious.

"See that." Lansana. "Need to work it out."

"Jacquelien's challenge. Let her do it." Either Anatoli or Andrey, who could tell? The corridors were darkened, or so they looked to anyone without eyeshine, and the men's faces were shadowed in the dim lights littering the edges of the floor.

"Right here?" Jacquelien drew a box shape on the wall with her hands. "We want on the other side of this spot? Are you certain?"

"Completely." Garik had walked the steps from turn to turn. He knew the distances. The picture in his head didn't lie.

"Lansana?" Jacquelien stepped back and motioned to her.

Lansana tilted her long neck, absorbing what she must do. Then she nodded, accepting the challenge. She stepped back and slammed into the wall with her shoulder. When it didn't break, she smiled apologetically.

"Melanie," Lansana said politely. "Glancing blow. At my shoulder."

Melanie groaned then walked a hundred steps down the corridor. When she turned, Lansana crouched as if prepared to impact the wall once more. Melanie began to run, blurred, and Lansana was slammed sideways. Dust flew, and when she pulled herself erect, the concrete block bore a series of distinct cracks. Lansana with her armored pangolin skin was unharmed.

She called to Melanie, "Again."

Melanie took a deep breath, jogged to her starting position, and began to run once more.

ONCE INSIDE, the room was completely dark, with only the glow from the utility corridor to provide any light. Garik could see fine. The others needed extra illumination to keep from bumping into things.

"Okay, Andrey. You're the one that described this place. Where do we look?" If Garik were Sunchaser, and the most important document for the electrified sword's cherished schematics couldn't fall into anyone's hands, what would be the obvious place?

About the time Andrey counted drawers, Garik already knew, and they reached for it at the same time.

"Locked." Andrey groaned. "I should have known."

"Would. Be." Melanie.

"Don'tcha think?" Anatoli.

"But the challenge!" Jacquelien took Anatoli and Andrey by the ears, and she said, "This is your fault. I refuse to lose. Show the birthmarks!"

Garik laughed. "I would rather have the schematic. I've got this." He grasped the drawer pull, twisted until the front of the drawer began to buckle, then with a yank, ripped it free. A leather folder rested inside. His heart raced, and he thought, *For you, Marisa,* and he lifted it out.

Inside, the printed design that revealed the true purpose of the sword leaped out at him. It clicked into place, lining up with the other fifty-nine pages. It was obvious, so simple. The sword was never designed to kill. He was right. It was a channel, a conduit. For what he wasn't sure but leaving this part of the design incomplete caused the sword's power to short from the blade, wreaking havoc on whatever it touched.

It was obvious, and it could never be allowed to happen again. There was only one thing to do.

"I need access to the sword." Garik looked up from the schematic, and he studied each person in the room, gauging their reactions.

"Always love a good joke." Anatoli chuckled.

"The. Paper. Reveals. What?" Melanie, with a frown.

"The man is serious." Lansana, taking up Garik's cause.

"More. Information." Melanie.

"I can get us to the storage room where it's kept. Stephen showed me." Garik considered his sudden need for access to the weapon. Repair? Destruction? He wasn't sure, but he had begun to breathe more rapidly with his need, drawing in more and more air. His heart, pumping more blood, preparing his body for any demand it might be called upon to meet. "If we can get inside."

"I am French toast, yes?" Lansana reached past Melanie and pushed on Garik's shoulder. The scarification around her eyes and up across her head seemed to glitter in the dim light. "The wall. That was me."

"And. I. Shared." Melanie.

"If you people are doing this, so are we." Anatoli and Andrey together.

"Challenge accepted." Jacqueline. "We must move now. Devon needs his key by nine."

Garik had a new pack. It seemed they had as much interest in assisting him as he did in protecting them. He grinned.

"Follow me."

"HOW DID I not see this?" The sword, just on the other side of the wall, and Garik couldn't get to it.

"My shoulder," Lansana said, "did not see it, either."

"Bet you felt it," Anatoli joked. The wall—beyond which Garik had assured them they would find the electrified sword—bore multiple imprints of her shoulder but no breakthroughs.

"Let me think." Garik's innate sense of actionable probabilities, his "prescience" ability, had become jumbled in the storm of his building excitement at gaining access to the sword. He pressed his hand to the wall. "This room wasn't on the original plans, so it must have been added later."

"With. Reinforcement." Melanie had run at Lansana repeatedly until she had claimed she could do no more.

"A vault," Anatoli offered.

"This, perhaps, is something?" Andrey knelt to a panel on the lower portion of the wall. He traced several words with a finger and read, "High voltage. Carriage drive access only. Last serviced—" and he read off several inked-in dates, the most recent one a year earlier. He flipped two catches along the top edge, and the panel lifted away. Inside were two breakers and a yellow and blue button, one labeled up and the other down, plus some other electronic components.

"Perhaps." Garik knelt beside Andrey and he stroked the yellow button. The future was sliding into place once more, his options forming before him, the path that was his *right now* branching out to *probabilities,* lesser *possibilities,* and finally a series of branching *options* that faded before him even as he reached for them. He glanced toward the ceiling. "The vault may be reinforced, but the path up and down, likely not. Here's what we're going to do."

He pushed the yellow button and cocked his head to listen to the lifting mechanism as it began to turn. A gear drive, the most dependable form of mechanical conveyance. He could hear the scissor-like arms pulling the ceiling of the vault aside and the glass case with the sword steadily rising. When he was satisfied, he pressed the button again, and the noise stopped.

"That. Helps. How?" Melanie.

"Yes, yes, I see." Jacquelien pressed her hand to the wall, looked toward the ceiling, and nodded. "This is reinforced. A floor up, access."

"If Stephen will help us." Garik pictured a door near the natatorium fronting a bump-out in a wide corridor. To the unschooled, it could be heating or cooling conduits. Now he placed it directly above the sword's vault. The shaft the sword traveled would need servicing occasionally. Stephen had access to the storage area, meaning he had a passkey that would open the door, that was if he could be trusted.

Tracking device. Why had he told Stephen that? Sometimes he was a fool even when he tried to be the best that he could be.

"CHILL, MY man. You're not the first to be tracked." Stephen, with his blond dreads, stood alongside Garik at the bump-out door, his passkey in his hand. The others lounged casually around them, a group of friends chatting, even if they were providing attentive cover for testing Stephen's key on the door.

"It didn't make me think nice things about you."

Stephen laughed aloud, to be shushed by Jacquelien's hand and looks from several of the others.

"That's funny?" The laugh pricked Garik's irritation.

"Lots of people don't think nice things about me."

"I expect they don't, not when you refuse to consider the feelings of others."

"Do you want me to insert this key or put it away until you quit insulting me?"

"I can't get past you blabbing to everyone."

"Just to the guys, and you can thank me. It makes you less Rodheimer's pet and more one of us."

"Pet? How's that? I don't get any special treatment from him."

"Jantzen's old suite at the top of the tower. Hmm, let's see, anything else? Yes. There's reinstatement into the program after breaking out *twice*. Plus praise every time he talks about you."

"And Sunchaser undermining every step I take." And my girlfriend being killed and my life stolen and all my friends gone, and that didn't touch the city being decimated because he was here. A real pet, yeah, a favorite of the guy in charge.

"Yeah, there's that, but the Director's the boss. He takes precedence over Sunchaser."

Lansana leaned in, "Still jawing? Thought we were doing something here. Tick tock. Devon needs his passkey back."

"Open it," Garik said.

Stephen's key, with his access to the storage and maintenance areas, worked, thunk, thunk, and he pulled the door back. It and the door opening were reinforced with metal plate. Light from behind Stephen and Garik fell into the opening.

It was the shaft they had expected to find, perhaps eight by eight in depth and width. Centering each wall, a well-lubricated gear track started below them and extended upward out of sight. And attached to it all, suspended in midair, a platform, the sword in its glass case in the middle, and room for two people to ride along on either side. It gleamed in the shadowed light, brighter than it ought, although the glass case was likely concentrating what light was available.

"The case. How do we access it?"

"That's the next challenge. Before, the Director has always done it. Lightning. Well, electricity, but it looks the same to me. We can create a committee to discuss it, but it wouldn't hurt to hurry."

Before they could decide on their next step, the overhead lights in the building dropped to half level, red emergency lighting spaced along the walls began to flash, and an alarm pulsed in a repeating pattern.

"Two minutes to lockdown," a voice intoned. "Move away from security doors and exit all elevators at the next floor. Remain where you are until you are okayed to return to your regular activities."

"I think they know we're here." Stephen stepped back and pushed the door to, sealing away the glass-encased sword. "We need to go."

"Where?" Garik asked.

"This way. We have to get upstairs." Stephen took off running northwest along the outside of the natatorium and away from the training area.

"How did I not see this?" Garik ran at Stephen's side, unclear on where they were headed. He was learning one thing: prescience was only as good as the information you could access. And today, he felt stupider than a rock.

EVERYONE CROWDED into a service elevator that ran from the storage area on Level 4 up to the research labs on Level 2. Without Stephen's passkey, it would have been impossible for them to gain access. Inside, another layer of required permission confronted them.

"Impending lockdown," the control panel said. "You will not have time to reach your destination. Override permission required."

The panel blinked for a hand scan, and Stephen placed his on the panel. It refused to scan and repeated, "Override permission required."

"Director Weston Rodheimer. Override permission granted."

"Thank you, Director Rodheimer. Have a good day."

The doors slipped shut with a ding, and the car began to move upwards one floor.

"Director Rodheimer?" Stephen looked behind him to see Anatoli grinning. "Which of you was Director Rodheimer?"

Andrey thumbed towards his brother, and Anatoli looked smug. He pumped a hand in the air. "Mockingbirds unite."

"So," Jacquelien said, "that's what he's good for. A chatterbox."

Anatoli struggled to reach her to pop her up beside the head, but his brother, Lansana, and Melanie managed to hold him back.

Garik laughed. He looked at the time displayed on the control panel. Fifteen of. They had time, and Devon wouldn't have to call security to get back into his apartment.

GARIK LAY in bed, his feet brushing the wall, and his head nearly touching on the opposite end. He now slept on his side or with his knees bent, a penalty for his extra DNA-driven height. He curled one arm around his pillow, and he worked his face into its softness. The scratch of hair on his cheek was new enough that it caught him off guard. He rolled to his back, looking at the ceiling.

He was partially pleased at his day.

Back by nine? Check, although Devon was already inside. When the warning sounded, he was on his way to the apartment. At a security guard's approach, he rummaged in his pockets as though searching for his passkey, and the guard offered his, warning him to keep inside until the lockdown was over.

Find the final layer of schematics to the electrified sword? Check. They hadn't brought it with them. Garik already had it in his head, and no, he wouldn't forget. That's what the *photographic* in *photographic memory* meant, he had assured everyone present.

Locate the sword to prevent Sunchaser from using it to wreak havoc on anyone else's life? Partial check. They had located it but were unable to access it, not fully. It remained somewhere in limbo between the Level 4 vault and the research center's main lobby. Whether that was what had triggered the campus lockdown, no one had bothered to say, and Devon hadn't heard.

He finally drifted off to an old dream, a nightmare, really. A giant silverback gorilla chased him, and a man in black held out a sword that could defeat it, but only while Garik held the sword in the air. Self-doubt always made the sword sag in his hands, and each time, the gorilla wrapped its fist around Garik and began to squeeze, jarring him awake.

Garik now knew the characters in the nightmare. The gorilla was the Director, DNA bonded with the beast. The man in black was Jantzen Hefferly, but he was gone and could no longer help him. The sword still confused him. He'd never held it in his hands and had only seen it wielded twice. He couldn't even get to it to make the corrections he'd seen in the final page of the schematics, the one that Marisa had known was missing so long ago.

If he could do that . . . if he could do that . . . if he could do that . . . and he drifted off to face the silverback one more time.

THE NEXT morning revealed the scope of what Garik and his pseudo pack had accomplished. At first, Devon struggled with opening the door.

"Hey, kiddo. This thing's stuck, you come give it a try."

"Wimp," Garik teased. "Maybe it wants your palmprint." His head still spun with dreams of holding the sword aloft and letting it fall every time, and he wore a false sense of bravado for his "roomie."

"Not working."

"And mine should?" His passkey was good for the Tower to access Jantzen's apartment and not much else. He couldn't even move about the research center without piggybacking on Devon's.

The door opened as Garik approached it and revealed Airman Shan Vang standing alongside someone Garik didn't recognize.

"Mr. Shayk, I see you are still with us. Ah, Mr. Maye. May I introduce Airman Collette Stephenson. Airman Stephenson will be assigned to you until the emergency is over."

"What emergency is that, Airman Vang?" Devon smiled.

"You are unaware?" Vang looked like he hardly believed it. "The sword has been stolen from its vault on Basement Level 4. Until it is recovered, no one can walk the premises without their assigned chaperone. Airman Stephenson will be ready to accompany you to breakfast when you are ready."

Stephenson greeted them. "Mr. Shayk, Mr. Maye," then turned her back to them and fell into parade rest, with her legs slightly apart and her hands behind her back.

Devon closed the door and turned to Garik. "You said you were looking for the final schematic, not to steal the sword."

"It was still there when I walked away. I swear." He held up his hand as a pledge of honesty, remembering the time he had pledged to behave with the same hand after having cut himself while breaking a mirror in frustration.

The sword. Stolen. Now he couldn't even repair or disable it. His last gift to Marisa, even that taken from him by the ineptitude of the Tower.

— 12 —

GARIK WAS back in Jantzen's apartment high in Corona Tower, banished by Weston Rodheimer.

He hadn't seen or spoken to Halo Sunchaser for the two weeks of his banishment, which was fine by him. His total link with humanity had been Kofi Mandela, meeting with him daily for physical training; and the delivery boy from the Stamford Suites Grill, Steve Tsuchiya, who rang his doorbell three times a day—whom Garik had learned almost nothing about, except that he was average height, had dark, very straight hair, and he wore the Corona Tower uniform very well. He was never creased and never stained.

Garik had also seen Dr. Jimenez every other day. Flexibility checks. Breathing capacity. The good doc had even ordered up a fancy treadmill so that he could run stress tests on his heart.

"You have all this equipment in the hospital. I ride the elevator very well. You can test me there." And get me out of this hamster cage, Garik thought. He could only look out the windows so many hours before he wanted to shake the dust of the Tower off his feet and be gone.

If there was any dust. He didn't know. Each day when he returned from his sessions with Kofi, his linens were freshened and the carpets vacuumed. And likely every item in the apartment searched for any contraband that Garik might have acquired THROUGH THE PLATE GLASS WINDOWS THAT DIDN'T OPEN.

Sheesh, this was getting old!

Dr. Jimenez had answered, "No, we can't," and he had refused to elaborate. Garik learned not to ask.

He had observed the portions of Bay City he could see from his windows, some towards the east but mostly south and west. The city had filled out with greenery. He could no longer see City View Apartments, his home for the first decade he'd lived in America. Bay City, once his home. It didn't feel much like home any longer.

Closer in, he'd spent hours watching the activity along Sycamore. From his height, the people along the sidewalks were very small, little more than ants. Several times he'd seen the ants moving very fast, skateboard fashion, and he'd remembered visiting the food court and Chow Down at the base of the Tower with his friends Ibn Hariri, Muhammad Saud, and Hayat al-Haber. It seemed a lifetime ago, even more, sometimes.

More unusually, in the first week, he had seen military transports making their way south from the Tower's base and down Sycamore. Most turned west at Ninth toward Argyle Station or possibly Interstate Transport; with others going north on Sycamore. The only reason for heading north was to access The Docks or Harbor Shipyards. After the first week, everything seemed to settle down.

He couldn't see the high school from his side of the building, but when he and Kofi were at the Stamford Suites pool, he tried to see if Colonel Brace's hybrid paramilitary troops were still stationed there. The glass wall along the pool was angled poorly to observe more than the roof, but he was no longer seeing young people on the streets during the day, and the white stylized eagle no longer flew from the school's flagpole.

His time with Kofi didn't even seem like training any longer, more like they were filling time until the next thing that happened.

Two weeks in was when it did.

DR. JIMENEZ reclined on Garik's couch—formerly Jantzen Hefferly's in a previous life—and observed Garik running on the treadmill. Garik wore shorts, socks and shoes, and leads with sticky pads attached to his chest and back.

"These are the same results we've seen the past two weeks. Is this all you have to give, Mr. Shayk?"

Garik continued to run, breathing evenly, not tired, and only perspiring enough to keep his body cooled to an optimal temperature.

He thought, *No, Dr. Jimenez, it's not. You wouldn't believe your machines if I gave you all I've got to give.* Instead, he remembered what Jantzen once told him, to not give away everything he could do.

He also noted the doctor's use of his last name. Not once in the previous two weeks had he called him Garik, and in retaliation, Garik had called him nothing at all, refusing to use either his first name or his last, only resorting to Doctor when forced.

"It is time, then, to alter what we do. If you will clean up and change, I wish us to visit the research center. You may find a few differences. I will wait here." The man pulled out his tablet and tuned out Garik as though no longer in the same room with him.

Garik stopped the treadmill and began removing the sticky pads. Not even Nurse Ratchett had been to visit him. The doctor had shown him how to attach the leads, and it had been Garik's responsibility each visit afterwards. He patted his face with a towel, left it draped over the treadmill, and headed for a shower.

He took his time under the water, letting it hit his back and shoulders until it burned. Why now? Why two weeks in? And why mention a few differences? How different could it be? People walking the corridors, the cafeterias serving up food, a few military types looking down on everyone else, and all the weird hybrid variations filling in the mix . . . life as normal in the Corona Tower basements.

Yet, on the way, it wasn't the same at all. Even with the Tower's super-purified air, the elevator smelled different. Unused. As if an element of humanity that couldn't be scrubbed from even the cleanest surface had been somehow removed.

Or maybe it was the lack of cleaning, the lack of the *necessity* of cleaning . . . an aroma missing . . . as much as he tried, Garik couldn't pinpoint it.

Reaching the hospital level, the sensation was stronger. The elevator doors opened to the ribbon-floored corridor that was Basement Level 4, with the blue stripes along each wall leading them forward.

Quiet. Everything so quiet.

"Where is everyone?" Garik knew it was the right question. He didn't hear . . . breathing, monitoring machines, footsteps, the rush of air as doors were opened and closed. His hearing was more acute than any human that had ever lived, and he realized he had adapted to the sounds of life as a backdrop that could be tuned out. Or better said, that he no longer had to tune out, but that he could hear selectively and pick up on individual sounds as he needed to hear them.

"So, you can tell?" The doctor paused and studied Garik for a moment. "Perhaps the Director is correct. There is the . . . slightest chance that you may be what he has been looking for all along." Then he shrugged. "It is not my call. Come. We have an appointment. Let's not keep them waiting. This way."

The doctor didn't motion, point, or pause. He simply moved forward, knowing Garik would follow.

GARIK WANTED to turn and walk out again when he saw the people waiting on him. Director Rodheimer across the room in a modern chair with thick arms. Halo Sunchaser behind him, her face hard. Colonel Brace, apart from them but still across the room from Garik. On the other side of the room, two bulky orderlies and Nurse Ratchett, all three prim and expressionless. In the center, a chair.

"For me, right?" It was the only option, and Garik lowered himself into it.

"So, my boy, the place to yourself." Rodheimer motioned around him. "Have you enjoyed it?"

"Enjoyed what? I've been in Jantzen's suite the entire time."

"Dr. Jamie?" Rodheimer looked at him and waited.

"I saw no need for him to move back and forth." The doctor shrugged.

"So be it. Now we are ready to move forward."

"And this is why you've emptied this facility, this boy?" Brace watched Garik with narrowed eyes.

"Hardly a boy, Colonel. He has evaded us in a full escape twice, and we are certain he was instrumental in stealing an artifact from the most secure vault in the most secure building in this city. All this and he left no trace of his presence."

"So you say." Brace didn't seem convinced.

"And he decimated your paramilitary on more than one occasion. You must give him that."

"I still do not understand why I am now responsible for all of your former experiments. You have room for them here."

"For two reasons, Colonel. The facility in Canada is now ready, and the Canadians wish it stocked with viable prospects for marketable skills. And as far as room, not for much longer. I am requesting three hundred of your men for volunteers. We can begin DNA sampling immediately."

Garik spoke up, "DNA sampling of what?"

"Of you."

"Like, cheek swabs?" Garik wasn't liking the sound of this.

"Please inform him now, Dr. Jamie. I had asked to have these explanations cleared up before my return."

"I understand, Director. However, I have been testing him over the previous two weeks, and I am of the opinion he is far stronger than we originally estimated. If he wanted to escape . . . well, this is a very secure room. It was better to wait."

"Tell me *what*." Garik spat it as a demand, not a question.

"The harvesting method is a little more than a cheek swab, Mr. Shayk. We need spinal fluid to concentrate the DNA enough to bring about the required hybrid adaptations in the new volunteers."

"Feed them wolf juice like you did me."

"Yes, this I am still unclear about." Brace leaned forward, his expression doubtful. "You say the boy is intractable. Why do I want soldiers who will not follow orders?"

"Not intractable. Strong willed. That's what we are resolving. He was undisciplined when we got him. Your men have years of training. We will be starting with different stock, one that is already compliant, all provided the same DNA blend, just as we did with your paramilitary team."

"Only without flaws."

"Zero flaws. As you can see, he is perfect."

"And we can't just give my men the DNA mixture you gave this boy? Surely they would turn out the same."

"Impossible. The DNA calibration is specific to each individual. The bonding has already happened with this one. No additional bonding required. Simply inject and wait for it to colonize the host body."

Brace fought a smile.

Garik tried to tamp down his breathing, settle his heart, but he didn't like this.

"How much spinal fluid?" He fought his voice as he said it, refusing to allow it to shake.

"All of it, my boy. That's why we can only move ahead with three hundred men at a time. We will take one from each group, and he will provide for the next three hundred."

"Not with me." Garik released the rainbows that hovered at the corners of his vision, but before they could fly, he felt something pierce his shoulder, and he slumped, the rainbows fading away.

"See, my boy, we know you better than you know yourself." The Director shook his head as if speaking to an imbecile. "Dr. Jamie, Nurse Leah, if you will direct your people to restrain the young man so he cannot escape this time. He's done that often enough. And you, Colonel, how soon can you provide your volunteers?"

"Three hundred, you say." He calculated. "Some will need to come overland. Three days. Will that do?"

"If this one doesn't escape before then." He walked to Garik who was now on a gurney with his arms, legs, and head strapped to the table. "You, Mr. Shayk, have outdone yourself. And don't pretend you can't hear me. The drug affects your muscles, not your mind. I wondered for a time if the damage to our facilities and our reputation—yes, I worried about that—was worth it, or if you would fail me as the rest have. Jantzen nearly pulled you away, but Halo resolved that. But you, you were amazing! To break into our most secure facility! Impressive! We have yet to locate the sword, but I'm certain it will turn up, and if not, then I will have to ask Halo to build another one, so nothing lost and everything gained." Rodheimer turned, and in the turning dismissed Garik as a tiresome matter over and done with.

Garik shook with fury and then realized he wasn't shaking at all. The orderlies were rolling him out of the room, and he had no control over his actions.

Revenge. Revenge would be sweet . . . if Nurse Ratchett didn't suck him dry first.

Book 10

The Russian's Revenge

GARIK SHAYK, survivor.

Well, sort of. If being the lone human hybrid remaining in the Corona Tower research facility counted as surviving . . . when they were about to remove his spinal fluid to enhance three hundred super soldiers and make them just like him, only more compliant to their demands . . . and didn't have intentions for him to survive the procedure.

He watched Dr. Jamie Jimenez move about the equipment-lined room in his white lab coat, checking readouts, adjusting several, at one point pulling a keyboard to him and adding information to a digital chart visible on the display.

"Canada, huh, Dr. Jamie?" Garik called to the man's back. Jimenez headed the hospital on Basement Level 4 of the underground research complex. Using the man's first name would appeal to his vanity. He liked to think of himself as a patient's doctor, a friend, even if the veneer was paper thin. "The Director said the new Canadian facility is open, so that must be where everyone is, right? It must be quite a place to absorb everyone from here."

"Yes." Jimenez paused in his busy activities and turned to Garik on the table, his arms and legs strapped firmly down with metal clamps. Satisfied he would not be in any danger, he approached. "I see you have come to terms with your situation. We do not wish you to suffer more than necessary. Your willing compliance will further our goals with the least disruption possible. And while we are waiting to move ahead, you will be given the best of care. We are not cruel. We want this to be easy for everyone with no further glitches."

The glitch in the process for Garik was that they needed to use his cranial-spinal fluid to concentrate the DNA enough to bring about the required hybrid adaptations in the three hundred new volunteers.

All of it, leaving him none.

"Three hundred, right?" Garik forced himself to show outward compliance. Inwardly, he burned. *It's my spinal fluid, and I'm supposed to have accepted my situation?* He pulled at the metal clamps. Even with his new levels of hybridized strength, they didn't budge.

"It is what the Director requested. I suppose we have you to thank for this leap forward." Jimenez moved closer to Garik and looked him over. He touched the clamp at one wrist, as if making sure it was secure. "Your theft of the sword so infuriated Halo that she forbade further research. Are we ready? Perhaps." He chuckled. "She hopes you to be our confirmation."

"I guess I would be proud to have helped out," Garik kept his voice level, but containing his anger was hard, "if I had actually stolen it."

After the alleged theft of Halo Sunchaser's electrified sword, the secretive underground Bay City research facility was emptied as Garik remained in isolation for two weeks in one of the penthouse apartments in the 40-story Tower. Garik knew very little, except that they considered his timber-wolf-and-human-hybrid mix to be the ultimate in DNA melding, and they planned to harvest his DNA to begin building a new level of soldier that could intermingle with normal humans yet disguise the skills that made them superhuman.

"Denials reflect a poor attitude. Not a good reflection on your change of heart, Mr. Shayk." Jimenez seemed to lose interest in the conversation. He only wanted compliance, not truth, and he stepped away.

Garik heard the use of his last name, a demotion, a black mark from Jimenez dropping him to the bottom of the doctor's value meter. He remembered an apology he gave Jimenez once, groveling to play the man's emotions to help save a fellow hybrid. The man had been lost, anyway. Garik would not grovel now.

Memories swept through him, flooding him with emotions.

Jantzen Hefferly, his mentor and father figure, lost to the sword. Paul Gberie and John Carter, left for dead on the parking garage floor. Stephen Klandermans, Jacquelien Van Kessel, Fabiola Bello, ripped up by the roots and likely transplanted in far-off Canada. Giselle Harmon, Paolo Leveen, Julia Cantos, broken by Sunchaser's electrically produced sonic boom. His girlfriend, Marisa Bruni, killed by the sword to trigger his final metamorphosis into his true hybrid form.

If this *was* his final form, eight inches taller, enlarged lung capacity, and a heart three times its normal size; and that didn't touch the things that couldn't be easily measured: his eyeshine; his capacity to read a scene from surrounding aromas; his hearing, more sensitive than even Jimenez could imagine.

And the rainbows ... his ability to move so quickly that time seemed to stand still, blurring the world into shimmering layers of refracted light—rainbows—and letting him do amazing things, all for about half a minute before it drained his body and left him exhausted and on the floor.

Restrained on the table, he gave in to his anger, and the room came to a standstill around him. Rainbows burst from every surface, the swirling refraction of oil on water, a dark, slick coating that made Dr. Jimenez and the machines and the room all blur together. The doctor held out a hand to a button, frozen, and the display at its side was in a half-on-half-off state, making it hard to read. The light overhead pulsed with a ring of colors, a full 360-degree waterfall of rainbow brilliance. Garik studied the metal rainbows at his wrists. He pulled, lifted, strained; twisted his wrists, compressed one hand, was even certain he broke a bone that healed too quickly for him to force his hand through the loop.

Another side effect of his DNA transformation: healing so rapidly that the knitting process was visible to the eye, with bone and skin reforming as you watched.

He wrestled and wrenched against his bonds, certain he could free himself. If only he were Jantzen, able to sublimate—morph— from solid to gas, he would be free and out of here.

Then his half minute was up, his resources were drained, and his anger was sliced from him, slumping to the floor in a crumpled heap, leaving him panting with exhaustion.

"Now, now, Mr. Shayk. We have pressure sensors on your restraints. No need to prove something everyone agrees you cannot do."

The man didn't even look at Garik when he spoke to him. It told one thing. They didn't know about the rainbows, about how fast he could move, even if it was only for a short time. He tried to formulate a plan, a way to get out of these cuffs and onto his feet. Out of this room. Exit this place so fast they wouldn't know he was gone until he was halfway across the world.

Houdini himself to a better place, one that had never heard of Corona Tower, Weston Rodheimer, or Halo Sunchaser.

The black god of exhaustion got the better of him. It swooped down like a bird, the heavens raining fire, a praying mantis with Popeye arms divided by extra joints in the forearms, one named Justin Kurtew, a man he used to know.

Used to know because Justin was now more mantis than man, hardly human at all.

As the darkness ate him up, Garik felt his hackles rise, and deep within him, his reasoning faded, a growl that was a basso rumble formed at the back of his throat, and he lifted his head and howled.

The sound was his need for revenge for all that he had lost. It was out there, and it would be his.

Then he collapsed into embers and ash, and the blackness of oblivion swallowed him whole.

DAY ONE, two, or three? Garik didn't know. He had pulled at the restraints several times, on each occasion felled by the ash god of oblivion. This time when he woke, he had a tube in his arm, and above him bags of energy leaked life into his veins.

"I would prefer pizza," he called into the room.

"Good, you're awake." Nurse Leah Fortinier walked from behind him into his line of sight. She reached to the bag, squeezed it gently, then pulled a marker from her pocket. She neatly printed *pizza* on the bag. "There, taste better?"

"Absolutely. I'm glad to see you've developed a sense of humor."

"I've always had a sense of humor. You've just failed to appreciate it."

"Tell me about Canada. Please."

"Please? Did I hear you correctly?" She stopped as if surprised.

"I'm appealing to your sense of humor. If I make you laugh, you might answer my question. Canada, please?"

"Certainly. It lies mostly above the forty-ninth parallel north, is the second largest country in the world, and holds over half of all the lakes in existence. There are two official languages—"

"Thank you, Coach Cates. He was my sixth-grade geography teacher, if you're asking, and he was more thorough than I wanted him to be. So, I know all that. Tell me about the Canadian research facility. How's it like this? Different, too?"

"Does it matter?" She pulled back the lapels of his pajamas and attached two sensors to his chest with sticky pads.

"I've got nothing else to do but listen." It hit him that he hadn't been wearing pajamas when he was first locked into the restraints. "The pajamas. How did you do that?"

"I didn't." She smiled. She worked another sensor under his pajama leg to the top of his thigh, and then produced two more for the inside of each elbow. "You must sleep sometime. We, meaning the hospital staff, took advantage."

"I hope not," he mumbled.

"Hope not what?" She worked the wires on the various sensors to a panel at the foot of the bed and began plugging them in.

"Nothing. If I slept, it's been a day at least. Correct?" Colonel Brace had said he would have his "volunteers" on site within three days. If Garik was to survive this, he had to come up with a plan, one that didn't include his brain and spinal juices being sucked from his body to enable three hundred soldiers to become DNA clones of him.

Why did being perfect—according to Director Rodheimer—have to be so difficult?

GARIK LEARNED to tell who walked into the room before he opened his eyes. Artificially applied scents, natural pheromones, even people's preferred hand soap. His ears told him nearly as much. Nurse Fortinier walked with a hard heel-first step, very precise and businesslike. Dr. Jimenez was softer, almost creeping, as though he wanted to observe without being observed. Brace had been in once, standing behind Garik, telling Jimenez in a low voice that the Canadians had a much more modern facility, and he could arrange for him to be transferred with a word. Garik recognized the man's smell before he began to speak.

"The city, Colonel. Can you offer me that?"

"Yellowknife is only an hour by plane. Anything you need, and I mean anything, can be shipped in for your convenience."

"And who would watch over your three hundred volunteers, Colonel? They must have the best care possible, and that is me."

"I am working on that. We have begun eliminating—"

Garik stopped listening at that point. *Eliminating!* Brace was referencing people he knew. He had studied the methods of Nazi Germany and the prison camps of the war. Experiment on people the rest of the world doesn't know or care about, and when you have used them up, eliminate them. The Nazis had used guns, gas, and ovens. The Tower had repurposed the hybrid failures for a living DNA bank, and once they had what they needed, they harvested reusable body parts. He remembered Chad Sherwin's legs, "donated" by another hybrid that couldn't use them.

Harvested was more like it.

"Are you sure the creature can't hear us?" Brace's words brought Garik back into the room.

"He is a man, Colonel, and he is sleeping."

"Those needles moved."

Garik didn't know the needles they were watching, but he forced his breathing and heart into a sleep-like rhythm. Slower, slower. He could do this.

"See, Colonel? Just dreaming. Everything has settled down. About Canada. Ask me again when we have your men fully hybridized. I might be agreeable."

Garik's anger was a rising storm. *Eliminating. I don't think so, Colonel Brace, not as I live and breathe.* Man or wolf, he would do whatever it took to get to his friends.

He locked onto one thing: Yellowknife. Then a second: one hour away.

That's where his pack was, and an alpha wolf never abandons the pack.

— 2 —

AN INVASION of suits and uniforms paraded through the door. They didn't ask and Garik couldn't have refused with his limbs firmly embedded into restraints that seemed stronger than steel.

"Am I the guest of honor?" Garik felt his situation like a vice, about to squeeze him in two. These people were the pinchers on one side, and his impending brain drain was on the other. They were coming together, and he was caught in the middle.

"As you will note, gentlemen, no dulling of mental sharpness or wit." Weston Rodheimer, with his broad shoulders derived from his silverback gorilla DNA, let the words rumble from him.

"This is our Action Plan?" Lt. Col. Marjorie Fair, wearing red hair and a dense pattern of freckles, looked doubtful. "Alfred, give us your input."

"Yes, ma'am." Major Alfred Lipstitch stepped forward. Tightly groomed dark hair told of his desire for perfection, to keep the program moving forward to complete and utter success. "First note, the men will not react well to the restraints on the prototype. They must be removed."

"I agree, Director." Fair. "We are under the oversight of Community Service, even within the auspices of this program. The well-being of each volunteer is at the heart of team morale."

"Brace?" Rodheimer by-stepped formalities and cut his question directly to the colonel. "We have consistently operated independently of oversight. Otherwise, we cannot successfully move forward."

"I understand, Director. Washington gives me no leeway in this." Colonel William Brace, a man with pretentions to Southern gentility, seemed almost apologetic.

"This is a new policy?" Rodheimer's words were hard.

"Not at all, Director. Your previous volunteers—" meaning everyone recently relocated to the new Canadian facility, "—were civilians or otherwise outside the U.S. military infrastructure. You have requested three hundred of our finest enlisted—"

"And this is different than the team we provided you with previously? They required no such Community Service." Rodheimer referenced the flawed paramilitary goons Brace had used to wrest control of Corona Tower from the Director when the power structure in Bay City had nearly collapsed under the weight of public protests, rioting, and terrorist activity. Brace's "goons" required oxygen concentrators to supplement their bodies' oxygen consumption during military exercises. They were frighteningly capable but flawed, and Garik was the pivot for creating the improved super soldier that would revolutionize military machines around the world.

"Ma'am, if I may." Lipstitch stepped forward slightly. "Director Rodheimer, the first team to be hybridized had the government's assurance that this was a tested and approved procedure with no possibility of side effects. But as you know—"

"Dr. Jamie," Rodheimer interrupted, now fully irritated, "please explain to this man that we gave them flawed men because Colonel Brace insisted that we come through with product. Rushed product. Incomplete product. This falls on the military's shoulders, not ours."

"Unimportant," Lipstitch said, brushing the interruption aside. "The first team entered this program with wide eyes expecting no issues. That's not what they got. This new team has seen the drawbacks of the first team's DNA enhancement. They have requested assurance that they will not suffer a similar drawback."

"Thank you, Alfred," Fair said. "And that is where Community Service comes into play. The men who have already arrived wish to meet with the prototype, see that he is fully functional, perhaps view his skills in action. The others on the way will likely have the same request."

"Director, is this possible?" Brace asked his question in a tone that indicated it had better be.

"Let me see what I can work out. The, um, *prototype* is our singular example, and to replicate the DNA melding process in a new prototype . . . I will have to work out how to meet your request without jeopardizing our end goals."

"Understood. Thank you, Director." Fair looked to Brace and Lipstitch. "We are through here? I have other duties on my plate. If I have your permission, Colonel?"

Garik watched the military fluffs file out, never having spoken to him or responded to his question, no more than a cipher in their day, a prototype to use up and discard at will.

As Rodheimer reached the door, he turned to study Garik, looked to Jimenez and nodded, then faced forward and was gone.

"Was I the guest of honor?" He prodded Jimenez, hoping to get him to acknowledge him as a real person.

"If you wish," the doctor said. He looked hard at Garik, evaluating, and not kindly. "If we must do as requested, there can be no errors. No escapes, no independent action. We will preview a plan, and we will stick to it. I hope that's clear."

"Clear," Garik said. The man nodded and moved away. He still hadn't used Garik's name, either first or last. And *prototype?* Whatever plan Jimenez and Rodheimer put into place, they might intend to stick to it, but Garik had other ideas. His hero, Harry Houdini, had been able to escape anything. Now it was Garik's turn, and he let the problem ping about in his brain. There was nothing else to do. He was strapped onto a table, again with fresh clothes, once again taken advantage of during the night. He suspected Nurse Ratchett's sleepy juice was involved. Otherwise, he would have noticed, you'd think, someone manhandling him to change his clothes. One thought rankled more than all the rest. *It was likely to happen again,* with or without his permission. He twisted his arms under his restraints, trying to force them free, only to admit he was trapped until he came up with a plan.

MORE SHACKLES, of a different sort, the kind with minders carrying dart pistols, as Garik was released to dress for the meet-and-greet with the men he would be sharing his LIFE WITH.

"Privacy? Or am I no longer allowed that?" Garik held the clothes he'd been given, a lightweight black turtleneck with long sleeves, gray slacks, polished black brogues, and socks and boxer briefs. Even a stick of deodorant. A belt was coiled and in one of the shoes. He recognized the things from his closet and knew they'd gone through everything he owned.

"I'm afraid not." Second Lt. Ron Wilder, a man with thinning hair and delicate features. His arms looked like they could bust bricks. "You may stand behind the chair if you feel the need."

Wilder held his hand just over the butt of his holstered gun, prepared, prepared. Something about the way he stood was off, and Garik let the image work through him as he stepped behind the chair and began to work his "lock-up" things off and kicked them to the side before selecting the briefs. He slipped them on, watching Wilder, and his memory linked a documentary he'd once watched about Israeli agents who'd hunted down Nazis in hiding after the war. Then another with real Mossad agents telling their story of pursuing the terrorist group Black September after they had killed eleven members of the Israeli Olympic team in Munich in the 70s.

The gears clicked, and Garik wondered if Colonel Brace knew one of his men was Mossad, likely with a degree from Harvard, a family on Long Island, adored nieces and nephews, and even pictures of them—all fictional. That's how it worked in the world of undercover.

Surely the man wasn't also hybrid. With those arms . . . was it possible that Israel had a program of their own, and Wilder was here to ensure that North America didn't best them at their own game?

Garik slipped his shirt over his head, his arms through the

sleeves, his eyes back on Wilder. They had met for the first time in the elevator. Airman Vang had been present, and Vang and Wilder had teamed up against him. A diversion? Garik had only seen him once more with Vang, never noticed him in a routine or even in the same location, and the man had pretended not to recognize Garik the last time they'd met.

The only thing Garik hadn't observed was the man slitting his plastic trash bags so his garbage couldn't be stolen from a dumpster. He smiled at that.

"Something amusing, Mr. Shayk?"

"Just picturing you cutting up your trash bags before dropping them in a dumpster."

"That's an odd thing to say." Wilder's hand lowered to his weapon, and his eyes narrowed.

"Only if you're—" Garik glanced at the two minders with the dart guns. They were trained on him.

"Only what, Mr. Shayk?"

"Only if you're a neat freak. Then it would be odd." Garik shrugged and he moved to the other side of the chair to sit and put on his shoes.

Wilder's hand relaxed, and he motioned to the two men with him. "He's ready. Shackles on, then let's move toward the training area."

Garik groaned. The men pulled out metal shackles that they fastened to his wrists and his ankles, with a chain connecting them.

"You've got to be kidding me."

"Director's orders." Wilder pulled a key from his pocket and showed it to Garik. "I have the only one, and it's right here."

"Won't the new volunteers see the chains?" He pulled his arms up as high as possible and shook them.

"Once we're on the elevator, the building will go into lockdown. Only my passkey will still permit movement around the facility. Remember that, Mr. Shayk, only my passkey. You will be released then. Not before."

"Small favors," Garik mumbled.

"Perhaps not so small," Wilder assured him, and they headed out the door, with Garik nearly tripping with every step he took.

ABOUT thirty men were gathered in the recreation area, this first group having flown in directly from the Canadian facility. When they arrived, a number were looking around, inspecting the amenities. Others were seated, bored, waiting on the display of Garik's skills to start. They carried a cross section of the world in their faces, many in bronze or coffee shades. The pale, blond faces were the fewest. Most were unlined, a few more mature, but all trim and fit.

A good thing, Garik considered, a leg up for those aspiring to become an improvement to what Colonel Brace's paramilitary already were.

Garik's arrival with Wilder changed the tone of the room. Men tapped shoulders, pointed, whispered, called to their friends, shifted chairs, moved to sit closer to the front. Garik realized he must present an appealing sight. Six-four, a thick chest, and powerful legs. What military man wouldn't wish to tower over almost everyone around him?

Wilder introduced him, asked them to hold off on their questions about his abilities, that Garik would provide some demonstrations later. Now was their time to find out about his experience going through the transformation. He directed Garik to a seat in front of the men, and he opened the floor for questions. The two dart guns, concealed from the crowd, were at his back.

The first question was from a blond man with buzzed hair. "We've seen some of the hybrids. Does the process hurt?"

"Only if you don't request sleepy juice," Garik responded. He heard chuckles in the crowd.

"Will we look like you after we change?" A coffee man with tight hair painted on his head. The implication was *or something weird like them?*

"Only if you want to become better looking." Garik grinned.

The questions began to come faster, from the length of time it had taken Garik to change, to the accommodations they could expect in the facility.

It was as they were moving toward the demonstration area that Garik overheard someone whisper, "Do you think he knows the guy with the purple eyes?"

"Who asked that?" He stopped and looked over the men, narrowing it down to one area. Three men were walking side by side.

"You could hear that?" The man was surprised.

"You said *knows*. What man with purple eyes?"

"Tim-o, you've met him. What's his name?"

"Hefferly, I think. Yeah, Jantzen Hefferly."

"He's alive?" Garik felt the floor rise up and hit him in the chest.

"Last time I checked," the man said, "and that was two days ago."

For Garik, this changed everything.

— 3 —

PROBABILITIES SWAM before Garik.

Rodheimer would call it prescience, even precognition, but it was neither. Garik observed, evaluated, and extrapolated. He followed the lines of probabilities until they were exhausted, understanding that choosing one altered all the others.

Even seeing the probabilities changed how he reacted to them, and that was another facet he had to consider.

Jantzen, able to morph—or sublimate—directly from a solid into purple smoke—a gas—and resolidify at will, a derivative of his squid DNA, was unique even among the human hybrids that had come out of the secretive basement research center underneath Corona Tower. How could he be alive? The sword . . . it was the only possibility.

Garik had located the final layer of the missing schematics and determined that the arcing lightning that spat from the end was due to a short in the system, an incomplete part of the design, a flaw intentionally incorporated into the prototype device for some reason of Halo Sunchaser's. With the final page of the schematics, Garik had intuited that the original design was some sort of conduit.

A mechanized teleportation device? The idea boggled his mind, but if Jantzen was in Canada after Garik had watched the electrical jolt from the sword slam into him and dismantle him molecule by molecule, atom by atom . . .

And that's when his mind put it together. That's exactly what the sword had done, disassembled Jantzen atom by atom, and he had been reassembled elsewhere. The obvious answer was the new Canadian facility.

Sublimation to the extreme. The ultimate process of shifting directly from a solid to a gas. Transferring to some sort of energy wave that could be reconstituted a thousand or two miles away.

What a coup this would be for Sunchaser and Rodheimer. No wonder they had disguised it from Colonel Brace and hidden the only copy of the final layer of the schematics in a secured room deep within the research facility. Moving weapons, troops, whatever they needed directly from one location to another. Even space travel, eliminating the need to lift every pound of supplies on rocket ships. Reassemble it from the surface of the planet directly onto an orbital station.

Any nation would pay an exorbitant fee to gain access to such game-changing technology.

Garik processed his revelation with one part of his mind, while his body exhibited his super-human, wolf-infused abilities to the men who had come to see the Tower's tame wolf perform. His fist, splitting a punching bag with one blow. Wrestling one of their strongest and laying him to the mat with ease. Lights down and still seeing like it was daylight. A level of flexibility that enabled him to force his body through confining mazes. Even stripping to a suit and entering the pool . . . five minutes . . . ten . . . fifteen, until he was asked to come up. He also got to show them the difficulty of clearing his lungs of pool water when he needed to breathe air once again.

All the time half of his mind was focused on Jantzen . . . alive . . . and in Canada. He had to get there, to Houdini out of this place, to . . . to do what, he didn't know. But it was Jantzen! He was alive!

At the end of his demonstration, still wearing his suit and his towel over one shoulder, he called to the man who said he'd met Jantzen.

"Tim-o, wait up!" He waved a hand, lifted the towel and rubbed it over his hair, and stepped his direction. He was stopped by one of the minders with the dart gun no one could see.

"Not so far, Shayk," the man growled.

"Mr. Shayk to you," Garik retorted. "Or use my first name. I'm not going anywhere. I understand my situation." Lockdown. Dart guns. They had all the power, and once again, like his entire life, he had none at all. "I just want to talk to the man."

"Okay, then." The minder gave a little bit, just enough for Garik to greet the man.

"Tim-o," Garik said, holding out a hand to shake. "Thanks for talking to me."

"It's Tim. Shane's a dork. All that was impressive. I'm looking forward to this. I suppose you'll be training us, you know, since you've gone through this. It takes an expert to make an expert." Tim smiled, open and friendly.

"Maybe." Actually not, especially as he would be DEAD. But

that revelation wasn't why he had called the man over. "You said you'd seen Jantzen Hefferly."

"Sure. What do you want to know?"

"Um, anything. How long's he been there? How did he arrive? How's he doing?" Did he ask about me? Did he send a message? Does he remember that I'm still here and care that I'm about to have my brain-juices sucked out and given to you people?

"I don't know about most of that. Sorry." Tim shrugged. "We know him because of his purple eyes, the only person I've ever seen like that."

"What's he doing there?"

"That I can answer. Not much. He's a space cadet, a zombie, an airhead—"

"Sure. I get it." Garik didn't, though. Jantzen was brilliant.

"I don't mean to offend, but he blanks out. That's when the purple eyes really shine. We like to talk to him just to watch it happen."

"Enough." The minder stepped closer. "Mr. Shayk, Lt. Wilder is signaling it's time."

"Thank you, Tim." Garik nodded.

"Anytime. Request me for training. I want on your team."

Garik smiled and nodded. They hadn't told these men that someone had to die for them to become super soldiers. No surprise there. Especially as they weren't the ones that had to do the dying part.

BACK AT the elevator, Wilder inserted his passkey to open the doors, then inside, he inserted it once again to close them. He didn't set a location but stepped out of the way as the minders with the dart guns pulled out the manacles and chains.

"Still can't trust me, huh?" And for good reason, Garik thought. Houdini, Houdini. It was the only thing on his mind, except that Jantzen was alive!

"The building is in lockdown. You do know what that means." Wilder stepped to the side as the two minders sorted out the restraints.

"Yes, yes, and only your passkey moves the elevator." When the man started to withdraw his key to the manacles, Garik tilted his head, rolled his eyes, and said, "And you have the only key to my freedom. I get it. I have no power at all, and I might as well get used to it."

"I'm glad to see you listen well."

The men had Garik's legs and one arm locked in, and one held his other wrist, preparing to latch it, when Wilder drew a third dart gun from inside his jacket, aimed it at the neck of the man to Garik's right and fired. Then, before the man to Garik's left could look up, he turned the dart gun and took him out, too.

Wilder put his finger to his lips, and he withdrew a cloth from a sealed bag, knelt, and held it over the men's noses until they passed out.

"My turn?" Garik could likely take the man, even with only one free hand, but the passkey was a bigger problem. Without Wilder's thumbprint, it wasn't taking him very far.

"Your turn?" Wilder stood. "Perhaps, but not the way you think. The dart is a muscle relaxant, only. I need them to not remember. The pad will blur the events just before and after. You. You said you remember what I told you?"

"Sure. I don't forget." Since his change into part werewolf, he couldn't forget, visual or auditory. Eidetic memory had been a gift of the DNA.

"Good." He pulled a small pouch from a pocket and worked out a single latex glove. "Hold out your hand. This has my prints embedded into each fingertip. You will need this to exit the facility."

"Exit the facility?"

"Still doing that, are you?"

"What?" Garik could hardly focus. This man was helping him escape? What luck! He hadn't seen this coming.

"Repeating people." He worked the glove over Garik's hand, adjusting each finger to align properly.

"Why are you doing this?"

"I need a reason?" Wilder stepped back and looked at Garik, wearing three manacles, with a chain linking one hand to his feet. "Why did you ask if I slashed my garbage bags?"

"Oh, that." Garik took a deep breath. "I read one time that agents do that to keep their trash from being stolen. It falls out if someone tries—"

"I know why I would slash my garbage bags. You said agents . . ." He paused and waited.

"Okay," Garik said, tired of the hints and innuendos, "you have to be Mossad. It fits. You don't even have a family on Long Island, do you?"

Wilder laughed.

"Are you hybridized, too? Those arms—"

"And you have guessed entirely too much. I have never been to Long Island, but yes, I have family pictures in my wallet, and yes, they are an invention. I tell you this to get you to do something for me."

"You're helping me escape, so shoot." Garik grimaced. "Poor word choice. Sorry."

"I have secured the sword—"

"You! And they blamed me!" Garik was stunned. The whole complex emptied by Sunchaser in revenge, and this man was at fault!

"Wait! Hear me out. The technology you see around you is shared between your country and mine. The Director and Ms. Sunchaser have chosen to abuse it for personal gain. You've seen the risks they've taken, the monstrosities—"

"My friends," Garik warned, unsure where he was headed.

"People they would eliminate. People you can save, the reason I pushed for them to be transferred to the new facility."

"And the sword?"

"A distraction. Eminently vital if the technology can be made useful, but for now, only a distraction to allow you to escape."

"And do what?" He had the final page of the schematics. He knew how to "fix" the sword. He was certain Wilder didn't know that.

"That answer is difficult. However, you are capable, everything this program has worked to achieve. The Canadians will be amenable." Wilder pulled out a thin leather document holder very much like a passport. "Show this at the border, then again at the facility. You must have the sword with you."

"There's a lot unexplained, but one thing I'll need is clothes. They'll be looking for me in this."

"Excellent thought. Here." Wilder worked one minder's dart gun from the man's waist and handed it to Garik. He talked as he began to work off his uniform. "You will need to anesthetize me to make this believable. Shoot me with this gun and leave it here. Take the unused one with you. Three shots, three darts used."

"The sword?" Garik hefted the gun. It was unfamiliar to him but seemed easy to use.

"I always carry the keys to my Jeep." He was to his shorts by then, and he held out his shirt, jacket, and pants. The metal in his pocket clinked.

"Which explains nothing. Can you unlock me first?"

"Good. If they question me, I can say you begged for your freedom. I must also be able to say you were still in restraints and that I did not offer you any assistance. On the neck, please. I want the dart in my skin when they find me. You would have to remove it with the clothes anywhere else."

"Okay. Ready?"

"From behind. They must think you a coward."

Garik lifted the gun, fired, and watched the man slump to the floor. He realized he didn't know where the man's car was. A Jeep. He could find a Jeep. He rustled through the pockets, found the key to the shackles, and unlocked them.

For you, Jantzen, he thought, as he stripped and pulled on Lt. Wilder's uniform. It was snug. His socks showed, and he was forced to wear his own shoes, but it was doable. Wilder's cap fit fine. He looked at the glove on his hand, pressed Wilder's thumbprint to the passkey, and watched the display light up.

Before choosing a destination, he dragged the three men out of the elevator and tossed the two used guns after them. He kept the unused one with him as Wilder had requested.

He almost pushed the button to take him to the mall. He could picture freedom from there. Yet, Wilder would have parked in the underground garage . . . where Paul Gberie and John Carter had fallen and Jantzen had been taken from him. His stomach churned at returning to that place, but he pressed. As the door closed, he listened to the ding that said he was on his way.

— 4 —

THE GARAGE.

Close in, the parking area was separated off for the exclusive Stamford Suites in the Tower. Beyond the concrete barriers set up to keep the richies from the riffraff, blocks of parking spaces reached into the distance. Cars peppered those closer in. Even with the research center mostly emptied, some people were required to keep the facility running, and the staff in the forty-story building needed somewhere to park.

Jeep. Where was it? Jeep, Jeep, come to me, Jeep.

The key had a remote fob, and he pressed the unlock button. A beep-beep echoed in the hard-ceilinged space, and he turned, looking. Another press, and a single beep narrowed his search. He pressed it again, this time catching the flashing lights as they painted the ceiling red.

He ran that way, aware of how outside the box his actions were. Darting someone, wearing a military uniform, out and about *during a building lockdown* . . . would Rodheimer ever be angry! He grinned. He loved it. Inside the Jeep, he hit the seat adjustment button to give his long legs room, touched the starter, and checked the gauges. It was only his second time to drive a car. The first was Kevin Lee's van, and that had been a disaster. This time, no busted windows!

Approaching the exit, the gates were closed, and he considered if they would open, or if he would need to use Wilder's passkey. With the place in lockdown . . . the gates moved aside as he approached. He breathed a sigh of relief. They were set to lock people out, not keep people in.

He drove up the ramp into the sun and sat, thinking of the tracking device inside him. It was linked to whoever was assigned to monitor him. He had Wilder's passkey, likely why no one was pursuing him already. When he drove away from the building, what would happen then? He guessed he would have to drive faster, but where? All he knew was Canada and Yellowknife. He typed in "Yellowknife" on the GPS screen, and one of the choices that pulled up was Yellowknife, Northwest Territories. Beside it, 39 hours, 2,290 miles. At least the Jeep wasn't total electric. No way would he find enough recharging stations in such a remote area.

Then the foundations for his plans began to crack. Gas cost money, and he had none. Yet, if Wilder had prepared all this, he must have made plans for that. Garik opened the console to find a thick packet of mixed bills, a valid-looking driver's license with his name and photo, and insurance on the Jeep in his name. Inside the glove box were travel documents, maps, and on one map, a red X in a red circle with no other information. Garik understood that was his destination.

Research labs. Why build only one, when the military will fund two at twice the price?

A pair of sunglasses on the dash seemed fitted just for him, and he slipped them on. He clicked Start on the navigation panel, and the image shifted, revealing the streets in Bay City, and said, "Make a right turn on Stamford Drive, then stay right to take Corona Street towards Sycamore." An arrow appeared showing his car turning right.

As the Jeep moved forward, the electric-only range showed 120 miles. The dinosaur tank was completely full. *Sorry, dinosaurs*, he thought. *You're gonna burn a second time today*. He hoped for a couple hours before he needed to suck them into the engine.

South on Sycamore took him to a left on First at the Old City Hall, past Park Avenue and the powerline right-of-way, and towards Bay City Medical and beyond to I-80 north. He was leaving his life behind, Muhammad, Ibn, Hayat, his Street Strider, his aunt, skating at the Connel Street Skate Park, his memories of Marisa, all of it. Thirty-nine hours. Could he do it?

Could he not?

Jantzen, transmorphized from Bay City to a place two thousand miles away. What had happened during that journey? A glitch in the system? A sword that Sunchaser refused to calibrate to a functional operating level because she wanted to claim the rights for her own?

How many had to suffer for the greed of people who were already rich by most people's standards?

He was just outside Bay City readying to accelerate onto the I-80 entrance ramp when a winged creature the size of a small car alighted on the roadway in front of him. He felt the Jeep slam on the brakes for him before he could react, and driver assist warnings flashed across the dash. The Jeep lurched to a stop feet before hitting the creature. Garik gulped air to calm himself before rolling down the window, leaning out, and yelling, "Justin, you idiot! I nearly hit you!"

"Yet, you didn't." The man's mantis-like jaw clacked twice when he finished speaking, a byproduct of his insect-infused bone structure giving him a jaw more suited to dismembering prey than speaking clear English.

"And, oh, my gosh, put on some clothes!" Garik leaned his head back and shut his eyes. Yet, what he had seen couldn't be unseen ever again. Eidetic. He could never forget, either visual or auditory. Curse Justin for a new memory he didn't want. The back of the Jeep opened and Justin began to rustle around.

"Did you look back here at all?" Clack, clack.

"I was running from men trying to suck out my brain. No, I

didn't look back there. I saved that for you."

"How does that uniform fit?" Clack, clack.

"Why?" Garik opened his eyes and saw Justin in the rearview mirror. He had folded in on himself, put on a black knit cap pulled low over his head, and he was pushing his long, thick arms into the sleeves of a leather duster.

"Thought it might be a bit snug, you know, where it counts." The clacks were infused with humor.

"Are you making fun of me?" Garik pushed open his door and exited the Jeep. Justin was right there, nose to nose, looking as normal as a human-hybrid praying mantis can look when wearing a leather duster and knit cap. They were about the same height, and Justin began to laugh.

"Lt. Wilder's not a big guy, I gather. Nice socks." Clack, clack.

"You're still an idiot. What are you doing here?" Garik tried to pull information from his memory explaining Justin's presence *on a random highway in the middle of nowhere.*

Yet, he had pulled clothes from the back of the Jeep, and that meant he knew they would be there. If Wilder was truly Mossad—which he hadn't admitted—and the Israeli government was also in the human-hybrid game . . . had Justin been recruited for a Mossad spy?

Garik blurted, "Are you Mossad, also?"

"Psst! As American as you." The clacks continued but less noticeable.

"Hello, Mossad agent. I'm Russian." Well, Armenian, but close enough. His parents lived in Russia, and he was born there.

"Hmm." Justin looked at Garik with new respect. "You've grown a bite with your new height. Ron told me to expect it—"

"Ron?" Repeating information, but Garik didn't care.

"Lt. Wilder. Get with me, my friend." Justin bumped a pincher-like hand against Garik's forehead. "You have clothes in the back that will fit. We need to find a rest stop—"

"I can change here." Wilder's uniform was indeed cutting off circulation, and Justin's reminder was making the tight fit more and more uncomfortable.

"But." Justin paused for effect. "I. Can't. Remove. Your. Tracking. Device. Here."

"Thank you." Relief flooded Garik. "I was worried about that."

"So are we. Rodheimer and Brace have to think you've disappeared, not that you're heading to Yellowknife. Get in. You can drive or I can."

"My driver's license and insurance. You ride shotgun."

"Fine with me."

As Justin turned, Garik noted how the wings fit nicely into the broad shoulders cut into the coat. Almost as if he were totally, completely, one-hundred-percent human.

Something neither of them could claim.

JUSTIN MADE sure Garik carried Lt. Wilder's passkey in with them. In a stall, he ran a scanning device over Garik, finally asking him to remove his shirt. The device beeped repeatedly at his lower back, just where Garik wouldn't be able to reach it easily if he wanted to remove the tracking beacon himself.

"Can't I just keep Wilder's passkey in my pocket?" Garik didn't like the size of the knife Justin held in his hand.

"When he is found and they can't locate his passkey, they will disengage it. They will begin searching for your beacon, and you are sending out to half of North America. It has to be out and now."

"Okay, but—" and Garik lurched as the knife buried into his back. "Yi-yi-yi, please finish!"

"When I find it." After another thirty seconds, Justin proclaimed, "Got it!"

"Let me see." Garik straightened. He placed his hand on the wound, only to feel smooth skin, the damage from the tracker already healed. The pain was with him forever, however. That's what eidetic meant . . . he never forgot.

A small device, a chip, likely, with a glowing red light and a tiny antenna. It and four inches of the knife's blade were stained red.

"Can I smash it?" Garik took his new shirt from a pile, worked his arms into the sleeves, and pulled it over his head. He dropped Wilder's pants and kicked them aside.

"Got something better." Justin handed him a worn pair of jeans. "These, and I have cloth boaters for you in the sack. We're changing your look."

"I like my look." Garik grinned as he slipped the jeans on. They buttoned at his waist, a perfect fit. "What are you doing with that?"

"I'm sending you south, hopefully as far as Mexico."

"How?" Garik was pretty sure Yellowknife and Canada were a long way to the north.

"A military-grade drone in the car. We're attaching this and Ron's passkey to it and sending it off. Where it crashes, no one knows."

"At least we won't. I'm sure the Director will."

"Distraction. Diversion." Justin gave him a clumsy thumbs up with his pincher-like hands. "And before you ask, you were right about Ron. And Mossad has made his Jeep as invisible as possible, so that should give us some protection. It's why we don't have watches or any other mobile devices with us." Justin had bagged the uniform, and he handed it to Garik.

"Except for the car's GPS." Garik had his shoes on and noted the worn look, like they had been his favorites for months. He approved.

"It runs on a virtual private network. It pings Europe if anyone's looking."

"Cool." One of his aunt's words. Irina had always liked old-fashioned terms. Using it reminded him of her. Good times that he could never bring back again.

"Ready?" Justin put his hand on the door latch.

Garik nodded, and they stepped out together into a stream of leather-covered, tattoo-inked bikers entering. The lead man, as tall as Garik and Justin, with a long beard and shoulders like a bear, took them in and nodded.

"My apologies for interrupting. No discrimination here. What you do on your time is your business." The others with him nodded their agreement.

"Thank you. I appreciate your open-minded attitude." Garik grinned, and he tugged Justin out the door.

"What?" Justin looked back to the restrooms, and he had a shocked expression. "Did he think . . . that we . . . how dare he!"

"It's funny. Laugh about it." Garik slapped him in the chest with the back of his hand. "Where's that drone? I want my tracking device in Mexico."

They found it in the back of the Jeep next to the electrified sword.

"Wilder said I had to have this. He didn't tell me where it was. He can truthfully say he told me nothing and didn't offer me any help. I hope he makes it okay."

"You darted him, right?" Justin was setting up the drone. It had a built-in tray for the passkey and the tracking device.

"Pow, pow, you're dead."

Justin looked at him hard.

"Well, anesthetized." Garik shrugged.

Justin's expression relaxed, and he started up the drone. It lifted and sped away towards the south. He set the control back into the car, told Garik he was driving, and they were off to Canada . . . by way of Nevada, Idaho, Montana, and every place in between.

— 5 —

GARIK OPENED his eyes to the glow of dash lights on Justin Kurtew's beak-like jaw. He still wore the knit cap and duster. His wrists extended from the sleeves, thickened, a Popeye caricature, and his hands seemed more pincers than fingers.

What was normal? How much could a man change and still remain who he was? Devon Maye's story of before and after, about his mother as an Olympic hopeful, to have her hopes dashed with a medical diagnosis that said she might not live to see her son married . . . yet, to Devon, she was the same person, someone who loved him more than life itself. Before and after, no difference.

Garik hadn't known Justin truly *before*, but he had seen the man make dramatic changes. He had been a man before, mostly, and now? Mantis almost completely. Yet, the bantering personality, the person that was static electricity in every conversation, the in-your-face response to things he didn't agree with hadn't changed. Justin was still Justin.

Garik wasn't sure he could say the same about himself. How far would his "after" take him? Was he there yet?

"You're awake." A single clack, subtle, as though Justin was trying to control it.

"Where are we?" Garik's voice was thick, and he cleared his throat, more of a rumble than a ripple.

"Idaho. Not much here, so I can't say much more. I just follow the little arrow on the screen. Did you growl at me?"

"I don't think so." Garik adjusted his position to relieve pressure on his back. His voice still felt thick. "Where you stabbed me is uncomfortable."

"I enjoyed that, by the way. Even-stevens for what you did to me in the ring."

"I'll do worse if you stab me again. Find somewhere to stop. I need to get out and stretch."

"Rest stop in thirty-seven miles. Are you good that long?"

"Sure." He reached behind the seat and rustled through several bags. They had stocked up for the road at a convenience store with a small ice chest, prepackaged meats, and other snackeries. A bag of chips rustled, and he pulled it into the front seat with him.

"Cheddar or vinegar?"

"Let me look." Garik held it up, read aloud, "Salt-and-vinegar," and popped the top of the bag to release a crisp, pungent aroma.

"Strong." Justin didn't indicate approval or disapproval, just a fact.

"You were with Joanie in the city. What happened?" The third person in Justin's group was last seen face down in the garage looking pretty dead.

"Like are we alive? Some of us." He clacked, less subtly, revealing emotion. "Giselle, Julia, and Paolo—"

"With Jantzen, I know." The memory haunted him.

"Your eyeshine really shows up at night. I've got the dash lights down, can barely see you, and you read that chip wrapper like it's daylight."

"Yeah." Glad to be distracted, he put a chip in his mouth and sat up, nearly spitting it out. He chewed it, cardboard, and swallowed with difficulty.

"What?"

"Who could eat this?" He held up the bag and looked for the expiration date, certain they had gone stale LIKE LAST YEAR.

"You picked them. Let me taste."

Garik held out the open bag, Justin groped for it, as though he couldn't find it in the dark, then worked out a chip. He crunched it, pronounced it stringently acidic, and said they tasted like normal vinegar-and-salt to him.

"I can't eat them. Do you want any?"

"Like I said, you picked them."

"Okay." Garik rolled the top, leaned over the seat, returned them to the sack, and dug in the ice chest for a package of bratwurst. He bit into one, and the flavor rolled down his throat like a sultry night in the desert, warm, comforting, and no distractions.

"Have you noticed that's all you're eating?"

"Not especially." Yet, he had. None of the grain-based snacks had appealed to him, but none had put him off like the chips. Yeah, Justin, he had noticed. "Let me know when we reach the rest stop."

"Like a bullhorn."

"Idiot." Garik laid his head against the door and let the motion of the car lull him into darkness.

THE REST stop was like daylight.

To Garik, anyway. As they pulled in, he came awake and tried to sit up. The Jeep rocked as Justin pulled over a speed hump, and Garik released a ragged breath.

"Sorry, man. I didn't pick the car."

"My back. I don't know why I hurt. I never have before."

"Lucky you." Justin pulled into a spot, killed the dinosaur engine, and said, "Bullhorn."

"I used to hate you." Garik worked his feet into his shoes.

"And I spoiled that how?"

"You haven't. I hurt too much to care right now."

"Baby. Take a walk."

"On the wild side?" Garik chuckled. He released the door, and the interior of the Jeep was like a strobe. He closed his eyes to let them adjust.

"To look at you, yeah. I didn't bring a shaving kit."

"It's a man's world. Preparing for Canada." Garik pulled himself from the car. "Don't leave without me."

He put his hand on his back where the knife had removed the tracker and realized that was only a small amount of it. Every part of him felt different, out of sorts, like when he was thirteen and growing, hurting all the time. He looked to the building, saw the men's sign, and stepped inside. In the mirror, he saw what Justin had seen. He was alone and stripped off his shirt, breathed in deeply, anger looking back at him in the image.

Wolf boy. Werewolf. Sideshow act. He looked at his fingers, searching for Christian's wolfhound hands. His nails, coarser, perhaps, but not claws, not yet.

"What have you people done to me?" he asked the mirror, balling his hand. He hardly recognized his voice, didn't want more changes, and smashed his fist into the glass, only to discover it wasn't glass but polished stainless steel. The metal deformed, dimpled the concrete block behind it, and held. Garik pulled his hand back, his throat giving off a whimpering sound that turned into a growl.

"Same old story." Justin stood at the door. "Don't mean to intrude, but this is the only restroom, and even us weirdos can't go in the open. Sorry. The highway department won't be happy about that mirror."

"You see me? Look at me."

"I'm not blind, just weird." Justin held up his hand and pretended to study it. "Yeah, still weird."

"Does it ever stop?" The changes, the distance between where he began and where he ended. The before and after. The losing everything he once treasured as important and having a future so unfamiliar he couldn't fathom it.

"Do you see me?" Justin snorted. "I *molt.* There is no stopping, not until what Corona Corporation has done to us runs its course."

"I'm supposed to be their super soldier."

"So was I. Welcome to reality. Since you're here, hold my coat." He began pulling off his duster.

"Nah, Justin!" Garik turned his head. He'd seen enough of the man on the road.

"Now who's the idiot? I have on clothes under this. What'd you used to say? Sheesh!" He tossed the duster to Garik and entered the stall.

Garik stepped outside. He didn't know what sounds mantises made when doing their business, and he didn't think he wanted to find out.

GARIK WAS surprised when they crossed into Canada. The border guards looked at his passport from Lt. Wilder, took a similar one from Justin, made some phone calls, noted the plates on the Jeep, and passed them through.

"How did that happen?" Garik had fully planned to skirt the checkpoint and had assumed that was the reason for the Jeep. Go anywhere through any terrain, then back on the road again.

"Mossad. There's mutual support between the countries." Justin brushed it off.

"Nah, this is about the program. After they called in, they never looked at you twice, and you're something to look at."

"Said the wolf with the big eyes to Little Red Riding Hood."

"Sheesh. Let me know when you want me to drive." Garik leaned his seat back. Now his legs hurt. What was going on with them?

There was no sleep to be found, and he watched the countryside evaporate behind them, in places revealing glinting patches of winter snow. He tried to see Jantzen but couldn't picture him without the purple mist. Would Jantzen know him? Or would he have changed so much that he would be just another Justin, a cast-off, a true cipher in the boundless Yellowknife wilderness?

THIRTY-NINE hours had turned into nearly forty-eight, with refueling stops, the border crossing, and Garik's increasing need to get out of the Jeep, move around, as Justin called it, pacing like a wolf, taking in the Canadian aromas, sniffing the air, learning of the new world around him. It was his first time this far north, wild country compared to Bay City, and he wanted to be out in it.

Not crammed into a Jeep that was feeling smaller by the mile.

By the time they reached Hwy 3—the Yellowknife Highway around Great Slave Lake—wood bison shared their journey, looking up as they passed, then ignoring the disruption and returning to grazing. A mile of steel girder bridge leapfrogged the Mackenzie River as they drove past lake after lake after lake.

After a night in Yellowknife, they headed out on Ingraham Trail, marked as Hwy 4, the reason for the Jeep, as Garik quickly realized. The pavement ran out less than an hour along the road, and then that turned to gravel. The red X on his map seemed truly to be in the middle of nowhere. The road ended at Tibbitt Lake, but a track cut off before then, the only possible path to the Canadian facility.

"They wanted to get away from it all, didn't they?" Garik was driving, and he navigated the Jeep like he stole it, often in 4-wheel low, gunning the engine over rutted sections, and working through snowmelt that seemed determined to swallow the tires for an afternoon snack.

"Just keep driving." Justin wasn't in a better mood. The trip had become a slog, from the sunny West Coast to the remains of a winter not long over. Coats were becoming necessary, and only Justin had one of those.

They topped a rise to find a stone and dirt embankment blocking their way. WARNING, a sign said. Underneath, written in smaller letters, GOVERNMENT FACILITY – NO ENTRANCE PERMITTED.

"This must be it." Garik searched for a gate, guards maybe, to whom they could show their identification and get inside.

"Seems so. I'll be right back." Justin opened the door, walked to the back of the Jeep, and rooted around. He returned with earbuds and a watch, which he was strapping to his thick wrist. The strap was especially long, meaning it was designed just for him.

"You had a watch." Meaning, *you had a phone.* "And you couldn't tell me."

"No, I couldn't," Justin said, and he tapped on the phone's face, waking it, and tapped again. He spoke, "We're here." After a moment, he spoke again, less polite. "Who do you think is driving for two days to get here and parked outside the gate? And yes, he has it. Open up, you fruitcake."

"Fruitcake?" Garik found reason to be amused.

"Ron set this up. They've surveilled us the past two hours. This is a Mossad-supplied vehicle with all the signatures that should provide them, and I'm tired. No offense, wolf boy, but the dog smell is about to get to me."

Dog smell. Something Garik hadn't noticed. What else had he missed? A section of the stone wall in front of them dropped into the ground, and Justin waved Garik ahead, telling him it was the point of the Jeep. Drive over the embankment. The other side revealed nothing except more trees, grass, and mounds of rotting snow.

"Now?" Garik watched behind them as the stone wall filled the gap once again.

"Go. Look for the red flare. It takes us underground."

Again. Garik was tired of being underground. Did no one like living in the sun? Sheesh! He pulled forward, finally locating the flare burning half a mile ahead.

— 6 —

GARIK SLAMMED the Jeep to a stop, called out, "I can't," and the world around him shifted to a kaleidoscopic rainbow of colors.

They were at the entrance to the underground complex. Justin sitting next to him froze, a rainbow man dressed in surprise. The trees in the landscape, poplar, spruce, pine, birch, and fir leapfrogged in fantastic rainbows to grasp the pristine Canadian sky. A man just ahead held a flare. He was stepping their way, forever with one foot in the air, ready to tread on the sturdy buffalo grass and sheep fescue that littered the walled-in compound.

Garik threw the door back, sending a wave of rainbows rippling through the air. He was beside the Jeep, then twenty feet away, then forty, breathing deep, taking in the forest aroma of poplar and pine and fir. It was if he had never lived, as if he needed this just to be alive. To drive below ground? It was an impossible request. Who could live in such a place? He would be crushed, his soul imprisoned, his spirit silenced forever.

He counted off without realizing he was doing so, sixteen, seventeen, eighteen . . . what was his life worth? How much did he have to pay to exact revenge for what had been done to him? Twenty-two, twenty-three . . . Mama, Papa . . . twenty-four . . . Jantzen, you abandoned me . . . twenty-five, twenty-six . . . his time was about up, and he released the rainbows, watched them evaporate into the clear Canadian sky, the wisps of their passing a longing he could never fulfill.

It was what he wanted to do, evaporate into the world around him, enter nature, never return. It called to him, the wilderness. He'd sensed it on the drive up, stronger and stronger, hadn't known what it was. Now he knew. This was where he was meant to be.

And no, not in the underground facility they'd driven forty-eight hours to reach. The wilderness, the wide-open landscape that ran as far as he could see, smell, hear, and taste.

Freedom. He'd always craved it. Now, there it was, just on the other side of the wall, even now being taken from him once again.

"HEY, GARIK, man, what was that?"

Garik turned to see Justin. He had pulled himself over the driver's seat and leaned halfway out of the door. In front of the Jeep, the man with the flare had dropped it and was raising his gun. Garik let the rainbows flare. Four seconds. That was what he had, plenty of time. In rainbow waves, the air moved out of his way, and he had the gun in his hand. He removed the ammunition and threw it far, far past the wall before returning the gun to the man's holster. Thirty, and he let the rainbows go once more, this time in the first ragged throes of pending exhaustion.

Thirty seconds. That's all he got before he had to recharge. Not worth much, was it, for a super soldier, the best of the best?

"Stop that, Garik!" This time, Justin made it all the way out of the Jeep. He called to the man with the gun, "Don't shoot—"

He already had the weapon located, had drawn it again, and with Garik suddenly at arm's length, he aimed the gun and pulled the trigger. The lack of a report surprised him, and he tried to fire again.

"You have no ammunition," Garik said, leaning over to rest his hands on his upper legs. "Justin, tell him I don't intend to get shot. Had that done, not fun."

Justin arrived about that time, took the gun from the man, and threw it to the side where it landed in the grass. A siren now wailed from underground.

"He could have kept the gun." Garik stood, feeling some of his energy returning. He looked at the man's name on his shirt. Williams.

"Not and shoot you."

"He had no ammunition. I removed it."

"No way," Williams said. "No effin' way!"

Several other men with weapons came running up the ramp, and they held their rifles while Williams retrieved his pistol and checked the ammunition.

"The entire magazine's gone. Where—"

"Over the wall," Garik said. "Where I want to be."

"Impossible," Williams insisted. "You didn't have time—"

"That's why your brass has worked so hard to get this man here. His DNA magic allows him to *make* the time." Justin asked Garik, "What do you need?"

"Food. Someplace to sit."

A man came striding out, and the soldiers holding the weapons made room for him. At a motion of his hand, they dropped their guns. He walked directly to Justin.

"Major Kevin Linkletter. You must be Justin. I'm glad to meet you. Did Lt. Wilder secure everything you needed?"

"We're here. Your man made us nearly dead." He nodded at Williams.

"Williams?" Linkletter's voice hardened. "Can you explain?"

"They were on their way in, sir, just as we expected. All they had to do was drive down the ramp. The hairy one got out of the vehicle . . . I take that back, Major. He didn't even get out. He was suddenly there, and there. He didn't move, just reappeared. I raised my weapon per procedure, and then he was in front of me. He did something with my pistol. I drew again and fired, only my magazine is somewhere beyond the perimeter."

"Explain *drew again*, soldier."

"I was lifting my pistol, and then it was back in my holster—"

Garik began to retch. He doubled over, held to Justin's arm, and fell to one knee.

"Food?" Justin knelt beside him.

"Yes. Doing that takes it out of me." It was worse than before, though. He was changing again. The soldier had summed it up. The hairy one. He might as well have said the werewolf. Garik felt the difference. The call of the wild. The need to be there and not here.

"This is the man Rodheimer and Sunchaser planned to cull?" Linkletter asked Justin.

"Crude, Major, but yes. Can we get him inside?"

"Inside," Garik managed to get out. He started to refuse, but the grass on the ground blurred, and he did a faceplant before he could say no.

"BACK UNDERGROUND again." Garik didn't need to open his eyes. He could smell it, the antiseptic cleanness of it all, unlike the Corona Tower facility, which prided itself on smelling like nothing at all. In addition, a whiff of brown soil, dead leaves, growing things, someone he knew. "Justin?"

"And someone else you want to see. Open your eyes, pretty boy."

"Snarky as always." Garik peeled his eyelids back as he drew himself up. A yawn overtook him, and he arched his back and stretched.

Like a dog would do.

He caught it, tried to stop it, instead drew in a deep breath through his nose, dissecting each portion of each aroma that assaulted him. Justin's mantis. His own, fur and dander, the rub of a hand against a favorite pet. A deep-sea saltiness, a touch of the shore, an ocean breeze.

"Jantzen?" It had to be.

"Almost. Don't expect too much." Justin called, "Jantz, come meet Garik."

Come meet? That was ominous. They already knew one another. He wanted to ask Justin to explain, then a trim man with a black beard and eyes with a purple tint walked into the room, held out a hand as if to shake and said, "Garik. Hello. I understand we know one another."

"Yes." Garik took the hand. The skin, familiar but different. The teasing, the challenges the man liked to dunk him in, the forcing him to be more than he wanted to be, smarter, quicker, more attentive.

That's what was missing.

"We worked together in the States at the other facility. Am I right?" He glanced at Justin as if making sure he had his information correct.

"Yes. You were my teacher." And friend and co-conspirator and anchor when my life was falling apart.

"Ah, then not together. Not as equals. Interesting. Perhaps—" Jantzen stopped, his expression frozen, and his eyes . . . this was what Tim-o had described to him. Jantzen's eyes blazed purple before fading, and he picked up where he left off. "—we will meet again. We can discuss it in more depth."

He was met by a woman who took his elbow and said, "This way, Dr. Hefferly. Dinner is waiting. You don't want to miss dinner, do you?"

"What happened?" Garik at least knew now why Jantzen hadn't returned to let him know he was alive. Because he wasn't, not really.

"They're not even sure why he's here. The sword shouldn't have worked at all. Yet somehow it did. Halfway, as you can see, but there's that."

"Yeah, there's that. Is outside time possible around here?"

"Want to see a mirror first? And the team here wants to check you out physically."

"You've got to be kidding me." Garik felt his lips pull into a snarl. "I've been checked to the core. They know everything there is to know about me."

"Maybe not. They tell me there's evidence that injury can jumpstart new DNA-induced transformations. Remember that tracker we took out?"

"The knife you stabbed in my back?"

"Yes, sorry." Justin didn't seem very sorry. "It looks like we have a good reason not to get injured. All the fights I got into? That's likely the reason my body has gone extreme."

"Should'a been a better person, huh?"

"Likely. Now, up from there. We've got someplace we need to be."

Garik tossed the blanket back, saw he was still fully clothed, and checked his arms for any attachments and found only two bandages.

"Already gone. Once you got filled up, I told them to take the bags away."

"Thank you, I guess." He tested sitting up, found it felt fine, and rose to his feet. "Outside's not a thing then."

"It can be, just not now. You know they've got a runway here. Not many people drive in like we did. Anyway, people do get outside, part of the reason for putting this facility here. Less chance for observation by the nosy neighbors."

"Quit trying to distract me. Why do I need to see a mirror?"

"You did notice your arms?"

"Somewhat." At the rest stop. Just now. And trying to ignore them.

"Sure then, let's do this cold turkey and hope people recognize you. Follow me." Justin led the way out of the room.

One thing Garik just realized. Justin wasn't in his duster. Shirt. Pants. And when he turned to exit the room, his neatly tucked wings were available for everyone to see.

What sort of place was this? Oh, right, Canada, where everyone accepts everyone else for exactly who they are, and no one steps on anyone's toes ever.

"KIDDO!" A tall, Nordic-featured man was the first to see Garik, and he ran to the door to greet him.

"Devo, how are you here?" Garik had pictured the move from the West Coast as a forced event for the hybrids alone. Devon, the activities director at the Corona Tower research center, was as un-hybrid as they came.

"Heard you might be joining us. How could I resist?"

"Heard from whom?" For two weeks, Garik had been stuck on the fortieth floor of Corona Tower with no information about what was happening in the basement facility that served as the research center for the human-hybrid project. Then he was given the terminal news that they intended to suck his brains to share it with three hundred volunteers who wanted to become him.

When did people plan to begin telling *him* something?

"Let's say word gets around."

"Wilder, right? I know he's Mossad."

"Kiddo, I knew you'd figure it out. Course, I didn't know any of it. No one tells me stuff. I'm just the hired hand. But, this is Canada! I've always wanted to come here!"

"Skiing, right?" Garik remembered the snow.

"For my mom. Now, let's get you to the party. You might know a few people."

And he did. Stephen to Veronika to Jacquelien and all the way to Raphaël, Joachim, and Melanie.

"Where's the twins?" He couldn't find them. They were like walking sore thumbs getting on everyone's nerves. They must be around.

"Yah, here!" In walked Andrey and Anatoli Burgorski carrying two kegs. "Anyone here under nineteen?"

"Sorry, kiddo," Devon said. "It's a joke on you."

Garik played along. A hybrid's body couldn't get high. For the rest of the party, the joke was on them.

— 7 —

"THERE'S A real chance this will work." Garik couldn't see how they could be so *dense*, so *hard-headed*, so unwilling to try something so *obvious*.

"We have only your word you can do this, and that's not enough." Dee Thomas, the senior outside project liaison, stood against an outsize monitor filling the wall. To the back of the room sat Major Linkletter, his legs crossed in a casual manner, alongside Shervaughnna Honda, assistant project scientist; Andrea Ho, assistant researcher; and Lauren Irons, assistant specialist for the AMS lab, or as Garik had learned, the American Mutant Services lab.

The screen showed the back of the Jeep, open with a bar of sky across the top and the bumper and part of a clump of buffalo grass below. Inside, the empty drone case. Next to it, the sword, surrounded by cloth, bunched where the sword had been unwrapped enough to identify it as real and present.

The Jeep was now parked underground with the sword being studied in an alternate location.

"You've already said you don't know what's wrong. I do. I can fix it." Garik was out of patience with these people. Sure, Canada, acceptance, and all that; and they had made room for his friends from the Corona Tower facility. Yet, his frustration mounted by the moment. Did he have to bash their heads to get them to understand? This concerned Jantzen, part of his pack. How could he not try anything to make sure this happened to no one else?

"James, will you please help Mr. Shayk understand how this works?" Thomas nodded to James Ku, a bland-faced man with an easy expression and dark, lifeless hair. He wore a white jacket with

Ku stitched onto the pocket and sat with everyone else around a U-shaped table.

"Yes, please. Thank you, Dee." He lifted a remote from the table and aimed it at the screen. The image changed to show a badly cropped photograph with several large machines, some with glowing lights, and an open area surrounded by a framework of bulky projector-style *things*. Ku indicated with a laser pointer as he spoke. "This is the receiving bay for incoming transmissions. In *theory* we can dematerialize any object and transport it any distance. It does require line of sight. It isn't magic."

"Satellites, sure. You say *in theory*. So, it doesn't work." Garik felt his frustration building. Plain, people. Quit with the half meanings. These are people we are talking about.

"Oh, yes." Ku's voice brightened with excitement. "It works well. Inanimate objects, we've done plenty of those. Successfully, though not over thousands of miles. That was the California end of the project. We've yet to understand why a *sword* was chosen. The transfer device could be designed in any shape."

"So *this* doesn't work." Garik stood, wrenched the remote from Ku's hand, and shifted the image to the sword in the back of the Jeep. "Yet, it got a man here. I saw the electricity from the end of the sword dismember him molecule by molecule."

"That's what makes this exciting—" Ku vibrated with enthusiasm.

"Exciting!" Garik slammed his hand on the table, leaving a dinner plate size impression.

"Mr. Shayk, if you will." Thomas held out her hand for the remote.

"Tell me about this." Garik walked to the screen, pressed the side of his fist against the picture of the sword, and held it there. "No theories, no explanations why it won't work. It got Jantzen Hefferly here. You've admitted that—"

"We've yet to confirm anything. He is here, yes. Why, we are unsure. The remote, please." Thomas still held out her hand.

"Here's what *I* can confirm. Sunchaser never completed the sword. She intentionally left it unfinished. To kill people? I can't say, but to retain the technology for herself, that's obvious."

"And yet you have no proof."

"Proof?" Garik heard the thickness in his voice, his anger reducing his words to a near growl, his eyes making the scene before him red around the edges. "There's a layer of schematics she never released. Let me have access to it—"

"The danger is unacceptable. We've yet to understand why it does not work properly—"

"*I* understand. Can't I get you to see that? This doesn't have to happen to anyone else." His words cracked. "And maybe it could help Jantzen . . ."

"We are uncertain how this could help him. There are rules we must follow—"

Garik cut off Dee Thomas, growling, "Then I must make my own rules," and he handed her the remote, now crushed against his fist of anger. When he reached the door, locked as always, he didn't hesitate. He twisted the handle until the stressed metal snapped in his hand, leaving a torn spot in the door and exposing the interior mechanism. Garik forced the metal back until he could reach his hand inside, pulled at the locking mechanism until it groaned and snapped. He threw the door wide and turned into the corridor with a sinewy grace that became a loping run the direction where he knew the sword was.

His hand? He had left blood behind, but it was healed before he was gone ten steps. It would take longer for his timber wolf DNA to initiate his next level of changes, but he could deal with that.

Someone had to do something, their rules or his. Even the sirens and blinking lights didn't slow him down.

"TRY TO stop me." Garik twisted his neck, lifted his head, and felt the changes in his jawline. Ripping through the door was already coming home. A growl, this time from within his chest, a new sound.

"The instrument is under study, Mr. Shayk." Aldo Ku, lookalike twin to James Ku from earlier, specialist in DNA mapping and sequencing, blocked his way into the research lab hiding the sword.

"My name is Garik. If you don't like that, your other option is Wolfman. Got it? I am going in."

Ku sighed. "You're the one from the West Coast, right?" He studied Garik's face. "My brother said . . . I didn't recognize you. The pictures were more, um—"

"Human?" The word was an angry slash. He caught *one*. Not man, not volunteer. Not person. Garik was none of those anymore.

"No, that's not what I meant. I expected a teenager."

"I'm what you got, thanks to timber wolf DNA that I didn't want and can't get rid of. I can take the door off the hinges if you need me to."

"So we know. Can I at least call someone?"

"Will they try to stop me?" The sirens and emergency lights still flashed along the corridors. No guns had shown up yet. Likely the Canadians were told to smile first and shoot later.

"Let me call. Maybe I can get the sirens silenced."

Please, Garik, thought. The high-pitched wail had his patience shattered, and he was afraid of what he might do if these people forced his hand. He stepped into the room, waited beside a desk while Ku lifted a corded phone and made a call. Across the room, the sword lay on a table with various tools around it. Thick power cables snaked across the floor, and two people, a man and a woman, studied schematic diagrams on a wall screen. They shuffled through a stack of paper, and occasionally they adjusted the image, compared the paper to the image, enlarged a section, only to make notes on the paper and go to another page.

Ku hung up the phone, and Garik noticed the sirens were gone.

"Thank you."

"I haven't told you the results of my conversation yet."

"Okay, then for the sirens." He didn't tell him he had overheard every word. He already knew they would allow him to "show" the missing schematic page "if he could." They wanted to demonstrate good faith before they kicked him out the door.

As if they had the power, he thought.

"We have fifty-nine schematic pages. The device was completed by Halo Sunchaser. None of us here worked on it, so we have to trust her—"

"Don't." Garik's chest rumbled at the thought of how the woman had lied to him over and over.

"Don't trust her? She is highly respected and very brilliant."

"And with a grandmother in South Africa suffering a blood disorder. She will do anything . . ." and the gears in Garik's head began to click and turn and give him a possible answer. "She never intended to sell the technology for the sword."

"How's that? The technology, when successfully tested, will be priceless on the world stage. When we learned she was keeping its advanced stage of completion from us, we all assumed—"

"Her grandmother. She intended to modify it as a device to heal her grandmother. It must be. She's already wealthy. The money can't be the driving force behind doing something so foolhardy. She had to know she would be found out. There must have been a personal motivation."

"It could be possible. The mechanism is designed to reassemble transported items in optimal condition."

"You've sent damaged things through to see?"

"No." Ku was walking Garik toward the sword and the two people working on the schematics. "There was no reason to. We were looking to see that items sent through did not suffer damage, not that the machine would repair it."

"Then let me show you what I know, things I suspect you haven't even thought of yet."

"Big words, Mr., um, Garik." Ku turned and introduced him to the other two people. "Damon Lonon, molecular biologist. He keeps your liver from winding up in your head. Jennifer Landa is our forensic pathologist. When your liver winds up in your head, she helps to tell us why. Damon, Jennifer, Garik says there's another page of schematics we haven't seen yet. We're hoping he can produce it for us."

Damon looked at Garik, and he grinned. "My grandfather used to listen to a Texas radio announcer named Wolfman Jack. Any relation?"

"Was he big and hairy?"

"Ah, man, you would ask that. A beard, maybe. He died a long time ago."

"I don't guess we'll ever find out."

Jennifer offered Garik a tablet and a stylus, saying, "A missing schematic page. Okay, then. Draw what you know."

"Do you have a pen and paper?"

Damon laughed. "Pen and paper? What? Were you raised by wolves?"

Garik smiled. It looked that way, didn't it? He decided Damon might be alright, for a mostly human guy who might one day keep his liver from winding up in his head.

Aldo Ku came up with the paper Garik requested, and of course they had pens. Garik looked through the papers with the schematics, and he sorted them out on a wide table, pointing out various parts and explaining what they did. From time to time, Jennifer said, "Oh, I see." Damon occasionally let out, "Hot dog!" Aldo Ku watched, took notes, and occasionally whispered into a black-faced smart watch on his wrist.

Eventually, Jennifer asked, "What about the schematic we don't have? I can see something's missing here," and she touched one page and sent it to the large monitor, "but what?"

"That's key, to first see what's missing. That's what I'm about to give you."

Garik began to draw, quickly, accurately, and with no hesitation. Eidetic. Photographic. He transferred the image in his head to the paper, easy as that. A printer he could plug into his brain would be quicker, but that's what his hands were for, that was, as long as they remained hands and not paws.

Christian Maguire flashed through his mind, a man who had been in Bay City, then here, and who had moved on before Garik got to see him, likely to Israel to participate in their human-hybrid program. Christian had been haunted by his wolfhound DNA, becoming more hound than human at the end, an archetype of what Garik might one day become. He shook it off. Worry didn't improve the future. Action did, and that's what he was doing, whatever it took to ensure the best outcome for his current endeavor.

Jennifer's eyes opened wide as the missing schematic reached completion. She touched one part, said, "Yes, I see," and seemed to be engrossed.

Damon kept grinning, unable to wipe his excitement off his face.

Aldo Ku was back on the phone. He said into the receiver, "Major, I think we have something here."

Garik thought, Of course you do. What do you think I am, only human? I'm better than that, any day of the week. Weekends? That was yet to be decided.

For you, Jantzen, he thought, as Damon clapped him on the back in excitement. If this helps anyone, I hope it helps you.

— 8 —

"WHAT DO you mean the sword has nothing to do with me? I'm the one who brought it to you. Have you forgotten that little detail?" Garik was livid, and after giving them the final page of schematics to finally bring it to working completion.

"And you have received sanctuary as promised to the Israeli government. And our gratitude, of course. This will mean a vast leg up to the Canadian program, and of course those countries we are aligned with." Major Linkletter sat behind a green, military-issue desk. The top was as cleared as the man was direct. One folder sat off to the side, and it was closed, the same as the man's mind.

"Do your people even understand it?" Garik did, inside and out. He could picture each page of the schematics in his head, overlay each on the previous one, and *feel* how it should work. Jennifer and Damon had been struggling just to understand the concepts until he had begun to explain.

"You seem to be misguided, Mr. Shayk. My people are not the ones with a lack of understanding. They are highly trained and the best in their fields. The device is an intricate piece of machinery, and it will take time to work out how your information fits into the whole, but we will do it." Linkletter stood, dismissing Garik, and he turned to a file cabinet at the side of the room and opened a drawer, thumbing through but not selecting anything to pull out.

Corporal Rory Williams, the man whose pistol Garik had disabled, stood from the chair at his side and motioned for Garik to also rise. Cpl. Williams wasn't a small man, but Garik felt outsized next to him. Garik had filed a protest when he was excluded from the laboratory working on the sword, and Williams had been his guide to meet with Linkletter. He wore a green patterned operational uniform with a khaki cap and black boots.

Once away from Linkletter's office, Garik offered a peace branch. "I like the uniform."

Williams cut him off sharply. "No, you cannot wear one. You are no longer in the States."

"Did I ask to? Sheesh. I was being nice. Are you still angry about the pistol?"

"The pistol." Williams stopped and turned to study Garik's face. "You embarrassed me in front of the Major, and you ask if I'm still angry. What do you think?"

"And I was supposed to let you shoot me?"

"You were supposed to drive down the ramp, not get out of the Jeep and do whatever it was you did. That's what you were supposed to do."

Another soldier, a woman, rounded a corner and walked toward them. Williams drew up, nodded as she passed, said, "Ma'am," and waited until she was out of sight.

"Fine," Garik said. He held out his arms with his wrists butted together. "Throw me in the brig. Then you can feel better about yourself."

Williams looked at him for a few moments, then shook his head and continued down the corridor.

"Wait, Corporal, or Williams, or whatever I should call you. You haven't handcuffed me yet. Let me pay my dues. I've been a bad boy, and I want to be your friend. Please?" Garik chased after him, dancing around him, while he continued to offer his wrists.

"Stop, please." Williams narrowed his eyes at him, then motioned for him to follow, and he opened a door, and they stepped inside. He closed the door.

"No lock," Garik said. He tried the door, it opened back up, and he latched it again. He did it once more before being satisfied.

"Are you teasing me?" Williams began to puff up.

"Seriously, no lock. In Bay City, every door was locked, and we had to have a passkey to move anywhere."

"We have locks here. Plenty of them." He pulled a lanyard from his shirtfront with a keycard on it then dropped it back inside.

"That door is not locked." Garik nodded his head its direction. "Enough of that. Why are we in here?"

"They kidnapped you when you were in high school?" Williams took on an expression of amazement.

Garik sighed. "It was the summer before my senior year, but yes. I found my way into the research center, and they refused to let me out."

"So, did you choose your wolf thing . . . or?"

Garik laughed.

"I've seen some of the others. Yours is the one I'd want, that is if that was something I ever wanted to do, which it isn't."

"I was knocked out, and when I woke up . . ." Garik shrugged. "Well, I woke up, and they said, 'Sorry, guy, you aren't you any longer,' and now I'm me."

"Man," Williams said with a whistle. "Sometime can you meet with a few of us? We've seen the people coming from there, and we've all got questions."

"The Major will let you?" Garik thought of Colonel Brace in Bay City. He'd slice some stuff off rather than be nice to people.

"He's a bit gruff but not a bad boss. Can I tell the others it's a go?"

"Okay. When and where?" The man looked so eager Garik couldn't say no.

"I'll request to be your escort—"

"Another guard? I had enough of that back home. Just put the cuffs on. You can lock me to this chair." He put his hands on the arm of a metal chair and waited.

"For a big guy, you have a sense of humor. Come on before someone decides I've kidnapped you." Williams took the door handle, waited until he was certain Garik was with him, and he opened it and stepped outside. A short distance down, two men dressed in a similar fashion met them. Williams pressed himself to the side, said, "Sirs," as they passed, and relaxed once they were gone.

"Aren't you boss of anybody?" Garik teased him.

"You'd think not, wouldn't you? Can you find your way to your quarters from here?"

"I'm free? Seriously?" Garik checked the signs on the walls and knew exactly where he was. "I don't think I'll get lost. Are you certain I don't need a key?"

"Not unless you're heading into any off-limits areas."

"Then I can borrow yours, right?"

"Funny guy. I'll let you know when and where." Williams pivoted on one foot and was gone.

Garik wondered what Devon was up to. No good, he hoped. He cocked his head, listening, then he sniffed. Trees and water, Devon's signature. He could pick it up anywhere.

Follow your nose, Garik. That's what all good wolves can do. Follow your nose.

"MARCO'S HERE?" Garik grinned. "How's the staff liking his marking trick?" Marco Lopez was DNA mated with a lemur, and he had developed a tail and an uncontrollable urge to mark places, items, and people with his distinctive scent.

"And Chad," Devon said. "He's asked about you. Wants to know if you have wings yet, or if you just like coming back to roost in the old hen house."

"He's an idiot." Chad was DNA-matched to a bat, only his transformation had taken him too far. He could only speak through a translator box that could interpret his high-pitched vocalizations. His box made him polite even when he was not.

"Here, someone wants to talk with you." Devon stood, still favoring the leg that had been broken in the car accident, and he called to someone on the other side of the room. "Marina, I've saved you a spot." He pointed and walked away with a grin.

"Garik," she said as she walked up to him. "What big eyes you have!"

"What sexy gills you have." He stood and invited her to join him. Marina Bruni's adaptations were aquatic, originally on one side of her body, but now spreading to both sides. "Have they provided you a place to hydrate?"

"The pool. I swim at night." She smiled, pushing the hair on one side behind her ear, much like her sister Marisa used to do. "I think about you when I'm with Jantzen. He thought so much of you, and I think you did about him."

"You serve as a caregiver for him, right?"

"Not all the time but when I can. I have to hydrate." She shrugged. She could be out of the water for extended times, but only by repeatedly applying high-moisture-content lotions.

"He didn't know me when I arrived." It had stabbed him in the heart, and the memory was nearly as bad.

"Sometimes he seems to remember things. I'm pretty sure he knows me from before, but I'm never certain. Spend time with him. He's the same person, just . . ." Her words trailed off as she searched.

"Incomplete?"

"I will say that is very close." She smiled. "I will see you with him? I feel certain he is in there. Perhaps he knows and cries out to us."

"Perhaps. Thank you, Marina. I will spend some time with him."

He stood as she excused herself. She didn't say where she was headed, but he thought the pool. Some things had been easier for some people in the Bay City facility. This one, while gleaming with newness, hadn't been designed with hybrids in mind.

He wondered what that had to say about their long-term welcome.

He wandered along one wall, touching it in places, looking up to see the ceiling that was like all the other ceilings here. Underground. Covered with dirt. Insulating him from the sun and the sky and whatever weather might come his way. He had begun to dream of trees and dirt and grass and running beneath the moon . . . and this place, no matter how welcoming and protected, was the opposite of all that.

The moon . . . it called to him. To howl? He didn't think so. Just to sit under it, like he used to do with Marisa on the roof of their apartment building. And maybe he would howl, just a little bit.

Just enough to let the moon know that it might be the only one of its kind, but it was never, never alone.

STEPHEN KLANDERMANS, fused with a narwhal for formidable bone regeneration, leaned in and said, "I'll do it."

"Not so fast," Garik cautioned the blond-haired man. His kinky locks were in a tangle of dreads that crashed past his shoulders. The dreads sparkled with medicinal amulets woven into them. "We don't need to break in. I have a key."

"A key?" Stephen smiled. "What about the print lock? How do we get past that?"

"Ever seen one of these?" Garik pulled out a lanyard and attached to it was a keycard.

"Chipped or metallic strip?"

Garik shrugged. "It works, that's all I know." The front said Rory Williams and boasted the man's photo.

"Still getting people in trouble, I see." Stephen reached for the card and looked at the name and the picture. "I know Rory didn't loan this to you."

"He's Rory to you." Garik considered that. It was harder to betray someone who was a friend. He had to trust Stephen in this.

"Drinking buddies. We drink, and he passes out. I remember when I once could." Stephen looked wistful. He hefted the key before holding it out to Garik. "This could make Jantzen's condition worse."

"And it could make him better." Garik had to hope.

"What would Jantzen do? Would he risk everything on a chance? That's what we're doing."

"A good chance. Get me in that lab, and I can repair that sword. Somehow, that sword took something away from Jantzen, and I believe it can give it back to him."

"Said the pied piper of Hamelin. Follow me, children, wherever I go, and I will lead you to fun and games and candy and everything you desire."

"I think you have that mixed with Pinocchio." Garik grinned. "But yeah, if that's what it takes, you, Stephen, can have everything you desire if you go with me tonight."

"Fun and games and candy?" Stephen grinned with enthusiasm.

"Fun and games, anyway. I didn't bring any candy."

"Two out of three ain't bad. An old Meat Loaf song."

"Oldies. I'm always around oldies. Okay, old man, let's get started."

Garik knew exactly where the sword was. Eidetic. Something burned into his brain was there forever, and he never forgot.

This was for Jantzen. *If they won't let me help you, Jantzen, then they'll play by my rules.*

Even if he had to make them up as he went along.

— 9 —

WITH RORY'S keycard, entering the lab was simple as rolling in new-mown hay. Or howling at the moon on a star-studded night.

Effecting repairs in the intricate machinery of the sword proved much more difficult.

Garik and Stephen found the nighttime corridors in what they had begun to call the Yellowknife Complex empty, but they expected that. This was Canada, land of kindness, trust, and goodwill, where doors were never locked and good behavior was expected because it was, well, *nice*. Once the lights were dimmed, no guards were posted, no cameras blinked red against the ceilings, and it seemed no alarms were set to go off if one of the rare locked doors was unlocked.

It was Canada in the wilderness. Who could find the place, anyway?

Lights revealed the same room Garik had seen earlier, only this time, the sword's casing was open. Large, lighted magnifying glasses on floor stands—now dark—hunched over the sword like greedy insects ready to pluck out and eat the best parts. The schematic diagrams were on the wall, lined up in order, with Garik's hand-drawn one in place at the end, number sixty. Someone with a red pen had made marks on it, adjusting several of Garik's notations. A sticky note attached read, "Must be an error. Look for alternatives."

Garik glanced at the sword as he walked to the wall of schematics. They were all in his head, layered on one another, clear and functioning. Seeing them in print told him more. The reality of the sword came from its physical makeup, not from how his brain organized the conceptual drawings. He had to adjust diodes, reroute capacitors, reset programing. Make sure not to blow up himself and a portion of the complex.

"Can you do this?" Stephen. He stood at the wall and went immediately to the hand-drawn page. He tapped it. "They don't have much confidence."

"I told them." Garik reached for the page and pulled it from the wall. "I drew it out for them, and still, they can't see it." The thought flashed through him, *only human*, but that was unkind, and he released it. My mind, my thoughts, my way. There was nothing to be gained from unkindness or cruelty.

He would have to remember that when his fury at Rodheimer and Sunchaser once more shifted the world into rainbows . . . if he could find his way through the red-hued landscape of his wolf half's frenzy state and control it.

"So, man, you can do what they can't. I get it. When do we start?" Stephen grinned.

THE LIGHTED magnifying glasses were crucial. Even though Garik could see every detail of the changes needed in his head, they were so tiny in the physical confines of the sword that the work was nearly impossible. He was forced to reference the paper versions over and over, only to face defeat even when he was certain he had done everything exactly as it should be.

Stephen, now sitting off to the side and bouncing a hollow rubber ball he had found off the wall, called out, "Too bad we can't go back and restart the night. Invite some fresh ideas. That's what we need."

"You can't restart—" and Garik's brain clicked with the words, the gears snapping into place, the machine in his head powering up as if it had been stuck in sleep mode. "That's brilliant, Stephen. I should have done that hours ago."

"What's brilliant?" He popped the ball against the wall, and he caught it on its return. Each hit had left a small mark, and one section was nearly black with hits.

"Have I told you about my Street Strider?" Garik was at the wall of schematics, and he searched.

"Your jet-assist bike, sure. What about it?" Smack, the ball hit again.

"It was junk, and the only way to get it to work sometimes was to reset the breakers. I think I've done everything correctly on the sword. I must have. I can see it in my head. I need to find something that would serve as a breaker, something that can reset the entire device."

"Oh, easy." Stephen popped the wall with the ball a final time, caught it, and stood. He walked to one sheet and pointed. "I saw it first thing."

"How . . . do you know . . . this?" Garik studied the symbol he was pointing to. And yes, what he pointed to made sense.

"I'm embarrassed to tell this, but I used to be a techie geek. Not now, but when I was a kid. I studied up on all this, had my parents buy me all sorts of techie stuff. Burned my parents' house down when I was thirteen. Never wanted to mess with it again."

"Interesting. Sure, let's reset the breaker. It works with computers. It's someone's solution, maybe ours."

Garik pulled the schematic from the wall, carried it to the table, and laid it beside the sword. He moved one of the magnifying glasses and it caught the diagram, making it huge, and he shifted the paper to the side, leaving just the sword under the glass. Each part of the intricate machine appeared outsized, clearly visible, and with Stephen's suggestion, obvious. Garik lifted a tiny pick from the table, and it became a massive lever under the glass. He located the switch, compared it to the diagram, and moved it to the right. It slid too easily, and he wondered whether he had made a mistake. Then he tried to move it back, and it was much harder.

"Trouble?" Stephen breathed down his neck.

"It doesn't want to reengage." He held the pressure on the switch, feeling for a click when it moved.

"I can help there." Stephen bumped Garik's elbow, forcing his hand forward.

"You idiot!" Garik jerked his hand back, and he jabbed an elbow into where he thought Stephen was. The man jumped, and his elbow just grazed him.

"Lucky jump, huh? Did it work?"

"Do you mean did you break it? Likely." Yet, Garik could see that the device was powering up, now emitting a pale blue glow. "Let me reassemble the casing. It seems to be doing something positive."

"Glad I could help." Stephen made his way to his chair and began to throw the ball once more. Thump, catch. Thump, catch. Thump, catch.

TRUST, EVEN in Canada, went only so far, Garik and Stephen found, when Cpl. Rory Williams and a team of fully weaponized soldiers burst into the lab.

"Step back," Williams demanded. "Both of you, hands away from your bodies, touch nothing."

"Oops," Stephen said. "We've been Canadasized."

"You think this is funny? Did you expect to break in here and no one would notice?" Williams, weapon in hand, moved to the table where the completed and fully operational sword glowed, and he lifted his keycard and lanyard. "Each time this is used, the system registers it. I cannot believe you thought you could take this and get away with it. I trusted you, Stephen."

"Me?" Stephen laughed. "You've got the wrong guy."

"Button it. The two of you are in more trouble than you know how to get out of. What have you done to that device? Why is it glowing?" He began to back away.

"It's repaired, I think." Garik lifted an arm, bringing Williams' weapon to bear on him. He lowered the arm. "Okay, I don't want to get shot."

"If you do that fast thing again, my men will shoot to stop you." Williams' gun twitched to tell Garik to keep his distance, and he took a step away from the table.

"So, you're finally the boss of someone."

"You could say that. Right now, I'm the boss of you." Williams' face looked as dark as it had the day of Garik's arrival. "We're putting you in detention until it can be determined you two have done nothing detrimental to the device. Move towards the door, slowly and with your hands away from your body. Now."

Williams' radio engaged, and he said, "Williams, here." He paused, looked to the table, and said, "Yessir, he has certainly done something with it, and it's now glowing." Another pause, listening, and he continued, "Yessir, the same color our machine uses." Pause. "Acknowledged."

"Not broken?" Garik smiled.

"Not my call. The Major wants to see you and it. Kumar, do we have a way to transport that thing?"

"Um," the man's voice wavered, "I can find something, I'm sure." It was clear he didn't want to touch it.

"You and Bashiir bring it up. We're headed to Theater A."

"Yessir."

OUTSIDE THE lab, Garik saw his mistake. He and Stephen had lost track of time, and the facility was alive with morning traffic. Constructed on one level spreading out under the parking garage and beyond, everyone kept track of everyone else's business by osmosis. What went on permeated the awareness of the occupants, and Garik and Stephen surrounded and marched along under guard drew a crowd, among them, the Bay City group who immediately recognized him.

"What did you do, Garik?"

"Hey, why is the man being locked away?"

"What's this, another escape?" That was from Chad Sherwin's mechanical translator box. "C'mon, Canadians, where's the smile?"

The Canadians working in the complex moved out of the way, making room for the group of weapons. Kumar and Bashiir brought up the rear of Cpl. Williams' group with the sword atop a wheeled cart.

"Hey, that looks like Sunchaser's sword. Never seen it glow blue before."

"Chris is right. Will you look at that?"

"Look at what?" Dark-haired, bearded Jantzen Hefferly appeared, seeming to step out of nowhere. He normally wandered the corridors without much interference, and this time he put himself in the way of the cart with the glowing sword.

"Pardon, sir." Kumar motioned to Bashiir to hold. "Please, sir, we need to get by."

"I know this." Jantzen seemed to light up with memories. "It . . . I helped create this, then, um, *someone* took it away and claimed it. I . . ." He seemed as puzzled as he was fascinated by the glowing device. He reached out a hand.

"No, Dr. Hefferly. Stand back."

Kumar lifted an arm to block him, but Jantzen was quicker. He placed one hand on the grip, the other on the blade, and he lifted and held it chest high, his eyes glowing with the reflected light from the sword.

Garik's group had stopped at the disruption, and he watched Jantzen with the sword.

"I know how this works," Jantzen murmured, and his hand moved on the hilt, shifting to the pommel.

No one else may have heard him, but Garik's hearing was better than most, and he knew exactly what Jantzen was about to do. With his other hand on the blade, if the sword engaged—

Garik yelled, "No, Jantzen," released the rainbows, and the room swirled. The men with their weapons trained on him had seen the shift in his expression, the compaction in his legs, and watched his throat as the words formed in his vocal cords. They had Cpl. Williams' clear instructions. Shoot if the man does anything untoward. The bullets were on the way before the rainbows could stop them, and Garik's body was pounded by multiple impacts. He staggered as the rainbows vanished, gasping with the pain, wondering if he would survive this time.

Across the room, Jantzen was oblivious, barely glancing away from the sword as the gunfire echoed around him. He engaged the sword, and the blue light brightened and swallowed him. Without warning, he vanished, leaving only wisps of purple smoke in the air, and the sword fell to the floor with a clatter. The casing split, something inside popped and fizzled, and the light faded.

"No!" Garik cried. Jantzen, lost to the sword again, and this time because of him.

"No kidding, you heal quick." Stephen cuffed him on the shoulder. "Your clothes are tattered. Where did the bullets go?"

"It doesn't matter." Dismay, anger at Williams, at Sunchaser, at Rodheimer pummeled Garik. He'd touched the sword, and now he wore Sunchaser's deathmaker mask. He wanted to Houdini out of this place, even the score. He could smell the pines and firs and poplars above ground, and they called to him. Then he pulled himself back to reality. He couldn't smell them at all. He was in here, and they were out there.

Williams nudged him with his weapon. "The Major still wants to see you. Move."

The bullets, he could feel them inside, rubbing, grating on bone with every step. Major Linkletter could do nothing to him now. Nothing that mattered, anyway. Somehow, some way, the people who had trapped him in this life would taste his revenge.

They would face him and see the limits of his anger unleashed. Then they would regret what they had done.

— 10 —

THE BED IN the detention section laughed at Garik. His body had gifted him another six inches in height, and the bed refused to allow his feet and head on the mattress at the same time. Sometimes, even when you think you're as low as you can go, people can still find something else to take away from you.

He had Stephen's rubber ball, and he tossed it against the wall, catching it when it came back to him. The light was adequate for his night-adapted wolfshine eyes, although most full humans would call it pitch black. Thump, catch. Thump, catch. He noticed a repetitive sound from across the room. He caught the ball, held it, and heard the thunk sound of the ball hitting the wall, then a polite, "I'm caught."

"Chad?"

"In the flesh." The words were spoken by Chad's interpretive translation device that voiced his high-pitched chirps and whistles.

"You can use the light. The switch is by—"

"Don't need it, bush boy." From anyone else, the slur would be harsh and unacceptable. Chad's box interpreted his voice into an invitation for cake and ice cream.

"Right. Echolocation. You know exactly where I am, even in the dark."

"And you, blind as a bat, yes? Why are you chucking that ball in the dark? Practicing midnight bank heist skills?" All said with the purr of polite conversation.

"Why are you bothering me?" Chad was a distraction. Garik's blood still steamed at the major's words: *You have destroyed the very thing we brought you here to save.* And he hadn't mentioned the man the sword took with it even once.

"Came to help you, if you want it."

"How? Echolocation is useless to me. I can see in the dark. You can't walk and have prosthetic arms. Even your voice is fake. What can you do to help me?"

"Ah, and there the big bad wolf is so wrong. The helpless mouse is the one that chews the rope that sets the captive wolf free."

"Okay, let's hear it." Garik sat up, his feet on the floor, and found Chad just inside the door. He was in his Invacare chair with something on his lap.

"First, this." Chad threw something at him, and Garik caught it. "Ooh, pretty boy. You really can see in the dark."

"A lanyard with a keycard. Williams." Garik glanced up. "This has already gotten me in trouble."

"So, what's a little more? Now this." He pushed the thing off his lap, his prosthetic arms whirring just enough Garik could hear, and it landed with a soft plop on the floor. The chair creaked and shifted, and slowly Chad stood. In the dim light, he looked very much like a normal human with two legs, two arms, and a normal size head. He kicked the package on the floor with the side of his foot. "It's a backpack. I'm not bringing it to you. I've just learned to stand."

"Congratulations. I didn't know you could." Garik reached to pick up the pack, and he felt Chad's hand on his back.

"Hold still. I need to sit."

"Sure." The hand shifted, shook, and shifted again. Then it was gone. Garik set the pack on his bed. "The reason for the demonstration?"

"Standing, people notice me. Sitting? I'm a nothing. Go anywhere, do anything, I'm invisible. People who do see me don't want to notice me, so I hardly ever get questioned. Look in the pack."

Inside, Garik found his passport, driver's license, the rolls of money, everything from the Jeep, including all the food the bag could hold. He pulled out several plant-based items and set them aside. He wouldn't bother with those.

"Are those the cookies?"

"Let me check. Yes."

"Toss them my way. I'll eat them. Here's your plan. At eight, you are to be shipped out to Israel. Linkletter feels you've outstayed your usefulness. Israel wants you for their human-hybrid program. I hear the U.S. version is sweet in comparison. At two every morning, this complex opens the vents above ground to replenish its air. It's one-thirty. You have thirty minutes. Don't come back this time. If any of us deserves freedom, it's you."

"Come with me." Garik offered, but he knew it was impossible. How could Chad survive out there?

"Sweet but no. Rodheimer took care of that. Make him pay. That's better than freedom for me."

Garik's eyes misted, and by the time he had them cleared, he was alone. It was time to move.

BOOTS. C'MON, Chad, you couldn't give me boots? Dawn was lighting the eastern sky behind him, and as far as he could see, the glimmer of water said the ground would be boggy for a long time to come.

A road. He needed a road, just not one close to the complex. He had no idea if anyone would be out looking for him, and the more lost he was, the harder he would be to find. He couldn't stay lost forever, but for a time, the trees, the dirt and grass and water. He wanted it all, and he never wanted to go south again.

He'd be back. The wilderness called him. It never had before, but now, he knew it was his home . . . would be his home, as soon as he evened the score for what had been taken from him.

A WEEK and a half of mud and sun and sleeping on the damp ground convinced Garik that the highway was a better option. The chance of being spotted was worth the risk. A trucker provided a ride for ten hours before pulling over, telling him he was welcome to stick with him, but he had to pay for his own meal and sleep in the back. Another five hours on the road, he put on his blinker for Vancouver, and Garik bid him farewell.

The border just south of Vancouver was a concern. His pack of money had thinned, and if his passport was flagged, where did that leave him? He breathed easier in Blaine, Washington, somewhere he'd never visited. A place to spend the night, shower, and wash his clothes consumed most of what was left, and he looked for help signs in storefronts and along the road. A kennel advertised DOG WALKER WANTED. Hungry, he pushed open the door and was employed for the first time in his life.

No worries. The dogs loved him. The sun was bright, and the kennel had a spare room at the back if he would also clean the cages in the mornings.

Five weeks later, summer was rolling in strong, and he was on the road again. Trucks rumbled past on the highway: with covers; open; rigs with long cradles of logs; none willing to take him along.

It was time to change the rules and take what no one wanted to give him. He needed a truck with a bed he could access but with cover for protection. He had over thirty seconds now, nearly forty-five, still a slim margin when doing something dangerous. Two rigs rolled by, the backs revealing metal doors. He could break through, but this wasn't about damaging something that wasn't his, rather about borrowing what someone else wasn't using.

Then a canvas-sided truck appeared. The heavy, vinyl fabric flexed in the wind, battering whatever was inside. A section at the back flexed more than the rest, and Garik decided to take it. He turned up the rainbows full force. The clouds stilled themselves, the trees no longer swayed in the wind, and the vehicles on the highway were very near frozen. As Garik ran toward the truck, the wheels inched forward at a snail's pace. He counted as he ran, eleven, twelve. He leaped up on the back bumper to untie the flap, sixteen, seventeen. He found the empty space, barely enough for him and his backpack, twenty-one, twenty-two. He slipped his pack off his back and worked it into the space, twenty-six, twenty-seven. He found a handhold and pulled himself up, thirty-one, thirty-two. He didn't really fit, but by adjusting the pack under his legs, he would survive, thirty-six, thirty-seven. He reached for the fastener and tried to get it to latch, forty-two, forty-three, but failed. The rainbows slipped away from him. The vinyl fabric now buffeted in the wind, creating a drumming sound that battered his ears. Not the best he could have asked for, but he'd take what he could get. He let himself drift into the upper edges of exhaustion, his margins trimmed about as close as he dared.

TWO RIDES later and three long nights of walking, and he could see the top of Corona Tower through the trees. He'd taken to doing that, riding when he could, but doing his walking at night. The stars, the moon, the smell of the dirt and grass and trees. It felt more home than he ever remembered the city being. Underground, how had he stood it?

Part of the change was him. He could hear a cricket in the woods and know if it was male or female and whether it was healthy enough to make a good snack if his food sources ran low. Squirrels, snakes, rabbits, all were out there, and he could hear the differences in each one.

His sense of smell, too. He wanted to pick up sticks just to breathe in their aromas. Nuts, berries, they were layered in information about the season, how much rain had fallen, even other animals that had come by, leaving a reminder of themselves.

He'd found he could tolerate plant-based foods to a degree, but meat was his preference. Often, he would purchase a burger and toss the bun. It was little more than cardboard to him.

His body had changed, too. His guard hairs were denser, prickling his back when the wind caught his shirt. He hadn't looked, but he knew what he'd find, and he wore long sleeves buttoned at the wrists and his collar pulled close to his neck. The backs of his hands, no one could miss that. And when he cleared his throat, like as not it came out a growl. Did it mean anything? Christian could answer that if he hadn't been harvested for parts.

He veered from the highway when he approached Bay City, finding his way into the forested area east of the industrial park. The hills rose to almost mountainous proportions, and he could see the bay out beyond The Docks and Harbor Shipyards. Waldorf's Department Store was hidden by tree-shrouded Shady Ridge Acres, an exclusive residential enclave just north of Ninth, but the flags at Argyle Station on the west side of town flapped in the breeze. It was nice to know someone was hoisting them and taking them down each day. Not everything in the city had broken down with the disaster that had terrorized his home.

A tornado of terror, the second worst thing Garik had ever endured.

Seeing Marisa buried under the falling storefront had been the worst. Then, the rioting, the stores burned, Marisa's family losing The Flower Shop where she had died. They had given up two daughters to Bay City and Corona Tower. He hoped they moved on to find a happier place to live. He didn't see how they could remain here. Everything would remind them of what they had lost.

He began his journey through the trees, the twigs breaking under his feet, the boots purchased in Blaine battered with the miles he'd traveled. He longed for a moment for his old bedroom at his aunt's apartment. He let the feeling go almost as quickly. She had moved on to Arik even before Garik left. Boyfriends can be lovers, nephews only friends.

He missed Marisa. Being back to Bay City flooded her memory over him. He wanted to reach out to her, do what he should have done then: told her how he felt, taken her hand, kissed her.

Who was that Garik, anyway? A child, a boy, a teen, a youth with unformed dreams and little ambition. He'd loved skating and his jet-assist bike. Nothing else had mattered. In a year it had vanished, gone, a dandelion blown apart in the wind.

He reached First, and he turned left. He passed Bay City Medical with its fancy entry gates and landscaped grounds. Cars and more cars, as if the lifeblood of the city flowed once more, oblivious to the damage that Corona Tower had caused in his life. At Coolidge, he looked south, the direction of the warehouse Dieter's father had converted into an indoor skate park. The passcode might still work. Nine blocks. It was worth a chance.

Garik hiked his backpack higher on his shoulders, looked uphill along Coolidge's unbending length, took in the red lights from First to Norfleet, and attempted to recall the graffiti he had once known on every building from Meyers south to Buda. As he walked, he tried to draw each one in his mind, surprised at how hard it was.

Then, he hadn't been wolf boy then . . . werewolf . . . lougarou . . . demon spawn . . . Frankenstein. He was all of those now, and more.

He had received a perfect memory. Eidetic. When he saw the graffiti images this time, he would own them forever.

— 11 —

HOW MANY months since he and Muhammad and Ibn had skated the ramps in Dieter's indoor park?

The passcode was good, the water on—and power. Likely Dieter's father had taken a year's lease, and when he had run with his son from the disaster in the Tower's basement, the rest of the lease was wasted.

Except not the previous night. Garik had enjoyed a bathroom, the small kitchenette, and a place to sleep insulated from the world. And it hadn't cost him any of his dwindling stash of cash.

He dropped off the halfpipe to the floor and looked underneath for an extra board. There had been several when he was here last, and he didn't expect they had been moved. Four, and he looked through them, all high-end boards, trucks, and wheels, just what he would expect from a man who would rent his son a warehouse just to build him an indoor skate park. He picked one with a sunflower on the top and Rock It! on the bottom. Father sun and mother earth. He carried it up the narrow steps to the top of the pipe and twirled it, one end in his hand and the other balanced on the loft's wooden surface. He pictured himself floating on the board, a handplant, the thrill, but he wore his boots from Blaine, and none of the shoes from under the pipe were sized for his feet, the penalty he paid for his phenomenal growth over the past year. He released the board into the pipe without him and watched it roll down, then back and forth until it came to a rest at the bottom. Even this was lost to him. He jumped into the pipe, a clean and easy leap into the center, landing just beside the board. He picked it up, returned it to its place under the pipe, and gathered his pack.

The Tower was waiting. It was time to make his peace. He looked around the space, a bit wistful for the friends he had seen here for the final time. Where were they now? Muhammed and Ibn were finishing up their senior year of school. John Carter was left on the parking garage floor, dead as far as he knew. Alyna, Amy, Marco. And Justin in Canada. Christian never made it this far, and Jantzen. He had been here that night. Garik's eyes burned for Jantzen, lost twice, the second time his fault. If he'd never touched the sword, never seen that final page of schematics, never tried to fix what he didn't know how to fix.

The memories reignited his anger, and it simmered just under his skin. He checked his pack, making sure he was prepared. Paul Gberie had suggested fruit bars. Garik had stocked up on beef sticks. The better to chew on, my dear. He could laugh at the old fairy tale. His plan was to walk to the Tower, and with beef sticks in hand, he would entangle the place with rainbows, shedding beef stick wrappers along the way, whatever it took to bring down Rodheimer and Sunchaser.

They didn't know about the rainbows, which meant it would work. It had to. It was the only plan he had to play.

THE DAY BEFORE, walking along Coolidge, he had studied the graffiti on the west side of the street. This morning, he took in the east. It was the last time he would walk this street, and he wanted to absorb the energy and fractured beauty of Uptown. He turned on First, walked west for three blocks and crossed the powerline right-of-way to Park Avenue before heading north towards Central Park. The burned cars were gone, but the charred asphalt mocked the city's efforts to make the past year disappear. The police department headquarters building was freshly scrubbed, and new paint covered part of the structure. Several store windows along his walk were filled in with plywood, painted with bright colors or murals to disguise the empty and blackened spaces hiding inside. The walls of one of the big houses in Pill Hill still stood, but its roof was missing. An overhanging tree was dead, its late-spring branches bare of leaves, killed by the heat of the flames.

Corona Tower dominated the sky long before he reached its base, a black fist that had smashed into him and crushed him. Now it was time for him to crush back. He walked with determined steps as he approached Rock Island, the street that would lead him to the back entrance of the Tower. He turned, his view a straight shot, expecting to see the scar left when the parking garage was bombed by Marisa, and surprised to see a nearly complete garage to replace it.

Even Marisa, her final fingerprint on the Tower, wiped away as if she'd never lived.

Nothing else. They would not have the chance to take anything else from him.

THE ENTRANCE to the garage was blocked with wood-and-fiberglass sawhorses, but the inside appeared fully functional, with gates and payment stiles in place. Garik leaped the sawhorses, easy as pie, and loped up the ramp leading to the Stamford Suites entrance where he would likely find Gunther Diehl. The concierge had always treated him kindly, and he didn't want him to suffer. He hoped he stayed out of his way. If Garik's plan worked, the man wouldn't see him until the damage to Rodheimer and Sunchaser was already done.

Through the glass doors into the Tower's lobby, it seemed business as usual. Charity Cellers at her desk. Choi Bak with a luggage cart, stopping to pull a cloth from his hip pocket to wipe down the brass rails on the cart before rolling it into a recess along the wall.

Wait, Garik, wait, he told himself, as he squatted and leaned with his back against a recess framed by two concrete columns. He didn't have a passkey, and to enter by force was to warn them. His retribution must come as a surprise. Someone would open the door. In five minutes, an hour. He had waited for weeks. He could wait half a day more.

BY NOON he realized the garage might not be his way inside. No one was using the door, in or out. Then Boris Lindemann of all people walked toward the door with a small dog on a leash. Boris lived in the Tower in Stamford Suites. He likely took his dog out every day. He pushed open the door without a passkey and stepped inside the garage just far enough to let the door close behind him. He studied his watch, tapped it several times, then pulled out a phone and began to talk. When the dog was finished, Boris reached for the door, opened it, and made his way inside . . . without a key!

"Hours wasted," Garik muttered as he stepped out of the shadows and shouldered his backpack. He sorted a handful of the beef sticks into various pockets. Ten beef sticks gave him ten minutes.

Twenty meant twenty minutes. He had a hundred with him. He figured he would be sick of beef sticks before he was finished, but that would give him an hour and a half of revenge.

He unzipped his anger as he stepped to the glass doors, letting his bottled fury batter at time, breaking into the shell of now and then and in a minute. *Marisa, John, Paul.* The anger bled from him, fueling the elation of his rising frenzy. *Jantzen, dead twice, and at his own hand.* Garik became two people, the youth—now a man—who had loved and lost. He could admit that now. Jantzen, his mentor, the man who had stepped in to save him, to become a father to him. Garik was also wolf, what the Tower had made him, no longer completely human, if human at all. Which would win in the end?

Garik wrested the rainbows from nothingness, controlled the rising tide around him by sheer will, a tornado vortex of colors twisting into every nook and cranny, turning the glass into shimmering, transparent rock candy, the door handles into glowing unicorn horns, and the lobby of the tower on the other side into a cascade of light, with color dripping from every surface.

He was through the doors, the air sucking in after him in a vortex of red, green, and violet, searching, searching, needing to find the people who had brought him to this. *Where are you? Where are you?* Gunther Diehl to the right, standing at his desk, lifting a sheet of paper, his eyes turned toward the private Stamford Suites elevator as if it had just dinged to indicate a passenger about to disembark. Color turned Gunther into a glowing lollipop, ready for Garik's anger to consume. Yet, Gunther wasn't his target, and Garik searched elsewhere.

Deeper into the lobby, the ornate sculptures, the elaborate furniture groupings, and people! Many people sitting here, visiting there, children in strollers, all alight in rainbow colors. They surprised Garik as he counted thirty-four, thirty-five, and his first wrapper fluttered from his fingertips and into the wasteland of real time, no longer enveloped in his vortex of speed.

Past Charity Cellers, leaving the woman mired in an easter egg cacophony of pink and yellow and blue; and the elevator, the door partially open and someone's hand reaching through. Color swirled out, tumbling onto the lobby floor into a liquid pool of effervescent time, colder and harder the faster Garik moved.

A second wrapper fluttered into real time, taking on its own little rainbow, frozen in a pool of light. Garik left it behind in his search, forgotten on his way to exact his revenge. He approached the door of the Director's office, with swirls of color leaking from the edges, blurring the name on the front. Still, he remembered Major Kennedy leading him inside, the tirade launched at him as he stood between Weston Rodheimer and Colonel Brace, becoming the center of their attack, and Brace's threats against Marisa's family before he was finally released.

Garik burned hot, another wrapper gone, and he wanted to lean against the door, feel it bow under the pressure of his shoulder, the satisfying crack as it gave way to his superior force. They would know he was no longer the boy they had trapped in this changing body, the timid youth who cowered when they threatened, the high school student no one would miss because he wasn't worth considering in Bay City's scheme of reckoning.

Yet, yet.

Garik turned, taking in what he hadn't yet absorbed. The people. A sign saying Welcome to Corona Tower. A new casualness to the furniture groupings. Sculptures that had been replaced with city-friendly designs, one of a life-size skater boy in bronze, his right hand holding the edge of a halfpipe, his feet pulled up under him, his left on a board floating beside him. The skater, a tangle of hair tied at the nape of his neck, now coming loose and flying free . . . the facial structure . . . familiar in a way that only a man who had once viewed that face in a mirror could know.

Garik forced his eyes away, tried to remember why his pockets bulged, and touched a beef stick. Eat, energy, it's time; and he opened one and released the wrapper as he searched for a way . . . and came up with nothing. He withdrew behind a grouping of small trees in one corner and fell back into real time. The groupings of people in the lobby were instantly boisterous, cheerful and friendly. Gunther set his paper down and smiled as a white-haired woman exited the Stamford Suites elevator. Charity stood and called a greeting to Choi Bak. The main elevator fully opened, and the hand became an arm, a person, a couple, and a family. Then out stepped Jantzen Hefferly.

Garik collapsed to the floor, his back hitting the wall hard, and his pack sliding up and off one shoulder. It was nothing to him against seeing the man he had come to vindicate walking into the room whole and alive. How? His mind clicked, the gears turned . . . gather, evaluate, extrapolate . . . the paths of probabilities painted themselves on the lobby floor, the opportunities he could choose, could walk, could cast aside, the branches that would evaporate as he made those choices.

It had to be the sword, not broken. Repaired! He had repaired it, and it had worked! Always, Jantzcn had reformed from his gaseous state into himself whole and undamaged. Why would this time be any different? He put his hand to the floor to stand, to call out to him, and heard Jantzen begin an address to the group in the lobby.

"Welcome, Citizens of Bay City. Corona Tower has been part of this city for many years, but I consider this to be our true opening day. The recent upset to our city is behind us, and Corona Tower guarantees its continued support of our beloved Bay City through healthcare initiatives and projects to maintain and improve the city's park system and more. As a pledge of the changes at Corona Tower, it's time we opened our facility to you. Bay City is our home, and we want you to share in the rebirth of Bay City and Corona Tower. Enjoy today's events."

Outside the windows, a massive release of colorful balloons, a rainbow of a different sort, brought oohs and aahs from the people. Garik was speechless. This violated everything he knew, and he watched as the paths in front of him narrowed to one.

Jantzen. He was the only one who could explain.

— 12 —

"YOUR PLANS?" Jantzen quizzed Garik as they exited the elevator into the subterranean warrens of Corona Tower's massive underground research center.

"My plans?" Garik laughed sourly. "I have no plans, except to return here and exact revenge on the two people I've come to hate most in my life. And now, you've taken even that from me."

"Is that a bad thing?" Jantzen was kind, warm, and seemed to want to engage with Garik, reconnect, renew some level of their earliest relationship. "I'm in the penthouse now that Weston is no longer part of the organization. My old apartment can still be yours. I've kept it vacant, hoping you would return."

"I saw the sculpture."

"Yes." Jantzen glanced away and ran his hand over his hair. "Does it bother you?"

"No. That's not me any longer." He pictured Dieter's warehouse that morning. He'd tried to regain that part of him, and it had already slipped away, gone forever. "What happened to Halo Sunchaser?"

"South Africa happened to her. Her brother Bongani is in the government, and when he discovered she was part of our program, he immediately recalled her."

"So, she got away scot-free."

"Hardly." Jantzen chuckled. "She will face worse penalties there than I could ever impose on her. Weston might be facing a trial for abuse, cruelty, and improper use of government funds, but he can rest easy that it's the U.S. government after him and not the South African one."

"And Colonel Brace. Protected by his own."

"That's life." He shrugged. "But the reason we're down here. Follow me."

The activity area. Memories, no longer quite real, attached themselves to every wall, every chair, everything they passed. Then they approached the glass-walled pool Marina had shown him the first day he had been able to get out and about. It was empty then. It wasn't now.

"Marina?" Garik stepped to the glass, pressed his hands to it. Inside, a beauty with layers of glistening scales, pulsing gills, and long black hair turned his direction.

"Garik." The words came from a speaker in the ceiling, but it was Marina's voice.

"You came back. I didn't expect to see you here." He smiled. She looked so much like Marisa, her expressive eyes, dainty chin, the smile that did something to him inside. "You are beautiful. Does anyone ever tell you that?"

"Yes, just now. And did you see this?" She pointed to the sides of her neck, her gills pulsing, the water creating small ripples of light on the pool floor.

"That's what makes you beautiful." He wanted to ask if she was lonely, if anyone ever swam with her. He could, let his lungs fill with water, his aquatic part of his body's ability to adapt to any environment . . . and live underground without the sun and sky and trees and dirt. "I'm glad to see you happy. Keep changing. You are more beautiful each time I see you."

"Thank you. You, also, are changing. Marisa would be proud of you. Her love from me to you." She placed one hand against his, the glass the barest of separation, and after a moment, she smiled and pushed away, gracefully withdrawing into another world.

"Come," Jantzen said, one hand on Garik's shoulder. "Let's head back upstairs. I want to know how you evaded us for nearly two months. We were notified when you crossed back into the States, but then you disappeared again."

"Mud, rain, living a dog's life." He shrugged it off. He remembered Cpl. Williams' bullets and his body expelling them during those weeks. It was an experience he'd rather forget.

"A dog's life." Jantzen nudged him. "That's funny. We contacted Yellowknife the next morning, and you were already gone. We scoured the highways, everywhere. You simply vanished. A dog's life."

"Seriously. I walked dogs for five weeks in Blaine." They were at the elevator, and Garik noticed Jantzen didn't use a passkey. The new Tower, all free and open to everyone.

"Then that's why we didn't find you south of the border. We had no idea you would stay there. You must have been totally off grid. You didn't pop up anywhere."

"I lived in the kennel. They had a room in the back I could use if I cleaned the cages. Of course, I'm half dog. Who else would want me?"

"About that." The elevator doors closed them in. "You will stay? Anywhere, my old apartment, anywhere in the basements, you choose. The penthouse—" longingly "—has plenty of room for two if that appeals to you. I remember some of my time in Canada, you showing up—"

"Do you really?" Garik remembered the blank looks. "You weren't there, not even a fragment of you. I tried to engage you, and you had to ask someone if you had my name right. This place—" He pictured Devon, the recreation director who had become his friend. Devo . . . Devon-o . . . *right-o, Devon-o* . . . and he smiled.

"What's the smile for?"

"A friend." He watched the elevator numbers click over. Without noticing, the car had carried them to the top of the Tower, no passkey required. "I need outside, Jantzen. Not any of this. Not the windows, not the views, not this city. You people changed me." He noticed his terminology. Jantzen no longer felt like *us* but had become *them*. Jantzen wanted all this. Garik didn't. He was no longer the youth that craved a mentor. He had become what he was supposed to be, a man who needed his freedom, independence, and to

679

figure out how to make his life work without someone standing over his shoulder.

The doors opened into the penthouse, the glass walls, the expansive views. The furniture was the same, something Garik saw as Jantzen's link to his childhood friend. Weston Rodheimer might have trashed their relationship, but Jantzen would always be intermingled with the man he had once been intimately bonded to.

Garik walked to the glass wall looking toward the water, the sun catching the waves and calling to him. *Freedom, Garik. Just one glass wall away. Step through. I'm here, ready to take you anywhere your dreams lead you.* He turned. "I need to go home."

"This is your home. I'll give you this place and move back into my old one. Whatever you want."

"No, *home.*" Trees, dirt, grass, sky. Outside, the smells and sounds. He realized his time on the road, walking during the nights, that was who he was. Not this, not carpets and chairs and windows. He was beyond that. The realization welled up in him. Beyond human, beyond boyhood crushes on men who could melt into purple vapor. Such tricks no longer fascinated him. He had earned enough of his own, and they had done nothing except steal away the things he held most dear in his life.

"Where is home for you?" Jantzen approached, then stopped before he reached him.

"I watched you die twice, Jantzen." Garik looked out the window again, not wanting to see the reactions on the man's face. He had needed Jantzen to want him, to treat him like a son, to need to spend time with him as much as Garik had needed him. "The first time I blamed it on Sunchaser. The second time I blamed it on me. I repaired the sword, and you picked it up, not knowing it was repaired, and you turned it on. You vanished, and the sword was broken. How was I supposed to handle that? I had become the murderer." He whispered, "I had become Sunchaser."

"I wanted . . . had hoped . . ." Jantzen hesitated, his eyes fixated beyond the glass, then he took a deep breath and his voice shifted to a brighter, more positive tone. "Perhaps Canada? Do you want to return to the facility there? I'm sure Major Linkletter would invite you back. Or Israel. Their programs are running down avenues we haven't considered. Lt. Wilder has extended an offer to open negotiations with the Israelis on your behalf—"

"Canada." The memories of the forests and the wild outdoors

were like fresh air on his tongue. Yet, he knew the realities of being in a foreign country. Canada, also, could never be home. "Not Israel. I need trees and growing things, more than they can provide." And they had offered to take him already, likely to cut him up for research.

"I can arrange Canada for you. Yellowknife, anywhere. What do you need from me?"

"My freedom. To cut the cords."

"You will carry a phone? Call? To lose you—"

"No phone. Just me. Alaska, perhaps. Mining, logging, maybe the oil fields. Just outside. That's where I need to be."

"Let me set that up for you. I can arrange the company jet to get you there—"

"You're not getting it." Garik thrust his hands deep in his pockets, his newly grown nails biting his palms, his voice taking an edge. "No cords, no help, just me. I'm not the kid who needs looking after any longer. I need to make it on my own."

"I deserved that." Jantzen stepped up to stand beside Garik, looking out, a margin of space between them. "My apologies. You are yourself, one hundred percent, and you have the right to live your life without me or anyone looking over your shoulder. I should have seen that before."

"I appreciate what you've done for me—" Garik wanted to trust Jantzen's words. Freedom, release, acceptance. Would the man follow through? *Could* he?

"Just don't do it anymore, right?"

"You mentored me though this. I couldn't have done it without you. At one point, I looked at you as my father—"

"Hey," Jantzen cautioned. "I'm not a graybeard yet. Don't give me crutches before I earn them."

Garik laughed, glad to see Jantzen teasing again. "Friend, then. Acceptable?" He truly liked the man, at one point admitted he might have loved him, but he had grown past him. Still, he didn't wish to hurt him.

"I'll take whatever I can get. When are you leaving?"

"A few days. Visit with Marina, see if there's anyone else in the city I might like to say goodbye to."

"Your aunt. She's still here."

"Iri." Garik considered the situation. "Not if she's with Arik."

"Done, if you'll let me do that for you."

681

"It won't change my mind. No cords, Jantz."

"Understood."

Garik didn't reply. He read the emotions behind the word in the man's heartbeat, his pheromones, the longing emanating from him. As Jantzen had taught him, you shouldn't give away everything you can do, especially when it would hurt a friend, one Garik had already left behind.

THE BIG DAY arrived a week later, the middle of May, with sunshine and wispy clouds in the sky. Garik sat in the penthouse lacing up new hikers, in heavy jeans and a flannel shirt. It was warm in Bay City, but where he was going, he expected winter year-round.

Backpack. Tent. The whole nine yards, Jantzen's gift to him. He stood, faced Jantzen, and said, "It's time."

"One last thing." Jantzen pulled out a slim leather wallet. He opened it to reveal a metal card inside, then closed it and held it out to Garik.

"I don't want that." Garik looked away and reached for his backpack.

"No limits. You don't have to use it, but if you need it . . . any amount. The card never expires."

"I won't use it."

"You won't take a watch or a phone—"

"I don't want to be tracked."

"I understand. This one thing, though. Emergencies only. Bus fare, plane fare, or buy the whole plane. This card will allow it. Carry it. For me."

"For you." Garik considered the card. "I want to disappear, Jantzen. Gone forever. That card can track me."

"Only if you use it, and only I will know."

That you're safe, but Jantzen hadn't needed to say that. Garik understood. He held out his hand, stroked the leather, and slid it into a pouch in his pack.

"Then I'm gone. North, somewhere. You'll be able to track when I cross the border, but don't. Please."

Garik hiked his pack and slipped it on, and he walked to the elevator without looking back. Making his way across the mall, he looked back at the Tower, wondering what had fascinated him about it for so long. It was a building, steel and glass. Where he was heading was so much better.

He faced east into the rising sun. A day's walk and he would turn north. How long until he got there? It didn't matter.

He had all the time in the world.

Thank You

Your readership is appreciated. Explore detailed maps of Bay City and delve into your favorite characters in *The Human-Hybrid Project*. All this and more at

www.TheHumanHybridProject.com

www.ingramcontent.com/pod-product-compliance
Lightning Source LLC
Chambersburg PA
CBHW071329020726
47502CB00001B/14